THE

LYLE
OFFICIAL
ANTIQUES
REVIEW 1993

THE

LYLE

OFFICIAL

ANTIQUES
REVIEW 1993

A PERIGEE BOOK

Perigee Books
are published by
The Putnam Publishing Group
200 Madison Avenue
New York, NY 10016

ISBN 0-399-51774-X
LC 74-640592

Cover design by Jack Ribik

Printed in the United States of America
1 2 3 4 5 6 7 8 9 10

This book is printed on acid-free paper.

Introduction

This year over 100,000 Antique Dealers and Collectors will make full and profitable use of their Lyle Antiques Review. They know that only in this one volume will they find the widest possible variety of goods – illustrated, described and given a current market value to assist them to BUY RIGHT AND SELL RIGHT throughout the year of issue.

They know, too, that by building a collection of these immensely valuable volumes year by year, they will equip themselves with an unparalleled reference library of facts, figures and illustrations which, properly used, cannot fail to help them keep one step ahead of the market.

In its twenty three years of publication, Lyle has gone from strength to strength and has become without doubt the pre-eminent book of reference for the antique trade throughout the world. Each of its fact filled pages are packed with precisely the kind of profitable information the professional Dealer needs – including descriptions, illustrations and values of thousands and thousands of individual items carefully selected to give a representative picture of the current market in antiques and collectables – and remember all values are prices actually paid, based on accurate sales records in the twelve months prior to publication from the best established and most highly respected auction houses and retail outlets in Europe and America.

This is THE book for the Professional Antiques Dealer. 'The Lyle Book' – we've even heard it called 'The Dealer's Bible'.

Compiled and published afresh each year, the Lyle Antiques Review is the most comprehensive up-to-date antiques price guide available. THIS COULD BE YOUR WISEST INVESTMENT OF THE YEAR!

Anthony Curtis

The publishers wish to express their sincere thanks to the following for their involvement and assistance in the production of this volume:

EELIN McIVOR (Sub Editor)
NICKY FAIRBURN (Art Director)
ANNETTE CURTIS (Editorial)
CATRIONA DAY (Art Production)
DONNA CRUICKSHANK (Art Production)
ANGIE DEMARCO (Art Production)
FRANK BURRELL (Graphics)
JAMES BROWN (Graphics)
DONNA RUTHERFORD
JACQUELINE LEDDY
EILEEN BURRELL

While every care has been taken in the compiling of information contained in this volume, the publisher cannot accept liability for loss, financial or otherwise, incurred by reliance placed on the information herein.

All prices quoted in this book are obtained from a variety of auctions in various countries during the twelve months prior to publication and are converted to dollars at the rate of exchange prevalent at the time of sale.

CONTENTS

9

Acknowledgements

AB Stockholms Auktionsverk, Box 16256, 103 25 Stockholm, Sweden
Abbotts Auction Rooms, The Auction Rooms, Campsea Ash, Woodbridge, Suffolk
Abridge Auction Rooms, Market Place, Abridge, Essex RM4 1UA
Allen & Harris, St Johns Place, Whiteladies Road, Clifton, Bristol BS8 2ST
Jean Claude Anaf, Lyon Brotteaux, 13 bis place Jules Ferry, 69456 Lyon, France
Anderson & Garland, Marlborough House, Marlborough Crescent, Newcastle upon Tyne NE1 4EE
Antique Collectors Club & Co. Ltd, 5 Church Street, Woodbridge, Suffolk IP 12 1DS
Auction Team Köln, Postfach 50 11 68, D-5000 Köln 50 Germany
Auktionshaus Arnold, Bleichstr. 42, 6000 Frankfurt a/M, Germany
Barber's Auctions, Woking, Surrey
Brian Bates, Fairview, Maer, Newcastle, Staffs
Bearnes, Rainbow, Avenue Road, Torquay TQ2 5TG
Biddle & Webb, Ladywood Middleway, Birmingham B16 0PP
Bigwood, The Old School, Tiddington, Stratford upon Avon
Black Horse Agencies, Locke & England, 18 Guy Street, Leamington Spa
Boardman Fine Art Auctioneers, Station Road Corner, Haverhill, Suffolk CB9 0EY
Bonhams, Montpelier Street, Knightsbridge, London SW7 1HH
Bonhams Chelsea, 65–69 Lots Road, London SW10 0RN
Bonhams West Country, Dowell Street, Honiton, Devon
British Antique Exporters, School Close, Queen Elizabeth Avenue, Burgess Hill, Sussex
William H Brown, The Warner Auction Rooms, 16–18, Halford Street, Leicester LE1 1JB
Butterfield & Butterfield, 220 San Bruno Avenue, San Francisco CA 94103, USA
Butterfield & Butterfield, 7601 Sunset Boulevard, Los Angeles CA 90046, USA
Central Motor Auctions, Barfield House, Britannia Road, Morley, Leeds, LS27 0HN
H.C. Chapman & Son, The Auction Mart, North Street, Scarborough.
Christie's (International) SA, 8 place de la Taconnerie, 1204 Genève, Switzerland
Christie's Monaco, S.A.M, Park Palace 98000 Monte Carlo, Monaco
Christie's Scotland, 164–166 Bath Street Glasgow G2 4TG
Christie's South Kensington Ltd., 85 Old Brompton Road, London SW7 3LD
Christie's, 8 King Street, London SW1Y 6QT
Christie's East, 219 East 67th Street, New York, NY 10021, USA`
Christie's, 502 Park Avenue, New York, NY 10022, USA
Christie's, Cornelis Schuytstraat 57, 1071 JG Amsterdam, Netherlands
Christie's SA Roma, 114 Piazza Navona, 00186 Rome, Italy
Christie's Swire, 1202 Alexandra House, 16–20 Chater Road, Hong Kong
Christie's Australia Pty Ltd., 1 Darling Street, South Yarra, Melbourne, Victoria 3141, Australia
A J Cobern, The Grosvenor Sales Rooms, 93b Eastbank Street, Southport PR8 1DG
Cooper Hirst Auctions, The Granary Saleroom, Victoria Road, Chelmsford, Essex CM2 6LH
Nic Costa, 166 Camden Street, London, NW1 9PT
The Crested China Co., Station House, Driffield, E. Yorks YO25 7PY
Clifford Dann, 20/21 High Street, Lewes, Sussex
Julian Dawson, Lewes Auction Rooms, 56 High Street, Lewes BN7 1XE
Dee & Atkinson, The Exchange Saleroom, Driffield, Nth Humberside YO25 7LJ
Garth Denham & Assocs. Horsham Auction Galleries, Warnsham, Nr. Horsham, Sussex
Diamond Mills & Co., 117 Hamilton Road, Felixstowe, Suffolk
David Dockree Fine Art, 224 Moss Lane, Bramhall, Stockport SK7 1BD
Dowell Lloyd & Co. Ltd, 118 Putney Bridge Road, London SW15 2NQ
Downer Ross, Charter House, 42 Avebury Boulevard, Central Milton Keynes MK9 2HS
Hy. Duke & Son, 40 South Street, Dorchester, Dorset
Du Mouchelles Art Galleries Co., 409 E. Jefferson Avenue, Detroit, Michigan 48226, USA
Duncan Vincent, 105 London Street, Reading RG1 4LF
Sala de Artes y Subastas Durán, Serrano 12, 28001 Madrid, Spain
Eldred's, Box 796, E. Dennis, MA 02641, USA
R H Ellis & Sons, 44/46 High St., Worthing, BN11 1LL
Ewbanks, Welbeck House, High Street, Guildford, Surrey, GU1 3JF
Fellows & Son, Augusta House, 19 Augusta Street, Hockley, Birmingham
Finarte, 20121 Milano, Piazzetta Bossi 4, Italy
John D Fleming & Co., 8 Fore Street, Dulverton, Somerset
G A Property Services, Canterbury Auction Galleries, Canterbury, Kent
Galerie Koller, Rämistr. 8, CH 8024 Zürich, Switzerland
Galerie Moderne, 3 rue du Parnasse, 1040 Bruxelles, Belgium
Geering & Colyer (Black Horse Agencies) Highgate, Hawkhurst, Kent
Glerum Auctioneers, Westeinde 12, 2512 HD's Gravenhage, Netherlands
The Goss and Crested China Co., 62 Murray Road, Horndean, Hants PO8 9JL
Graves Son & Pilcher, 71 Church Road, Hove, East Sussex, BN3 2GL
Greenslade Hunt, 13 Hammet Street, Taunton, Somerset, TA1 1RN
Peter Günnemann, Ehrenberg Str. 57, 2000 Hamburg 50, Germany
Halifax Property Services, 53 High Street, Tenterden, Kent
Halifax Property Services, 15 Cattle Market, Sandwich, Kent CT13 9AW
Hampton's Fine Art, 93 High Street, Godalming, Surrey
Hanseatisches Auktionshaus für Historica, Neuer Wall 57, 2000 Hamburg 36, Germany
Andrew Hartley Fine Arts, Victoria Hall, Little Lane, Ilkely
Hauswedell & Nolte, D-2000 Hamburg 13, Pöseldorfer Weg 1, Germany
Giles Haywood, The Auction House, St John's Road, Stourbridge, West Midlands, DY8 1EW

13

ANTIQUES REVIEW

Heatheringtons Nationwide Anglia, The Amersham Auction Rooms, 125 Station Road, Amersham, Bucks
Muir Hewitt, Halifax Antiques Centre, Queens Road/Gibbet Street, Halifax HX1 4LR
Hobbs & Chambers, 'At the Sign of the Bell', Market Place, Cirencester, Glos
Hobbs Parker, Romney House, Ashford, Ashford, Kent
Hotel de Ventes Horta, 390 Chaussée de Waterloo (Ma Campagne), 1060 Bruxelles, Belgium
Jacobs & Hunt, Lavant Street, Petersfield, Hants. GU33 3EF
James of Norwich, 33 Timberhill, Norwich NR1 3LA
P Horholdt Jensens Auktioner, Rundforbivej 188, 2850 Nerum, Denmark
Kennedy & Wolfenden, 218 Lisburn Rd, Belfast BT9 6GD
G A Key, Aylsham Saleroom, Palmers Lane, Aylsham, Norfolk, NR11 6EH
Kunsthaus am Museum, Drususgasse 1–5, 5000 Köln 1, Germany
Kunsthaus Lempertz, Neumarkt 3, 5000 Köln 1, Germany
Lambert & Foster (County Group), The Auction Sales Room, 102 High Street, Tenterden, Kent
W.H. Lane & Son, 64 Morrab Road, Penzance, Cornwall, TR18 2QT
Langlois Ltd., Westway Rooms, Don Street, St Helier, Channel Islands
Lawrence Butler Fine Art Salerooms, Marine Walk, Hythe, Kent, CT21 5AJ
Lawrence Fine Art, South Street, Crewkerne, Somerset TA18 8AB
Lawrence's Fine Art Auctioneers, Norfolk House, 80 High Street, Bletchingley, Surrey
David Lay, The Penzance Auction House, Alverton, Penzance, Cornwall TA18 4KE
Brian Loomes, Calf Haugh Farm, Pateley Bridge, North Yorks
Lots Road Chelsea Auction Galleries, 71 Lots Road, Chelsea, London SW10 0RN
R K Lucas & Son, Tithe Exchange, 9 Victoria Place, Haverfordwest, SA61 2JX
Duncan McAlpine, Stateside Comics plc, 125 East Barnet Road, London EN4 8RF
John Maxwell, 75 Hawthorn Street, Wilmslow, Cheshire
May & Son, 18 Bridge Street, Andover, Hants
Morphets, 4–6 Albert Street, Harrogate, North Yorks HG1 1JL
D M Nesbit & Co, 7 Clarendon Road, Southsea, Hants PO5 2ED
Onslow's, Metrostore, Townmead Road, London SW6 2RZ
Outhwaite & Litherland, Kingsley Galleries, Fontenoy Street, Liverpool, Merseyside L3 2BE
J R Parkinson Son & Hamer Auctions, The Auction Rooms, Rochdale, Bury, Lancs
Phillips Manchester, Trinity House, 114 Northenden Road, Sale, Manchester M33 3HD
Phillips Son & Neale SA, 10 rue des Chaudronniers, 1204 Genève, Switzerland
Phillips West Two, 10 Salem Road, London W2 4BL
Phillips, 11 Bayle Parade, Folkestone, Kent CT20 1SQ
Phillips, 49 London Road, Sevenoaks, Kent TN13 1UU
Phillips, 65 George Street, Edinburgh EH2 2JL
Phillips, Blenstock House, 7 Blenheim Street, New Bond Street, London W1Y 0AS
Phillips Marylebone, Hayes Place, Lisson Grove, London NW1 6UA
Phillips, New House, 150 Christleton Road, Chester CH3 5TD
Pinney's, 5627 Ferrier, Montreal, Quebec, Canada H4P 2M4
Pooley & Rogers, Regent Auction Rooms, Abbey Street, Penzance
Harry Ray & Co, Lloyds Bank Chambers, Welshpool, Montgomery SY21 7RR
Rennie's, 1 Agincourt Street, Monmouth
Riddetts, Richmond Hill, Bournemouth
Ritchie's, 429 Richmond Street East, Toronto, Canada M5A 1R1
Derek Roberts Antiques, 24–25 Shipbourne Road, Tonbridge, Kent TN10 3DN
Rogers de Rin, 79 Royal Hospital Road, London SW3 4HN
Russell, Baldwin & Bright, The Fine Art Saleroom, Ryelands Road, Leominster HR6 8JG
Sandoes Nationwide Anglia, Tabernacle Road, Wotton under Edge, Glos GL12 7EB
Selkirk's, 4166 Olive Street, St Louis, Missouri 63108, USA
Skinner Inc., Bolton Gallery, Route 117, Bolton MA, USA
Southgate Auction Rooms, 55 High St, Southgate, London N14 6LD
Henry Spencer, 40 The Square, Retford, Notts. DN22 6DJ
Spink & Son Ltd, 5-7 King St., St James's, London SW1Y 6QS
Street Jewellery, 16 Eastcliffe Avenue, Newcastle upon Tyne NE3 4SN
Stride & Son, Southdown House, St John's St., Chichester, Sussex
G E Sworder & Son, Northgate End Salerooms, 15 Northgate End, Bishop Stortford, Herts
Taviner's of Bristol, Prewett Street, Redcliffe, Bristol BS1 6PB
Tennants, 27 Market Place, Leyburn, Yorkshire
Thomson Roddick & Laurie, 24 Lowther Street, Carlisle
Thomson Roddick & Laurie, 60 Whitesands, Dumfries
Timbleby & Shorland, 31 Gt Knollys St, Reading RG1 7HU
Venator & Hanstein, Obenmarspforten 7-11, 5000 Koln 1, Germany
T Vennett Smith, 11 Nottingham Road, Gotham, Nottingham NG11 0HE
Duncan Vincent, 105 London Road, Reading RG1 4LF
Wallis & Wallis, West Street Auction Galleries, West Street, Lewes, E. Sussex BN7 2NJ
Ward & Morris, Stuart House, 18 Gloucester Road, Ross on Wye HR9 5BN
Warren & Wignall Ltd, The Mill, Earnshaw Bridge, Leyland Lane, Leyland PR5 3PH
Dominique Watine-Arnault, 11 rue François 1er, 75008 Paris, France
Wells Cundall Nationwide Anglia, Staffordshire House, 27 Flowergate, Whitby YO21 3AX
Woltons, 6 Whiting Street, Bury St Edmunds, Suffolk IP33 1PB
Peter Wilson, Victoria Gallery, Market Street, Nantwich, Cheshire CW5 5DG
Woolley & Wallis, The Castle Auction Mart, Salisbury, Wilts SP1 3SU
Austin Wyatt Nationwide Anglia, Emsworth Road, Lymington, Hants SO41 9BL

14

ANTIQUES
REVIEW 1993

T HE Lyle Official Antiques Review is compiled and published with completely fresh information annually, enabling you to begin each new year with an up-to-date knowledge of the current trends, together with the verified values of antiques of all descriptions.

We have endeavored to obtain a balance between the more expensive collector's items and those which, although not in their true sense antiques, are handled daily by the antiques trade.

The illustrations and prices in the following sections have been arranged to make it easy for the reader to assess the period and value of all items with speed.

You will find illustrations for almost every category of antique and curio, together with a corresponding price collated during the last twelve months, from the auction rooms and retail outlets of the major trading countries.

When dealing with the more popular trade pieces, in some instances, a calculation of an average price has been estimated from the varying accounts researched.

As regards prices, when 'one of a pair' is given in the description the price quoted is for a pair and so that we can make maximum use of the available space it is generally considered that one illustration is sufficient.

It will be noted that in some descriptions taken directly from sales cataloges originating from many different countries, terms such as bureau, secretary and davenport are used in a broader sense than is customary, but in all cases the term used is self explanatory.

Brown & Polson's: counter sign *Sleep My Little One*, pressed cardboard with ogee border, multicolored, 49 x 62cm. (Phillips) **$89**

Painted and decorated painter's sign, America, late 19th century, painted red and embellished with white, yellow and blue flourishes, 32¼ x 28½in. (Skinner Inc.) **$1,320**

Schweppes counter sign, *Are You A Schweppicure? Schweppervescence Lasts The Whole Drink Through*, 30 x 35cm. (Phillips) **$169**

Edward Henry Potthast (American, 1857–1927), *The July Number – The Century/* An advertising poster for the July 1896 issue, 21¼ x 16in. (Skinner Inc.) **$275**

A William IV painted coat-of-arms of the Livery Company of Butchers, with a pair of winged bulls flanking a cartouche beneath a helmet, 42 x 36½in. (Christie's) **$1,884**

Duke, Waring, Crisp & Co., London Trade Catalog: Wire Goods, cloth back, 179 pages. (Phillips) **$373**

'Star Wind Mill' advertising poster, 20th century, depicting a windmill inscribed *FLINT AND WALLING M.F.G. CO., KENDALLVILLE, IND.*, 14 x 11in. (Butterfield & Butterfield) **$550**

Painted and decorated rubber trade sign, Ales Goodyear Shoe Co., Nagatuck, Connecticut, late 19th century, painted red and enhanced with white and blue, 35¼in. high. (Skinner Inc.) **$935**

A good cartridge display board, the center with a *Kynoch Loaded Cartridges* box lid decorated with a falcon and its prey, within four colored labels, glazed, 63 x 73cm. (Phillips) **$2,666**

For All Repairs There's A Great Run On Redfern Rubber Heels and Soles, enamel sign featuring a policeman chasing a boy, blue, white and orange on yellow, 51 x 76cm.
(Phillips) $178

'Ruskin Pottery', high-fired stoneware lettering, speckled green glaze with areas of cloudy blue, mounted on copper panels, circa 1905, 113cm. long.
(Christie's) $5,907

A painted and stenciled wooden trade sign, American, early 20th century, bearing an oil rig and motor-driven transport truck on a mustard ground within a green-painted and gold-stenciled frame, 35¼in. long.
(Christie's) $3,520

Huntley & Palmer: sign, *Huntley & Palmer Ginger Nuts,* in a circle with central figure of John Ginger, multicolored on a green background, 47 x 46cm.
(Phillips) $533

Sunlight: enamel sign, in the form of a baker's boy holding a £1,000 bag of money with the label *Guarantee of Purity,* 86cm. high, 83cm. wide.
(Phillips) $835

Dewar's: enamel sign, *By Royal Warrant To Her Majesty The Queen Dewar's Perth Whisky,* blue and red on white with thistle motif, 102 x 92cm.
(Phillips) $124

A reverse color printed bevel glass panel incorporating to the centre an aneroid barometer, inscribed *Pacific Line of Royal Mail Steamers,* 55 x 35cm.
(Phillips) $924

Quaker Oats: enamel sign, *Eat Quaker Oats In Packets Only,* featuring a packet, in blue, yellow, brown and black on white, 106.5 x 60cm.
(Phillips) $133

Alphonse Mucha: "Job", 1898, an Art Nouveau girl with long black hair, printed to the border *Imp F. Champenois, 66, Bould. St. Michel, Paris,* 140 x 92cm.
(Phillips) $3,644

A North British black scottie dog advertising figure holding a dimple ball in his mouth by Sylvac, 28cm.
(Phillips) $830

A 1920's metal-body hanging advertising sign in the shape of a film box with hanging panel and mounted bracket.
(Christie's) $285

A Carlton ware Guiness advertising table lamp base in the form of a toucan standing by a glass, 23.2cm.
(Bearne's) $370

Fill Your Sump From The Castrol Pump, pictorial printed tinplate, 46 x 34cm.
(Onslow's) $432

A good ammunition display board, the center with the trade mark of Nobel Industries Ltd. encompassed by a circle of cartridges and a further circle of brass cased ammunition, 79 x 64cm.
(Phillips) $3,111

Associated Motorways: enamel sign, *Its Cheaper And More Enjoyable By Road*, black and orange on green and orange, 76 x 51cm.
(Phillips) $213

Dunlop Stock, circular enamel sign, 61cm. diameter.
(Onslow's) $116

A Penfold man advertising figure in papier mâché, with outsized cap, 51cm.
(Phillips) $490

Mobiloil Save Money!, pictorial printed tinplate sign, 49 x 37cm.
(Onslow's) $249

18

Beswick ware pottery ornament, made for Double Diamond, inscribed *A Double Diamond Works Wonders*, 8in. (G.A. Key)　　$168

A large exhibition multi-blade knife with thirty-two various blades stamped *Wlaszlovits Stos*, 8in. long. (Christie's)　　$2,035

A Dunlop man advertising figure in papier mâché, with dimple ball head, and carrying a bag of clubs, 39cm. (Phillips)　　$850

A good ammunition display board, the center with Eley trade mark encompassed by a circle of cartridges and a further circle of brass cased ammunition, glazed, 80.5 x 65cm. (Phillips)　　$2,489

Guest, Keen & Nettlefolds Ltd., an impressive fastenings display board featuring a central device of a lion's head with a massive screw through its jaws, entirely composed from screws in different materials, 137cm. square. (Phillips)　　$7,288

A glazed wall display cabinet of I. Sorby 'Punch' Brand Tools, including hand and tenon saw, 43½ x 39in. (Christie's)　　$3,350

A tyre and inner tube with Englebert in a panel, yellow, red, black and gray on green, pressed tin, 55 x 79cm. (Phillips)　　$249

A carved and painted cigar store Indian, American, late 19th century, carved in the form of an Indian princess with a gold feather headdress above long groove-carved black hair and carved gold earrings, 72½in. high. (Christie's)　　$13,200

A set of five educational dental views *Made for the Dental Board of the United Kingdom by Educational & Scientific Plastics Ltd Croydon Surrey*, 13 x 18in. (Christie's)　　$325

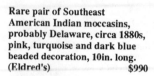

Rare pair of Southeast American Indian moccasins, probably Delaware, circa 1880s, pink, turquoise and dark blue beaded decoration, 10in. long. (Eldred's) $990

Acoma polychrome pottery jar, with wide flaring sides and tapering rim, a geometric band at top, 10¼in. high. (Butterfield & Butterfield) $1,980

Pair of Athabaskan boots, circa 1910, with beadwork decoration. (Eldred's) $193

Hopi Kachina doll representing Heheya, shown with arms pressed to the midriff, the red and yellow torso supporting a pale blue casemask, 9¾in. high. (Butterfield & Butterfield) $715

Pair of Crow beaded gauntlets, partially beaded on hide, with stars on the hands, the cuffs filled by an elaborate floral configuration in polychrome beads, 16in. long. (Butterfield & Butterfield) $660

Sioux beaded panel from the Battle at Little Big Horn, consisting of a trapezoidal hide panel taken from a cradle cover, fully beaded with stepped triangles, diamonds and a roll-beaded edge, 16in. long. (Butterfield & Butterfield) $6,600

Northern Plains beaded yoke, fully beaded on buffalo hide, depicting a four-directional diamond medallion flanked by two corner stars, 16½in. long. (Butterfield & Butterfield) $935

Ojibwa beaded bandolier bag, consisting of a loom-beaded geometric panel with tab and tassel suspensions, fastened to a cloth background, 46in. long. (Butterfield & Butterfield) $1,980

Rare Navajo Germantown sampler, mixed recarded background with blue, white and yellow geometric decoration, 21in. square. (Eldred's) $605

Pair of Santee Sioux moccasins, circa 1870s, with floral decoration, 7in. long.
(Eldred's) $468

Washo polychrome basket of flattened hemispherical form, carrying staggered rows of feather tip triangles, 8¼in. diameter.
(Butterfield & Butterfield)
     $8,800

Makah wood wolf headdress, having allover relief-carved ovals and characteristic motifs, 22in. long.
(Butterfield & Butterfield)
     $770

Northwest Coast bentwood box, the square container painted on opposing sides with elaborate traditional renditions of supernatural beings or animals, 25¼in. high.
(Butterfield & Butterfield)
     $4,950

Apache basket, with central solid four-petal device, surrounded by double-banded and solid zig-zags in a diamond lattice pattern, 18¼in. diameter.
(Butterfield & Butterfield)
     $1,540

Woodlands Indian mittens, circa 1890, with floral beadwork decoration, 11in. long.
(Eldred's) $770

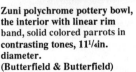

Zuni polychrome pottery bowl, the interior with linear rim band, solid colored parrots in contrasting tones, 11¼in. diameter.
(Butterfield & Butterfield)
     $8,800

Hopi Kachina doll representing Hututu, standing with arms close to the body, the case mask with domed top, semi-circle ear and one long horn, 14¼in. high.
(Butterfield & Butterfield)
     $3,025

Pima miniature basket, very finely woven, the slightly flaring sides drawn with concentric angular box meanders, 5¼in. diameter.
(Butterfield & Butterfield)
     $825

Maidu basket, with concentric serrated and stepped triangle devices flanked by a variety of eccentric floating motifs, 10¼in. diameter.
(Butterfield & Butterfield)
$550

Apache olla, woven with vertical rows of connected outlined diamonds, zig-zags and stripes, 13in. high.
(Butterfield & Butterfield)
$1,100

American Indian woven basket, circa 1900, black motif in stepped block configuration, 18in. diameter.
(Du Mouchelles) $3,500

Large Acoma pottery jar, painted overall in a fine-line repeat compartment pattern, 19in. high.
(Butterfield & Butterfield)
$770

Navajo Germantown rug, the field divided into two panels, showing various diamond, plant life and lightning bolts, 3ft. 2in. x 2ft. 3in.
(Butterfield & Butterfield)
$1,540

Anasazi cradle, Four Mile culture, circa 1375–1450 A.D., consisting of two parallel flat wood slats, supporting a slightly concave and rounded seat of plaited fibres, 30in. long.
(Butterfield & Butterfield)
$4,675

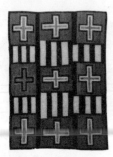

Navajo chief's style rug, in a nine-spot box pattern, each compartment centering concentric crosses, 4ft. 11in. x 7ft.
(Butterfield & Butterfield)
$4,125

Apache polychrome basket, the solid and checkered center ringed by multi-banded zig-zags, 19in. diameter.
(Butterfield & Butterfield)
$2,475

Navajo Germantown blanket, the banded pattern alternating panels of connected stepped diamonds, diamond halves, zig-zags and stripes, 6ft. 7in. x 4ft. 9in.
(Butterfield & Butterfield)
$11,000

Mesa Verde black on white
pottery mug, the loop handle
painted with a diamond lattice
and pierced to resemble a
keyhole, 4^1/$_2$in. diameter.
(Butterfield & Butterfield)
$770

Navajo pictorial rug depicting
three human figures, each
wearing striped conical hats and
jewelry, within a reciprocal
stepped zig-zag border, 4ft. 2in.
x 6ft. 2in.
(Butterfield & Butterfield)
$3,300

Panamint polychrome pictorial
bottleneck basket, of
characteristic form, deer and
appended hourglass devices on
the sloping shoulder, 4^1/$_4$in. high.
(Butterfield & Butterfield)
$5,225

Zia polychrome pottery jar,
painted in two panels of
scalloped bands, stylized
floriforms and geometrics,
10^1/$_4$in. high.
(Butterfield & Butterfield)
$2,420

Northeast California
polychrome basketry pitcher,
the globular body drawn with
zig-zag bands of quail topknot
motifs and floating diamonds,
14^1/$_2$in. high.
(Butterfield & Butterfield)
$1,100

Pima polychrome olla with
straight flaring sides, drawn
allover in a diamond lattice
pattern, each compartment with
smaller diamonds, 12in. high.
(Butterfield & Butterfield)
$1,650

Zuni polychrome pottery jar,
painted with volutes, rosettes
and a narrow band of scrolls
over traditional deer with heart
lines, 10^1/$_2$in. high.
(Butterfield & Butterfield)
$4,950

Navajo Germantown rug with a
central row of concentric solid
and serrated diamond lozenges
and complementary diamond
halves, 5ft. 4in. x 3ft. 3in.
(Butterfield & Butterfield)
$4,125

Hopi polychrome pottery bowl,
painted on the interior with an
asymmetrical arrangement of
swimming tadpoles below
stepped panels, 13^3/$_4$in.
diameter.
(Butterfield & Butterfield)
$495

Dice-O-Matic amusement machine made in the U.K., circa 1930.
(Costa/Bates) $270

A 'Novelty Merchantman' crane by the Exhibit Supply Co. Chicago, the crane takes the form of the bow end of a merchant ship with the grab as a derrick, 71in. high.
(Bonhams) $853

'Towerbridge' amusement machine made in the U.K., circa 1950.
(Costa/Bates) $540

An early 20th century oak cased 'Shooting Star' pinball machine, 92cm. high.
(Spencer's) $424

'Sneezy' dice shaker amusement machine made in the U.S.A., circa 1930.
(Costa/Bates) $270

Your Horoscope amusement machine 'Is this Your Lucky Day?', made in the U.K., circa 1930.
(Costa/Bates) $270

A Bryans Quadmatic Allwin, having two Elevenses Allwins, a seven cup Allwin and a U-Win Allwin with one large U-shaped winning cup, 66in. high.
(Bonhams) $853

'Twenty One' amusement machine made in the U.S.A., circa 1930.
(Costa/Bates) $450

'El-Chic-Chic' brass dice shaker amusement machine, made in Spain, circa 1910.
(Costa/Bates) $810

AMUSEMENT MACHINES

'Clairvoyance' amusement machine 'The Secrets of Clairvoyance and Mesmerism', made in the U.K. by Illusion Machines, circa 1890.
(Costa/Bates) $3,600

A coin operated Dalek kiddies ride, the six foot Dalek has a seat inside for the passenger, made by Edwin Hall & Co., London.
(Bonhams) $938

Mills amusement machine, with Mystery Payout, made in the U.S.A., 1960's.
(Costa/Bates) $450

An early 20th century coin operated 'Playball' game with eight winning shots, 71cm. high.
(Spencer's) $300

'Egg laying hen' early stamped metal vending machine made by C F Schulze & Co Berlin. The hen sits on an oval basket and on insertion of 10pfg in her comb and turning of the handle a 12 part container for 59 eggs is moved so that an 'egg' (containing confectionery) is laid. Fully operational, circa 1900. (Auction Team Köln)
$4,725

'British Beauties Bureau' amusement machine made in the U.K., circa 1900.
(Costa/Bates) $2,700

Film Star Gum Vender, made in Belgium, circa 1950.
(Costa/Bates) $225

A late Victorian cast-iron platform weighing machine, labelled *Salter 1897*, to weigh 24 stone, with elaborate all over decoration, approx. 66in. high.
(Bonhams) $1,876

'Automatic Doctor' vending machine 'For the convenience of visitors' made by the Allied Chemical Co. Ltd., 1930's.
(Costa/Bates) $450

A finely detailed wooden panel mummy portrait of a young woman with open eyed gaze and wearing a thin loop chain necklace, Roman Egypt, 2nd-3rd century A.D., 10$\frac{1}{2}$in. high. (Bonhams) $2,600

A late Etruscan hollow bronze votive boot, with high instep and heavy hob-nailed soil, 3rd-2nd century B.C., 5$\frac{1}{4}$in. long. (Bonhams) $2,775

Mochica figural pottery vessel, circa 200 500 A.D., the rectangular base surmounted by a fierce looking human head, having long fangs, 8$\frac{3}{4}$in. high. (Butterfield & Butterfield) $715

Jalisco kneeling pottery female figure, circa 150 B.C.–250 A.D., the short bend legs covered by a skirt and supporting a massive torso, 11$\frac{1}{2}$in. high. (Butterfield & Butterfield) $220

Mayan polychrome pottery cylinder vase, circa 550–950 A.D., painted allover in a repeat panel pattern of bat face profiles, 8in. high. (Butterfield & Butterfield) $770

A Roman heavy bronze hollow votive hand, with extended fingers, and a late Roman thin gold ring, 3rd-4th century A.D., 5$\frac{3}{4}$in. high. (Bonhams) $3,700

An Apulian black-glazed hydria decorated with the draped standing figure of a winged Nike, early 4th century B.C., 11$\frac{3}{4}$in. high. (Bonhams) $4,000

Veracruz seated pottery figure, circa 550–950 A.D., with legs crossed and hands to the knees, 14$\frac{1}{2}$in. high. (Butterfield & Butterfield) $1,980

A large Apulian black-glazed bell krater with red-figure decoration of a seated nude female gazing into a mirror, Greek South Italy, late 4th century B.C., 12$\frac{1}{2}$in. (Bonhams) $2,000

One of a pair of terracotta half capitals, each of two sections with grotesque masks between scroll angles, damages, late 19th century, 30½in. wide. (Christie's) (Two) $1,113

Architectural ornament, America, 19th century, the full-bodied molded copper figure of an eagle with outspread wings perched on hemispherical base, 27½in. high. (Skinner Inc.) $2,750

A George III statuary marble chimneypiece tablet, depicting St. George slaying the Dragon, carved in high relief, 18th century, 13½ x 31½in. (Christie's) $3,137

A Regency wrought-iron rectangular panel, centered by a roundel of acanthus and interlocking darts within a 'lace' and bobbin surround, early 19th century, 32¼in. wide. (Christie's) $1,096

A pair of carved stone sphinxes, each with an elaborate tasseled headdress and saddles by a raised floral ornament band, 24in. high. (Christie's) $2,009

A pair of walnut and marquetry doors, each with five molded rectangular panels to either side, the front inlaid with foliate marquetry, 19th century, 33½ x 111in. (Christie's) $3,643

The Grocers' Company Coade stone camel, with a roped bale, standing beside rockwork, on an oval base signed *COADE--99*, late 18th century, 53in. wide. (Christie's) $25,300

A gray-painted carved oak lunette of Louis XV style, the panel centered by a triumphant vase with a shell cartouche on claw feet, a pair of putti to either side, late 19th century, 59 x 112¾in. (Christie's) $4,565

One of a pair of cast-iron gargoyles, each formed of two sections, with grotesque features and outstretched wings, late 19th century, 20in. high. (Christie's) (Two) $639

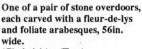

One of a pair of stone overdoors, each carved with a fleur-de-lys and foliate arabesques, 56in. wide.
(Christie's)   (Two)
$2,024

A Japanese granite lantern, with pagoda top, the pierced octagonal shaft decorated with raised carved naturalistic scenes on stepped base, 69in. high.
(Christie's) $2,374

A green patinated copper lunette, by Edward William Wyon, cast in high relief, centered by two pheasants, their young and a squirrel, signed *E.W. Wyon. Sc 1860*, 57in. wide.
(Christie's) $8,501

A pair of substantial wrought-iron doors, each centered by a foliate brass roundel within a circular surround, each door, 82¹/₂in. high; 26³/₄in. wide.
(Christie's) $1,720

A Coade stone keystone, 'The Laughing Philosopher', of tapering form, the leering face shown bearded and wearing the floppy turban, the base signed *Coade London, 1790*, late 18th century, 13in. wide at top.
(Christie's) $2,834

A pair of Louis XV style doors, paneled and carved with trophies including the flaming torch, a cornucopia, a drum and bells, traces of parcel-gilt, late 19th century, 49 x 134¹/₂in.
(Christie's) $3,441

An Istrian marble Corinthian capital, of three sections, 17th/18th century, each section: 32¹/₂in. wide; 22in. high.
(Christie's) $2,024

A monumental William IV carved stone royal coat of arms, inscribed *HONI SOIT QUI MAL Y PENSE*, quartered with the arms of England, Scotland, Ireland and Wales, Irish, circa 1837, 85in. high.
(Christie's) $1,826

A pair of Vicenza stone sea-horses, each carved riding on the 'waves' with scaled fish-like tail, on a rectangular base, 20th century, 31¹/₂in. wide.
(Christie's) $1,518

ARMOR

A WWI tank driver's mask, leather covered metal frame, narrow eye-slits, chinmail mouth guard, chamois lined.
(Wallis & Wallis) $229

A pair of late 18th century copies of gothic gauntlets, very fine throughout.
(Bonhams) $1,020

A right handed elbow gauntlet, circa 1640, probably English, 18$^{1}/_{2}$in. overall, raised medial ridge, roped turned over border, 6 plate articulated back of hand.
(Wallis & Wallis) $641

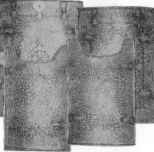

Fine lacquered suit of armor, sixty-two plate kabuto with five-lame shikoro, crescent maedate and gold lacquer kuwagata.
(Skinner Inc.) $17,600

A rare Indian full armor for a man and horse, all finely damascened in gold with scrolling foliage and flower-heads, partly 17th/18th century.
(Christie's) $16,434

A composite German full armor, of bright steel, each cuff struck with the Nuremberg mark, the helmet and gauntlets mid-16th century, the remainder in 16th century style, on wooden figure mounted on a wooden plinth.
(Christie's) $14,608

A 19th century Indian part suit of gold damascened armor, including fluted khulah khud with sliding nasal bar and plume sockets, fabric lined with butted link camail.
(Wallis & Wallis) $1,283

ARMOR

An Italian breast-plate of rounded form with low medial ridge cut off straight at the waist and with a bold angular outward turn at the neck, early 16th century, 25¹/₂in. high. (Christie's) $2,922

A very fine Ottoman gilt-copper chanfron, formed of a single piece of mercury-gilded copper with shaped flange around each nostril, eye and ear, struck with the Ottoman (St. Irene) arsenal mark, second half of the 16th century, 23in. long. (Christie's) $118,690

A rare German 'Maximilian' chanfron, in two halves riveted together horizontally, shaped to the front of the horse's head and decorated with radiating flutes, circa 1520, 24in. long. (Christie's) $17,490

A boldly modeled russet-iron mempo with one-piece nose and fangs (onimen), with a four-lame yodorekake covered in black leather, the facepiece early 16th century, the mounting 17th century. (Christie's) $4,026

A reinforcing plackart, of great weight and flattened form with low medial ridge, single line border to the arms, supplied in 1673, 11¹/₂in. high. (Christie's) $875

An early 19th century officer's steel cuirass of the Household Cavalry, morocco lining and crimped blue velvet edging, leather bound borders and brass studs. (Wallis & Wallis) $2,932

An unusual moyegi-ito-odoshi tosei-gusoku with a fine associated kabuto comprising a sixty-two-plate russet-iron sujibachi, unsigned, probably 18th century. (Christie's) $12,078

A post-1902 Household Cavalry trooper's plated cuirass, leather lining with blue cloth edging, brass bound borders and studs, leather backed brass scales with ornamental ends. (Wallis & Wallis) $779

A German half-chanfron, comprising a single main plate shaped to the front of the horse's head to just above the nostrils, embossed over the eyes, circa 1560, probably Brunswick, 16¹/₂in. long.
(Christie's) $3,498

A German gorget, of exceptionally large size, comprising front and back-plates of bright steel pivoted together, bluntly pointed and struck with Nuremberg mark, early 17th century, 6¹/₂in. high.
(Christie's) $1,735

A rare Gothic falling bevor composed of three plates with medial ridge, the top plate with angular outward turn and released by a spring catch, late 15th century, 13¹/₂in. high.
(Christie's) $1,826

A German burgonet and almain collar from a black and white armor, the former with one-piece four-sided skull drawn up to a point with an acorn finial, circa 1560.
(Christie's) $4,198

An extremely rare Ottoman chanfron, formed of a single piece of steel with a horizontal flange at the top and shaped flanges round the eyes, circa 1517–20, 18³/₄in.
(Christie's) $96,195

A post-1902 Household Cavalry trooper's plated cuirass, leather lining with blue cloth edging, brass bound borders and studs.
(Wallis & Wallis) $1,008

A moyegi-ito-odoshi gold lacquered domaru, comprising a fine russet-iron sixty-two-plate koboshi bachi, the interior gilt, signed *Myochin Shigenobu*, second half 16th century.
(Christie's) $18,519

A good post-1902 major's plated cuirass of the Royal Horse Guards, morocco lining with crimson velvet edging, brass bound borders and studs, shoulder cords and aiguilette.
(Wallis & Wallis) $2,474

CASED SETS

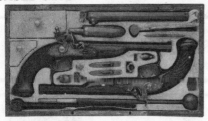

An unusual pair of German target pistols, the locks with interchangeable flint and percussion parts, the interchangeable smooth and rifled rebrowned octagonal sighted barrels signed in full and dated in silver on the top flats, by Franz Ulrich In Stuttgart, dated *1828*, 14½in. long.
(Christie's)   **$5,597**

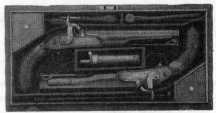

A pair of percussion officer's pistols with browned octagonal sighted barrels signed on the top flats, engraved case-hardened breeches with platinum line and plug, engraved case-hardened tangs, signed engraved case-hardened bolted locks, by Westley Richards, Birmingham proof marks, circa 1850, 13½in. long.
(Christie's)   **$2,973**

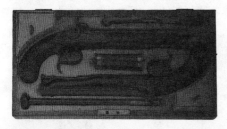

A pair of percussion officer's pistols, converted from flintlock, with browned twist sighted barrels each engraved *London* on the top flat, platinum line, engraved case-hardened tangs, signed case-hardened bolted locks engraved with a trophy of arms on the tails, by Beckwith, London, Birmingham proof marks, early 19th century, 14½in. long.
(Christie's)   **$2,274**

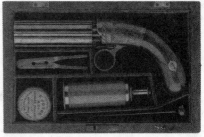

A Blunt & Syms under-hammer six-shot percussion pepperbox revolver with blued fluted barrels, blued rounded action engraved with open scrolling foliage, ring-trigger, figured walnut grips, and much original finish, unsigned, mid-19th century, 7¾in. long.
(Christie's)   **$1,826**

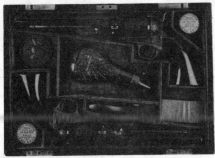

Deluxe engraved cased pair Colt model 1860 army percussion revolvers, .44 caliber, serial numbers 151388 and 151389, 7½in. barrels, marked *Address Col. Saml. Colt New York, U.S. America.*
(Butterfield & Butterfield)   **$286,000**

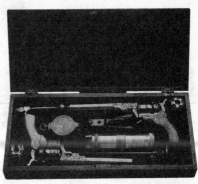

Pair of cased belt Model Paterson revolvers (No. 2), Patent Arms Manufacturing Company, circa 1837–40, serial No. 626 and 678, in untouched condition, engraved *Abraham Bininger*, barrel 5½in. long.
(Skinner Inc.)   **$242,000**

CASED SETS

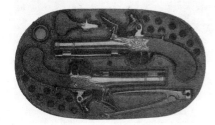

An unusual pair of Flemish flintlock box-lock pistols with brass cannon barrels and actions of one piece, the latter engraved with a floral and musical trophy on each side, thumbpiece safety-catches also locking the steels, early 19th century, 10in. long.
(Christie's) $3,652

A 54-bore Tranter patent five-shot self-cocking percussion revolver, with blued octagonal sighted barrel engraved at the muzzle and breech, the top-strap signed *B. Cogswell, 224 Strand, London*, patent rammer, case-hardened cylinder, London proof marks, 11³/₄in. long.
(Christie's) $2,009

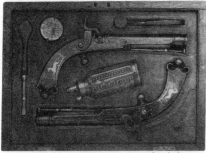

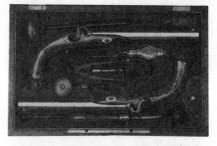

A pair of Highland all-metal percussion belt pistols with reblued three-stage barrels engraved with thistles, engraved faceted breeches, engraved flat locks, engraved stocks inlaid with an engraved silver panel on each side of the fore-end, Birmingham proof marks, mid-19th century, 10in. long.
(Christie's) $3,104

A pair of Continental percussion target pistols with etched twist octagonal polygroove rifled sighted barrels, case-hardened breeches, engraved tangs each with folding back-sight, case-hardened back-action locks, highly figured walnut half-stocks with carved scallop fore-end caps, each pistol stamped *J. Brunel*, mid-19th century, 15³/₄in. long.
(Christie's) $5,247

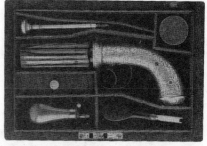

A pair of French percussion target pistols with minor differences, the three-stage partly fluted blued octagonal sighted barrels of hog's back form and rifled with twelve grooves, signed *Fⁿⁱ Par Gastinne Renette à Paris* and numbered 1 and 2 at the case-hardened scroll engraved faceted breeches, second half of the 19th century, 16¹/₂in. long.
(Christie's) $5,478

An unusual self-cocking six-shot percussion pepperbox revolver with reblued fluted barrels engraved at the muzzles and numbered from 1 to 6, by Joseph Wood, Lewes, London proof marks, mid-19th century, 8³/₄in. long.
(Christie's) $3,104

33

CASED SETS

Deluxe cased and engraved Colt model 1860 army percussion revolver with matching shoulder stock, .44 caliber, 8in. barrel marked *Address Col. Samuel Colt, New York, U.S. America.*
(Butterfield & Butterfield) $308,000

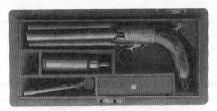

A Belgian Mariette patent four-shot percussion pepperbox revolver with long etched twist turn-off barrels numbered from 1 to 4, case-hardened rounded action engraved with scrolling foliage, signed on top within a bright oval *Ad. Jansens Arq. er du Roi à Bruxelles*, Liège proof mark, circa 1845, 9^{1}/$_{2}$in. long.
(Christie's) $2,191

A rare Colt Hartford-English dragoon percussion revolver, No. 477 for 1853, the blued barrel with New York address, blued cylinder with traces of roll-engraved Texas Ranger and Indian scene, case-hardened frame and rammer, the lid with trade label of *I. Murcott, 68 Haymarket, London*, London proof marks, 14^{1}/$_{4}$in. long.
(Christie's) $11,869

A pair of flintlock dueling pistols with rebrowned octagonal sighted barrels signed in full on the top flat, engraved tangs, gold vents, signed locks with safety-catches, figured walnut full stocks, checkered butts with conventional flower-head pommels, by H.W. Mortimer, London, Gun Maker To His Majesty, circa 1790, 15^{3}/$_{4}$in. long.
(Christie's) $6,122

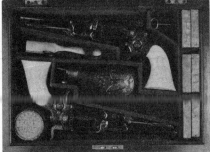

Outstanding cased pair of engraved presentation Colt Root model 1855 percussion revolvers, circa 1863, .31 caliber, 4^{1}/$_{2}$in. barrels marked *Address Col. Colt New York, U.S.A.*
(Butterfield & Butterfield) $220,000

Cased Colt new police 'Cop and Thug' model revolver, British proofed, 4^{1}/$_{2}$in. barrel with two line Pall Mall address, 38 CF caliber, rare nickel finish with blued hammer, checkered hard rubber grips, serial No. 17879.
(Butterfield & Butterfield) $6,050

CASED SETS

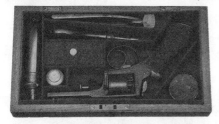

Cased Remington New Model police revolver, serial number 7168, factory converted to .38 rimfire caliber, 3¹/₂in. octagonal barrel marked with Remington address, patent dates and *New Model.*
(Butterfield & Butterfield)   **$8,800**

A scarce 6-shot .455in. Cordite Webley Fosbery automatic cocking revolver number 3159, 10³/₄in. overall, barrel 6in., Birmingham proofs, side of top strap stamped *Webley Fosbery.*
(Wallis & Wallis)   **$2,199**

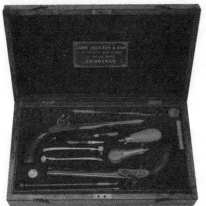

A fine pair of D.B. flintlock pistols with heavy browned twist barrels signed in full on the rib, silver fore-sights, scroll engraved case-hardened breeches and breech tangs, the former with gold vents and the latter also engraved 1 and 2, by John Dickson & Son, 63 Princes Street, Edinburgh, London proof marks, nos. 4590/1 for 1893, 14³/₄in. long.
(Christie's)   **$9,130**

A pair of Royal over-and-under flintlock carriage pistols with rebrowned twist octagonal barrels signed in gold on the top flats and with gold lines at the breeches, gold fore-sights, platinum vents, engraved case-hardened tangs, signed engraved case-hardened locks with blued steel-springs and top jaws, by Durs Egg, No. 132 Strand, London, No, 700, circa 1815, 8³/₄in. long.
(Christie's)   **$13,992**

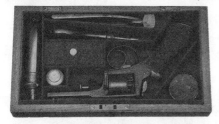

A 5 shot 120 bore model 1851 Adam's patent self cocking percussion revolver made under licence by Francotte of Liege, No. 16851, 8in., octagonal barrel 3¹/₄in. engraved *A. Francotte a Liege.*
(Wallis & Wallis)   **$1,054**

A Colt-Root 1855 model .31 percussion pocket revolver, No. 12864E for 1868, with blued two-stage sighted barrel engraved with London address, in original lined and fitted oak case with full accessories, London proof marks, 9in. long.
(Christie's)   **$7,871**

DAGGERS & KNIVES

A good Victorian silver mounted officer's Scottish dirk, spear point blade 12in., single back fuller, finely corded wood hilt; with plain silver mounts, in its blind tooled leather sheath with silver mounts.
(Wallis & Wallis) $1,250

A good 18th century Persian dagger pesh kabz, 14in. long, recurved T section blade 9¹/₂in., finely watered with raised central rib and edges, applied with shaped device on each side.
(Wallis & Wallis) $769

A good Indian gold damascened dagger pesh kabz circa 1800, 13¹/₂in., finely watered recurved single edged blade 8³/₄in. of dark tight whorled pattern, large steel hilt thickly gold damascened with flowers and foliage in panels and borders, faceted button to pommel.
(Wallis & Wallis) $389

A good late Victorian Bowie knife, pronounced clipped backed blade 8¹/₂in. by J. Rodgers & Sons No. 6 Norfolk St. Sheffield England, oval German silver guard with ball finials, staghorn grips.
(Wallis & Wallis) $248

A good Russian 19th century nielloed silver mounted kindjal, 18¹/₄in., straight polished blade 13in. with deep off set fullers, two piece horn grips, nielloed silver fittings including grip strap and inlaid strips to horn, ornamental rivet heads, back of ferrule with nielloed Arabic inscription.
(Wallis & Wallis) $496

A rare German Hauswehr with heavy single-edged blade curving up to meet the decoratively notched point, struck at the base on one face with two orb and cross marks, iron handle conforming to the shape of the tang and comprising deep rectangular ferrule, early 16th century, 16³/₄in. long
(Christie's) $2,556

A good Victorian Scottish officer's dirk set of the Seaforth Highlanders, scallop back blade 10in., with broad and narrow fullers, retaining all original polish, etched with crown, *V.R.* Thistles, foliage, crown, *"L"*, Elephant "Assaye" and *"Cuidich'n Righ"*.
(Wallis & Wallis) $2,016

DAGGERS & KNIVES

A good 19th century Indo Persian scissors dagger, 10¹/₂in., fluted steel blades gold damascened with foliage, scroll pierced brass handles with traces of gilding.
(Wallis & Wallis) $266

A scarce Nazi NPEA student's dagger, by Karl Burgsmuller, plain hilt with plated mounts, in its bright steel sheath, with K98 type leather frog.
(Wallis & Wallis) $1,374

An Ngombe tribal war knife Welo from Ubangi Province of Zaire, circa 1900, pierced swollen blade 19¹/₂in. with geometric tooled ribs and 2 copper inlays, brass and copper wound wooden hilt with leather covered pommel.
(Wallis & Wallis) $664

A fine quality 18th century Indo-Persian dagger pesh kabz, 13³/₄in., recurved blade 9in. of hollow ground T section, finely watered dark kirk nardaban pattern, fluted back edge, thickened armor piercing top.
(Wallis & Wallis) $1,054

A Nazi Luftwaffe officer's 2nd Pattern dagger, by Eickhorn, gray metal mounts, silver wire bound yellow grip, in its gray metal sheath with original bullion dress knot and hanging straps.
(Wallis & Wallis) $319

A Nazi naval officer's dirk, by Eickhorn, blade etched with fouled anchor, entwined dolphins, and foliage, brass mounts, brass wire bound white celluloid grip, in its brass sheath.
(Wallis & Wallis) $211

A fine quality Japanese dagger tanto, blade 28.7cm., signed *Mito Yokoyama Suke Mitsu*, dated Meiji 2nd year (= 1869 A.D.), unokubizukuri, gunome hamon, bold nie, itame hada.
(Wallis & Wallis) $4,123

ARMS & ARMOR

An early 19th century Afghan khyber knife, "T" section blade 27in. with narrow fullers, faceted steel ferrules with gold damascened flowers and foliage, gripstrap gold damascened with Persian inscriptions, large 2-piece ivory grips.
(Wallis & Wallis) **$161**

A bowie style hunting knife circa 1900, broad straight blade 9³/₄in. with false edge, stamped *Singleton & Priestman Sheffield*, natural staghorn grip.
(Wallis & Wallis) **$246**

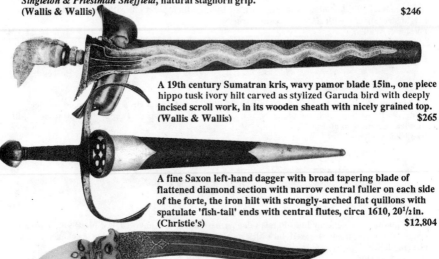

A 19th century Sumatran kris, wavy pamor blade 15in., one piece hippo tusk ivory hilt carved as stylized Garuda bird with deeply incised scroll work, in its wooden sheath with nicely grained top.
(Wallis & Wallis) **$265**

A fine Saxon left-hand dagger with broad tapering blade of flattened diamond section with narrow central fuller on each side of the forte, the iron hilt with strongly-arched flat quillons with spatulate 'fish-tail' ends with central flutes, circa 1610, 20¹/₂in.
(Christie's) **$12,804**

An Indian khanjar with finely watered recurved double-edged blade with three gold-damascened lines over nearly its entire length on both sides, the forte chiseled in low relief on each side with arabesques and flowering foliage, 18th/19th century, 15³/₄in. long.
(Christie's) **$8,217**

A good 19th century silver mounted Moro sword barong, swollen single edged heavy blade 19in., hilt of nicely shaped form of iridescent grained wood, large silver ferrule.
(Wallis & Wallis) **$189**

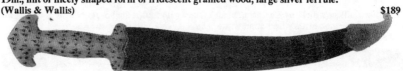

An Indian dagger with watered slightly curved double-edged blade cut with lines forming ridges along its entire lengths on both sides, mutton-fat jade hilt with fish-tail pommel and swelling grip, 19th century, 16¹/₂in. long.
(Christie's) **$6,391**

DAGGERS & KNIVES

A 19th century Russian nielloed silver mounted kindjal, 18¼in., broad double edged tri fullered blade 11½in., deeply struck with maker's name in Cyrillic. Silver hilt with ornament filigree rivet heads, silver wire work borders nielloed with foliage and arabesques.
(Wallis & Wallis) $567

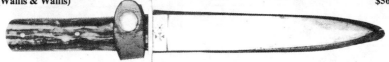

A bowie type hunting knife, straight tapered double edged blade 6¾in., stamped *J Rodgers & Sons No 6 Norfolk St Sheffield England* with GR and crown, and makers stamps.
(Wallis & Wallis) $95

A silver mounted Burmese dagger dha, blade 8¼in., one piece octagonal ivory hilt, sheet silver ferrule and sheath with filigree bands.
(Wallis & Wallis) $113

A good 17th century Indian Moghul inlaid thrusting dagger katar, 14¾in., double edged blade 8½in., with swollen tip and raised ribs, steel hilt with swollen grip bars and flared wings, inlaid overall with copper gilt flowers and foliage chiseled in relief.
(Wallis & Wallis) $387

An Indian dagger with watered slight curved double-edged blade reinforced towards the point, rock-crystal hilt decorated with shaped gold panels set with green foiled cabochon gems, probably 17th century, 12in. long.
(Christie's) $1,607

An unusual and good quality late 19th century English hunting knife in the form of an Eastern dagger, by Hill & Son, London, heavy recurved single edged blade 12in. with narrow fuller and bowie style tip.
(Wallis & Wallis) $454

A Spanish 1889 pattern naval boarding knife, recurving blade 10in., etched at forte *Artilleria Fabrica De Toledo 1881*, brass hilt, short crosspiece shaped ribbed grip, in its brass mounted leather sheath.
(Wallis & Wallis) $483

HELMETS

A close-helmet with one-piece skull with high roped comb, pointed visor with single vision-slit and lifting peg, circa 1560, probably Italian, 11¾in. high.
(Christie's) $13,695

A North Italian 'Spanish' morion, in one piece, with skull rising to a stalk, the base encircled by a row of brass lining rivets with rosette-shaped washers, late 16th century, 11½in. high.
(Christie's) $10,243

A cuirassier helmet, of bright steel, with fluted ovoidal two-piece skull rising to a ring finial on star-shaped rosette, early 17th century, probably German, 12in. high.
(Christie's) $4,055

A composite German ('Maximilian') close helmet with one-piece globular fluted skull cut out at the back for one plain and two fluted neck-plates, early 16th century, 12in. high.
(Christie's) $7,256

A burgonet, the two-piece skull with roped comb, riveted pointed fall, single riveted neck-plate and deep hinged cheek-pieces, mid-17th century, German or Dutch, 10¼in. high.
(Christie's) $787

A German foot-combat close-helmet with one-piece skull with low file-roped comb, brass plume-holder, bluntly pointed visor and upper and lower bevors pivoted at the same points on either side, circa 1630, 12½in. high.
(Christie's) $12,804

An Imperial Austrian army officers shako, black patent leather crown and peak, black cloth covered body with yellow cloth band, gilt brass Imperial eagle.
(Wallis & Wallis) $367

A Prussian Mounted Rifles other ranks helmet, a wartime issue in grey metal skull fitted with eagle plate, top spike, roundels, leather chinstrap, dated 1916.
(Phillips) $644

A post-1902 royal Horse Guards trooper's helmet, plated steel skull with brass plate applied with garter star, plume holder with red horsehair plume.
(Phillips) $988

HELMETS

An Italian 'Spanish morion' of one piece, with tall pointed skull surmounted by a stalk, encircled at the base by holes for lining rivets, circa 1580, 7½in. high.
(Christie's) $1,826

An Argentinian Cavalry trooper's helmet, the steel skull with brass fittings including Argentine arms front plate, comb embossed with foliage and head of Minerva.
(Phillips)   *'* $573

A sallet of great weight, made from a single piece, the rounded skull with low keel-shaped comb pierced for a crest-holder, perhaps 15th century Italian, 9in. high.
(Christie's) $5,478

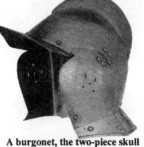

A Saxon Electoral Guard comb morion, of one piece, with roped comb and brim, the base of the skull encircled by sixteen gilt-brass lion-masks capping the lining rivets, the brim struck with the Nuremberg mark, circa 1580, 11¾in. high.
(Christie's) $23,474

A burgonet, the two-piece skull with roped comb, riveted pointed fall, single riveted neck-plate and deep hinged cheek-pieces, painted inside *SO 87*, mid-17th century, German or Dutch, 10½in. high.
(Christie's) $1,049

A post 1902 RAMC Captain's uniform, comprising blue cloth ball topped helmet, shoulder belt and pouch; full dress blue tunic, mess jacket with matching dull cherry waistcoat and pair breeches.
(Wallis & Wallis) $1,134

A very rare Milanese sallet, of one piece, the rounded skull arched over the face, with low-keel-shaped comb, short pointed tail and narrow outward turn along the lower edge, late 15th century, 10¾in. high.
(Christie's) $34,980

A French 3rd Republic Cuirassier officer's helmet, the silver plated skull with gilt fittings including front plate embossed with foliage and flaming grenade.
(Phillips) $1,253

An Imperial German Hesse Infantry officer's Pickelhaube gilt helmet plate, leather backed chinscales and mounts, fluted spike, both cockades, leather and silk lining.
(Wallis & Wallis) $890

HELMETS

An Imperial German Prussian Landwehr OR's shako (re issued M 1866 pattern) oval metal badge in state colors with Landwehr cross.
(Wallis & Wallis) $348

A Cromwellian lobster tail helmet, ribbed skull with suspension loop, the peak with traces of armorer's mark and initial *F*, sliding nasal bar.
(Wallis & Wallis) $1,191

A Victorian officer's blue cloth ball topped helmet of The R. Artillery, gilt mounts, velvet backed chinchain and ear rosettes.
(Wallis & Wallis) $385

A good Victorian officer's silver plated helmet of the Royal Horse Guards, gilt peak binding, ornaments, top mount, leather backed graduated link chinchain and simple-petal ear rosettes.
(Wallis & Wallis) $4,215

A close burgonet, the heavy two-piece rounded skull with low rolled-over comb with iron plume-pipe at the base containing an iron candlestick nozzle, circa 1630, probably Dutch, 15in. high.
(Christie's) $2,099

A post 1902 officer's silver plated helmet of The Life Guards, gilt peak bindings and ornaments, silver plated spike, gilt and silver plated helmet plate with good red and blue enameled center.
(Wallis & Wallis) $2,535

A good officer's bearskin of the Irish Guards, St. Patrick's blue feather plume, velvet backed graduated link gilt chinchain.
(Wallis & Wallis) $779

A Victorian officer's lance cap of the 16th (The Queen's) Lancers, black patent leather skull, blue cloth sides and top, embroidered peak, gilt lace trim and cords.
(Wallis & Wallis) $2,566

A good post 1902 OR's white metal helmet of the Royal Horse Guards, brass peak binding and mounts, leather backed chinchain and ear rosettes.
(Wallis & Wallis) $1,080

HELMETS

A Prussian Infantry NCO's Pickelhaube, brass helmet plate and mounts, leather backed brass chinscales.
(Wallis & Wallis) $458

A Cromwellian lobster tail steel helmet, the skull with six flutes, four piece articulated neck lames with large steel rivets.
(Spencer's) $1,382

A post 1902 officer's full dress uniform of a Territorial Bn. The Queen's (R. West Surrey) Regt., comprising: blue cloth spiked helmet, scarlet tunic, and pair overalls.
(Wallis & Wallis) $660

A Victorian OR's Albert pattern white metal helmet of the 1st (Royal) Dragoons, brass mounts, leather backed chinchain and large ear rosettes, brass helmet plate, black hair plume with brass rosette.
(Wallis & Wallis) $1,100

A Civil War steel helmet, with peaked hinged visor applied with large brass rivets, a single ridge to the skull extending down to a single socket plume holder.
(Spencer's) $1,472

A good Victorian officer's silver plated helmet of the Hertfordshire Yeomanry, gilt ornaments, top mount and spike, velvet backed chinchain and large ear rosettes.
(Wallis & Wallis) $1,833

A Victorian officer's silver plated helmet of the 1st (Royal) Dragoons with gilt peak binding, mounts, ball and spike, red leather backed chinchain and ear rosettes.
(Wallis & Wallis) $2,199

An officer's 1817 pattern steel helmet of the Household Cavalry, brass binding to front and rear peaks, skull embellished with acanthus foliage.
(Wallis & Wallis) $7,330

An officer's fur busby of the 19th (Queen Alexandra's Own) Royal Hussars, triple gilt cord, gilt gimp cockade, white busby bag with gilt braid trim and purl button.
(Wallis & Wallis) $1,741

A fine Collier patent second model five-shot flintlock revolver,
No. 89, with octagonal browned twist sighted barrel signed and
engraved with scrollwork on the sighting rib and fitted with
engraved case-hardened patent priming magazine with roller, by
E.H. Collier, London, circa 1825, 14¼in. long.
(Christie's) $18,260

A fine Saxon wheel-lock holster pistol of the Trabantan Guard,
with three-stage barrel retaining traces of original blue and
struck with a mark (New Støckel 5422) at the breech, plain lock-
plate with traces of color, engraved gilt-brass wheel-cover, the
safety-catch spring and dog incised with scrolls, late 16th century,
24¾in. long.
(Christie's) $20,988

A 24-bore Tower Heavy Dragoon flintlock holster pistol to the
3rd Dragoon Guards, 18½in. overall, barrel 12in. with Tower
proofs and engraved *3d D. Gds*, rounded lock with swan-neck
cock, the plate engraved with crowned *GR* and *Tower*, walnut
full-stocked with 1780 ordnance mark on butt.
(Wallis & Wallis) $1,649

Rare and unique cased Colt Paterson belt model percussion
revolver, engraved and silver banded, .34 caliber, 4⅝in. barrel
marked *Patent Arms M'g Co. Paterson N.J. Colts Pt.*
(Butterfield & Butterfield) $770,000

A rare German repeating air pistol on the Girandoni system,
with octagonal barrel rifled with six grooves, later folding rear-
sight, the breech with sliding transverse breech-block and
octagonal steel magazine mounted on the right, Mainz, mid-19th
century, 14¾in. long.
(Christie's) $1,574

Historic Colt Whitneyville Walker model 1847 Dragoon
percussion revolver, .44 caliber, 9in. half round octagon barrel
marked *Address Sam'l Colt, New York City* and *U.S. 1847* over
wedge.
(Butterfield & Butterfield) $275,000

PISTOLS

A very rare French long wheel-lock holster pistol with slender two-stage barrel with a ribbed molding at the muzzle and stepped breech, the rear section fluted and struck with a mark, full-length border engraved tang, flat lock of French form with chamfered borders, struck with maker's mark *HF*, circa 1600–10, probably Sedan, 32¾in.
(Christie's) $51,128

Rare Colt single action new army revolver, caliber 41, 6in. barrel marked *Colt D.A. 41* on left side, blued finish, walnut grips, serial No. 1, produced in the 1890s.
(Butterfield & Butterfield) $8,800

A very rare Bohemian flintlock three-shot revolving pistol with sighted barrel, three hand-rotated steel chambers each fitted with a pan and steel, and locked by a spring-catch with trigger-guard release, unsigned, circa 1740, 19in. long.
(Christie's) $4,748

A superbly decorated matchlock gun, the russet iron octagonal barrel fitted with a set sight on the peep line and a bar sight on the flared muzzle which also bears five gilt applied Tokugawa aoimon, signed *Kunitomo Heiji Shigetoshi, working in Omi*, and dated *March 1820*, late 19th century.
(Christie's) $70,455

Rare Collier patent flintlock revolver, circa 1824, .48 caliber, 8¼in. brown octagonal barrel engraved with military motifs, signed *E.H. Collier London*, and fitted with priming magazine.
(Butterfield & Butterfield) $44,000

A rare Flemish four-barrel turn-over flintlock box-lock pistol with rifled turn-off cannon barrels released by the trigger-guard, border engraved action decorated with flowers and foliage on each side and inscribed *Segallas London*, late 18th century, 10⅜in. long.
(Christie's) $1,461

45

ARMS & ARMOR

A Colt 1851 model navy percussion revolver, No. 204033 for
1868, the octagonal sighted barrel with New York address,
cylinder with naval engagement scene, brass trigger-guard and
back-strap, 13in. long.
(Christie's) $1,242

A good brass framed brass barreled boxlock flintlock
blunderbuss pistol with bayonet by Waters circa 1790, of the type
favored by Naval officers, 13in., swollen barrel 7in. with
reinforced muzzle, Tower proved.
(Wallis & Wallis) $1,695

One of a pair of double barreled flintlock box-lock pistols with
plain barrels each engraved with a foliate band at the muzzles,
border engraved actions signed in full and engraved with a
trophy of flags to one side, by Bennett, Royal Exchange, London,
Birmingham private proof marks, Birmingham silver hallmarks
for 1791, maker's mark of Charles Freeth, 10³/₄in. long.
(Christie's)   (Two) $2,624

A Spanish miquelet-lock belt pistol the two-stage barrel with
turned girdle and molded muzzle, the forward stage with raised
rib and engraved with flower-heads and foliage, plain patilla
lock, wooden full stock entirely covered with brass embossed and
chased with scrolling foliage of Moorish design, circa 1700,
almost certainly Ripoll, 12¹/₂in. long.
(Christie's) $4,897

A rare Viennese repeating air pistol on the Girandoni system
with swamped twist octagonal multigroove rifled sighted barrel
signed in silver, the breech inlaid with silver foliage and with
sliding transverse breech-block and silver-inlaid tubular steel
magazine on the right, signed *Joseph Oesterleinsche Fabrique*,
mid-19th century, 11¹/₄in. long.
(Christie's) $2,739

A rare Nuremberg self-spanning wheel-lock officer's pistol with
iron barrel turned and molded at the muzzle, flat beveled lock
(dog replaced) struck on the inside with Nuremberg mark and
maker's mark *CR*, circa 1620–30, 24¹/₂in. long.
(Christie's) $3,323

PISTOLS

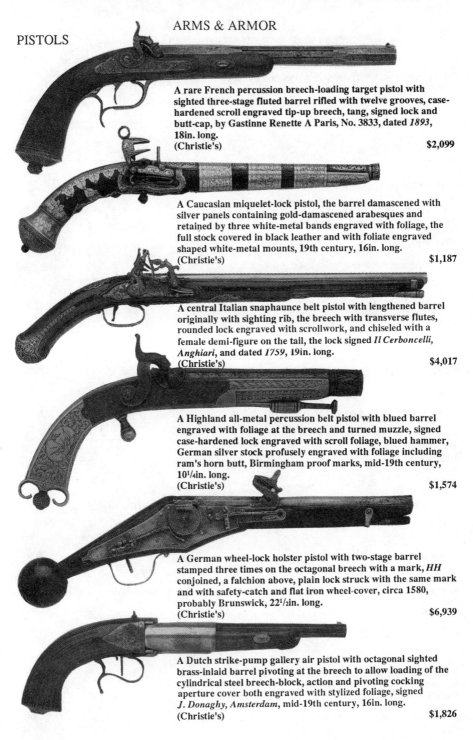

A rare French percussion breech-loading target pistol with
sighted three-stage fluted barrel rifled with twelve grooves, case-
hardened scroll engraved tip-up breech, tang, signed lock and
butt-cap, by Gastinne Renette A Paris, No. 3833, dated *1893*,
18in. long.
(Christie's)   **$2,099**

A Caucasian miquelet-lock pistol, the barrel damascened with
silver panels containing gold-damascened arabesques and
retained by three white-metal bands engraved with foliage, the
full stock covered in black leather and with foliate engraved
shaped white-metal mounts, 19th century, 16in. long.
(Christie's)   **$1,187**

A central Italian snaphaunce belt pistol with lengthened barrel
originally with sighting rib, the breech with transverse flutes,
rounded lock engraved with scrollwork, and chiseled with a
female demi-figure on the tail, the lock signed *Il Cerboncelli,
Anghiari*, and dated *1759*, 19in. long.
(Christie's)   **$4,017**

A Highland all-metal percussion belt pistol with blued barrel
engraved with foliage at the breech and turned muzzle, signed
case-hardened lock engraved with scroll foliage, blued hammer,
German silver stock profusely engraved with foliage including
ram's horn butt, Birmingham proof marks, mid-19th century,
10¼in. long.
(Christie's)   **$1,574**

A German wheel-lock holster pistol with two-stage barrel
stamped three times on the octagonal breech with a mark, *HH*
conjoined, a falchion above, plain lock struck with the same mark
and with safety-catch and flat iron wheel-cover, circa 1580,
probably Brunswick, 22½in. long.
(Christie's)   **$6,939**

A Dutch strike-pump gallery air pistol with octagonal sighted
brass-inlaid barrel pivoting at the breech to allow loading of the
cylindrical steel breech-block, action and pivoting cocking
aperture cover both engraved with stylized foliage, signed
J. Donaghy, Amsterdam, mid-19th century, 16in. long.
(Christie's)   **$1,826**

PISTOLS

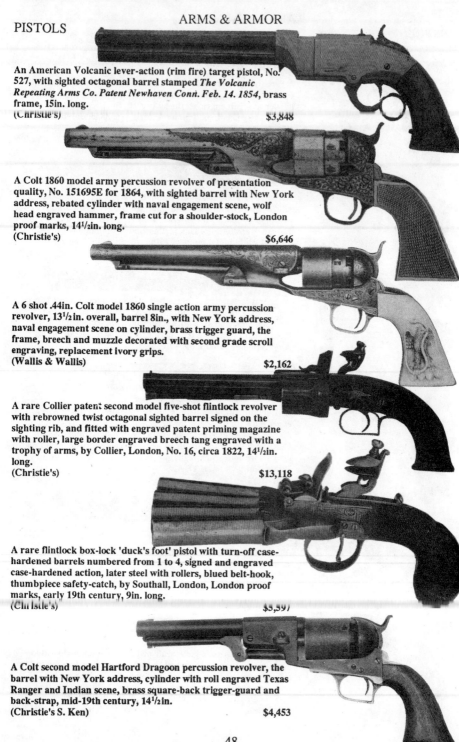

An American Volcanic lever-action (rim fire) target pistol, No. 527, with sighted octagonal barrel stamped *The Volcanic Repeating Arms Co. Patent Newhaven Conn. Feb. 14. 1854*, brass frame, 15in. long.
(Christie's) $3,848

A Colt 1860 model army percussion revolver of presentation quality, No. 151695E for 1864, with sighted barrel with New York address, rebated cylinder with naval engagement scene, wolf head engraved hammer, frame cut for a shoulder-stock, London proof marks, 14^{1}/$_{2}$in. long.
(Christie's) $6,646

A 6 shot .44in. Colt model 1860 single action army percussion revolver, 13^{1}/$_{2}$in. overall, barrel 8in., with New York address, naval engagement scene on cylinder, brass trigger guard, the frame, breech and muzzle decorated with second grade scroll engraving, replacement ivory grips.
(Wallis & Wallis) $2,162

A rare Collier patent second model five-shot flintlock revolver with rebrowned twist octagonal sighted barrel signed on the sighting rib, and fitted with engraved patent priming magazine with roller, large border engraved breech tang engraved with a trophy of arms, by Collier, London, No. 16, circa 1822, 14^{1}/$_{2}$in. long.
(Christie's) $13,118

A rare flintlock box-lock 'duck's foot' pistol with turn-off case-hardened barrels numbered from 1 to 4, signed and engraved case-hardened action, later steel with rollers, blued belt-hook, thumbpiece safety-catch, by Southall, London, London proof marks, early 19th century, 9in. long.
(Christie's) $3,597

A Colt second model Hartford Dragoon percussion revolver, the barrel with New York address, cylinder with roll engraved Texas Ranger and Indian scene, brass square-back trigger-guard and back-strap, mid-19th century, 14^{1}/$_{2}$in.
(Christie's S. Ken) $4,453

POWDER FLASKS

19th century Norwegian powder horn with chased decoration and lid in the form of a mythical beast, 18.5cm. long.
(Auktionsverket) $418

An Italian all-steel powder-flask of curved faceted conical form with tapering two-stage nozzle octagonal at the base, curved into belt hook, early 17th century, 9³/₄in. long.
(Christie's) $1,187

An all-steel combined priming-flask and wheel-lock spanner with curved body flattened on one side, 17th century, probably German, 6³/₄in. long.
(Christie's) $1,187

An embossed copper three horses heads gun sized powder flask 8¹/₄in., G&JW Hawksley common white metal top with nozzle graduated 2¹/₄–3 drams.
(Wallis & Wallis) $250

A copper bodied 3 way flask, 4³/₄in. overall, fixed nozzle, blued spring, hinged cover for balls, screw on base cap.
(Wallis & Wallis) $150

An embossed copper pistol flask, 5¹/₂in., body with shaped foliate design, patent brass top stamped *Fred Griffiths Patent, Late T Collins*, adjustable nozzle.
(Wallis & Wallis) $213

A scarce copper powder flask embossed as entwined dolphins, 8¹/₄in. long, twin steel hanging rings, common brass top stamped *Bartram & Co.*, nozzle graduated from 2–2¹/₂ drams.
(Wallis & Wallis) $550

A Continental silver-mounted priming-flask, with brass mounts, and four rings for suspension, early 18th century, possibly Dutch, 4¹/₄in. long.
(Christie's) $1,096

A brass mounted military gunner's priming horn circa 1820, 9¹/₂in., sprung brass charger with lever, brass end cap with unscrewable base for filling.
(Wallis & Wallis) $239

An engraved map powderhorn, inscribed and dated *Joseph Clayton, 1761*, decorated with British arms above the inscription *New Yorke*, 11³/₄in. long.
(Christie's) $5,280

Engraved powder horn, Bolton, Massachusetts, dated 1874 inscribed *Albert J. Houghton Bolton, Mass. Feb. 27 1874* 15in. long.
(Skinner Inc.) $400

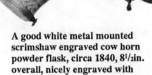

A good white metal mounted scrimshaw engraved cow horn powder flask, circa 1840, 8¹/₂in. overall, nicely engraved with very early steam train, line engraved with adjustable nozzle.
(Wallis & Wallis) $266

49

A 10 bore Volunteer Brown Bess flintlock musket by D. Egg, 55in. overall, barrel 39in. with Tower private proofs, rounded lock with swan neck cock, the plate with line engraved border, walnut fullstock with regulation brass mounts.
(Wallis & Wallis) $1,008

Elaborate silver mounted German or Austrian double barrel tube-lock percussion fowling gun, early 19th century, 30in. two stage 20 gauge barrels with gilt muzzles, sight rib and polygonal breech section, balance blued.
(Butterfield & Butterfield) $17,600

A .577in. Volunteer Enfield 2 band percussion rifle, 48¾in. overall, barrel 33in. with Tower proof, plain lock with engraved date *1859*, walnut stock with steel barrel bands and mounts, steel ramrod, sling swivels.
(Wallis & Wallis) $708

Rare iron frame Henry rifle, caliber 44 RF, 24in. barrel with fifteen shot tubular magazine, cleaning rod in butt, blued finish, walnut stock, serial No. 192.
(Butterfield & Butterfield) $34,100

Rare Winchester 'One of One Hundred' model 1873 rifle, caliber 44–40, 24½in. octagonal barrel, first type with mortised dust cover, engraved and banded on breech and muzzle, top of barrel engraved *One of One Hundred*, deluxe checkered stock and forearm, made in 1876.
(Butterfield & Butterfield) $60,500

Winchester model 1876 rifle, second model, caliber 50 express (50–95), 26in. round barrel with half magazine, blued finish, case hardened frame, forecap and lever, checkered deluxe stock and forearm, shot gun butt, standard address, serial No. 9901, made in 1880. (Butterfield & Butterfield)   £9,400 $16,500

A Norwegian 14 bore Scheel breech loading underhammer military percussion rifle of Larsen type, 49^{1}/$_{2}$in. overall, barrel 30^{1}/$_{4}$in., the breech stamped with crowned *K* and dated *1860*. (Wallis & Wallis)   **$686**

Volcanic carbine, manufactured by New Haven Arms Company, caliber 38, 16^{1}/$_{2}$in. octagonal barrel, blued finish unengraved brass frame and butt plate, walnut stock, case hardened hammer, blued lever, serial No. 86. (Butterfield & Butterfield)   **$23,100**

A very fine 22 bore German flintlock sporting rifle by Christianus Wolff of Ulm dated 1685, 46^{1}/$_{4}$in., stamped octagonal browned barrel 31in., stamped (CH), *Ristianus*Wolff*VLM** and engraved **1685**, engraved standing open sight. (Wallis & Wallis)   **$3,665**

A 26 bore Kurdish miquelet flintlock rifle, 19th century, 38in., swamped octagonal barrel 36in., fullstocked, lock with some engraved silver inlay silver faced and engraved bridle, button trigger. (Wallis & Wallis)   **$1,484**

Rare historic engraved first model Colt Lightning saddle ring carbine, serial number 3543, .44 caliber, 20in. barrel with carbine sight and marked with early Hartford address, sliding safety lock in trigger guard bow, frame, tangs, trigger guard and butt plate scroll-panel engraved by Cuno Helfricht. (Butterfield & Butterfield)   **$52,250**

Rare Colt double rifle, caliber 45–70, 28in. round side by side barrels, double trigger and double hammer, case hardened frame, hammers and butt plate with brown damascus finish on barrels, oil stained checkered walnut stock and forearm, blued trigger guard, lever and rear and front sight. (Butterfield & Butterfield)   **$20,900**

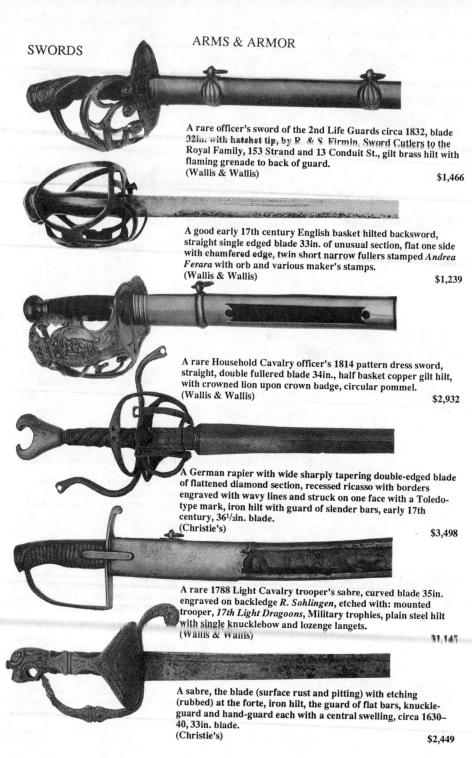

A rare officer's sword of the 2nd Life Guards circa 1832, blade 32in. with hatchet tip, by R. & S. Firmin, Sword Cutlers to the Royal Family, 153 Strand and 13 Conduit St., gilt brass hilt with flaming grenade to back of guard.
(Wallis & Wallis) $1,466

A good early 17th century English basket hilted backsword, straight single edged blade 33in. of unusual section, flat one side with chamfered edge, twin short narrow fullers stamped *Andrea Ferara* with orb and various maker's stamps.
(Wallis & Wallis) $1,239

A rare Household Cavalry officer's 1814 pattern dress sword, straight, double fullered blade 34in., half basket copper gilt hilt, with crowned lion upon crown badge, circular pommel.
(Wallis & Wallis) $2,932

A German rapier with wide sharply tapering double-edged blade of flattened diamond section, recessed ricasso with borders engraved with wavy lines and struck on one face with a Toledo-type mark, iron hilt with guard of slender bars, early 17th century, 36½in. blade.
(Christie's) $3,498

A rare 1788 Light Cavalry trooper's sabre, curved blade 35in. engraved on backledge *R. Sohlingen*, etched with: mounted trooper, *17th Light Dragoons*, Military trophies, plain steel hilt with single knucklebow and lozenge langets.
(Wallis & Wallis) $1,145

A sabre, the blade (surface rust and pitting) with etching (rubbed) at the forte, iron hilt, the guard of flat bars, knuckle-guard and hand-guard each with a central swelling, circa 1630–40, 33in. blade.
(Christie's) $2,449

An interesting Georgian experimental naval boarding cutlass circa 1820, broad straight single edged 28¹/₂in. with crowned *GR* 3 inspector's stamp and government disposal marks, boat shaped steel guard stamped *BO* with broad arrow, pierced twice with diamond shaped brass label.
(Wallis & Wallis)
$549

An EIIR RAF officer's dress sword, blade 32in., by Wilkinson Sword, retaining much original polish, etched with Royal Arms, blank scrolls and laurel sprays, gilt hilt, with royal cypher, eagle's head pommel, original bullion dress knot, gilt wire bound white fishskin covered grip.
(Wallis & Wallis)
$389

A scarce 2nd Life Guards officer's dress sword circa 1832, plain blade 40in., brass hilt, scrolled guard, flaming grenade to pommel and reverse of guard, brass wire bound grip, associated bullion dress knot, in its steel scabbard with brass suspension ring mounts. (Wallis & Wallis)
$974

A 19th century Ngombe tribal executioner's sword, Mbulu, from Ubangi Province, iron blade 21in. with sickle shaped bottom section, simple decoration, double wooden baluster grip with iron band bound base mount.
(Wallis & Wallis)
$177

A fine German combined hunting sword and flintlock pistol with straight tapering blade of flattened diamond section, flat disc guard of copper with engraved borders on the inner side, two-stage barrel chiselled on top of the breech with symmetrical scrollwork, by Picart a Freudenthal, early 18th century, 23³/₄in. blade.
(Christie's)
$10,956

A Turkish shamshir with curved single-edged blade with blunt yelman and cut with two deep fullers within lines on both sides, the forte struck on one side with the Mamluk (St. Irene) arsenal mark, the hilt and scabbard 19th century, the blade circa 1501–1516, 33in. blade.
(Christie's)
$29,733

TSUBAS

An inome-ni aoigata migakiji tsuba, cherryblossom and clouds in gilt nunomezogan, unsigned, Awa Shoami or Sendai school, 19th century, 8cm.
(Christie's)　　　$1,610

A large kyo-sukashi tsuba of stylized chrysanthemum form, 17th century, 8.8cm.
(Christie's)　　　$1,308

A mokko sentoku tsuba, the ishimeji cushioned plate decorated with a bell cricket and gilt vine leaves in takazogan, 18th century, 7.2cm.
(Christie's)　　　$1,207

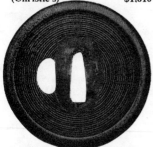

A rare Muromachi Period circular bronze kagamishi (mirror-makers) tsuba, with kozuka-hitsu, early 15th century, 7.2cm., in wood box with descriptive hakogati by Sasano Masayuki.
(Christie's)　　　$3,220

A rounded-rectangular iron yakite-shitate tsuba with radiating spokes and bekko pattern, the wide shallow rim with a long-eared rabbit, bird and paulownia designs, signed Naoaki, mid 19th century, 8.6cm.
(Christie's)　　　$1,409

A rare Muromachi Period oval yamagane ko-kinko tsuba, the plate with a simple punched pattern, late 15th/early 16th century, 6.7cm., in wood box with descriptive hakogati by Sasano Masayuki.
(Christie's)　　　$1,409

An oval dark shibuichi migakiji tsuba, takabori and iroe takazogan, Yoritomo hiding in a hollow tree and Kagetoki driving out two wood pigeons, signed Shojuken Hamano Haruteru, 19th century, 6.9cm.
(Christie's)　　　$1,505

An aorigata iron tsuba, decorated in takabori and iroe takazogan with the Chinese Emperor Meiko watching his ghostly protector Shoki, signed Katsunobu, late 19th century, 9.1cm.
(Christie's)　　　$1,881

A futatsu-mokkogata tsuba, sentoku with leaves inlaid in gilt and shakudo hirazogan, applied shibuichi rim, signed Kataoka Tachibana Tadayoshi (Shoami school), worked in Kyoto, circa 1716-35, 7.5cm.
(Christie's)　　　$7,649

TSUBAS

An otafukumokkogata tsuba, a hat and bag in shinchu takazogan, signed *Yatsushiro Jingo saku*, 1746–1823, 7.4cm. (Christie's)　　　　$846

A broad oval iron migakiji tsuba, kirimon scattered inside a scrolling ropework border in gilt nunomezogan, unsigned, Edo Higo style, circa 1850. (Christie's)　　　　$1,007

A circular iron heianjozogan tsuba with brass inlay forming a circle of chrysanthemum clumps, 17th century, 8.6cm. (Christie's)　　　　$564

A lacquer tsuba decorated in Shibayama style and gold and silver hiramakie on a kinji ground with birds among tree peony and a fallen fisherman losing his eels, late 19th century, 10cm. wide. (Christie's)　　　　$4,703

A broad oval sentoku tsuchimeji tsuba, marumimi, grapevine and trellis in shakudo hirazogan, signed *Hisanori*, 18th century, 8.4cm. (Christie's)　　　　$12,078

A circular shakudo-nanakoji tsuba, the face with six sunk roundels containing flowers in shishiaibori, decorated in similar style on the reverse, unsigned, Goto school, 17th century, 7.4cm. (Christie's)　　　　$2,415

An otafuku-mokkogata shakudo migakiji tsuba on omote, shibuichi on ura, copper, gilt and silver hirazogan and takazogan, signed *Kakusensai Yoshimune* and *Kao*, late 19th century, 7cm. (Christie's)　　　　$4,026

A large rounded square mi-parti tsuba of iron and rogin, iroe hirazogan and takazogan, the migakiji iron plate decorated with the ceremony of Setsubun on the eve of Risshun, late 19th century, wood box, 8.5cm. (Christie's)　　　　$6,240

A hachimokkogata iron migakiji tsuba decorated in silver and gilt nunomezogan with chrysanthemum flowers, unsigned, Awa Shoami or Sendai style, 19th century, 7.5cm. (Christie's)　　　　$1,409

ARMS & ARMOR

WEAPONS

A 17th century polearm partizan, head 9³/₄in. including baluster turned socket, side wings with shaped edges, raised central rib and swollen tip.
(Wallis & Wallis) $204

A good and unusual 19th century Indian axe zaghnal, 25in., thick heavy steel head 10³/₄in. including pagoda finial, pierced with foliate sides and a little silver damascened ornament.
(Wallis & Wallis) $283

A massive and rare 19th century Hindu sacrificial axe, probably from Chota Nagpur, 41in., moustache shaped blade 23in., central column applied with brass device of trisula upon mound with flag.
(Wallis & Wallis) $92

A halberd, with very long tapering spike of stiff diamond section, flat crescentic axe-blade pierced with key-hole shaped holes, two long straps, and wooden staff, late 16th century, probably German or Swiss, 34in. head.
(Christie's) $525

A fine 19th century Indian steel axe, 30in., blade of elephant's ear form 10in. finely pierced with a tiger springing onto two elephants in silhouette, thickly silver damascened overall with foliate and geometric ornaments.
(Wallis & Wallis) $354

A good 18th century Rajput gold and silver damascened elephant goad Ankus, 22in., cagework haft gold and silver damascened and filled with small bells, broad top spike and hook, baluster neck with swollen pommel.
(Wallis & Wallis)   0779

A very rare German combined four-barreled matchlock gun, mace and spear with wooden cylindrical head stained black and containing four iron barrels, bound on the outside with three iron bands, circa 1600, 34in. long.
(Christie's) $9,130

56

WEAPONS

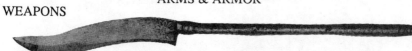

An all steel Indian axe Bhuj, 28in., recurved swollen watered blade 11in., chiselled with palmette at forte, steel haft.
(Wallis & Wallis) $220

An early 18th century partizan, head 9¼in. with slightly thickened tip, baluster socket, on later brass studded wooden haft with elaborate silk tassels woven around gilt octagonal ferrule.
(Wallis & Wallis) $230

A 19th century Persian Qjar all steel axe, 27¾in., crescent head 8in. chiseled with Islamic inscriptions and some damascened embellishment, steel haft of part faceted part spiral section.
(Wallis & Wallis) $318

A Saxon horseman's hammer, entirely from iron, with small turned hammer head balanced by a long beak-shaped fluke of stiff diamond section and with spherical finial, slender haft of circular section with thicker wire-bound grip, early 17th century, 21½in. long.
(Christie's) $2,922

A 17th century halberd, 90in. long, head 25in. overall, pierced backspike and crescent shaped blade, tall square section top spike, on its brass studded velvet covered haft with cotton tassels.
(Wallis & Wallis) $445

A mace, the head with eight lobed-shaped flanges each pierced with seven circular holes, octagonal haft with bulbous capital and central and basal molding, brass and iron wire-bound grip, 16th century, 23¼in. long.
(Christie's) $1,749

A small Continental bronze cannon barrel of tapering multi-stage form decorated with moldings in relief, those at the muzzle separated by a band of acanthus leaves, finely cast in relief, circa 1750, 18¼in. barrel, 1in. bore.
(Christie's) $2,798

Thomas Edward Lawrence (1888–1935), a 2pp. a.l.s., by Lawrence, writing as T.E. Shaw, to H.M. Tomlinson, dated *R.A.F. Mount Batten, Plymouth, 3.V.30*, discussing his reluctance to write prefaces.
(Christie's)   **$3,203**

An autographed 'Coutts' check by Charles Dickens, dated *Gad's Hill, thirtieth October 1860*, for wages amounting to fourteen pounds, ten shillings; together with an envelope signed *Charles Dickens*.
(Christie's)   **$561**

Elizabeth W. Shutes (Survivor of the Titanic), a post-card from the "Carpathia" dated April 16th from Elizabeth Shutes to Mrs. Irving G. Mills saying *Safe again after a horrible experience.*
(Christie's)   **$1,602**

Three Abraham Lincoln autograph letters and a gold handled cane, the letters dated Executive Mansion Washington, July 25, 1864.
(Skinner Inc.)   **$66,000**

Rex Whistler (1905–44); Edwin Lutyens (1869–1944) a 2pp. a.l.s., by Rex Whistler, addressed *20 Fitzroy Street, W.1.*, to Mrs Porcelli, with a pen and ink drawing at the head of the paper of a figure crouched over a desk covered in a sackcloth and burning embers.
(Christie's)   **$701**

George Bernard Shaw (1856–1950), a 2pp. printed journalist's application questionnaire in French, evidently given to Shaw by the Belgian writer (?) Dotremont, which *Bernard Shaw, Vieillard sans future* has taken literally, and responds with wit and flippancy.
(Christie's)   **$841**

AUTOMATONS

A bisque-headed clockwork musical automaton, modeled as a standing man wearing 18th century style pink satin fancy dress, 24in. high, by Lambert, early 20th century.
(Christie's) $5,966

A carved wooden-headed electric automaton, modeled as a silversmith, sitting at a table and working with a hammer, 17in. high, by David Secrett of Diss, Norfolk.
(Christie's) $709

Bébé niche, a clockwork musical automaton modeled as a girl standing holding a kennel-shaped basket, 21¹/₂in. high, probably by Lambert.
(Christie's) $4,475

Fruit Seller, a leather-headed clockwork musical automaton modeled as a Negro holding a tray, as the music plays, he turns and bows his head, opens his eyes while the fruits lift to reveal dancing dolls, a circling mouse and a monkey, 24in. high, by Vichy.
(Christie's) $14,916

A bisque-headed clockwork automaton, modeled as a woman lying in bed with a baby, as the music plays she sits up, opens her eyes, rocks the baby and lies down again, 13¹/₂in. long.
(Christie's) $1,678

Soubrette, a bisque-headed clockwork musical automaton tea drinker, with closed mouth, and original silk and lace frock, 18in. high, the head stamped *tete Jumeau*, by Roullet and Decamps.
(Christie's) $5,221

An unusual composition headed clockwork musical automaton, modeled as a seated man playing a violin while the child dances, 17in. high, (re-dressed).
(Christie's) $5,221

A black bisque-headed clockwork musical automaton smoker, with wooden hands, glass eyes, cigarette holder, original trousers and shirt, 18in. high, probably by Phalibois.
(Christie's) $5,966

A clockwork automaton of a white rabbit in a cos lettuce, with jaw movement when head emerges from leaves, 7in. high, by Roullet & Decamps.
(Christie's) $1,678

French gilt bronze musical
automaton, circa 1900, with
single drawer and singing bird,
4¼in. wide.
(Skinner Inc.) $935

A singing bird in cage, the
octagonal gilt wire cage on
giltwood base, with three-cam
movement operating the bird's
head, beak and tail, 20½in. high,
circa 1900.
(Christie's) $2,725

A bisque-headed clockwork
musical automaton, modeled as
a woman sitting at her dressing
table with closed mouth, fixed
blue eyes, and original silk
dress, 15in. wide, by Phalibois.
(Christie's) $3,356

Peasant and baby, a rare
composition-headed clockwork
musical automaton, modeled as
a man seated on the back of a
rush chair holding a pig on his
left knee, 30in. high, by Vichy/
Triboulet, circa 1910.
(Christie's) $46,613

Pierrot serenading the Moon, a
composition-headed clockwork
musical automaton, with fixed
brown eyes, metal hands, orange
waistcoat and black tights, 22in.
high, by G. Vichy.
(Christie's) $54,071

A bisque-headed clockwork
musical automaton, modeled as
a boy sitting on a tree stump
playing a mandolin, as the music
plays he turns his head from
side to side, 14in. high, head
impressed *F1G by Vichy circa
1890*.
(Christie's) $5,966

A singing bird automaton,
French, last quarter 19th
century, the glass case
containing a tree with silk leaves
and flowers and a total of seven
birds and two large beetles.
(Tennants) $1,767

A Martin painted tinplate and
fabric 'Le Pianiste', with
musical mechanism, 5in. wide.
(Christie's) $783

A good French twin singing bird
automaton, the brass wire
domed cage containing a bird on
a perch, with a companion
below, 22in. high overall, second
half 19th century.
(Tennants) $3,348

A musical automaton of a Negro gentleman, circa 1900, with nodding composition head, the square base with two key-wound movements, 33in. tall.
(Tennants) $2,790

A gilt and enamel singing bird box, the bird with moving body, wings and metal beak, 4in. wide, in leather traveling case.
(Christie's) $6,620

An RCA mechanical speaking dog of painted papier mâché having moveable head and fitted for sound in the rear and at base, 39½in. high.
(Butterfield & Butterfield) $1,650

A composition-headed clockwork musical automaton, modeled as a standing Negro banjo player, as the music plays he strums his instrument while turning and nodding his eyes and closing his eyes, 18in. high, by Vichy.
(Christie's) $5,221

Tireur Automate, an extremely rare bisque headed clockwork toy, modeled as a Zouave soldier with molded brown mustache, 10in. wide, stamped on the base *J. Steiner*.
(Christie's) $5,966

An early French keywind automaton and music-box, consisting of a beautifully dressed monkey, feeding her baby from a bottle, nodding her head, and closing her eyes, 22in. high.
(Christie's) $6,050

Little Girl Magician, a bisque-headed clockwork musical automaton, with fixed brown eyes, and original black velvet bolero, 16½in. high, by Renou, circa 1900.
(Christie's) $11,187

An automaton of two blacksmiths, probably German, circa 1900, the two figures stand hammering a horseshoe upon an anvil with the forge and bellows beyond, 14½in. high.
(Tennants) $1,488

A musical automaton of a female flute player, French, last quarter 19th century, with composition moving head and arms and playing two airs on the key-wound movement, 16½in. high.
(Tennants) $1,302

A George I ebony and silver-mounted stick barometer, circa 1725–30, signed *Delander Fecit*, 43¹/₂in. high. (Christie's)
$389,400

William IV mother-of-pearl inlaid rosewood wheel barometer, circa 1830, J. Cetta, London, 46in. high. (Skinner Inc.)
$1,045

An early Victorian rosewood stick barometer, inscribed *H. Hughes, 59 Fenchurch Street, London.* (Christie's)
$653

Admiral Fitzroy oak cased barometer (Royal Polytechnic), in apparently complete condition. (G.A. Key)
$1,150

A 19th century mahogany and boxwood strung wheel barometer signed *Lione & Somalvico*, 4ft. 1¹/₂in. high. (Phillips)
$2,960

A Victorian flame mahogany stick barometer with engraved ivory scale, the trunk inset with a thermometer, 35¹/₂in. high. (Christie's)
$1,212

A 19th century mahogany wheel barometer, the 10in. silvered dial with hygrometer, thermometer and with level, signed *P. Intross*, 3ft. 7³/₄in. high. (Phillips)
$555

A George II mahogany stick barometer by F. Watkins, London, signed on the silvered barometer scale, 41in. high. (Christie's)
$11,616

Antique banjo barometer in mahogany frame with shell and line inlays, inscribed *G Rossi of Norwich*.
(G.A. Key) $800

A late George III mahogany and checker strung stick barometer by John Evans, London, 39in. high. (Christie's) $1,342

An early George III mahogany-cased wheel barometer, circa 1760–72, signed *Geo. Adams*, 41in. high. (Christie's) $62,304

A George II walnut cased wheel barometer, circa 1740, signed *Jno. Hallifax, Barnsley*, 53in. high. (Christie's) $62,304

A Queen Anne ivory double-sided column barometer, circa 1710, signed *Invented and made by D. Quare, London*, 36³/₄in. high. (Christie's) $70,092

A 19th century mahogany wheel barometer, by James Grimshaw, London, with hygrometer, thermometer and spirit level scales, 39in. high. (Christie's S. Ken) $910

An early 18th century style red lacquered column barometer, in the style of Daniel Quare or John Patrick, 40³/₄in. high. (Christie's) $11,682

A William III silver-mounted ebonized siphon tube barometer of royal provenance, circa 1700, signed *D. Quare Lond Fecit*, 39in. high. (Christie's) $603,570

A Regency mahogany bow-front stick barometer with ogee top, glazed Vernier scale signed *G C Dixey London*, 38¹/₂in. high. (Christie's) **$3,150**

A French mahogany and boxwood inlaid stick barometer, the dial signed *Charpentier, Paris, 1789*, 3ft. 6¹/₂in. high. (Phillips) **$1,080**

A 19th century mahogany and edgeline wheel barometer, signed on the level *I. Dubini*, 3ft. 2in. long. (Phillips) **$575**

An oak stick barometer, signed on the ivory scale *Josh. Somalvico, 2 Hatton Garden, London*, 3ft. 5in. high. (Bonhams) **$864**

A 19th century mahogany and boxwood mercury and glycerine double barometer, by *Josh Somalvico & Co., London*, 2ft. 2¹/₂in. long. (Phillips) **$650**

A George III mahogany wheel barometer, signed *J. Verga St. Ives warranted* on the silvered disc housing the spirit level beneath the silvered register scale, 42¹/₂in. high. (Christie's) **$1,735**

A rare double barometer, the paper register plate signed *Prandi & Co., Fecit, Sheffield* in a cartouche above the mercury and oil double tube, 2ft. high. (Bonhams) **$1,364**

A George II walnut cased wheel barometer; circa 1740, the dial signed *Jno. Hallifax, Barnsley*, on a silvered disc in the arch above the silvered 'chapter ring', 50¹/₄in. high. (Christie's) **$71,434**

BAROMETERS

A George II mahogany stick barometer with later wood finial to cavetto arched top, the dial with foliate border engraving, 38in. high.
(Christie's) $886

A 19th century round top mahogany stick barometer, signed *Marratt, King William St, City*, 3ft. 1in. long.
(Phillips) $1,440

A George III wheel barometer, the boxwood lined case with spirit level below silvered register scale with pierced blued steel and brass hands.
(Christie's) $795

A good mahogany bow fronted stick barometer, signed on the silvered register plate *G. Adams, London*, 3ft. 4in. high.
(Bonhams)
$5,456

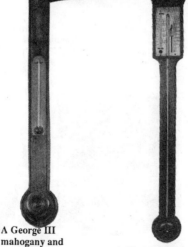

A 19th century mahogany and edgeline wheel barometer, with 10in. silvered dial, signed on the level *F. Bernascone, Devizes*, 3ft. 7¼in. long.
(Phillips) $540

A George III mahogany and boxwood angle barometer with molded cistern cover, the thermometer scale signed *Josho. Knight Fecit*, 32in. the vertical.
(Christie's)
$5,907

A Victorian mahogany barometer, the boxwood and ebony strung case signed *L. Boffy Hastings*, 38in. high.
(Christie's) $628

A Queen Anne walnut column barometer with integral watch; circa 1710, the watch above with glazed hinged bezel signed *Charles Cabrier London*, 41in. long.
(Christie's)
$50,424

Nantucket basket, Nantucket
Island, Massachusetts, late 19th
century, with turned and incised
wooden base, 13¹/₂in. diameter.
(Skinner Inc.) $935

Yokut polychrome pictorial
friendship basket.
(Butterfield & Butterfield)
$24,200

Miniature melon basket,
America, late 19th/early 20th
century, 4¹/₄in. high.
(Skinner Inc.) $935

Nantucket basket, Nantucket
Island, Massachusetts, late 19th
century, with shaped handle,
brass ears, 6³/₈in. high.
(Skinner Inc.) $660

Open-carved whalebone
mahogany sewing basket, second
half 19th century, 6¹/₂in. high.
(Skinner Inc.) $2,970

Maidu twined burden basket of
characteristic conical form,
decorated with three serrated
zig-zag bands, 18¹/₂in. high.
(Butterfield & Butterfield)
$1,320

A mahogany and cane
newspaper basket, designed by
Sir Edwin Lutyens, with carved
'rope' decoration and cane
panels, 81cm. wide.
(Christie's) $7,876

One of a pair of mahogany
octagonal waste paper baskets
each with molded top above
pierced gothic fretwork, 13¹/₄in.
high.
(Christie's) $6,776

Nantucket covered work basket,
A.D. Williams, Nantucket
Island, Massachusetts, 20th
century, wooden base with
partial paper label, 8¹/₂in. high.
(Skinner Inc.) $1,210

A Derbyshire fluorspar or
'bluejohn' goblet on knopped
stem and circular foot, 17cm.
high.
(Phillips) $3,382

A pair of English bluejohn urns
each with stepped turned finial
and on turned socle, 19th
century, 13¹/₂in. high.
(Christie's) $6,195

A bluejohn cup with circular
tapering body on ring-turned
tapering shaft and spreading
circular base, 6¹/₂in. high.
(Christie's) $3,203

A pair of Derbyshire fluorspar
or 'bluejohn' obelisks, raised on
alabaster and black slate
mounted plinths, 42cm. high.
(Phillips) $6,408

A Derbyshire fluorspar or
'bluejohn' turned cup raised on
a fluted stem and domed foot,
11cm. diameter.
(Phillips) $641

A pair of 19th century
Derbyshire fluorspar or
'bluejohn' urns with fruiting
cone finial, on spreading brass
foot and square plinth, 21cm.
high.
(Phillips) $2,544

A Derbyshire fluorspar
campana-shaped urn, on black
slate and gray marble stepped
square base, 19th century,
13³/₄in. high.
(Christie's) $925

A Derbyshire fluorspar or
'bluejohn' urn with turned
finial, raised on an alabaster and
black slate mounted plinth,
27cm. high.
(Phillips) $3,026

A George III ormolu-mounted
bluejohn perfume burner
attributed to Matthew Boulton,
the circular top with pierced
beaded collar, lacking cover,
7in. high.
(Christie's) $4,145

BRONZE

Le Conte, nineteenth century French bronze figure of a girl with a broken pitcher, signed, 30cm. high.
(Langlois) $548

A bronzed and parcel-gilt Napoleonic eagle with outstretched wings and clutching a ribbon-tied laurel wreath, 19th century, 38¹/₂in. wingspan.
(Christie's) $3,762

A fine bronze of a young boy, in running pose, 21¹/₂in. high, the base signed *J. Injalbert.*
(Canterbury) $653

A bronze fountain group of a putto holding a fish, after Andrea del Verrocchio, (weathered), 28¹/₄in. high.
(Christie's) $3,300

A 19th century large cold painted Austrian bronze inkstand modeled as a group of a bear fending off two attacking hounds, 15in. high.
(Christie's) $7,500

A Japanese bronze tazza, the circular top incised with lotus and supported on a tapering cylindrical waisted stepped base, 16¹/₄in. high.
(Christie's) $2,750

A bronze fountain group of a monkey and two snakes, cast from a model by Juan Passani, Argentine, early 20th century, 20³/₄in. high.
(Christie's) $2,750

A pair of bronze figures of Saint Elizabeth of Hungary and Saint Helena of Constantinople, cast from a model by Anna Coleman Ladd, American, early 20th century.
(Christie's) $4,400

A Japanese bronze figure of a laughing man standing leaning forwards, his kimono decorated in gilt hirazogan and takazogan, 9¹/₂in. high.
(Christie's) $3,500

A large Japanese bronze model of a standing warrior dressed in robes decorated in relief with dragons among clouds, 24in. high.
(Christie's) $850

Gilt-splashed bronze censer (Gui), 17th/18th century, bombé form with loop handles, spurious Xuande six-character mark, 7¹/₂in. wide.
(Skinner Inc.) $3,850

'Horse trainers of Marly', one of a pair of bronze groups, inscribed *Coustou*, 22¹/₄ x 20³/₄in.
(Christie's) (Two)
$6,600

A 19th century French bronze bust of Napoleon as Emperor, wearing cocked hat, signed and dated *P. Colombo, 1885*, 14in. high, overall.
(Christie's) $2,500

A lifesize bronze head of a horse after the Antique, 30⁵/₈in. high, weathered brown patina.
(Christie's) $3,850

An Italian bronze of a boy standing beside a spirally-fluted column topped by the head of a man, stamped *NELLI ROMA*, late 19th century, 22¹/₂in. high.
(Christie's) $1,223

A 19th century French bronze group of a fallen Amazonian warrior holding the reins of her attentive steed, signed *GECHTER*, circa 1840, 15¹/₄in. wide.
(Christie's) $2,800

'Moth Girl', a bronze and ivory figure, carved and cast from a model by Ferdinand Preiss, of a girl poised holding up a glass, wearing a blue and gold elaborate costume, 40.5cm. high.
(Christie's) $6,620

A nineteenth century Russian bronze group, mounted trooper's farewell, signed *A.B.D. C.F. Woerfpel? Petersburg*, with founders mark and cyrillic inscription, 25cm. high.
(Langlois) $1,405

BRONZE

A Komai vase two-handled tripod vase decorated with a dragon on various brocade designs, signed *Kyoto ju Komai Moto sei*, late 19th century, 17cm. high.
(Christie's) $5,643

An unusual Art Deco group depicting three leaping antelope, each with gilt patination, 26in. long.
(Bearne's) $688

Emile Corillan Guillemin, French, (1841–1907), cast metal figure, 'What a Fly', signed in metal, 29in. high.
(Selkirk's) $4,000

A French green patinated bronze figure of the bathing Venus, her hair elaborately tied, her left leg raised on a rocky base with drapery over her thigh, on square base, 24in. high.
(Christie's) $1,113

Gilt-bronze two-piece garniture in the baroque taste, second half 19th century, supported by a figure of a nereid and a triton sounding a conch and riding on a dolphin, 14$\frac{1}{2}$in. high.
(Butterfield & Butterfield) $4,950

Fine gilt bronze figural group of two immortals, Ming Dynasty, the fickle immortal Lu Dong Bin depicted in the clutches of inebriation, supported by a demonic attendant wearing a mugwort skirt, 8$\frac{5}{8}$in. high.
(Butterfield & Butterfield) $9,350

An Italian patinated bronze bust of Brutus, after Michelangelo, with a robe about his shoulder and tied to the right with a brooch, 20th century, 22$\frac{3}{4}$in. high.
(Christie's) $1,113

A pair of cast bronze figures of well-groomed hunting dogs, seated and alert, hand finished brownish-green patina, 24in. high.
(Selkirk's) $1,800

A Roland Paris cold-painted and ivory figure, modeled as a comical jester with hands behind his back, he wears a jester's hat with bells and matching tunic, 36.5cm. high.
(Phillips) $1,517

Paul Jean Baptiste Gasq, French (1860–1944), cast bronze figure, allegorical female bust on a red marble plinth, 24in. high. (Selkirk's) $1,500

Edouard Letourneau, French (–1907), cast bronze figure of an Indian on horseback, dark brown patina, signed, 23in. high. (Selkirk's) $3,000

Austrian bronze figure of a harem dancer, after Carl Kauba, late 19th century, nude with elaborate belt, 7½in. high. (Skinner Inc.) $1,500

Continental gilt-bronze-mounted brown onyx footed basin, late 19th century, the coved socle surrounded by a wreath of gadrooning and stiff leaves on a square base, 13in. high. (Butterfield & Butterfield) $1,870

Pair of Empire bronze-mounted rouge marble five-light candelabra, circa 1810, raised on four anthemion and flowerhead-cast scrolled feet, 27in. high. (Butterfield & Butterfield) $2,475

Nepalese bronze figure of Dharmapala and Consort, 19th/ 20th century, in yab-yum and each wearing dharmapala ornaments and stepping in pratyalidhasana on an anthropomorphic garuda, 15in. high. (Butterfield & Butterfield) $1,760

'Les amis de toujours', a bronze and ivory group, cast and carved after a model by Demetre Chiparus, modeled as a lady flanked by two borzoi, 11in. high. (Christie's) $9,648

Italian School, 19th century, cast bronze figure of a standing female nude figure of a Greek goddess, 31in. high. (Selkirk's) $1,200

A bronze teapot and cover modeled as an aubergine, decorated in iroe hirazogan with birds and butterflies among flowering branches, signed *Miyabo zo*, late 19th century, 15.5cm. high. (Christie's) $1,599

A stylish bronze and ivory figure, cast and carved from a model by Demetre Chiparus, she wears an elaborate beaded costume with a layered and hooped skirt, 33.5cm. high. (Phillips) $12,059

A cold-painted bronze and ivory figure, cast and carved in the manner of Ferdinand Preiss, as a young girl wearing a blue siren suit, cap and shoes, 21.5cm. high. (Phillips) $895

A gilt bronze figure, by H. Keck, cast as a naked maiden dressed only in stockings, garters and high heel shoes, 33cm. high. (Phillips) $1,517

A late 19th century Polish bronze figure of a young discalced, whistling urchin, signed and dated, *V. SZCZEBLEWSKI, 1889*, 17in., on a marble plinth. (Christie's) $1,300

Large Korean silver inlaid bronze sacrificial vessel, Yi Dynasty, based on a Koryo Dynasty prototype with a wide everted rim above a deep straight-sided body resting on a high pedestal foot, 8^1/$_8$in. high. (Butterfield & Butterfield) $33,000

A 19th century Italian bronze figure, of the Dancing Faun of Pompeii, on a rectangular base, 31in. high, overall. (Christie's) $783

'Russian Dancer', a gilt bronze figure, by P. Phillipe, modeled as a woman in long pleated dress with sash, 37.5cm. high. (Phillips) $1,751

A pair of German bronze figures of Virtues, the two maidens shown standing with heads bowed, in classical robes, early 20th century, 27^1/$_2$in. high. (Christie's) $1,317

A 19th century French animalier bronze figure of a cockerel, the naturalistic oval base signed *P.J. Mêne*, 5in. high, overall. (Christie's) $895

A gilded bronze figure of Venus, by J.L. Gerome, depicting Venus dancing clutching Paris' prize apple in one hand, her other hand raised, holding her billowing dress.
(Phillips) $1,848

A 19th century French bronze animalier figure of an alert pointer, signed *Fratin*, 9in. wide.
(Christie's) $466

'Balancing', a cold-painted bronze and ivory figure, cast and carved from a model by Ferdinand Preiss, as a young woman wearing a green tinted bathing costume, 38cm. high.
(Phillips) $12,837

Japanese mixed metal vase on stand, Meiji period, signed *Dai Nihon Tei Koku Toyama Ken Takaoki Shi Ohashi San'emon Sei Zo*, formed as rough pottery vase with printed wrapping, 14in. high.
(Skinner Inc.) $20,000

A pair of Empire mantel ornaments depicting Venus advised by Cupid, and Venus chastising Cupid, 13¼in. high.
(Christie's) $18,810

Georg Kolbe, German (1877–1947), bronze, Crouching Girl 1925, golden brown patina, signed with monogram, 11¼in. high.
(Selkirk's) $9,250

A patinated bronze figure of a paperboy, a bundle of newspapers under one arm, retailed by Etling, Paris, 13½in. high.
(Bearne's) $550

'Sonny Boy', a painted bronze and ivory figure, cast and carved from a model by Ferdinand Preiss, as a young boy wearing a greenish-silver shirt, dark blue trousers and tie, 20.7cm. high.
(Phillips) $3,601

A Roland Paris cold-painted bronze and ivory figure, modeled as a pierrot in traditional pleated cloak with ruff collar, 35.5cm. high.
(Phillips) $1,517

French silvered and patinated-bronze and cast brass figural centerpiece, third quarter 19th century, raised on the backs of three black-patinated and silvered-bronze blackamoor figures, 8¹/₂in. high.
(Butterfield & Butterfield)
$4,400

A bronze panel by Doris Flynn, rectangular, cast decoration of people queueing, mounted in wooden frame, signed in the bronze *Flynn*, 88cm. wide.
(Christie's) $985

A rare French bronze model of a sleeping jaguar, cast from a model by Antoine-Louis Barye, signed *BARYE* and inscribed *F BARBEDIENNE, FONDEUR*, 19th century, 3³/₈ x 12¹/₄in.
(Christie's) $1,826

A Victorian cast seal modeled as a putto, naked except for a strategically draped leafy vine, munching on a bunch of grapes held in one hand, by Francis Higgins, 1872, 8.5cm. high.
(Phillips) $644

A pair of bronzed resin busts of Charles Stewart Rolls and Frederick Henry Royce, 8¹/₂in. high.
(Christie's) $1,210

'Patience'. A bronze and ivory figure cast and carved from a model by Demetre Chiparus, the barefooted young lady stands in her nightgown her hands clasped her eyes averted, 37.5cm. high.
(Phillips) $10,348

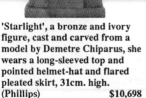

'Starlight', a bronze and ivory figure, cast and carved from a model by Demetre Chiparus, she wears a long-sleeved top and pointed helmet-hat and flared pleated skirt, 31cm. high.
(Phillips) $10,698

Large bronze vase, Japan, late 19th century, on circular foot with concentric ring design, 12¹/₄in. high.
(Skinner Inc.) $600

French patinated bronze figure of a bulldog cast after a model by Valton, circa 1900, the excited dog with snarling barking face, 18¹/₄in. high.
(Butterfield & Butterfield)
$2,750

Art Deco sculpture with lady and goat, gilt and painted bronzed metal scene arranged atop faux stone bridge, 31in. long.
(Skinner Inc.) $550

A 19th century gilt bronze figure of Cupid reclining on a draped basket, on malachite veneered base, probably Russian, 15cm. wide.
(Phillips) $731

A Charles X ormolu surtout-de-table with circular mirrored plate, the pierced frieze cast with scrolling anthemia, 28in. diameter.
(Christie's) $15,840

'Girl with a Cigarette', a black patinated bronze figure by Bruno Zach, of a young woman wearing lounging pyjamas and mules, 28in. high.
(Christie's S. Ken) $8,712

A pair of Charles X bronze and parcel gilt six-light candelabra, the leaf cast arms with subsidiary scrolls issuing from an urn of flowers and fruit, 77cm. high.
(Phillips) $3,560

A fine French bronze figure of Diana Victorious, cast from a model by Albert-Ernest Carrier-Belleuse, the goddess of hunting shown standing, lightly draped, a hunting horn over her right shoulder and a bow in her left hand, late 19th century, 31½in. high.
(Christie's) $22,800

'Ayouta', a cold-painted bronze and ivory figure, cast and carved from a model by Demetre Chiparus, she wears a beaded and textured top with matching head-dress, 29cm. high.
(Phillips) $5,640

A fine French gilt bronze group of the birth of Venus, entitled *Venus à la coquille*, cast from a model by Jean-Jacques Pradier, signed *J. PRADIER*, mid 19th century, 9in. high.
(Christie's) $17,869

Life-size patinated bronze figure of Mercury, cast after a model by Giambologna, late 19th/early 20th century, 6ft. 2in. high.
(Butterfield & Butterfield) $11,000

Don Wiegand, American, cast bronze figure, Mark Twain, brown patina, signed and dated 1985, 16in. high.
(Selkirk's) $3,800

A fine French bronze model of 'The Accolade', cast from a model by Pierre-Jules Mêne, the Arab mare and stallion shown with their necks interlocked, circa 1850, 13¹/₄in. high.
(Christie's) $9,636

A George III ormolu perfume-burner by Matthew Boulton, the domed circular pierced lid with fruiting finial on an acanthus cap, 10³/₄in. high.
(Christie's) $19,470

An Italian bronze bust of a gentleman, cast from a model by Giuseppe Renda, shown with a large mustache, on molded socle, late 19th century, 19³/₄in. high.
(Christie's) $2,374

An Italian bronze equestrian portrait of Wellington, cast from a model by Carlo Marochetti, the general shown seated upon his favorite horse Copenhagen, 19th century, 17in. high.
(Christie's) $2,191

A French bronze figure of Henri IV, cast from a model by Baron François-Joseph Bosio, shown as a child, dressed in contemporary breeches and doublet, mid 19th century, 49¹/₄in. high.
(Christie's) $5,113

A French bronze figure of a judge, cast from a model by R. Colombo, shown standing in contemporary costume, his head downcast as he reads a sealed document, late 19th century, 21¹/₂in. high.
(Christie's) $1,461

A mid-19th century Russian gilt bronze figure, of a bearded peasant hauling a sled loaded with a churn, on malachite veneered base, 16cm. wide.
(Phillips) $1,749

A late 19th century French bronze group of a Bacchanalian term embracing a naked female, a putti to their feet, his hair tied at the back, 28¹/₂in. high.
(Christie's S. Ken) $1,884

A bronze statuette of Napoleon, on circular gilded base and rectangular plinth, applied with his cypher within a garland surmounted by an eagle, 30cm. high.
(Phillips) $1,193

A French bronze group of a pointer and a retriever, cast from a model by Pierre-Jules Mêne, the two hounds pointing a partridge, 19th century, 8³/₄in. high.
(Christie's) $2,739

A large bronze hexagonal long-necked vase, cast with deer, rabbit and other animals amidst rocks and divided by vertical flanges, 15th/16th century, 55cm. high.
(Christie's) $7,256

An English Art Union bronze figure of a boy at a stream, cast from a model by John Henry Foley, the naked youth shown standing against a tree trunk, mid 19th century, 21¹/₂in. high.
(Christie's) $3,287

A pair of French gilt bronze figures of sphinxes, the graceful figures shown seated, their heads adorned with Egyptian headdresses and long plaits, early 20th century, 18¹/₈in. high.
(Christie's) $3,652

A 19th century bronze statuette, of a classical maiden stooping at a plinth, 28cm. high, on a later marble base.
(Phillips) $763

A French bronze figure of a nymph, entitled 'Le Rêve', cast from a model by Hippolyte Moreau, shown seated on a rock, her robes fallen off her shoulders, second half 19th century, 22¹/₄in. high.
(Christie's) $3,287

An ormolu encrier, the shaped top of scrolls and acanthus centered by a naked female figure seated on a draped foliage-cast plinth, assembled second quarter 19th century, 20in. wide.
(Christie's) $1,004

A French bronze group of Maternity, cast from a model by Paul Dubois, the tender mother seated on a rocky outcrop, on infant suckling at her breast, the other child asleep, 19th century, 18³/₄in. high.
(Christie's) $1,643

BRONZE

French patinated bronze and carved marble group of Venus at her toilette, cast and carved from a model by L. Chalon, late 19th century, 23¹/₂in. high. (Butterfield & Butterfield)

$4,675

Japanese mixed metal vase, Meiji Period, finch on a prunus branch, stylized animal base, signed, 13in. high. (Skinner Inc.) $19,000

Fine French patinated bronze group, 'Caresse de L'Amour', cast after a model by Albert-Ernest Carrier-Belleuse, third quarter 19th century, 35³/₄in. high. (Butterfield & Butterfield)

$8,800

Bronze figure of deity on a brass stand, 20th century, wearing regal ornaments and a diaphanous dhoti with the legs drawn up towards the body in a posture of royal ease, 19¹/₈in. high. (Butterfield & Butterfield)

$550

A French bronze jardinière, entitled 'Les Maraudeurs', cast from a model by Frédéric-Auguste Bartholdi, in the form of an oval wicker basket supported at either end by a faun, signed A Bartholdi, 19th century, 8 x 10¹/₄in. (Christie's) $1,967

Fine gilt bronze figure of Guanyin on a lotus pedestal, Ming Dynasty, the deity seated dhyanasana and wearing thick robes with chased floral borders accented with regal jewelry, 20¹/₂in. high. (Butterfield & Butterfield)

$6,050

'Lady Golfer', a patinated bronze and ivory figure, cast and carved from a model by Chiparus, 14in. high. (Christie's S. Ken)

$5,900

Italian gilt-bronze handle, circa 1600, cast as a pair of serpents entwined at the tails, each coiling upwards to grasp at one side the foliate fringes of a grotesque mask, 3¹/₄in. high. (Butterfield & Butterfield) $1,100

A finely modeled cast statuette of a maiden, proffering a caudle cup and cover, on a wooden octagonal plinth, 18cm. high, 1924. (Phillips) $805

BRONZE

Bronze Art Deco figure, after Bruno Zach, semi clad flapper with outstretched arms partially cold painted, 14in. high. (Skinner Inc.) **$990**

Large patinated bronze figural group of the Youth of Athens being sacrificed to the Minotaur, late 19th century, 24¼in. high. (Butterfield & Butterfield) **$3,850**

Italian bronze bust of a Hellenistic general, after the Antique, late 19th century, wearing a baldric over his shoulder, 26in. high. (Butterfield & Butterfield) **$3,025**

French gilt-bronze figure of a knight, Barbedienne Foundry, cast after a model by Jean Larrive, late 19th century, 25in. high. (Butterfield & Butterfield) **$990**

Pair of patinated bronze figures of a Harlequin and Columbine, cast after models by Paul Dubois, 32¾in. high. (Butterfield & Butterfield) **$7,150**

Fine Korean large gilt bronze figure of Sakyamuni Buddha, Yi Dynasty, the thickset figure standing in monastic robes covering both shoulders and falling in rhythmic folds to his bare feet, 45½in. high. (Butterfield & Butterfield) **$16,500**

Bronze temple bell, late 17th/ early 18th century, tapering form with serpentine rim, banded rib decoration and panels of inscriptions, 25in. high. (Skinner Inc.) **$2,860**

A Tiffany Studios 'Zodiac' gilt bronze rectangular photograph frame, the broad edge embellished with the twelve signs of the Zodiac, 20.5cm. high. (Phillips) **$700**

Bronze figure of a Bodhisattva, Ming Dynasty, seated in dhayanasana and garbed in heavy robes partially open to reveal a beaded necklace, 8⅜in. high. (Butterfield & Butterfield) **$660**

A Georgian mahogany and brass bound peat bucket, of tapering ribbed form with brass swing handle, 40cm. high.
(Phillips) $2,784

A mahogany plate-bucket, the octagonal sides pierced with Chinese fretwork bound with brass and with brass carrying-handle, 12¹/₂in. high.
(Christie's) $4,089

A Regency brass-bound mahogany plate bucket, with brass liner and carrying-handle, the ribbed sides with U-shaped aperture, 15³/₄in. diameter.
(Christie's) $5,034

An early 19th century brass bound mahogany peat bucket of oval form, with brass swing handle and liner, 34cm. high.
(Phillips) $783

Firkin, 19th century, in pine, stamped *C. Wilder & Son, So. Hingham, Mass*, 10in. high.
(Eldred's) $110

A brass-bound mahogany bucket, with gadrooned rim , the sides with lion-mask and ring-handles, 13³/₄in. high.
(Christie's) $2,093

A George III brass-bound mahogany plate bucket with slatted sides with brass carrying-handle and brass liner, 11¹/₂in. diameter.
(Christie's) $1,936

A George III mahogany and brass bound peat pail of navette shape, with liner and swing handle, 13¹/₂in. wide.
(Christie's) $746

A George III mahogany octagonal plate pail with brass swing handle above a narrow brass band and with vertical pierced sides, 12³/₄in. high.
(Tennants) $2,232

Oval Micmac quillwork and birch bark box, late 19th century, wooden bottom, 8½in. wide.
(Eldred's) $743

Yellow painted oval Shaker carrier, probably Harvard, Massachusetts, late 19th century, three fingered box with carved handle.
(Skinner Inc.) $6,600

Inlaid camphorwood lap desk, dated *1840*, inlaid with whalebone presentation plaques inscribed *Rosetta Reynolds Made in the Year 1840*, 17³/₄in. wide.
(Skinner Inc.) $1,980

An Indian teak revolving cigar cabinet carved with foliage and scrolling tendrils, the stand with cabriole legs joined by an undertier, 26in. square.
(Bearne's) $396

A Japanese lacquer cabinet decorated with birds in a mountainous landscape, applied throughout with engraved brass corner mounts, hinges and escutcheons, 36in. wide.
(Bearne's) $1,204

A Regency tortoiseshell tea caddy of bowed octagonal form, the interior with two lidded compartments, 6½in. wide.
(Bearne's) $1,290

A mid-19th century rectangular three division tea caddy, veneered in scarlet tortoiseshell and inlaid with brass en premier et contre-partie, 12in. wide.
(Christie's) $1,025

An early 19th century tea caddy in the form of a house with two dormer windows and chimney, the interior with two lidded compartments, 17cm. high.
(Phillips) $950

A Tunbridgeware domed tea caddy inlaid with a view of Dover Priory within a mosaic border, fitted interior, 9³/₄in. wide.
(Bearne's) $602

A good William IV papier-mâché tea caddy, of rectangular form, the front of arc en arbalette section, with splayed apron, the lid painted with a spray of summer flowers, 12¹/₂in. wide.
(Phillips)   **$884**

A late Regency tortoiseshell veneered and ivory strung tea caddy, the canted lid inset with a silver plaque, the bowed sides with cast loop handles, 31cm. wide.
(Phillips)   **$1,749**

A late 18th century German kingwood-veneered, walnut-banded and inlaid casket, the lid with a spray of flowers within an oval, 41cm. wide.
(Phillips)   **$1,326**

A 19th century mahogany domestic medicine chest, the lid rising to reveal compartments for fourteen bottles, 8¹/₄in. high.
(Christie's S. Ken)   **$964**

Rosewood cased surgical set, circa 1870, by G. Tiemann Co., 67 Chatham Street, N.Y., NY, containing approximately sixty-eight instruments in fitted velvet compartments.
(Eldred's)   **$1,980**

A George III mahogany, kingwood banded and herringbone strung knife box, with sloping lid and arc en arbalette front.
(Phillips)   **$572**

A William and Mary oyster olivewood veneered table cabinet, the rectangular top, sides and pair of doors geometrically inlaid with boxwood lines, 1ft. 8in. wide.
(Phillips)   **$1,988**

A George III mahogany and ebony strung cutlery urn, the domed cover with urn finial, the tapering body with triple boxwood strung supports, 61cm. high.
(Phillips)   **$1,511**

An early 19th century polychrome paper scroll tea caddy of hexagonal outline, with lidded interior, 7in. wide.
(Christie's S. Ken)   **$815**

George III etched and engraved
ivory tea caddy, circa 1800, in
the neoclassical taste, decorated
with checker and line borders,
7¼in. wide.
(Butterfield & Butterfield)
$880

A good Regency penwork tea
caddy, extensively decorated
with neo-classical figures and
motifs, 1815, 33cm. wide.
(Phillips) $1,335

A Regency rosewood and brass
inlaid tea caddy, of sarcophagus
form, the interior fitted with
three lidded canisters, all raised
on bun feet, 33cm. wide.
(Phillips) $972

An Edwardian mahogany
decanter box, with crossbanding
and inlaid shell patera to top and
front.
(Bonhams) $1,035

A late 17th/early 18th century
Indo-Colonial hardwood and
ivory inlaid traveling writing
cabinet, the fall front, top and
sides decorated all over with a
profusion of arabesque scrolls,
1ft. 3in. wide.
(Phillips) $1,908

A 19th century mahogany
domestic medicine chest, the lid
rising to reveal compartments
for sixteen bottles, 8¾in. high.
(Christie's S. Ken) $1,606

A 19th century Continental
painted casket, 11in. wide, with
pierced brass gallery.
(Dreweatt Neate) $5,850

A Regency tortoiseshell tea-
caddy, with domed octagonal
top, the sides carved with blind
Gothic arcading and quatrefoils,
on ivory bun feet, 6¼in. high.
(Christie's) $2,826

Fine jewelry chest in rosewood
with mother-of-pearl inlaid bird
and flower decoration, circa
1840, 15in. long.
(Eldred's) $935

A Regency rosewood-veneered and multiple banded tea caddy, of rectangular form, having lion-mask handles and paw feet, the interior adapted with a metal liner, 30cm. wide.
(Phillips) $460

Antique oak spice cupboard with 11 interior drawers, 16in. wide.
(Jacob & Hunt) $683

A Louis XV straw-work casket with domed double-opening lid and fitted interior, each compartment inset with a reverse painted glass panel, 20cm. wide.
(Phillips) $707

A Chippendale inlaid walnut desk-box, Salem, Massachusetts, 1750–80, the hinged molded rectangular top decorated with stringing and centered by a compass star over a conforming case enclosing an elaborately fitted interior, 22¹/₂in. wide.
(Christie's) $6,050

A mahogany domestic medicine cabinet, early/mid 19th century, the mahogany case with brass bail handle above, 34cm. wide.
(Allen & Harris) $1,778

An Anglo-Indian ivory and tortoiseshell table-cabinet, enclosing a fitted interior of nine various-sized hardwood-lined drawers, late 17th century, possibly Dutch or Portuguese Colonial, 15in. wide.
(Christie's) $4,897

A Federal inlaid ash and mahogany document box, probably Pennsylvania, 1790-1810, elaborately inlaid with bands of diagonal inlay centring a compass star and two fans in a shaped reserve, 20in. wide.
(Christie's) $2,420

Carved, turned, painted and gilded cenotaph, New England, 1800, decorated with green bannerole inscribed *Washington*, 35in. high.
(Skinner Inc.) $25,300

A rare late Regency hardstone veneered tea caddy, the canted lid and tapering sides with geometric decoration in the form of mainly English hardstones, 11¹/₂in. wide.
(Phillips) $2,828

An early Georgian walnut violin-case, the domed hinged lid centered by a brass carrying-handle and an oval plaque engraved *James Dixon*, 30¹/₄in. wide.
(Christie's) $3,498

A George III tortoiseshell veneered tea caddy, 8in. wide.
(Dreweatt Neate) $1,131

Joined oak and yellow pine box, Connecticut or Massachusetts, circa 1700, 27in. wide.
(Skinner Inc.) $12,100

An 18th century German lacquered table writing desk, the panels decorated with chinoiseries, the sloping fall enclosing two pairs of drawers flanking three compartments above a long drawer, 46cm. wide.
(Phillips) $1,352

An Anglo-Indian ivory, tortoiseshell and sandalwood folding gaming-board in the form of two bookspines, late 18th/early 19th century, probably Vizagapatam, 18¹/₂in. wide.
(Christie's) $5,947

An Anglo-Indian Vizigapatam ivory and sandalwood table-bureau banded overall with scrolling foliate decoration, the sides formerly with carrying-handles, late 18th century, 20¹/₂in. wide.
(Christie's) $2,449

A late 17th/early 18th century kingwood veneered and brass bound coffret, the hinged lid and front with radiating veneers, probably Dutch, 39cm. wide.
(Phillips) $2,226

A pair of Regency japanned chestnut urns of tapering form, the navette section lids with spire finial, 32cm. high.
(Phillips) $1,602

A Queen Anne walnut tea-caddy inlaid overall with geometric fruitwood banding, the hinged stepped rectangular top enclosing an interior with two divisions, 10³/₄in. wide.
(Christie's) $1,602

A Regency brass-mounted rosewood bookstand, the rectangular top with pierced foliate gallery and raised sides with carrying-handles, on bun feet, 14in. wide.
(Christie's) $1,594

A George III mahogany traveling medicine chest, the double hinged fascia opening to reveal five fitted drawers with turned ivory handles and seventeen compartments for bottles, 29cm. wide.
(Spencer's) $360

William IV Sterling and fabric jewel casket by Robert Garrard, London, 1838, the domed green velvet top secured at the edge by dentilated silver border above the lid framing, 6³/₄in. wide.
(Butterfield & Butterfield) $2,750

A fine Victorian traveling toilet box, the veneered rectangular case with brass mounts, the lid with leather towel case and mirror, 12in., maker Frances Douglas 1854.
(Woolley & Wallis) $2,905

Gothic style champlevé enamel casket, late 19th century, the corners with female therms, raised on four C-scroll, fruit, and mask-cast feet, 15³/₄in. wide.
(Butterfield & Butterfield) $3,300

A George III rectangular silver-mounted shagreen etui, the hinged cover inset with a mirror, containing two glass scent bottles, circa 1800, 2⁵/₈in. high.
(Christie's) $3,344

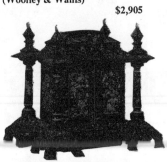 

A gold, silver and mother-of-pearl-inlaid brown tortoiseshell table-cabinet inlaid overall with foliate scrolls, first half 19th century, probably English, 23¹/₂in. wide.
(Christie's) $12,870

George III pearwood teacaddy, late 18th century, 7in. high.
(Skinner Inc.) $1,760

Early two-tiered traveling liquor case, oak with original red paint geometric design, the lower section with twenty rectangular decanters with stoppers, Spain, 1790–1810.
(Skinner Inc.) $2,200

A rare William and Mary oblong silver-mounted shagreen instrument case, the elaborate hinges and lock plate engraved with stylized flowers and pierced with kidney-shaped motifs, circa 1695.
(Christie's) $5,653

'Papillions', a Lalique rectangular burr walnut veneered box with hinged cover, the top and sides with mirrored glass panels, 11¹/₂in. wide.
(Christie's) $10,514

A 19th century Chinese export lacquer rectangular box, heightened in gilt and painted with figures in landscapes, on winged dragon feet, 13¹/₂in. wide.
(Christie's) $559

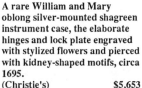

A George III rectangular gold-mounted shagreen writing set, the hinged cover and front wall applied with a cagework of putti, birds and scrolls, circa 1770, 2¹/₂in. wide.
(Christie's) $3,520

An important Swiss necessaire with singing bird automaton and twin musical movements, by Frères Rochat, Geneva, circa 1825, the implements with restricted warranty mark for gold, Paris, 1819–1839.
(Christie's) $175, 230

Napoleon III boulle liqueur case, third quarter 19th century, the top lifting and the sides opening to an interior with a removeable tray fitted with four fluted square decanters and fourteen faceted liqueurs, 13¹/₂in. wide.
(Butterfield & Butterfield) $3,300

A mahogany cheese coaster of dished outline, the scrolled division and frieze edged with chainlink above rockwork and acanthus-carved frieze, 20¹/₄in. wide.
(Christie's) $3,098

A crocodile traveling dressing case opening to reveal silver mounted fitted interior, 8in. wide.
(Hy Duke & Son) $409

A Victorian coromandel wood traveling dressing case, by Thomas Johnson, 1861, William Leuchars, 1886, Charles Asprey and George Asprey, 1899, 20¹/₂in. wide.
(Christie's) $10,650

A 35mm. Janua camera with a
San Giorgio Essegi f/3.5 5cm.
lens.
(Christie's) $1,271

A 5 x 12cm. stereoscopic
binocular camera with
removable plate magazine
section, simple sector shutter,
right-angle viewfinder and lens
sections engraved W. *Watson &
Sons.*
(Christie's) $2,346

A 35mm. Leica Ia camera No.
8558 with a Leitz Elmar f/3.5
50mm. lens.
(Christie's) $1,075

J. Lancaster & Son,
Birmingham, half-plate polished
mahogany-body Rover detective
camera with a brass bound lens
with integral see-saw shutter
and leather case.
(Christie's) $939

A quarter-plate folding Frena
camera with removable camera
section, a Beck-Steinheil
Orthostigmat 4¼ inch lens in a
rotary shutter and Frena film
magazine section.
(Christie's) $508

A 5 x 4 inch tropical Improved
Artists Reflex camera with
polished teak body, red leather
bellows and viewing hood,
lacquered brass fittings, 1911.
(Christie's) $1,955

A 16mm. RCA Sound
cinematographic camera Type
PR–25 No. 1156 with a Taylor-
Hobson Cooke Cinema 1 inch
f/3.5 lens, in maker's fitted
leather case.
(Christie's) $1,271

A 13 x 18cm. tropical Tropica
folding baseboard camera with
polished teak body, black
leather bellows and a Carl Zeiss,
Jena Tessar f/6.3 21cm. lens.
(Christie's) $4,302

A 5 x 5 inch mahogany-body
transitional wet/dry-plate
bellows camera with red square-
cut leather bellows, a brass
bound lens with rack and pinion
focusing.
(Christie's) $2,955

E. Leitz, Wetzlar, a 35mm. Leica IIId camera, with a Leitz Summitar 5cm. f/2 lens, in maker's leather ever ready case.
(Christie's) $3,824

A 2 x 1¹/₂ inch Piccolo-type camera with black leather covered body, ivorine fittings, sportsfinder, wheel stops and sector shutter.
(Christie's) $355

A 35mm. black Leica M4 camera No. 1181552.
(Christie's) $1,271

A 120-rollfilm Zeca-Flex twin lens reflex camera with a Sucher-anastigmat f/2.9 viewing lens, in maker's leather case.
(Christie's) $1,466

A 127-rollfilm Vollenda camera with a Leitz Elmar 5cm f/3.5 lens in a rimset Compur shutter, in maker's leather case.
(Christie's) $254

Franke and Heidecke, Braunschweig, a 6 x 6cm. tele-Rolleiflex camera with a Heidosmat f/4 135mm. viewing lens and a Carl Zeiss Sonnar f/4 135mm. taking lens.
(Christie's) $1,564

A 35mm. twin lens Contaflex camera with a Carl Zeiss Jena Sucher objectiv f/2.8 8cm. viewing lens.
(Christie's) $2,542

A mahogany box with tripod screw and camera mounting plate containing a quarter-plate mahogany-body and brass-fitted folding camera.
(Christie's) $1,857

Eastman Kodak Co., Rochester, U.S.A., 120-rollfilm Boy Scout Brownie camera with green body covering, olive green paint and chrome styled front with Boy Scouts of America emblem.
(Christie's) $235

CAR MASCOTS

A chromium-plated Minerva, circa 1935, 6in. high. (Christie's) $445

A 1930's chromium plated car mascot modeled as The Submarine S6B single seat, high speed racing sea plane, with moving propellor, 16cm. wide. (Spencer's) $483

A brass seated cat, the base inscribed *Bofill*, 4in. high. (Christie's) $365

A car mascot in the form of a cross-legged Pierrot playing a mandolin, the face and hands in simulated ivory, mounted on a radiator cap, 4¹/₂in. high. (Christie's) $1,210

A brass circus elephant standing on its two front legs with trunk raised, 7¹/₂in. long. (Christie's) $470

Etling nude automobile mascot, the molded fiery opalescent figure with arm outstretched, holding drape and standing on raised platform, 8³/₄in. high. (Skinner Inc.) $1,500

A chromium-plated Art Deco style winged goddess mascot, 7¹/₄in. high. (Christie's) $245

'Tête d'Aigle', a Lalique mascot, the clear and satin-finished glass molded in the form of an eagle's head, 11cm. high. (Christie's) $2,726

A nickel-plated skipping girl with painted bikini, signed *P. Porsairil* (skipping rope missing), 8in. high. (Christie's) $245

Carved and painted outside row armored jumper, C.W. Parker, circa 1920, original paint, 57in. long.
(Skinner Inc.) $1,540

Carved and painted carousel bull, late 19th/early 20th century, the full body with horns and sweeping tail in a running position, 39in. long.
(Butterfield & Butterfield) $1,760

Carved and painted elephany carousel figure, attributed to Bayol, France, circa 1920, 25in. high.
(Skinner Inc.) $1,925

Carved and painted jumper, Charles Marcus Illions, circa 1910, original paint, horsehair tail.
(Skinner Inc.) $7,700

A carved wood leaping frog, the figure with whimsical expression, carved saddle vest and bow tie, 41in. long.
(Christie's East) $15,400

Carved and painted outside row prancer, Rederich Heyn, Germany, circa 1900, 55¹/₂in. high.
(Skinner Inc.) $2,200

Carved inside row prancer, Dentzel, circa 1900, stripped and primed, 53in. high.
(Skinner Inc.) $7,700

Carved and painted rooster carousel figure, attributed to Coquereau and Marechal, France, circa 1900, 51in. high.
(Skinner Inc.) $3,300

Painted and carved jumper, Charles Marcus Illions, circa 1920, with original paint, horsehair tail.
(Skinner Inc.) $7,700

Continental wrought-iron and clear and colored glass twenty-light chandelier, of cage form, 38in. high.
(Butterfield & Butterfield)
$6,600

Baroque style gilt-metal twelve-light chandelier, 19th century, the fluted baluster-form shaft applied with gilt-bronze foliate-and-scroll-and-therm-cast mounts, 42in. high.
(Butterfield & Butterfield)
$4,950

A George III crystal chandelier, having two tiers of eight faceted arms with stellar grease pans, all linked by beaded swags and hung with pendant drops, 1.05m. drop.
(Phillips)
$20,470

An English glass chandelier, by F & C Osler and the pair of wall lights en suite, the chandelier of six lights with a central spiral twist shaft, 42in. high.
(Christie's)
$1,826

A Biedermeier gilt wood six-light chandelier, the scroll upswept arms issuing from a central petaled bowl surmounted by a tiered fruiting finial, 60cm. wide.
(Phillips)
$2,298

An early 19th century tôle peinte hanging ceiling lamp, the six burners each surmounted by conical shades with glass bowls beneath, 62cm. diameter.
(Phillips)
$3,026

Louis XV style six-light gilt-bronze and rock crystal chandelier, of open cageform suspending overall pear-shaped drops, 32in. high.
(Butterfield & Butterfield)
$3,025

An early Victorian ormolu six-light chandelier, the upright foliate corona above a beaded vase surrounded by putto heads mounted on channeled scrolls, 48in. high.
(Christie's)
$18,365

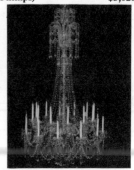

A mid-Victorian cut-glass twenty-four light chandelier probably by Perry & Co., the corona with two levels of spirally-twisted scrolling canes hung with swags of drops, 96in. high.(Christie's)
$43,725

One of a set of four late 19th century cut-glass four-branch wall-lights, each with obelisk atop a dished corona hung with faceted drops and bulbous stems cut with stars, 36in. high. (Four)
(Christie's) $22,737

An Empire ormolu ten-light chandelier with flaming finial and spreading shaft cast with lotus leaves above a band of bees and cornucopia garlanded with laurel wreaths and anthemia, 41in. wide.
(Christie's) $75,845

A brass twelve-light chandelier with baluster shaft and two tiers of S-scroll branches each with circular dished drip-pan, 18th/19th century, 26in. high.
(Christie's) $4,250

Gilt-bronze and crystal chandelier in the Regency taste, of cage form enclosed by chains of faceted beads, 32in. high.
(Butterfield & Butterfield) $4,125

Fine American Renaissance parcel-gilt and patinated bronze twenty-four-light chandelier and two matching sconces, circa 1872, 4ft. 7in. high.
(Butterfield & Butterfield) $14,300

A Meissen six-light chandelier modeled in three tiers around a central rococo-scroll-molded and pierced baluster column, mid-19th century, 39in. high.
(Christie's) $5,113

A brass twelve-light chandelier with two tiers of scrolling branches each with dished drip-pan, 19th century, 33$^{1}/_{2}$in. high.
(Christie's) $4,522

A cut-glass six-light chandelier with dished circular corona cut with latticework hung with faceted drops and swags, late 19th century, fitted and drilled for electricity, 63in. high.
(Christie's) $19,239

Rare Swedish neoclassical gilt-bronze, cranberry and clear glass chandelier made for the Russian market, stamped *I.A.S. Fischer St. Peterburg* (sic), *1795*, 35in. high.
(Butterfield & Butterfield) $27,500

AMERICAN

CHINA

Chelsea Keramic Art Works vase, Massachusetts, late 19th century, with relief decoration of squirrels and oak branches, 12in. wide.
(Skinner Inc.) $1,400

Anna pottery snake jug, with four snake heads and lower torso of man, with initials *A.M.A.B.* and *C2WK Anna ILL 1881*, 9in. high.
(Skinner Inc.) $2,750

Wheatley pottery bowl, Cincinnati, Ohio, circa 1900, relief decorated with open petaled flowers and leaves, 7½in. diameter.
(Skinner Inc.) $800

Important pottery vase, by Fritz Wilhelm Albert (1865–1940), circa 1906, 14½in. high.
(Skinner Inc.) $25,000

Paul Revere Pottery decorated vase, Boston, with incised and painted band of trees, hills and sky, 8½in. high.
(Skinner Inc.) $700

Parian pitcher, America, 19th century, with figures of George Washington in relief, 10in. high.
(Skinner Inc.) $935

An Omega earthenware vase by Roger Fry, covered in a finely crackled white tin glaze with yellow ocher and blue abstract decoration, circa 1914, 16.5cm. high.
(Christie's) $1,674

San Ildefonso Blackware pottery plate, Maire, painted in a large-scale repeat feather pattern within a triple perimeter band, 11in. diameter.
(Butterfield & Butterfield) $2,090

Santa Clara Blackware pottery jar, Christina Naranjo, carved to depict an Avanyu below a rim band of parallel linear devices, 9¼in. high.
(Butterfield & Butterfield) $1,100

94

Fulper pottery buttress vase, with glossy streaked glaze in muted green and metallic brown flambé, 8in. high. (Skinner Inc.) $385

Acoma pottery olla, circa 1920, with black, white and orange stylized decoration, 6in. high. (Eldred's) $275

Weller pottery vase, Zanesville, Ohio, circa 1914, "Camelot" funnel shape neck on squat bulbous body, 7³/₄in. high. (Skinner Inc.) $275

Double handled pottery floor vase, probably Zanesville Stoneware Co, Ohio, early 20th century, 18¹/₂in. high. (Skinner Inc.) $200

Marblehead pottery three color vase, circa 1907, by Arthur Irwin Hennessey, decorated with five oval medallions depicting grape clusters and leaves, 3¹/₂in. high. (Skinner Inc.) $1,100

Santo Domingo pottery olla, circa 1910, black and white geometric decoration, 11in. high. (Eldred's) $440

San Ildefonso blackware pottery plate, Maria/Popovi, the shiny black surface with a repeat feather pattern within three encircling bands, 14in. diameter. (Butterfield & Butterfield) $5,500

Ernst Wahliss Art Nouveau pottery plaque, with portrait of an appealing young couple holding musical score, 21 x 18in. (Skinner Inc.) $2,420

San Ildefonso pottery jar of hemispherical form, painted on the body, lip and both sides of top, in black on red, 11¹/₄in. high. (Butterfield & Butterfield) $9,900

ARITA

A large Arita blue and white apothecary bottle, decorated with four panels of birds amongst peonies, divided by lotus flower heads and swirling karakusa, late 17th century, 43.5cm. high.
(Christie's) $9,240

A pair of Arita blue and white baluster jars overlaid with gold and colored lacquer decoration, the porcelain painted overall with flowering peonies and foliage, 26¹/₂in. high.
(Christie's) $9,250

An ormolu-mounted Arita blue and gilt vase decorated overall with shrubs and bamboo, now transformed into a lamp, 17th century, 19¹/₂in. high.
(Christie's) $3,350

An Arita blue and white bottle decorated with chrysanthemums among rockwork beneath lotus sprays, late 17th century, 26.5cm. high.
(Christie's) $6,019

A pair of Arita blue and white deep dishes decorated with pomegranates in finger citron, the reverse with branches of peaches, late 17th century, 35cm. diameter.
(Christie's) $12,150

Good Arita carp-form vase in gilt bronze mounts, late 17th century, molded as a large carp leaping out of cresting waves, 7³/₈in. high.
(Butterfield & Butterfield) $8,250

An Arita blue and white charger painted with a central roundel enclosing the letters *V.O.C.*, surrounded by two Ho-o birds, late 17th century, 14¹/₂in. diameter.
(Christie's) $22,500

A pair of large Arita blue and white bottles decorated with buildings in mountainous landscapes beneath a band of foliate design, late 17th century, 44.5cm. high.
(Christie's) $22,250

An Arita blue and white vase decorated with three shaped panels containing peonies among rockwork, divided by lotus sprays, late 17th century, 41.5cm. high.
(Christie's) $13,475

BERLIN

A finely painted Berlin topographical cup, cover and stand, painted with views of a palace at Koblenz and the castle of Stolzenfels above the Rhine.
(Phillips) $4,800

A Berlin casket and hinged cover in the form of a commode, the corners molded with foliate scrolls enriched in gilding and surmounted with two cherub heads on the front corners, blue scepter and iron-red *KPM* and globe marks, circa 1895, 20³/₄in. wide.
(Christie's) $11,500

An interesting and finely painted Berlin cabinet cup and saucer, painted with a view of Windsor Castle.
(Phillips) $2,400

A Berlin rectangular plaque painted by R. Dittrich with a portrait of Ruth in the cornfields, impressed KPM and scepter marks, 19¹/₄ x 11³/₄in.
(Christie's) $9,500

A pair of Berlin rectangular plaques painted with head and shoulders portraits of young girls, each with long brown hair, signed *L. Schinnel*, impressed KPM and scepter marks, circa 1880, 12³/₄ x 10¹/₂in.
(Christie's) $30,096

A Berlin rectangular plaque painted with a young girl reclining on a couch in an interior before orange drapery and beside a box of scrolls, circa 1880, framed, 9¹/₄ x 6in.
(Christie's) $3,425

A Berlin rectangular plaque painted by G.L. Schinzel after C. Kiesel with a bust-length portrait of a young girl facing right, her dark-brown hair en chignon, impressed *KPM*, circa 1880, 12³/₄ x 10¹/₄in.
(Christie's) $8,765

A finely painted Berlin Easter egg, with a view of Werdesdie Kirche in Berlin, flanked by a house and with figures under a tree, 6.5cm. high.
(Phillips) $4,800

A Berlin rectangular plaque painted with a portrait of Princess Louise descending a stone staircase, impressed KPM and scepter mark, circa 1880, 9¹/₄ x 6¹/₄in.
(Christie's) $2,985

BOW

A Bow figure of a bagpiper in pink hat, blue jacket and yellow breeches with a hound at his feet, 15cm. high.
(Phillips) $1,275

A pair of 18th century Bow figurines of female figures 'The Seasons', the bases impressed with letter *B*, 8¹/₂in. high.
(Greenslades) $2,900

A fine Bow sweetmeat figure of a Turkish lady seated and holding a flower-painted shell dish edged in puce, 16.5cm. high.
(Phillips) $2,040

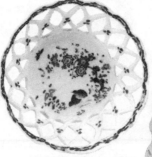

A pair of Bow figures of dancers after the models by J.J. Kändler, he standing before a tree-stump wearing a pale-yellow hat, his blue-lined white jacket applied with blue bows and ribbons, circa 1758, 19cm. high.
(Christie's) $5,513

A Bow pierced circular basket painted in the Kakiemon palette with The Quail pattern, the border with a band of iron-red foliage, circa 1758, 18cm. diameter.
(Christie's) $1,409

Two Bow figures of a youth and companion, he standing before a tree-stump playing the bag-pipes, his companion holding a posy, circa 1760, 15cm. high.
(Christie's) $2,817

A Bow figure of Kitty Clive in the role of 'The Fine Lady' from Garrick's farce 'Lethe', standing holding a spaniel beneath her right arm, circa 1750, 25.5cm. high.
(Christie's) $14,767

A Bow white squat baluster bowl and cover with loop handles, applied with prunus sprigs, the cover with branch finial, circa 1752, 13cm. diameter.
(Christie's) $3,544

A Bow figure of Euterpe by the Muses Modeller, her pink-lined dress painted with flowers and with pale-yellow drapery, 1750–52, 16cm. high.
(Christie's) $2,954

BOW

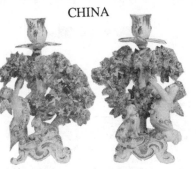

A Bow figure of a sportsman, standing holding a gun in his left hand and with a seated dog at his feet, circa 1758, 22cm. high. (Christie's) $1,477

A pair of well colored Bow groups each with a winged putto reaching up to a bird perched in the flower-encrusted bocage, 25.5cm. high. (Phillips) $2,720

A Bow group, of Spring, a lady seated on a bank with a basket of flowers on her arm and by her feet, 4³/₄in. high. (Woolley & Wallis) $992

A pair of Bow figures of a youth and companion, he seated on a tree-stump, his seated companion with a basket of grapes on her lap, circa 1762, 14cm. high. (Christie's) $1,950

A Bow blue and white pierced circular basket painted with a version of The Pinecone and Foliage pattern, circa 1765, 17cm. diameter. (Christie's) $931

A pair of Bow figures of a shepherd and shepherdess, he leaning against a flower-encrusted tree-stump playing the clarinet, she in a dancing pose with a recumbent lamb at her feet, circa 1770, 18.5cm. high. (Christie's) $1,409

A Bow figure of a nun, standing reading from an iron-red-bound book, her right hand held to her bosom, wearing a mauve veil, circa 1756, 16.5cm. high. (Christie's) $1,241

A Bow lobed oval teapot and cover in a Kakiemon palette with blue-branched iron-red prunus and chrysanthemum issuing from blue and turquoise rockwork, circa 1753, 8.5cm. high. (Christie's) $2,275

A Bow white model of an owl with molded and incised feather markings, perched on a tree-stump applied with three flowers, circa 1758, 19.5cm. high. (Christie's) $3,901

BRITISH

CHINA

A pair of Coalport outside-decorated plates, the centers painted in a bright palette with country churches, circa 1810, 23cm. diameter.
(Christie's) $1,095

Fine tobacco leaf charger, 18th century, the interior painted overall in vivid shades of yellow, green, turquoise, blue, brown and iron-red with gilt-edged overlapping leaves, 15in. wide.
(Butterfield & Butterfield)
                              $7,700

A Staffordshire redware pecten-shell-molded teapot and cover with scroll handle, the snake's spout molded with flowering foliage, circa 1755, 12.5cm. high.
(Christie's) $6,940

Liverpool transfer decorated and handpainted creamware pitcher, England, early 19th century, handpainted in polychrome with Caleb Bate's ship, "Venilia", 10½in. high.
(Skinner Inc.) $39,600

A pair of Bristol hexagonal slender tapering vases and covers, the decoration of each vase differing slightly with four sides painted predominantly in green and in colors with trees and shrubs, circa 1775, 44.5cm. high.
(Christie's) $17,350

A large and important Pilkington Lancastrian lustre vase, painted by Gordon Forsyth to commemorate the Brussels International Exhibition of 1910 where the British and Belgian sections burned, 51cm. high.
(Phillips) $18,825

A creamware mug printed and colored with *THE COCK-PIT* within a flower and foliage cartouche and *Come fifty Guineas I will lay That Ginger beats your bonny Gray*, 7in. high.
(Christie's) $783

A large stoneware vase by Janet Leach, swollen cylindrical form with inverted rim, brown glazed body beneath mottled speckled olive green with wax resist 'scars', 35.2cm. high.
(Christie's) $2,009

A pearlware commemorative jug molded in relief with a bust-length portrait of the Duke of York in military costume, circa 1810, 8in. high.
(Christie's) $744

BRITISH

A Della Robbia twin-handled vase decorated by Liz Wilkins, with incised and slip decoration of daffodils framed within leafy border, 40.5cm. high.
(Christie's) $886

An H. & R. Daniel blue-ground oviform jug, painted with a view of Teddesley Hall, the reverse with a gentleman dressed in a coachman's uniform in conversation with a peasant woman, circa 1835, 23cm. high.
(Christie's) $5,475

John Stinton, an ovoid vase and cover painted with Highland cattle in a mountainous landscape, the reverse with a view of a lake, date code for 1910.
(Phillips) $3,080

A Coalport gold-ground two-handled 'jeweled' and reticulated vase and domed cover of baluster form, the body enriched with turquoise and gilt 'jewels' beneath a cream band at the shoulder, circa 1895, 10in. high.
(Christie's) $1,590

A George Jones majolica punch-bowl modeled as Mr. Punch lying on his back, being crushed beneath the weight of a large bowl, the surface molded and colored to simulate orange-rind, circa 1874.
(Christie's) $4,750

A Della Robbia vase decorated by Liz Wilkins, with incised and slip decoration of frogs amongst lily-pads, flowers and grasses, yellow, green, blue and brown, dated 1903, 38.5cm. high.
(Christie's) $1,280

A Spode lavender-ground potpourri-vase and pierced cover with gilt dragon handles and finial, painted with shells and seaweed, circa 1825, 21cm. high.
(Christie's) $3,275

A finely painted English 'Honeysuckle Group' box, the cover painted with a man in classical dress reading the hand of a young lady, her friend at her side, 9.5cm. wide.
(Phillips) $1,485

A creamware baluster coffee pot and cover with flower finial, printed in black with figures taking tea in a garden landscape, circa 1775.
(Christie's) $431

BRITISH

Parian bust of Shakespeare, England, circa 1875, mounted on a raised circular base, Robinson and Leadbeater mark, 12³/₄in. high.
(Skinner Inc.) $715

A Davenport blue and white oval footbath, impressed mark, 21in. wide.
(Dreweatt Neate) $1,326

An English pottery model of a lion standing with a yellow globe under his front paw and before a flowering tree, 12cm. high.
(Phillips) $714

A Winchcombe Pottery earthenware pitcher by Michael Cardew, with applied strap handle, covered in a translucent brown glaze beneath yellow ocher, with bands of brown decoration, 28.3cm. high.
(Christie's) $394

A pair of tiles designed by George Frampton, with molded decoration, one depicting the profile of the God of Music, the other the God of Poetry, circa 1900, 30 x 15.1cm.
(Christie's) $295

An attractive and brightly colored Musselburgh toby jug with individualistic facial features, seated wearing a chocolate brown coat, 23cm. high.
(Phillips) $2,720

An attractive early English 'blue dash' tulip charger painted with a blue and yellow tulip flanked by green leaves and other blue and red flowers, 34cm. diameter.
(Phillips) $1,105

Parian figure of John A. Andrews, England, circa 1867, fine quality full modeled figure mounted atop a cut-corner square base, impressed marks *M. Milmore S.C.*, 21in. high.
(Skinner Inc.) $1,210

English lusterware pitcher, decorated with a pink molded deer in a pink and green landscape, 5¹/₄in. high.
(Eldred's) $88

BRITISH

An important Limehouse model of a cat, modeled and seated upright with its whiskers and paws picked out in underglaze blue and with a solid wash of blue between the paws, 16.3cm. (Phillips) **$8,160**

An unusual Bretby jardinière, 21in. wide, impressed mark. (Dreweatt Neate) **$546**

A Carlton Ware vase and cover, covered in a lustrous orange glaze, decorated in gilt and polychrome glazes with Egyptian figures and motifs, 31.5cm. high. (Christie's) **$1,707**

A creamware toby jug and cover, the smiling man seated holding a jug of frothing ale, wearing dark-blue hat, his brown jacket with blue button-holes, perhaps Yorkshire, circa 1790, 25.5cm. high. (Christie's) **$1,137**

A Jessie Marion King christening mug, for 'Adam', Eve with a spinning wheel, inscribed *When Adam delved and Eve span who was then the gentleman*, signed, circa 1921, 3in. high. (Christie's) **$748**

An early Victorian Copeland Parian bust of Clytie, raised upon a waisted socle, impressed *C. Delpech*, 1855, 15in. high. (Spencer's) **$528**

A creamware pink luster jug printed in black with a scene of Peterloo and a bust of Henry Hunt, 15cm. (Phillips) **$613**

A Walton model of the royal lion seated, with naturalistically colored body, wearing a crown above its curly mane, 14cm. high. (Phillips) **$1,445**

A Copeland & Garrett large stirrup-cup modeled as a hound's head with gray and black fur markings, wearing a light-brown collar, circa 1840, 17cm. high. (Christie's) **$1,735**

CANTON

A famille rose Canton enamel and gilt-bronze model of a jardinière, the knobbly bonsai tree with gilt branches, set with metal and hardstone leaves and blossoms, 58cm. high.
(Christie's) **$5,907**

Canton 'famille rose' covered warming dish, late 18th century, executed in the characteristic Canton 'famille rose' palette, the oval warming dish decorated to the well with a bird and flower medallion, 15³/₄in. wide.
(Butterfield & Butterfield)
$1,210

A massive Canton enamel temple tripod incense burner and cover, raised on monster-mask legs and fitted with box-section upright bracket handles, Qianlong seal mark, 110cm. high.
(Christie's) **$20,000**

A rare famille rose Canton enamel large baluster vase, Qianlong seal mark and of the period, 18¹/₂in. high.
(Christie's) **$60,000**

A pair of ormolu-mounted Chinese (Canton) baluster vases, each with everted lip and scrolled handles, painted in bright colors on a celadon ground with peony, fruit and other flowers, 19th century, 27in. high.
(Christie's) **$12,400**

A fine famille rose Canton enamel slender baluster vase, ruby enamel Qianlong seal mark and of the period, delicately decorated with three cartouches of lady immortals standing among turbulent waves, 9³/₈in. high.
(Christie's) **$28,387**

CHELSEA

A Chelsea bowl with slightly flared rim, painted with five naked iron-red putti, one with a basket of grapes and another with a bunch of grapes, circa 1755, 15.5cm. diameter.
(Christie's) **$4,750**

A pair of Chelsea mazarine-blue ground tapering square vases, the sides painted with Oriental figures with birds and parasols, the sloping shoulders with exotic birds, circa 1765, 31.5cm. high.
(Christie's) **$9,130**

A Chelsea silver-shaped oval dish with molded thumbpieces, painted in a vibrant Kakiemon palette with a red tiger looking up towards a sinuous red-scaled dragon, circa 1750, 25cm. wide.
(Christie's) **$14,600**

CHELSEA

A Chelsea salt of compressed oval form, painted with scattered flowerheads and ladybirds, the interior with a moth and similar flowerheads, circa 1745, 8cm. wide.
(Christie's) $9,000

A Chelsea fable-decorated silver-shaped plate painted in the manner of Jefferyes Hammett O'Neale with the fable of The Fox and the Monkey, circa 1752, 22.5cm. diameter.
(Christie's) $26,884

A Chelsea botanical pierced oval dish, the center painted with pale-pink cistus and with scattered moths, insects and a caterpillar, circa 1756, 31cm. wide.
(Christie's) $6,900

A Chelsea botanical octagonal teabowl and saucer, the teabowl with trailing blue convolvulus, the reverse and interior with two specimen flowers, circa 1753.
(Christie's) $8,200

A Chelsea kakiemon lobed and flared beaker painted in a vibrant palette with a Ho Ho bird perched on pierced turquoise rockwork, circa 1750, 7cm. high.
(Christie's) $3,650

A Chelsea 'Hans Sloane' botanical plate painted with a branch of fruiting mulberry and with a leaf-spray, butterfly and insect, circa 1756, 24cm. diameter.
(Christie's) $5,840

A Chelsea teaplant coffee-pot, with spirally-molded brightly colored teaplants, 1745–49, 13.5cm. high.
(Christie's) $8,200

A 'Girl in a Swing' white Holy Family group after Raphael, the Virgin Mary wearing flowing robes seated on rockwork before a tree-stump, her left arm encircling the Infant Christ Child, circa 1750, 21cm. high.
(Christie's) $51,700

A Chelsea figure of a Chinaman wearing a pink-lined yellow conical hat and long-sleeved white coat painted with iron-red flowers, his hands tucked in his sleeves, circa 1755, 11cm. high.
(Christie's) $2,900

A Chelsea petal molded bowl of lobed outline, painted in colors with flower sprays and scattered sprigs, 17cm., red anchor mark.
(Phillips) $4,183

A pair of Chelsea flowersellers with open panniers, wearing florally painted and colored clothes, 15cm. high.
(Phillips) $2,210

A Chelsea porcelain thimble, brightly painted with birds and a conifer branch within gold line bands, inscribed *Souvenez vous de moy*, 2.2cm.
(Bearne's) $3,938

A Chelsea strawberry-leaf dish with incised vein markings enriched in puce, painted with a loose bouquet and with scattered flowers and foliage, red anchor mark, circa 1756, 22.5cm. long.
(Christie's) $1,575

A Chelsea melon-tureen and cover naturally modeled and enriched in yellow and green, the cover with curled branch finial with foliage and flower terminals, circa 1756, 17cm. long.
(Christie's) $7,482

A Chelsea 'Hans Sloane' botanical lobed plate painted with a yellow tulip, fern, lilac, a caterpillar and insects, circa 1756, 25cm. diameter.
(Christie's) $4,726

A Chelsea lobed circular shallow dish painted with a loose bouquet and with scattered flowers and insects beneath a brown line rim, circa 1753, 26.5cm. diameter.
(Christie's) $1,674

A pair of Chelsea figures of a shepherd and shepherdess, he leaning on a staff filling a satchel with wool, she with a garland of flowers over her shoulder, gold anchor marks, circa 1768, 28cm. high.
(Christie's) $4,922

One of a pair of Chelsea finger bowls painted in colors with flower sprays and scattered springs including a striped tulip and rose, 7.5cm. high.
(Phillips) $2,380

CHINESE

Green Fitzhugh oval platter, China, 19th century, with pierced liner, 17¹/₂in. wide. (Skinner Inc.) $1,100

Pair of famille verte Fu lions, 19th century, each creature ferociously bearing its fangs, each supported on a separated fashioned rectangular pinth, 19in. high. (Butterfield & Butterfield) $6,050

Chinese export porcelain masonic punch bowl, circa 1810, the interior with central medallion of pillars, 11¹/₄in. diameter. (Skinner Inc.) $3,190

A Chinese export porcelain covered bowl, circa 1810, decorated in sepia with a bucolic figure leaning on a cow with a dog at his feet, 5³/₄in. high. (Christie's) $935

Pair of Mandarin garden seats, China, 19th century, 19in. high. (Skinner Inc.) $2,640

Rose Mandarin temple jar and cover, China, circa 1830, brass bound rim and hinged cover, paneled figural courtyard scenes between ornaments, 16¹/₂in. high. (Skinner Inc.) $2,475

A large Han period horse's head of burnt grey tone, and wooden socle, 22.5cm. high. (Galerie Koller) $2,816

Pair of Chinese export porcelain vases, late 18th century, enamel decorated figural courtyard scenes, 11¹/₄in. high. (Skinner Inc.) $1,870

Rose Mandarin wash basin and matching water bottle, China, mid 19th century, decorated in typical palette with figural courtyard scenes, 15¹/₂in. high. (Skinner Inc.) $1,210

A fine blue and white cup, encircled Kangxi six-character mark, finely penciled to the exterior with a continuous mountainous landscape and huts obscured behind willow, 3in. high.
(Christie's) $43,750

A pair of Louis XV ormolu-mounted turquoise-glazed models of parrots on aubergine rockwork bases, the porcelain Kangxi, 9³/₄in. high.
(Christie's) $25,000

A Transitional blue and white jar painted with a dragon chasing a flaming pearl amongst clouds, the short neck with pendent stiff leaves, Shunzhi, 27cm. high.
(Christie's) $2,000

A Chinese export porcelain hot-water plate, early 19th century, decorated in polychrome with the arms of the state of New York, 11¹/₄in. diameter.
(Christie's) $2,860

A highly important large Geyao octagonal vase, Ba Fanghu, Song dynasty, the thinly-potted vase imitating an archaic bronze shape of oblong octagonal section, 10¹/₂in. high.
(Christie's)
$1,480,918

A fine Transitional blue and white brush-pot, circa 1635, painted on the exterior with a scholar seated at a rootwood table shaded by a pine tree, 7⁷/₈in. diameter.
(Christie's) $9,935

A Louis XVI ormolu-mounted Chinese porcelain vase decorated with bamboo shoots and shrubs and a bird on a light-blue ground, the porcelain Qianlong and repaired, 11¹/₂in. high.
(Christie's) $11,000

A pair of ormolu-mounted Chinese blue porcelain peacocks, each with tail feathers up and seated on a naturalistic base, the porcelain Kangxi, 9¹/₂in. wide.
(Christie's) $11,000

A Sancai tilemaker's figure of a Lokopala standing with his legs apart and his arms clenched at his waist, wearing elaborate ribbons, armor and waist sash, Ming Dynasty, 49cm. high.
(Christie's) $12,799

CLARICE CLIFF

A 'Bizarre' grotesque mask designed by Ron Birks, the features painted in panels of orange, yellow and black, 11in. long.
(Christie's) $2,035

A 'Bizarre' Flora wallmask painted in shades of orange, yellow and black, rubber stamp mark, 14¹/₂in. long.
(Christie's) $1,630

A 'Bizarre' model of a laughing cat, after a design by Louis Wain, the orange body with black spots, and green bow tie, 6in. high.
(Christie's) $1,525

A Bizarre twin-handled lotus jug, in 'Autumn crocus' pattern, 29cm. high.
(Allen & Harris) $460

A 'Bizarre' Bonjour teapot and cover, painted in bright colors on a yellow ground with scenes of a Slavonic peasant couple, 5in. high.
(Christie's) $1,625

'Age of Jazz', a 'Bizarre' table decoration modeled as two musicians in evening dress, rubber stamp mark, 6in. high.
(Christie's) $4,475

A'Bizarre' Chahar wallmask, painted in colors, printed factory marks, 10¹/₂in. long.
(Christie's) $1,725

A 'Bizarre' Stamford trio in the 'Tennis' pattern, painted in colors with red banding, height of teapot 4¹/₂in. high.
(Christie's) $4,475

A Bizarre 'orange roof cottage' cylindrical biscuit jar and cover, with wicker handle, 15cm. high.
(Allen & Harris) $535

Delft blue and white flower brick, England, mid 18th century, 6¼in. long. (Skinner Inc.) $605

An exceptional delft bottle, probably London, of rare mallet shape, painted in blue with a seated Chinese lady playing a dulcimer, 26cm. high. (Phillips) $5,550

Delft blue and white bulb bowl, England, circa 1750, 8½in. diameter. (Skinner Inc.) $1,045

A pair of Dutch delft polychrome hounds, their coats splashed in manganese with their tails curled over their flanks and their ears flapping behind their heads, mid-18th century, 21cm. high. (Christie's) $8,500

An English delft blue and white drinking-vessel modeled as a spurred boot, inscribed beneath the flared rim *OH. MY HEAD* above a wide blue band, Southwark, circa 1650, 17.5cm. high. (Christie's) $21,659

A pair of fine Dutch delft polychrome figures of a lady and gentleman, on green washed bases with chamfered corners, 21cm. high. (Phillips) $8,500

Delft blue and white bowl, England, circa 1760, inscribed in center *One Bowl More & Then*, 10½in. diameter. (Skinner Inc.) $1,760

Delft blue and white barber bowl, England or Continental, 13¼in. diameter. (Skinner Inc.) $825

Delft bowl, England or Continental, 18th century, with fluted edge, 12ln. diameter. (Skinner Inc.) $1,100

DERBY

Derby 'brocade' pattern lozenge-shaped dish, third quarter 18th century, painted in underglaze blue with a shaped 'brocade' border, 9¹/₂in. long. (Butterfield & Butterfield)
$800

19th century Derby blue, gilt and iron red flower and foliage decorated dessert service. (Ewbank)
$2,000

A finely painted Derby ovoid pedestal vase and cover, with scroll handles, signed *Leroy*, date code for 1897, 8in. high. (Bonhams)
$1,300

A Derby yellow-ground botanical dessert-service painted in the manner of John Brewer with specimen flowers, named on the reverses in Latin and English, the wells gilt with stylized pendant ornament, within bright yellow borders between gilt lines, circa 1800. (Christie's)
$100,000

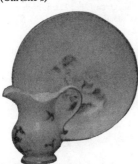

Derby cream jug and saucer, third quarter 18th century, painted in rose camaieu, 2⁷/₈in. high. (Butterfield & Butterfield)
$800

Derby 'Japan' pattern plate, third quarter 18th century, centrally painted with stylized floral and foliate forms in orange and dark-blue, 8¹/₄in. diameter. (Butterfield & Butterfield)
$1,000

Royal Crown Derby 'Billy' Dean, flattened ovoid vase, painted with fishing smacks within a raised gilt scroll cartouche, date code for 1883, 3³/₄in. high. (Bonhams)
$480

An attractively painted Derby
basket, the base painted by 'The
Moth Painter' with a leafy
branch of cherries, 23cm. wide.
(Phillips) $2,720

A Derby butter tub and cover,
painted in colors with birds in
branches and scattered
butterflies and insects, 13.5cm.
wide.
(Phillips) $1,275

A rare Derby teapot and cover
with an unusual handle molded
from a ribbon tied bouquet of
flowers, 14cm. high.
(Phillips) $1,190

An important Derby Royal
Presentation gum container
modeled as a circular turret
raised on the backs of four
gilded elephants, 14.5cm. high.
(Phillips) $3,675

A boldly painted Derby ice pail
of 'U' shape with double scroll
handles outlined in gilding,
painted on both sides with a
central exotic bird, 24cm. high.
(Phillips) $1,750

A pair of Derby figures of
blackamoor dancers, each
holding a posy of flowers, he
with his left hand on his hip, his
companion holding out the edge
of her cape, Wm. Duesbury &
Co., circa 1758, 22cm. high.
(Christie's) $3,741

A Derby coffee cup, probably
painted by William Billingsley,
with roses within a gilt edged
rectangular and circular-shaped
panels, 6.8cm. high, circa 1790.
(Phillips) $1,550

A pair of Derby biscuit figures
of a shepherd and his
companion, probably modeled
by J.J. Spangler, 24.5cm. and
26.5cm. high.
(Phillips) $2,720

A Derby coffee can, painted by
Richard Askew, with a female
figure, a sketch in her hand,
seated by a classical style tomb,
6cm. high, 1794-98.
(Phillips) $3,700

DERBY

A small Derby rectangular box and cover, the cover painted, probably by George Complin, with a still life of a butterfly amongst fruit, 1789-1795. (Phillips) **$6,225**

A Derby cabaret set, each piece painted, probably by Zachariah Boreman, with named Derbyshire views reserved with simulated pearl borders, circa 1790. (Phillips) **$19,450**

A Derby coffee can and saucer, the can probably painted by George Complin, with a finch perched on a still life of fruit, 7.5cm. high, 1789-95. (Phillips) **$28,200**

A Derby biscuit figure of a shepherd, probably modeled by J.J. Spangler, seated on a leafy rock and playing a pipe, 20cm. high. (Phillips) **$3,060**

A set of four Derby figures emblematic of the Elements, painted in colors and enriched in gilding, standing before bocage, on pierced scroll-molded bases, Wm. Duesbury & Co., circa 1770, about 23.5cm. high. **$4,332**

An early Derby 'dry edge' figure of Winter in white, the old woman standing and leaning against a tree trunk, 16.5cm. high. (Phillips) **$2,720**

A Derby two-handled chocolate cup, cover and stand, painted on one side, probably by George Complin, with two finches perched amongst fruit, 1789-95. (Phillips) **$20,425**

A Derby coffee can and saucer, the can probably painted by James Banford or Richard Askew, with a winged putto, a falcon on his arm, 7.5cm. high. (Phillips) **$6,225**

A Derby trout's head stirrup-cup naturally modeled and colored, the rim reserved and inscribed in gilt *THE ANGLER'S DELIGHT*, circa 1800, 10.5cm. high. (Christie's) **$1,969**

A Bunnykins Ware teapot and cover modeled as a crouching animal with its head for a spout, 4³/₄in. high.
(Christie's) $1,328

'Gwyneth' H.N.1980, a bone china figure, printed and painted marks, 7¹/₄in. high.
(Christie's) $285

A Flambé figure of an elephant, printed factory marks, 5¹/₂in. high.
(Christie's) $190

A Chang cylindrical beaker, covered in a thick glaze in shades of red, ocher and white, signed *Noke and Harry Nixon* monogram, 2¹/₂in. high.
(Christie's) $342

A pair of stoneware vases by Mark V Marshall, tube lined with arched panels of flowers and foliage, 11³/₄in. high.
(Christie's) $1,044

A Lambeth earthenware circular dish by Linnie Watt, printed in colors with a rustic scene of two young girls resting on the grassy verge, 13in. diameter.
(Christie's) $474

A Burslem Rembrandt Ware vase, decorated with an oval portrait of a man between swags of eagles, 10¹/₂in. high.
(Christie's) $854

'Grossmith's Tsang Ihang', a polychrome painted pottery advertising figure in traditional dress standing with fan, 11¹/₂in. high.
(Christie's) $531

'Toothless Grannie' D.5521, a character jug, printed factory marks, 6¹/₂in. high.
(Christie's) $474

DOULTON

'The Calumnet' H.N.1428, a pottery figure, printed and painted marks, 6in. high.
(Christie's) $361

A Flambé tobacco jar and cover modeled as a pipe, with silver mounts to rim and handle, London 1910, 12¹/₂in. high.
(Christie's) $474

'Molly Malone' H.N.1455, printed and painted marks, 7in. high.
(Christie's) $1,859

A silver-mounted Athenic-pattern ceramic vase, maker's mark of Gorham Mfg. Co., Providence, circa 1905, the vase marked *Royal Doulton*, 11³/₄in. high.
(Christie's) $1,430

A pair of Mark V Marshall stoneware baluster vases, each decorated in relief with arched panels of dessicated foliage, 15¹/₂in. high.
(Christie's) $1,233

An unusual Lambeth slip-molded stoneware jug by Frank Butler, the body decorated with incised bands of stylized foliage and applied beading, dated *1883*, 8¹/₂in. high.
(Christie's) $721

'Sweet and Twenty' H.N.1360, a bone china figure, printed and painted marks, 5³/₄in. high.
(Christie's) $474

'Old Mac', a musical character jug, printed factory marks, 6¹/₄in. high.
(Christie's) $247

'The Flower Seller's Children', a bone china group, printed and painted marks, 7³/₄in. high.
(Christie's) $474

DOULTON

A Royal Doulton figure, 'A Yeoman of the Guard', HNL122, 6in. high.
(Dreweatt Neate) $644

Doulton Lambeth Hannah B. Barlow jardinière, England, dated *1883*, with an incised frieze of a coach being pulled by a team of horses towards grazing sheep and cattle, 7³/₄in. diameter.
(Skinner Inc.) $1,870

A Royal Doulton figure entitled 'The Pied Piper', H.N.2102, withdrawn 1976.
(Bearne's) $202

A Royal Doulton 'Chang' vase, with inverted rim, covered in a thick crackled mottled white, black, red, ocher glaze running over mottled shades of ocher, red, blue and black, 11cm. high.
(Christie's) $788

A Royal Doulton 'Reynard the Fox' coffee service, printed marks and pattern number H4927.
(Dreweatt Neate) $507

Doulton Lambeth Hannah B. Barlow pitcher, England, circa 1895, incised cat frieze enameled in light blue, 9¹/₄in. high.
(Skinner Inc.) $2,860

Doulton Lambeth stoneware pilgrim vase, England, circa 1885, serpent handles, impressed marks and *Frank A. Butler* signature, 12³/₄in. high.
(Skinner Inc.) $1,210

An unusual white Royal Doulton Simon the Cellarer character Jug, 2⁷/₈in. high.
(Dreweatt Neate) $215

Doulton Lambeth Hannah B. Barlow pitcher, England, dated *1876*, with incised goats running, a dog tied to the base of the handle, 9¹/₂in. high.
(Skinner Inc.) $1,540

DOULTON

A Royal Doulton figure entitled 'Dorcas', H.N.1558, withdrawn 1952.
(Bearne's) $465

Doulton Lambeth Hannah B. Barlow vase, England, circa 1880, with shaped bead framed panels incised with deer in various scenes, 14in. high.
(Skinner Inc.) $1,760

A Royal Doulton figure entitled 'The Young Miss Nightingale', H.N.2010, withdrawn 1953.
(Bearne's) $566

Doulton Lambeth Hannah B. Barlow pitcher, England, circa 1895, with incised hounds and pâte-sur-pâte quail on a stippled background, 9in. high.
(Skinner Inc.) $2,090

A pair of Doulton Lambeth stoneware vases by Florence E. Barlow, deeply incised with a continuous band of finches flying amongst rushes, 13in. high.
(Spencer's) $1,493

Doulton Lambeth Hannah B. Barlow vase, England, dated 1880, with incised decoration of a young girl surrounded by goats, donkeys, cattle and geese, 14¹⁄₂in. high.
(Skinner Inc.) $3,740

A Doulton and Watts stoneware flask modeled as Lord Brougham holding a scroll inscribed 'The True Spirit of Reform', 18cm.
(Phillips) $817

A Royal Doulton pottery character jug 'Arry', with buttons, printed mark in green, 7in. high.
(Spencer's) $906

A Doulton Lambeth stoneware jug of tapering form 'in Commemoration of the Hoisting of the Flag at Pretoria, June 5th 1900', 21cm.
(Phillips) $531

EUROPEAN

An Amphora polychrome painted pottery figure of a motorist wearing green cap and black goggles, 14in. high.
(Christie's) $545

A Zsolnay Pecs green luster pottery figure of a stylized fish, printed factory marks, 4¹/₂in. high.
(Christie's) $58

A Katshütte Thuringia polychrome painted figure of a young girl wearing floral patterned fluted dress, dancing with large fan, 20¹/₂in. high.
(Christie's) $1,168

'Felix the Futurist Cat', an Amphora pottery vase designed by Louis Wain, the body incised with *Miaow Miaow* notes, 9¹/₂in. high.
(Christie's) $3,115

A pair of Vienna-style dark-blue-ground plates painted by Wagner with portraits of young girls wearing broad-brimmed bonnets, one entitled *Flieder*, the other entitled *Rosen*, circa 1900, 10in. diameter.
(Christie's) $3,044

An Aladin polychrome painted porcelain box and cover, modeled as an Egyptian seated with knees drawn up, in exotic pattern robes in yellow, rust and black, 8in. high.
(Christie's) $175

'Manuelita', a Manna polychrome painted pottery figure, of a young woman wearing floral patterned dress and headscarf, 11in. high.
(Christie's) $253

A group emblematic of Plenty in a pink robe holding a cornucopia, seated on a lion surrounded by putti on a rockwork base, circa 1890, 10in. high.
(Christie's) $1,468

A Sitzendorf polychrome painted pottery figure of a bare breasted dancer wearing blue and green skirt, 9¹/₂in. high.
(Christie's) $234

FAMILLE ROSE

A fine famille rose yellow-ground bowl, Qianlong seal mark and of the period, densely enameled on the exterior with a continuous band of scrolling peony, chrysanthemum, lotus and hibiscus, 7³/₄in. diameter.
(Christie's) $35,557

A rare large famille rose kneeling boy pillow, Qianlong, the plump infant crouching on all fours with a smiling face raised to the left and his feet in the air, 15in. long.
(Christie's) $39,000

A fine Famille Rose bowl, Jiaqing seal mark and of the period, the rounded sides rising to a slightly flaring rim, painted with clusters of fruiting pomegranate vines entangled with bamboo, 4½in. diam.
(Christie's) $5,973

A rare famille rose long-necked oviform vase, iron-red Xianfeng six-character mark and of the period, enameled on the broad body with two clusters of flowering chrysanthemum, peony and magnolia, 12in. high.
(Christie's) $18,452

A pair of Famille Rose blue-ground double-gourd vases, iron-red Qianlong seal marks, Daoguang, each raised on a flaring foot and surmounted by a tall neck with a floral rim, 8³/₄in. high.
(Christie's) $7,111

A fine famille rose baluster vase, iron-red Daoguang seal mark and of the period, delicately enameled on the broad body with a procession of Chinese and European figures, 11¹/₄in. high.
(Christie's) $56,774

A fine and very rare famille rose celadon-ground molded lobed vase, underglaze-blue Qianlong seal mark and of the period, the slightly-flattened gourd-shaped vase with splayed foot and flaring neck, 14¹/₄in. high.
(Christie's) $384,028

A fine and rare famille rose yellow-ground bowl, blue enamel Qianlong four-character seal mark and of the period, densely enameled on the exterior with four large flower-heads amongst elaborate scrolling foliage, 5⁷/₈in. diameter.
(Christie's) $14,194

A famille rose 'figural' vase, Huairentang Zhi mark, 20th century, finely painted to the exterior with Shoulao and a young attendant offering a ripe peach to a dancing maiden beside a flower basket, 10⁷/₈in. high, box.
(Christie's) $8,121

FRENCH

Alphonse Mucha portrait plaque, colorful handpainted woman in the Art Nouveau manner after the 1899 color lithograph 'La Primevere Polyanthus', 16$^{1}/_{2}$in. diameter. (Skinner Inc.) **$1,210**

A pair of massive French colored biscuit busts, signed *Paul Duboy*, of two blonde ladies with roses in their hair, 59cm. high. (Phillips) **$3,400**

A French porcelain cabinet-plate painted by Wagner with a head-and-shoulders portrait of Napoleon I in half-profile to the left within a ciselé gilt cartouche, circa 1880, 9$^{3}/_{4}$in. diameter. (Christie's) **$1,315**

A French faience caricature figure of a brown whippet, seated on its haunches and holding a flowered rectangular tray on his outstretched forepaws, circa 1899, 21$^{1}/_{2}$in. high. (Christie's) **$1,735**

Pair of French gilt-bronze-mounted porcelain covered urns, circa 1900, with two mask handles in the form of maidens with ears of wheat in their coiled hair, 18$^{1}/_{2}$in. high. (Butterfield & Butterfield) **$2,475**

A Gallé faience model of a cat, its yellow body decorated in blue and white with heart shapes and roundels, 34cm. high. (Phillips) **$2,600**

A large Clément Massier ceramic jardinière. (Christie's) **$5,730**

Pair of Paris porcelain vases with floral panels, 40cm. high, circa 1825. (Christie's) **$4,947**

A very large Moustier dish, first half of 18th century, 21$^{1}/_{2}$in. diameter. (Dreweatt Neate) **$1,170**

FRENCH

A French faience shaped oval dish, the handles painted with butterflies, the exterior painted with a seated Chinaman, 36.5cm., 18th century.
(Bearne's) $322

A rare and attractive Saint Cloud spice box and cover, painted in a bright underglaze blue with Berainesque designs, 14cm. diameter.
(Phillips) $5,780

A Jacob Petit porcelain inkstand painted with flowers on an emerald green and gilt ground, circa 1840.
(Duran, Madrid) $1,391

Clement Massier art pottery vase, pinched oval clay body with handpainted decoration of two dragonflies among cat-tails and grasses, 7¹/₂in. high.
(Skinner Inc.) $450

A pair of French gilt-metal-mounted white-ground inverted pear-shaped vases and covers, the bodies painted in the style of Wouvermans with figures beside encampments, circa 1910, 33in. high.
(Christie's) $8,217

Gilt-bronze-mounted Samson porcelain covered bowl, mid-19th century, painted on front and back with exterior scenes of peasants dancing, separated by sprays of flowers, 21in. high.
(Butterfield & Butterfield) $3,025

Sarreguemines majolica centerpiece, France, circa 1875, the bowl with pierced ringlets to the sides and supported by a center stem flanked by sea nymphs, 14³/₄in. high.
(Skinner Inc.) $880

A pair of French polychrome biscuit figures of a lady and her gallant on square plinths, circa 1845, 47.5cm. high.
(Duran, Madrid) $3,479

A biscuit porcelain figure group of Louis XVI and Benjamin Franklin, Niderville Factory, France, circa 1785, on a draped red and white marbleised base, 12⁷/₈in. high.
(Christie's) $50,600

121

A Sceaux faience cabbage-tureen and cover naturally modeled, the outer overlapping gray-green leaves with pale-green midribs and veins, circa 1755, 32cm. wide.
(Christie's)   **$12,500**

Pair of French flower encrusted figures of a boy and a girl carrying baskets, on round bases, 10¹/₂in. high.
(Ewbank) $260

French flower decorated pot pourri jar with pierced cover, the supports in the form of three dolphins, gilt pierced cover, 8¹/₂in. high.
(Ewbank) $350

A French Art Deco porcelain night light, from a model by M. Béver, in the form of a young girl, dressed in pink, rust and blue harlequin costume, 9¹/₄in. high.
(Christie's) $354

A pair of Chantilly white wolves naturalistically modeled seated on their haunches looking to left and right, with ferocious looking teeth, pricked ears, long curly coats and bushy tails forming the bases, circa 1740, 21cm. high.
(Christie's) $17,000

A French gilt-metal-mounted tapering oviform vase and domed cover, the white ground enriched in a lustrous pink and gray and painted with a woman holding an iris, wearing an anthemion headdress, circa 1910, 30¹/₄in. high.
(Christie's) $6,000

A pair of Sèvres-style turquoise ground oviform vases with rams head and grape handles, painted in colors with maidens in landscape, circa 1860, 14¹/₂in. high.
(Christie's) $1,273

A rare and unusual Gallé pottery centerpiece modeled as an elderly man in brown robe tied to the middle, he crouches while supporting a large twin-handled basket on his back, 36.5cm. high.
(Phillips) $1,665

A pair of French pink-ground baluster vases, painted with continuous friezes of mythological figures in wooded landscapes, circa 1860, 20¹/₂in. high.
(Christie's) $3,980

FRENCH

French shell vase with two cherubs seated on one edge, 7in. (Ewbank) $220

Pair of French 19th century vases decorated with hunting trophies and dead game, gilt highlighted borders and ring handles, 9$^{1}/_{2}$in. high. (Ewbank) $480

A Vincennes tureen, cover and stand of oval form, gilt with panels of birds in flight within scrolling gilt cartouches, 25.5cm. wide. (Phillips) $7,820

A Mennecy silver-mounted snuff-box modeled as a seated Buddha patting his tummy in a puce-flowered open-necked robe with a fur collar, décharge for Éloy Brichard, Paris 1756–1762, circa 1755, 5.5cm. high. (Christie's) $2,830

An ormolu encrier with two wells contained in a gabled niched summerhouse framing a turquoise-glazed Vincennes porcelain model of a pug with a puppy, the pug, circa 1750, 7in. high. (Christie's) $5,000

A Vincennes large pot-pourri vase and a cover, the shoulders with puce and gilt foliage scrolls with harebells suspending sprays of flowers, between seven pierced holes molded with gilt cartouches, circa 1752, 32cm. high. (Phillips) $34,500

A pair of Jacob Petit oviform ewers, painted with panels of figures and flowers, the handles molded with flowers, blue *J.P* mark circa 1850, 14in. high. (Christie's) $1,077

A Paris porcelain turquoise ground oviform two-handled pot pourri vase and cover, painted with figures in landscapes within a cartouche of scrolls in gilding, circa 1880, 14$^{1}/_{2}$in. high. (Christie's) $509

A pair of Sèvres-style tapering cylindrical gilt-metal mounted vases and covers, painted in colors with lovers in landscape, circa 1880, 18$^{3}/_{4}$in. high. (Christie's) $3,329

GERMAN

A Böttger chinoiserie saucer painted with a figure standing and holding a staff and leaning on a table, circa 1725. (Christie's) $1,034

An Ansbach bullet-shaped teapot and cover with a dog's head spout and foliate scroll handle, painted in puce camaieu with bouquets of flowers, circa 1770, 7.5cm. high. (Christie's) $2,363

A German group of a hunchback and three children in colored and patterned clothes, the hunchback with a stick and carrying one child in a sling on his back, perhaps Limbach, circa 1775, 16.5cm. high. (Christie's) $2,954

A pair of Bock-Wallendorf baluster vases and covers, the finials modeled with crowned Arms applied with flowers and with cherub supporters, the handles modeled as maidens seated wearing flowered robes, circa 1905, 24³/₄in. high. (Christie's) $5,478

A pair of rare Ludwigsburg tureens and covers, painted with sprays of flowers in colors, surmounted by finials of cabbage, onion and garlic, 25cm. wide. (Phillips) $3,740

Pair of German gilt-bronze-mounted porcelain covered urns, mid 19th century, painted on the front and back with scenes of eighteenth century lovers and musicians in a garden setting, 27¹/₈in. high. (Butterfield & Butterfield) $5,500

Pair of German porcelain figures of a couple from the Malabar Coast, after a Meissen model by F.E. Meyer, circa 1900, 12in. tall. (Butterfield & Butterfield) $935

A German porcelain plaque depicting Amor and Psyche, each scantily clad, flying above the clouds, 25.3cm. x 17.8cm., in a gilt Florentine frame. (Bearne's) $1,848

A pair of Thuringian figures of a shepherd and shepherdess, he in a long coat, she in a black and red hat, white bodice with a purple edge, circa 1770, 14cm. high. (Christie's) $2,166

124

GERMAN

A Thuringian figure of a lady, possibly Wallendorf, holding her black apron in one hand, wearing a lace collar, a red bodice and a floral skirt, 13cm.
(Phillips) $825

A J. von Schwarz earthenware and nickle-plated brass tray, the base with impressed and polychrome glazed decoration of a maiden's profile, 46cm. long.
(Christie's) $974

A Böttger two-handled chinoiserie slender beaker and saucer painted in the manner of J.G. Höroldt with figures at various pursuits, one chopping teabricks, one with a table fountain and another drinking tea, circa 1725.
(Christie's) $2,445

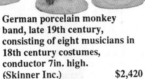

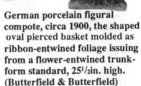

A Höchst figure emblematic of Winter modeled by J.P. Melchior, as a putto wrapped in an ermine-lined cape with a muff seated on a grassy hummock, circa 1760, 16.5cm. high.
(Christie's) $1,067

German porcelain monkey band, late 19th century, consisting of eight musicians in 18th century costumes, conductor 7in. high.
(Skinner Inc.) $2,420

German porcelain figural compote, circa 1900, the shaped oval pierced basket molded as ribbon-entwined foliage issuing from a flower-entwined trunk-form standard, 25½in. high.
(Butterfield & Butterfield) $1,540

A pair of Potschappel (Carl Thieme) baluster vases, covers and stands, enriched with gilt caillouté and on footed shaped-square stands applied and painted with bouquets and edged with molded scrolls and shells, late 19th century, 32¾in. high. (Christie's) $11,869

A German porcelain figure emblematic of Smell modeled as a naked putto taking snuff, with a purple drape and holding a brown snuff-box, perhaps Kassel, circa 1770, 10.5cm. high.
(Christie's) $896

Pair of Furstenberg porcelain figures of a young man and woman, circa 1770, each on a low shaped oval base mottled in green, 7¼in. high.
(Butterfield & Butterfield) $9,900

GERMAN

A pair of Potschappel (Carl Thieme) vases and covers, the shoulders applied on each side with two seated putti holding bouquets and wreaths of flowers, 20th century, 40in. high.
(Christie's) $11,400

A German porcelain rectangular plaque painted by Wagner after Asti with a bust-length portrait of a young woman facing left, with long flowing brown hair, circa 1880, 8¹/₂ x 5¹/₂in.
(Christie's) $4,565

A pair of Potschappel (Carl Thieme) two-handled vases, covers and stands, the covers modeled with two cherubs flanking a crowned coat of arms, blue cross and T marks, circa 1880, 41¹/₂in. high.
(Christie's) $11,400

A Böttger pagoda figure wearing an unusual tall purple hat with deeper purple scrolls and flowerheads between iron-red ribs, with brown hair, eyebrows, eyes and curling mustache, circa 1715, 13cm. high.
(Christie's) $13,783

A Nymphenburg white figure of a beggar modeled by Franz Anton Bustelli, wearing tattered clothes, in a contra-posto pose holding out an empty tattered hat in his right hand, circa 1760, 17cm. high.
(Christie's) $39,380

A Böttger red-stoneware coffee-pot and cover made for the Turkish market, the onion-shaped domed cover cut with straps of diaper and a Turkish crescent and pendant, circa 1712, 17cm. high.
(Christie's) $14,767

A pair of Potschappel (Carl Thieme) pot-pourri vases, modeled in high relief with two seated maidens, circa 1880, 35¹/₂in. high.
(Christie's) $5,700

One of a pair of Dresden chinoiserie vases and covers, with crown and cushion finials and female-mask handles 16¹/₂in. high. (Christie's)   (Two)
                $1,800

A pair of Ludwigsburg figures of a gallant and companion modeled by Franz Anton Pustelli, circa 1760, 13cm. high.
(Christie's) $5,710

GOLDSCHEIDER

A Goldscheider polychrome-painted pottery figure, modeled by Dakon, of a dancer dressed in spotted blue bodice, 16in. high. (Christie's) **$935**

Goldscheider wall mask with stylized ringlets, terracotta, 8¹/₂in. high, 1930s. (Muir Hewitt) **$650**

A Goldscheider polychrome painted pottery table lamp, modeled as a pair of blonde women dancing together, 19in. high. (Christie's) **$1,110**

A Goldscheider polychrome painted pottery figure of a young female dancer, wearing blue dress painted with bubbles and vines, 15¹/₄in. high. (Christie's) **$1,300**

A pair of Goldscheider pottery bookends, in the style of Wiener Werkstätte, each modeled as a kneeling girl with head turned to the side, 8in. high. (Christie's) **$2,531**

A Goldscheider polychrome painted pottery figure of a ung girl in bat costume, printed factory marks, 18¹/₂in. high. (Christie's) **$1,750**

A Goldscheider polychrome painted pottery figure of a Spanish dancer, wearing a short flounced yellow dress, 18in. high. (Christie's) **$876**

A Goldscheider polychrome painted pottery group from a model by Bouret, of two children walking arm in arm, 9in. high. (Christie's) **$876**

A Goldscheider ceramic figure of a negro dandy, dressed in three piece suit, wing collar and tie, with a glass monocle, 20¹/₂in. high. (Christie's) **$4,440**

IMARI

A large and massive Imari vase and cover, decorated with a continuous panel of bijin beside flower carts, late 17th/early 18th century, 103cm. high.
(Christie's) $16,929

A pair of fine Imari octagonal vases and covers decorated with various shaped panels of landscapes and foliage, late 17th/early 18th century, 51cm. high.
(Christie's) $13,167

Late 17th century Imari vase, richly decorated in iron red, blue and gold with flowering bushes on a terrace, Genroku period, 63cm. high.
(Christie's) $26,615

A large Imari vase and cover decorated with panels of chrysanthemum sprays among informal gardens, beneath a band of irises and other foliage, late 17th century, 71cm. high.
(Christie's) $10,722

A pair of Imari models of actors, the robes with roundels containing the character ju among sprays of flowers, foliage and blossom, late 17th century, 31.8cm. high.
(Christie's) $8,700

An Imari octagonal tureen and cover decorated with panels of karashishi and cranes (cover and bowl with extended crack and chips), late 17th/early 18th century, 41cm. high.
(Christie's) $4,514

An Imari tureen and cover decorated with stylized chrysanthemum flowerheads with geometric and floral patterns surrounded by flowers and scrolling foliage, late 17th century, 38cm. high.
(Christie's) $6,070

A pair of octagonal Imari vases and covers decorated with shaped panels of birds among flowers and foliage, late 17th/ early 18th century, 63.5cm. high.
(Christie's) $12,227

A fine Imari charger decorated with three lobed panels containing a ho-o bird hovering above waves beside various flowers and foliage amongst rockwork, late 17th/early 18th century, 54.7cm. diameter.
(Christie's) $6,772

ITALIAN

CHINA

A Castelli plate painted in yellow, brown, manganese, ocher and blue with seven blonde cherubs entwined, 23.5cm. diameter.
(Phillips) $2,380

A Ferniani coffee pot and cover, painted in blue, red, yellow, olive green, brown and manganese, with a Japanese Imari style garden landscape with giant flowers, 34cm. high.
(Phillips) $782

A finely painted Urbino Istoriato dated dish with The Adoration of the Magi, a mountainous landscape in the background with hill-top towns, 29cm. diameter.
(Phillips) $8,840

A maiolica group of the Virgin and Child seated holding the Christ Child on her knee, her features enriched in blue, wearing an ocher veil and ocher-trimmed blue cloak, most probably Faenza, circa 1540, 40cm. high.
(Christie's) $27,000

A Deruta blue and gold lustered dish, the center painted with a winged mythical beast with the naked torso of a woman and the lower part of a hoofed monster with a divided tail, circa 1525, 43cm. diameter.
(Christie's) $55,132

A Naples (Real Fabbrica Ferdinandea) figure of a dancing lady, her pale-brown hair tied in a bun, wearing a green and puce striped bodice over a white blouse, circa 1790, 17.5cm. high.
(Phillips) $9,600

An interesting small Castel Durante dish with sunken center painted with a coat of arms of a standing figure of a negro inscribed *V: Sapes: Forts*, 17cm. diameter.
(Phillips) $850

An Italian rectangular casket and cover with a detachable surmount formed as a youth and maiden embracing, holding a goblet and bunch of grapes, attended by a putto, circa 1880, 12½in. high.
(Christie's) $3,044

A massive Montelupo dish boldly painted with the interior of a bakery with figures kneading dough and removing bread and cakes from the oven, late 16th century, 50.5cm. diameter.
(Christie's) $19,690

ITALIAN

A white maiolica group of two putti symbolic of Autumn, one lying on the ground and holding a goblet into which the standing putti is squeezing a bunch of grapes, 26.5cm. high.
(Phillips) $680

A Lodi ichthyological shaped oval dish painted with a pike with naturally colored light and dark-brown scales, fins and tail, Ferretti's factory, circa 1750, 43.5cm. wide.
(Christie's) $3,650

A Savona blue and white armorial ewer of waisted baluster form, the loop handle with mask terminal, the body with the quartered Arms flanked by foliage, circa 1740, 28.5cm. high.
(Christie's) $4,200

Large faienza oviform wine jar, 18th century, painted with a roundel of leaves and fruit enclosing a cherub's head with halo and blue and green wings below, 22¼in. high.
(Butterfield & Butterfield)
                           $1,650

A Bassano plate painted in the manner of Bartolomeo Terchi with numerous figures at discussion before turreted buildings on a hilly promontory before the sea, circa 1740, 22.5cm. diameter.
(Christie's) $2,757

A pair of Doccia figures of Harlequin and Columbine from the Commedia dell'Arte, in black masks and iron-red and yellow checkered theatrical costumes, circa 1770, 12.5cm. high.
(Christie's) $13,150

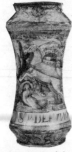

An istoriato armorial waisted albarello painted with Aurora in her chariot in a continuous mountainous landscape, Urbino or Castel Durante, circa 1563, 30.5cm. high.
(Christie's) $4,200

A Savona blue and white oviform wet-drug jar, titled in manganese *S. de Pharfara* between bands of foliage, circa 1720, 7¼in. high.
(Christie's) $548

An Italian trefoil rim jug, the globular body inscribed in Greek within a scroll cartouche, circa 1780, 9in. high.
(Christie's) $548

JAPANESE

A Kinkozan vase decorated with detailed figurative scenes, divided by scattered brocade designs, stamped *Kinkozan zo*, late 19th century, 27cm. high.
(Christie's) $4,514

A Hirado blue and white temple bell decorated with Raijin and ho-o birds among clouds, late 19th century, 24.5cm. high.
(Christie's) $4,138

A Kiyomizu sake bottle, decorated in iron-red, green and blue enamels and gilt with scrolling foliage, early 19th century, 20cm. high.
(Christie's) $2,539

A Ryozan vase decorated with a figurative scene divided by a panel of flowers and grasses, signed *Kyoto Ryozan*, late 19th century, 21.5cm. high.
(Christie's) $3,762

A fine Ko-Kutani deep dish with slightly inverted rim and ring foot, enameled in green, blue, yellow and black, the center with a rocky landscape bordered by six medallions, Fuku mark, late 17th century, 28cm. diameter.
(Christie's) $97,000

A Kinkozan vase decorated with numerous revelers, the shoulder with a band of brocade designs, signed and sealed *Kinkozan sei* and *Masayasu*, 17.4cm. high.
(Christie's) $3,950

Large studio ware ovoid vase, Sumidagawa, late 19th century, the slender ovoid vase applied to the exterior with a continuous band of horde of monkeys in high relief, 17³/₄in. high.
(Butterfield & Butterfield) $2,750

Ki-Seto model of a koma-inu, 19th century, the mythical beast seated on its rear haunches and with its straight forelegs resting to the front of the oval base, 11⁷/₈in. high.
(Butterfield & Butterfield) $1,320

A Yabu Meizan koro and cover decorated with a continuous procession of courtiers and samurai, signed *Yabu Meizan*, late 19th century, 10.5cm. high.
(Christie's) $7,148

KAKIEMON

A rare Kakiemon oviform ewer of Islamic form, decorated in iron-red, green, aubergine, yellow and black enamels and molded in low relief, late 17th/early 18th century, 30cm. high.
(Christie's) $15,180

A pair of Kakiemon cockerels, vividly decorated in iron-red, green, blue, yellow and black enamels, late 17th/early 18th century, mounted on wood stands, 28cm. high.
(Christie's) $99,693

A Kakiemon vase and cover, the shoulder with geometric and foliate designs including hanabishi, the domed cover with flattened knop finial, late 17th century, 32.5cm. high.
(Christie's) $64,750

LEACH

A St. Ives stoneware vase by Bernard Leach, with flange rim, incised linear motifs, covered in a speckled oatmeal glaze beneath brushed white with rust red and blue brushwork floral decoration, 15cm. high.
(Christie's) $1,378

A fine stoneware charger by Bernard Leach, the cream glazed ground with wax-resist decoration of a bird in flight, the rim with diagonal bands, 36.5cm. diameter.
(Christie's) $16,434

A St. Ives stoneware hexagonal vase by Bernard Leach, with everted rim and circular aperture, covered in a blue and iron brown mottled speckled glaze, 20.4cm. high.
(Christie's) $1,181

LENCI

A Lenci pottery model of a young naked girl, kneeling on two large fish and holding a fish above her head, 18¼in. diameter.
(Christie's) $2,954

A Lenci pottery model of a naked female, dancing with arms outstretched, on a black mound base, 11½in. high.
(Christie's) $1,811

A Lenci pottery model of a young naked girl wearing a black and white checkered tammie, holding a book, and with a dog on top of a globe, 19½in. high.
(Christie's) $8,270

CHINA

LUCIE RIE

A porcelain inlaid and sgraffito bottle vase by Dame Lucie Rie, covered in a pitted matt manganese glaze, the shoulder and neck brushed beige with vertical sgraffito, circa 1908, 24.5cm. high.
(Christie's)　　　　　$4,648

A porcelain bowl by Dame Lucie Rie, covered in a translucent finely crackled yelow glaze with lustrous bronze run and fluxed glaze to rim, circa 1980, 16.6cm. diameter.
(Christie's)　　　　　$2,922

A stoneware sgraffito bottle vase by Dame Lucie Rie, the bulbous body with tall cylindrical neck and flared rim, mushroom-gray glaze inlaid with green sgraffito to rim and shoulder, 27.2cm. high.
(Christie's)　　　　　$5,907

MACINTYRE

A Macintyre Florian 'Poppy' pattern preserve jar on saucer, with domed cover, white ground with raised slip decoration of blue poppies, with brown printed Macintyre stamp, circa 1904, 14cm. diameter.
(Christie's)　　　　　$591

A Macintyre 'Claremont' pattern bowl, streaked blue and green ground with decoration of pink, green and blue mushrooms, circa 1903, 12cm. high.
(Christie's)　　　　　$1,477

A Macintyre Florian 'Poppy' pattern vase designed by William Moorcroft, white ground with raised slip decoration of blue poppies, with brown printed Macintyre stamp, circa 1904, 31cm. high.
(Christie's)　　　　　$2,560

MARTINWARE

A Martin Brothers vase, with incised floral decoration, covered in a matt brown glaze with painted brown, green, white and blue, dated 1887, 20.1cm. high.
(Christie's)　　　　　$985

A small Martin Brothers grotesque bird, mounted on oval ebonized wooden base, the head incised *R.W. Martin Bros, London & Southall, 19.8.1913*, 16.5cm. high.
(Christie's)　　　　　$1,181

An R.W. Martin and Brothers stoneware jug in the form of a grotesque animal squatting on four feet with scaled body, 21cm. high.
(Bearne's)　　　　　$5,104

MEISSEN

A Meissen porcelain thimble painted with an encircling scene of soldiers in a camp, the top painted with a gold flower head, circa 1740.
(Bearne's) $4,296

Meissen footed bowl, late 19th century, pierced basketweave sides, enamel and gilt decorated floral panels, 10¼in. wide.
(Skinner Inc.) $935

A Meissen figure of Winter modeled as an old man in a simple fur-lined cloak painted with formal flowers, 12cm., crossed swords mark.
(Phillips) $646

Meissen porcelain bust of a 'jeweled' Renaissance lady, late 19th century, depicted wearing a purple bodice with a high ornate collar of ruffled lace, 12¾in. high.
(Butterfield & Butterfield) $1,430

A pair of Meissen dark-blue-ground 'Limoges enamel' vases of amphora shape, the handles with anthemion terminals, the bodies painted in white, shaded in dark blue, with mythological scenes, circa 1865, 15¾in. high.
(Christie's) $15,521

A Meissen figure of a cavalier, sanding wearing a plumed, broad-brimmed brown hat, purple cloak, ocher jacket with white lace collar and gilt-fringed turquoise sash, circa 1890, 8½in. high.
(Christie's) $730

A Meissen chinoiserie group of three figures, modeled as a young woman wearing a yellow robe and blue-lined flowered cloak, holding a double-spouted kettle and pouring milk from a jug, 20th century, 8¼in. high.
(Christie's) $1,278

A Meissen figure allegorical of Europe, modeled as a young woman wearing a crown, holding an orb and scepter and seated beside a standing white stallion, circa 1880, 10in. high.
(Christie's) $3,287

A Meissen figure emblematic of Winter modeled by J.F. Eberlein as an old man with his arms folded and scantily clad in a fur-lined blue cloak, circa 1750, 26.5cm. high.
(Christie's) $2,112

MEISSEN

An early Meissen teapot and cover with yellow ground, painted in Oriental style with two panels of birds perched on a tree, 10cm. high.
(Phillips) **$1,700**

A Meissen figure of a traveler, the gentleman carrying a bag and holding a staff, 14cm. high, early 19th century.
(Phillips) **$510**

A fine Meissen porcelain oval plaque in the Sèvres manner, painted with a view of Pillnitz on the River Elbe, 15.2cm. wide.
(Bearne's) **$2,464**

A Meissen white model of a royal eagle, vigorously modeled with crouching legs and outspread wings, wearing a 'jeweled' gilt crown with white bosses, its beak open aggressively and with boldly painted features, circa 1880, 20¼in. high.
(Christie's) **$4,119**

A pair of Meissen portrait busts of Prince Louis Charles and Princesse Marie Zéphirine de Bourbon, after the original models by J.J. Kändler, blue crossed swords marks, circa 1880, 6in. high.
(Christie's) **$1,552**

A Meissen pedestal jar and cover with handles in the form of writhing snakes, painted in green enamel and gold with figures in gardens, 31.5cm. high, 18th century.
(Bearne's) **$950**

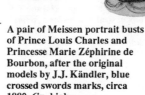

A Meissen octofoil teabowl and saucer painted with scattered insects in the manner of J.G. Klinger, including a large moth, the interior of the cup with a flower sprig, circa 1738.
(Christie's) **$1,411**

A Meissen group of the triumphal procession of Amphitrite after the original model by J.J. Kändler, formed in three detachable sections, circa 1880, 19in. high.
(Christie's) **$10,043**

Meissen porcelain figure of a young cupid, after a model by Pollack, late 19th century, the child holding a large flaming heart in his left hand, 12½in. high.
(Butterfield & Butterfield) **$1,210**

MEISSEN

A Meissen group of a goat and four putti, the figures lightly clad in loose flowered and spotted robes holding bunches of grapes, circa 1880, 6¹/₂in. high. (Christie's) $2,191

A Meissen group of three cherubs allegorical of Architecture, after the original model by M.V. Acier, the figures scantily clad and modeled constructing a Corinthian capital, circa 1880, 9in. high. (Christie's) $2,374

A Meissen figure of a seated harlequin with a bird-cage after the model by J.J. Kändler and J.F. Eberlein, in a pink hat, and playing-card jacket over yellow trousers, circa 1745, 13.5cm. high. (Christie's) $19,008

A Meissen group of the Eavesdropper at the Fountain after the original model of J.J. Kändler. on a shaped-oval grassy base molded with white and gilt scrolls, circa 1880, 8³/₄in. high. (Christie's) $3,104

A Meissen royal presentation gold-mounted armorial snuff-box of oval bombé form, painted by J.G. Herold with a portrait of Augustus the Strong, the front with the Arms of Saxony and Poland surmounted by a crown, circa 1730, 7cm. wide. (Christie's) $379,000

A Meissen figure of a lady of the Mopsorden modeled by J.J. Kändler, in a puce dress with a crinoline skirt enriched with gilding and a turquoise flowered underskirt, circa 1745, 28.5cm. high. (Christie's) $10,138

A large Meissen baluster vase and domed cover, the front and back painted with scenes after Watteau with quatrefoil cartouches, the sides with smaller panels painted with Venetian scenes after Melchior Küsel, circa 1740. 39cm. high. (Christie's) $63,360

A Meissen (Augustus Rex) yellow-ground coffee-cup painted with a mustached chinoiserie figure bending forwards and beckoning with his hand and standing on a terrace before a fence, circa 1730, 7cm. high.(Christie's) $23,000

A Meissen white bust of Carolus VII from the series of busts of Holy Roman Emperors (Kaiserbusten), made for the House of Habsburg and modeled by J.J. Kändler and P. Reinicke, 1743–46, 38cm. high. (Christie's) $23,232

MEISSEN

A Meissen group of Venus, Cupid and a nymph, after the original model by Schoenheit, on a rocky oval base molded with a band of yellow and gilt lozenges, circa 1880, 8¹/₄in. high. (Christie's) $2,739

A Meissen box and cover modeled as a tortoise probably by Georg Fritzsche, with a yellow head and tail with black and iron-red markings and four yellow feet with black claws, circa 1725, 19.5cm. long. (Christie's) $38,000

A Meissen salt modeled as a centaur and Cupid supporting a scallop shell, the beast recumbent to the left, smiling and holding one end of the shell on his upraised right arm, circa 1880, 10¹/₄in. high. (Christie's) $1,461

A Meissen Augustus Rex beaker-vase painted by J.E. Stadler, divided into three sections, the flaring top painted with two chinoiserie figures, AR mark, circa 1730, 39cm. high. (Christie's) $48,906

A Meissen armorial circular dish from the Swan Service modelled by J.J. Kändler and J.F. Eberlein for Count Brühl, the shell-patterned surface molded with swans among bulrushes, herons, fish and shells, 1737–41, 42cm. diameter. (Christie's) $63,360

A Meissen figure of Harlequin playing the bagpipes in a green pointed hat with a black bow, iron-red mask, yellow-patterned jacket and blue-patterned breeches, circa 1735, 14cm. high. (Christie's) $8,870

A Meissen figure of a lady beside a spinning-wheel wearing a lace-trimmed spotted white bonnet tied with blue ribbon, a yellow-lined flowered pink jacket, and blue shoes, circa 1880, 6³/₄in. high. (Christie's) $2,008

A Meissen tea canister of rectangular shape, painted in the manner of C.F. Heroldt with shipping and harbor scenes, 10.5cm. high. (Phillips) $4,250

A Meissen group of three musicians modeled as a young woman playing the harp, a young man seated opposite her holding an open score wearing a pink-lined blue coat, circa 1880, 7¹/₂in. high. (Christie's) $2,922

A fine Ming-style yellow and green-glazed blue and white dish, encircled Yongzheng six-character mark and of the period, 10⁵/₈in. diameter.
(Christie's) $99,355

A rare early Ming blue and white jar, encircled Xuande six-character mark and of the period, painted around the body with two long-tailed phoenixes in flight amidst leafy vines, 5¹/₄in. high.
(Christie's) $94,779

A Ming imperial yellow dish potted with well-rounded sides rising to an everted rim, all under an even egg-yolk yellow glaze, Zhengde six-character mark and of the period, 20.3cm. diameter.
(Christie's) $10,000

A fine Ming blue and yellow saucer-dish, encircled Zhengde four-character mark and of the period, painted in underglaze-blue with a central hibiscus branch of two flowers and one bud among leaves, 7³/₄in. diameter.
(Christie's) $70,968

A fine early Ming blue and white 'Dice' bowl, Xuande six-character mark below the rim and of the period, the heavily-potted rounded sides painted to the exterior with a leafy peony scroll above a band of upright lotus panels, 11³/₈in. diameter.
(Christie's) $241,290

A fine small late Ming Wucai bowl, encircled Wanli six-character mark and of the period, painted and enamelled on the exterior with three figures and a caparisoned deer in a landscape, 4³/₈in. diameter.
(Christie's) $22,710

A very fine Ming-style blue and white moon flask, Qianlong seal mark and of the period, painted to each side in rich cobalt-blue with eight petals, 19¹/₄in. high.
(Christie's) $192,519

A dated late Ming blue and white cylindrical censer with molded lion-masks around the base, painted with dragons among fire-scrolls, 25.5cm. diameter.
(Christie's) $3,600

An early Ming blue and white small jar painted with a band of four blooming lotus flowers on a continuous leafy vine below closed flower buds, 13cm. high.
(Christie's) $44,000

CHINA

A Minton majolica circular pigeon-pie tureen and cover molded to simulate yellow wicker-work, the tureen supported on the tails of three fan-tailed pigeons, circa 1864. (Christie's) $8,000

A Minton majolica monkey teapot and cover, the smiling creature's head forming the detachable cover and its curling tail forming the handle, date code for 1874, 6in. high. (Christie's) $2,000

A Minton majolica oval seafood dish, the cover modeled as a large crab resting on a bed of green seaweed, the fronds curling up its back to form a loop handle, date code for 1859, 15³/₄in. wide. (Christie's) $6,600

A Minton majolica ewer and stand after a model by Hughes Protât, the tapering dark-brown body with a knopped shoulder moulded with bands of gadroons and applied with the seated figures of a putto riding a dolphin, impressed date code for 1859, 24¹/₂in. high. (Christie's) $2,985

A massive Minton majolica group of two frogs courting under a bunch of leaves, their faces turned towards each other with fond devotion and their hands entwined around the stem of the leaves, date code for 1876, 48in. high. (Christie's) $31,042

A Minton majolica dark-blue-ground jardinière and stand with two bamboo-moulded handles extending to encircle the rim and foot, date code for 1870, 9in. high. (Christie's) $2,190

A large Minton majolica flower vase in the form of a fawn after a model by Paul Comolera, the young animal with a matt gray-brown body and white spotted markings, circa 1875, 32³/₄in. high. (Christie's) $13,695

A Minton majolica lamp base modeled as a boy and a girl putto scantily clad in manganese drapes tied in ocher, date code for 1872, 13³/₄in. high. (Christie's) $1,990

A Minton majolica jardinière in the form of a nautilus shell resting on coral and rocks, the shell with a whitish glaze on the exterior splashed with manganese beads, date code for 1873, 26in. high. (Christie's) $6,600

A Minton majolica dish modeled as a white rabbit with pink and black ears and tail, nibbling the edge of a large cabbage-leaf, date code for 1869, 9¼in. wide.
(Christie's) $1,490

A Minton majolica blackamoor in liveried costume wearing a green and ocher jacket, red boots and lion-skin cloak, circa 1877, 17¼in. high.
(Christie's) $3,524

A Minton majolica-ware game pie dish and cover, with double tied-twig handles, supported on four paw feet, 36cm. wide, date code for 1882.
(Phillips) $1,870

A Minton majolica cheese-dish and domed cover in the form of a bee-skep with a branch-molded loop handle, molded on the exterior with fruiting blackberry branches, date code for 1865, 13¾in. high.
(Christie's) $4,017

A Mintons majolica fluted jardinière, the dimpled dark-brown ground molded in relief with leafy sprays of pink and white foxgloves and overlapping fern-leaves, date code for 1873, 13in. high.
(Christie's) $2,985

A Minton majolica-ware 'Baroque vase', molded with four grotesque bacchanalian satyr masks linked by rope festoons, 32cm. high, 1873.
(Phillips) $1,020

A Minton majolica 'Lazy Susan', the flat circular tray with 'encaustic' decoration, the central white flowerhead enclosed within a purple-ground disc including quatrefoils, circa 1873, 18¼in. diameter.
(Christie's) $1,187

The Octoroon, a Minton parian model of a young girl after an original sculpture by John Bell, modeled standing naked, her head lowered modestly, date code for 1868, 17½in. high.
(Christie's) $511

A Minton stoneware bread plate designed by A.W.N. Pugin, with molded decoration of stylized foliage and wheat ears, the rim with inscriptions *Waste Not, Want Not*, 33.1cm. diameter.
(Christie's) $1,969

MINTON

A Minton Parian figure of Ariadne and the Panther after a model by John Bell, the naked maiden with her hair en chignon adorned with a wreath of acanthus, date code for 1862, 14¹/₂in. high.
(Christie's) $1,045

A Minton majolica green and treacle glazed teapot and cover with shell finial, modeled as a tortoise, circa 1878 impressed *Minton*, 8¹/₄in. long.
(Christie's) $4,112

A Minton figure of a girl in loosely draped robes holding a wreath of flowers beside rock work on an oval base, circa 1860, 22in. high.
(Christie's) $592

A Minton majolica turquoise-ground vase and cover, the finial modeled as a putto blowing the horn, the drum-shaped body molded with a band of fret-pattern and applied in high relief with three seated maidens, date code for 1863, 22in. high.
(Christie's) $5,750

A pair of Minton figures of the Coachee and Easy Johnny with nodding heads, circa 1860, 7¹/₂in. high.
(Christie's) $1,223

Minton oriental style vase, England, 1888, pierced scroll-formed ivory ground body with raised ribbon, 8¹/₂in. high.
(Skinner Inc.) $935

One of a set of twelve Mintons pâte-sur-pâte service plates, decorated by R. Bradbury, retailed by Tiffany & Co., New York, 1937, 10⁵/₈in. diameter.
(Butterfield & Butterfield) $4,400

A Minton porcelain vase designed by Dr. Christopher Dresser, with painted bands of stylized decoration in gold, green, yellow, blue, black and orange enamels, 29cm. high.
(Christie's) $3,347

A Minton's Art Pottery circular wall plaque, the design attributed to William S. Coleman, painted with a young girl in tunic and loose fitting mauve dress, 42.5cm. diameter.
(Phillips) $1,100

MOORCROFT

A baluster vase decorated in the 'Eventide' pattern, in shades of ocher, pink, green and blue, 13in. high.
(Christie's) $1,216

A large twin-handled vase, decorated with a band of plums and foliage, in shades of pink, mauve and green on a dark blue ground, 12½in. high.
(Christie's) $2,549

A Liberty vase, of tapering waisted cylindrical form, decorated in the 'Hazledene' pattern, in shades of blue and green, printed factory marks, signed in green, 9in. high.
(Christie's) $1,333

A Moorcroft 'Pomegranate' pattern two-handled vase, mottled dark blue ground with decoration of pomegranate amid foliage, in pink, amber, purple and green, 27cm. high.
(Christie's) $1,575

A pair of cylindrical candlesticks decorated in the 'Pomegranate' pattern, in shades of pink, ocher and green on a mottled green and blue ground, 8in. high.
(Christie's) $1,765

A dimpled oval section vase of finely ribbed form, decorated with a fish amongst waterweeds, in shades of red, yellow, green and blue under a light flambé glaze, impressed factory and facsimile signature, signed in blue, 11½in. high.
(Christie's) $824

A Moorcroft 'Chrysanthemum' pattern two-handled vase, blue-green raised slip decoration of chrysanthemums in amber, yellow, green and purple, 31cm. high.
(Christie's) $3,544

An oviform vase decorated with a band of vine leaves and berries, in shades of yellow, pink and green on a deep blue ground, 12in. high.
(Christie's) $686

A Moorcroft 'Pansy' pattern vase, white ground with decoration of yellow and purple pansies amid green foliage, circa 1916, 23cm. high.
(Christie's) $1,378

QIANLONG

A guan-type square vase, Cong, Qianlong seal mark and of the period, each side molded with the eight Daoist trigrams, all under a widely crackled pale grayish-blue glaze, 11in. high.
(Christie's) $17,772

A Ming-style yellow-ground blue and white dish, Qianlong seal mark and of the period, 21.2cm. diameter.
(Christie's) $6,892

A fine celadon-glazed globular vase, Hu, Qianlong archaistic seal mark and of the period, the globular body molded with three horizontal ribs, all under an even pale celadon glaze, 16¹/₈in. high.
(Christie's) $39,742

A fine and rare 'Robin's egg'-glazed bottle vase, impressed Qianlong seal mark and of the period, the compressed globular body surmounted by a thick cylindrical neck terminating in a flared everted rim, all covered in a finely crackled thick milky-turquoise glaze, 8³/₈in. high.
(Christie's) $111,069

A pair of famille rose lotus-petal dishes, Qianlong seal marks and of the period, each enameled to the exterior to simulate a lotus blossom with three layered lotus petals over the yellow stigma, 6³/₄in. diameter.
(Christie's) $15,645

A fine and rare blue and yellow vase, early Qianlong, painted on the globular body with formal scrolling lotus, each flower-spray divided by kui dragons, all between bands of ruyi-heads, 10¹/₂in. high.
(Christie's) $70,968

A fine robin's-egg-glazed oviform vase, impressed Qianlong seal mark and of the period, covered overall with a mottled glaze of turquoise and rich blue tone, 9¹/₄in. high, box.
(Christie's) $24,179

A fine Ming-style yellow-ground green-glazed blue and white dish, decorated in the centre with a bouquet of ribbon-tied lotus and water weeds, Qianlong seal mark and of the period, 21.2cm. diameter.
(Christie's) $53,163

A fine celadon-glazed moulded vase, Meiping, impressed Qianlong seal mark and of the period, relief-molded on the body with sprays of the sanduo, fruiting peach, finger citrus and pomegranate, 9in. high.
(Christie's) $36,903

ROBJ

Robj French porcelain inkwell, figural blackamoor in gold trimmed white turban and costume, 6¼in. high. (Skinner Inc.) $275

A Robj polychrome painted porcelain box and cover modeled as a black sultan in green striped robes and turban, 6in. high. (Christie's) $545

French porcelain perfume burner by Robj, white robed Oriental gentleman sitting cross-legged on gold accented stepped platform, 8¼in. high. (Skinner Inc.) $550

ROCKINGHAM

A Rockingham dated claret-ground cylindrical mug, painted with a horse with jockey up, inscribed in gilt *First Year of WATH RACES, MDCCCXXXI,* 1831, 13cm. high. (Christie's) $7,482

A very rare Rockingham empire-style coffee-pot and cover, the ovoid body enameled in colors on either side with a bouquet of flowers, 7¾in. high, 1826–30. (Tennants) $731

A Rockingham polychrome porcelain figure of a girl feeding a lamb, seated in puce bodice and white skirt, circa 1830. (Tennants) $866

ROOKWOOD

Rookwood pottery vase, Cincinnati, Ohio, 1915, with incised line and petal decoration in matte brown glaze, impressed mark 12½in. high. (Skinner Inc.) $350

Rookwood pottery scenic vellum plaque, Frederick Rothenbusch, 1915, "Late Autumn" woodland with light snowfall, 10 x 14in. (Skinner Inc.) $1,760

Rookwood pottery vase standard glaze ewer, Cincinnati, Ohio, 1896, by Matthew Daly, underglaze decoration of open petaled white roses against shaded brown green ground, 9¾in. high. (Skinner Inc.) $375

ROYAL DUX

A pair of Royal Dux painted bisque figures modeled as a harvest girl and a reaper, 16½in. high.
(Christie's) $876

A pair of Royal Dux figures of a near eastern desert dweller and fishergirl, both wearing green and apricot rustic dress, pink triangle pad mark, 20th century, 24¼in. high.
(Christie's) $1,425

Pair of Royal Dux porcelain figural vases, late 19th century, mid Eastern couple standing beside palm trees, 36in. high.
(Skinner Inc.) $715

ROZENBURG

Earthenware vase with basket handle, by J.L. Verhoog, manufactured at the Hague by Rozenburg, date-coded 1898, 13in. high.
(Skinner Inc.) $1,600

Rozenburg thistle wall plate, the Hague, date coded 1898, hand painted with stylized thistle flowers in earthy tones of brown, rust and lavender-gray, 10¾in. diameter.
(Skinner Inc.) $700

Large earthenware two-handled vase, Rozenburg, produced at the Hague, date coded 1903, decorated by H.G.A. Huyvehaar, bold polychrome designs of flowers and foliage, 13½in. high.
(Skinner Inc.) $1,400

A Rozenburg porcelain box and cover by Samuel Shellink, of gently tapering rectangular section, 8½in. high.
(Christie's) $6,230

Unusual pair of Rozenburg pottery vases, the Hague, date coded 1898, decorated with polychrome floral and dragon motif on brown ground, 9½in. high.
(Skinner Inc.) $1,300

A Rozenburg eggshell porcelain vase painted by R. Schenken, painted in shades of red, green, brown, lilac and yellow, 31.5cm. high, 1902.
(Phillips) $4,420

145

A small Ruskin Pottery high-fired bowl, with flared circular foot, gray ground with mottled liver red and purple glaze speckled with green, 8.6cm. high.
(Christie's) $788

A Ruskin Pottery high-fired stoneware bowl, with three pulled notches, gray ground beneath mottled liver red with cloudy purple and turquoise and pitted green-black speckles, 21cm. high.
(Christie's) $1,969

A Ruskin Pottery high-fired ginger jar on stand, with domed cover, on tripod stand, covered in a gray with mottled liver and purple-red and green-black speckling, 11.2cm. high.
(Christie's) $1,378

A Ruskin Pottery high-fired stoneware vase and cover, with short cylindrical neck, the domed cover with knopped finial, dove gray ground fragmented with random gray and green 'snake-skin' patterning.
(Christie's) $9,845

A Ruskin Pottery high-fired eggshell stoneware bowl, pierced with floral roundels, red-purple glaze fading to mottled mauve and green towards the well, impressed *Ruskin England 1924*, 15cm. diameter.
(Christie's) $1,378

A Ruskin Pottery high-fired stoneware vase, with flared cylindrical neck, white ground beneath mottled green with slight red veining, impressed *Ruskin England 1914*, 17.6cm. high.
(Christie's) $1,477

A large Ruskin Pottery high-fired stoneware vase, with mottled white and dove gray ground beneath clouded with swirling bands of liver red, purple and blue, impressed *Ruskin England 1925*, 46.2cm. high.(Christie's) $4,529

A Ruskin Pottery high-fired stoneware vase, swollen form tapering to cylindrical neck, covered in a mottled gray glaze, impressed *Ruskin England 1927*, 9.5cm. high.
(Christie's) $236

A large Ruskin Pottery high-fired stoneware vase on stand, the white ground mottled with liver red, blue and purple beneath speckled green, on ornate tripod stand, impressed *Ruskin, 1914*, 44.5cm. high.
(Christie's) $6,301

RUSKIN

A Ruskin Pottery high-fired
stoneware vase, with flared rim,
covered in a mottled dove gray
speckled glaze, impressed
Ruskin, 24cm. high.
(Christie's) $1,969

A Ruskin Pottery high-fired
stoneware bowl, the white
exterior with mottled gray, the
interior with mottled liver red
and purple with speckled well,
impressed *Ruskin England,
1927*, 24.2cm. diameter.
(Christie's) $1,378

A rare Ruskin Pottery high-
fired stoneware vase, tall mallet-
shaped, mottled gray ground
with areas of cloudy and mottled
blue, impressed *Ruskin England,
1924*, 37cm. high.
(Christie's) $3,544

A Ruskin Pottery high-fired
stoneware vase, the white
ground covered in a dark red
speckled glaze shaded with
purple towards the foot,
stamped *Ruskin England, 1926*,
40cm. high.
(Christie's) $4,726

A Ruskin Pottery high-fired
eggshell stoneware bowl, the
interior covered in a mottled
jade green glaze, the exterior
mottled liver red speckled with
green, 17cm. diameter.
(Christie's) $2,757

A Ruskin Pottery high-fired
stoneware vase, with matt white
ground, mottled purple beneath
fragmented duck egg speckled
with green-black, impressed
pottery seal *Ruskin Pottery West
Smethwick*, dated *1908*, 31.6cm.
high. (Christie's) $2,363

A Ruskin Pottery high-fired
stoneware vase, with everted
rim, white ground beneath liver
red and dove gray streaked
glaze, 23.6cm. high.
(Christie's) $1,969

A Ruskin Pottery high-fired
vase, with tapering neck and
flared rim, band of molded
floral decoration, covered in a
mottled oatmeal glaze, 27cm.
high. (Christie's) $591

A Ruskin Pottery high-fired
stoneware vase, white ground
covered in mottled greenish buff
glaze beneath clouds of dark
maroon and blue, impressed
Ruskin England 1922. 22.5cm.
high. (Christie's) $2,363

SATSUMA

Small Kinkozan caddy with inner lid and outer cover, the body with fine panels of figures or birds.
(Graves, Son & Pilcher)
$2,200

A Kyo Satsuma bowl decorated in colored enamels and gilt with an ebi amongst seaweed and crashing waves, early 19th century, 26cm. diameter.
(Christie's)
$2,257

A large Satsuma two-handled tripod-footed koro and cover decorated with a border of butterflies and flowers, signed *Fujo Satsuma Kinran-toki, Tokozanzo* and *Satsuma mon*, 19th century, 48cm. high.
(Christie's)
$18,200

A Satsuma tripod-footed koro, the bronze cover decorated with takaramono and aoimon, surmounted by a chrysanthemum finial, signed *Dai Nihon Satsuma Ishui-in, Hozan*, late 19th century, 21.9cm. high.
(Christie's)
$4,000

A very large Satsuma vase decorated in various colored enamels and gilt, with two elegantly decorated carts in formal garlands of chrysanthemums, wild pinks and bamboo fences, signed *Keishu ga*, late 19th century, 61.5cm. high.
(Christie's)
$38,500

A Satsuma koro and cover decorated in various colored enamels and gilt with panels depicting scenes of a pavilion among trees in a mountainous landscape, signed and stamped *Kinkozan zo*, late 19th century, 5.6cm. high.
(Christie's)
$2,600

A Satsuma vase decorated in various colored enamels and gilt with ho-o birds among flowers and foliage, the shoulder with a band of chrysanthemums, signed *Satsuma Meizan*, late 19th century, 32cm. high.
(Christie's)
$9,700

A Satsuma two-handled tripod koro and cover decorated in various colored enamels and gilt with various figurative scenes, signed *Dai Nihon Yokohama Hododa seizo*, late 19th century, 17.5cm. high.
(Christie's)
$3,198

Satsuma covered urn, 19th century, signed *Kyoto Yasuda zo kore*, ovoid form with molded handles and raised base, each side decorated with three figures, 24in. high.
(Skinner Inc.)
$1,400

SATSUMA

A Satsuma square vase, the body with a continuous decoration of bijin with children in an extensive landscape on the banks of a stream, late 19th century, 22cm. high, wood stand. (Christie's) $2,384

Satsuma bowl, interior with wisteria blossoms, impressed and enameled signatures, 8³/₈in. high. (Skinner Inc.) $2,000

19th century Satsuma porcelain figure of a boy playing a drum, his gilded robe richly decorated in black, red, white and blue, 38cm. high. (Finarte) $5,726

Fine Kinkozan Satsuma vase, 19th century, signed *Dai Nihon*, tapering globular form, reserves of eight immortals and samurai, 15in. high. (Skinner Inc.) $9,500

Satsuma tea bowl, 19th century, inscribed *Tokuzan Zo*, with figural reserves and diaper pattern exterior, thousand butterflies interior, 3¹/₄in. high. (Skinner Inc.) $4,000

Satsuma globular-shaped vase, Japan, mid to late 19th century, gilt and enamel decorated scenes of warriors within bamboo framed panels, 8¹/₂in. high. (Skinner Inc.) $1,900

SATURDAY EVENING GIRLS

Saturday Evening Girls pottery bowl, green glazed half-round with sgraffito interior border of yellow nasturtium blossoms, 8¹/₂in. diameter. (Skinner Inc.) $935

Decorated Saturday Evening Girls pottery pitcher and bowl, Boston, 1918, both with rabbit and turtle border. (Skinner Inc.) $450

Decorated Saturday Evening Girls motto mug, Boston, 1918, with motto *In The Forest Must Always Be A Nightingale and In The Soul a Faith So Faithful That It Comes Back Even After It Has Been Slain*, 4in. high. (Skinner Inc.) $800

SEVRES

A pair of gilt-metal-mounted
Sèvres-pattern vases and covers,
the dark-blue grounds painted
with mythological scenes, late
19th century, 39½in. high.
(Christie's) $16,434

A Sèvres coffee cup from the
Catherine the Great service,
painted in colors with a panel
of white classical figures on a
brown ground.
(Phillips) $476 ·

A pair of gilt-metal-mounted
Sèvres-pattern oviform vases
and covers painted by H.
Desprez with battle scenes, late
19th century, 51½in. high.
(Christie's) $32,868

A Sèvres oval plaque painted by
Pauline Laurent after F.X.
Winterhalter with a three-
quarter length portrait of Queen
Victoria in ceremonial regalia,
circa 1858, 7½in. high.
(Christie's) $7,669

A Sèvres snuff box of
rectangular form, painted in the
manner of André-Vincent
Vielliard with panels of Teniers-
style figures and garden scenery,
8cm. wide.
(Phillips) $1,020

A Sèvres sucrier and cover
painted in colors with
Watteauesque scenes of figures
in landscapes, 8cm., date letter
for 1756.
(Phillips) $1,275

A pair of Sèvres gilt-metal-
mounted green-ground
tapering-oviform vases and
covers with white and gilt solid
strap handles, the bodies
painted in the style of Boucher,
date codes for 1862, 14½in.
high.
(Christie's) $3,652

A pair of gilt-metal-mounted
Sèvres-pattern dark-blue-
ground oviform vases and
covers painted by J. Pascault
with Le Mariage, the other after
David with Le Sacre, late 19th
century, 43¼in. high.
(Christie's) $23,738

A pair of gilt-metal-mounted
Sèvres-pattern two-handled
vases and covers of tapering
oviform, painted by Desprez
with battle scenes, late 19th
century.
(Christie's) $40,172

SEVRES

A gilt-metal-mounted Sèvres-pattern two-handled oval center-dish, the pale-blue ground reserved with a medley of garden-flowers within a white-ground oval cartouche, 20th century, 21in. wide. (Christie's) $1,520

A composite garniture of three large gilt-metal-mounted Sèvres-pattern vases and covers of slender tapering oviform, the white grounds painted by J. Pascault, late 19th century, 62in. high. (Christie's) $58,432

A gilt-metal-mounted Sèvres-pattern two-handled oval center-dish, the claret ground painted by Guy with Napoléon rallying his generals before a shadowy army, 20th century, 18¹/₂in. wide. (Christie's) $1,900

A pair of gilt-metal-mounted Sèvres-pattern green-ground vases, the bodies of tapering oviform and each painted with a scene of Amphitrite, attended by nymphs, tritons and cherubs, late 19th century, 43¹/₄in. high. (Christie's) $16,434

'Sèvres' gilt-bronze-mounted porcelain centerbowl, late 19th century, painted on one side with a pastoral scene of a man presenting a reclining woman with flowers, 24¹/₂in. high. (Butterfield & Butterfield) $6,050

A pair of gilt-metal-mounted Sèvres-pattern green-ground vases and covers, painted in muted colors with scenes of medieval knights, one with a warrior knighting another attended by a multitude of spectators before pavilions and a castle, late 19th century, 50¹/₂in. high.(Christie's) $43,824

A pair of gilt-metal-mounted Sèvres-pattern pale-blue-ground oviform vases and covers painted by D.P. Boucher with pastoral scenes of children in idyllic rural landscapes, circa 1895, 35³/₄in. high. (Christie's) $19,900

A gilt-metal-mounted Sèvres-pattern two-handled jardinière, the front with six playful putti around a felled tree-trunk, circa 1860. (Christie's) $4,185

A pair of ormolu-mounted Sèvres-pattern dark-blue-ground oviform vases and covers, painted by Maxnot in a pale palette with lovers seated at leisure in Arcadian landscapes, late 19th century, 51¹/₂in. high. (Christie's) $40,172

SEVRES

An attractive Sèvres sucrier and cover painted in colors with harbor scenes within cisele gilt borders, 17cm., date letter for 1778.
(Phillips) $1,870

'Sèvres' porcelain-mounted parcel-gilt and silvered brass jewel casket, second half 19th century, opening to a red velvet-lined interior, 11¹/₂in. wide.
(Butterfield & Butterfield)
                              $825

Large 'Sèvres' bleu-céleste-ground vase, late 19th century, painted with a large oval panel depicting a garden scene centered by three ladies and a gentleman, 31in. high.
(Butterfield & Butterfield)
                              $1,760

A gilt-metal-mounted Sèvres-pattern tapering oviform vase and cover painted by J. Pascault with a continuous bacchanalian scene of a maiden seated before a distant forest, late 19th century, 58¹/₄in. high.
(Christie's) $13,695

Pair of Sèvres gilt-bronze-mounted porcelain urns, late 19th century, painted on the front with a different eighteenth century scene of a woman with two toddlers and a sleeping infant, 28in. high.
(Butterfield & Butterfield)
                              $3,850

A gilt-metal-mounted Sèvres-pattern dark-blue-ground vase and cover, the urn-shaped body molded with vertical gadroons, on a waisted stem attached to the square metal base, circa 1880, 27¹/₄in. high.
(Christie's) $5,478

'Sèvres' gilt-bronze-mounted center bowl, late 19th century, the oval bleu-du-roi-ground bowl reserved on either side with a painted panel, 13¹/₂in. high.
(Butterfield & Butterfield)
                              $2,750

A pair of Sèvres biscuit figures of Spring and Autumn, possibly modeled by Falconet, she with incised *F* mark.
(Phillips) $1,020

Sèvres gilt-bronze-mounted porcelain covered urn, late 19th century, painted in pastel tones with a continuous scene of putti in a landscape, 17¹/₈in. high.
(Butterfield & Butterfield)
                              $4,950

SEVRES

A Sèvres Louis XVIII cabinet cup and saucer, Tasse Jasmin, painted by Mme Adelaide Ducluzeau with a quarter length titled portrait of Mme de Maintenon.
(Phillips) $2,550

Pair of Sèvres porcelain urns and covers emblematic of the Four Seasons, late 18th century, decorated with a broad band composed of four white bisque panels, 30in. high.
(Butterfield & Butterfield) $19,800

'Sèvres' biscuit porcelain bust, signed *Vavasseur*, 19th century, the lady with flowers and pearls in her elaborately dressed hair, 31in. high.
(Butterfield & Butterfield) $3,300

Pair of Sèvres gilt-bronze-mounted porcelain urns, circa 1900, painted with a pair of eighteenth century lovers in a pastoral setting, one signed *E. Pernodet*, 22¹/₂in. high.
(Butterfield & Butterfield) $2,475

A large Sèvres-style vase and cover, painted in colors with a scene of Napoleon and his army in battle, signed *Verney*, 72cm. high.
(Phillips) $1,190

A pair of gilt-metal-mounted Sèvres-pattern vases and covers of slender oviform, the cream grounds painted by H. Poitevin in a soft palette with nymphs wearing loose robes and swirling drapery, circa 1910, 40¹/₂in. high.
(Christie's) $10,956

Sèvres porcelain green-ground footed vase, 18th century, painted with a pair of rustic lovers in a pastoral setting, 14³/₈in. high.
(Butterfield & Butterfield) $7,700

Two Sèvres gilt-bronze-mounted porcelain urns, late 19th century, the sides with pan masks, raised on a socle over an octagonal base, 25in. high.
(Butterfield & Butterfield) $3,300

A gilt-metal-mounted Sèvres-pattern vase of broad and squat form, the body painted with figures wearing 18th century dress at a marriage banquet, late 19th century, 28¹/₂in. high.
(Christie's) $8,217

STAFFORDSHIRE

A 'Pratt' creamware cow creamer, sponged and painted in black and ocher, set on a green shaped base, 14cm. high.
(Bearne's) $634

A Neale & Co. creamware toby-jug modeled as a seated jovial man holding a mug of frothing ale, impressed mark and incised *15*, circa 1795, 25cm. high.
(Christie's) $1,477

A creamware fox head stirrup cup, with grinning expression, decorated in brown and buff glazes, 5in. long.
(Spencer's) $504

Yellow-glazed Staffordshire satyr jug, England, circa 1810, enamel decorated relief with silver luster sprigwork, 5¹/₂in. high.
(Skinner Inc.) $605

A pair of Pratt type small figures of birds, 3¹/₂in. high.
(Dreweatt Neate) $1,365

A rare mid Victorian Staffordshire figure of John Brown, standing in bright blue coat with two black girls, 13¹/₂in. high.
(Tennants) $1,360

An interesting and attractive prattware toby jug of ordinary type, seated and holding a foaming jug on his knee, 24.5cm. high, possibly Yorkshire.
(Phillips) $884

A Staffordshire pink luster Royal Wedding Commemorative jug, molded with named bust portraits of Princess Charlotte and Prince Leopold, 6⁵/₈in. high, circa 1816.
(Tennants) $446

A fine Prattware toby jug, the ruddy-faced toper firmly grasping his jug and goblet, his pipe of coiled snake type resting against his chest, 9³/₄in. high, circa 1800–20.
(Tennants) $1,395

STAFFORDSHIRE

A Staffordshire saltglaze drab-
ware small globular teapot and
cover with crabstock handle and
spout, circa 1750, 9.5cm. high.
(Christie's) $748

A Staffordshire saltglaze bear-
jug and cover, its head forming
the cover, a young bear
suspended between its forepaws,
circa 1750, 21cm. long.
(Christie's) $2,953

A Staffordshire creamware
dated cylindrical teapot and
cover, inscribed in iron-red
Mifs. Hannah.Haris (sic)/*1775*,
12.5cm. high.
(Christie's) $1,575

A rare Victorian Staffordshire
figure of the Rev. C.H.
Spurgeon, standing in black coat
and white trousers, 12¹/₄in. high
(Tennants) $1,020

Pair of Prattware figures of
Elijah and the Widow of
Zarephath, England, late 18th
century, 9¹/₂in. high.
(Skinner Inc.) $660

A mid 19th century
Staffordshire railway group, as
an arch with clock face, flanked
by girls in Highland dress,
10¹/₂in. high.
(Tennants) $714

Staffordshire satyr jug,
England, circa 1815,
polychrome enamel decorated
with black feathered field, 4¹/₂in.
high.
(Skinner Inc.) $110

A historical Staffordshire wash
basin and pitcher by Ralph
Stevenson, Cobridge, England,
circa 1825, with a foliate band
over a view of the Deaf and
Dumb Asylum, Hartford,
Connecticut, 14in. diameter.
(Christie's) $3,740

A Wilkinson Ltd. toby jug,
designed by Sir F. Carruthers
Gould, in the form of Marshal
Joffre, sitting with a shell on his
knee, 26.3cm. high.
(Bearne's) $563

STAFFORDSHIRE

A pink luster creamware puzzle jug, printed with the word *'Reform'* and flanked by bust portraits of Earl Grey, and Lord Brougham and Vaux, 17cm.
(Phillips) $1,124

A pair of Wood style pearlware groups, titled 'Rualer and Pastime', the brightly coloured figures seated before flowering bocage, circa 1815, 8in. high.
(Bonhams) $333

Pratt-type cow creamer with milkmaid, England, circa 1800, with yellow and black sponged cow and maid, 5¼in. high.
(Skinner Inc.) $440

A rare Staffordshire group, depicting Romeo at the balcony with Juliet, 11½in. high.
(Bonhams) $686

Four Staffordshire figures of the Apostles, Saints Mark, Matthew, Luke and John, all standing and each with his appropriate emblem, 19cm. high.
(Phillips) $1,573

A Walton group, 'Songsters', modeled as boy and girl musicians on a rocky base with bocage behind, circa 1820, 9in. high.
(Bonhams) $882

A Staffordshire group, depicting King John sitting in a tented pavilion signing the Magna Carta, 12¼in. high.
(Bonhams) $216

A pair of Staffordshire equestrian portrait figures, 'King William III and Queen Mary', 10¼in. high.
(Bonhams) $314

Pratt-type toby jug, England, circa 1810, attributed to Yorkshire Pottery, molded caryatid handle, 7¾in. high.
(Skinner Inc.) $825

STAFFORDSHIRE

A pearlware model of a cow with orange and brown markings with a seated milkmaid at its side, circa 1800, 7¼in. long.
(Christie's) $790

A fine pair of Staffordshire models of rabbits, with white bodies with black markings, their floppy back ears with pale apricot interiors, 24.5cm. long.
(Phillips) $4,810

A creamware arbor group of Whieldon type, modeled as a garden shelter, a woman in a crinoline sitting on either side of the curved seat, 14.5cm. high.
(Bearne's) $27,750

A Staffordshire dog clock group, the clock face surmounted by a poodle and flanked by red and black coated spaniels, 9½in. high.
(Bonhams) $333

A rare pair of Staffordshire groups of the flight into and return from Egypt, with Mary riding on a gray ass and Joseph holding the animal's head, 24cm. high.
(Phillips) $2,498

A Staffordshire portrait figure, 'Prince of Wales', in military attire standing beside a chair, 10½in. high.
(Bonhams) $314

A Pratt type pearlware clock-group modeled as a grandfather clock painted in blue, yellow and green with panels of flowers, circa 1800, 10in. high.
(Christie's) $889

A pair of models of zebras, on green oval bases with gilt-line borders, circa 1900, 9in. high.
(Christie's) $1,185

A pearlware toby-jug, the smiling man seated holding a jug of frothing ale, a barrel between his feet and a pipe at his side, circa 1780, 26cm. high.
(Christie's) $984

Antique three-gallon stoneware crock with cobalt decoration.
(Eldred's) $176

A pair of Compton Pottery stoneware bookends, each trefoil form with relief decoration of a butterfly, on semi-circular base, circa 1945, 12.2cm. high.
(Christie's) $197

Cobalt decorated one-gallon stoneware batter jug, America, 19th century, with tin cover and spout cap, 9ln. high.
(Skinner Inc.) $880

A tall stoneware vase by Richard Batterham, with incised bands of linear decoration, covered in a crackled olive green ash glaze stopping short of the foot, 79.5cm. high.
(Christie's) $1,181

Pair of English stoneware Japan pattern pot-pourri jars and covers, Samuel Alcock & Co., circa 1869, the sides applied with flanking dragons' masks, 23¹/₂in. high.
(Butterfield & Butterfield)
                                     $4,400

A rare stoneware funnel-shaped vase by Hans Coper, on conical-shaped foot, covered in a matt buff glaze burnished and textured to reveal matt manganese beneath, 21cm. high.
(Christie's) $4,923

Cobalt decorated stoneware crock, probably Ohio or Pennsylvania, circa 1860, the four-gallon crock inscribed *Hurrah for Abe Lincoln*, 11¹/₂in. high.
(Skinner Inc.) $4,400

A Dreihausen stoneware Ringelkrug, with bands of incised decoration, the upper part applied with three tiered multiple loops, 27cm. high.
(Phillips) $3,060

A saltglaze stoneware two-handled 'Farmer Giles' mug, the merry man with brown curly hair wearing a hat, 22cm. high.
(Bearne's) $387

STONEWARE

A stoneware swollen sack form by Elizabeth Fritsch, the front decorated with aubergine, terracotta, buff and mustard angular panels, over which mid and light blue geometric design, 1983, 41cm. high.
(Christie's) $11,737

A small stoneware cut-sided bowl by Katharine Pleydell-Bouverie, with incised decoration, covered in a dark brown glaze, impressed *KPB*, 8cm. diameter.
(Christie's) $158

An ash-glazed stoneware face-jug, attributed to Evan Javan Brown, Georgia, 20th century, the handle pulled from the back and ceramic chards for eyes and teeth, 6¼in. high.
(Christie's) $2,420

A St. Ives stoneware pitcher, with pulled lip and applied handle, covered in a pale sage green glaze over iron brown body, impressed with St. Ives seal, England, 20.7cm. high.
(Christie's) $197

An incised and cobalt-decorated stoneware harvest jug, New York, 1805, decorated on the obverse with incised floral vine below a fish, the reverse with a Masonic apron, inscribed and dated *J. Romer, 1805*, 7in. high.
(Christie's) $6,050

A large stoneware bottle vase by Janet Leach, the cup-shaped rim applied with lug handles, covered in a pitted matt olive green and brown glaze with translucent olive green running, 48.5cm. high.
(Christie's) $886

Two-gallon stoneware jug, inscribed in cobalt *E.A. & H. Hildreth, Southampton*, 14in. high.
(Skinner Inc.) $880

Bailey stoneware vase, England, circa 1875, incised leaf and floral design, 9½in. high.
(Skinner Inc.) $440

A saltglazed stoneware baluster shaped character jug, 4¾in. high, circa 1800.
(Dreweatt Neate) $234

SUSIE COOPER

A squat octagonal bowl with electroplate rim painted with a geometric pattern of overlapping squares, triangular *SCP* mark, 10in. diameter. (Christie's) $305

An earthenware figure of a fox, on curved base, naturalistically painted, incised signature, 5in. long. (Christie's) $710

An oval dish painted in orange, black, yellow, grey and green, triangular *SCP* mark, 8¼in. high. (Christie's) $445

A cylindrical vase with inverted rim decorated with applied crescent motifs, incised signature, 7¾in. high. (Christie's) $195

A Gloria luster pear-shaped vase, with scrolling flowers and foliage in gold, printed factory mark, painted Susie Cooper monogram, 7½in. high. (Christie's) $500

A Carved Ware baluster vase, with a continuous frieze of stylized leaves, incised signature and *592*, 9¼in. high. (Christie's) $225

A Gloria luster waisted cylindrical vase painted in pink, lilac and gilt, painted Susie Cooper monogram, 12in. high. (Christie's) $1,300

A cylindrical biscuit barrel and cover in the 'Seagull' pattern, with a stylized gull above blue and green waves, printed facsimile signature, 5¼in. high. (Christie's) $810

'Skier', a Crown Works Nursery Ware Kestrel cocoa pot and cover, gazelle *SCP* mark, 5in. high. (Christie's) $1,220

A Sancai equestrienne group, the female rider wearing an amber and cream tunic and a long-sleeved green and amber shirt, Tang Dynasty, 34.5cm. diameter.
(Christie's) $13,000

A Sancai pottery model of an ox and cart, the cuboid cart with an arched roof, the back pierced with a rectangular door, Tang Dynasty, 23cm. long.
(Christie's) $8,861

A rare white-glazed kundika with tall waisted neck, ovoid body and spreading foot, under an even ivory glaze over a looping white slip, Tang Dynasty, 28.5cm. high.
(Christie's) $3,544

A red painted pottery standing horse and a groom, the horse with plain saddle and brick-red painted body, the groom with clenched wrists and looking upwards, Tang Dynasty, the groom 28cm. high.
(Christie's) $9,845

A rare brown-glazed ewer of ovoid shape on a short foot, surmounted by a slightly tapered cylindrical neck applied with a molded loop handle and short cabriole spout, Tang Dynasty, 13.5cm. high.
(Christie's) $2,685

A large painted pottery horse standing foursquare on a rectangular base, the saddle draped with a knotted cloth falling in folds above a striped saddle blanket, Tang Dynasty, 41cm. high.
(Christie's) $5,600

A painted pottery equestrienne group, the lady wearing a short jacket over a tunic with long sleeves, her hair braided and pinned above her head, Tang Dynasty, 40cm. high.
(Christie's) $12,000

A pale-glazed Sancai horse, naturalistically modeled and standing foursquare on a rectangular base, the saddle unglazed, Tang Dynasty, 31.5cm. high.
(Christie's) $6,000

A Sancai equestrian figure, the figure wearing a green-glazed flowing coat and trousers, with his cream-glazed sleeves and pierced hands before him, Tang Dynasty, 40.5cm. high.
(Christie's) $13,389

TECO

Teco pottery handled vase, decorated by four angular quatriform handles extending to base rim, 13½ in. high. (Skinner Inc.) **$1,320**

Teco pottery wall pocket, green matt glaze on hanging vase with angular top over molded roundel, 5¼ in. wide. (Skinner Inc.) **$385**

Teco Pottery vase, Terra Cotta, Illinois, circa 1909, square-shaped mouth on modeled elongated neck flaring to form bulbous base, 16½ in. high. (Skinner Inc.) **$1,100**

TIFFANY

Tiffany pottery bowl, raised rim bulbed pot of white clay fired with amber, blue, gray and green drip glaze overall, 6in. high. (Skinner Inc.) **$600**

Tiffany pottery vase, with mottled earth tone brown-tan-amber glaze overall, 9½ in. high. (Skinner Inc.) **$1,980**

Tiffany pottery flower bowl, heavy walled jardinière form of white clay decorated in blue, 5¼ in. high. (Skinner Inc.) **$1,650**

VAN BRIGGLE

Van Briggle Pottery vase, Colorado Springs, Colorado, circa 1909, striated brown matte glaze, incised marks, 9¾ in. high. (Skinner Inc.) **$225**

Van Briggle pottery vase, Colorado Springs, Colorado, after 1920, relief decorated with cranes in turquoise matte glaze, 16¾ in. high. (Skinner Inc.) **$550**

Van Briggle Pottery vase, Colorado Springs, circa 1904, decoration of narcissi, matte green glaze with yellow accents, 9⅝ in. high. (Skinner Inc.) **$700**

A Vienna-style yellow-ground circular plaque painted by F. Wagner after Peter Paul Rubens with Decius standing on a pedestal conversing with four Roman warriors, circa 1880, 19in. diameter.
(Christie's) $4,945

A Vienna-style dark-blue-ground rectangular tray painted after Peter Paul Rubens with Die Opferschau, a sacrificial presentation to the Consul Decius Mus, circa 1880, 12¹/₂ x 16¹/₂in.
(Christie's) $13,320

A Vienna-style plate painted by Scholz with Diana and Venus reclining on furs and drapery beside a pond in a woodland glade attended by Cupids, circa 1880, 9¹/₂in. diameter.
(Christie's) $723

A Vienna cylindrical coffee-pot and domed cover, painted with Hectors Aschied, Hector bidding farewell to Andromache and his son, Astyanax, 1796, 20.5cm. high.
(Christie's) $9,845

A Vienna gold-ground cabaret reserved with bouquets including roses, tulips, canations, peonies, anenomes and forget-me-nots and the borders with bands of chased gilt scrolls, date code for 1790.
(Christie's) $6,120

Extremely fine pair of Continental porcelain vases, bearing the Vienna beehive mark, 18¹/₂in. high, early 19th century.
(G.A. Key) $4,779

A Vienna-style gold-ground circular plaque painted by E. Forster with a scene of mythological revelers in and around a pool before classical ruins and entitled *Märchen*, circa 1880, 16¹/₄in. diameter.
(Christie's) $4,750

A Vienna (Du Paquier) two-handled circular écuelle and cover molded and colored with prunus within half-peony and blue scroll borders, circa 1730, 12cm. wide.
(Christie's) $1,181

A Vienna-style plate painted with a Roman centurion seated in an extensive barren landscape with distant mountains, with a maiden appearing in a vision among clouds, circa 1880, 9³/₄in. diameter.
(Christie's) $608

WEDGWOOD

Wedgwood porcelain Fairyland luster footed punch bowl, 1920's, decorated on the exterior with the 'Poplar Trees' pattern of trees before buildings, bridges, and fairies, 11in. diameter.
(Butterfield & Butterfield)
$2,200

Wedgwood majolica game pie dish, England, 1868, complete with queensware liner, 11in. wide.
(Skinner Inc.) $3,575

A Wedgwood 'fairyland' luster octagonal bowl, the 'drake neck green' ground painted in dark blue and gold with Firbolgs, 3¼in. high.
(Bonhams) $550

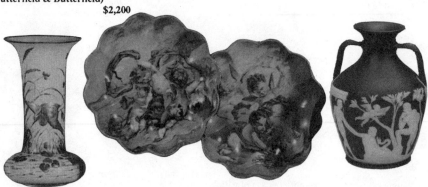

A Wedgwood bone china onion vase with a flared trumpet neck, molded gilt and silvered with two herons amongst bulrushes and lily pads, circa 1890, 8¼in. high.
(Bonhams) $370

A pair of Wedgwood earthenware scalloped dishes painted with putto symbolic of the elements fire and water, 9in. wide.
(Bonhams) $740

A Wedgwood black and white solid jasper copy of the Portland or Barberini vase by Thomas Lovatt, of conventional type, the base with Paris wearing the Phrygian cap, circa 1880, 26cm. high.
(Christie's) $1,871

A Wedgwood creamware oviform teapot and cover painted in the manner of David Rhodes with vertical bands of stylized ornament, circa 1768, 14cm. high.
(Christie's) $3,347

Wedgwood basalt figure "Nymph at Well", England, circa 1840, modeled as a female figure holding a shell, 11in. high.
(Skinner Inc.) $1,045

A Wedgwood creamware teapot and cover decorated in Leeds in the Rhodes workshop with a flower spray on either side.
(Phillips) $650

WEDGWOOD

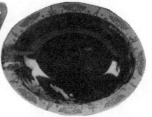

A Wedgwood majolica oval fish-platter, molded in relief on a pale-turquoise ground with a salmon lying on a bed of green ferns with ocher tips, circa 1876, 25¼in. wide.
(Christie's) $694

'Ferdinand the Bull' a Wedgwood figure of a bull modeled by Arnold Machin, 12½in. long.
(Christie's) $392

A Wedgwood rosso antico oval settling-pan made for Lady Anson's dairy at Shugborough, the rim with wide pouring-lip and molded with 'Egyptian' reliefs in black, 1807, 54.5cm. wide.
(Christie's) $3,650

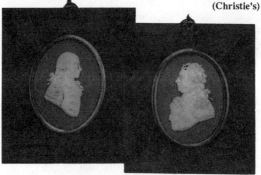

A Wedgwood coral and bronze 'Fairyland Luster' baluster vase and domed cover, decorated in the 'Jeweled Tree' pattern, 9¾in. high.
(Christie's) $2,900

A pair of Wedgwood blue and jasper oval portrait medallions molded in relief with Admiral Earl Howe and Admiral Viscount Duncan, circa 1800.
(Christie's) $570

A Wedgwood black basalt vase, applied in relief with a series of continuous figures including a mother and child and children, 37cm. high.
(Phillips) $560

A Wedgwood 'Fairyland Luster' Florentine vase, decorated in the 'Goblins' pattern, 6½in. high.
(Christie's) $2,600

'Bull', a Wedgwood black basalt figure designed by John Skeaping, impressed factory marks and facsimile signature, 5¼in. high.
(Christie's) $941

A Wedgwood Fairyland Luster oviform vase, painted with three panels of fairies, elves and birds before river landscapes, 8½in. high.
(Christie's) $1,378

WEDGWOOD

A Wedgwood creamware sauce tureen and cover with a fixed stand, together with a lozenge shape dish on a ball foot and a navette shaped dish.
(Lawrence) $630

A Wedgwood Creamware oviform teapot and a cover, painted in the manner of David Rhodes in iron-red, green and black, circa 1768, 14.5cm. high overall.
(Christie's) $1,480

A Wedgwood small fairyland luster bowl, decorated with imps and goblins at play on a green ground, 13cm. diameter.
(Phillips) $750

A large Wedgwood and Bentley black basalt vase of shouldered ovoid form, with Bacchus head terminals with their horns forming handles, 36cm. high.
(Phillips) $2,650

A Wedgwood redware teapot, cover with crocodile finial and stand, molded in black with Egyptian motifs, a two-handled sugar-bowl and cover, and a milk-jug, impressed mark.
(Christie's) $593

A Wedgwood blue jasper zodiac vase of shield shape on a square plinth, applied in white relief with scenes of classical maidens, 28cm. high.
(Phillips) $350

A pair of Wedgwood blue jasper urns and covers, with mask handles and decorated with classical maidens, on square bases, 16.5cm. high.
(Allen & Harris) $306

A Wedgwood fairyland luster vase with 'flame' background, decorated with 'Boys on a Bridge' design in bright lime-green, 26cm.
(Phillips) $2,450

A pair of Wedgwood and Bentley black basalt urn-shaped vases and covers, the latter with Sybil finials, 28cm. high.
(Phillips) $4,500

WEDGWOOD

A Wedgwood fairyland luster bowl, decorated with groups of poplars and a lake on a midnight blue ground, 21.5cm., Portland vase mark.
(Phillips) $1,890

A Wedgwood 'Queens ware' teapot, painted in colors with a cockerel amongst paeony and chrysanthemum, 5½in. high.
(Bonhams) $275

A Wedgwood anti-slavery Cream-ware teapot and cover, of oviform with scrolling handle, probably decorated in the David Rhodes workshop, 13cm. high.
(Phillips) $1,850

A Wedgwood 'fairyland' luster 'Melba Cup', the ogee bowl externally painted with dancing fairies and goblins, 3in. high.
(Bonhams) $1,100

A Wedgwood Fairyland luster plate, the centre painted in predominant shades of blue, purple, claret and green and enriched in gilding with goblins crossing a bridge, 1920's, 27.5cm. diameter.
(Christie's) $1,965

A Wedgwood pottery 'Boat Race' cup, designed by Eric Ravilious, the footed vessel decorated with three oval panels to the exterior, 25.5cm. high.
(Phillips) $520

A pair of Wedgwood Fairyland luster 'Torches' vases, printed in gold and painted on the exterior in Flame Fairyland tones with 'Torches', 28.5cm. high.
(Phillips) $3,500

A rare Wedgwood blue jasper astrological vase and cover supported by three classical figures on a triangular base, 15¾in. high.
(Bonhams) $1,300

A garniture of two Wedgwood crocus pots and covers and a small flower vase each colored in cream and brown, with relief molded cream ribbon-tied swags, 14cm. to 16cm.
(Phillips) $460

A Wemyss (Bovey Tracey) large pig, made for Jan Plichta, painted in pink and green with sprays of clover, 28cm. wide.
(Phillips) $1,030

Wemyss biscuit pot and cover, decorated with Scottish thistles and stamped *T Good & Co, South Audely Street, London.*
(G.A. Key) $298

Roses, an ewer and basin, 39cm. diameter, both with painted *Wemyss* mark.
(Phillips) $1,100

A Wemyss ware commemorative goblet printed with *V R* below a crown and flanked by thistles, roses and shamrock, the reverse dated *1897*, 5¹/₂in. high.
(Christie's) $783

Carnations, a combé flower pot, 17.2cm. high, impressed *Wemyss* mark.
(Phillips) $1,480

A Wemyss (Bovey Tracey) model of a cat after a Gallé original, seated upright, with green glass eyes and a smug expression, 32cm. high, mark *Wemyss* in dark green.
(Phillips) $2,625

A Wemyss (Bovey Tracey) model of a pig, seated on its haunches, decorated with large black patches, 28cm. high.
(Phillips) $1,850

A pair of Wemyss candlesticks painted with the rose-pattern, impressed marks, 12in. high, circa 1900.
(Christie's) $352

A small Wemyss model of a pig, its coat decorated with shamrocks, the ears, snout and trotters in pink, 10cm. high.
(Phillips) $630

WESTERWALD

A Westerwald stoneware silver-mounted cylindrical mug with loop handle, the body incised and enriched in blue with stylized foliage flanked by two flowerhead medallions, mid-18th century, 19cm. high.
(Christie's) $1,000

A Westerwald stoneware spirit-barrel of ribbed form, the blue ground incised with bands of scrolling stylized foliage, the ends with winged cherubs' heads and flowers, 18th century, 33cm. long.
(Christie's) $1,530

A Westerwald stoneware globular jug with loop handle, the mottled blue ground applied with navette-shaped molded medallions of stylised masks and grasses, late 17th century, 26cm. high.
(Christie's) $1,000

WOOD

A toby jug and cover of Ralph Wood type, seated with a jug of generously frothing ale and smoking a pipe, 9¹/₂in. high, circa 1780.
(Tennants) $1,488

A Ralph Wood oval plaque portrait of a woman, perhaps Charlotte Corday, circa 1780, 20cm. high.
(Christie's) $1,250

A Ralph Wood Bacchus mask jug, circa 1775, 23.5cm. high.
(Christie's) $850

A Ralph Wood figure of an old woman feeding birds, wearing a pale-brown dress and with a white shawl over her head, three birds feeding from a circular green bowl at her feet, circa 1780, 20cm. high.
(Christie's) $3,300

A Ralph Wood figure of a recumbent ram, on an oval green rockwork base molded with foliage, circa 1770, 18.5cm. wide.(Christie's)$5,000

A Ralph Wood group of the Vicar and Moses of conventional type, circa 1770, 21.5cm. high.
(Christie's) $1,000

WORCESTER

A Chamberlain's Worcester shallow bowl and cover, the center to the interior painted with a loose bouquet within a gilt scroll well, circa 1840, 16cm. diameter.
(Christie's) $2,559

James Hadley, a fine large pair of figures of eastern water carriers, the lady holding the vase on her shoulder, the man with a large jug slung over his right shoulder, 43cm. high, date code for 1911.
(Phillips) $1,575

A Worcester blue and white fluted oviform teapot and cover painted with The Prunus Root pattern, circa 1756, 12.5cm. high.
(Christie's) $1,772

A Royal Worcester ivory-ground globular 'Persian' ewer prints in colors and raised gilding with two parrots perched on pine branches beneath a tall flared quatrefoil neck, 1883, 17$^{1}/_{2}$in. high.
(Christie's) $876

A pair of Royal Worcester ring-necked pheasants, modeled by R. Van Ruyckevelt.
(Bearne's) $1,267

A rare Worcester vase of baluster shape and quatrefoil section, painted in colors with a central floral bouquet and scattered sprigs, 16cm. high.
(Phillips) $935

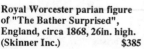

Royal Worcester parian figure of "The Bather Surprised", England, circa 1868, 26in. high.
(Skinner Inc.) $385

A pair of Royal Worcester spirally-molded candlesticks of squat form, the shaded yellow and apricot bodies with knopped stems and circular feet, 1892, 4$^{1}/_{4}$in. high.
(Christie's) $402

A Royal Worcester model of Marion by Ruth Van Ruyckevelt, dressed for tennis with a racket and a ball in her hands, 19.2cm. high.
(Bearne's) $352

WORCESTER

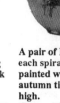

A Worcester blue and white lobed bowl painted with The Prunus Root pattern extending into the interior, painter's mark to footrim, circa 1758, 16cm. diameter.
(Christie's) $945

A pair of Royal Worcester vases, each spirally molded body painted with leaves and ferns in autumn tints and gold, 27.3cm. high.
(Bearne's) $493

A Worcester globular teapot and cover painted in a pale famille rose palette with flowering peony and chrysanthemum issuing from rockwork, circa 1755, 13cm. high.
(Christie's) $2,757

A Worcester quatrefoil pierced chestnut-basket and cover, molded with yellow-centered puce flowerheads, the centers to the stands painted with a loose bouquet and scattered flowers, circa 1765, the stand 26cm. wide.
(Christie's) $2,363

A rare Flight, Barr and Barr cottage pastille burner and nightlight in the form of a rustic half-timbered house with a gabled thatched roof, 17cm. high.
(Phillips) $578

A Worcester small baluster mug with grooved loop handle, painted with a loose bouquet and scattered flowers, circa 1760, 8.5cm. high.
(Christie's) $886

A larger Worcester basket, the center painted with a spray of fowers in colors within gilt scroll work and a scale blue border, 21cm. diameter.
(Phillips) $2,890

A pair of Worcester (Flight & Barr) oviform vases, painted with The Queen Charlotte pattern, with short flared necks and on spreading circular stems, circa 1800, 51cm. high.
(Christie's) $9,845

A Worcester mask-jug, the oviform body molded with stiff leaves enriched in yellow, puce and purple, circa 1770, 19cm. high.
(Christie's) $1,969

WORCESTER

A remarkable early Worcester hexagonal teapot and cover of small size, the press-molded body sharply modeled with panels of single flowering plants, 9.75cm. high.
(Phillips) $13,125

Eileen Soper, a very rare Worcester group of 'Take Cover' from the Wartime Series, showing a little girl, her brother beside her holding a puppy in his arms, both looking skywards in fear and apprehension, 15.5cm., date code for 1941.
(Phillips) $700

George Moseley, a teapot and cover of globular shape with gilt scroll handle and finial, painted with apples and blackberries,, 13.5cm., date code for 1930.
(Phillips) $805

A pair of Worcester oviform vases with short waisted necks, painted with exotic birds and with birds, butterflies and insects in flight, circa 1755, 12.5cm. high.
(Christie's) $15,752

A Royal Worcester figure of Mary Queen of Scots standing wearing a crucifix, a black-trimmed gilt snood, holding a handkerchief and 'jeweled' rosary, date code for 1917, 8$^{1}/_{4}$in. high.
(Christie's) $475

A pair of Royal Worcester tapering oviform ewers with trefoil lips, painted by G. Johnson on an azure ground with four swans in flight, date codes for circa 1909, 10$^{1}/_{2}$in. high.
(Christie's) $9,950

A large Worcester coffee or chocolate cup painted in famille rose enamels with a Chinese lady standing near a tree, a small boy running towards her, 7.4cm. high.
(Phillips) $960

A Royal Worcester circular plaque painted by John Stinton with Highland cattle among tufts of grass and heather, 1910, framed and glazed, 8$^{1}/_{4}$in. diameter.
(Christie's) $4,380

A Worcester baluster sparrow beak jug with a grooved loop handle, painted in colors with three chinoiserie figures and a boy in a landscape with a tree and house, 8cm. high.
(Phillips) $630

CHINA

YI

Blue and white decorated jar, Yi Dynasty, the body freely painted in underglaze blue with a pair of sparrows perched on a branch of flowering prunus, 5⁵/₈in. high. (Butterfield & Butterfield) $1,540

Underglaze blue decorated vase, Yi Dynasty, the body decorated in underglaze blue with leafy blossoming branches and hovering bats on a white ground, 10³/₄in. high. (Butterfield & Butterfield) $27,500

A Korean underglaze-blue and iron-spotted peach-shaped waterdropper, naturally molded in an upright position issuing from a carved leafy stalk serving as the foot of the vessel, Yi Dynasty, 19th century, 9cm. high. (Christie's) $7,203

YONGZHENG

A fine and rare 'Green dragon' baluster jar and cover, encircled Yongzheng six-character mark and of the period, crisply painted in underglaze-blue around the body with two five-clawed dragons, 8³/₈in. high. (Christie's) $63,871

A blue and white saucer-dish, encircled Yongzheng six-character mark and of the period, painted at the center in vivid blue tones with a ferocious four-clawed dragon writhing amongst clouds and fire scrolls, 6in. diameter. (Christie's) $3,690

A fine and rare blue and white pear-shaped vase, encircled Yongzheng six-character mark and of the period, painted around the body in pencil style and brilliant blue tones with the three friends, sanyou, pine, prunus and bamboo, 13in. high. (Christie's) $283,871

YUAN

A very rare blue and white vase, Yuhuchun, Yuan dynasty, freely painted to the body in deep purplish tone with two figures within a rocky landscape divided by a willow tree, 9³/₈in. high. (Christie's) $133,283

A Yuan blue and white dish, the interior painted with a central medallion of phoenixes in flight amid scrolling clouds, below a chrysanthemum scroll around the well, Yuan dynasty, 28.5cm. (Christie's) $15,752

A Yuan blue and white pear-shaped vase, Yuhuchunping, painted in brilliant tones of cobalt blue with a continuous lotus scroll between bands of detached lappets and upright leaves, 26cm. high. (Christie's) $10,920

BRACKET CLOCKS

An 18th century ebonized bracket clock, signed *Alex' Cumming, London*, the twin fusée movement with signed and engraved backplate and with verge escapement, 1ft, 9¹/₂in. high.
(Phillips) $3,133

A Regency brass inlaid mahogany bracket clock, signed *Thos. Halder, Arundel*, the twin fusee movement with anchor escapement, striking the hour on bell, circa 1820, 19³/₄in. high.
(Christie's) $1,760

A Victorian carved oak quarter chiming bracket clock, the case with carved wood dolphin finials to domed scale-carved top, signed *T. Bassnett Liverpool*, 29³/₄in. high.
(Christie's) $2,798

A small ebony silver-mounted striking bracket clock, circa 1708, the 4³/₄ x 5¹/₄in. dial signed *Tho: Tompion & Edw: Banger London*, 9in. high.
(Christie's)
                    $1,012,440

A highly unusual early ebony bracket clock by Simon Bartram, the corners of the 5¹/₂ inch square gilt dial engraved with winged masks, the escapement with pendulum fixed to pivoted verge arbor, circa 1660–1665, 12¹/₄in. high.
(Christie's) $14,300

A Charles II ebony Dutch striking small bracket clock by Joseph Knibb, London, within a phase III case with gilt foliate scroll escutcheons to the door and foliate mounts to the caddy top, circa 1680s, 11in. high.
(Christie's) $46,200

German ebonized bracket clock by Friedrich Heinrich Ahrens, dated 1792, the eight-day half-hour strike with repeat and alarm, on gilded-brass ogee bracket feet, 18¹/₄in. high.
(Butterfield & Butterfield)
                    $2,475

A George III mahogany striking bracket clock, the 8in. white painted dial signed *Willm Fidgett, London*, with anchor escapement, in a molded break arch case, 1ft. 5in. high.
(Bonhams) $1,449

A George III ebonized quarter chiming bracket clock, the case with handle and four flambeau finials to inverted bell top, the dial signed *Graham's Nephew & Successor Puckridge London*, 20¹/₂in. high.
(Christie's) $5,247

BRACKET CLOCKS

A William III ebony striking bracket clock, circa 1700, the 7¹/₄ x 8in. dial signed *Tho: Tompion Londini fecit*, 15¹/₂in. high.
(Christie's)   **$136,290**

A George II ebony bracket timepiece with alarm and original wall bracket, circa 1750, unnumbered, the dial signed *Geo: Graham London*, 21in. high.
(Christie's)   **$81,774**

A George I ebony striking bracket clock with alarm, circa 1725, the dial signed *Geo: Graham London*, 14in. high.
(Christie's)   **$146,025**

Benj. Barber London, a fine George III tortoiseshell and ormolu mounted musical bracket clock, the case with ogee top surmounted by urn-and-flambeau finials and applied with foliate ormolu mounts.
(Christie's)   **$31,482**

Josephus Pryor, a Charles II ebony striking bracket clock of large size, the plinth shaped case with gilt carrying handle to cushion molded top, glazed sides, the 10in. square skeletonized dial with silvered chapter ring.
(Christie's)   **$17,490**

Ellicott London, a fine George III musical striking bracket clock, the case with foliate urn finials to bell top, handles and cast pierced sound frets to side doors, 32in. high.
(Christie's)   **$19,239**

A good George II ebonized striking bracket clock with moonphase, the brass-lined case with handle to inverted bell top, signed *John. Hodges St. Clemt. Lane London*, 18¹/₂in. high.
(Christie's)   **$7,346**

A good Regency rosewood striking bracket clock, the Indo-gothic lancet case on brass pad feet with turned moldings, signed *Brockbank and Atkins London 1902*, 20¹/₂in. high.
(Christie's)   **$2,798**

A late 18th century mahogany quarter chiming bracket clock, the case with inverted bell top, signed on a recessed cartouche *Higgs Y Diego Evans Bolsa Real Londres*, 2ft. 2¹/₂in. high.
(Phillips)   **$5,713**

BRACKET CLOCKS

An early 18th century ebony veneered pull quarter repeat alarum bracket clock, the fusée movement with five finely finned pillars, signed *William Post, London Bridge*, 20¹/₂in. high.
(Lawrence) $6,930

An unusual Scottish Regency mahogany striking bracket clock, the case with cushioned molded top and gilt wire lattice sound frets to sides, signed *David Whitelaw Edinburgh*, 33³/₄in. high.
(Christie's) $3,498

A 19th century mahogany bracket clock, the case with chamfer top, surmounted by a finial, raised on four brass ball feet, the circular painted dial signed *Frodsham*, 18¹/₂in. high.
(Phillips) $1,350

Thomas Tompion London, an ebony veneered quarter repeating bracket clock, circa 1700, the caddy top case surmounted by a carrying handle, 15¹/₂in. high.
(Phillips) $126,000

Dan: Quare London 62 (Graham No. 550), a George I ebonized striking bracket clock of small size, the case with large giltmetal handle to cushion molded top, circa 1715, 11⁷/₈in. high.
(Christie's) $104,940

Henry Massey, London, a late 17th century ebonized basket top bracket clock, the square brass dial with signed silvered chapter ring, 16in. high.
(Phillips) $4,320

A 19th century Chinese hardwood bracket clock, the rectangular case decorated with carved motifs, the twin fusée movement with verge escapement, striking on a bell, 1ft. 3in. high.
(Phillips) $684

A George III inlaid mahogany small bracket clock, the white dial within brass bezel above inlaid panel, turned acorn finials now fitted with 19th century French countwheel striking movement, 14in. high.
(Christie's) $3,300

A Regency mahogany striking bracket clock, the boxwood lined arched case with fish-scale frets and lion-mask-and-ring handles, signed *Perigal & Duterrau*, 17¹/₄in. high.
(Christie's) $1,749

CARRIAGE CLOCKS

A miniature French oval gilt brass and porcelain paneled carriage timepiece, with lever platform escapement, the porcelain dial decorated with a young girl and boy, 4in. high.
(Phillips) $3,060

An unusual 19th century gilt brass French carriage clock, the movement with lever platform escapement, push repeat and alarm, signed *Lucien, A. Paris*, 9¹/₂in. high.
(Phillips) $6,480

A miniature French gilt brass and enamel paneled carriage timepiece, bearing the *Drocourt* trade mark, and signed for *Klaftenberger, Paris*, 3³/₄in. high.
(Phillips) $2,160

A fine parcel gilt silver grande sonnerie carriage clock signed *Tiffany & Co., New York*, the movement probably by Drocourt, circa 1883, 8¹/₂in. high.
(Christie's) $8,250

A gilt brass grande sonnerie striking carriage clock, the massive going barrel movement having duplex escapement with cut bimetallic balance on large gilt platform, with blued Breguet hands and silvered alarm hand, 7¹/₂in. high.
(Christie's) $25,597

A French gilt brass carriage clock, with lever platform and helical hairspring, push repeat, alarm, striking on a gong and signed *Baschet & Baullet, Paris*, 7in. high.
(Phillips) $828

A good 19th century French gilt brass grande sonnerie carriage clock, signed *Klaftenberger* on the edge of the plate, 7in. high.
(Phillips) $6,300

A French gilt brass carriage clock, with lever platform escapement and push repeat, striking on a gong, with enamel dial signed for *T. Martin*, 7¹/₂in. high.
(Phillips) $864

A French gilt brass and porcelain paneled carriage clock, with replaced lever platform escapement, alarm, push repeat and striking on a gong, 7¹/₂in. high.
(Phillips) $2,070

CARRIAGE CLOCKS

A French miniature brass carriage timepiece, the lever movement bearing *DC* trademark, in a numbered pillared case, 10.5cm. high.
(Phillips) $865

A 19th century French gilt brass and enamel carriage clock, striking on a gong, with push repeat, the silvered chapter within a gilt mask, 6³/₄in. high.
(Phillips) $1,332

A 19th century French gilt carriage clock, the lever movement striking on a gong with push repeat, dated *1874*, 7¹/₄in. high.
(Phillips) $1,418

A French miniature brass carriage timepiece, the circular enamel dial within a florally decorated silvered mask, in a caryatid case, 4¹/₄in. high, together with a traveling case.
(Phillips) $1,261

A silver and enamel miniature one-piece carriage timepiece in the Oriental taste with platform lever escapement, the backplate with stamp of *L'Epeé Made in France 11 jewels*, 3¹/₄in. high.
(Christie's) $875

A gilt brass and enamel carriage timepiece with later platform lever escapement, backplate stamped *France*, silvered chapter ring with Arabic chapters, 5¹/₄in. high.
(Christie's) $1,084

A giltmetal grande sonnerie striking carriage clock with cut bimetallic balance to silvered lever platform, the backplate with stamp for *Margaine*, 7in. high.
(Christie's) $3,673

A rare chased gilt carriage clock with singing bird automaton, signed *Japy Freres & Cie.*, surmounted by glazed virtrine with rising handle displaying the bird perched within realistic silk and feather foliage, circa 1860, 12³/₄in. high.
(Christie's) $18,700

A Victorian parcel-gilt and silver-mounted carriage timepiece, the case with large baluster finial to fish-scale pierced molded top with two amorous angels seated above, by John Mortimer and John S. Hunt, 1842, 8¹/₂in. high.
(Christie's) $14,960

CARRIAGE CLOCKS

A French gilt brass grande sonnerie carriage clock, the lever movement striking on two gongs with alarm and push repeat, signed for *Sennet Freres Paris Chnie*, 6³/₄in. high.
(Phillips) $1,477

An eight-day repeating carriage clock with alarm, the white enamel dial signed *Chas. Frodsham, Clockmaker to the Queen*, 6¹/₄in. high.
(Bearne's) $1,290

A silver jubilee small silver carriage timepiece with gilt lever platform, white enamel Roman dial signed *Chas. Frodsham London* with blued hands, 3¹/₄in. high.
(Christie's) $962

A 19th century French brass carriage clock by Paul Garnier, Paris, with two-plane escapement, striking on a bell with push repeat, signed on the backplate, 6¹/₂in. high.
(Phillips) $2,659

A French brass and champlevé enamel carriage clock, the lever movement, with alarm and push repeat striking on a bell, signed for *L Urard & Co., Tientsin*, 8in. high.
(Phillips) $2,660

An Art Nouveau tortoiseshell and silver carriage timepiece, with uncut bimetallic balance to silvered lever platform, silvered Roman chapter disc signed *George Edward & Sons Buchanan St. Glasgow*, 4¹/₂in. high.
(Christie's) $1,312

A gilt engraved brass striking oval carriage clock with alarm on gong, white enamel Roman chapter disc with blued moon hands, alarm disc below VI 6¹/₄in. high.
(Christie's) $2,099

A 19th century brass carriage clock, the lever movement striking on a gong, bearing the *Margaine* trade mark, with enamel dial, in an engraved gorge case, 7in. high.
(Phillips) $1,390

A gilt brass striking carriage clock with brass balance to silvered cylinder platform, strike on bell, corniche case, with brown leather traveling case, 5³/₄in. high.
(Christie's) $525

CLOCK SETS

Fine Louis XV style gilt-bronze and cloisonné three-piece clock garniture by Vincent and Cie, retailed by Tiffany and Co., New York, circa 1900, with eight-day time and half-hour strike on a coiled gong, 28¼in. high.
(Butterfield & Butterfield) $23,100

A French ormolu and Sèvres-pattern turquoise ground garniture, the clock surmounted by an urn, with a mask-head and swag handle to each side, decorated with a woman and putti, late 19th century, 19in. high.
(Christie's) $5,843

A French gilt brass and champlevé enamel clock garniture, the arched case of four glass form, surmounted by a twin handled urn and four finials, 1ft. 8in. high, together with a matching pairs of urns.
(Phillips) $3,152

A 19th century ormolu and porcelain mounted mantel clock case, of arched form surmounted by an oval enamel panel, with foliate swags, on four turned feet and mounted with twelve floral panels, together with two associated side pieces.
(Phillips) $990

A French ormolu and Sèvres-pattern blue ground garniture, the mantel clock of square outline surmounted by an urn with flaming finial, a female mask head to each corner, the dial decorated with a cherub, late 19th century, 18in. high.
(Christie's) $5,478

A French gilt brass and bronzed garniture, comprising a clock surmounted by an urn with foliate swags, the arched case with addorsed dolphins and flaming finials, the dial with twelve enamel numeral plaquettes, late 19th century, 26¾in. high.
(Christie's) $3,287

CLOCK SETS

Brass garniture set, Europe, circa 1915, in the style of Onder den St. Marten, comprising an elongated pendulum clock and matching double arm candlesticks with pierced designs on the front of the cases, 14¹/₂in. high.
(Skinner Inc.) $700

A French porcelain mounted clock garniture, the two-train movement in a drum case, putto decorated dial, 1ft. 3in. high, flanked by a pair of four-light candelabra, decorated with putti and musical trophies.
(Bonhams) $1,044

A French porcelain and ormolu clock garniture, two-train movement by Henri Marc, with dial decorated with birds, flanked by a pair of bulbous urns, 11¹/₂in. high.
(Bonhams) $2,340

A 19th century ormolu and porcelain mantel clock, the decorated dial with Roman numerals, the twin train movement stamped *Ch. Vcne*, together with a pair of associated candlesticks, 16in. high.
(Phillips) $1,475

Extremely fine Napoléon III parcel-gilt and patinated bronze three-piece clock garniture, signed *Raingo Frères*, Paris, third quarter 19th century, the case surmounted by a group of a classically robed reclining woman and three children, 31¹/₂in. wide.
(Butterfield & Butterfield) $22,000

A bronzed and gilt metal clock garniture, the clock with circular gilt foliate stamped dial set in a horizontal cylindrical drum as a houdah, surmounted by a chinoiserie figure holding a feather fan, 23in. high, flanked by a pair of two branch candelabra.
(Spencer's) $4,847

A late 17th century brass lantern clock, the frame surmounted by a later bell, the signed florally engraved dial inscribed *S F * K*, with brass chapter, 1ft. 4in. high. (Phillips) $9,000

An unusual George III gilt brass watch lantern in the gothic manner, the upper part with pagoda pediment and pierced square cover, originally hung with bells, on paw feet, 16¹/₂in. high. (Canterbury) $1,250

Nicholas Coxeter Londini Fecit, a Charles II lantern clock with alarm, the movement with large diameter balance to verge escapement, countwheel strike on bell above, 15¹/₂in. high. (Christie's) $5,597

A brass striking lantern clock, the case of typical form with florally engraved dial center signed *Morguet A H'Oudain*, with galleried front fret, 12³/₄in. high. (Christie's) $1,068

A brass lantern clock, the frame surmounted by a bell, the 17th century engraved brass dial inscribed *John Hilderson, Londini Fecit*, with brass chapter ring and single steel hand, 1ft. 2¹/₂in. high. (Phillips) $1,440

Thomas Loumes, at the Mermayd in Lothbury, a 17th century brass lantern clock, the case surmounted by a bell with turned corner posts, 1ft. 1¹/₂in. high. (Phillips) $4,680

A 17th century brass lantern clock, the posted frame surmounted by a bell with engraved dial plate signed *John Pennock in Lothbury, Londini*, 1ft. 5in. high. (Phillips) $2,160

A Japanese striking lantern clock with alarm, the case of standard form with twin foliot verge movement, black painted dial with Japanese chapters, lacking hand, 9¹/₂in. high. (Christie's) $2,935

A George I miniature brass lantern timepiece with alarm, the arched dial signed *Massey London* on a disc within foliate engraving, lacking gallery frets and one side door, 8in. high. (Christie's) $2,264

LANTERN CLOCKS

A Chares II brass striking lantern clock, with original verge escapement and bob pendulum, the florally engraved dial signed *Tho. Wintworth, Sarum Fecit*, 14³/₄in. high.
(Christie's) **$5,090**

A brass lantern clock with adapted thirty hour movement, incorporating a mid-17th century dial with floral engraving, signed *John Langley*, 10in. high.
(Phillips) **$810**

A brass lantern clock with alarm of standard form, now with early anchor escapement and countwheel strike on bell above, narrow silvered chapter ring, 15¹/₂in. high.
(Christie's) **$2,449**

Robert Robinson, Londini, a 17th century brass lantern clock, the signed florally engraved dial,with silvered chapter ring and alarm set disc to the center, 1ft. ¹/₂in. high.
(Phillips) **$2,520**

A Viennese gilt metal miniature striking lantern clock, the movement with tic-tac escapement, the gilt case with trellis-work engraving to side doors, 6in. high.
(Christie's) **$4,300**

A Charles II brass miniature lantern timepiece case signed *Windmills London* on the foliate engraved dial center with alarm disc, 9¹/₄in. high.
(Christie's) **$1,137**

Benjamin Hill in Fleete Streete, a late 17th century brass lantern clock, the frame surmounted by a later bell and cage with turned corner posts, 1ft. 3in. high.
(Phillips) **$3,420**

A Swiss iron weight driven clock in the manner of Erhard Liechti, the wrought iron frame surmounted by a decorated strap and bell, 1ft. 3in. high.
(Phillips) **$10,800**

A gilt brass striking lantern clock of standard form with anchor escapement and countwheel strike on bell above, the dial signed *John Lisborrow Ashen,* 15in. high.
(Christie's) **$2,297**

LONGCASE CLOCKS

An early Victorian longcase clock, by Francis Abbott, Manchester, 104in. high, circa 1840. (Tennants)
$3,400

A George II mahogany month-going longcase regulator, circa 1755, signed *Ellicott London*, 87³/₄in. high. (Christie's)
$136,290

A 19th century Scottish longcase clock, by Winter, Edinburgh, 87¹/₂in. high, circa 1840. (Tennants)
$1,530

George III japanned and chinoiserie decorated tall case clock, late 18th century, 88in. high. (Skinner Inc.)
$1,980

A Chippendale cherrywood tall-case clock, dial signed *Nathan Dean, Plainfield, Connecticut,* late 18th century, 86¹/₂in. high. (Christie's)
$4,180

A three-train eight day long case clock, by the Northern Goldsmiths Co, Newcastle on Tyne, dated *1920*, 7ft. 7in. high. (Tennants)
$1,860

A William and Mary floral marquetry longcase clock, signed *Wm. Cattle in fleet Street Londini fecit* at VI o'clock, 1680s, 78¹/₂in. high. (Christie's)
$19,800

A Federal inlaid cherrywood tall-case clock by Christian Eby, Manheim, Pennsylvania, circa 1810, 107¹/₂in. high. (Christie's)
$49,500

LONGCASE CLOCKS

Italian Renaissance style walnut tall case clock, A. Cheloni, Firenze, 1889, 110in. high. (Skinner Inc.) **$9,350**

An eight day long case clock, the silvered and brass square dial inscribed *John Nethercott, Chipping Norton*, 7ft. 5in. high. (Tennants) **$930**

Chippendale mahogany carved tall case clock, Newport, Rhode Island, 1760–85, 86in. high. (Skinner Inc.) **$73,700**

A fine Queen Anne burl walnut longcase clock by Thomas Tompion, circa 1710, 92in. high. (Christie's) **$181,500**

A Federal carved mahogany tall-case clock, by Isaac Reed, Frankford, Pennsylvania, circa 1800, 91¹/₂in. high. (Christie's) **$9,900**

A George II long case clock, the eight-day movement with brass and silvered dial signed *Wm Chase Derby*, circa 1740, 7ft. 5¹/₂in. high. (Tennants) **$4,092**

A Charles II walnut longcase clock, circa 1685, the 10in. square dial signed *John Knibb Oxon fecit*, 6ft. 6in. high. (Christie's) **$93,456**

A Chippendale mahogany tall-case clock, dial and case signed *Nathaniel Mulliken, Lexington, Massachusetts*, circa 1754, 91¹/₂in. high. (Christie's) **$33,000**

Federal mahogany veneer tall case clock, Simon Willard, Roxbury, Massachusetts, circa 1800, 98¹/₄in. high. (Skinner Inc.)

$29,700

Federal cherry inlaid tall case clock, Concord, Massachusetts, 1800–1815, 90in. high. (Skinner Inc.)

$4,400

A Charles II parquetry longcase clock by Johannes Fromanteel, London, circa 1680, 75in. high. (Christie's)

$20,900

Mahogany carved tall case clock, Benjamin Willard, Grafton, Massachusetts, 1770, 89in. high. (Skinner Inc.)

$48,400

An early Victorian Scottish mahogany longcase clock, the drumhead hood with glazed bezel to circular silvered engraved dial signed *Whitelaw Edinburgh*, 6ft. 6in. high. (Christie's)

$2,090

An early 18th century walnut longcase clock, with silvered chapter ring, signed *Wm. Crow, London*, with subsidiary seconds and date aperture, 6ft. 10in. high. (Phillips)

$2,685

A mahogany longcase clock, hood with swan neck pediment surmounted by three gilt eagle finials, signed *Thomas Brown, Chester*, 93¹/₂in. high. (Christie's S. Ken)

$4,869

A green lacquer longcase clock, signed on a raised silvered disc *Danl. Torin, London*, strike/silent ring in the arch flanked by dolphin spandrels, 88¹/₂in. high. (Christie's S. Ken)

$2,431

LONGCASE CLOCKS

Grained tall case clock, Aaron Miller (d. 1777), Elizabethtown, New Jersey, 91in. high. (Skinner Inc.)
$6,270

Federal walnut inlaid tallcase clock, Pennsylvania, circa 1770–1810, 7ft. 11in. high. (Butterfield & Butterfield)
$5,225

An Arts and Crafts black painted oak electric longcase clock, with a stained and leaded glass door, 76in. high. (Christie's)
$591

Dutch rococo marquetry longcase clock, the dial signed *H. Smitt, Amsterdam,* 7ft. 10in. high. (Butterfield & Butterfield)
$5,225

George II walnut eight-day longcase clock by Joseph or Joshua Morgan, London, second quarter 18th century, 7ft. 9¹/₂in. high. (Butterfield & Butterfield)
$7,150

Tall case clock, circa 1800, in mahogany with wooden works, bonnet top, reeded quarter columns, turned feet, 93in. high. (Eldred's)
$1,320

George I Circassian walnut eight-day longcase clock, labeled *Joseph and Thomas Windmills, London,* circa 1714, 6ft. 10¹/₂in. high. (Butterfield & Butterfield)
$14,300

Late George III inlaid mahogany longcase clock, the dial signed *Barry, Leigh,* first quarter 19th century, 7ft. 11¹/₂in. high. (Butterfield & Butterfield)
$3,575

LONGCASE CLOCKS

George III scarlet japanned chinoiserie decorated tall case clock, James Jackson, London, third quarter 18th century, 90in. high.
(Skinner Inc.)
$2,750

Fine Louis XV style gilt-bronze-mounted parquetry regulateur, late 19th century, 8ft. 5in. high.
(Butterfield & Butterfield)
$13,200

An antique Scottish George III mahogany longcase clock, maker's name *John Peatt, Crieff*, (circa 1800), 6ft. 11in. high.
(Selkirk's)
$2,600

Arts and Crafts oak tall case clock, circa 1910, brass numerals and dial over leaded glass cabinet door, 75$\frac{1}{2}$in. high.
(Skinner Inc.)
$935

A fine George II burl walnut musical longcase clock by John Hodges, Clements Lane, London, rack striking the hour and playing one of 12 tunes, circa 1730, 110in. high.
(Christie's New York)
$24,200

Chippendale mahogany tall case clock, Pennsylvania, late 18th century, inscribed *Geo Lively, Baltimore*, 7ft. 7in. high.
(Butterfield & Butterfield)
$2,475

Swedish neoclassical painted thirty-hour longcase clock, late 18th century, now painted Venetian red with pale gray detail, 8ft. 7in. high.
(Butterfield & Butterfield)
$4,950

A late 19th century nine-tube chiming mahogany longcase clock, signed *Granshaw, Baxter, & J.J. Elliot Ltd*, the massive three-train movement striking the quarters on eight tubes and the hours on a ninth, 91in. high.
(Christie's S. Ken)
$4,426

LONGCASE CLOCKS

A German Renaissance Revival carved walnut and elm Standuhr, two-train chiming movement, 8ft. 5in. high. (Selkirk's)

$3,500

Queen Anne japanned tall case clock, Gawen Brown (1749–1773), Boston, circa 1760, 87in. high. (Skinner Inc.)

$4,510

Mahogany tall case clock, William Claggett (1695–1749), Newport, Rhode Island, 1725–40), 88¼in. high. (Skinner Inc.)

$25,300

Dutch baroque burl walnut tall case clock, H.P. Karbentus, Hage, mid 18th century, 93in. high. (Skinner Inc.)

$4,675

A George III Scottish flame mahogany longcase clock, signed *Sam. Collier Eccles* on the arch above the painted moonphase, the four pillar rack striking movement with anchor escapement, 7ft. 7½in. high. (Christie's)

$2,508

Louis XVI fruitwood and parquetry longcase clock, the nine and one half inch brass arched dial repoussé with cherub's head spandrels, 7ft. 11in. high. (Butterfield & Butterfield)

$7,700

A George III mahogany longcase clock, the 12in. arched brass dial with silvered chapter ring, subsidiary seconds and date aperture, signed *Joshua Arnold, London*, with painted seascape in the arch, 8ft. 2½in. high. (Phillips)

$5,365

An early 18th century walnut and floral marquetry longcase clock, the 11in. square brass dial with silvered chapter ring, signed *Natha. Pyne Londini fecit*, with subsidiary seconds, date aperture and with ringed winding holes, 6ft. 5½in. high. (Phillips)

$7,770

MANTEL CLOCKS

An unusual French brass and black marble automaton band saw mantel timepiece, two-train movement by C.L.T. Paris, 1ft. 4in. high.
(Bonhams) $3,580

Louis XVI style gilt-bronze-mounted porphyry pendule à cercles rolant, mid-19th century, of urn-form richly embellished with applied swags of berried foliage and flowers, 16in. high.
(Butterfield & Butterfield) $7,700

A good Louis XVI white marble and ormolu calendar mantel clock, circular white enamel dial signed *Furet a Paris*, the top surmounted by a seated female figure embraced by a winged cherub, 1ft. 9in. high.
(Bonhams) $6,820

Unusual Renaissance design gilt-brass mantel clock, late 19th century, the domed case surmounted by an urn with lotus bud finial supported by four winged snarling animal mask monopodia, 26¹/₂in. high.
(Butterfield & Butterfield) $1,320

A French Directoire ormolu and marble mantel clock, the case depicting 'La Lecture', the female figure seated before a draped table with a lamp, 1ft. 1in. high.
(Phillips) $4,137

A Victorian carved walnut shelf-clock by Seth Thomas Company, Thomaston, Connecticut, circa 1890, of violin form carved with foliage centering a glazed cupboard door painted in gilding with musical motifs, 29in. high.
(Christie's) $4,180

An English ormolu and black marble mantel timepiece, single train fusée movement signed *Lamb, 86 Newman St.*, 7¹/₂in. high.
(Bonhams) $682

A 19th century Continental gilt brass and enameled mantel timepiece, the case in the form of a ship's wheel, signed on a shaped cartouche for *Tiffany & Co.*, 8in. high.
(Phillips) $394

A Scottish Regency mahogany balloon mantel regulator of large size, with handles to sides and on brass ball feet, the backplate signed *Ian. Dalgleish Edinburgh*, 25¹/₂in. high.
(Christie's) $2,099

MANTEL CLOCKS

An enameled silver Renaissance revival clock in the form of a camel, the case by Hermann Bohm, Vienna, the oval base finely painted with mythological scenes with ground of leafy scrolls, circa 1880, 9³/₄in. high.
(Christie's) $7,150

James Fr. Cole London, an important and early silver-cased, minute repeating, perpetual calendar, astronomical traveling timepiece with alarm, London 1823, unnumbered, 6in. high.
(Christie's) $271,095

A Second Empire yellow marble, ormolu and bronze striking mantel clock, the case with ormolu foliate mounts and surmounted by a bronze lion, 15in. high.
(Christie's) $875

A black slate perpetual calendar and equation striking mantel clock, the twin going barrel movement striking on bell on backplate stamped *Drielsma Liverpool*, 16¹/₂in. high.
(Christie's) $1,399

A Eureka mantel timepiece, the 4¹/₂in. circular enamel dial signed *Eureka Clock Co. Ltd, London*, the large bimetallic balance wheel visible beneath, 1ft. 1in. high.
(Bonhams) $1,108

An Edwardian silver cased mantel timepiece, in plain balloon case with tied reed borders upon ogee bracket feet by W. Comyns, London 1909, 8³/₄in.
(Tennants) $1,275

Federal mahogany pillar and scroll clock, Eli Terry and Sons, Plymouth, Connecticut, circa 1820, 30-hour wooden movement, 32in. high.
(Skinner Inc.) $990

A Second Empire porcelain and brass elephant clock, for the Turkish market, the elephant with turquoise glaze and with royal blue and gilt decoration, 11¹/₂in. high.
(Christie's) $1,890

A 19th century satinwood mantel clock, the rectangular case surmounted by a sphinx, the florally engraved square gilt brass dial signed *Walter Yonge*, 10¹/₂in. high.
(Phillips) $4,334

MANTEL CLOCKS

Federal mahogany inlaid shelf timepiece, probably Massachusetts, circa 1810, eight day weight driven movement, 8¹/₂in. high.
(Skinner Inc.)   **$3,575**

Louis XV style gilt-bronze mantel clock, retailed by Tiffany & Co., New York, circa 1900, the circular white enameled clock face with Arabic hours and minutes with floral garlands, 24in. high.
(Butterfield & Butterfield)
                              $3,300

An ormolu and cloisonné enamel four glass mantel clock, the twin-train movement with off-white enamel dial, decorated with floral swags, on paw feet, 17¹/₂in. high.
(Christie's)   **$1,132**

A Regency tortoiseshell, and boulle and ormolu mounted bracket clock, signed on an enamel cartouche below the six, *Le Boeuf, Paris*, the two-train movement with outside countwheel strike on a bell, 34in. high.
(Christie's S. Ken)
                              $2,926

Louis XVI style gilt-bronze and white marble figural mantel clock by S. Marti et Cie, Paris, late 19th century, 12¹/₂in. high.
(Butterfield & Butterfield)
                              $2,750

A 19th century French boulle and polychrome enamel striking bracket clock in Louis XVI style, the waisted case applied with giltmetal foliate mounts on scroll feet surmounted by the winged figure of Peace, 35¹/₄in. high overall.
(Christie's)   **$1,672**

Napoleon III gilt-bronze figural mantel clock, Japy Frères, third quarter 19th century, surmounted by a group of a young girl and hound on a knoll, 19in. high.
(Butterfield & Butterfield)
                              $1,760

Empire mantel clock by Samuel Terry of Bristol, reverse painted upper tablet flanked by stenciled columns, carved eagle cornice, carved paw feet, 29¹/₂in. high.
(Eldred's)   **$413**

A French gilt bronze and bronze sculptural mantel clock with pietra dura panels, with Brocot suspension, bell striking and bearing the stamp of Vincenti, 16¹/₂in. high.
(Lawrence Fine Art)
                              $2,134

MANTEL CLOCKS

Louis XVI style gilt-bronze
mounted white alabaster lyre
clock, Japy Frères, late 19th
century, the white enameled
dial painted with floral festoons,
24in. high.
(Butterfield & Butterfield)
$1,980

Federal mahogany pillar and
scroll clock, Riley Whiting,
Winchester, Connecticut, circa
1825, thirty-hour wooden
movement, 30in. high.
(Skinner Inc.) $935

'Metropole', a Memphis clock,
designed by George J. Sowden,
1982, wood and plastic laminate,
finished in shades of gray, green,
yellow and mauve, with metal
plaque, *Memphis, Made in Italy*.
(Christie's) $2,588

Important Chinese export
porcelain clock case, 18th
century, with green and white
polychrome floral decoration,
13¹/₂in. high.
(Eldred's) $550

Weller Dickensware art pottery
mantel clock, housed in
elaborated pottery frame
decorated with yellow pansies,
10in. high.
(Skinner Inc.) $440

A chased and engraved gilt
metal quarter striking
Türmchenuhr, now striking
hours on bell in lower colonnade,
and quarters on bell in upper
colonnade, German, circa 1600,
14¹/₂in. high.
(Christie's New York)
$30,800

Louis XV style parcel-gilt and
patinated bronze figural clock,
19th century, raised on a
support cast with palm fronds, a
seated putto at its base holding a
tablet, flanked by two putti,
25¹/₂in. high.
(Butterfield & Butterfield)
$3,300

Federal mahogany pillar and
scroll clock, Bishop and Bradley,
Waterbury, Connecticut, circa
1825.
(Skinner Inc.) $1,650

A Liberty & Co. Tudric pewter
clock designed by Archibald
Knox, decorated with
rectangular panels of abalone,
circular dial with Roman
chapters, circa 1902, 16.7cm.
high.
(Christie's) $2,700

193

MANTEL CLOCKS

A 19th century Austrian silver and enamel timepiece, the case in the form of a twin handled urn, surmounted by a floral spray and decorated with classical scenes, 9in. high.
(Phillips) $3,600

A 17th century German quarter striking table clock, decorated with the figure of a hound with automated eyes and tail, the dial to the side with silvered chapter and center alarm set, 8in. high.
(Phillips) $9,720

A Martin Brothers stoneware mantel clock, the base decorated to each corner with fierce griffin-like heads, the arched pediment raised off twin griffin supports with applied lizard above, 31.5cm. high.
(Phillips) $1,801

A fine and rare Louis XV celadon craquelure glazed and ormolu mounted mantel clock of urn form with horizontal chapter ring, signed on the backplate *Masson à Paris*, 1ft. 11½in. high, circa 1765.
(Bonhams) $37,800

A Biedermeier ormolu mounted walnut and parquetry automaton table clock with organ, the front with an automaton representing a garden grotto with rotating glass rods simulating water jets spouting into the mouths of dolphins, 22¼in. high.
(Christie's) $24,880

A French boudoir combined timepiece, barometer and thermometer with cream enamel dials and silvered-metal scale, 12in. high.
(Bearne's) $520

A late 18th century French white marble and ormolu mantel clock, the case surmounted by a twin handled urn flanked by columns wrapped with leaves, 15½in. high.
(Phillips) $900

An early 18th century gilt brass Continental table clock, the square case with glazed apertures to the sides and winged paw feet, 13cm. square.
(Phillips) $3,600

An Empire ormolu grande sonnerie striking pendule d'officier, the foliate cast case on chased paw feet, signed *Auguste Droz*, 8½in. high.
(Christie's) $4,529

MANTEL CLOCKS

A French boulle mantel clock, two-train movement and white enamel dial signed *Leroy à Paris*, in a waisted brass and tortoiseshell case, 12in. high.
(Bonhams) $936

A two-day marine chronometer, the movement with Earnshaw-type spring detent escapement, signed *Charles Frodsham, London.*
(Phillips) $2,364

A 19th century French ormolu and porcelain mounted mantel clock, the case surmounted by a gilt urn with ram's head supports, 14¹/₂in. high.
(Phillips) $1,044

An enamelled silver Renaissance Revival jewel casket fitted with a watch, the case by Simon Grünwald, Vienna, on winged paw feet, the side panels and broken arch pediment set with panels painted with mythological scenes, circa 1880, 5in. high.
(Christie's) $4,180

An unusual rosewood quarter chiming small mantel clock signed *Gibbs, 38 Banner St. London*, the shaped arched dial with Roman chapters, blued-steel Breguet hands, purpose made for the late 18th century miniature triple fusée movement now fitted with chains, 11in. high.
(Christie's) $4,400

An enameled silver Renaissance revival figural clock, Viennese, surmounted by a caricature of a violinist in frock coat and wide brimmed hat, the plinth painted with a scene of peasants dancing in rustic landscape, circa 1880, 10¹/₂in. high.
(Christie's) $4,950

A 19th century gilt brass strut timepiece in the manner of Thomas Cole, the shaped rectangular case with engraved decoration, 6in. high.
(Phillips) $2,340

An important silver mounted gilt table clock, the movement signed *D. Buschman [Augsburg]*, raised on four paw feet each chased with winged mask, circa 1660, 6in. high.
(Christie's) $9,350

Victorian gilded spelter mantel clock, with pink and white polychrome decorated reserve panels and face, early 19th century, 15in. high.
(G.A. Key) $645

MANTEL CLOCKS

Louis XV ormolu and patinated bronze figural mantel clock, the dial signed *Antoine Thiout*, mid-18th century, 21³/₄in. high. (Butterfield & Butterfield)
$8,250

A Regency ormolu-mounted griotte marble mantel clock by Benjamin Lewis Vulliamy, the milled circular Roman-chaptered dial in a serpent bezel, 16in. wide.
(Christie's)
$8,131

Louis XVI bronze and white marble mantel clock, early 19th century, urn finials and circular dial, 25in. high.
(Skinner Inc.)
$2,200

A 19th century French mahogany and ormolu mounted mantel clock of lyre shape, the twin train movement striking on a bell, 19¹/₂in. high.
(Christie's)
$2,237

A late Federal mahogany pillar and scroll shelf clock, Seth Thomas, Plymouth, Connecticut, circa 1820, with a glazed cupboard door flanked by colonettes and enclosing a white dial with Arabic chapter ring, 31in. high.
(Christie's)
$1,540

A late 19th century French mantel timepiece, the circular ormolu dial with Roman numerals, within a cartouche shaped champèvé enamel case, 10¹/₂in. high.
(Christie's)
$839

A fine modern perpetual calendar and moonphase chronometer four-glass clock by Sinclair Harding, Cheltenham, in ebony and gilt brass glazed case, 14in. high.
(Christie's S. Ken)
$12,173

A Victorian gilt metal strut timepiece, the easel with pierced foliate decoration, the rear inscribed *HOWELL & JAMES REGENT ST. LONDON.*, 12¹/₂in. high.
(Christie's)
$601

A late Victorian three-train oak mantel clock, the fusée anchor movement with silvered dial, the case with break-arch top, circa 1880, 20in. high.
(Tennants)
$850

MANTEL CLOCKS

A gilt metal figural stackfreed clock, the figure, in classical armor, standing next to an engraved shaft supporting a wreath and scroll mount to silver time ball, circa 1580, 11³/₄in. high.
(Christie's) **$11,000**

Patinated metal clock, Amsterdam School, (1915–30), bulbous teardrop shape with round dial, 11in. high.
(Skinner Inc.) **$530**

A 19th century French bronze and parcel gilt mantel clock with Cupid surmount, the twin train movement striking on a bell, 13¹/₂in. high.
(Christie's) **$559**

A 19th century French bronze and ormolu mantel clock, the rectangular case with acanthine borders, surmounted by the figure of an infant bacchanal, 19in. high.
(Christie's) **$1,585**

Charles X gilt-bronze figural clock, circa 1830, the engine-turned circular clock face within an ivy frame set in a rectangular case surmounted by a ewer, 14³/14³/₄in. high.
(Butterfield & Butterfield) **$1,320**

Empire ormolu mantel clock, early 19th century, rectangular cornice on four columns above a circular dial, 21in. high.
(Skinner Inc.) **$1,870**

A Victorian three-train ebonized mantel clock, the fusée anchor movement with brass and silvered dial inscribed *Deacon, Swindon,* 29¹/₂in. high.
(Tennants) **$1,700**

René Lalique Deux Figurines clock, with recessed molded design of two women in diaphanous gowns, 14in. high.
(Skinner Inc.) **$9,900**

A gilt quarter striking mantel clock on molded base, the case glazed with four beveled panels, the rounded angles, supporting plain cornice, English/French, mid 19th century, 15in. high.
(Christie's) **$2,750**

MANTEL CLOCKS

An unusual French four-glass mantel clock, two-train movement by Vincenti & Cie, white enamel dial with red numerals, 1ft. 5¹/₂in. high.
(Bonhams) $1,260

A French ormolu and bronze mantel clock, two-train movement by S. Martin with silk suspension, embossed gilt dial with white enamel numeral reserves, 1ft. 11in. wide.
(Bonhams) $1,620

A Regency rosewood striking mantel clock of lyre form, circular 3in. white enamel dial signed *Thwaites & Reed, London*, 8in. high.
(Bonhams) $2,070

An ormolu grande sonnerie mantel clock with calendar, the molded ebonized base raised on toupie feet, with applied gryphons and scrolls, Vienna, circa 1810, 19in. high.
(Christie's) $7,150

A 19th century ormolu mantel timepiece, the rectangular case with brickwork corners on ball feet, the circular silvered dial, signed *Wildenham*, 9in. high.
(Phillips) $1,080

A 19th century Austrian quarter striking mantel clock, the mahogany case flanked by gilt wood dolphins and applied with gilt mounts, signed *Johann Kralik in Wien*, 1ft. 11in.
(Phillips) $684

An ormolu and painted musical pagoda clock, the tiered case on stepped base with oriental fretwork to the plinth, the balustraded pagoda top supported on dragons at each angle, 18¹/₂in. high.
(Christie's) $2,954

A Second Empire ormolu striking mantel clock, the case on milled sconce feet, the pedestal flanked by a column with incense urn atop and an angel strumming a lyre, 14in. high.
(Christie's) $1,574

A 19th century mahogany nightwatchman's timepiece, the silvered dial with outer recording ring and with plunger above, the fusée movement with anchor escapement.
(Phillips) $630

MANTEL CLOCKS

An Empire ormolu grande sonnerie striking pendule d'officier, signed *Louis Duchène*, with pierced blued hands, the circular movement with chain fusée, 8¼in. high.
(Christie's) $5,316

An ormolu and porcelain French mantel clock, the shaped case decorated with swags and foliage and surmounted by two doves, 11in. high.
(Phillips) $792

A Louis XVI ormolu and bronze mantel clock, the two-train movement with silk suspension in a drum case mounted on a bronze horse, 1ft. 1in. high.
(Bonhams) $9,360

A French porcelain and ormolu mantel clock, two-train movement with white enamel dial, in a bow-ended case cast with acanthus, 1ft. 2in. high.
(Bonhams) $1,170

An Empire ormolu and marble striking mantel clock with green marble base on toupie feet, a lady seated in a bergère reading at a draped table on paw feet with oil lamp atop, signed *Leroy & Fils Hgers. du Roi A Paris No. 1065*, 12³/₄in. high.
(Christie's) $4,023

An unusual 19th century Austrian miniature porcelain timepiece, the shaped case decorated with flowers on paw feet, signed *Doker, in Wien*, 55mm. high.
(Phillips) $828

A Regency ormolu and marble mantel timepiece, the case on milled bun feet supporting the rectangular white marble base applied with a ribbon-tied fruiting swag, signed *Webster London*, 8in. high.
(Christie's) $2,461

A 19th century French white marble, ormolu and bronze mantel clock, surmounted by two naked putti, signed *Aubanel & Rochat, A. Paris*, 1ft. 6in. high.
(Phillips) $810

A Victorian burr walnut mantel clock, 6in. foliate engraved gilt dial, trefoil hands, two-train chain fusée movement with anchor escapement, 12in. high.
(Bonhams) $2,700

SKELETON CLOCKS

A 19th century brass skeleton timepiece, the shaped plates with silvered chapter ring, the fusée movement with five spoked wheels and anchor escapement, 10³/₄in. high.
(Phillips) $936

A Victorian brass skeleton clock with a single fusée movement and painted chapter and second ring inscribed *Widenham London*, under glass dome, 17in. high.
(G.A. Sworder) $1,037

A 19th century brass skeleton timepiece, the shaped plates with silvered chapter, the fusée movement with five spoked wheels and anchor escapement, 1ft. 1in. high.
(Phillips) $1,225

A 19th century brass skeleton clock, the pierced shaped plates in the gothic style with pierced and engraved silvered chapter ring, 1ft. 8in. high.
(Phillips) $4,140

A Great Exhibition alarum skeleton timepiece, annular white enamel chapter ring with concentric alarum setting disc, 9³/₄in. overall.
(Bonhams) $810

A Victorian brass striking skeleton clock, the six pillar twin chain fusée movement with anchor escapement, the wheels with five crossings, 21in. high.
(Christie's) $2,972

A rare early 19th century floor standing skeleton timepiece, signed *Inventum a Jocobo Wright, Quondam Coll: Hert et Nuper Aul: Mag: Oxon: 1826 Jepson Fecit.*
(Phillips) $4,200

A 19th century brass skeleton timepiece, the fusée movement with five spoked wheels and anchor escapement, 10³/₄in. high.
(Phillips) $684

WALL CLOCKS

An 18th century traveling wall timepiece with alarm, the engraved brass dial with silvered chapter ring, signed in the arch, *Willm. Allam, London*, 5in. high.
(Phillips) $4,320

An Austrian parcel-gilt cartel clock, the circular enamel dial signed *Toban Vellauer a Vienne*, the shaped case surmounted by a vase flanked by seahorses, 30in. high.
(Christie's) $2,772

A Louis XVI ormolu cartel clock with circular enamel dial signed *Baret A Breuvanne*, in a cartouche-shaped case surmounted by a flaming urn, 29in. high.
(Christie's) $6,930

An 18th century mahogany hooded wall clock by Ellicott, London, the shallow arched case decorated with three finials, the five pillared twin fusée movement with verge escapement, 2ft. 7in. high.
(Phillips) $9,900

A fin-de-siècle mahogany and boxwood gaming wall clock, the framed and glazed baize lined dial with checkerboard chapter disc with raised Arabic chapters, the frame 20 x 20in. square.
(Christie's) $1,378

A 19th century Black Forest Trumpeter wall clock, the carved case decorated with a stag's head and a door below opening to reveal two trumpeters, 2ft. 10in. high.
(Phillips) $4,320

A Victorian Gothick quarter chiming wall clock, the case with soundfrets to the pedimented top, doors to sides, the front applied with carved wood trefoil spandrels, signed *W. Potts & Sons Leeds*, 35in. high.
(Christie's) $3,347

A Viennese picture clock, depicting an inland river scene, the Roman enamel dial set into the clock tower, the going barrel movement with pierced-out plates and lever escapement, 29 x 24¹/₂in.
(Christie's) $1,608

An 18th century Continental thirty-hour wall clock, the shaped pierced painted dial with single hand, the posted frame movement with verge escapement.
(Phillips) $1,890

WALL CLOCKS

An antique French Louis XVI style gilt-bronze cartel clock with urn-form finial festooned with laurel wreath, inscribed *Lanier*, 28in. high.
(Selkirk's) $1,900

Handpainted opal glass hanging clock, Wavecrest-type circular frame housing, Welch Company, Forestville, Connecticut, 6in. high.
(Skinner Inc.) $275

George III giltwood wall clock, Henry King, Lincoln's Inn, third quarter 18th century, eagle crest above a silvered circular dial, 31in. high.
(Skinner Inc.) $880

A George III 'Act of Parliament' clock signed *Justin Vulliamy, London*, the timepiece movement with tapered rectangular plates, spring suspended pendulum to anchor escapement, last quarter 18th century, 58in. high.
(Christie's) $9,350

A Viennese quarter striking picture clock depicting carousing cavaliers at a tavern with lakeland views and castle, with silk suspended pendulum in carved giltwood frame, circa 1850, 39¹/₂ x 29in.
(Christie's) $5,947

Louis XV style gilt-bronze-mounted ebony clock and thermometer, signed *J. Molteni et Cie, Paris*, the ebony case applied with pierced foliate-and-scroll cast gilt-bronze edges, 45in. high.
(Butterfield & Butterfield) $2,750

A giltwood Vienna regulator, 6¹/₂in. circular white enamel dial (cracked), with subsidiary seconds, brass bezel and dead-beat escapement, 3ft. 2in. high.
(Bonhams) $1,535

A George III scarlet japanned Act of Parliament clock signed *Owen Jackson Cranbrook*, on the shaped 26in. green repainted dial with Roman and Arabic chapters, 58in. high.
(Christie's) $1,749

Welsh calendar clock with case painted to simulate rosewood, spring driven pendulum movement, 33in. high.
(Eldred's) $660

WALL CLOCKS

Régence style gilt-bronze cartel clock, circa 1900, the circular dial cast in low relief with foliate scrolls and shells, 30in. high. (Butterfield & Butterfield) **$1,980**

Hen. Mowtlow Londini Fecit, a rare Charles II ebonized wall timepiece with alarm, the 5¹/₂in. square dial signed on the brass chapter ring, alarm disc to the matted center, 17¹/₂in. overall. (Christie's) **$5,247**

American banjo clock by J.N. Dunning (Joseph Nye Dunning), black and gilt reverse painted tablet and throat glass, painted dial, 52in. high. (Eldred's) **$3,300**

An attractive early 19th century mahogany 'Tavern' wall clock, the eight day movement rack striking on a single bell, the hood with broken arched pediment, 59in. high. (Spencer's) **$1,221**

Classical shelf clock, Isaac Packard, North West Bridgewater, Massachusetts, circa 1825, 30-hour wooden "Torrington-type" movement, 23¹/₄in. high. (Skinner Inc.) **$990**

A fine inlaid walnut grande-sonnerie Lanterndluhr with calendar, Fertbauer in Wien, the waisted glazed case with ebony moldings, striking grande sonnerie on two bells, circa 1800, 57in. high. (Christie's) **$74,800**

Classical gilt and mahogany lyre-form banjo timepiece, probably Massachusetts, circa 1820, 40in. high. (Skinner Inc.) **$2,310**

An unusual Regency wall timepiece, the 14-inch brass dial inscribed *Greenwood, York*, the anchor movement with tapering plates, circa 1820, 32in. high. (Tennants) **$2,325**

Antique American banjo clock in mahogany, by A. Willard, Boston, gilt acorn finial, painted dial, reverse painted throat and tablet, 33¹/₂in. high. (Eldred's) **$2,640**

A fine early 19th century gold, enamel and seed pearl quarter repeating open-face pocket watch, the reverse with a Mediterranean harbor scene with seed pearl decoration to the rim and bezel, 60mm. diameter.
(Christie's) $13,118

An 18ct. gold dress watch, silvered dial, signed *Cartier*, damascened nickel keyless lever movement signed *European Watch and Clock Co., 1929*.
(Bonhams) $1,194

Fontac London No. 227, an unusual gilt, silver and enamel verge pocket watch in consular case, the silver back cover with blue enamel scene depicting Aesop's fable The Fox and the Crow, 57mm. diameter.
(Christie's) $1,224

A gold and Huaud enamel verge watch, the case signed *Fratres Huaud Pinxerunt*, the reverse painted with a polychrome enamel of the Virgin Mary and St. Elizabeth holding Christ and St. John the Baptist, circa 1750, 37mm. diameter.
(Christie's) $10,494

Patek Philippe, a rare early 1920s keyless gold open-faced pocket watch with up-and-down indication in plain case, the white enamel dial with Arabic numerals, subsidiary seconds, power reserve indication at twelve, 49mm. diameter.
(Christie's) $17,490

A fine and rare late 18th century gold, enamel and seed pearl quarter repeating and musical open-face pocket watch, the reverse with an enameled scene of Belisarius receiving alms, 59mm. diameter.
(Christie's) $69,960

An early 18th century gold, gilt metal and tortoiseshell pair cased verge watch, the movement with Egyptian pillars, signed *Paul Beauvais*, 59mm. diameter.
(Phillips) $985

An early 18th century gold, gilt metal and shagreen pair cased quarter repeating verge watch, signed *Pet Garon, London*, with silver dust ring, 57mm. diameter.
(Phillips) $1,970

A gold pair cased verge watch, the movement with pierced and engraved cock and diamond endstone, signed *Tho. Reid, Edinburgh*, 1790, 53mm. diameter.
(Phillips) $1,537

WATCHES

John Roger Arnold No. 1956, a rare 18ct. gold pocket chronometer in plain consular case, the white enamel dial with Roman numerals and large subsidiary seconds, gold hands, *London 1805*, 57mm. diameter.
(Christie's) $22,737

A fine enameled gold verge watch, the case signed *Huaud le Puisne fecit*, the purpose made movement signed *Hoendshker, Dresden*, finely painted with "Roman Charity" after Simon Vouet, 40mm. diameter.
(Christie's) $38,500

An 18th century silver pair cased quarter repeating verge watch, the movement with pierced tulip pillars, signed *Windmyller, London*, 57mm. diameter.
(Phillips) $1,576

Robert & Courvoisier:fine and rare gold bras en l'air verge pocket watch in engine-turned case, a gilt automaton indicating the time with its arms by depressing the pendant, 56mm. diameter.
(Christie's) $21,250

A rare 19th century gold, enamel and seed pearl musical and automata open-face pocket watch, the reverse with a painted enamel scene of a landscape, the foreground in multicolored gold high relief with three automata figures, 38mm. diameter.
(Christie's) $47,223

An enameled gold center seconds watch, the movement signed *Ilbery, London, No. 6652*, the enamel signed *Richt*, the engraved gilt and partly skeletonized duplex movement with going barrel, Geneva, circa 1810, 57.5mm. diameter.
(Christie's) $26,400

A finely enameled gold center seconds watch by Ilbery, London, the engraved gilt partly skeletonized duplex movement with going barrel, Geneva, circa 1820, 57.5mm. diameter.
(Christie's) $33,000

An 18 carat gold watch, the movement with 'Savage' two pin lever escapement, signed *Hampson & Shelwell*, 1817, 54mm. diameter.
(Phillips) $1,280

A gold and enamel cylinder watch, enameled on the machined cuvette *Ami Sandoz & Fils, Geneve*, silvered dial, case back with multi-colored enameled flowers, 44mm.
(Bonhams) $477

WATCHES

A Swiss 18 carat gold hunter cased minute repeating keyless lever chronograph, the movement jeweled to the center, marked for London 1909, 60mm. diameter.

(Phillips) **$5,122**

A fine gold hunter cased carillon minute repeating watch with triple automaton, the nickel movement jeweled through the hammers, bimetallic balance and counterpoised escapement, Swiss, circa 1885, 57mm. diameter.

(Christie's) **$8,250**

A Swiss gold hunter cased minute repeating keyless lever Jacquemart watch, the movement jeweled to the center and with jeweled repeat train, 51mm. diameter.

(Phillips) **$6,120**

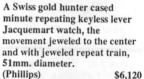

An engraved silver paircase verge watch by Peter Garon, London, the cock and back plate furniture pierced and engraved with leafy scrolls and mask, circa 1705, 53mm. diameter.

(Christie's) **$1,430**

An unusual eight-day alarm Masonic traveling clock with giltmetal bezel, the white enamel dial with colored Masonic symbols, in triangular folding leather case, 81mm.

(Christie's) **$1,224**

An early 18th century gold pair cased verge watch, the movement with pierced Egyptian pillars and pierced engraved cock, signed *Brounker Watts, London.*

(Phillips) **$7,560**

A silver oignon with alarm, Sourdeval a Paris, the movement with Egyptian pillars, pierced bridge chased with scrolls, strapwork and birds, the barrel of the alarm train chased with leafy scrolls on matted ground, 18th century, 60mm. diameter.

(Christie's) **$2,200**

Vulcain: a 1920s white gold and sapphire keyless dress watch in square case with cabochon winder and sapphires set to the band, the brushed silvered dial with raised Arabic numerals and subsidiary seconds, 40mm. square.

(Christie's) **$1,189**

An enameled gold verge watch, the bridge pierced with scrolls spelling *Chevalier*, white enamel dial with Arabic chapters, gold beetle-and-poker hands, the back enameled with scene of children playing in the woods, circa 1790, 53mm. diameter.

(Christie's) **$4,400**

WATCHES

A unique gold hunter cased chronograph, cast and chased in the form of a buffalo, the case and movement by Nicole, Nielsen & Co., London, for Edward and Sons, London and Glasgow, 60mm. diameter.
(Christie's) **$26,400**

Julien Leroy, Paris, an 18th century silver pair-cased pull quarter repeat calendar and alarm coach-watch in pierced metal outer case, pierced, chased and engraved inner case with gimbaled pendant, with white enamel dial.
(Christie's) **$7,871**

A silver gilt and enamel hermetic bag watch, champagne dial signed *Movado Ermeto*, the slide winding movement in case with black enamel bands, 47mm., circa 1933.
(Bonhams) **$324**

JS. Patron, Geneve, a late 18th century gold, enamel and seed pearl verge pair-cased pocket watch, the decorative outer case with enameled scene of a couple in a garden to the reverse, 49mm. diameter.
(Christie's) **$4,722**

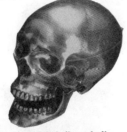

A finely modeled silver skull watch opening to reveal the engraved silver chapter ring with Roman numerals and Arabic five-minute divisions, signed *Pete. Garon, London*, 75mm. long.
(Christie's) **$2,798**

A silver Masonic dress watch by Solvil Watch Co., G. Schwab-Loeille, Geneve, with 15-jewel keyless lever movement, mother-of-pearl dial with chapters formed from the working tools of the various degrees of Freemasonry, 1930s, 55mm. long.
(Christie's) **$1,760**

A rare silver openface self-winding watch, the dial signed *Loehr Patent*, the square gilt lever movement with compensation balance and flat blued hairspring, 1880s, 48mm. wide.
(Christie's) **$2,200**

An engraved gold early digital watch, the gilt keyless cylinder movement jeweled to the third wheel, within an 18ct gold case, the upper lid engraved with scrolls and flowerheads, 1880s, 38mm. diameter.
(Christie's) **$1,320**

Dunhill: an unusual 9ct gold petrol burning lighter with a watch mounted in the front wound automatically on operating the lighter, in engine turned case with wind guard, 47 x 42mm.
(Christie's) **$4,023**

WRIST WATCHES

A rare tonneau-shaped single button chronograph wristwatch, signed *Cartier, European Watch & Co.*, **circa 1935.**
(Christie's)   **$104,280**

Cartier, an 18ct gold chronograph wristwatch model Pasha, the rotating bezel with five-minute marks, the white dial with raised luminous dot five-minute marks, 38mm. diameter.
(Christie's)   **$6,296**

A platinum tonneau-shaped jump hour wristwatch, signed *Patek Phillipe & Co., Geneve, No. 752957, 1989.*
(Christie's)   **$104,280**

An 18 carat gold perpetual calendar wristwatch with moonphases and chronograph, signed *Patek Phillipe & Co., Geneve, No. 863178*, **circa 1944.**
(Christie's)   **$108,625**

Longines, a modern steel pilot's automatic hour-angle watch in circular case, the rotating bezel engraved with hours and quarters, the white enamel dial with Roman numerals, 36mm. diameter.
(Christie's)   **$665**

An 18 carat white gold perpetual calendar wristwatch with moonphases and chronograph, signed *Patek Phillipe & Co., Geneve, No. 875348, Ref. 3970.*
(Christie's)   **$78,210**

A Swiss gold circular automatic gentleman's wristwatch by Vacheron & Constantin, Genève, with signed gilt dial with center seconds and Roman numerals, 36mm. diameter.
(Phillips)   **$2,831**

Patek Philippe, a fine and rare gold wristwatch in turtle case with wire lugs, the matt white dial with black enamel Arabic numerals, 26 x 26mm.
(Christie's)   **$10,494**

Cartier, a gentleman's gold wristwatch in 'turtle' case with cabochon winder, the white enamel dial with Roman numerals and secret signature at VII, 33 x 27mm.
(Christie's)   **$6,646**

WRIST WATCHES

Universal, a pink gold triple calendar and moonphase chronograph wristwatch, the silvered dial with outer tachymetric scale, alternating raised pink dagger and Arabic numerals, 36mm. diameter.
(Christie's) $2,449

Rolex, a gold quarter Century Club wristwatch in flared case, the two-tone silvered dial signed *Eaton*, the signed *Ultra Prima* chronometer movement with eighteen jewels and timed to six positions, 42 x 23mm.
(Christie's) $4,547

Cartier, a ladies gold and diamond-set quartz wristwatch in rectangular case, the shoulders set with diamonds, the white enamel dial with Roman numerals and secret signature at X, 28 x 21mm.
(Christie's) $3,498

Cartier, a 1930s 18ct gold 'tank' wristwatch with ruby cabochon winder, white enamel dial with Roman numerals, the back secured by four screws in the band, 31 x 23mm.
(Christie's) $5,247

Eberhard, a gilt/steel limited edition chronograph and calendar with moon phase wristwatch with gilt bezel, the matt silvered dial with tachymetric scale, 40mm. diameter.
(Christie's) $1,049

An 18 carat pink gold perpetual calendar chronograph wristwatch with moon phases, signed *Patek Phillipe & Co.*, *Geneve, No. 868248*, circa 1950.
(Christie's) $213,840

Omega, a stainless steel automatic calendar diver's watch, model Seamaster 600 Professional, the rotating bezel calibrated in five-minute marks, 55 x 45mm.
(Christie's) $875

Navitimer, a stainless steel Breitling chronograph wristwatch with milled rotating bezel, the signed black dial with outer calculating scales, 40mm. diameter.
(Christie's) $787

Cartier, an 18ct gold automatic calendar wristwatch model Pasha, with gold grill to the dial, the rotating bezel with ten-minute calibrations, 38mm. diameter.
(Christie's) $7,871

WRIST WATCHES

Uhrenfabrik Glashütte, a World War II military chronograph wristwatch with rotating bezel, the black dial with luminous Arabic numerals, 38mm. diameter.
(Christie's) $962

Tavannes, an early gold wristwatch in elliptical case, the white enamel dial with Arabic numerals, the nickel-plated bar movement jeweled to the third under snap-on back, 45 x 27mm.
(Christie's) $1,487

Movado, a pink gold and steel wristwatch with stepped pink gold bezel and faceted lugs, the two-tone silvered dial with Arabic numerals and outer seconds ring, 29mm. diameter.
(Christie's) $700

International Watch Co., a gold waterproof wristwatch in tonneau case, the brushed gilt dial with raised baton numerals and sweep center seconds, 40 x 33mm.
(Christie's) $962

An 18 carat gold circular keyless lever wristwatch, by Chas. Frodsham & Co., London, with gold cuvette, 1912.
(Phillips) $335

A gold wristwatch by Patek Philippe & Co., Geneve, the nickel adjusted 18-jewel movement with black dial, gold raised Arabic chapters and hands, subsidiary seconds.
(Christie's) $6,600

An 18 carat gold 'Eclipse', wristwatch by Cartier, the rectangular case with circular movement, signed *European Watch and Clock Co. Inc.*, 35 x 19mm.
(Phillips) $13,500

A Swiss gold curved rectangular wristwatch by Cartier, the signed dial with Roman numerals, the numbered case also marked *1326*, with cabochon winder.
(Phillips) $6,480

Glycine, a 1930s white and pink gold digital wristwatch in rectangular case, the pink gold top cover with apertures for hours, minutes and seconds, the case with hinged back, 37 x 23mm.
(Christie's) $5,597

WRIST WATCHES

A Swiss gold circular wristwatch by Patek Philippe, Geneve, with signed silvered dial, applied batons and subsidiary seconds, 29mm. diameter.
(Phillips) $2,880

Patek Philippe, a fine 18ct gold officer's campaign watch made as a limited series of 2,000 pieces for the company's 150th anniversary in 1989, maker's attestation and commemorative medal, 33mm. diameter.
(Christie's) $12,243

A Swiss gold circular Rolex wristwatch, the signed white dial marked in $1/5$th seconds, with Arabic numerals and red sweep seconds, 29mm. diameter.
(Phillips) $1,080

A Swiss steel Oyster Perpetual GMT Master by Rolex, the signed black dial with center seconds and additional twenty-four hour hand, 39mm. diameter.
(Phillips) $900

A 19th century gold and enamel ladies bracelet watch in circular case with seed pearl-set bezel, the white enamel dial with Roman numerals, 30mm. diameter.
(Christie's) $3,498

A steel triple calendar and moonphase wristwatch made for Tiffany by Record Watch Co., the brushed steel dial with Arabic numerals, 34mm. diameter.
(Christie's) $525

Longines, a steel military wristwatch, the rotating bezel calibrated in minutes with a locking screw in the band, the silvered dial with Arabic numerals and sweep center seconds, 33mm. diameter.
(Christie's) $735

A gentleman's rectangular Swiss gold wristwatch by Longines, the signed movement numbered 3739388, 30 x 25mm.
(Phillips) $756

A gold wristwatch by Audemars Piguet, Geneve, the nickel adjusted 19-jewel movement with gold train, silvered dial, raised Arabic and abstract chapters and hands, dial and movement, 1940s.
(Christie's) $1,540

CLOISONNE

A silver, cloisonné and russet iron tripod koro, the body decorated with two shaped and pierced panels with a ho-o bird among paulownia and a karashishi among peonies, late 19th century, 12cm. high.
(Christie's) $10,120

A cloisonné enamel and gilt-bronze recumbent mythical lion, the rich black body set with white, yellow, turquoise and iron-red details, 18th century, 18cm. long.
(Christie's) $4,332

One of a pair of gilt-bronze and polychrome cloisonné enamel vases, each of baluster form decorated all over with peonies and with two panels depicting a mythical dragon, 26¼in. high.
(Christie's) (Two)
$1,900

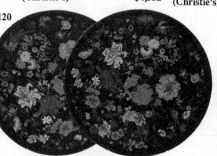

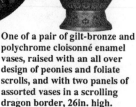

Fine Canton enamel tripod censer and cover, Qianlong mark and period, painted with lotus flowers interwoven with leafy tendrils and assorted flowers bracketed by a stylized plantain leaf and a ruyi-lappet band, 8½in. high.
(Butterfield & Butterfield) $3,575

A pair of massive cloisonné chargers decorated in vibrant colored enamels and various thicknesses of wire, with dense profusions of flowers and foliage, late 19th century, 92.5cm. diameter
(Christie's) $19,250

One of a pair of gilt-bronze and polychrome cloisonné enamel vases, raised with an all over design of peonies and foliate scrolls, and with two panels of assorted vases in a scrolling dragon border, 26in. high.
(Christie's) (Two)
$1,900

A pair of cloisonné vases decorated in various colored enamels and thicknesses of wire depicting alternate panels of ducks, egrets amongst reeds and Mount Fuji, Gonda Hirosuke, late 19th century, 41cm. high.
(Christie's) $5,460

A foliate-shaped silver and cloisonné box and cover with a central roundel decorated in high relief with various shells with a karashishi under a waterfall, late 19th century, 11cm. wide.
(Christie's) $3,450

A massive pair of Japanese cloisonné vases, the bodies decorated with four red-capped cranes and birds amidst flowering branches, 53¼in. overall.
(Woolley & Wallis) $11,770

212

A fine large cloisonné enamel and gilt-rectangular baluster vase and cover, all decorated with turquoise and enriched with gilt key-pattern cloisons, Qianlong, 53cm. high.
(Christie's) **$11,814**

A pair of cloisonné enamel turquoise-ground standing duck vessels, their plumage detailed in wire, Qianlong/Jiaqing, 21.5cm. long.
(Christie's) **$7,482**

A cloisonné oviform vase decorated with a shallow perched by wisteria, a narrow band of lappets to the foot and under the rim, late 19th century, 18.4cm. high.
(Christie's) **$975**

A Hayashi kodenji cloisonné vase decorated in various colored enamels and thicknesses of silver wire on a deep blue ground with sparrows, signed *Nagoya Hayashi saku*, late 19th century, 31.5cm. high.
(Christie's) **$8,085**

A pair of Japanese cloisonné vases, each finely decorated with birds amongst wisteria on a bamboo trellis, 7¼in. high.
(Bearne's) **$946**

One of a pair of gilt-bronze and polychrome cloisonné enamel vases, each of baluster form, with two bordered panels depicting birds, butterflies and spring flowers, 20³/₄in. high.
(Christie's) (Two) **$2,090**

A cloisonné vase decorated in various colored enamels and thicknesses of gold and silver wire in the Namikawa style with a ho-o bird and a dragon, late 19th century, 15.5cm. high.
(Christie's) **$1,223**

Pair of massive cloisonné enamel vases, Meiji Period, featuring a pair of peacocks perched on the trunk of a flowering cherry tree, 35¹/₈in. high.
(Butterfield & Butterfield) **$9,900**

A Namikawa Sosuke vase of baluster form finely worked in silver wire and musen-jippo with a magpie in plum blossom, signed *Sosuke*, late 19th century, 29.5cm. high.
(Christie's) **$86,526**

A Regency brass kettle-on-stand, the shaped carrying-handle of reeded ebony, the ovoid kettle with domed stepped lid, on foliate cabriole legs and pad feet, 18¹/₂in. high.
(Christie's) $1,195

A bell-metal posnet by Lawrence Langworthy, Newport, Rhode Island, 1731–1739, the flaring cylindrical pot with molded lip, on three feet, 10⁷/₈in. high.
(Christie's) $6,600

A 17th century style brass alms dish of Nuremberg type, the center raised with the figures of Adam and Eve, 16¹/₂in. diameter.
(Christie's) $1,350

A very fine gilt-copper pear-shaped ewer and cover, 16th century, probably circa 1550, modeled after a near eastern metalwork shape, relief cast with petal-shaped panels at either side depicting dignitaries, 11⁷/₈in. high.
(Christie's) $31,226

Pair of North African brass and ivory-inlaid large urns, early 20th century, inlaid with various star and geometric motifs, raised on a spreading circular base, 42¹/₂in. tall.
(Butterfield & Butterfield) $2,750

A brass stool, the reeded X-frame cast with acanthus and headed by elbow rests with rounded terminals, circa 1830, possibly North European, 25in. wide.
(Christie's) $6,021

A brass jardinière with rounded rectangular top above a trellis-etched slightly tapering body flanked by lion-masks, on claw-and-ball feet, 19th century, 28¹/₄in. wide.
(Christie's) $3,584

An inlaid hammered copper vase by Paul Mergier, with inlaid white-metal decoration of leaping antelope amid foliage, with inlaid signature *P. Mergier*, 30cm. high.
(Christie's) $2,920

A silver-applied copper inkwell, maker's mark of Tiffany & Co., New York, 1902, the copper body applied with silver strapwork with applied flowerheads, 6³/₄in. high.
(Christie's) $3,520

A Perry, Son & Co. copper hot water jug designed by Dr. Christopher Dresser, with angled spout and loop handle, 19cm. high.
(Christie's) $1,083

A 19th century French gilt-brass encrier, the cover set with a reclining dog, on animal mask supports with claw feet, 10¼in. wide.
(Bearne's) $722

A Victorian brass and copper oyster bucket and liner, the sides formed of vertical brass spindles joined by copper bands, 40cm. high.
(Phillips) $3,294

A pair of George III brass candlesticks, each with quatrefoil drip-pan and ring-turned nozzle, above a gadrooned rounded square platform and turned shaft, 11in. high.
(Christie's) $11,548

Talwin Morris, two embossed brass finger plates each with a central motif of a heart imposed on a stylized foliate grid of blooming and budding roses, circa 1893, 11 x 5in.
(Christie's) $650

A matched pair of Charles X gilt brass curtain ties, of oval form with hinged clasp, having continuous stamped florette decoration, 22cm. and 23cm.
(Phillips) $713

A Benham & Froud copper coffee-pot designed by Dr. Christopher Dresser, globular form with tapering cylindrical neck and hinged cover, circa 1884, 22cm. high.
(Christie's) $1,378

W.M.F. brass coffee set, Germany, circa 1910, Wuerttembergische Metal Fabrik, wicker covered handles with manufacturers mark.
(Skinner Inc.) $500

Hammered copper fruit cooler, probably Austria, circa 1905, with geometric detail, raised on four cut-out and stepped feet, 15in. high.
(Skinner Inc.) $275

America, late 18th century, man's homespun cotton double breasted tailcoat.
(Skinner Inc.) **$660**

Gentleman's dress waistcoat, late 18th century, satin weave silk embroidered with silk and metallic threads and heightened with spangles.
(Skinner Inc.) **$605**

A rare child's linen suit comprising chemise and pantaloons, early 19th century.
(Christie's) **$792**

A purse in the form of a bunch of grapes, the grapes worked in many coloured silks and silver gilt threads, 3in. long, English, early 17th century.
(Christie's) **$5,150**

Winston S. Churchill (1874–1965), a grey Homburg by *Lincoln Bennett & Co., by appointment to her Majesty the Queen*, initialed in gold *W.S.C.*, the up-turned brim with ribbon trim.
(Christie's) **$13,213**

A wide brimmed straw hat with shallow crown, lined with red silk brocaded with flowers, with original green silk ribbons, 1765–70.
(Christie's) **$3,366**

A gown of ivory satin, printed with undulating bands of pink columbines against seagreen and lilac heart shaped leaves.
(Christie's) **$7,788**

Pair of child's western chaps, circa 1920, label reads, *A.J. Williamson, Casper, Wyo.*
(Eldred's) **$220**

A dress of blue and white striped satin, the cuffs and front trimmed with ivory satin and blue satin ribbons, with pleated train, late 1870's.
(Christie's) **$412**

COSTUME

A Victorian linen smock, the bodice, sleeves, collar, cuffs and pockets embroidered with blue cotton.
(Bonhams) **$128**

A dress of fine wool, printed with stripes of slate gray alternating with striped cones, V-shaped bodice, 1840's.
(Christie's) **$399**

A nobleman's coat of purple velvet, embroidered in metal thread with crescents below stylized floral motifs, second half of 19th century, Bokharan.
(Christie's) **$660**

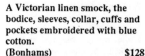   

A pair of kid gloves, the cuffs of pink silk embroidered in gold thread and sequins and edged with gold lace, early 17th century.
(Christie's) **$2,441**

A gentleman's nightcap of linen worked in cutwork with vines, the cuff also edged with lace, English, circa 1610.
(Christie's) **$6,625**

A pair of ladies shoes of ivory silk applied with ivory silk braid, the tongue lined with blue silk damask, English, early 18th century.
(Christie's) **$6,102**

A Chinese kossu robe embroidered overall in gilt and silver wire with a design of emblems, 55in. high.
(Bearne's) **$1,110**

A late 19th century lady's dolman of dark brown plush, elaborately decorated with black lace and bobble braid, circa 1880.
(Phillips) **$214**

A Chinese kesi blue-ground dragon robe woven predominantly in gilt-wire with dragons, flaming pearls, precious objects and clouds, 58in.
(Bearne's) **$415**

A wax-headed pedlar doll, with bead eyes, down turned mouth, printed cotton open-robe, quilted petticoat, and a basket of wares, 9¹/₂in. high, circa 1840. (Christie's) $1,212

A bisque-headed child doll, with blue lashed sleeping eyes, original pink silk and lace trimmed dress and bonnet, 21in. high, impressed *DEP 9* stamped in red *Tete Jumeau*. (Christie's) $1,678

A bisque-headed bébé, with closed mouth, blue yeux fibres, feathered brows, pierced ears, blonde mohair wig, 10¹/₂in. high, marked *J Steiner Fre A 3*. (Christie's) $3,170

Hopi Kachina doll representing a Black Ogre, with pop-eyes, tubular snout and semi-circle ears, with hair in disarray, 12in. high. (Butterfield & Butterfield) $550

A rare bisque-headed character doll, with open/closed mouth, blue sleeping eyes, deeply molded features, white gown and underwear, 15in. high, impressed *1428 9*, by Simon & Halbig. (Christie's) $2,797

A bisque shoulder-headed musical marotte, with fixed blue eyes, white mohair curls, and cap with red bows and pom-pom, 15in. high, the head marked *S PB* in star H. (Christie's) $848

A bisque-headed child doll, with blue sleeping eyes, fair mohair wig, and original outfit of red cotton bonnet, frock, stockings and shoes, 16in. high, marked *DEP R O A*. (Christie's) $559

A mask-face cloth baby doll, with blue sleeping eyes, original sewn-on knitted clothes and white plush hood, 13in. high. Chad Valley "Carese". (Christie's) $839

A bisque-headed doll with blue paperweight eyes, painted lashes, closed mouth, pierced ears and light brown wig, stamped *Le Petit Parisien, BEBE STEINER*, 10¹/₂in. high. (Christie's) $2,410

DOLLS

A bisque-headed character doll, with blue sleeping eyes, dressed in spotted muslin with lace insertions, 19in. high, impressed *1299 SIMON & HALBIG S & H 8*.
(Christie's S. Ken) $1,048

A rare bisque-headed character doll, with open/closed mouth, brown intaglio eyes, and composition body, 21in. high, marked *181*, by Kestner.
(Christie's) $5,966

A bisque-headed bébé, with open/closed mouth, fixed blue eyes, bisque shoulder-plate and arms, 19in. high, impressed *Bru Jne 6*, circa 1880.
(Christie's) $26,103

A bisque swivel-headed fashionable doll, with closed mouth, blue insert eyes, gusseted kid body and bisque lower arms, 16in. high.
(Christie's) $1,864

A boxed set of German bisque-head dressed aviator figures, circa 1920, consisting of two adult uniformed pilots, a man and a woman, and two children, 10¹/₂ x 6¹/₂in.
(Christie's) $5,280

Hopi Kachina doll representing a Hemis, wearing stepped polychrome tableta, painted sash and moccasins, 13¹/₂in. high.
(Butterfield & Butterfield)
$1,210

An Armand Marseille 'Scowling Indian' bisque head doll with black mohair wig, fixed brown glass eyes, marked *AMO*.
(Phillips) $421

The Bisto Kids, a pair of composition headed advertising dolls, with cloth bodies and original clothes, 12in. high, in original box.
(Christie's) $895

A François Gaultier bisque shoulder head Polcinello puppet with fixed blue glass eyes, 16¹/₂in.
(Phillips) $421

Felt girl, no marks visible, painted features on felt face, mohair wig, fully jointed, cloth body with felt limbs, 21in. high. (Butterfield & Butterfield)

$275

An Armand Marseille bisque socket head girl doll, with dark brown wig, painted features, closing blue glass eyes with eyelashes, 60cm. tall. (Spencer's) $433

Bisque child, incised *A 980 M Germany 7 D.R.G.M*, blue glass sleep eyes, open mouth with teeth, replaced wig, 26in. high. (Butterfield & Butterfield)

$550

Bisque bébé with paperweight eyes, closed mouth, and human hair wig, kid body with label, 24in. high. (Butterfield & Butterfield) $23,100

A Schoenau and Hoffmeister bisque socket head girl doll with dark brown straight long wig, painted features, closing brown glass eyes and eyelashes, 60cm. tall. (Spencer's) $300

A Minerva tin shoulder headed doll, having set blue glass eyes, open mouth with teeth, molded and painted short curly blonde hairstyle, on a later cloth body, 22in. high. (Butterfield & Butterfield)

$99

Bisque baby incised *16 Made in Germany 16 J.D.K. 211*, blue glass sleep eyes, meld wig, open mouth with teeth, papier mâché bent limb body, 20in. high. (Butterfield & Butterfield)

$385

An Armand Marseille bisque socket head girl doll, with curled mid-brown mohair wig, painted features, closing blue glass eyes, open mouth with four upper teeth, 59cm. tall. (Spencer's) $333

An Armand Marseille bisque socket head character doll, with dark brown wig, painted features, closing blue glass eyes with eyelashes, 43cm. tall. (Spencer's) $566

A mulatto bisque-headed doll, with brown lashed flirting eyes pierced ears, brown wig, and composition body, 13in. high, marked *1039 Simon & Halbig 4*. (Christie's) $597

A Simon and Halbig bisque and socket head character baby doll, with cropped mid brown wig, painted features, and flirty brown glass eyes, 40cm. tall. (Spencer's) $599

An early 20th century bisque socket head doll with tightly curled blonde wig, painted features, wearing full Scottish Highlanders costume, 29cm. tall. (Spencer's) $300

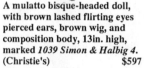

Bisque boy, incised *A.B.G. 1322/ 1*, brushed stroked hair, intaglio eyes, open/closed mouth with teeth, papier mâché body, 12in. high. (Butterfield & Butterfield) $413

An Armand Marseille/ Koppelsdorf bisque socket head character doll, with blonde mohair wig, painted features, closing blue glass eyes with eyelashes, 48cm. tall. (Spencer's) $333

Felt boy, no visible marks, painted features on felt face, mohair wig, fully jointed, cloth body with felt limbs, 15in. high. (Butterfield & Butterfield) $248

A fine J.D. Kestner bisque head 'Googly' eyed character doll, with brown hair wig, weighted blue eyes and closed 'watermelon' mouth, 16in. high. (Bonhams) $6,650

Bisque baby, incised *AM Germany 341/4*, molded painted hair, brown glass sleep eyes, cloth body with composition hands, 18in. high. (Butterfield & Butterfield) $138

A Simon and Halbig, Kammer & Reinhardt bisque head doll, having blonde wig, closing brown glass eyes, open mouth with four teeth showing and with pierced ears, 22^{1}/₂in. high. (Bearne's) $686

ENAMEL

Copper and enamel box, Buffalo, New York, circa 1910, red enamel floral decoration with stylized motifs in green and black enamel, 7in. wide. (Skinner Inc.) $400

A Staffordshire enamel etui, painted in colors with scenes of figures in landscapes and flower sprays, 7.5cm. high. (Phillips) $578

Plique à jour bowl, 20th century, decorated overall with leafy blossoms in translucent colors on a white-flecked light green glass ground, 4⅞in. diameter. (Butterfield & Butterfield) $770

An antique Viennese enamel vase featuring six finely executed oval allegorical reserves on a gold background with polychrome scrolling foliage, 19th century, 14in. high. (Selkirk's) $6,500

Louis XVI style onyx and champlevé enamel three-piece table garniture, circa 1900, each decorated en suite with an enameled band around the amber streaked cream body, 17½in. high. (Butterfield & Butterfield) $5,500

Viennese enamel and gilt-bronze ewer, circa 1900, the slender ovoid body with a shaped flaring mouth and the domical base all painted in polychrome with mythological figural scenes, 8in. high. (Butterfield & Butterfield) $2,200

A south Staffordshire white ground enamel tea caddy, the cover painted with shepherds and their flock by a river, circa 1770, 8in. long. (Christie's) $7,040

A pair of champlevé enamel and gilt bronze candlesticks, the square domed foot rising to a stepped waist below a deep drip pan, mid Qing Dynasty, 48cm. high. (Christie's) $4,322

A very attractive Staffordshire enamel writing box, painted with a lady seated playing a lute and a man standing at her side playing a violin, 8.5cm. wide. (Phillips) $850

A Staffordshire enamel oval patch box with a pink base, the white cover inscribed *Love constitutes the Value* within a jeweled border, 4.5cm. wide. (Phillips) **$578**

A Staffordshire enamel masonic snuff box, the cover painted with masonic insignia divided by a flower spray, 5.5cm. wide. (Phillips) **$1,190**

A 19th century Viennese enamel and ormolu mounted model of a coach, the pink ground painted with reserves of figures in landscapes, 8in. long. (Christie's) **$2,574**

Small plique à jour ovoid vase, 20th century, decorated with a continuous design of leafy blossoms executed in translucent multicolored glass on a light green ground, 3³/₄in. high. (Butterfield & Butterfield) **$1,100**

Pair of Viennese enamel miniature figures of musicians, 19th century, each in Renaissance style dress of colorful hat, jacket with wide or cut-out sleeves, pantaloons, and slippers, 8in. high. (Butterfield & Butterfield) **$3,850**

A Staffordshire enamel circular box, transfer-printed and colored with The Haymakers, 6.5cm. wide. (Phillips) **$442**

An interesting Staffordshire enamel George III snuff box printed and colored with a profile portrait of the King in ermine-collared cloak, below the 'All-seeing eye', 5cm. high. (Phillips) **$544**

A fine south Staffordshire rectangular blue ground enamel tea caddy, the cover painted with three herdsmen and their cattle by a river, circa 1770, 8¹/₂in. long. (Christie's) **$31,680**

A Staffordshire enamel ballooning patch box printed and colored with a figure in a hot air balloon, turquoise base, 5cm. high. (Phillips) **$1,190**

A fan, the leaf painted with the Jews asking Queen Esther for their Freedom, the verso painted with a lady on a daybed watched by putti on an island, 12in., circa 1750. (Christie's) $3,390

A fan, the leaf painted with the Finding of Moses, the verso with a King and Queen before a castle, 11½in., circa 1740, probably for the Spanish market. (Christie's) $1,412

A bamboo fan decorated in gold, silver and black hiramakie, with cranes among grasses in the foothills of Mount Fuji, the reverse with branches of wisteria and tree peony, late 19th century, 45cm. open. (Christie's) $1,444

A fan, the chicken skin leaf hand-painted with maidens in classical dress amidst flowers and leaves, signed A. Lafève, 25cm. long, circa 1910's. (Phillips) $846

A Canton brisé fan painted and lacquered with figures in a garden against a red lacquer ground, 8in., circa 1820. (Christie's) $1,876

A fan, the leaf painted with peasants in an interior, the reserves with a trompe l'oeil of lace against a blue ground, 11in., circa 1760. (Christie's) $3,563

A fan, the leaf painted with figures drinking and fighting at an inn by a river, the verso with fishermen by a well, made for the Spanish market, circa 1740. (Christie's) $2,448

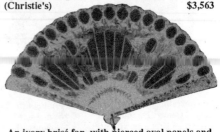

An ivory brisé fan, with pierced oval panels and lacquered in gold with figures and buildings, the guardsticks decorated with Shibayama work, 10in., Japanese, circa 1880. (Christie's) $3,939

A fan, the leaf painted with a classical scene, probably Esther and Ahasuerus, the verso with a lady and a shepherd, by ruins, 11in., French, circa 1740.
(Christie's) $1,507

A fan, the leaf painted with Maria Leszczynska, daughter of King Stanislas of Poland, arriving at Versailles to meet Louis XV before their marriage in 1725, 10in., French, circa 1750.
(Christie's) $20,715

A fine fan, the leaf painted with two maidens by a bridge in an autumnal landscape with putti, signed *F. Houghton*, the smokey gray mother of pearl sticks pierced, 12¹/₂in., circa 1880.
(Christie's S. Ken) $1,255

A mid-19th century Mandarin fan, originally made for export, having ivory sticks and guards densely carved with figures in a garden setting, 28cm. long, with tassel and white feather trim, Canton, circa 1860's.
(Phillips) $1,132

A fine fan, the lace leaf of Brussels point de gaze with three shaped silk insertions painted with elegant figures, signed *F. Houghton*, 14in., circa 1885.
(Christie's) $5,439

A fan, the leaf painted with the Rape of the Sabine Women, with ivory sticks, 10¹/₂in., Rome, circa 1700.
(Christie's) $2,063

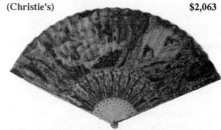

A fan, the leaf painted with a lady and gentleman in Turkish dress drinking coffee, the reserves with portrait miniatures against a silver ground, circa 1760.
(Christie's) $1,688

A fan, the leaf painted with two asymmetrical vignettes of villages, the verso with farm buildings, the ivory sticks carved, pierced and painted with rabbits and birds, 11in., circa 1750.
(Christie's) $1,407

A velvet and felt Dean's Mickey Mouse with yellow felt hands, yellow cardboard-lined feet, red shorts, felt ears and printed smile, 11¹/₂in. high, early 1930s.
(Christie's) $194

A set of sixteen Mazda Mickey Mouse Lights, each colored plastic Christmas tree light transfer-printed with Disney characters, made in England by The British Thomson-Housten Co. Ltd. in original box, 9¹/₂ x 16¹/₂in.
(Christie's) $133

An illustrated premiere programme for Walt Disney's Snow White and the Seven Dwarfs, Cathay Circle Theatre, Los Angeles, California, December 21st, 1937.
(Christie's) $288

Jean Simmons, a close-fitting, trained evening dress of ruby red crêpe-de-Chine, designed by R. St. John Roper and worn by Jean Simmons in Steven Sondheim's production A Little Night Music, 1975.
(Christie's) $350

A printed souvenir menu for the Grand Order of Water Rats House Dinner, Savoy Hotel, London, September 21st 1947, with illustrated cover featuring cartoon portraits of guests of honor Laurel and Hardy, autographed by subjects in blue ink, 6³/₄ x 14³/₄in.
(Christie's) $1,954

Wizard of Oz, a guardsman's bearskin cap with metal plume-ring on left side, 15in. high, thought to have been worn by one of the Wicked Witch's Winkie guards, in the 1939 M.G.M. film The Wizard of Oz, 8¹/₄ x 10¹/₄in.
(Christie's) $3,703

A pair of painted rubber pointed ear tops, 2¹/₄in. high, worn by Leonard Nimoy to create the appearance of Mr Spock's Vulcan ears in the T.V. series, 5¹/₄ x 9¹/₄in. framed.
(Christie's) $1,646

A Wadeheath nursery bowl, featuring Mickey Mouse and Pluto, 6¹/₂in. diameter.
(Christie's) $103

Bruce Davidson, "The new face of Marilyn Monroe", circa 1960, gelatin silver print, 6³/₄ x 9⁷/₈in.
(Butterfield & Butterfield)
                                 $880

Liberty, MGM, 1929, one-sheet, linen backed, 41 x 27in.
(Christie's) **$6,600**

A painted plaster portrait model of Christopher Reeve as Superman in a flying pose, 26in. long.
(Christie's) **$494**

A plush and velvet Dean's Donald Duck with white hands, yellow cardboard-lined feet, blue velvet hat and jacket trimmed with ribbon and glass eyes, 8in. high.
(Christie's) **$288**

A cloth Mickey Mouse dressed as a cowboy with sheepskin and leather chaps, original swing-tag ticket and *Knickerbocker Toy Co.* printed label glued to Mickey's right foot, 11in. high, circa 1935.
(Christie's) **$453**

Jessica Tandy, a pair of gilt frame spectacles, signed *Imperial G.F.*, worn by Jessica Tandy in the 1989 Warner Brothers film, Driving Miss Daisy.
(Christie's) **$720**

An American one sheet poster for The Empire Strikes Back, Twentieth Century Fox, 1981, signed by *Harrison Ford, Dave Prowse, Billy Dee Williams, Carrie Fisher, Mark Hamill, Peter Mayhew, Anthony Daniels, Kenny Baker* and *George Lucas*, framed, $40^{1}/_{2}$ x $26^{3}/_{4}$in.
(Christie's) **$1,748**

Mickey Mouse, a rare early 1930s German lithographic tinplate mechanical bank with lever action eyes and extending tongue operated by pressing Mickey's right ear, probably made by Saalheimer & Strauss, 7in. high.
(Christie's) **$15,427**

Walt Disney, a piece of card signed and inscribed, *To Marie Rose, Our Best Walt Disney*, $3^{1}/_{2}$ x $4^{3}/_{4}$in.
(Christie's) **$391**

A velvet and felt Dean's Mickey Mouse with white felt hands and yellow leather-soled feet, white shorts, felt ears, printed smile and comic eyes, $8^{1}/_{2}$in. high, early 1930s.
(Christie's) **$247**

A George Formby banjo, the skin stamped with Formby's facsimile signature and additionally signed and inscribed, *Good Luck George Formby 1939* in black ink, 22in. long.
(Christie's) $2,263

An American one sheet poster for Lolita, Metro-Goldwyn-Mayer, 1962, framed, 41¼ x 26½in.
(Christie's) $535

An Angus McBean head and shoulders portrait photograph of Olivier as Othello, signed and inscribed, *All wishes and kind remembrances, L. Olivier... 1966,* 9¾ x 7¾in.
(Christie's) $267

A prototype robotic head of painted gold rubber for the character C-3.P.O. from the film Star Wars, 1977, incised at the base of the neck *C-3.P.O. 20TH CENTURY FOX 1977,* 12 x 9in.
(Christie's) $494

A rare school year book for the 'Class of 1949', Fairmount High School, Fairmount, Indiana, U.S.A. published by the school's Journalism Department, featuring James Dean in the graduating year.
(Christie's) $4,114

A re-issued promotional thermometer for the United Artists film Some Like It Hot of bright orange and white enamel and printed metal decorated with a caricature of Marilyn Monroe, 39 x 8in.
(Christie's) $329

A head and shoulders portrait photograph, signed and inscribed on margin *To S.M. Swamy with my best wishes Charlie Chaplin 1.9.42,* 12¼ x 8¾in.
(Christie's) $370

A bowler hat lined in silk with manufacturer's details *G.A. Dunn & Co. Ltd,* additionally signed *Malcolm McDowell* and inscribed in a separate hand, worn by McDowell in the leading role of the 1971 Warner film A Clockwork Orange.
(Christie's) $3,703

A Souvenir of New York calendar for 1953 featuring a color reproduction of the famous nude portrait of Marilyn Monroe by Tom Kelly, titled *Golden Dreams,* 15½ x 9½in.
(Christie's) $329

Michael J. Fox/Back to the Future Part II, a Mattel Hoverboard of fluorescent pink plywood covered in pink three-dimensional effect vinyl decorated with various Mattel stickers, 19¹/₂in. long.
(Christie's) $4,937

Jailhouse Rock, MGM, 1957, three-sheet, linen backed, 81 x 41in.
(Christie's) $1,045

Aliens, a grotesque Alien creature head of polyurethane foam with isoclylate coating finished in acrylic airbrush, 36¹/₂in. long, used in the 1986 Twentieth Century Fox film Aliens.
(Christie's) $1,646

Noel Coward, a full-length dressing gown of black and gold silk, accompanied by a letter of authenticity stating that the robe was given to fellow actor Ronnie Ward at Drury Lane when Ward shared a dressing room with his friend Noel Coward.
(Christie's) $2,468

A novelty souvenir clock for the film Indiana Jones & The Last Crusade, made out of a film box, signed by *Steven Spielberg, George Lucas, Alison Doody, Denholm Elliott, Tom Stoppard, Harrison Ford* and eleven other members of the cast and crew, 11³/₄ x 11³/₄in.
(Christie's) $987

A red and white striped cotton jacket fastening with three white buttons, stamped *M.G.M. WARDROBE* and inscribed *Gene Kelly* inside collar, possibly worn by Kelly in the 1952 M.G.M. film Singing In The Rain.
(Christie's) $370

A late Regency stained satin birch spoonback chair, marked with Paramount Studios invoice number *A 5158* and stencilled with artist's name *Marlene Dietrich*.
(Christie's) $5,760

The Last Sitting, a set of ten limited edition Bert Stern colour portrait photograps taken in 1962, six weeks before Marilyn Monroe's death, printed in 1978.
(Christie's) $4,114

A single-breasted tailcoat of charcoal gray wool, with *Metro-Goldwyn-Mayer* woven label inscribed with production number and artist's name *Groucho Marx*.
(Christie's) $3,497

A fine George III brass basket grate of serpentine section, having pierced apron with continuous husk, scroll and acanthus motifs, with central basket flanked by urn finials, 92cm. wide.
(Phillips) $8,750

A George III steel firegate in the Adam style with rectangular back and curved, railed basket flanked by a pair of urns, 36¼in. wide.
(Christie's) $9,293

A Regency cast iron and ormolu mounted fire grate, in the manner of George Bullock, with applied palmette motifs, on paw feet, 36in. wide.
(Christie's) $7,145

A George III paktong and steel basket-grate with serpentine railed basket and lift-off front, 32½in. wide.
(Christie's) $40,887

A Victorian brass and cast iron fire grate, the railed bowed basket above a Vitruvian scroll frieze, 30in. wide.
(Christie's) $1,222

A steel basket-grate of serpentine outline, the frieze pierced with fluting on engraved tapering supports, late 18th century, 30in. wide.
(Christie's) $2,531

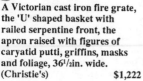

A Victorian cast iron fire grate, the 'U' shaped basket with railed serpentine front, the apron raised with figures of caryatid putti, griffins, masks and foliage, 36½in. wide.
(Christie's) $1,222

A cast iron and polished steel fire grate of serpentine outline, the tapering cylindrical standards with urn finials, the backplate with a rustic scene, 27in. wide.
(Christie's) $1,316

A 19th century Dutch polished steel fire grate, the barred front and sides above a fret pierced frieze, the tapering standards with urn finials, 29in. wide.
(Christie's) $4,702

A George III carved white marble chimneypiece, the fluted frieze centered by a tablet carved with three trophies in relief and flanked by twin-handled urns, 5ft. 8in. wide.
(Phillips) $16,814

A George II Siena, jasper and statuary marble chimneypiece, attributed to Sir Henry Cheere, Bt., the conjoined Ionic columns supporting the entablature embellished with a flower head to each end, centered by a projecting bas-relief carved tablet of a pastoral scene, circa 1755, 79¹/₂in. wide.
(Christie's) $40,480

A George II Siena, jasper and statuary marble chimneypiece, attributed to Sir Henry Cheere, Bt., the conjoined Ionic columns supporting the entablature embellished with a flower head to each end, centered by a projecting bas-relief tablet, depicting a winter landscape with children attending a fire, circa 1755, 87¹/₂in. wide.
(Christie's) $105,248

A fine George III carved statuary marble and Spanish brocatelle chimneypiece, the frieze of arcaded form with husk spandrels, centered by palmette motif, the carved central tablet depicting 'The Marriage of Cupid and Psyche', circa 1775, 64in. wide.
(Christie's) $32,868

One of a pair of parcel-gilt and white-painted rococo style chimneypieces, with integral overmantels, in the Chinese taste after a design by Matthias Lock, each looking-glass with arched frame centered by a lattice-framed pavilion, late 19th/early 20th century, 57in. wide.
(Christie's) (Two) $13,156

A George III Siena and statuary marble chimneypiece, the frieze inset with Siena flutes and centered by a projecting tablet carved with an acanthus-supported vase with foliate scrolls, circa 1780, 82in. wide.
(Christie's) $21,912

A Victorian cast-iron fire surround, with a molded shelf and rounded corners, the fluted pilasters surmounted by a female figure, emblematic of Peace and Plenty, second half 19th century, 67in. wide.
(Christie's) $810

A white marble chimney-piece, inlaid in the Bossi style, the frieze centered by a vase of strawberries, grapes and cherries suspending husk garlands and with ribbon-tied crossed thyrsi, 74¹/₂in. wide.
(Christie's) $73,986

A carved pine and marble fire surround, the white-painted frieze centered by a strapwork cartouche, the liver colored veined marble arched inset deeply molded, on block feet, 79¹/₄in. wide.
(Christie's) $1,826

A George III statuary marble and Siena chimneypiece, the central tablet carved with an oval medallion depicting a classical female figure, late 18th century, 72in. wide.
(Christie's) $36,520

American Renaissance stained maple faux bamboo mantel, circa 1872, the jambs decorated with foliate pendants, all bordered in faux bamboo, 6ft. 11¹/₂in. wide.
(Butterfield & Butterfield) $2,090

232

Italian neoclassical parcel-gilt and painted mantel, last quarter 18th century, the rectangular outstepped white faux marbre shelf over a faux Siena marble frieze carved with a gilt foliate vine centered by a mask, 8ft. 4½in. wide.
(Butterfield & Butterfield) $16,500

A late Victorian white marble chimneypiece, with a molded rectangular shelf above a frieze carved with a panel of ribbon-tied flowers, the jambs similarly carved with foliage, on block feet, 74in. wide.
(Christie's) $972

A French gray veined white marble chimneypiece of Louis XVI design, the frieze centered by a rosette with floral motifs, the jambs each head by a rosette, on block feet, 19th century, 49¾in. wide.
(Christie's) $2,191

A French gray-veined white marble chimneypiece, of Louis XVI style, the jambs each headed by a square foliate rosette above a tapering fluted pilaster, on block feet, late 19th century, 57½in. wide.
(Christie's) $2,024

A Regency statuary marble chimneypiece, the frieze centered by a carved mask of Mercury and anthemion to each side, on block feet, 57½in. wide.
(Christie's) $14,610

American Renaissance maple and walnut mantel by Herter Brothers, New York, circa 1872, the jambs mounted with replicas of opposed winged lions, 6ft. 5in. wide.
(Butterfield & Butterfield) $2,090

A pair of polished steel firedogs attributed to Alfred Bucknell, each bud finial above hammered and fluted perpendicular, on trestle feet, 57.5cm. high.
(Christie's) $1,280

Fine pair of Louis XV ormolu and patinated bronze chenets, mid-18th century, in the form of a black patinated boar rising to its feet or a reclining stag, 19in. wide.
(Butterfield & Butterfield) $16,500

A set of polished steel fireirons, attributed to Thornton & Downer, comprising a poker, a pair of tongs, a shovel, a brush, supported on square-section stand with three arched legs, 63.5cm. high.
(Christie's) $2,166

A pair of Chippendale brass andirons, American, late 18th century, each with a ball-and-flame finial over a baluster and ring-turned support, 21¹/₂in. high.
(Christie's) $9,350

Pair of large patinated bronze figural andirons of American Indians by Louis Potter, first quarter 20th century, Roman Bronze Works, New York, 22in. high.
(Butterfield & Butterfield) $4,950

A set of three George IV steel and brass fire-irons, each with seated-lion finial, the shovel 31in. long.
(Christie's) $1,240

A set of three Regency brass fire-irons each with chamfered domed finial, comprising: a shovel with trellis-pierced pan, a pair of tongs and a poker.
(Christie's) $1,884

Pair of Louis XV style bronze figural chenets, 19th century, each with musical putto on leafy scroll base, 14in. high.
(Skinner Inc.) $1,870

A pair of brass andirons, probably New York, 1790–1810, each with steeple-top above a ball with mid-band over a faceted hexagonal plinth, 22in. high.
(Christie's) $1,320

A pair of engraved brass andirons by Richard Whittingham, New York, 1800–1820, on spurred arched legs, 20in. high.
(Christie's) $3,850

A pair of gilt brass andirons marked *Bradly and Hubbard*, cast as a pair of dolphins with scrolled tails, 14in. high.
(Christie's) $1,540

A pair of George III seamed brass andirons, each with ball finial on turned and faceted baluster shaft, 18in. high.
(Christie's) $3,392

A set of Regency ormolu and steel fire-irons, each with dragon-head finial and faceted baluster shaft, 31in. long.
(Christie's) $5,417

Pair of Louis XVI style bronze chenets, 19th century, with male and female classical figures, 19in. high.
(Skinner Inc.) $1,430

A pair of Chippendale brass and iron firetools attributed to Daniel King, Philadelphia, circa 1760, the tongs with penny grips, 28in. high.
(Christie's) $2,860

A pair of George III seamed brass andirons, each with ring-turned baluster shaft on hipped downswept legs, 18³/₄in. high.
(Christie's) $2,355

An attractive Pontypool toleware coal scuttle, with slightly domed hinged cover, foliate cast loop handles to the sides, and raised upon four lion paw feet, 22in. wide over handle.
(Spencer's) $1,560

Pair of Italian baroque style patinated bronze grotesque andirons, second half 19th century, each in the form of a serpent-tailed many-breasted long-necked chimera, 28in. high.
(Butterfield & Butterfield) $5,225

235

Gustav Stickley day bed, circa 1902–03, no. 216, wide crest rail over five vertical slats, with cushion, signed with large red decal, 31in. wide.
(Skinner Inc.) $2,400

A 17th century-style oak cradle with arched canopy, paneled sides and ball finials, 33½in. high.
(Bearne's) $894

Empire mahogany and ormolu lit en bateau decorated with sirens, stars, arabesques and mythological figures.
(Finarte) $26,308

Federal mahogany tall post bed, New England, circa 1800, square tapering headposts flank head board, reeded footposts, 55in. wide.
(Skinner Inc.) $2,310

Important Moorish style gilt-metal-mounted, mother-of-pearl and ivory inlaid ebony bedstead and pair of matching nightstands, circa 1878.
(Butterfield & Butterfield) $90,750

An Anglo-Dutch mahogany metamorphic wing open armchair, the back with hinged support, opening to become a daybed, on cabriole legs with pad feet, mid-18th century, 88in. long.
(Christie's) $10,835

Italian baroque style carved walnut posted bed, the massive cylindrical posts carved with three bands of vertical acanthus, 6ft. 9in. long.
(Butterfield & Butterfield) $4,950

Italian Empire carved and painted pine daybed, first quarter 19th century, with paneled scrolled ends, the sides of the headboard each carved in relief with a recumbent leopard-headed sphinx, 5ft, 7½in. long.
(Butterfield & Butterfield) $2,750

A red painted ebonized and parcel-gilt boat shaped daybed of antique Egyptian style, the dished seat covered in black horsehair, 76in. wide.
(Christie's S. Ken) $3,218

FURNITURE

A Regency brass-mounted mahogany cot, the arched canopy hung with orange silk, on four spreading turned supports each with vase-shaped finials, 57in. wide.
(Christie's) **$4,840**

Piedmontese giltwood center-bed, second half 18th century, 180cm. long.
(Finarte) **$6,351**

Extremely fine Victorian figured walnut half tester bedstead, the foot of serpentine form with applied paneled designs.
(G.A. Key) **$5,280**

'The Yatman', a half-tester bed, designed by William Burges, the walnut paneled footboard and framework surmounted by an elaborate and ebonized frieze and dentillated cornice, 157.5cm. wide.
(Christie's) **$51,000**

19th century canopy bed, the upholstery with colored bunches of flowers with braided edges.
(Finarte) **$6,812**

Fine American Renaissance figured maple and rosewood three-piece bedroom suite comprising a bedstead, nightstand, and dresser, by Herter Brothers, New York, circa 1872.
(Butterfield & Butterfield) **$12,100**

Fine 19th century mahogany four poster bedstead, the foot post carved with The Prince of Wales Feathers and reeded, 6ft. 9in. wide.
(G.A. Key) **$3,363**

Fine Aesthetic inlaid, gilt-incised and carved walnut and burled walnut three-piece bedroom suite by Herter Brothers, New York, circa 1880.
(Butterfield & Butterfield) **$22,000**

A mahogany and cream-painted four-poster bed with cream floral chintz upholstery, the front-posts and headboard 18th century, 66in. wide.
(Christie's) **$5,653**

BOOKCASES

An early 20th century banded mahogany circular revolving bookstand, the radially-veneered top centered by a small inlaid florette motif, 34¹/₂in. high.
(Tennants) $1,105

An impressive George IV-early Victorian mahogany breakfront library bookcase, the architectural cornice above four doors with gothic-arch astragals and four paneled doors, 145in. wide.
(Bearne's) $14,276

A late George III mahogany and satinwood banded bookcase, the lower section with rectangular top above two marquetry eared paneled doors with classical urns and swags, 44¹/₂in. wide.
(Christie's) $4,799

George III style mahogany breakfront bookcase, late 19th century, the lower section with acorn pendant-carved frieze over six panelled cupboard doors, raised on a plinth base, 11ft. 3¹/₂in. wide.
(Butterfield & Butterfield) $9,900

A classical mahogany library-case, New York, 1810–1830, on foliate-carved and gadrooned bun feet, 47¹/₂in. wide.
(Christie's) $3,850

Louis XV style gilt-bronze-mounted inlaid tulipwood bibliothèque, late 19th/early 20th century, the coved rectangular top surmounted by a brèche marble slab, 46³/₄in. wide. (Butterfield & Butterfield) $3,850

An early Victorian mahogany breakfront bookcase with molded bolection cornice and pediment above a frieze applied with the letters XYZ, 129in. wide.
(Christie's) $23,232

A Victorian mahogany library bookcase with rounded rectangular and molded cornice above three arched glazed paneled doors, on plinth base, 84in. high.
(Christie's) $2,276

A mid-Victorian oak bookcase, the upper section with three glazed doors enclosing eleven later shelves, the base with three glazed doors enclosing five later shelves, 78in. wide.
(Christie's) $1,948

BOOKCASES

A Heal & Son oak bookcase, the domed superstructure with three shelves above single paneled cupboard door, on platform base, 53.3cm. wide.
(Christie's) **$590**

A William IV breakfront bookcase, on a plinth base, 64in. wide.
(Dreweatt Neate) **$1,521**

A George III mahogany bookcase, the upper part with dentil molded cornice above a pair of astragal glazed doors, 55in. wide.
(Spencer's) **$1,792**

An antique English William IV mahogany breakfront bookcase with molded cornice above four glazed doors, circa 1830, 6ft. 5in. wide.
(Selkirk's) **$3,200**

An early 19th century pine open bookcase, with brass carrying handles, 18^1/$_2$in. wide.
(Dreweatt Neate) **$1,014**

A George III mahogany tambour cylinder front bookcase, of breakfront outline, the upper part with a dentil cornice and pear drop frieze, 6ft. 11^1/$_2$in. wide.
(Phillips) **$11,489**

Empire style gilt-bronze-mounted mahogany bibliothèque, circa 1900, the stepped and thumb-molded top above a frieze mounted with gilt-bronze palmettes, 6ft. 2in. wide.
(Butterfield & Butterfield) **$5,225**

Louis XIV carved, painted and mirrored bookcase, the setback upper part with an arched cornice above a pair of mirrored doors, resting on short leaf-carved supports, 4ft. 5in. wide.
(Butterfield & Butterfield) **$27,500**

Empire style gilt-bronze-mounted mahogany bibliothèque, circa 1900, of slight breakfront outline, the shaped top above an elaborate gilt-bronze frieze, 6ft. 6in. wide.
(Butterfield & Butterfield) **$3,850**

A George III mahogany breakfront bookcase with molded cornice above two pairs of rectangular-glazed doors enclosing shelves. (Christie's) $10,950

An early Victorian rosewood dwarf bookcase with rectangular top and molded cornice above two sets of two shelves, 72in. wide. (Christie's) $7,915

A George III mahogany bookcase with molded rectangular cornice above a band of entrelac and a pair of geometrically-glazed doors, 80in. wide. (Christie's) $8,479

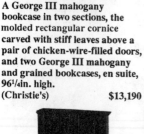

A George III mahogany bookcase in two sections, the molded rectangular cornice carved with stiff leaves above a pair of chicken-wire-filled doors, and two George III mahogany and grained bookcases, en suite, 96¼in. high. (Christie's) $13,190

Fine George III inlaid mahogany breakfront bookcase, circa 1790, the glazed doors with 'Gothik' mullions enclosing shelves, the lower section with four paneled cupboard doors, 8ft. 10in. wide. (Butterfield & Butterfield) $33,000

One of a pair of Irish George III mahogany library bookcases, each with rectangular dentiled cornice above a pair of geometrically-glazed doors enclosing four shelves, 78³/₄in. wide. (Christie's) (Two) $39,919

A mid-Georgian oak bookcase in two sections, with molded rectangular cornice, on shaped bracket feet, 50¹/₂in. wide. (Christie's) $5,653

A Regency mahogany breakfront bookcase, with stepped cornice above two pairs of horizontally-glazed doors each enclosing four shelves, on plinth base, the locks stamped *TURNERS*, 97¹/₄in. wide. (Christie's) $14,932

A George IV rosewood bookstand, the rectangular black leather-lined top with gadrooned edge above three shelves to front and back, 26in. wide. (Christie's) $10,085

BOOKCASES

One of a pair of Regency mahogany bookcases each with molded rectangular top and two glazed doors enclosing four shelves, 53in. wide.
(Christie's) (Two) $14,520

A Regency mahogany secretaire breakfront-bookcase, with molded cornice above four glazed doors with arcaded glazing bars headed by acanthus, 113in. wide.
(Christie's) $33,231

An Irish William IV mahogany bookcase by Williams & Gibton, the bolection molded inverted-breakfront cornice carved with Greek key, on plinth base, 62in. wide.
(Christie's) $14,867

A Federal mahogany bookcase, Philadelphia, 1790–1810, the two bookcase sections each with double cupboard doors glazed in a Gothic-arch pattern enclosing adjustable shelves, on a molded base, 119in. wide.
(Christie's) $24,200

A Regency rosewood and simulated rosewood small bookcase with three-quarter brass scroll-galleried portor marble top, the frieze centered by anthemia and a patera above two open shelves and a door simulated as two shelves filled with books, 15in. wide.
(Christie's) $21,010

A George III mahogany breakfront bookcase, the molded cornice above a pair of geometrically-glazed doors flanked by two doors enclosing shelves, 93³/₄in. wide.
(Christie's) $32,033

A George III mahogany breakfront library bookcase attributed to Thomas Chippendale, the center with scrolled pediment outlined with ebony and with ebony dentils, 79in. wide.
(Christie's) $661,980

A mid-Georgian mahogany bookcase with molded cornice above a pair of geometrically-glazed doors, on bracket feet, 63in. wide.
(Christie's) $40,656

A Regency mahogany bookcase with molded eared rectangular cornice with central arch above three long geometrically-glazed cupboard doors, each enclosing shelves, 75in. wide.
(Christie's) $10,494

BUREAU BOOKCASES

A Victorian mahogany cylinder bureau bookcase, the ogee molded cornice above a pair of arched glazed doors.
(Bonhams) $3,110

Federal cherry desk and bookcase, Southern New England, early 19th century, two-shelved divided upper interior, 41¹/₂in. wide.
(Skinner Inc.) $3,300

An antique American Renaissance Revival figured walnut cylinder desk and bookcase, the top member with architectural pediment, circa 1880, 8ft. 1in. high.
(Selkirk's) $1,900

A Queen Anne walnut, crossbanded and feather strung bureau cabinet, the upper part with a molded cornice and fitted interior with folio compartments, on bracket feet, 3ft. 2in. wide.
(Phillips) $25,311

A black japanned and gilt chinoiserie decorated double-domed bureau cabinet of Queen Anne design with overall scenes of figures and pagodas in foliate landscapes, on bun feet, 44in. wide.
(Christie's S. Ken) $11,083

A mahogany bureau bookcase with a pair of astragal glazed doors and geometrically inlaid fall enclosing fitted interior, late 18th century, 52in. wide.
(Christie's S. Ken) $2,887

A good Gordon Russell English walnut yew and ebony bureau bookcase, the paneled doors inlaid with yew banding and ebony stringing and enclosing shelves, 1.90m. high.
(Phillips) $10,736

A George III mahogany bureau bookcase, the fall enclosing a central cupboard, drawers and pigeonholes above four long graduated drawers on ogee bracket feet.
(Bonhams) $2,920

George I walnut bureau-bookcase, with a molded stepped cornice above a pair of shaped arched mirrored doors over two candle slides, on turnip feet, 38¹/₂in. wide.
(Butterfield & Butterfield) $8,800

BUREAU BOOKCASES

A George III style mahogany bureau bookcase, the fall front enclosing a fitted interior above two short and three long drawers.
(Bonhams) $3,864

George III style mahogany secretary bookcase, circa 1900, the base with a fall-front enclosing a writing surface and various compartments, 37¹/₂ in. wide.
(Skinner Inc.) $6,750

A walnut and burr walnut-veneered bureau cabinet, with cavetto cornice, two astragal-glazed doors, two candle slides, and a well, 41in. wide.
(Bearne's) $4,644

An 18th century South German walnut bureau cabinet, the upper part with a molded cornice above a pair of doors enclosing an interior of fifteen drawers, on bracket feet, 3ft. 6in. wide.
(Phillips) $6,814

George III mahogany secretary bookcase, late 18th century, the fret-carved rectangular cornice above a pair of glazed doors opening to shelves over small drawers and pigeonholes, raised on bracket feet, 42in. wide.
(Butterfield & Butterfield) $6,600

George III mahogany secretary bookcase, circa 1790, the lower section with a slant front opening to drawers and fitted compartments, raised on bracket feet, 37in. wide.
(Butterfield & Butterfield) $8,800

A George I walnut bureau-cabinet with two arched glazed doors, each with later plate, above two candle slides, on later bracket feet, 41³/₄ in. wide.
(Christie's) $7,084

An Edwardian mahogany and satinwood banded bureau bookcase, the fall front enclosing a simple interior, with four long drawers below, on bracket feet, 36in. wide.
(Bonhams) $1,609

A 19th century Dutch stained oak cylinder bureau cabinet outlined throughout with carved and recessed dentil banding, 47¹/₂ in. wide.
(Bearne's) $1,342

BUREAU BOOKCASES

A George I black japanned and parcel gilt bureau cabinet, the fall front enclosing drawers and pigeonholes around a cupboard door, above a well, 28in. wide. (Bonhams) $13,300

A South German walnut and ebonized bureau-cabinet in three sections inlaid overall with geometrical stringing in stained wood, with arched molded cornice above a door inlaid with a double-headed eagle, mid-18th century, 48in. wide. (Christie's) $7,128

A George III mahogany bureau bookcase, in four sections, the breakfront central section with arched cornice headed by an acanthus-scrolled cresting, probably North Country, 50½in. wide. (Christie's) $9,680

An Anglo-Dutch figured-walnut bureau-cabinet feather-banded and inlaid overall with bands and panels of seaweed marquetry, with later waved apron and shaped bracket feet, 18th century, the marquetry 19th century, 43¼in. wide. (Christie's) $12,248

A George I walnut crossbanded and feather strung bureau cabinet, the upper part with an ogee molded cornice and angular arched sides centered by a mirrored panel in the frieze, 3ft. 5in. wide. (Phillips) $49,490

An early Georgian burr walnut and walnut bureau-cabinet inlaid overall with featherbanding, the molded rectangular cornice above two mirrored doors enclosing shelves, on bracket feet, 42¾in. wide.(Christie's) $15,928

William and Mary walnut veneered double-domed bureau cabinet, circa 1700, in three sections, the upper part enclosed by a pair of shaped arched mirrored doors, raised on bun feet, 40½in. wide. (Butterfield & Butterfield) $17,600

A South German walnut, fruitwood and marquetry bureau-cabinet in three sections, the hinged flap enclosing a fitted interior, the concave-fronted waved base with three long drawers, on bun feet, 47¾in. wide. (Christie's) $25,740

A Queen Anne walnut bureau cabinet, inlaid overall with feather-banding, the double dome cornice with vase-shaped finials, above two mirrored doors each with beveled plate, on later bracket feet, 38in. wide. (Christie's) $27,104

BUREAU BOOKCASES

A George III mahogany bureau bookcase with a pair of geometrically-glazed doors enclosing three shelves, on shaped bracket feet, 42in. wide. (Christie's) $16,456

A black and gilt-japanned bureau cabinet decorated overall with chinoiserie scenes, with arched molded cornice centered by a scallop shell flanked by shrubs, part early 18th century, 40½in. wide. (Christie's) $52,272

A George I walnut and parcel-gilt bureau-cabinet with a pair of later mirror-glazed doors enclosing two shelves, pigeon-holes and four drawers, the candle-slides and feet possibly replaced, 38¾in. wide. (Christie's) $60,896

A George I red and gilt-japanned bureau-cabinet decorated overall with chinoiserie figures in European poses hunting, riding and drinking tea, the upper section with broken arched cresting with cavetto cornice, 40¾in. wide. (Christie's) $117,656

South German baroque inlaid walnut secretary bookcase, first quarter 18th century, in three parts, the center section with a slant-lid centering a scene of hunters and a boar, raised on compressed-ball feet, 4ft. 1in. wide. (Butterfield & Butterfield) $24,750

A George I brass-mounted figured and burr-walnut bureau-cabinet, the cavetto cornice above a pair of doors, the later mirror plates engraved with arches, on shaped bracket feet, 40in. wide. (Christie's) $58,828

A walnut bureau bookcase, with two candle-slides, the lower section with fall-front enclosing a fitted interior above four graduated long drawers, on shaped bracket feet, basically early 18th century, 39in. wide. (Christie's) $13,992

A George I figured walnut bureau-cabinet, with broken semi-circular pediment centered by a plinth above a pair of later mirror-glazed doors, 39½in. wide. (Christie's) $60,929

A George III mahogany bureau-cabinet, the upper section with broken triangular pediment carved with foliage, egg-and-dart and dentiling, above a pair of glazed, shaped paneled doors, on ogee bracket feet, 45in. wide. (Christie's) $14,520

An antique English George III inlaid mahogany slantfront desk with four graduated cockbeaded drawers, circa 1790–1800, 3ft. 6in. wide.
(Selkirk's) **$1,100**

Chippendale tiger maple slant front desk, New England, late 18th century, the lid with thumb-molded-edge, opening to a compartmentalized interior with six valenced pigeonholes, 37in. wide.
(Butterfield & Butterfield) **$4,400**

A George I walnut bureau, the sloping flap enclosing a fitted interior of seven drawers and pigeonholes around a central cupboard, on bracket feet, 3ft. 1in. wide.
(Phillips) **$6,678**

An early Georgian burr walnut bureau, the top section with rectangular top and hinged flap with reading shelf enclosing a fitted interior with slide and secret drawers, 34in. wide.
(Christie's) **$8,580**

George III mahogany slant-front desk, the rectangular top above a slant-front enclosing a central prospect door flanked by small drawers, 4ft. 1¹/₂in. wide.
(Butterfield & Butterfield) **$3,025**

A walnut bureau of small size with a crossbanded top and sloping feather strung flap enclosing an interior of pigeonholes, on bracket feet, parts 18th century, 2ft. 2in. wide.
(Phillips) **$6,960**

An early 18th century walnut crossbanded and feather strung bureau, the sloping fall enclosing a fitted interior with central enclosed cupboard, 3ft. wide.
(Phillips) **$5,220**

A late 18th/early 19th century Continental birchwood cylinder bureau, the superstructure with a rectangular oak top, above a tambour shutter enclosing pigeonholes, 3ft. 4in. wide.
(Phillips) **$6,360**

A George I oak bureau, the sloping fall enclosing a stepped interior of drawers and pigeonholes above a well, on bracket feet, 35³/₄in. wide.
(Bonhams) **$1,743**

BUREAUX

Chippendale mahogany block front desk, late 18th century, base restoration including four repaired feet, 36¹/₂in. wide. (Skinner Inc.) $2,800

A Victorian lady's walnut cylinder bureau with a fitted interior. (Greenslades) $2,008

An antique Federal period mahogany slantfront desk of desirable small size, decorated with line inlay, the flap enclosing a fitted interior, 34in. wide. (Selkirk's) $3,000

Portuguese rococo style serpentine-fronted padouk slant-front desk, 19th century, raised on a projecting coved ebony base on compressed ball feet, 37in. wide. (Butterfield & Butterfield) $2,200

A Federal inlaid cherrywood slant-front desk, Maryland or Pennsylvania, circa 1790, the rectangular top above a slant lid with line inlay centering an inlaid patera opening to a fitted interior with a corner fan-inlaid prospect door, 38in. wide. (Christie's) $11,000

Chippendale maple and cherrywood slant front desk, New England, late 18th century, the thumb-molded edge slant lid enclosing a compartment interior with six valenced pigeonholes centering two document drawers, 40¹/₄in. wide. (Butterfield & Butterfield) $3,025

Antique American Chippendale slant lid desk in tiger maple, fitted interior with six drawers and seven pigeon holes, four drawers with molded fronts, 40in. wide. (Eldred's) $5,940

Edwardian mahogany four drawer bureau with falling front, having crossbanding and shell inlay, basically fitted interior, 2ft. 6in. wide. (G.A. Key) $479

Chippendale walnut slant-front desk, Pennsylvania, circa 1770–1790, the thumb-molded edge slant lid opening to a compartmentalized interior, 41in. wide. (Butterfield & Butterfield) $3,850

247

BUREAUX

A Chippendale mahogany reverse serpentine slant-front desk, Massachusetts, 1760–1780, on short cabriole legs with ball-and-claw feet, 43¾in. wide.
(Christie's) $4,950

A Dutch mahogany and floral marquetry bombé bureau, the hinged fall enclosing a fitted interior, on claw-and-ball feet, late 18th/early 19th century, 41in. wide.
(Christie's) $12,477

A Queen Anne walnut and feather banded bureau, the sloping flap enclosing an interior of four drawers and pigeonholes above a well, on later bun feet, 3ft. 2in. wide.
(Phillips) $4,984

Antique American Chippendale slant lid desk in mahogany, seashell, herringbone and line inlay, four graduated drawers, fitted interior with an inlaid prospect door and four small drawers, 37in. wide.
(Eldred's) $1,210

Austrian Empire part-ebonised walnut cylinder desk, early 19th century, the rectangular top above three drawers over a cylinder front opening to reveal drawers and a shelf, 4ft. 4in. wide.
(Butterfield & Butterfield) $4,400

Federal style cherrywood slant-front desk, Pennsylvania, 19th century, the thumb-molded edge slant-lid opening to a compartmentalized interior with eight small drawers, 39¾in. wide.
(Butterfield & Butterfield) $1,870

Chippendale sycamore slant lid desk, New England, late 18th century, a stepped interior of small drawers, 36in. wide.
(Skinner Inc.) $3,080

Dutch rococo walnut and marquetry roll-top desk, mid 18th century, raised on hairy paw feet, 55in. wide.
(Skinner Inc.) $15,400

Chippendale tiger maple slant lid desk, New England, circa 1800, the interior has small drawers and open valanced compartments, 40½in. wide.
(Skinner Inc.) $5,500

248

BUREAUX

A Chinese export padouk wood bureau, the rectangular top and hinged slope enclosing a fitted interior with well, mid 18th century, 37¼in. wide.
(Christie's) $2,517

A George IV brass-inlaid and mahogany rosewood bureau-on-stand with rectangular top and paneled hinged flap, with fitted interior, on column supports, 36in. wide.
(Christie's) $2,834

A Dutch marquetry mahogany bombé bureau with scrolling foliate and bird motifs, the sloping fall front enclosing fitted interior, 19th century, 40in. wide.
(Christie's) $8,809

Federal walnut inlaid slant-front desk, Pennsylvania, early 19th century, the thumb-molded edge top with string quarter fan-inlay opening to a compartmentalized interior, 42in. wide.
(Butterfield & Butterfield) $2,200

A George III mahogany bureau outlined throughout with stringing, the sloping fall front inlaid with kingwood banding, 41in. wide.(Bearne's) $2,726

Chippendale carved tiger maple slant lid desk, New Hampshire, late 18th century, stepped interior of small drawers and valanced compartments, 37½in. wide.
(Skinner Inc.) $9,900

A George III oak bureau, the fall enclosing drawers and pigeonholes above two short and three long drawers, on bracket feet.
(Bonhams) $1,610

Chippendale maple desk, New England, late 18th century, replaced hardware, 35¼in. wide.
(Skinner Inc.) $3,520

A George III mahogany bureau with sloping flap enclosing small drawers and a cupboard, on later bracket feet, 34in. wide.
(Bearne's) $2,580

CABINETS

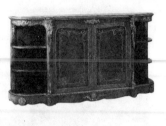

An important 17th century Italian tortoiseshell, ivory, ebony and gilt bronze mounted architectural cabinet of impressive proportions and accentuated perspective, the whole inset with gilt metal classical relief panels, 6ft. 4in. wide.
(Phillips) $461,100

An 18th century South German walnut and marquetry cabinet on stand, inlaid with lines and panels of flower sprays, on a walnut veneered and beechwood stand, 2ft. 10in. wide.
(Phillips) $2,314

A mid Victorian burr-walnut, tulipwood banded and ormolu-mounted credenza, the serpentine and eared top above two shaped paneled doors, flanked by open shelves, 76¼in. wide.
(Christie's) $8,638

A mid-Victorian mother-of-pearl-inlaid black and gilt-japanned side cabinet, decorated overall with floral bouquets within gilt scrolls, on plinth base, 45in. wide.
(Christie's) $6,730

One of a pair of early Victorian giltmetal-mounted table-cabinets, crossbanded in kingwood, on tapering acanthus-cast feet, 31in. wide.
(Christie's)   (Two)
$7,160

A 'Dieppe ivory' architectural cabinet on stand, carved and engraved all over, the cabinet surmounted by a crenellated cornice and eight tapering finials, fitted with seven concealed drawers, second half 19th century, the cabinet 25¼in. wide. (Christie's) $33,300

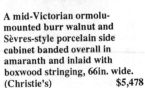

A Regency ormolu-mounted ebonized, parcel-gilt and Chinese lacquer side-cabinet, the two paneled doors each inset with a panel of 18th century Somada-style Chinese lacquer, 57¾in. wide.
(Christie's) $29,040

An ormolu-mounted brass, brown tortoiseshell and ebony boulle side cabinet in the manner of A-C Boulle with molded rectangular breakfront top, late 19th century, 71in. wide.
(Christie's) $5,478

A mid-Victorian ormolu-mounted burr walnut and Sèvres-style porcelain side cabinet banded overall in amaranth and inlaid with boxwood stringing, 66in. wide.
(Christie's) $5,478

CABINETS

A Napoleon III ormolu-mounted brass-inlaid ebony and simulated tortoiseshell side cabinet, the breakfront black marble top above an acanthus-cast frieze, 66in. wide.
(Christie's)　　　　$5,843

A Viennese ebonized and polychrome enamel table cabinet, mounted all over with plaques depicting mythological scenes, late 19th/early 20th century, 13¹/₂in. wide.
(Christie's)　　　　$7,304

A tortoiseshell, ivory and mahogany cabinet with a paneled fall-front enclosing six variously-sized mahogany-lined drawers, the interior and panels Colonial, 18th century, in a William IV exterior, 11¹/₂in. wide.
(Christie's)　　　　$2,073

A rare late 17th century Iberian tortoiseshell and mother of pearl two-tier cabinet on stand of trapezoidal form, on octagonal section fluted knopped and ring turned legs, 5ft. 6in. wide.
(Phillips)　　　　$18,559

A pair of side cabinets, rectangular overhanging molded top above single banded cupboard door with brass drop handles, on baluster turned legs, 34.7cm. wide.
(Christie's)　　　　$9,845

A late 18th century North Italian walnut, fruitwood, tulipwood crossbanded and marquetry side cabinet, in the manner of Maggiolini, on square tapered legs, 1ft. 10in. wide.
(Phillips)　　　　$7,950

One of a pair of Napoleon III ormolu-mounted tulipwood and rosewood wall-cabinets each with two shaped mirror-backed glass shelves, 24in. high.
(Christie's)　(Two)
　　　　$2,922

Fine Regency rosewood, parcel-gilt and gilt-brass side cabinet, circa 1810, with an orange scagliola top surmounted by a galleried three-division mirrored back superstructure, 5ft. 11³/₄in. wide.
(Butterfield & Butterfield)
　　　　$9,900

A Charles II black japanned and chinoiserie decorated cabinet on a contemporary carved and silvered stand, the upper part containing eleven drawers, 5ft. high.
(Phillips)　　　　$12,720

A mid-Georgian lacquered
brass-mounted black and gilt-
japanned cabinet-on-stand
decorated overall with flowers,
foliage, birds and landscapes,
with repository label, 40¹/₂in.
wide.
(Christie's) $4,840

A Milanese ebonized cabinet
decorated overall with carved
and pierced ivory and bone
arabesque panels, on inverted
plinth base, mid 19th century,
43³/₄in. wide.
(Christie's) $14,396

A William and Mary
polychrome and white-japanned
cabinet-on-stand, with giltmetal
escutcheon, hinges and corners,
fitted with a pair of doors
decorated with a Japanese-style
panoramic scene of figures,
possibly Dutch, 43³/₄in. wide.
(Christie's) $64,713

An amusing Scandinavian
cabinet on stand, designed by
Osten Kristiannson, in oak,
modelled as an army officer, his
flies opening to reveal a
mechanical curiosity, 169cm.
high.
(Phillips) $6,548

A pair of brass-inlaid rosewood
side cabinets, each inlaid overall
with foliage, anthemia and
banding, on claw feet, basically
early 19th century, 38in. wide.
(Christie's) $16,959

An amusing Scandinavian
cabinet, designed by Osten
Kristiannson, in oak, modeled
as a Scandinavian woman with
hat, her tunic opening to reveal
a naked body, 170cm. high.
(Phillips) $4,092

A mid Victorian harewood,
marquetry and giltmetal
mounted credenza of broken D-
shaped outline, inlaid overall
with a dot-trellis, 48in. wide.
(Christie's) $4,799

A Dutch walnut and marquetry
cabinet, decorated overall with
birds and flower filled urns, on
hairy paw feet, damage to
cornice, mid 18th century,
85¹/₂in. wide.
(Christie's) $23,034

An ebonized and painted corner
cabinet, designed by Charles
Rennie Mackintosh, with
painted panels by Margaret
Macdonald Mackintosh, the two
cupboard doors with pierced
hinge plates, circa 1897, 183cm.
high.(Christie's) $23,000

CABINETS

A Spanish gilt-metal mounted walnut vargueno, the interior with twelve doors and a central drawer enclosing three further drawers, 43in. wide.
(Christie's) $9,504

A fine mid-Victorian ebonized and brass inlaid side cabinet with gilt bronze and hardstone mounts, with turned and fluted projecting column supports above a shaped apron on disc feet, 79in. wide.
(Tennants) $4,092

Fine Napoleon III gilt-bronze and Sèvres porcelain mounted tulipwood serre à bijoux, third quarter 19th century, mounted with Sèvres porcelain plaques, 16³/₄in. wide.
(Butterfield & Butterfield) $12,100

Extremely fine Italian Renaissance style hardstone, marble and bronze-mounted ebonized cabinet, Florence, circa 1860, the cupboard doors opening to an architectural interior with an arrangement of drawers enclosing secret drawers, 4ft. wide.
(Butterfield & Butterfield) $93,500

A pair of French ormolu and porcelain mounted mahogany corner cabinets, the drawer mounted with two shaped Sèvres style porcelain plaques painted with flowers, 27in. wide.
(Christie's) $7,678

One of a pair of black-japanned and simulated bamboo side cabinets of Regency style, each with a rectangular eared and concave-fronted verde antico marble top, 20th century, 25¹/₄in. wide.
(Christie's) (Two) $6,199

An 18th century German oak fruitwood banded and marquetry buffet in two parts, decorated with roundels and green stain heightened foliate vases and birds, 4ft. 2in. wide.
(Phillips) $8,838

Fine Italian late Renaissance carved walnut cabinet of large size, circa 1600, the upper part enclosed by a pair of doors inset with wrought-iron scrollwork, 6ft. 9in. wide.
(Butterfield & Butterfield) $20,900

A late 18th century Dutch walnut and marquetry strung display cabinet, decorated with foliate scrolls, floral stems, masks and urns of flowers with birds and butterflies, 6ft. 6in. wide.
(Phillips) $28,280

CABINETS

A Goanese hardwood brass mounted and ivory inlaid cabinet, fitted with six drawers above a frieze drawer, on bobbin-turned uprights with bun feet, early 18th century, 28in. wide.
(Christie's) $5,097

An Edwardian mahogany and marquetry side cabinet inlaid overall with satinwood bands and ebony and boxwood stringing, 30¼in. wide.
(Christie's) $2,879

A yew and brass mounted cabinet-on-stand surmounted by rectangular rouge marble top above a pair of doors inset with oval Sèvres-style porcelain panels, 41in. wide.
(Christie's) $4,607

Ceylonese carved rosewood four door cabinet made for the English market, second quarter 19th century, raised on tapering ring-turned feet, 47¾in. wide.
(Butterfield & Butterfield) $1,980

Pair of Louis XIV style marquetry cabinets, third quarter 19th century, each polished slate rectangular top with outset rectangular corners above a frieze drawer over a cupboard door enclosing a shelf, 29in. wide.
(Butterfield & Butterfield) $9,350

Italian Renaissance walnut credenza, rectangular molded top over a paneled case fitted with a small frieze drawer, on bracket feet, 27½in. wide.
(Skinner Inc.) $2,970

A walnut cabinet in two sections with molded cornice above central arched glazed compartments flanked by open compartments, mid 19th century, possibly Colonial, 100in. high.
(Christie's) $10,557

A French mahogany purpleheart and walnut D-shaped cabinet with giltmetal mounts and inlaid overall, on gilt toupie feet, 48in. wide.
(Christie's) $6,718

Flemish baroque style oak cabinet, 19th century, enclosed by two pairs of paneled doors applied with mitred geometric moldings centered by cherubs' heads, 4ft. 4in. wide.
(Butterfield & Butterfield) $4,400

CANTERBURYS

A George III mahogany four-division canterbury, the bowed slatted compartments above a drawer, on turned legs, 46cm. wide.
(Phillips) $1,958

A Victorian burr-walnut canterbury whatnot with pierced scroll galleried oval eared top on spiral-twist supports, on bun feet and castors, 23³/₄in. wide.
(Christie's) $1,821

A Victorian rosewood canterbury, the upper section with Prince of Wales' feathers decoration above a frieze drawer, on baluster turned legs.
(Bonhams) $1,632

A Regency mahogany four-division canterbury with flattened baluster slats, containing an ebony strung drawer, on ring turned feet, 1ft. 8in. wide.
(Phillips) $3,309

A mahogany gothic canterbury, the dished rectangular top with gothic arches, paneled pillar-angles, five divisions and a scrolled carrying handle, 19th century, 19¹/₂in. wide.
(Christie's) $2,834

A Regency mahogany canterbury, the pierced rectangular top with three divisions and a carrying-handle, on ring-turned legs, 20in. wide.
(Christie's) $3,896

Federal mahogany canterbury, probably New York, 1820's, pulls appear original, 19in. high.
(Skinner Inc.) $1,650

An early Victorian rosewood canterbury, the foliate carved four-division top above a base drawer on turned baluster legs, 20in. wide.
(Christie's S. Ken) $1,502

A late George III mahogany canterbury, the four divisioned slatted top above a drawer on square tapered legs, 18in. wide.
(Christie's) $3,455

DINING CHAIRS

One of a set of eight Italian walnut dining-chairs including an associated armchair, on turned tapering fluted legs and pointed feet, early 19th century. (Christie's) (Eight)

$14,850

One of a pair of 18th century Venetian decorated and parcel gilt salon chairs, in the Louis XV taste, on cabriole legs with shell carved knees and scroll feet. (Phillips) $2,226

One of a set of eighteen George IV mahogany dining-chairs attributed to Gillows of Lancaster, each with a semi-balloon back, on turned and reeded tapering legs. (Christie's) (Eighteen)

$36,784

One of a pair of George I walnut chairs with slightly curved backs and solid baluster splats carved with foliage and rosettes, the crestings centered by shells framed by foliate scrolls, 40³/₄in. high. (Christie's) (Two)

$93,456

A painted Windsor fan-back side-chair, New England, 1780–1800, the serpentine bowed crestrail with shaped ears above seven spindles flanked by baluster-turned stiles, 37¹/₄in. high. (Christie's) $990

One of a set of eight George III mahogany dining-chairs with lobed shield-shaped backs carved with flowerheads and foliage with foliate lunette bases, 37³/₄in. high. (Christie's) (Eight)

$33,099

One of a fine set of six antique American Federal mahogany scrollback dining chairs in the manner of Duncan Phyfe, on reeded splayed legs, probably New York, circa 1810. (Selkirk's) (Six) $5,100

A fine early 18th century walnut and burr walnut chair, the back with inscrolled uprights and cresting carved in high relief with rocaille rockwork and leaf scrolls, possibly Dutch, or North German. (Phillips) $1,335

One of a set of eighteen George IV oak dining-chairs, the padded seat covered in close-nailed striped material on turned tapering reeded legs. (Christie's) (Eighteen)

$19,239

DINING CHAIRS

One of a set of eight walnut dining-chairs, each with waved toprail, on cabriole legs headed by scallop-shells and claw-and-ball feet, part-18th century.
(Christie's)   (Eight)

$20,727

One of a set of four late George II mahogany hall chairs, the shaped solid seats on cabriole legs joined by turned stretchers, 36in. high.
(Christie's)   (Four)

$25,311

One of a set of eight George III Scottish mahogany dining chairs, including two open armchairs, each with shield-shaped back with pierced vase-shaped splat.
(Christie's)   (Eight)

$10,648

One of a set of fourteen early Victorian oak dining-chairs by Holland & Sons, and designed by A.W.N. Pugin, each with padded rectangular back and seat covered in nailed red leather.
(Christie's)   (Fourteen)

$20,114

One of a set of three Queen Anne walnut and marquetry dining chairs, on tapered legs united by turned and curved stretchers terminating in pad feet.
(Phillips)   (Three)

$7,155

A Chippendale mahogany side-chair, Newport, 1760–1780, the serpentine crestrail centered by diapering flanked by molded scrolling ears over a scrolling, pierced vase-shaped splat, 37¼in. high.
(Christie's) $4,400

One of a set of six George III mahogany dining-chairs each with rectangular back with pierced vertical-railed splat and leafy capitals.
(Christie's) (Six) $8,479

One of a set of eight William IV rosewood dining-chairs, on turned tapering acanthus-carved legs and turned feet.
(Christie's)   (Eight)

$10,494

One of two black-painted Queen Anne side-chairs, New York, late 18th century, each with yoked crestrail over a vase-shaped splat, 41½in. high.
(Christie's)   (Two) $1,760

DINING CHAIRS

One of a set of six Regency mahogany dining chairs, the scroll tablet top rails above bar splats and overstuffed seats, on saber legs.
(Bonhams)   (Six)
$2,576

A pair of mahogany chairs, designed by George Walton, the curved backs with vase-shaped splats pierced with a heart, circa 1900, 48in. high.
(Christie's)
$1,772

Grained Windsor chair for stand-up desk, New England, early 19th century, original red and black graining, 46in. high.
(Skinner Inc.)
$522

Antique American Queen Anne side chair in maple, vase shaped back splat, rush seat, turned legs ending in Spanish feet, 42½in. high.
(Eldred's)
$275

One of a set of six Regency beechwood, simulated rosewood and rosewood brass inlaid dining chairs, on saber legs.
(Phillips)   (Six)
$2,544

Queen Anne walnut carved side chair, Newport, Rhode Island, circa 1760, refinished, 38in. high.
(Skinner Inc.)
$7,150

One of a set of six George III style mahogany dining chairs, the arched toprails above pierced splats centered by paterae, on square chamfered legs, late 19th century.
(Bonhams)   (Six)
$1,239

One of a set of six late 18th/early 19th century Dutch carved mahogany and floral marquetry dining chairs, in the Queen Anne taste, on cabriole legs with shell carved knees.
(Phillips)   (Six)
$10,812

One of a pair of James II oak side chairs, each with high arched cane-filled back and seat on C-scroll legs joined by turned stretchers.
(Christie's)   (Two)
$3,392

DINING CHAIRS

One of a set of six George III mahogany and inlaid dining chairs, in the Sheraton taste, the backs with curved bar toprails with satinwood veneered panels.
(Phillips)   (Six) $3,005

One of a set of six late 18th/early 19th century German carved walnut dining chairs, in the Louis XV taste, on cabriole legs with cabochon incised decorated feet.
(Phillips)   (Six) $2,862

One of a set of three Dutch 19th century floral marquetry side chairs, the arcaded top rails with barley twist central supports.
(Tennants)   (Three) $930

Chippendale mahogany carved side chair, Massachusetts, 1775–85, needlepoint slip seat, 38in. high.
(Skinner Inc.) $2,420

One of an unusual pair of Regency carved mahogany hall chairs, the wide oval panel backs with radiating reeded ornament, having solid seats, on turned tapered legs.
(Phillips)   (Two) $2,067

One of a set of six Italian walnut Renaissance Revival dining chairs, with arched upholstered backs and seats on scale carved square tapering legs.
(Bonhams)   (Six) $864

Painted fan-back Windsor side chair, New England, 1780–1800, black paint, 35³/₄in. high.
(Skinner Inc.) $330

Two of a set of six George I style needlepoint upholstered carved walnut sidechairs, 19th century, raised on shell-carved molded front supports.
(Butterfield & Butterfield) $12,100

One of a pair of Regency mahogany hall chairs each with waisted arched back and dished shaped seat on eared solid supports.
(Christie's) $1,319

DINING CHAIRS

One of a set of four Regency white painted and gilt decorated elbow chairs, the cane seats with horsehair cushion squabs on saber legs.
(Phillips)   (Four) $5,724

A George II mahogany open armchair, the arched tapering back centered by a shell cresting with pierced interlaced knot-pattern splat headed by rosettes, 37½in. high.
(Christie's) $70,092

A George II mahogany open armchair with waved foliate toprail, and pierced vase-shaped splat carved with interlaced tiered C-scrolls and foliage, on cabriole legs carved with acanthus sprays, 38½in. high.
(Christie's) $101,244

A Federal white-painted and parcel-gilt armchair, Philadelphia, circa 1790, the arching molded crestrail decorated with acorns amid oak leaves over a padded tapering back flanked by reeded baluster-turned stiles, 36in. high.(Christie's) $52,800

Two of a set of six Regency black and gilt-japanned dining-chairs, and two similar open armchairs, each with scrolled back and shaped toprail painted with eagle-masks.
(Christie's)   (Six) $10,364

One of a pair of George II mahogany open armchairs with arched tapering heart-shaped backs, molded and beaded toprails and crestings carved with fruiting vines issuing from flowerheads, 36in. high.
(Christie's)   (Two) $486,750

A James I oak open armchair, the rectangular back with waved scrolled cresting and pointed finials above a band of stylized flowerhead-filled guilloche.
(Christie's) $9,421

One of a set of eight Regency mahogany dining chairs, the backs with curved bar top rails and rope twist horizontal splats.
(Phillips) $4,984

One of a pair of George II black and gilt-japanned open armchairs by William and John Linnell, each with stepped rectangular back filled with black and gold Chinese paling.
(Christie's) $292,050

DINING CHAIRS

A mahogany open armchair, the arms with lion-mask terminals, on cabriole legs carved with acanthus issuing from a lion-mask on claw-and-ball feet.
(Christie's) $7,163

One of a set of eight Regency blue-painted and parcel-gilt open armchairs in the manner of Henry Holland, each with channeled toprail.
(Christie's) (Eight) $113,685

A George I walnut and burr walnut open armchair, the arched back with tablet cresting centered by a scallop shell and vase-shaped splat.
(Christie's) $63,888

A blue-painted Windsor sack-back armchair, New England, late 18th century, the arching crestrail above seven spindles and shaped arms over baluster-turned supports and a shaped plank seat, retains 19th century paint, 43½in. high.
(Christie's) $10,450

Two of a set of fourteen William IV mahogany dining-chairs including two open armchairs, with molded seat-rail on channeled saber legs, later blocks. (Christie's) (Fourteen) $16,456

A George II mahogany open armchair with arched back, rockwork and foliage cresting, solid vase-shaped splat, shepherd's crook arms and drop-in grospoint needlework seat, 41¼in. high.
(Christie's) $35,046

One of a set of five George III later white painted and gilt decorated elbow chairs, in the Sheraton taste, with column splats having padded arm supports and stuffover seats.
(Phillips) (Five) $4,949

One of a pair of George III mahogany Gothic open armchairs in the manner of Robert Manwaring, the rectangular crenellated back carved with a pierced cusped rose centered by spandrels.
(Christie's) $16,616

A Regency mahogany metamorphic library step chair, after a patent by Morgan & Saunders, the padded seat folding out to form four steps on saber legs.
(Phillips) $5,000

DINING CHAIRS

One of a set of three English oak side chairs, each with shaped raised cresting centered by a flowerhead, with 19th century patched-needlework squab cushions.
(Christie's)   (Three)

$1,355

Two of a set of four Japanese bamboo and lacquer sidechairs, late 19th century, each with a rounded-arched top.
(Butterfield & Butterfield)

$4,400

One of a set of six Regency mahogany dining-chairs each with curved paneled toprail with brass roundel terminals, the padded drop-in seats covered in brown leather.
(Christie's)   (Six)

$6,582

One of a set of six oak side chairs designed by A.W.N. Pugin, on turned and chamfered legs joined by chamfered stretchers.
(Christie's) $2,363

Very important inlaid walnut and ebony chair, designed by Greene & Greene, executed in the workshop of Peter Hall for the living room of the Robert R. Blacker house, Pasadena, California, circa 1907.
(Skinner Inc.) $34,000

One of a set of four mid Victorian mahogany gothic revival side chairs, after a design by Charles Bevan, each with red leather upholstered outswept back.
(Christie's)   (Four)

$1,728

One of a set of six antique English Chippendale style mahogany dining chairs with pierced backs boldly carved with shell and foliate motifs.
(Selkirk's)   (Six)
$3,600

A pair of Italian rococo carved walnut side chairs, third quarter 18th century, each with floral-carved serpentine crestrail centered by a carved flowerhead.
(Butterfield & Butterfield)
$1,870

One of a set of twelve Federal maple side-chairs, New York, 1790–1810, each with a scrolling concave crestrail over a conforming slat and caned trapezoidal seat, $33^{1}/_{2}$in. high.
(Christie's)   (Twelve)
$5,500

DINING CHAIRS

A Federal mahogany side-chair, New York, 1790–1810, the molded serpentine crestrail above a shield-shaped back, 37³/₄in. high.
(Christie's) $2,640

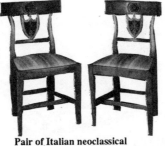

Pair of Italian neoclassical carved walnut side chairs, circa 1800, each with a broad bowed crestrail centered by a floral medallion above a pierced urn-form splat.
(Butterfield & Butterfield)
                            $660

One of six antique English Régence rosewood dining chairs, the concave top rails and splats inlaid with brass marquetry, circa 1815. (Six) $1,440
(Selkirk's)

One of a pair of oak side chairs, designed by J.P. Seddon, the chamfered curving legs supported by carved brackets, joined by chamfered stretcher, upholstered backs and seats.
(Christie's)   (Two)
                          $3,150

A pair of Milanese ebonized hall chairs with ivory and bone intarsia panels, the crested C-scroll backs above premier and contrepartie paneled seats.
(Christie's) $1,344

A fine Chippendale carved walnut side chair, Philadelphia, circa 1760, with a serpentine crest-rail centered by a shell flanked by foliate boughs and shell-carved ears over fluted stiles, 41³/₄ in. high.
(Christie's) $110,000

One of a set of six Edwardian painted satinwood dining chairs, each with stepped and finialed toprail above a pierced lattice lower rail, on square tapering saber legs.
(Christie's)   (Six)
                          $6,142

Pair of George II carved mahogany side chairs, each with serpentine crestrail carved with leafage and flowerheads over a pierced and carved baluster-form splat.
(Butterfield & Butterfield)
                          $3,575

An early George III carved mahogany dining chair, after a design in Chippendale's Director, on molded chamfered square legs united by 'H'-stretchers.
(Phillips) $1,602

EASY CHAIRS

George II mahogany wing chair, second quarter 18th century, the bowed seat raised on shell-carved cabriole legs ending in pad feet.
(Butterfield & Butterfield)
$1,980

A late 19th century Foot's patent invalid's winged armchair, upholstered in leather.
(Dreweatt Neate) $1,950

Antique American Chippendale wing chair in mahogany, square legs.
(Eldred's) $660

Louis XV Provincial carved walnut bergere, third quarter 18th century, the shaped seat raised on scroll-carved cabriole legs.
(Butterfield & Butterfield) $1,650

American iron campaign folding arm chair, 19th century, with pale gray buttoned leather upholstery.
(Butterfield & Butterfield) $550

Stainless steel and leather lounge chair, with head roll, supported by leather buckled straps on X-shape stainless steel frame, $29^{1}/_{2}$in. high.
(Skinner Inc. $550

An early Georgian wing armchair, on cabriole legs carved with scallop shells on claw-and-ball feet, one front leg replaced, rerailed.
(Christie's) $1,716

A Victorian walnut nursing chair, with needlework upholstery, the carved top rail with gilt metal cresting above a bowed seat on turned legs.
(Bonhams) $673

Fine antique American Chippendale wing chair with mahogany frame, chamfered straight legs with stretchers, red brocade damask upholstery, 44in. high.
(Eldred's) $3,410

EASY CHAIRS

One of a pair of Louis XV style needlepoint-upholstered painted bergères, mid-19th century, raised on cabriole legs.
(Butterfield & Butterfield)
$4,400

One of a matched pair of mid-Victorian ebonized bergères of shell shape, each covered in floral silk brocade with turned tapering legs.
(Christie's)   (Two)
$2,922

Louis XIV carved walnut tapestry upholstered fauteuil, on scroll supports united by flattened wavy X-form stretchers.
(Butterfield & Butterfield)
$6,600

Italian rococo carved walnut armchair, third quarter 18th century, the scrolled arms above a serpentine-fronted seat, raised on cabriole legs ending in hoof feet.
(Butterfield & Butterfield)
$2,475

Italian rococo walnut bergère, late 18th century, the out-scrolled arms with caned sides, the shaped seat raised on molded cabriole legs.
(Butterfield & Butterfield)
$1,100

Louis XIV style walnut needlepoint upholstered fauteuil, the raking domed back and square seat upholstered in tones of blues, beige and red with stylized flowering plants.
(Butterfield & Butterfield)
$880

A Queen Anne walnut wing armchair covered in later yellow and purple patterned needlework on cabriole legs joined by a turned H-shaped stretcher.
(Christie's) $3,861

Empire style carved mahogany fauteuil, the serpentine crestrail carved with opposed scrolls and foliate sprigs.
(Butterfield & Butterfield)
$880

A good early George III mahogany 'Gainsborough' armchair, the arm supports carved with crisp outscrolling and continuing to the molded square front legs.
(Tennants) $10,587

EASY CHAIRS

A Charles X mahogany bergère with outswept toprail, the arms with lappeted and anthemion decoration on slight saber legs headed by anthemia.
(Christie's) $1,920

A Victorian walnut armchair, the curved top rail with central strapwork cartouche flanked by ribbed carving, on leaf carved and fluted tapered legs.
(Bonhams) $746

A George II mahogany wing armchair, the serpentine back, outscrolled arms, padded seat and squab cushion upholstered in gray velvet, on cabriole legs.
(Phillips) $3,916

A Federal inlaid mahogany lolling-chair, Massachusetts, 1790–1810, with downswept line-inlaid supports above a padded trapezoidal seat, 46in. high.
(Christie's) $10,450

Two similar Louis XV carved walnut fauteuils en cabriolet, third quarter 18th century, on cabriole supports.
(Butterfield & Butterfield) $2,750

A late 18th/early 19th century carved beechwood elbow chair with a guilloche frame, the oval upholstered panel back with riband cresting and stuffover seat.
(Phillips) $1,034

A Regency mahogany bergère, the rectangular caned back, arms and seat with squab cushion covered in ivy-patterned chintz.
(Christie's) $4,023

A George III mahogany wing armchair, the padded rectangular back, arms and seat covered in close-nailed green leather, on square chamfered legs.
(Christie's) $5,947

A George II mahogany wing armchair, the rectangular back, outscrolled arms, seat and cushion upholstered in stuffover green velvet, on cabriole legs.
(Phillips) $3,498

EASY CHAIRS

A late Regency mahogany bergère with caned slightly bowed panel back, arms and seat within a reeded frame, on turned legs and castors.
(Christie's) $7,294

A late 19th century pink upholstered chair, on turned legs, in the form of a scallop shell.
(Bonhams) $463

A George III giltwood open armchair with oval padded back, arms and bowed seat covered in light blue silk, the frontrail re-supported, stamped *T M* and with ink inscription.
(Christie's) $2,710

A Georgian style wingback armchair, on claw and ball feet with needlework upholstery.
(Bonhams) $890

Pair of Italian baroque giltwood armchairs, early 18th century, each with a domed tapering tall back and molded outswept arms.
(Butterfield & Butterfield)
$13,200

A Regency rosewood side chair with scroll back and seat covered in gros-point foliate needlework, on ring-turned tapering legs and brass caps.
(Christie's) $1,736

A Victorian walnut armchair, with needlework upholstery, the top rail curving down into arms with carved scrolled supports on cabriole legs.
(Bonhams) $708

An early Georgian walnut armchair, the padded rectangular back, outward scrolling arms and seat covered in blue velvet, on cabriole legs headed by scallop shells.
(Christie's) $6,376

One of a pair of Directoire white painted and gilt heightened fauteuils, the rectangular padded backs, open arms and bowed stuffover seat with anthemion and rosette decoration.
(Phillips)   (Two) $6,764

EASY CHAIRS

One of a pair of George IV white-painted and parcel-gilt bergères attributed to George Seddon, covered in black-ground 'Adamite' silk. (Christie's) (Two) $12,243

One of a pair of early Victorian giltwood side-chairs, the arched backs and squared seats upholstered with silk strapwork appliqué on a dark green silk velvet ground. (Christie's) (Two) $4,428

A fine George II carved mahogany open armchair, having a stuffover seat and carved undulating seat rail with rocaille ornament, on cabriole legs. (Phillips) $23,850

A late Victorian mahogany and leather campaign chair, the folding rectangular back with ring-turned side supports, on turned baluster legs and brass caps. (Christie's) $1,417

Louis XV style painted and parcel-gilt fauteuil à la reine, circa 1860–1880, with cartouche paneled back, centerpad arms and serpentine feet. (Butterfield & Butterfield) $1,980

One of a pair of George III mahogany open armchairs in the French manner with arched padded back, outward scrolling arms and serpentine seat covered in associated 18th century Aubusson tapestry. (Christie's) (Two) $29,040

One of a pair of George IV rosewood spoonback library open armchairs with arched curved padded back, bowed seats and padded arms covered in close-nailed brown suede. (Christie's) (Two) $14,520

A George II mahogany small sofa with high padded back, upholstered in floral cut-velvet on cabriole legs headed by shells and husks, 38in. wide. (Christie's) $12,584

One of a pair of George III later decorated open armchairs, in the French taste, having padded scroll arm supports and stuffover seats with palmette decorated seat rails, on cabriole legs. (Phillips) (Two) $5,656

EASY CHAIRS

A Regénce style walnut fauteuil à l'oreilles, the padded back and arms within a rocaille carved frame, on cabriole legs.
(Bonhams) $745

One of a pair of mid-Victorian ebonised spoon-back chairs, each with padded buttoned arch back and seat covered in yellow damask.
(Christie's)   (Two)
             $6,195

A Queen Anne walnut wing armchair with padded back, outscrolled arms, bowed seat and squab cushion covered in gros-point needlework.
(Christie's) $15,074

One of a pair of George II mahogany library armchairs, the curved padded arms ending in out-turned realistically carved dolphins' heads, 41in. high.
(Christie's)   (Two)
         $506,220

A William IV mahogany reclining open armchair, on ring-turned tapering legs and brass caps, stamped twice *R Colvil* at the base of the arms, the slide front possibly reveneered.
(Christie's) $2,479

One of a pair of mahogany and parcel-gilt open armchairs of George II style, the arm terminals with ormolu tips, the eared cabriole legs carved with acanthus and flower-heads, on hairy paw feet, 19th century.
(Christie's) $29,040

A Georgian mahogany frame wing armchair, the back, scroll arms and stuffover seat upholstered in 18th century hookstitch and gros point needlework.
(Phillips) $5,656

A Regency mahogany open armchair by Gillows, the high curved padded back, arms and seat covered in beige patterned cotton, on turned legs.
(Christie's) $797

One of a pair of early George III mahogany library armchairs covered in nailed pale olive green floral silk damask, the outscrolled arms carved with foliage, blind fretwork and scrolls, 38³⁄₄in. high.
(Christie's) $223,905

EASY CHAIRS

George III beech open armchair in the French taste, circa 1780, raised on stiff-leaf carved and fluted turned tapering supports. (Butterfield & Butterfield) $1,650

Chippendale mahogany and walnut easy chair, Southern New England, 1760–90, 45in. high. (Skinner Inc.) $12,100

Venetian rococo painted and parcel gilt armchair, mid 18th century, 44in. high. (Skinner Inc.) $2,200

L. & J.G. Stickley armchair, No. 420, circa 1910, four horizontal back slats, leather upholstery spring cushion seat, 42in. high. (Skinner Inc.) $550

A mid-Victorian walnut music-bergère of Louis XV style with padded back, arms and serpentine seat covered in close-nailed striped velvet with silk brocade. (Christie's) $1,355

An oak armchair of Queen Anne style with padded back, arms and seat sewn with needlework flowers on eared cabriole legs. (Christie's) $968

A William IV mahogany bow-back library armchair, the scrolling acanthus carved back and arms above a bowed seat on reeded tapering legs. (Christie's) $1,274

Queen Anne walnut carved easy chair, Pennsylvania, circa 1740–60, shell-carved knees and pad feet with carving, 20th century upholstery, 41in. high. (Skinner Inc.) $53,900

One of a pair of Directoire walnut fauteuils, late 18th century, each with a bowed fan-shaped back and outcurved arms. (Butterfield & Butterfield) $3,850

EASY CHAIRS

A Victorian walnut nursing chair with original Berlin woolwork upholstery, on cabriole legs.
(Bearne's) $1,084

A George III mahogany tub bergere, the deeply curved padded back, seat and squab cushion covered in white calico.
(Christie's) $2,130

A Victorian rosewood-framed armchair, the oval padded back with flower head cresting.
(Bearne's) $1,410

George III mahogany and needlepoint upholstered wing chair, third quarter 18th century, on carved chamfered legs joined by stretchers, 46in. high.
(Skinner Inc.) $3,300

Venetian rococo giltwood armchair, mid 18th century, serpentine upholstered seat raised on cabriole legs, 34³/₄in. high.
(Skinner Inc.) $1,870

Spanish baroque carved walnut armchair, the square panel back and seat upholstered in floral cut silk velvet, the downswept arms ending in foliated scroll finials.
(Butterfield & Butterfield) $935

A 19th century Anglo-Indian coromandel open armchair carved with a shell, scrolling foliage, flowers and fruit, on cabriole legs.
(Bearne's) $1,307

Italian Renaissance style walnut and green-cut velvet upholstered armchair, 37in. high.
(Skinner Inc.) $495

Continental rococo walnut armchair, mid-18th century, the cartouche-paneled back, center-pad arms and serpentine seat upholstered in green velvet.
(Butterfield & Butterfield) $2,750

George I walnut and needlepoint upholstered wing chair, first quarter 18th century, on cabriole legs ending in pointed feet, 48³/₄in. high.
(Skinner Inc.) $4,400

A Regency mahogany tub bergère, the arched padded back, arms and slightly bowed seat covered in close-nailed brown leather.
(Christie's) $4,722

One of a set of green and grey-painted seat furniture of Transitional style comprising four bergères and a canapé each with padded curved back, late 19th century.
(Christie's)   (Five)

$6,939

One of a pair of mahogany chairs of early George II style, upholstered in close-nailed floral needlework, the downswept arms carved with berried foliage, on cabriole legs, early 20th century.
(Christie's)   (Two)

$8,131

Pair of Louis XV carved polished beech fauteuils à la reine, third quarter 18th century, on molded cabriole supports, brown leather upholsteries.
(Butterfield & Butterfield)

$13,200

A fine George III carved giltwood open armchair, attributable to Thomas Chippendale, the oval upholstered panel back with pierced riband and laurel swag cresting within a guilloche border.(Phillips) $28,620

Biedermeier walnut wing armchair, German, circa 1810–1820, with flaring arms and scrollover padded arms, raised on square tapering supports.
(Butterfield & Butterfield)

$1,430

One of a pair of William IV mahogany library armchairs, each with buttoned crested bow back with three pierced tear drop splats.
(Christie's)   (Two)

$3,071

Directoire walnut bergère, late 18th century, with a raking tall back and square seat above a reeded seatrail raised on turned tapering supports.
(Butterfield & Butterfield)

$3,025

ELBOW CHAIRS

A Regency simulated rosewood spoon-back side chair, with padded seat and on saber legs with brass caps, lacking covering.
(Christie's) $708

Queen Anne maple carved arm chair, Connecticut River Valley, 18th century, 36in. high.
(Skinner Inc.) $4,950

A mahogany open armchair of George II style with pierced curved back with vase-shaped and columnar splats, 19th century.
(Christie's) $1,549

A late Victorian painted satinwood bergère, the cane back centered by an oval portrait medallion, the downswept arms continuing into tapering turned legs.
(Bearne's) $1,514

A Regency mahogany library reading-chair in the manner of Morgan & Saunders, the deeply curved back with scroll terminals and adjustable sliding reading-slope.
(Christie's) $5,947

One of a matched pair of Anglo-Dutch mahogany metamorphic wing-backed open armchairs, on cabriole legs and pad feet, opening to become a daybed, mid-18th century, 84¼in. long, extended.
(Christie's)   (Two) $36,784

One of a set of nine late George III mahogany dining chairs, with rectangular bowed toprail and horizontal splats between reeded arms, on square tapering legs.
(Christie's)   (Nine) $7,678

Antique American plank seat Windsor armchair with bamboo turnings.
(Eldred's) $99

A late Elizabethan oak X-frame chair carved with scrolling foliage within a double-guilloche arch, with molded sides, hipped scrolling arms and planked seat.
(Christie's) $7,160

ELBOW CHAIRS

One of a set of eight George III style mahogany shield-backed dining chairs, on square section tapered legs.
(Bonhams)   (Eight)
$1,424

Two of six L. & J.G. Stickley chairs, circa 1912, comprised of one armchair, no. 802, and five side chairs, no. 800, 36½in. high.
(Skinner Inc.) $1,700

Gustav Stickley reclining chair, No. 346, circa 1905, four horizontal back slats, flat arms over square post legs, 30in. wide.
(Skinner Inc.) $1,100

A pair of Directoire style parcel-gilt and carved walnut fauteuils, late 19th century, the downswept arms above urn-form supports.
(Butterfield & Butterfield)
$2,750

A Yorkshire ash panel-back open armchair, the rectangular paneled back with waved scroll-carved cresting flanked by scrolls, mid-17th century.
(Christie's) $3,769

Two of a set of ten Federal carved mahogany chairs, Philadelphia or Baltimore, circa 1800–1810, on square tapering legs joined by H-stretchers.
(Butterfield & Butterfield)
$8,800

A Chippendale walnut armchair, Pennsylvania, 1750–1780, the serpentine crestrail with scrolling ears centering a shell above a spurred vase-shaped splat and serpentine, scrolling arms, 41½in. high.
(Christie's) $27,500

Pair of neoclassical style parcel-gilt and cream-painted armchairs, 19th century, the rectangular arms above a caned seat, raised on tapering square legs.
(Butterfield & Butterfield)
$2,750

A George III mahogany open armchair with waved eared toprail and pierced vase-shaped splat, on canted square legs joined by an H-shaped stretcher.
(Christie's) $1,413

ELBOW CHAIRS

A Federal carved mahogany armchair, with scrolling molded tablet crestrail flanked by reeded stiles over X-shaped molded ribs, 35in. high.
(Christie's) $2,420

Two of a set of six antique English George II mahogany dining chairs comprising one armchair and five side chairs, circa 1760.
(Selkirk's) (Six)
          $3,750

A Regency armchair, the turned top rail above a horizontal tablet splat and a turned splat.
(Bonhams) $320

Two of six "Linear" chairs, attributed to Luigi Tagliabue, Italy, two armchairs, four side curved plank-back, 27in. high.
(Skinner Inc.) $2,400

A Charles I oak open armchair, the rectangular paneled back with raised cresting incised *RM 1640*, with carved apron.
(Christie's) $1,413

Two of four satinwood dining-chairs including two open armchairs, each with pierced shield-shaped back painted with an oval.
(Christie's) $4,706

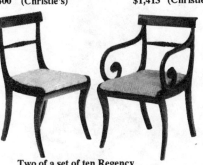

A James II oak open armchair, the paneled rectangular back carved with strapwork, the toprail carved *1686* flanked by animal scrolls.
(Christie's) $3,580

Two of a set of ten Regency carved mahogany dining chairs, first quarter 19th century, comprising eight side chairs and two armchairs.
(Butterfield & Butterfield)
          $6,600

Shaker maple armed rocker, New Lebanon, New York, circa 1850, old splint seat over-upholstered, 44¾in. high.
(Skinner Inc.) $10,450

ELBOW CHAIRS

A Queen Anne walnut armchair, Pennsylvania, 1740–1760, the scrolling arms with incurved supports above a trapezoidal slip seat concealing the support for a chamber pot, 42½in. high. (Christie's) $3,080

Handcraft Furniture slant back Morris chair, circa 1910, No. 497, stationary back with wide arms over five vertical slats, 41in. high. (Skinner Inc.) $2,310

An important antique Italian Louis XV parcel-gilt creme lacqué fauteuil, the cartouche shaped back inset with cane and carved foliate motifs, circa 1750. (Selkirk's) $2,300

An English walnut open armchair with arched back and oval cane-filled splat, the toprail carved with acanthus, on keeled scroll legs headed by acanthus, basically late 17th century. (Christie's) $2,145

Stickley Brothers inlaid settle, Grand Rapids, Michigan, circa 1901, inlaid with flowers, leaves, grasses and other naturalistic motifs, unmarked, 51¾in. high. (Skinner Inc.) $3,000

A 19th century mahogany 'curule' open armchair after the design of Thomas Hope, the wide top rail with tapered finials and carved with a central roundel. (Tennants) $2,976

A Chippendale carved walnut roundabout chair, Rhode Island, 1760–1780, with a serpentine slip-seat and cabriole front leg carved with a scallop shell and pendant bellflower, 31¾in. high. (Christie's) $49,500

One of a pair of Liberty and Co. large oak armchairs, with rectangular upholstered red leather backs and seats, the wings carved with mythical beasts. (Christie's) (Two) $4,092

A Robert 'Mouseman' Thompson oak armchair, the horseshoe-shaped arm and back with carved splats bearing carved shield. (Christie's) $985

ELBOW CHAIRS

A Charles II oak open armchair with rectangular paneled back carved with scrolls and flowerheads and *THOMAS IEPSON*, on baluster legs.
(Christie's) $4,145

An Italian throne chair in walnut, gilt and other woods, with twin curled leaf crests, upholstered rectangular back and seat on plain square legs, 17th century and later.
(Tennants) $1,302

Antique American corner commode chair in maple, square legs, slip seat, 32in. high.
(Eldred's) $248

A Bohemian satin birch armchair, with downcurved arms, on scrolling supports, with upholstered seat, on square section tapered legs.
(Bonhams) $484

A Regency simulated-bamboo low chair with spindle back and arms, the rectangular seat covered in later needlework woven with a dog within a red velvet border, 24³/₄in. wide.
(Christie's) $1,507

An English walnut open armchair with rectangular cane-filled back and toprail carved with putti supporting a laurel wreath, lacking part of front feet, incorporating some 17th century carved elements.
(Christie's) $1,073

Antique American sack-back Windsor armchair, Rhode Island, 18th century, in pine, maple and other woods.
(Eldred's) $468

Adjustable-back Morris chair, circa 1910, flat arms supported by short corbels over three vertical slats, unsigned, 40¹/₂in. high.
(Skinner Inc.) $1,600

An oak Liberty & Co. Moorish side chair, the plain seat with elaborately carved apron, on turned column legs.
(Christie's) $1,432

ELBOW CHAIRS

An Empire mahogany and giltmetal mounted fauteuil, the toprail with gilt classical maidens above a bowed padded seat flanked by Egyptian stiles. (Christie's) $1,728

A pair of Clisset Highback ash armchairs designed by Ernest Gimson, with ladder backs above rush seats. (Christie's) $1,181

A George III mahogany open armchair (lacking upholstery) with an oval fluted back and serpentine seat rail, on square tapering channeled legs. (Phillips) $1,335

One of a pair of yew and elm Windsor chairs with hooped spindled back and pierced violin-splat above a solid seat, early 19th century. (Christie's)   (Two) $1,440

A pair of Gordon Russell turned yew armchairs, the spindle filled back with two tall bun finials, on turned legs with bar stretchers. (Christie's) $1,772

One of a pair of Regency ebonized and parcel-gilt open armchairs, on ring-turned tapering legs, re-decorated, minor differences in seat rail construction and proportions. (Christie's)   (Two) $3,072

A George III gothic green, white and red-painted open armchair decorated overall with vine-leaves, on square chamfered legs joined by an H-shaped stretcher. (Christie's) $3,098

Two of a set of ten Colonial hardwood and brass-mounted dining chairs including two open armchairs, on saber legs, late 19th century. (Christie's)   (Ten) $4,102

One of a set of six mahogany dining chairs, of mid Georgian design, with a drop-in seat, on square chamfered legs joined by stretchers. (Christie's)   (Six) $3,839

FURNITURE

ELBOW CHAIRS

A yew wood and elm Windsor arm chair, early 19th century, the low back with pierced splat, solid seat and turned legs united by a crinoline stretcher.
(Tennants) $1,023

Two of a set of five 19th century Dutch mahogany and marquetry dining chairs, decorated with trailing floral tendrils, the backs with shaped arched top rails.
(Phillips)   (Five) $3,916

A Regency mahogany caned library bergère, the bowed back with hide cushion seat on turned reeded legs.
(Christie's) $4,607

A mid-Georgian walnut corner chair, the curved back with scrolled arm-supports and pierced vase-shaped splats, on turned supports.
(Christie's) $1,771

Two of a set of fourteen mahogany dining chairs, each with oval back and pierced uprights, on square tapering legs.
(Christie's)   (Fourteen)
                            $4,475

Charles II walnut armchair, second half 17th century, rectangular pierced foliate-carved back centered by a caned panel, 46in. high.
(Skinner Inc.) $495

Dutch baroque walnut and marquetry armchair, mid 18th century, on cabriole legs ending in ball and claw feet, joined by stretchers, 44¼in. high.
(Skinner Inc.) $2,420

Two of a set of eight William IV mahogany dining chairs, each with bowed bar toprail carved with gadrooning, on reeded tapering legs, possibly Scottish.
(Christie's)   (Eight)
                            $7,831

One of a pair of late George III grained and parcel-gilt open armchairs, each with arched caned back and ball decorated splat above bowed caned seat.
(Christie's)   (Two)
                            $5,759

CHESTS OF DRAWERS

A walnut chest with herringbone bandings, fitted with two short and three long drawers, on ogee bracket feet, 31in. wide, part 18th century.
(Bonhams) $850

A late Federal mahogany veneer chest-of-drawers, New York, 1810–1820, the rectangular top above a conforming case fitted with a crossbanded long drawer veneered in imitation of three short drawers, 46½in. wide.
(Christie's) $2,200

Antique American Hepplewhite bowfront chest in cherry, cock beaded drawer fronts, French feet, brass knobs, 41in. wide.
(Eldred's) $1,540

A Federal inlaid mahogany chest-of-drawers, New York, 1790–1810, on flaring bracket feet, appears to retain original brasses, 45¼in. wide.
(Christie's) $2,200

A Makers of Simple Furniture birchwood chest of drawers designed by Gerald Summers, on platform base, 68.5cm. wide.
(Christie's) $709

A Federal mahogany bow-front chest-of-drawers, Eastern Connecticut, 1790–1810, the rectangular top with bowed front over a conforming case, on French feet, 43½in. wide.
(Christie's) $2,640

Chippendale mahogany reverse serpentine chest of drawers, Massachusetts, 1760–80, drawers with cockbeaded surrounds, 39¼in. wide.
(Skinner Inc.) $13,200

A Federal mahogany and figured maple veneered chest-of-drawers, Boston, Massachusetts, 1790–1810, on bracketed turned tapering feet, 42in. wide.
(Christie's) $5,500

Painted Chippendale chest of drawers, New England, mid 18th century, document drawer, old red paint, 37¾in. wide.
(Skinner Inc.) $2,200

Child's whalebone and exotic woods inlaid mahogany chest of drawers, America, 19th century, 27¹/₂in. wide.
(Skinner Inc.) $4,950

South German baroque inlaid walnut serpentine-fronted chest of drawers, early 18th century, the shaped top with two panels inlaid with a bird perched before a floral sprig, 4ft. wide.
(Butterfield & Butterfield) $10,450

William and Mary oak chest of drawers, fitted with two short over three geometrically fronted drawers, on bracket feet, 40in. wide.
(Butterfield & Butterfield) $1,650

Antique American Sheraton four-drawer bureau, circa 1800, in mahogany and maple, back splash, cock beaded drawers, shaped apron, peg feet, 39¹/₂in. wide.
(Eldred's) $605

Painted birch chest of drawers, Northern New England, circa 1800, drawers beaded, all over original red paint, 43³/₄in. wide.
(Skinner Inc.) $3,850

George II walnut chest of drawers, the cross-banded rectangular top with canted corners above two short and three graduated long drawers, 39¹/₂in. wide.
(Butterfield & Butterfield) $3,025

Federal bird's-eye maple and mahogany veneered bow-front bureau, New England, early 19th century, 41¹/₄in. wide.
(Skinner Inc.) $1,045

Maple and pine tall chest, New England, circa 1800, refinished, replaced brasses, 36in. wide.
(Skinner Inc.) $3,300

Federal mahogany veneer and cherry chest of drawers, Connecticut River Valley, circa 1800, brasses replaced, 41in. wide.
(Skinner Inc.) $2,310

CHESTS OF DRAWERS

A late George III inlaid mahogany serpentine chest, the later eared top with central shell motif, on later bracket feet, 36in. wide.
(Christie's) $2,610

Fine pine grained and bird's-eye maple painted apothecary chest, New England, 19th century, with rectangular gallery above thirty-two small graduated drawers, 6ft. ¹/₂in. high.
(Butterfield & Butterfield) $27,500

A Chippendale maple chest-of-drawers, New England, 1760–1780, the molded rectangular top above a conforming case fitted with four thumbmolded graduated long drawers, 38¹/₂in. wide.
(Christie's) $1,320

Continental rococo inlaid walnut small chest of drawers, possibly Dutch, third quarter 18th century, surmounted by a brocatelle marble top of shaped outline, 26³/₄in. wide.
(Butterfield & Butterfield) $3,025

Pair of Swedish Biedermeier figured maple chests of drawers, second quarter 19th century, raised on bracket feet, 35in. wide.
(Butterfield & Butterfield) $11,000

A mid Victorian walnut and rosewood banded Wellington chest, the rectangular top above six drawers flanked by a locking stile, 16¹/₂in. wide.
(Christie's) $2,367

A George III mahogany serpentine chest with eared top above four graduated long drawers and on later shaped bracket feet, 39¹/₄in. wide.
(Christie's) $3,098

Chippendale painted tall blanket chest, New England, circa 1800, the top opens to a well with three drawers below, old dark red paint, 37¹/₂in. wide.
(Skinner Inc.) $3,025

A walnut and oak chest, the coffered rectangular top above four long fielded, graduated drawers on bun feet, late 17th century, 42in. wide.
(Christie's) $2,879

CHESTS OF DRAWERS

Flemish rococo carved oak chest of drawers, Liège, second quarter 18th century, of slightly serpentine outline with fielded panel sides, 4ft. 8³/₄in. wide. (Butterfield & Butterfield)
$6,600

An oak ebonized low chest designed by Denham MacLaren, the rectangular top above two long drawers with rectangular slit hand grips, 106.7cm. wide. (Christie's)
$1,969

Chippendale carved walnut highboy base, Pennsylvania, 18th century, 20th century top, refinished, replaced brasses, 38¹/₂in. wide. (Skinner Inc.)
$800

A William and Mary walnut-veneered chest, with crossbanding and ebony stringing, ovolo carcase moldings and on later bun feet, 39in. wide. (Bearne's)
$998

A Chippendale mahogany block-front chest-of-drawers, Boston, Massachusetts, 1760–1780, the molded rectangular top with blocked and shaped front above a conforming case, on bracket feet, appears to retain original brasses, 36in. wide. (Christie's)
$55,000

A Chippendale cherrywood block-front chest-of-drawers, Connecticut, circa 1775, with blocked front edge above a conforming case fitted with four graduated long drawers above a molded base, on ogee bracket feet, 37¹/₂in. wide. (Christie's)
$9,900

Antique American Chippendale six-drawer tall chest in maple, graduated drawers, molded cornice, bracket base, 38in. wide. (Eldred's)
$1,870

An American Federal mahogany and maple dressing bureau in the manner of John and Thomas Seymour of Boston, on turned tapering reeded legs, 38¹/₂in. wide. (Christie's)
$5,759

A Dutch mahogany and marquetry chest, variously inlaid with a basket of flowers and foliage, on tapering square feet, 37¹/₄in. wide. (Bearne's)
$5,332

A George III mahogany chest with molded canted serpentine top, on angled bracket feet, 41in. wide.
(Christie's) $5,034

Italian neoclassical painted chest of drawers, late 18th century, fitted with three long drawers painted with cornucopiae, baskets of fruit and scrolls, 4ft. ³/₄in. wide.
(Butterfield & Butterfield)
                               $23,100

Chippendale mahogany veneer serpentine chest of drawers, Philadelphia, circa 1789, probably the work of Jonathan Gostelowe (1744–1795), 48in. wide.
(Skinner Inc.) $23,100

A Chippendale mahogany veneer chest-of-drawers, Salem, Massachusetts, 1760–1780, the molded serpentine top over a conforming case fitted with four cockbeaded graduated long drawers, on ogee bracket feet, 42in. wide.
(Christie's) $11,000

A 17th century North Italian ebonized and ivory inlaid chest, containing three long molded panel drawers with filigree scroll roundels, Lombardy, possibly Venetian, 4ft. 10in. wide.
(Phillips) $8,745

A Chippendale carved cherrywood serpentine chest-of-drawers, probably Lyme, Connecticut, 1780–1800, with serpentine front and molded edges, on ogee bracket feet with elaborately double-scrolled brackets, 39¼in. wide.
(Christie's) $28,600

A George III oak chest crossbanded overall, the retangular top above two short and three graduated long drawers, on later bracket feet, 37in. wide.
(Christie's) $1,063

Fine American Renaissance inlaid maple and rosewood tall chest of drawers by Herter Brothers, New York, circa 1872, 37in. wide.
(Butterfield & Butterfield)
                               $20,900

A George III dark-stained harewood and marquetry chest crossbanded overall with rosewood and inlaid with fruitwood lines, on splayed legs, 46in. wide.
(Christie's) $11,369

CHESTS OF DRAWERS

A George III mahogany chest with molded eared serpentine top with slide and four graduated mahogany-lined drawers, on shaped bracket feet, 38in. wide.
(Christie's) $15,488

A Chippendale mahogany serpentine chest-of-drawers, Massachusetts, 1760–1780, on short bracketed cabriole legs with ball-and-claw feet, appears to retain original brasses, 38in. wide.
(Christie's) $30,800

A mahogany chest with moulded serpentine top carved with flower-applied entrelac above a green leather-lined slide and four graduated long drawers, on ogee bracket feet, 39in. wide.
(Christie's) $17,424

A George I walnut and burr-walnut bachelor's chest, the hinged rounded rectangular quarter-veneered top with re-entrant corners above two short and three graduated long drawers, 25³/₄in. wide.
(Christie's) $48,972

A William and Mary oyster-veneered walnut chest, banded overall with fruitwood, the molded rectangular top inlaid with concentric circles and geometric pattern, on later bun feet, 37¹/₄in. wide.
(Christie's) $11,893

An early Georgian walnut chest, the molded rectangular re-entrant top above four graduated long drawers, on shaped bracket feet, 29¹/₂in. wide.
(Christie's) $16,456

A William and Mary walnut chest, crossbanded overall, the molded rectangular quarter-veneered top inlaid with a shaped oval, above three graduated drawers, 36³/₄in. wide.
(Christie's) $9,045

A George III mahogany, boxwood and ebonized serpentine chest with eared cross-banded molded top above a mahogany and oak-lined later-fitted drawer and three graduated drawers, 47in. wide.
(Christie's) $19,360

One of a pair of George III mahogany and crossbanded serpentine front chests, fitted with brushing slides and containing four graduated and cockbeaded drawers, on swept bracket feet, 3ft. 2in. wide.
(Phillips) (Two) $10,335

CHESTS ON CHESTS

Chippendale maple carved chest on chest, New England, circa 1780, old refinish, some original brass, 38³/₄in. wide.
(Skinner Inc.) $13,200

A George I burr walnut and walnut tallboy chest, crossbanded and feather strung, the base with a slide above three long drawers, on shaped bracket feet, 3ft. 6in. wide.
(Phillips) $6,408

A walnut tallboy with a molded cornice above two short and three graduated long drawers between fluted quarter angles, on bracket feet, early 18th century, 42in. wide.
(Christie's S. Ken) $7,979

George III mahogany chest on chest, circa 1770, the drop-fronted secretaire drawer with fitted interior flanked by fluted quarter-round stiles, 4ft. 1in. wide.
(Butterfield & Butterfield) $5,225

Queen Anne maple tall chest, Salisbury, New Hampshire area, School of Bartlett Cabinetmaking, circa 1800, refinished, 36in. wide.
(Skinner Inc.) $4,000

George III mahogany chest-on-chest, late 18th century, with a cavetto-molded cornice, on ogee bracket feet, 40¹/₄in. wide.
(Butterfield & Butterfield) $4,400

George III mahogany chest-on-chest, circa 1800, the thumb-molded denticulated top above two short and two long drawers flanked by canted and fluted stiles, 40in. wide.
(Butterfield & Butterfield) $4,400

Chippendale mahogany carved chest on chest, New London County, Connecticut, 1760–80, on a serpentine lower case, 44¹/₄in. wide.
(Skinner Inc.) $30,800

Late George III mahogany chest-on-chest, first quarter 19th century, the top drawer of the lower section fitted with a later leather-inset writing slide, 40¹/₄in. wide.
(Butterfield & Butterfield) $2,750

CHESTS ON CHESTS

A George I burr-walnut secretaire-tallboy inlaid overall with feather-banding, the base with fitted secretaire-drawer above three graduated long drawers, on bracket feet, 41in. wide.
(Christie's) $50,622

An early 18th century walnut tallboy chest, with burrwood drawer fronts, the upper part with cavetto molded cornice, on later ogee bracket feet, 3ft. 7in. wide. (Phillips) $9,222

Chippendale carved cherrywood and birch bonnet-top chest on chest, New England, late 18th century, on ball-and-claw feet centering a foliate-carved pendant, 38in. wide. (Butterfield & Butterfield) $4,125

A Chippendale figured maple chest-on-chest, New Hampshire, 1760–1790, carved with a fan centered by a pair of short drawers over four long drawers, the lower section with four long drawers, 34¼in. wide.
(Christie's) $17,600

A George III mahogany chest-on-chest, the serpentine front with two short and seven graduated long drawers divided by reeded bands, on short cabriole legs ending in scrolled feet, 47¼in. wide.
(Christie's) $77,880

An early Georgian walnut chest-on-chest, inlaid overall with feather-banding, with molded rectangular cornice above two doors enclosing drawers of various sizes, on later bracket feet, 44in. wide.
(Christie's) $9,422

Chippendale maple tall chest of drawers, Rhode Island, late 18th century, the molded cornice above the thumb-molded edge, on bracket feet, 39¼in. wide.
(Butterfield & Butterfield) $3,575

A George III Welsh oak chest on chest, the upper part with molded cornice and flute molded frieze above, the whole raised on bracket feet, 41in. wide.
(Spencer's) $1,536

George III mahogany chest-on-chest, circa 1800, in two parts, the molded cornice above a cock-beaded divided top drawer over three similar long drawers, 43½in. wide.
(Butterfield & Butterfield) $2,475

CHESTS ON STANDS

A William and Mary oak high chest-of-drawers, English, late 17th century, on six spiral-turned legs joined by shaped stretchers with compressed ball feet, 38¹/₂in. wide.
(Christie's) $3,300

Queen Anne cherry high chest of drawers, Rhode Island or Connecticut, 1750–70, brasses appear original, 46in. wide.
(Skinner Inc.) $8,800

A Queen Anne walnut veneered high chest-of-drawers, Massachusetts, 1730–1750, on cabriole legs with pad-and-disc feet, signed in chalk on lower background *J. Davis [?]*, 39in. wide.
(Christie's) $38,500

A William and Mary black and gilt-japanned chest-on-stand, decorated with birds, figures and buildings within chinoiserie landscapes, the base part late 17th century, 40in. wide.
(Christie's) $6,595

A walnut and marquetry chest-on-stand crossbanded and inlaid overall with floral panels and boxwood and ebonized lines, on spirally-turned legs joined by waved stretchers, late 17th century, 38¹/₂in. wide.
(Christie's) $7,915

A William and Mary oyster-veneered chest, the top geometrically inlaid with boxwood lines, on a later stand with twist-turned supports, bun feet and flat stretchers, 33¹/₂in. wide.
(Bearne's) $3,440

A William and Mary oyster-veneered walnut chest-on-stand inlaid overall with sycamore, the rectangular top with circles and scrolls, on later barley-twist legs, 41in. wide.
(Christie's) $6,021

A William and Mary walnut chest-on-stand, with molded cornice above a pair of doors enclosing seven variously-sized drawers around ̶ ̶ ̶ ̶tral door, 28¹/₄in. wide.
(Christie's) $7,438

Queen Anne maple chest on frame, New Hampshire, circa 1760, old refinish, brasses probably original, 38in. wide.
(Skinner Inc.) $7,700

CHIFFONIERS

A Regency giltmetal-mounted brass-inlaid rosewood and simulated rosewood bonheur-du-jour in the manner of John McLean, 32³/₄in. wide.
(Christie's) $12,370

An Edwardian rosewood and marquetry side cabinet, with broken scroll pediment, spindle-turned uprights and pair of glazed hinged compartments, 60¹/₂in. wide.
(Christie's) $1,865

A William IV rosewood chiffonier, the mirrored back carved with lotus, acanthus and scrolls, on a concave plinth base, 54in. wide.
(Bearne's) $1,686

A William IV mahogany chiffonier, the single shelf superstructure on turned front supports, on a plinth base, 41¹/₂in. wide.
(Bonhams) $1,780

A classical mahogany and parcel-gilt sideboard, New York State, first quarter 19th century, the rectangular molded top with upswept scrolling three-quarter splashboard over a conforming case fitted with a pair of bolection-molded short drawers, 49¹/₂in. wide.
(Christie's) $2,860

A Regency brass-mounted red ebony chiffonier with three-quarter scroll-galleried rectangular top above a shaped shelf, 33in. wide.
(Christie's) $6,661

A Regency rosewood and banded chiffonier, the rectangular brass three-quarter galleried mirrored ledged back top with turned supports, 36³/₄in. wide.
(Christie's) $2,303

A late Victorian walnut coromandel and inlaid sideboard by Gillows, the raised back with a rectangular plate flanked by blind fret panels, 65³/₄in. wide.
(Tennants) $2,232

A Regency rosewood chiffonier, the shelved superstructure with a pierced brass gallery above a beaded frieze and a pair of upholstered paneled doors, 33in. wide.
(Christie's S. Ken) $3,768

289

COMMODES & POTCUPBOARDS

A George III mahogany tray top night commode.
(Dreweatt Neate)   **$1,268**

A pair of Italian walnut and parquetry bedside commodes, the doors, back and sides with rectangular panels of parquetry squares, 2ft. 3in. high.
(Phillips)   **$7,424**

A George III mahogany bedside commode, the sides pierced with carrying-handles, above a pull-out-section with later green leather-lined top and waved apron, 21in. wide.
(Christie's)   **$1,328**

A George III mahogany tray top bedside cupboard, 15³/₄in. wide.
(Dreweatt Neate)   **$1,209**

A pair of late Regency mahogany bedside tables, each with a folded rectangular twin flap top, stamped *Gillows Lancaster*, 32in. wide open.
(Christie's)   **$7,294**

A George III mahogany bedside cupboard attributed to Thomas Chippendale, on tapering legs headed by roundel bosses, 29in. high.
(Christie's)   **$58,410**

A Regency mahogany bedside commode by Gillows of Lancaster, with a drawer and a door and a pull-out section on legs enclosing a bidet, on turned reeded legs, 20in. wide.
(Christie's)   **$3,896**

A pair of mid Victorian mahogany bedside cupboards with slightly raised backs, molded tops and with opposed panel doors, 15¹/₂in. wide.
(Tennants)   **$1,395**

An early George III mahogany tray top commode, with a shaped three-quarter gallery and pierced carrying handles above a pair of cupboard doors and fitted pull-out commode drawer, 1ft. 9in. wide.
(Phillips)   **$2,314**

COMMODE CHESTS

A late 18th century Milanese walnut and marquetry commode, the rectangular quarter veneered top with a pastoral scene of a figure and oxen within an oval, on square tapering legs (water damaged), 4ft. 2in. wide.
(Phillips) $12,816

A George III harewood, rosewood and marquetry commode, the banded eared serpentine top inlaid with a bird eating at a basket of fruit, on splayed feet, 49½in. wide.
(Christie's) $27,110

Louis XV/XVI transitional style marquetry commode of slight breakfront outline, the breche d'Alep marble top above a drawer mounted with gilt-bronze entrelac frieze, 4ft. 5in. wide.
(Butterfield & Butterfield) $3,575

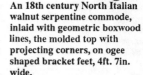

A George III mahogany commode with eared molded serpentine top above four graduated long drawers flanked by scrolled canted angles carved with acanthus, possibly 19th century, 45in. wide.
(Christie's) $16,456

A small Continental kingwood commode in Louis XV style, the bombé front fitted with two drawers, divided by inlaid brass fluting, on cabriole legs, 19½in. wide.
(Tennants) $5,952

An 18th century North Italian walnut serpentine commode, inlaid with geometric boxwood lines, the molded top with projecting corners, on ogee shaped bracket feet, 4ft. 7in. wide.
(Phillips) $7,120

One of a pair of Italian neoclassical walnut and parquetry small commodes, late 18th century, on square tapering legs, 23in. wide.
(Skinner Inc.) (Two) $6,600

Régence gilt-bronze-mounted inlaid kingwood galbé commode, stamped *J.M. Chevalier*, mid-18th century, surmounted by a brèche marble top with a molded edge, 36¼in. wide.
(Butterfield & Butterfield) $15,400

A Louis XV-style kingwood and marquetry bombé commode, the pink veined marble serpentine top above drawers inlaid sans travers with scrolling foliage and flowers.
(Bearne's) $1,582

COMMODE CHESTS

A 19th century French ormolu mounted black lacquer and mother-o'-pearl inlaid bombé commode, in the manner of Dubois, surmounted by a molded gray braccia serpentine top, 5ft. 1/2in. wide. (Phillips) $9,540

Louis XV Provincial walnut commode, mid 18th century, on short cabriole supports ending in scrolled feet, 4ft. 8 1/2in. wide. (Butterfield & Butterfield) $9,900

Régence inlaid tulipwood and gilt-bronze-mounted bombé commode, circa 1725, the angled projecting stiles applied with gilt-bronze foliate mounts continuing to conforming sabots, 4ft. 3 1/2in. wide. (Butterfield & Butterfield) $20,900

Louis XV ormolu-mounted kingwood and tulipwood marquetry bombé commode, stamped *W. Thomas, JME*, circa 1789, raised on cabriole legs ending in cast sabots, 39 1/2in. wide. (Butterfield & Butterfield) $14,300

Fine Louis XVI style gilt-bronze-mounted parquetry commode, after J.F. Leleu, stamped *Beurdeley, Paris*, late 19th century, raised on tapering cylindrical legs headed by ormolu foliage, 35 3/4in. wide. (Butterfield & Butterfield) $12,100

Louis XV tulipwood and kingwood commode, stamped *Schlichtig, JME*, circa 1770, the rectangular mottled gray, brown and white marble top with rounded edge, 30in. wide. (Butterfield & Butterfield) $6,600

A Régence rosewood, crossbanded and brass mounted serpentine commode of small size, veneered à quatre faces and applied with gilt metal cartouche key plate and handle, 3ft. wide. (Phillips) $5,406

A George III mahogany commode attributed to Thomas Chippendale, the eared concave-sided rectangular top with molded edge above two cupboard doors, 62 1/4in. wide. (Christie's) $1,654,950

A French Provincial oak commode, on foliate headed cabriole legs with scroll feet, late 18th/early 19th century, possibly adapted, 26in. wide. (Christie's) $950

COMMODE CHESTS

A Louis XV kingwood commode, by Jean Charles Saunier, of serpentine bombé shape with a molded brèche d'Alep marble top, 2ft. 5in. wide.
(Phillips) $26,513

A French ormolu-mounted mahogany commode, after the model by Guillaume Beneman and Joseph Stöckel, with eared rectangular white marble top, late 19th/early 20th century, 72in. wide.
(Christie's) $12,782

An 18th century Lombardy walnut serpentine commode of bombé form, crossbanded and inlaid with boxwood lines, on cabriole legs with pointed feet, 4ft. 10in. wide max.
(Phillips) $37,118

One of a pair of George II mahogany commodes of serpentine outline, each fitted with three graduated long drawers mounted with foliate rococo gilt-lacquered brass handles and lock-plates, 31¼in. wide.
(Christie's) (Two) $447,810

Italian rococo painted commode, third quarter 18th century, decorated with Oriental figures and pavilions in landscape setting and tones of red, yellow, green, blue and brown on a pale yellow ground, 4ft. 3in. wide.
(Butterfield & Butterfield) $19,800

Louis XV/XVI Transitional kingwood and tulipwood commode, stamped *Jovenet*, third quarter 18th century, raised on cabriole legs ending in later gilt-bronze sabots, 31½in. wide.
(Butterfield & Butterfield) $3,575

Régence carved elm commode, circa 1720, the top en arbalette, over a long and short frieze drawer above a double-fronted long drawer, 4ft. 2¼in. wide.
(Butterfield & Butterfield) $7,700

A Louis XV kingwood and crossbanded bombé petite commode surmounted by a serpentine gray marble top, on splayed legs, 2ft. 8in. wide.
(Phillips) $6,717

Italian rococo inlaid walnut marquetry bombé commode, third quarter 18th century, the rectangular top with rounded corners, inlaid with a scrolled border, 47in. wide.
(Butterfield & Butterfield) $38,500

COMMODE CHESTS

Louis XV provincial fruitwood commode, mid 18th century, serpentine top above three drawers and scrolled feet, 50in. wide.
(Skinner Inc.) $4,000

A 19th century French Provincial decorated commode, the serpentine breccia molded marble top above three long drawers, on cabriole legs, 2ft. 10in. wide.
(Phillips) $3,026

A French mahogany ormolu-mounted mahogany and marquetry bombé commode with white-veined liver marble serpentine top, late 19th/early 20th century, 52¹/₂in. wide.
(Christie's) $4,747

A Régence rosewood commode, the molded serpentine breccia marble top above two short and two long pewter banded drawers veneered à quatre faces, 38in. wide.
(Bonhams) $12,591

A Napoleon III tulipwood serpentine meuble d'appui, the cupboard door inlaid with a flower filled jug on an ebonized reserve, 42in. wide, circa 1850.
(Bonhams) $4,202

A French giltmetal-mounted rosewood and marquetry inlaid bombé commode of Louis XV style with eared serpentine liver mottled top, 20th century, 36in. wide.
(Christie's) $2,739

An Italian walnut and parquetry commode with overall zig-zag inlay within banded borders, the rectangular top above two short and two graduated long drawers, 48in. wide.
(Christie's S. Ken) $7,536

An 18th century Continental rosewood and marquetry bombé petite commode, surmounted by a contemporary molded serpentine top containing two drawers inlaid à travers with a bucket of flowers, 2ft. wide.
(Phillips) $3,498

A 19th century mahogany and brass mounted rectangular commode, in the Directoire style, surmounted by a peach grained marble top with three-quarter brass gallery, 4ft. 5in. wide.
(Phillips) $3,180

COMMODE CHESTS

An antique French Empire flame-figured mahogany commode of three drawers with gray marble top, on ebonized bun feet, circa 1800, 38in. wide.
(Selkirk's) $1,900

One of a pair of North Italian walnut, burr-walnut and ebonized commodes, each with eared-molded serpentine top above two long drawers, made from a single mid-18th century commode, 57³/₄in. wide.
(Christie's)
(Two) $14,085

Venetian rococo style parcel-gilt and silvered bombé commode, 19th century, the undulating corners carved with shells and flowerheads, 4ft. 2in. wide.
(Butterfield & Butterfield) $2,200

A late 18th century Schleswig Holstein walnut and carved giltwood commode, the burr figured and crossbanded top with a foliate decorated edge, 2ft. 9¹/₂in. wide.
(Phillips) $15,000

Directoire mahogany commode, circa 1800, raised on tapering square legs ending in square-cast sabots, 28¹/₂in. wide.
(Butterfield & Butterfield) $1,650

A giltmetal-mounted rosewood and kingwood miniature commode, feather-banded overall, the canted rectangular top above three long drawers on cabriole legs, 12¹/₂in. wide.
(Christie's) $3,467

Louis XV Provincial carved walnut commode, third quarter 18th century, the later rectangular top with molded edge over three bow-fronted drawers, a scalloped apron below, 4ft. ¹/₂in. wide.
(Butterfield & Butterfield) $3,575

Louis XV style gilt-bronze-mounted burled fruitwood commode, circa 1900, raised on cabriole legs with gilt-bronze mask-form espagnolettes, ending in animal paw sabots, 4ft. ¹/₂in. wide.
(Butterfield & Butterfield) $2,750

Louis XV Provincial inlaid walnut serpentine-fronted commode, mid-18th century, the shaped top with inlaid central large star above three short and two long drawers, 45in. wide.
(Butterfield & Butterfield) $7,150

CORNER CUPBOARDS

Classical carved walnut veneered glazed corner cabinet, Ohio, 1830–40, refinished, brass replaced, 55in. wide.
(Skinner Inc.) **$4,125**

A Heal & Son oak corner cabinet, triangular top with canted corners, above three partitioned shelves, on plinth base, 54cm. wide.
(Christie's) **$669**

A lemonwood and marquetry corner cupboard, the doors inlaid in boxwood, English, 19th century.
(Duran, Madrid) **$4,280**

A Dutch walnut and marquetry standing bowfront corner cupboard, the cavetto molded cornice with a carved foliate pediment, on bracket feet, early 19th century, 34in. wide.
(Christie's S. Ken) **$8,455**

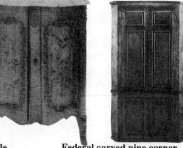

Pair of Louis XV style marquetry encoignures, stamped *Nogaret a Lyon*, third quarter 19th century, raised on shaped cross-banded feet ending in cast hoof-form sabots, 28$\frac{1}{2}$in. wide.
(Butterfield & Butterfield) **$1,870**

Federal carved pine corner cupboard, mid-Atlantic States, early 19th century, the lower molded panel doors opening to one shelf over a molded base, 46$\frac{1}{2}$in. wide.
(Butterfield & Butterfield) **$2,475**

Late Federal carved birch corner cupboard, early 19th century, with swan's neck cresting centering three urn-shaped finials, 45in. wide.
(Butterfield & Butterfield) **$3,300**

Cherry corner cupboard, Ohio, circa 1840, glazed doors open to a two-shelved interior above a single drawer, 56in. wide.
(Skinner Inc.) **$1,650**

Federal cherrywood corner cupboard, mid-Atlantic States, early 19th century, the two hinged glazed doors opening to three shelves above a molded waist, 4ft. 3in. wide.
(Butterfield & Butterfield) **$2,750**

CORNER CUPBOARDS

A George III fruitwood corner cupboard in two sections, with molded cornice above a dentil molding and two paneled doors enclosing an arched blue-painted interior, 57in. wide. (Christie's) $8,712

Louis XV kingwood parquetry hanging corner cupboard, circa 1760, the graduating scalloped sides enclosing three graduated tiers of serpentine outline, 34in. high. (Butterfield & Butterfield) $1,100

Federal cherry glazed corner cupboard, probably Fairfield County, Ohio, circa 1820–35, the lower case with a single shelf, replaced brasses, 41¹/₂in. wide. (Skinner Inc.) $4,400

Federal pine corner cupboard, New England, early 19th century, the hinged paneled doors opening to shelves, on bracket feet, 47in. wide. (Butterfield & Butterfield) $2,090

A pair of green lacquer and chinoiserie decorated hanging bowfront corner cupboards each with tiered gallery, late 18th century, 24in. wide. (Christie's S. Ken) $2,574

A Federal red-painted corner-cupboard, Northern New England, early 19th century, the upper section bowed with molded cornice hung with spherules over a frieze , 56¹/₂in. (Christie's) $11,000

An early 18th century walnut hanging corner cupboard with re-entrant top corners enclosing three shaped shelves within reeded canted corners, 39³/₄in. high. (Tennants) $2,325

George III pine corner cupboard, last quarter 18th century, with a stepped and dentiled cornice above an arched aperture disclosing a blue painted interior, 4ft. 2¹/₂in. wide. (Butterfield & Butterfield) $3,300

A Chippendale mahogany corner-cupboard, Philadelphia, 1760–1780, the upper section with broken pitched pediment with molded dentiled cornice filled with lattice-work, on ogee bracket feet, 54¹/₂in. wide. (Christie's) $33,000

CUPBOARDS

An oak court cupboard inlaid with parquetry bands and applied with split moldings, on block feet, parts 17th century, 50in. wide.
(Christie's) $1,536

An antique French ebonised fruitwood buffet inlaid with amboyna wood and kingwood, with gilt bronze mounts and Sèvres pattern Paris porcelain plaques, 19th century.
(Selkirk's) $3,600

Pine paneled cupboard, North America, first half 19th century, the two doors on rat-tail hinges, 46in. wide.
(Skinner Inc.) $3,080

Antique American kitchen cupboard in pine, backsplash top, two small drawers over two paneled cupboard doors, bracket feet, 48in. high.
(Eldred's) $660

A George III inlaid mahogany portable croft, with a frieze drawer and paneled door enclosing twelve small drawers, 20in. wide.
(Christie's S. Ken) $2,781

Louis XIV provincial oak pannetiere with a pierced circular rondel above paneled rondels and a fielded panel within a floral-carved reserve, 41½in. wide.
(Butterfield & Butterfield) $3,850

An oak cupboard with molded canted rectangular top and sides carved with Romayne panels flanked and divided by foliate capitals, basically mid-16th century, 34in. wide.
(Christie's) $2,826

A Charles II walnut, elm and ash hanging-cupboard, the rectangular top with later molded cornice and bolection-molding frieze above a pierced door, 33in. wide.
(Christie's) $7,160

Antique American two-part step-back cupboard in pine, upper section with two glazed doors, lower section with two paneled doors, 76in. high.
(Eldred's) $1,100

CUPBOARDS

Painted cupboard, probably Georgia, mid 19th century, opens to a two-shelved interior, all over original red paint and pulls, 59½in. wide.
(Skinner Inc.) $4,950

Louis XV Provincial fruitwood buffet with shaped paneled doors with ebonized outline, raised on simple shaped feet, 4ft. 7in. wide.
(Butterfield & Butterfield) $2,750

A paneled oak press cupboard, the projecting frieze carved with initials and the date 1728, on stile feet, 59in. wide.
(Bearne's) $1,617

A William and Mary gumwood kas, New York, 1725–1755, the upper part with an elaborately molded bold cornice above two fielded panel double cupboard doors enclosing two shelves, 65½in. wide.
(Christie's) $4,950

Pair of Italian neoclassical walnut and marquetry small cupboards, late 18th century, the single crossbanded frieze drawer over a horizontal tambour shutter, 13⅞in. wide.
(Butterfield & Butterfield) $8,250

Louis XV transitional stripped pine buffet à deux corps with a cavetto molded cornice above a pair of fielded and shaped arched doors carved with sprays of cereal, 4ft. 5½in. wide.
(Butterfield & Butterfield) $3,025

Louis XIV carved walnut buffet à deux corps, each part enclosed by a geometrically molded and grotesque mask-carved double-fronted door, 37¾in. wide.
(Butterfield & Butterfield) $4,675

Chippendale carved pine cupboard, probably Canadian, 18th century, the molded cornice above two hinged paneled doors opening to three shelves, 4ft. 1¾in. wide.
(Butterfield & Butterfield) $1,540

Joined, paneled and painted oak court cupboard, probably Massachusetts, 17th century, refinished, 50in. wide.
(Skinner Inc.) $12,100

DAVENPORTS

A late Victorian burr walnut inlaid davenport with hinged leather lined top above scrolled supports with drawers to the side.
(Bonhams) **$1,901**

An Irish Killarney arbutus davenport inlaid with scenes of ruins, Irish motifs and foliage, on dark stained foliate carved mahogany supports and inverted plinth base, 32¹/₄in. wide.
(Christie's) **$4,748**

A Victorian rosewood davenport with shaped gallery, sloping flap with tooled leather insert, hinged pen and ink drawer, 21in. wide.
(Bearne's) **$1,892**

A mid Victorian walnut davenport with tulipwood radial inlay, the brass three-quarter galleried pen compartment above a hinged leather-lined slope, 21¹/₄in. wide.
(Christie's) **$2,983**

A George IV ormolu-mounted bird's eye maple and amaranth davenport, the sides with candle-slides and a hinged secret drawer, on plinth base, 18¹/₂in. wide.
(Christie's) **$5,947**

A George IV rosewood davenport inlaid overall with boxwood lines, with rectangular top above a green leather-lined hinged slope, enclosing a mahogany-lined interior, 18in. wide. (Christie's) **$2,638**

An Anglo-Japanese davenport, ebonized, the drawers at either side (one set dummy) and front columns decorated with floral inlay and supported by Japanese fretwork, 1.04m. high.
(Phillips) **$1,400**

A late Victorian walnut and ebonized davenport, the top with three quarter gallery above a hinged leather lined slope, supported by scrolling corbels, 28¹/₂in. wide.
(Bonhams) **$1,788**

A Victorian burr-walnut davenport, with an open fretwork gallery above a serpentine writing slope, enclosing a satin-birch interior, 23in. wide.
(Bonhams) **$2,483**

DISPLAY CABINETS

A Louis Philippe tortoiseshell display cabinet-on-stand with a pair of glazed doors enclosing shelves, on scroll supports joined by stretchers, 33in. wide. (Christie's) $2,975

One of a pair of ormolu-mounted amaranth, amboyna, burr oak and parquetry display cabinets, in the manner of Adam Weisweiler, late-19th century, 36in. wide. (Christie's) $18,260

An Italian painted display cabinet carved with putti and fruit garlands, the cartouche cresting above a glazed paneled door, 19th century, 50^1/₂in. wide. (Christie's) $5,759

A Dutch walnut and marquetry bombé display cabinet with overall checker and floral inlay, the arched cresting above a pair of astragal glazed doors, 19th century, 72^1/₂in. wide. (Christie's) $21,021

American Aesthetic movement rosewood, marquetry and parcel gilt side cabinet, circa 1875–85, Herter Brothers, New York, 66^3/₄in. wide. (Skinner Inc.) $19,800

An Edwardian mahogany breakfront display cabinet, the molded cornice above a glazed cupboard door with applied astragals. (Bonhams) $1,892

A George III mahogany display cabinet with molded rectangular top, and pierced fretwork gallery above two glazed doors, on block feet, 37in. wide. (Christie's) $12,584

A mid Victorian French Provincial oak cabinet of Louis XV design, with arched scroll crested cornice above two glazed double paneled doors, on cabriole legs, early 19th century, 56in. wide. (Christie's) $3,455

A Chinese hardwood display cabinet having overall pierced floral carving with figures and foliage to the uprights, 49^1/₂in. wide. (Christie's) $1,001

DISPLAY CABINETS

A Glasgow style mahogany display cabinet, the rectangular top with mirror back above a pair of stained and leaded glass doors, 69in. high.
(Christie's) **$1,969**

An Edwardian mahogany display cabinet inlaid overall with satinwood banding and sunburst motifs, on bracket base, 35in. wide.
(Christie's) **$4,607**

A Glasgow style mahogany display cabinet, with a pair of leaded glass doors divided by a stained and leaded glass foliate panel, 46in. wide.
(Christie's) **$3,741**

An 18th century Dutch oak china cabinet, the upper part with an arched molded cornice centered with a 'C'-scroll flowerspray above a pair of arched geometrically glazed doors, 5ft. wide.
(Phillips) **$3,916**

Biedermeier cherry display cabinet, circa 1810, with a tablet top above a chamfered frieze projecting above a pair of geometrically glazed doors, 5ft. 7³/₄in. wide.
(Butterfield & Butterfield) **$3,300**

An attractive Dutch walnut bombé display cabinet in the 18th century style, the upper section with broken arched cresting carved with acanthus leaves and flowerheads, 4ft. 2in. wide.
(Spencer's) **$7,898**

A red japanned cabinet on giltwood stand, the sides and spandrels with gilt chinoiserie decoration, on foliate headed cabriole legs with hairy paw feet, early 18th century, 47¹/₂in. wide.(Christie's) **$2,495**

19th century lyre shaped walnut vitrine, the shelves supported on internal columns, on bun feet, 172cm. high.
(Finarte) **$6,258**

A French satinwood and ormolu-mounted vitrine of Transitional design, the onyx marble top with concave frieze, 28¹/₄in. wide.
(Christie's) **$3,455**

DISPLAY CABINETS

A Continental Renaissance Revival walnut vitrine, crisply carved with foliate motifs and facial mascarons, circa 1895, 39in. wide.
(Selkirk's) $2,500

L. & J.G. Stickley china closet, circa 1912, no. 746, overhanging top above two doors with six smaller panes above single glass panel, 62in. high.
(Skinner Inc.) $4,750

An Edwardian mahogany and marquetry display cabinet, the upper section with broken scroll pediment, on square tapering legs with spade feet, 50in. wide.
(Christie's) $5,375

Louis XIV style gilt-bronze-mounted boulle vitrine, late 19th century, the glazed door with boulle framework, enclosing a mirrored interior with glass shelves, 34³/₄in. wide.
(Butterfield & Butterfield) $3,300

A Dutch satinwood and ebony display cabinet-on-chest with arched foliate carved cresting above cartouche-shaped glazed doors and sides, on angled paw feet, late 18th/early 19th century, 35¹/₂in. wide.
(Christie's) $4,991

An ormolu-mounted plum-pudding mahogany vitrine-cabinet, with stepped eared rectangular breakfront top, the frieze with blue glass panel painted with children, 46¹/₂in. wide.
(Christie's) $4,702

An Edwardian inlaid satinwood and mahogany cabinet with kingwood crossbanding, the rectangular molded cornice above two glazed paneled doors, 37³/₄in. wide.
(Christie's) $6,142

A French Louis XV style bronze-mounted mahogany vitrine with Vernis Martin lacquer decoration in a single convex glazed door, circa 1890–1910, 58in. high.
(Selkirk's) $1,500

An Edwardian mahogany and marquetry display cabinet-on-stand, the base with central classical urn, on square fluted tapering legs with spade feet, 35in. wide.
(Christie's) $2,610

DRESSERS

A mid-Georgian oak dresser banded overall in mahogany, the rounded rectangular top with re-entrant corners, on ogee-bracket feet, 79¹/₂in. wide. (Christie's) $5,276

A George II oak dresser with molded rectangular top above three drawers and two paneled doors, on stile feet, on foot repaired, 53¹/₂in. wide. (Christie's) $9,009

A George III oak dresser with three long drawers and an arcaded gallery with column supports on bracket feet, formerly with superstructure, Shropshire, 73¹/₂in. wide. (Christie's) $9,009

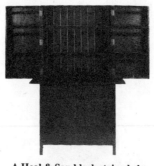

Italian Renaissance style walnut credenza, late 19th century, signed *Professor M. Franchi*, 52¹/₂in. wide. (Skinner Inc.) $1,870

A Heal & Son black stained elm dresser, designed by Sir Ambrose Heal, the rectangular superstructure with two cupboard doors enclosing three shelves, circa 1914, 123.3cm. wide.(Christie's) $2,954

A mid-Georgian oak dresser, with molded cornice above two shelves, the lower section with three drawers above two fielded arched paneled doors, 62³/₄in. wide. (Christie's) $3,365

George III Provincial inlaid oak Welsh dresser in two parts, the upper section with molded top over a stylized floral and foliate-pierced apron, raised on cabriole legs ending in pad feet, 5ft. 10¹/₂in. wide. (Butterfield & Butterfield) $1,650

A George III oak dresser, crossbanded overall in mahogany, the superstructure with molded rectangular cornice above a pierced foliate frieze, on square tapering legs with block feet, 76in. wide. (Christie's) $7,964

Chippendale walnut step back cupboard, possibly Pennsylvania, late 18th/early 19th century, in two parts, the upper section with molded cornice above two glazed doors, 6ft. 8in. wide. (Butterfield & Butterfield) $4,675

DRESSERS

A George II Irish oak dresser base with molded rectangular top, above three long and two short drawers each crossbanded with fruitwood, 86¹/₂in. wide.
(Christie's) $7,084

An early Georgian oak low dresser with molded rectangular top above three paneled drawers each simulated as two drawers, above two paneled doors each enclosing a shelf, 74in. wide.
(Christie's) $11,594

A late George III oak dresser base with rectangular molded top above three frieze drawers and shaped apron, on cabriole legs, 75in. wide.
(Christie's) $5,375

Pine glazed stepback cupboard, Pennsylvania, circa 1840, refinished, replaced pulls, 51in. wide.
(Skinner Inc.) $2,475

A mid Georgian oak dresser, with a later plate rack, the lower section with three drawers, on cabriole legs, 75in. wide.
(Bonhams) $5,320

An antique carved oak buffet in Louis XV style in two parts, the top member with canted glazed sides and a single glazed door, 19th century, 4ft. 4in. wide.
(Selkirk's) $2,000

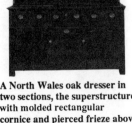

A North Wales oak dresser in two sections, the superstructure with molded rectangular cornice and pierced frieze above three plate racks, on waved end-supports, mid-18th century, 64in. wide.
(Christie's) $13,190

An oak dresser, designed by George Walton, the curved splash board on a rectangular shelf above a pair of open shelves , 55in. wide.
(Christie's) $3,741

A J.P. White 'Daffodil' oak dresser, designed by M.H. Baillie-Scott, the superstructure with rectangular top above two open shelves flanked by single cupboard doors, 153.5cm. wide.
(Christie's) $8,950

305

A mid-Victorian mahogany partner's desk with rectangular leather inset top, with opposing paneled doors to each pedestal, on plinth bases, 60in. wide.
(Christie's) $5,606

A George III mahogany partners' desk, the rectangular red leather-lined top with three frieze drawers and three dummy drawers, on plinth base, the frieze drawer locks numbered and stamped, 73in. wide.
(Christie's) $8,745

A Victorian mahogany kneehole desk, the three-quarter galleried top above one long and two short frieze drawers, on pedestals of three graduated drawers with plinth bases.
(Bonhams) $1,598

A George II mahogany kneehole desk, having a molded edge, containing a long frieze and an arched apron drawer, fitted with six short drawers about a central enclosed recessed cupboard, 3ft. 1in. wide.
(Phillips) $4,628

A Chippendale carved mahogany block-front and shell-carved bureau-table, Goddard or Townsend Workshops, Newport, Rhode Island, 1750–1760, with a coved frieze and long blocked drawer carved with three shells above a recessed kneehole, 36³/₄in. wide.
(Christie's) $115,500

A late George II mahogany kneehole dressing- and writing-table, the rectangular molded top with serpentine front and canted angles edged with ribbon-and-rosette ornament, 41in. wide.
(Christie's) $66,198

A William IV Welsh oak double-sided desk, the design attributed to Thomas Hopper with rectangular Welsh grey-green Penmon limestone top above an arcaded frieze, 53¹/₄in. wide.
(Christie's) $32,912

George III mahogany dressing table, third quarter 18th century, fitted with a slide over a central drawer and cupboard, 42in. wide.
(Skinner Inc.) $9,900

A mahogany small pedestal desk with rectangular red leather-lined top above three mahogany-lined frieze drawers, 39in. wide.
(Christie's) $1,239

KNEEHOLE DESKS

A Regency mahogany library desk, on four paneled pedestals, two enclosing three drawers, one enclosing six pigeon-holes, and one a removable double-divide folio section, 73in. wide.
(Christie's) $24,486

A walnut-veneered pedestal desk inlaid with panels of seaweed marquetry, the top with tooled leather insert, 51½in. wide.
(Bearne's) $2,150

A late Victorian mahogany partner's desk, on pedestals of three drawers opposing paneled cupboard doors, 66in. wide.
(Bonhams) $1,770

An early Victorian burr walnut writing-desk, the molded rounded rectangular top with leather-lined reading slope with ledge, the frieze with single drawer, 41½in. wide.
(Christie's) $19,305

An attractive Edwardian mahogany cylinder bureau, with a paneled fall enclosing drawers and pigeonholes and a leather inset writing surface.
(Bonhams) $2,576

A German oak and parcel ebonized piano front desk, the superstructure with three short drawers, above the fall front enclosing a rosewood interior, 55½in. wide, circa 1860.
(Bonhams) $4,202

A George III mahogany pedestal secrétaire library desk, in the manner of Gillows, the leather lined hinged double ratcheted slope with a hinged pen and ink tier, 4ft. 1in. x 2ft. 1in.
(Phillips) $8,366

A George II mahogany or 'red walnut' kneehole desk, having a central recessed cupboard enclosed by fielded panel door between six short drawers, on bracket feet, 2ft. 8½in. wide.
(Phillips) $4,134

A late George II mahogany kneehole desk, the rectangular molded top above a frieze drawer and ogee arched apron drawer, on ogee bracket feet, 3ft. wide.
(Phillips) $5,303

LINEN PRESSES

A William IV mahogany linen press, the molded cornice above a pair of paneled doors enclosing drawers, on turned feet.
(Bonhams) **$1,068**

A George III mahogany linen-press in two sections, with molded rectangular top above two long paneled doors, on bracket feet, 50in. wide.
(Christie's) **$7,357**

A late George II mahogany linen press, the base with a long drawer and slide (possibly of late date) above six various drawers on ogee bracket feet, 4ft. 3in. wide.
(Phillips) **$4,628**

A Chippendale figured maple linen-press, Pennsylvania, 1760–1780, the upper section with elaborately molded cornice about two arched paneled cupboard doors fitted with three shelves, on bracket feet, 48in. wide.
(Christie's) **$14,300**

A handsome George III mahogany linen press, with a pair of oval paneled cupboard doors, crossbanded in satinwood, the lower section with two short and two long drawers, 49³/₄in. wide. (Bonhams) **$2,674**

A George III mahogany linen press, the lower section with two false drawers and a long drawer below, on bracket feet, 39³/₄in. wide.
(Bonhams) **$676**

A late George III mahogany linen press, the doors with tulipwood banded oval panels, with two short and two long drawers below, on bracket feet, 50in. wide.
(Christie's) **$2,185**

A 19th century Dutch marquetry press or cupboard on chest, decorated with scrolling foliage and oval panels centered with birds, urns and floral bouquets, on bracket feet, 4ft. wide.(Phillips) **$6,052**

A William IV mahogany linen press with crossbanded doors set with molded panels, four graduated long drawers below with lotus-carved knob handles, 58¹/₂in. wide.
(Bearne's) **$1,376**

LOWBOYS

A George III mahogany lowboy, the rectangular top with deep crossbanding, thumb molded edge, a long drawer to the frieze, 2ft. 8in. wide.
(Spencer's) $1,494

An attractive early George III mahogany low boy, the top with molded edge and re-entrant corners above an arrangement of three drawers with brass handles, 31¹/₂in. wide.
(Tennants) $1,674

A Dutch walnut and marquetry serpentine lowboy, decorated with birds amongst scrolling foliage, on husk carved cabriole legs and claw-and-ball feet, mid 18th century, 33in. wide.
(Christie's) $5,375

An oak and red walnut lowboy, on cabriole legs with pad feet, basically 18th century, 30in. wide.
(Christie's S. Ken)
                              $4,529

George II inlaid walnut lowboy, circa 1730, with re-entrant front corners above an arrangement of three crossbanded drawers, 26¹/₂in. wide.
(Butterfield & Butterfield)
                              $3,575

A walnut and feather-banded lowboy with rounded rectangular molded top above two graduated drawers on cabriole legs with pointed pad feet, early 18th century, 30¹/₂in. wide. (Christie's S. Ken)
                              $2,574

PRIE DIEU

An 18th century Italian carved giltwood prie dieu, in the baroque taste, with stuffover bar top rail and foliate scroll uprights, on scroll and paw supports.
(Phillips) $954

Italian baroque ivory-inlaid walnut prie-dieu, the kneeling rail inlaid with a star, a long drawer below, 28¹/₂in. wide.
(Butterfield & Butterfield)
                              $3,575

Italian Renaissance walnut prie-dieu, late 16th century, square plinth base with a hinged compartment, 35³/₄in. high.
(Skinner Inc.) $1,760

SCREENS

A Portuguese Colonial red and gilt-painted six-leaf screen, decorated overall with cartouches variously painted with figures of ladies and gentlemen and hunters in landscapes and domestic scenes, circa 1730, each leaf 76 x 21³/₄in. (Christie's) **$38,720**

An 18th century tapestry panel, depicting a vase with flowers and fruit, with two parakeets, within a mahogany stand, 3ft. 9in. tall. (Phillips) **$884**

Charles X paper four-panel floorscreen, second quarter 19th century, grisaille decoration, 84in. high. (Skinner Inc.) **$1,320**

A Chinese coromandel and painted six-leaf screen, the four central panels with paintings of birds in landscapes, the reverse painted and applied with exotic birds among trees, each leaf 105in. high., 20³/₄ in. wide. (Christie's) **$7,623**

A painted four-leaf screen decorated with a scene in the manner of Francis Barlow of a spaniel and a goose arguing in an idyllic pastoral landscape with other birds, each leaf 86¹/₄ x 26¹/₂in. (Christie's) **$13,552**

A George II mahogany and needlework cheval fire-screen with a petit point needlework scene depicting The Rape of Proserpine in a chariot, 32in. wide. (Christie's) **$107,085**

A Chinese red and two-tone gold lacquer six-leaf screen decorated with a panoramic Chinese landscape with pavilions, mounted warriors and domestic scenes, 19th century, each leaf: 81¹/₄in. x 22¹/₂in. (Christie's) **$25,168**

Two screens by Sue Golden, undulating molded plywood, the larger black lacquered, the other gilded and patinated, 180cm. high. (Christie's) **$3,938**

SCREENS

Louis XVI style giltwood four-panel floor screen, panels painted with neoclassical motifs, 68½in. high.
(Skinner Inc.) **$1,650**

Painted three panel floor screen, depicting an elephant family moving through the jungle, signed *Ernest Brierly*, 8ft. wide.
(Skinner Inc.) **$2,500**

A late Federal rosewood firescreen, probably Boston, mid-19th century, with three hinged rectangular panels over trestle supports with hipped downswept legs, 40½in. high.
(Christie's) **$1,320**

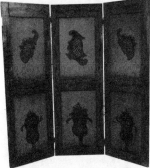

Paint decorated three-paneled folding screen, America, 19th century, each section decorated with rocaille and a laden compote within scrolled border, 5ft. high.
(Skinner Inc.) **$330**

A mahogany and needlework pole-screen with adjustable rectangular petit point floral needlework panel worked with two birds perched on flowering branches and a dog below, partly mid-18th century, 60½in. high.
(Christie's) **$23,364**

An Arts and Crafts mahogany-framed four-fold draught-screen, decorated and gilt with pomegranates and meandering foliage, 75in. high.
(Christie's) **$1,083**

A late 18th/early 19th century Dutch decorated embossed leather six-leaf screen with chinoiserie scenes, waterfowl and other polychrome birds, each leaf 6ft. 6in. x 1ft. 10in.
(Phillips) **$5,340**

A walnut firescreen of Régence style, with rectangular gros-point needlework panel, in a molded frame carved with scrolls and foliage on scroll feet, 29in. wide.
(Christie's) **$886**

A Chinese red and gilt-lacquer six-leaf screen decorated overall with chinoiserie figures and courtiers within a walled palace, 19th century, each leaf 85 x 22in.
(Christie's) **$8,131**

SECRETAIRE BOOKCASES

Regency mahogany secretary-bookcase, circa 1825, 46in. wide. (Skinner Inc.) $3,300

A George III mahogany secretaire-cabinet attributed to Thomas Chippendale, the breakfront upper part with arched center and molded cornice, 45^{1}/2in. wide. (Christie's) $95,403

A George III mahogany secretaire-bookcase, the lower section with fitted green leather-lined secretaire drawer simulated as two drawers, on later shaped bracket feet, 33in. wide. (Christie's) $6,021

A Federal inlaid mahogany secretary-bookcase, North Shore, Massachusetts, 1790–1810, the shaped cornice flanked by reeded plinths surmounted by two brass urn finials above two glazed cupboard doors with geometric line-inlaid mullions, on French feet, 43in. wide. (Christie's) $12,100

A George III brass-inlaid mahogany breakfront secretaire-bookcase, with four glazed doors filled with gothic arcading bars and lined with pleated green silk, 100in. wide. (Christie's) $15,488

A classical mahogany desk-and-bookcase, probably New York, circa 1820–1840, the upper section with cove-molded pediment above a crossbanded frieze over a pair of Gothic-glazed cupboard doors, on acanthus-carved paw feet, 45^{1}/2in. wide. (Christie's) $4,180

A late George III mahogany secrétaire cabinet, the base with a secrétaire drawer enclosing a fitted interior of eight drawers, pigeonholes and a central cupboard, 4ft. 3in. wide. (Phillips) $5,088

A late George III mahogany secretaire bookcase, the upper section with shallow swept molded cornice over shelves enclosed by a pair of arched astragal glazed doors, 4ft. 6in. wide. (Spencer's) $3,770

A Queen Anne walnut secretaire cabinet, with molded rectangular top above two mirrored doors each with later beveled plate, on later bun feet, 44in. wide. (Christie's) $25,168

SECRETAIRE BOOKCASES

A George III mahogany secrétaire bookcase, enclosed by a pair of molded astragal glazed doors, the lower section with a secrétaire drawer enclosing drawers and pigeonholes, 4ft. 2in. wide. (Phillips) $3,975

Federal mahogany veneered glazed secretary, New England, 1830's, interior with four open compartments above small drawers, 37¹/₂in. wide. (Skinner Inc.) $2,200

An American maple Federal secretaire bookcase, the raised cornice with three urn finials above a pair of arched glazed doors, with hinged baize-lined writing slope below, 19th century, 31in. wide. (Christie's) $3,455

A mid Victorian mahogany bowfront secretaire bookcase, the breakfront lower section with fall front secretaire drawer enclosing a fitted leather-lined interior, 57¹/₄in. wide. (Christie's) $7,678

A George III satinwood secretaire-bookcase inlaid overall with checker stringing and boxwood and ebonized lines, the oval glazing bars joined by floral tablets enclosing a green velvet-lined interior with three shelves, 31in. wide. (Christie's) $10,648

A George III mahogany and boxwood strung secrétaire bookcase, the lower section with dummy drawer fall front enclosing a fitted interior with drawers and pigeonholes about a central cupboard, 3ft. 6in. wide. (Phillips) $8,700

A Regency Egyptian-Revival mahogany secretaire-bookcase, the upper part with a pair of glazed doors below a pediment with ebony-inlaid acroteria, 42in. wide. (Tennants) $2,720

A George III mahogany and satinwood banded secrétaire bookcase, the lower section with a secrétaire drawer fitted with drawers and pigeon holes. (Bonhams) $1,449

A Regency mahogany secretaire bookcase, with secretaire drawer enclosing a part satinwood-lined interior with eight mahogany-lined drawers and pigeon-holes, 36¹/₂in. wide. (Christie's) $9,680

SECRETAIRES

A German mahogany secretaire with eared rectangular top above frieze drawer and hinged fall enclosing fitted interior with baize-lined slide, mid 19th century, 39½in. wide.
(Christie's) $2,704

A George III mahogany secrétaire chest, the molded rectangular top above a secrétaire drawer enclosing boxwood strung drawers and pigeonholes.
(Bonhams) $1,175

A mid-George III mahogany secretaire chest-on-chest, the molded dentil cornice with a blind-fret frieze, the hinged fall enclosing a fitted interior, on bracket feet, 44in. wide. (Christie's S. Ken)
$5,763

An antique French Empire flame-figured mahogany secretaire à abattant, the flap enclosing a fitted interior of calamander wood above a pair of cupboard doors, circa 1810, 41in. wide.
(Selkirk's) $3,200

Biedermeier mahogany and part ebonized fall-front secretary, probably German, second quarter 19th century, on shallow block feet, 46in. wide.
(Butterfield & Butterfield) $3,025

A Biedermeier mahogany secrétaire, the upper part of breakfront outline with stepped dentil cornice fitted with cupboards enclosed by panel doors, with classical figures, 3ft. 9in. wide.
(Phillips) $7,954

An Empire mahogany and brass mounted secrétaire à abattant, the fall with tooled leather panel to the reverse enclosing eight drawers, 3ft. wide.
(Phillips) $2,862

A Federal mahogany butler's-desk, New York, early 19th century, fitted with a pair of cockbeaded short drawers above a crossbanded secretary drawer, on turned tapering reeded legs and brass ball feet, 51½in. wide.
(Christie's) $3,850

A Louis XVI tulipwood, purpleheart and marquetry secrétaire à abattant, surmounted by a brèche d'Alep marble top, the fall inlaid with a vase of flowers and writing utensils, 2ft. 7in. wide.
(Phillips) $13,256

SECRETAIRES

Early Gustav Stickley drop front desk, 1902–04, step-down gallery, chamfered drop front with copper strap hinges over two open shelves, 52in. high. (Skinner Inc.) $6,000

A Victorian mahogany secretaire campaign chest, the central drawer fitted with four bird's-eye maple-veneered drawers and pull-out writing slide, 39in. wide. (Bearne's) $2,236

A Queen Anne walnut-veneered secrétaire with molded cornice, the fall front enclosing pigeon holes and small drawers around a central cupboard, 45¼in. wide. (Bearne's) $4,472

A Queen Anne walnut escritoire of small size, inlaid with boxwood and ebony lines, the fall front enclosing twelve various small drawers and pigeonholes around a central cabinet, 3ft. wide. (Phillips) $5,340

A late George III mahogany secretaire chest, the upper fall front drawer with applied molding and concealing an arrangement of drawers and pigeon holes, 45in. wide. (Tennants) $2,046

A Louis XVI tulipwood, crossbanded and inlaid secrétaire à abattant, the fall front veneered 'à quatre faces' and enclosing a fitted interior, on later tapered feet, 3ft. 1½in. wide. (Phillips) $4,242

Louis Philippe boulle marquetry, ebonized and gilt-bronze-mounted secrétaire, mid-19th century, raised on square cabriole supports applied with female therm chutes continuing to foliate sabots, 33½in. wide. (Butterfield & Butterfield) $8,250

A Biedermeier figured mahogany secretaire chest, circa 1820, the top with molded edge concealing secret compartments above a drop-front drawer, 38¼in. wide. (Tennants) $1,581

Napoleon III inlaid and ebonised secrétaire à abattant, third quarter 19th century, the rectangular grey marble top above a frieze drawer over a fall front opening to a bird's-eye maple interior, 28in. wide. (Butterfield & Butterfield) $4,400

SETTEES & COUCHES

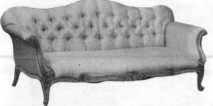

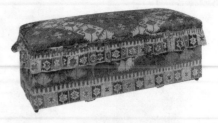

An Italian cream painted and parcel-gilt sofa, the shaped button back, serpentine seat and outswept scroll arms with pale blue upholstery, mid 19th century, 86in. wide.
(Christie's) **$2,111**

A Kelim upholstered Ottoman.
(Bonhams) **$392**

Louis XV style tapestry-upholstered carved walnut canape a orielles, the tapestry 18th century, the frame circa 1900, raised on cabriole legs, 6ft. 2in.
(Butterfield & Butterfield) **$4,125**

Fine small classical carved and parcel gilt mahogany and marble sofa, Philadelphia, circa 1820–1830, on Ionic marble columns with gilt capitals and bases on turned feet, 4ft. 7in. long.
(Butterfield & Butterfield) **$3,850**

A Danish ormolu-mounted mahogany sofa, with curved arms and front rail with mythological mounts, on splayed legs, 19th century, 74in. wide.
(Christie's) **$2,125**

A William IV mahogany sofa, the crested back, scroll arms and buttoned seat upholstered in green striped moire above a rope-twist apron on splayed legs, 81$^{1}/_{2}$in. wide.
(Christie's) **$3,071**

George III mahogany sofa with a high square back sloping down to downswept upholstered arms, on four square tapering front supports joined by H-form stretchers, 6ft. 10in. wide.
(Butterfield & Butterfield) **$3,300**

Classical carved mahogany sofa, Boston, circa 1820–1825, the molded and concave shaped crest terminating in rosette and punchwork scrolls, 6ft. 10in. long.
(Butterfield & Butterfield) **$990**

SETTEES & COUCHES

A Kelim upholstered three seater sofa.
(Bonhams)   **$801**

Italian rococo carved walnut window seat, the
scroll ends each with a fluted crestrail above two
arched pierced rungs, 7ft. 3¹/₂in. long.
(Butterfield & Butterfield)   **$1,980**

Italian neoclassical gray painted settee, circa
1790, the channel-molded frame with dark gray
line borders, the straight back with shallow
downswept sides ending in scroll finials, 6ft. 1in.
long.
(Butterfield & Butterfield)   **$2,475**

An Empire gilt-bronze mounted 'lit bateau', the
swept ends and front support applied with a
band of trailing poppies and foliage, raised on
scroll feet, possibly Portuguese.
(Tennants)   **$6,696**

A good painted satinwood triple chair back
settee, late 19th century in the Hepplewhite style,
each splat pierced with a classical twin handled
urn with a large painted floral bouquet issuing
from the narrow neck, 51³/₄in. wide.
(Tennants)   **$4,464**

An 18th century Italian carved giltwood settee,
the undulating arms, seat rails and cabriole legs
carved with strapwork, shells and pendant
foliage joined by acanthus carved scrolling
stretchers, 7ft. wide.
(Phillips)   **$3,535**

A late Victorian grained knole settee, the
rectangular padded back and ratchet-sides with
turned finials, with squab cushion and on turned
legs, 85in. wide.
(Christie's)   **$6,199**

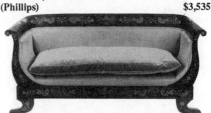

A 19th century Dutch mahogany and marquetry
scroll-end sofa, decorated with foliate scrolls,
and floral tendrils, on outswept legs, 6ft. 5in.
wide. (Phillips)   **$3,560**

SETTEES & COUCHES

A Regency cream and gilt painted dual scroll end sofa, the seat rail carved with roundels on splayed legs headed by scrolls, later decorated, 86in. wide.
(Christie's) $1,365

A William IV rosewood window seat with carved scrolling ends, on turned tapered reeded legs headed by rosettes, 54½in. wide.
(Christie's) $8,062

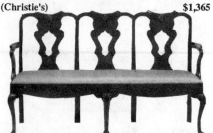

A mahogany triple chair back sofa, each with a shell carved shaped toprail and pierced vase splat above a drop-in seat, mid 18th century, 66in. wide.
(Christie's) $3,071

Empire style ormolu mounted mahogany settee, 56in. wide.
(Skinner Inc.) $2,750

Italian neoclassical walnut sofa, late 18th century, the slightly arched backrail continuing to downswept sides ending in outscrolled knuckled terminals over inswept uprights, 4ft. 8in. wide.
(Butterfield & Butterfield) $3,025

A late Victorian painted satinwood double chairback settee, the back with cane panels centered by cherubs, on tapering turned legs with brass castors.
(Bearne's) $3,612

A Regency carved rosewood chaise longue with single scroll end and downswept back carved with acanthus leaves, the seat rail and turned tapering legs with lotus carved decoration, 79in. wide. (Christie's) $3,455

A late Federal carved mahogany sofa, New York, circa 1825, the upswept crestrail carved with a basket of fruit flanked by griffins and tasseled swags over a padded back, on cornucopia-bracketed paw feet with casters, 86in. wide.
(Christie's) $11,000

318

SETTEES & COUCHES

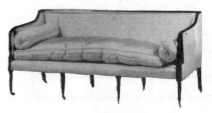

Classical mahogany veneered and carved sofa, Boston, circa 1830, embossed green velvet upholstery, old refinish, 72in. wide.
(Skinner Inc.) $2,860

A Regency mahogany sofa, the arms with reeded vase-turned supports on reeded tapering legs headed by paterae, 78in. wide.
(Christie's) $3,729

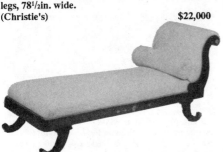

A Federal inlaid mahogany sofa-frame, Baltimore, 1790–1810, the serpentine crestrail curving to molded downswept arms above a serpentine seatrail flanked by oval reserves inlaid with shaded foliage over square tapering legs, 78$^{1}/_{2}$in. wide.
(Christie's) $22,000

A mid Victorian satinwood sofa, with vase-turned arm supports and square tapering legs headed by paterae, 66in. wide.
(Christie's) $2,303

A mahogany and brass mounted daybed with single scroll end and padded seat on reeded scroll legs, 19th century, 74in. wide.
(Christie's) $2,424

An Italian gray-painted settle, the arched back painted with putti and a winged angel with a horn supporting an armorial cartouche, late 17th century, 84in. wide.
(Christie's) $25,740

A classical mahogany and parcel-gilt recamier, New York, 1810–1820, with serpentine-molded crestrail terminating in a rosette over a padded back and flaring molded arms carved with rosettes, on gilt foliate bracketed hairy paw legs and casters, 83$^{1}/_{2}$in. wide.
(Christie's) $3,300

A George IV white-painted and parcel-gilt sofa, the scrolled padded back, outward-scrolling arms and seat with squab cushion and two bolsters covered in pink and white striped silk, 91in. wide.
(Christie's) $10,494

SETTEES & COUCHES

Painted and decorated settee, Pennsylvania, 1830–50, all over old light green paint with stencil decoration and striping, 75¼in. wide.
(Skinner Inc.) **$1,760**

Federal mahogany carved sofa, Salem, Massachusetts, circa 1810, refinished, 75¾in. wide.
(Skinner Inc.) **$1,320**

An antique American Classical Revival carved mahogany upholstered settee carved with cornucopia and foliate motifs with molded seat rail on paw feet, 7ft. 5in. wide.
(Selkirk's) **$1,650**

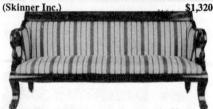

Classical carved mahogany veneer sofa, New York, circa 1820–30, molded veneer crest rail with scrolled arms above leaf carved arm supports, 71½in. wide.
(Skinner Inc.) **$1,540**

An antique baroque revival walnut chairback settee with three oval padded backrests within carved motifs of scrolls, grapevines, birds and cartouche crestings, 19th century, 68in. wide.
(Selkirk's) **$1,000**

An antique Italian neoclassical parcel-gilt creme lacqué upholstered settee, the fluted armrests terminating in boldly carved eagle heads, circa 1800, 4ft. 7in. long.
(Selkirk's) **$1,500**

Napoleon III walnut confidante, third quarter 19th century, two opposing long seats with seats at either end, raised on cabriole legs, 80in. wide.
(Skinner Inc.) **$3,750**

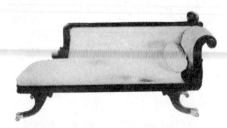

A late Regency rosewood chaise longue, the scrolled carved top rail above an upholstered seat with scrolled back rest, on saber legs.
(Bonhams) **$1,682**

320

SETTEES & COUCHES

Late classical mahogany carved sofa, probably New York, mid 19th century, green and gold silk upholstery, 84in. wide.
(Skinner Inc.) $1,045

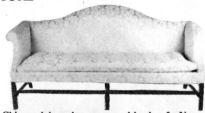

Chippendale mahogany camel-back sofa, New York, 18th century, refinished, 76in. wide.
(Skinner Inc.) $8,250

A Louis XV walnut and beechwood canapé à oreilles, the molded frame carved with flowerheads, the undulating padded back and seat upholstered in gros and petit point needlework, 6ft. 5in. wide.
(Phillips) $5,303

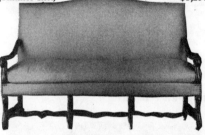

Louis XIV style walnut settee, 19th century, with a camelback and straight seat raised on eight S-scroll supports, 5ft. 8in. wide.
(Butterfield & Butterfield) $1,980

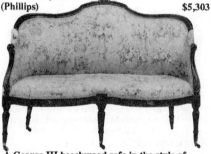

A George III beechwood sofa in the style of Thomas Chippendale, on six stop-fluted turned tapering legs carved with long leaves and headed by paterae, the castors stamped COPE & COLLINSON PATENT STRONG, 53in. wide. (Christie's) $14,520

Federal carved mahogany triple chairback settee, early 19th century, the triple shield back with carved and pierced urn-shaped splats with outstretched shaped arms, 4ft. 6in. wide.
(Butterfield & Butterfield) $3,025

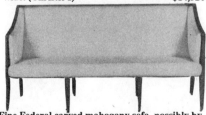

Fine Federal carved mahogany sofa, possibly by Slover and Taylor, New York, circa 1800–1815, on square tapering reeded legs ending in brass and wood wheel casters, 6ft. 6in. long.
(Butterfield & Butterfield) $14,300

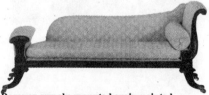

Regency ormolu-mounted grain-painted recamier, circa 1815, the supports mounted with ormolu plumes and foliate scrolls, raised on lobe-carved out-scrolled legs ending in foliate brass feet on casters, 6ft. 4in. wide.
(Butterfield & Butterfield) $4,125

Fine Louis XVI style gilt-bronze-mounted mahogany console desserte, the rectangular mirror plate with downswept sides and gilt-bronze framework, the green marble top above three frieze drawers, 7ft. 9½in. wide.
(Butterfield & Butterfield) **$5,500**

George III style mahogany pedestal sideboard, mid-19th century, the serpentine-edged top above three frieze drawers, one pedestal with a cupboard door enclosing slides, the other with a shelf and a drawer, 6ft. 1in. wide.
(Butterfield & Butterfield) **$2,750**

A Regency parcel-gilt rosewood side cabinet inlaid overall with boxwood lines, on hairy paw feet, bearing a label *Hugh Cecil Earl of Lonsdale* with coat-of-arms; and a Chinese Kangxi blue and white covered porcelain vase, 66½in. wide.
(Christie's) **$174,240**

Gustav Stickley sideboard, circa 1902, No. 967, gallery top over two short drawers and single long drawer, two cabinet doors below, iron hardware, 60in. long.
(Skinner Inc.) **$6,050**

A Hille sideboard, the rectangular superstructure with three sliding glass doors each enclosing single glass shelf, on four bowed carved legs, 167.5cm. wide.
(Christie's) **$1,083**

A burr-maple Art Deco sideboard, the design attributed to Ray Hille, the rounded rectangular top above deep frieze with vertically fluted panel and two short drawers, 137cm. wide.
(Christie's) **$1,181**

SIDEBOARDS

A classical parcel gilt mahogany sideboard, New York, 1820–1830, the rectangular top backed by a splashboard with broken pediment centering a pinecone finial over a pair of crossbanded short drawers, on paw feet, 61³/₄in. wide.
(Christie's) $3,080

George III style inlaid mahogany pedestal sideboard, third quarter 19th century, the rectangular top with outset ends and concaved splashboard, the frieze fitted with two drawers, 7ft. 6in. wide.
(Butterfield & Butterfield) $3,300

A burr maple Art Deco sideboard, the design attributed to Ray Hille, rectangular top above single fluted drawer, flanked by rectangular sides supporting single glass shelf, 113cm. wide.
(Christie's) $1,083

L. & J.G. Stickley sideboard, circa 1910, no. 738, rectangular plate rack on corresponding top, two long drawers flanked by cabinet doors, 60in. wide.
(Skinner Inc.) $4,100

George III inlaid mahogany serpentine-fronted sideboard, early 19th century, raised on molded tapering square legs ending in spade feet, 6ft. long.
(Butterfield & Butterfield) $2,200

A Liberty & Co. break-front cabinet, shaped central glazed cupboard doors above rectangular top, flanked on each side with arched and columned open recesses and adjustable shelves, 122.5cm. wide.
(Christie's) $985

A mahogany sideboard of George III style, on channeled legs carved with satyr masks and acanthus and headed by paterae on block feet, 80¼in. wide.
(Christie's) $7,970

Edwardian inlaid and penwork decorated mahogany sideboard in the neoclassical taste, circa 1900, the whole on a plinth base, 6ft. 9½in. wide.
(Butterfield & Butterfield) $4,675

A George III-style semi-circular sideboard inlaid throughout with boxwood and ebonized stringing, the central frieze drawer above an arched recess, 60in. wide.
(Bearne's) $5,504

Federal carved mahogany sideboard, New York, circa 1815–1820, the rectangular top with Palladian arched splashboard flanked by reeded columns with acorn finials, 6ft. ½in. wide.
(Butterfield & Butterfield) $1,650

A Federal mahogany sideboard, New England, 1790–1810, the serpentine top above a conforming case fitted with a serving slide lined with stenciled leather, on Marlborough legs with pendant husk and cuff inlay, 61in. wide.
(Christie's) $60,500

A Federal inlaid mahogany sideboard, Mid-Atlantic States, 1790–1810, the rectangular top with serpentine front edge, on square tapering legs with pendant husks and cuff-inlay, 65½in. wide.
(Christie's) $8,800

SIDEBOARDS

George III inlaid mahogany sideboard of large size, circa 1800, the top crossbanded in rosewood within boxwood strung borders, 7ft. 11¼in. wide.
(Butterfield & Butterfield) $2,475

William IV brass-mounted mahogany pedestal sideboard, second quarter 19th century, the bowed cross-banded rectangular top with arched splashboard, 8ft. 1½in. wide.
(Butterfield & Butterfield) $2,750

Unusual Limbert sideboard, Grand Rapids, Michigan, circa 1903, gallery top, three short drawers over three cabinet doors, single long drawer below, round copper and brass pulls, 59¼in. wide.
(Skinner Inc.) $1,600

A late George III mahogany bow-front pedestal sideboard, the back with double brass rail, the crossbanded top above three frieze drawers, on slender bracket feet, 72½in. wide.
(Bearne's) $3,612

A George III mahogany bowfronted sideboard with a mahogany-lined drawer in the arched center flanked by oval-inlaid cupboard door on the left and a cellaret drawer on the right, 60¼in. wide.
(Christie's) $25,311

A Regency mahogany pedestal sideboard, supported by two pedestals, each with one top drawer above a convex paneled door with two twisted side columns.
(Bonhams) $979

A Regency mahogany breakfront sideboard banded overall with fruitwood and ebonized lines with one long drawer above two concave-sided spandrels flanked by two drawers to either side, 75in. wide.
(Christie's) $3,564

A George III mahogany bowfront sideboard with five drawers around a waved kneehole, on square section legs terminating with spade feet.
(Bonhams) $2,408

A late George III mahogany breakfront sideboard, the rectangular top above an arcaded frieze fitted with two drawers flanked by a pair of bowed simulated drawers, 96¼in. wide.
(Christie's S. Ken) $7,979

George III style satinwood inlaid mahogany bow-front sideboard, second quarter 19th century, on six tapering legs of square and diamond shape, 5ft. wide.
(Butterfield & Butterfield) $3,575

One of a pair of George III mahogany bow-fronted sideboards, each with two lead-lined doors flanking a kneehole drawer on square tapering legs, 42in. wide.
(Christie's)
(Two) $7,430

A George III mahogany, tulipwood crossbanded and inlaid serpentine sideboard, containing a central drawer in the arched apron between deep drawers, on square tapered legs, 4ft. 7in. wide.
(Phillips) $4,984

A George III mahogany and inlaid demi-lune sideboard, with boxwood stringing, containing a central drawer flanked by a pair of deep drawers and cupboards with dummy drawer fronts, 5ft. wide.
(Phillips) $9,570

A Heal & Son oak sideboard with quarter-galleried rectangular top above two short and one long drawers and original curtain rail, 122.3cm. wide.
(Christie's) $827

A George III mahogany tulipwood crossbanded and inlaid bowfront sideboard with ebony and boxwood stringing, on square tapered legs terminating in spade feet, 4ft. 11in. wide.
(Phillips) $4,134

STANDS

A late Victorian mahogany folio stand with slatted adjustable sides on dual reeded scroll uprights joined by a flattened stretcher, 29in. wide.
(Christie's) **$2,111**

A pair of George II walnut and parcel-gilt candle-stands, on tripod cabriole base carved with acanthus and C-scrolls ending in scrolled feet, 42¹/₂in. high.
(Christie's) **$175,230**

A set of George III mahogany library steps with molded rail and baluster banisters divided by stop-fluted columns above pierced risers, 67in. wide.
(Christie's) **$97,350**

A Federal inlaid mahogany two-drawer stand, Portsmouth, New Hampshire, 1790–1810, the rectangular top with outset rounded corners over a conforming case fitted with two crossbanded drawers, 18³/₄in. wide.
(Christie's) **$26,400**

A late Victorian ebonized and ivory two-tier trolley by Howard & Sons, the rectangular top with balustrade gallery and ring-turned finials, 30¹/₂in. wide.
(Christie's) **$7,438**

A George III mahogany tripod caddy-stand, the circular top with baize-lined well, fitted with an associated contemporary circular silver caddy, by William & Aaron Lestourgeon, 1777, 23¹/₄in. high.
(Christie's) **$70,092**

A George III mahogany tripod stand, the circular top edged with ribbon-and-rosette and pendant lozenges, on triple scrolled supports of double C outline, 31in. high.
(Christie's) **$56,463**

A George III set of mahogany metamorphic library steps, the rectangular green baize-lined top with three-quarter spindle gallery, 18³/₄in. wide.
(Christie's) **$4,198**

A George III mahogany gold-fish bowl stand of triangular outline, on cabriole legs carved with acanthus ending in scrolled feet, 26¹/₄in. high.
(Christie's) **$19,470**

STANDS

A Chippendale cherrywood candle-stand, New England, 1760–1780, the circular top above a column and urn-turned pedestal and tripartite base with cabriole legs, 28in. high.
(Christie's) **$3,080**

A George IV rosewood folding folio stand with turned supports and stretchers, on pedestal legs with bun feet, 28½in. wide.
(Christie's S. Ken) **$3,768**

Federal tiger maple candlestand, New England, early 19th century, refinished, 27½in. high.
(Skinner Inc.) **$1,500**

American Renaissance inlaid maple and rosewood nightstand by Herter Brothers, New York, circa 1872, the later faux marble top within a molded walnut border, 17in. wide.
(Butterfield & Butterfield) **$990**

A set of Regency rosewood library steps with six fluted treads, brass hand-supports (partly deficient) and turned supports, 51in. wide.
(Christie's) **$44,528**

An ebonized and parcel-gilt umbrella-stand, the rectangular top above a vertical-railed slightly-tapering body, on a molded stepped plinth base, 32in. high.
(Christie's) **$2,450**

Open-sided music stand, circa 1907, similar to Gustav Stickley no. 670, four tapering posts, centering four shelves with gallery, unsigned, 39in. high.
(Skinner Inc.) **$1,000**

A William IV rosewood and simulated rosewood folio stand adjustable by ratchet supports and raised on trestle end supports, 32in. wide.
(Tennants) **$4,092**

A Federal mahogany stand, Salem, Massachusetts, 1790–1810, on square tapering molded legs joined by X-stretchers, 14¼in. wide.
(Christie's) **$2,090**

328

STANDS

Chippendale mahogany dish top inlaid candlestand, Connecticut River Valley, late 18th century, 26in. high.
(Skinner Inc.)   **$5,225**

Art Nouveau marquetry corner stand, France, early 20th century, floral and foliate inlay, green marble top, brass hardware, 42in. high.
(Skinner Inc.)   **$2,000**

A Regency satinwood and parcel gilt torchère stand, on reeded shaft with foliate ornament and tripod splayed supports, 2ft. 11in. high.
(Phillips)   **$2,651**

A mid-Georgian mahogany dumb-waiter, the three graduated circular tiers on an urn-shaped shaft with arched cabriole tripod base, 23in. diameter.
(Christie's)   **$6,930**

An early Victorian mahogany telescopic dumb waiter on carved volute feet with castors, the mechanism for the lower tier presently inoperative, 45in. wide.
(Tennants)   **$1,023**

Extremely fine Empire ormolu-mounted mahogany meuble d'entre deux d'horloge, in the manner of Jacob Desmalter, circa 1800–1820, raised on bun feet, 35¹/₂in. wide.
(Butterfield & Butterfield)   **$16,500**

Painted and mahogany veneer stand, Massachusetts or New Hampshire, 1800-15, top and base painted with original red stain, 18in. wide.
(Skinner Inc.)   **$4,840**

A Victorian rosewood folio stand, with two adjustable slatted panels resting on carved brackets, 112cm. wide.
(Allen & Harris)   **$2,426**

A George III mahogany urn stand, on tapered legs, 12¹/₄in. wide.
(Dreweatt Neate)   **$2,925**

STOOLS

A late 18th century Continental giltwood and gesso stool, with a tapestry cover depicting an angelic lady pointing to a peacock, possibly Scandinavian, 1ft. 11in. wide.
(Phillips) **$890**

Pair of Italian neoclassical carved giltwood stools, late 18th century, each with a square brocaded and cut velvet upholstered seat above a paneled frieze, 16in. wide.
(Butterfield & Butterfield) **$4,400**

An Empire giltwood tabouret pliant with padded rectangular seat covered in close-nailed blue watered silk, on channeled X-shaped supports carved with paterae, 25^1/$_2$in. wide.
(Christie's) **$14,850**

A walnut stool of Queen Anne style, the rectangular seat with squab cushion, on cabriole legs and pad feet, late 19th century, 21in. wide.
(Christie's) **$1,258**

One of a pair of early George III mahogany stools, on cabriole legs headed by scallop-shells, scrolls and acanthus ending in scrolled feet, 26^1/$_4$in. wide.
(Christie's) (Two) **$165,495**

Gustav Stickley footstool with cross stretcher base, circa 1902, no. 725, arched sides with leather upholstery and tacks, 16^1/$_2$in. wide.
(Skinner Inc.) **$1,200**

A carved mahogany oval stool with 18th century needlework panel, on cabriole legs with scallop shell and pendant decorated knees.
(Phillips) **$1,590**

A pair of 18th century Italian carved giltwood stools, in the Régence taste, on acanthus scroll carved legs and paw feet, 1ft. 3in. square.
(Phillips) **$3,026**

A black-painted Windsor footstool stamped *J. Stanyan*, Pennsylvania, 1790–1820, on bamboo-turned splayed legs joined by stretchers, 12^3/$_4$in. wide.
(Christie's) **$550**

330

STOOLS

Roycroft "Ali Baba" bench, circa 1910, oak slab seat with some exposed bark underneath, plank ends joined by long center stretcher, 42in. long.
(Skinner Inc.) $1,500

A pair of late Federal mahogany foot-stools, New England, 1800–1820, each with padded rectangular top above a reeded apron with baluster and ring-turned legs, 12in. wide.
(Christie's) $660

An Italian walnut stool, a foliate scroll bar to each end on bearded satyr supports with later turned feet, late 19th century, 40in. wide.
(Christie's) $2,303

A mahogany stool, the dished rectangular paneled seat with acanthus-carved apron on channeled cabriole legs joined to the front by a waved stretcher, 22³/₄in. wide.
(Christie's) $8,745

A late 18th century Italian carved giltwood neo-classical window seat, having a stuffover seat, on square tapered legs, with trailing husks, 4ft. 8in.
(Phillips) $2,298

A mahogany stool of George I design, the inset rectangular upholstered seat on cabriole legs with pad feet joined by stretchers, 21in. wide.
(Christie's S. Ken) $2,817

A Chinese hualiwood stool with pierced frieze and bowed supports joined by a shaped stretcher, 16¹/₂in. wide.
(Christie's S. Ken) $642

A pair of Willam IV mahogany stools with rectangular needlework tops on baluster turned legs, 11in. wide x 9in. high.
(Christie's S. Ken) $728

An early Victorian oak gout stool, the hinged and ratcheted close-studded green leather rest on baluster-turned front legs, 22¹/₄in. wide.
(Christie's S. Ken) $385

SUITES   FURNITURE

Harden three-piece suite, circa 1910, including settee, armchair and rocker, concave crest rail
over five vertical slats, bent arm over four vertical slats, spring cushion seat.
(Skinner Inc.) $1,000

A mid Victorian carved walnut salon suite comprising a scrolling floral and foliate carved sofa
with shaped crested toprail, on cabriole legs, and four side chairs with pierced balloon back.
(Christie's) $6,142

An Edwardian mahogany inlaid and boxwood strung part salon suite, comprising: a settee and
two side chairs.
(Bonhams) $773

SUITES

A set of George II mahogany seat furniture comprising four chairs and a double-back settee, each with dished scrolled toprail and pierced vase-shaped splat.
(Christie's) $14,520

Fine and important Moorish style ivory-inlaid carved ebony and pearwood seven-piece parlor suite, circa 1878, comprising a settee and six side chairs.
(Butterfield & Butterfield) $74,250

Suite of Third Republic giltwood seat furniture, comprising a canapé and two graduated pairs of armchairs, each with coral red and green sprig decorated gray satin upholsteries.
(Butterfield & Butterfield) $4,125

BREAKFAST TABLES

A mid Victorian walnut breakfast table with quarter-veneered shaped oval tip-up top on four splayed scroll legs, 57in. wide.
(Christie's) $2,983

A George III mahogany breakfast table with rounded rectangular tilt top on baluster shaft and quadripartite base, 54in. wide.
(Christie's) $2,657

A Victorian burr-walnut breakfast table, on a carved baluster-turned shaft and quadripartite hipped splayed legs with foliate headings, 56½in. wide.
(Christie's) $2,367

George IV rosewood breakfast table, circa 1825, the circular top with a paneled frieze tilting above a fluted shaft raised on fern-leaf carved and molded quadruple supports, 4ft. 2¼in. diameter.
(Butterfield & Butterfield) $7,700

A George III mahogany breakfast-table, the crossbanded oval tilt-top inlaid with fruitwood stringing, on turned shaft and quadripartite base, 59½in. wide.
(Christie's) $5,421

George III mahogany breakfast table, first quarter 19th century, on a high arched molded quadruple base ending in foliated and shell-cast gilt-bronze cappings on castors, 4ft. 2½in. wide.
(Butterfield & Butterfield) $1,650

A satinwood breakfast table, the canted tip-up top banded in tulipwood, on turned simulated fluted shaft and four splayed legs, 42½in. wide.
(Christie's) $1,920

A George III fiddleback mahogany breakfast table with well-figured rounded rectangular tip-up top, on turned stem and splayed feet, 68¾in. wide.
(Christie's) $20,444

Regency rosewood brass mounted and inlaid breakfast table of large size, the circular snap top with a border of stylized foliate cut brass marquetry, 4ft. 5½in. diameter.
(Phillips) $11,489

CARD & TEA TABLES

Federal mahogany inlaid card table, Massachusetts, circa 1810, refinished, 35½in. wide. (Skinner Inc.) **$2,640**

A mid Victorian walnut card table, on a bulbous carved column support, on downswept scroll feet, 36in. wide. (Bonhams) **$1,251**

A George III mahogany tea-table, the shaped frieze centred by a crisply carved foliate clasp and carved with fruiting vines and flowerheads, on square legs, 35½in. wide. (Christie's) **$25,311**

One of a pair of George III satinwood and rosewood card-tables, each inlaid overall with amaranth bands and ebonized and fruitwood lines, on turned tapering baluster legs and turned feet, 36in. wide. (Christie's) (Two) **$14,867**

A boulle serpentine card table of Louis XV design, the fold-over top with central figure playing a lyre flanked by caryatids, urns and butterfly motifs, 19th century, 34¼in. wide. (Christie's) **$3,263**

A Federal inlaid mahogany card-table, Rhode Island, 1790–1810, the hinged D-shaped top with lightwood banding over a conforming frieze centered by a fluted vase issuing bellflowers and rosettes, 36¼in. wide. (Christie's) **$13,200**

Federal mahogany inlaid card table, Newport or Providence, Rhode Island, circa 1790, 36in. wide. (Skinner Inc.) **$2,750**

A George II Colonial mahogany and mother-o'-pearl inlaid card table, the crossbanded baize lined top with projecting corners with mother-o'-pearl inlaid counter recesses, 3ft. wide. (Phillips) **$4,110**

A George III mahogany tea-table, the frieze applied with blind fretwork and centered by a satinwood tablet, on square channeled chamfered legs, 34in. wide. (Christie's) **$2,073**

CARD & TEA TABLES

Dutch rococo walnut games table, 18th century, needlepoint lined playing surface, 35¼in. wide.
(Skinner Inc.) $3,080

A Regency rosewood card table, the hinged rounded rectangular crossbanded top on a square chamfered column support.
(Bonhams) $1,104

A George II mahogany card-table with eared rectangular hinged top with green baize-lined interior, on cabriole legs headed by scallop shells, 35¾in. wide.
(Christie's) $6,195

A Dutch hardwood tea-table with eared serpentine top, the waved frieze carved with C-scrolls and rockwork, on cabriole legs headed by acanthus, mid-18th century, 34in. wide.
(Christie's) $7,744

One of a pair of George III satinwood card-tables inlaid overall with ebonized stringing, each with hinged rectangular baize-lined top inlaid with chevron banding and crossbanded in amaranth, 37in. wide.
(Christie's) (Two) $17,490

One of a pair of George III satinwood and marquetry card-tables, each with D-shaped hinged top crossbanded in rosewood and inlaid with oval panel with musical and martial trophies, 36in. wide.
(Christie's) (Two) $22,737

An early George III mahogany concertina-action card-table, the hinged green velvet-lined rectangular top with foliate-carved rim, on channelled cabriole legs, 36in. wide.
(Christie's) $18,392

A Regency mahogany card-table crossbanded in a different mahogany, banded overall in satinwood and inlaid with ebonized lines, on saber legs, 32¾in. wide.
(Christie's) $3,365

A Queen Anne cherrywood tea-table, probably Northampton or Hatfield, Massachusetts, 1740–1760, the deeply scalloped moulded top above a rectangular frame, 35in. wide.
(Christie's) $38,500

CARD & TEA TABLES

A George II mahogany tea-table with D-shaped twin-flap top enclosing a semi-circular well, with panelled frieze and gateleg action, on cabriole legs, 27¼in. wide.
(Christie's) $7,744

A Regency brass-inlaid rosewood and simulated rosewood card-table, on turned spreading partially-fluted shaft, gadrooned socle and circular quadripartite platform base, 36in. wide.
(Christie's) $2,302

A fine antique English George I concertina action walnut tea table of desirable small size, on shell-carved cabriole front legs, circa 1720, 28in. wide.
(Selkirk's) $4,750

A mid Victorian walnut card table with serpentine eared swivelling top and scroll carved frieze on four scroll uprights, 36½in. wide.
(Christie's) $2,003

A George III satinwood half round card table, the hinged baize lined top with a wide crossbanded border, on square tapering legs with ebonized spade feet, 3ft. wide.
(Phillips) $4,272

A French ormolu-mounted tulipwood and kingwood card-table with rectangular banded quarter-veneered top with foliate edge, late 19th century, 32½in. wide.
(Christie's) $1,771

A William IV rosewood D-shaped tea table on turned lotus-carved shaft with gadrooned base and four acanthus carved splayed legs, 36in. wide.
(Christie's) $2,495

An Irish mid-Georgian yew-wood card-table, the shaped frieze centered by a lion-mask with bared teeth, flanked by flowerheads, on tapering cabriole legs, 34½in. wide.
(Christie's) $62,304

A Victorian walnut card table with serpentine-sided fold-over top, on four splayed 'S'-scroll legs carved with strapwork and foliage, 35½in. wide.
(Bearne's) $1,238

Napoleon III boulle center table, the top of undulating outline with an egg-and-leaf-cast edge and brass-inlaid boulle reserve of arabesques and foliate-scrolls centered by a medallion, 4ft. 10½in. wide.
(Butterfield & Butterfield)
$2,200

A late Victorian satinwood and marquetry table, the circular top centered by a sun-burst with radiating fan-pattern and green-stained demi-lunes, 54in. diameter.
(Christie's) $7,915

Continental marble center table, resting on an unpolished white marble balustrade urn relief-carved with swags and pendants, 29in. high.
(Butterfield & Butterfield)
$14,300

Italian Empire walnut center table, circa 1800–1810, the circular top veneered in radiating section of Circassian walnut above a plain deep frieze fitted with a single drawer, 27½in. diameter.
(Butterfield & Butterfield)
$2,475

Carolean oak and elm credence table, raised on barleytwist suports above blocked feet joined by a molded stretcher, 44in. wide.
(Butterfield & Butterfield)
$2,475

Italian baroque carved walnut center table, the octagonal top raised on a faceted attenuated baluster standard flanked by four inverted dolphins, 31¾in. high.
(Butterfield & Butterfield)
$1,210

One of a pair of Anglo-Indian ebony center tables each with gadrooned rectangular top on turned fluted legs and H-shaped platform, 19th century, 38¼in. wide.
(Christie's)   (Two)
$6,595

Amusing Dutch colonial carved hardwood center table, second half 19th century, on splayed tripod supports in the form of three human legs, 42in. diameter.
(Butterfield & Butterfield)
$2,200

Flemish baroque carved oak center table, the flattened oval top above a deep scalloped frieze fitted with a geometrically-fronted drawer, 40¼in. wide.
(Butterfield & Butterfield)
$1,760

CENTER TABLES

Italian rococo style carved, silvered and giltwood and scagliola center table, raised on a baluster and ring-turned standard, 31¹/₂in. high. (Butterfield & Butterfield) $4,125

An ormolu-mounted ebonised and boulle center table, the waved frieze with a drawer inlaid with scrolling foliage in contra-partie marquetry, mid-19th century, 58¹/₂in. wide. (Christie's) $4,565

A Biedermeier burr-elm and ebonized center table with circular quarter-veneered top and faceted shaft, first quarter 19th century, 54in. diameter. (Christie's) $6,718

An early 19th century Dutch mahogany and marquetry center table, the circular top with cornucopia, birds and butterflies, on a splayed trefoil pedestal, 3ft. 4in. diameter. (Phillips) $4,984

Biedermeier inlaid mahogany center table, Austrian, second quarter 19th century, on a hexagonal line-inlaid pedestal supported by six C-scroll brackets terminating on a six-sided flanged base, 30in. wide. (Butterfield & Butterfield) $3,300

Classical mahogany veneer center table, New York, 1810–30, marble top on a conforming skirt with canted corners over a four-column pedestal, 33¹/₂in. wide. (Skinner Inc.) $1,100

George III Irish mahogany center table, acanthus carved knees, cabriole legs on scrolled feet, 33¹/₂in. wide. (Skinner Inc.) $3,025

A mahogany circular center table with gadrooned edge, on rectangular platform with paw feet, mid 19th century, 45in. diameter. (Christie's) $1,728

An antique French Régence oak center table with shaped top and intricately carved frieze on scroll legs, circa 1730, 28in. high. (Selkirk's) $1,100

CONSOLE TABLES

Régence carved oak console, first quarter 18th century, the rectangular mottled and figured brown and gray marble top above a frieze centered by a pierced shell-and-scroll-carved cartouche, 47¹/₂in. wide. (Butterfield & Butterfield)
$15,400

A Louis XVI decorated console table, with an elliptical molded red and gray marble top, on a ribbon carved and acanthus scrolling support, 1.01m. wide. (Phillips) **$2,314**

Italian rococo stripped pine console table, with a rectangular verde antico marble top above a shell and scroll-carved cavetto apron, 4ft. 3¹/₂in. wide. (Butterfield & Butterfield)
$6,600

An 18th century carved giltwood console table, in the Louis XV taste, surmounted by a later simulated marble top of arc en arbalette serpentine outline, 3ft. 2in. wide. (Phillips) **$7,950**

A classical mahogany pier-table, probably New York, circa 1825, the rectangular crossbanded top above a frieze with brass string inlay and a mirrored back-plate, 42³/₄in. wide. (Christie's) **$2,640**

Italian rococo parcel-gilt and polychromed console table, mid 18th century, the blue marbleized top of shaped outline with inswept sides above a conforming frieze carved with rocaille, 40¹/₂in. wide. (Butterfield & Butterfield)
$5,500

George III inlaid mahogany console table, circa 1790–1800, raised on fluted and reeded turned tapering supports, 36in. wide. (Butterfield & Butterfield)
$3,575

An antique French Louis XV oak console with shaped apron on scrolled legs and having a marble top, circa 1760, 37in. wide. (Selkirk's) **$2,000**

Rococo pine console table, possibly German, mid 18th century, raised on carved cabriole legs, ending in a waterfall, 31in. wide. (Skinner Inc.) **$3,300**

CONSOLE TABLES

Italian baroque parcel-gilt and painted console, the shaped triangular scagliola top with a molded outline above a parcel-gilt and painted foliate-scroll frieze, 46in. wide.
(Butterfield & Butterfield)
$6,600

A French serpentine fronted giltwood console table of Louis XV design, the molded Carrara top above a paterae and guilloche molded frieze with central foliate cartouche, 19th century, 71³/₄in. wide.
(Christie's) $2,731

A 19th century German rosewood and oak console table, of demi-lune form, the deep frieze applied and carved with heraldic crests, 4ft. 3in. wide.
(Spencer's) $1,592

Continental neoclassical style inlaid marble, painted and parcel-gilt console table, the semi-circular white marble top inlaid in the Adam taste, 34³/₄in. wide.
(Butterfield & Butterfield)
$4,400

American Renaissance carved walnut pier mirror and console, executed for the south wall of the main floor hall, Thurlow Lodge, Menlo Park, California by Herter Brothers, New York, circa 1872, 15ft. 6in. high.
(Butterfield & Butterfield)
$22,000

A neo-classical Italian cream painted and parcel gilt half-round pier table, surmounted by a volute molded top with projecting angles, 4ft. 2¹/₂in. wide.
(Phillips) $2,703

One of a pair of George II style parcel-gilt mahogany eagle-form consoles each with rectangular salmon marble top within a parcel-gilt and floral-carved border, 4ft. wide.
(Butterfield & Butterfield)
$6,600

George I style silvered wood and molded gesso console table, second half 19th century, with a gray slate rectangular slab top, 37in. wide.
(Butterfield & Butterfield)
$3,025

A Napoleon III ormolu-mounted red tortoiseshell and boulle console table and pier glass en suite, the serpentine top inlaid with a Berainesque design above a waved frieze, 43¹/₂in. wide.
(Christie's) $10,043

Rococo pine console table, possibly German, rectangular egg and dart and Vitruvian scroll frieze, 52in. wide. (Skinner Inc.) $3,410

Rococo giltwood console table, possibly German, shaped foliate-pierced apron carved with acanthus leaves, 42in. wide. (Skinner Inc.) $7,700

A Victorian serpentine fronted steel console table with eared Carrara marble top above a shaped frieze with central bust, on cabriole legs, date mark 14 May 1846, 55¹/₂in. wide. (Christie's) $3,459

A classical gilt-stenciled mahogany pier-table, New York, 1815–1830, the rectangular white and gray marble top with canted corners over a conforming bolection-molded frieze centered by a rosette, 45in. wide. (Christie's) $6,600

A 19th century Swedish Empire white painted and gilt heightened console table and pier glass, the egg and dart molded cornice surmounted by a large eagle with outspread wings, 2ft. 11in. wide. (Phillips) $7,120

A William IV mahogany console table with rectangular molded white marble top on column uprights with foliate capitals, 45in. wide. (Christie's) $1,547

One of a pair of Milanese ebonized console tables, each supported by a kneeling blackamoor and scrolling back panel, mid 19th century, 40¹/₄in. wide. (Christie's) (Two) $7,294

One of a pair of Regency giltwood console tables attributed to Marsh & Tatham, the design attributed to C.H. Tatham, each with later rectangular white marble top, the frieze carved with egg-and-dart above foliage, 54¹/₄in. wide. (Christie's) (Two) $594,660

A George I gilt-gesso pier table attributed to James Moore and John Gumley, the removable rectangular top with re-entrant corners decorated in low relief with ribbon-tied laurel around the ensigned *RC* cypher of Richard Temple. (Christie's) $349,800

DINING TABLES

L. & J.G. Stickley dining table, circa 1912, no. 720, circular top, straight apron, supported on five tapering legs, with four extension leaves, 48in. diameter. (Skinner Inc.) $1,800

Italian baroque carved walnut draw-leaf table, raised on turned cylindrical legs headed by Ionic columns, 47in. wide. (Butterfield & Butterfield) $825

L. & J.G. Stickley dining table, circa 1912, no. 722, round top, straight apron cross stretcher base tenoned through square legs, with three leaves, 48in. diameter. (Skinner Inc.) $1,300

A Regency mahogany extending dining table, the rounded rectangular top including five extra leaves with a reeded edge and plain frieze, 12ft. long. (Phillips) $10,605

A Robert 'Mouseman' Thompson oak dining table, on chamfered column trestle ends joined with single chamfered square section stretcher, 183cm. wide. (Christie's) $3,347

A Dutch oak draw-leaf table with rectangular twin-flap top, on baluster legs joined by box stretchers and on block feet, 17th century, 79¹/₂in. wide. (Christie's) $6,783

"Bonnie" dining table, designed by Ferruccio Tritta, produced by Studio Nove, New York, on three columnar supports, 56in. diameter. (Skinner Inc.) $2,600

Large Burmese carved and pierced hardwood circular tilt-top dining table, second half 19th century, the top carved with a broad border of exotic birds and foliage over a swelling scalloped pierced conforming frieze, 4ft. 5in. (Butterfield & Butterfield) $2,750

A mahogany dining table with Cumberland action on canti-levered quadripartite baluster-turned supports and splayed legs, early 19th century, 49¹/₂in. wide. (Christie's) $4,991

343

DRESSING TABLES

A 19th century Dutch mahogany and marquetry dressing chest, decorated with trailing floral sprays and festoons with ribbons. the rectangular molded top surmounted with a rectangular plate, 3ft. 3in. wide. (Phillips) **$3,026**

An Edwardian satinwood and inlaid dressing table, the oval plate above two small drawers, the lower section with five drawers around the kneehole. (Bonhams) **$1,331**

Charles X ormolu mounted mahogany dressing table, circa 1825, 55in. high. (Skinner Inc.) **$2,310**

A Chippendale carved walnut dressing-table, Philadephia area, 1760–1780, on cabriole legs with carved knees and ball-and-claw feet, 33½in. wide. (Christie's) **$46,200**

A Federal carved mahogany dressing table, New York, 1800–1815, the stepped rectangular top with four short drawers surmounted by a rectangular frame containing a conforming plate on serpentine dolphin supports, 63¼in. high. (Christie's) **$2,200**

A Queen Anne cherrywood dressing table, New England, 1740–1760, with a molded rectangular top above a long drawer and three short drawers over an arched apron, 32½in. wide. (Christie's) **$8,800**

An Empire mahogany and giltmetal mounted dressing table, the arched rectangular swing-plate above a single frieze drawer, 32in. wide. (Christie's S. Ken) **$3,282**

Queen Anne cherry dressing table, Connecticut, 1750–80, brass replaced, 33in. wide. (Skinner Inc.) **$17,600**

Federal mahogany carved and inlaid dressing bureau, Boston or North Shore, Massachusetts, circa 1810, supported by fluted posts and scrolled side arms, 38½in. wide. (Skinner Inc.) **$15,400**

DRESSING TABLES

A Victorian burr walnut dressing table with matching wash stand, 48in. wide. (Dreweatt Neate)　**$1,170**

A Chippendale carved mahogany dressing-table, Philadelphia, 1760–1780, on cabriole legs headed by shells with ball-and-claw feet, 34in. wide. (Christie's)　**$22,000**

A heat-treated sheet steel dressing table with chair en suite by Tom Dixon, with raised rectangular platform inset with marble, solder heightened with gilt, 125.5cm. wide. (Christie's)　**$2,954**

George I burl walnut dressing table, the rectangular top with molded edge and notched front corners, raised on cabriole legs ending in pad feet, 31½in. wide. (Butterfield & Butterfield)　**$4,400**

Italian baroque style ivory-inlaid walnut chest, 19th century, the superstructure with swiveling mirror above two small drawers, raised on turtle-form feet, 4ft. 3½in. wide. (Butterfield & Butterfield)　**$4,400**

Chippendale carved walnut dressing table, Pennsylvania, circa 1770, with shaped skirt and shell carved legs ending in trifid feet, 35in. wide. (Skinner Inc.)　**$4,125**

A 19th century mahogany and walnut crossbanded dressing table, 48in. wide. (Dreweatt Neate)　**$2,925**

Dutch neoclassical satinwood and amboyna dressing table, fourth quarter 18th century, fitted interior, 24¾in. wide. (Skinner Inc.)　**$1,320**

An early 19th century mahogany tray top dressing table, 38½in. wide. (Dreweatt Neate)　**$895**

DROP LEAF TABLES

A rare George III mahogany drop leaf table, raised on cabriole legs with molded and carved knees, terminating on hoof feet, the top 40¹/₂ x 35³/₄in.
(Tennants) $8,556

Queen Anne painted maple drop leaf dining table, New England, 1760–80, extended 42¹/₄in.
(Skinner Inc.) $3,575

A Queen Anne mahogany drop-leaf table, New England, circa 1750, the hinged oval top with twin drop-leaves over a flat-arched apron and cabriole legs, 46¹/₂in. wide.
(Christie's) $2,420

Chippendale cherry drop leaf table, New England, circa 1780, with beaded edges and replaced brass, refinished, 36in. wide.
(Skinner Inc.) $550

A Victorian walnut Sutherland table, the molded rectangular top on baluster turned legs with down curved feet.
(Bonhams) $976

A late 18th/early 19th century Dutch mahogany and marquetry drop-leaf table, with all over profusion of floral and riband twist inlay, on square tapering legs, 3ft. 6¹/₂in. extended.
(Phillips) $1,958

Federal mahogany carved and veneered drop leaf table, Rhode Island, circa 1815, one working and one simulated drawer, 45¹/₄in. wide.
(Skinner Inc.) $1,320

Fine American custom-made butterfly table in the 17th century style, one drawer, 28in. high.
(Eldred's) $523

A Victorian walnut Sutherland table with quarter-veneered burr-walnut oval top, on splayed legs, 42in. wide.
(Bearne's) $1,032

DRUM TABLES

A Victorian mahogany drum-top library table, the revolving top with tooled leather insert, on a scroll-carved tripod base with brass castors, 48in. diameter.
(Bearne's) $2,666

A Regency mahogany drum-table, on gadrooned baluster shaft and quadripartite support with fluted leaf-headed scroll legs, 27¼in. diameter.
(Christie's) $26,235

A George III rosewood drum-table, the frieze with four mahogany-lined drawers and four simulated drawers, 39in. diameter.
(Christie's) $21,863

A William IV carved mahogany drum-top library table, the revolving crossbanded top inset with a panel of green tooled leather containing four short and dummy drawers in the frieze, 3ft. 6in. diameter.
(Phillips) $7,830

A Regency rosewood library drum table banded overall in tulipwood, the frieze with four mahogany-lined drawers and four hinged doors simulated as drawers, 29¾in. high.
(Christie's) $19,360

George IV mahogany drum table, second quarter 19th century, the cross-banded circular revolving top above a frieze fitted with alternating drawers and false drawers, 44in. diameter.
(Butterfield & Butterfield)
                             $3,575

A good George IV mahogany drum table, the tooled leather inset top within an ebony inlaid border of scrolling foliage, upon a plain turned lotus capped column and tri-form base with scroll feet, 49¾in. diameter.
(Tennants) $3,348

Regency style mahogany drum table, second half 19th century, the circular cross-banded top above a frieze alternating drawers and false drawers, 45½in. diameter.
(Butterfield & Butterfield)
                             $3,575

A William IV mahogany library drum table, the circular top inlaid with a star-shaped patera with gadrooned rim and paneled frieze, 51¼in. diameter.
(Christie's) $23,232

GATELEG TABLES

A William and Mary walnut gateleg dining table with oval twin-flap top on spiral-twist supports joined by stretchers, 62¼in. wide.
(Christie's) $2,495

A Charles II oak oval gateleg table with a boldly figured top, frieze drawer and slender turned legs, joined by molded stretcher, 59½ x 46in.
(Tennants) $2,790

A George II walnut gateleg table with oval twin-flap top on turned spreading legs joined by box stretchers and on scroll feet, 57¼in. wide.
(Christie's) $5,653

A walnut gateleg table with oval twin-flap top and single end-drawer on fluted column legs and splayed feet joined by plain stretchers, 30in. wide.
(Christie's) $1,452

A Charles II oak gateleg table with oval twin-flap top, on turned slightly-spreading supports joined by stretchers, 49½in. wide.
(Christie's) $3,392

A George II mahogany spider-leg table, the rectangular twin-flap top on ring-turned legs, 34in. wide.
(Christie's S. Ken) $2,738

Mid to late 19th century mahogany Sutherland table, standing on turned ringed legs and stretchers, 3ft. wide.
(G.A. Key) $622

A mahogany and walnut gateleg dining table, the rounded rectangular top crossbanded in satinwood, on baluster turned supports tied by similar stretchers, the top 18th century.
(Bonhams) $1,505

Painted maple gateleg table, New England, 18th century, dark red stain, beaded skirt, 29¾in. wide.
(Skinner Inc.) $3,850

FURNITURE

LARGE TABLES

A mahogany dining-table in three sections, the end-sections with rectangular single drop-leaf, the central section with two drop-leaves, on square tapering reeded legs, 160in. long. (Christie's) **$2,657**

Federal mahogany veneer two-part dining table, circa 1815, refinished, 93in. long. (Skinner Inc.) **$2,090**

Federal carved mahogany two-part dining table, New England, circa 1815–1825, the D-shaped top with one drop leaf, on ring-turned and foliate carved legs, length extended 7ft. 9in. (Butterfield & Butterfield) **$1,540**

A George IV mahogany extending dining table with rounded rectangular top on reeded turned tapering legs, includes four extra leaves, 128in. wide. (Christie's) **$4,319**

A Regency mahogany D-end extending dining table with reeded edge and sliding action, on reeded tapering legs, includes three extra leaves, 124in. wide. (Christie's) **$10,557**

A mid George III mahogany D-end dining table in three sections with central rectangular drop-leaf section and two D-ends, on square tapering legs, 136in. wide. (Christie's) **$6,910**

Spanish baroque walnut and oak refectory table, circa 1700, the one-piece rectangular top on baluster, ring-turned and blocked trestle supports, 6ft. 8¹/₂in. long. (Butterfield & Butterfield) **$9,350**

A mahogany triple pedestal D-end dining table with reeded edge, on vase-turned shaft and reeded splayed legs, basically late 18th century, 157in. wide, extended. (Christie's) **$12,012**

Italian Renaissance style walnut refectory table, 94in. long.
(Skinner Inc.) $1,650

A large and early refectory table, the massive three-plank top supported on solid trestle ends joined by two 'beam' stretchers, 119in. long.
(Tennants) $8,500

An oak refectory table with rectangular plank top on baluster-turned uprights joined by stretchers, the top 18th century, 121in. wide.
(Christie's) $4,607

Shaker cherry ministry dining table, probably Enfield, New Hampshire or Harvard, Massachusetts, first half 19th century, the cherry two-board scrubbed top above an arched maple base, 84in. long.
(Skinner Inc.) $82,500

A Federal inlaid mahogany two-part dining table, probably Baltimore, 1800–1810, in two parts, each with D-shaped ends and rectangular drop leaves, on five square tapering legs edged with stringing, 48in. wide.
(Christie's) $14,300

A George III mahogany dining table in three parts inlaid with boxwood and ebonized lines, with a central drop-leaf section and 'D'-shaped ends, 8ft. 6in. x 3ft. 6in. wide.
(Phillips) $6,678

Queen Anne maple dining table, probably Rhode Island, circa 1760, old refinish, 47¼in. wide.
(Skinner Inc.) $3,000

Drop-leaf table, George Nakishima for Widdicomb Furniture, Grand Rapids, Michigan, circa 1955, 73¾in. wide.
(Skinner Inc.) $1,500

LARGE TABLES

A Victorian Anglo-Indian rosewood dining table, the coffered rectangular top on lappeted carved tapering turned legs with castors, extending to 215 x 68¼in.
(Christie's S. Ken) $10,196

A George IV oak dining-table by Alexander Norton, with rectangular central section and two rectangular end-sections, on turned tapering arcaded legs carved with acanthus and headed by paterae, 216in. long.
(Christie's) $8,479

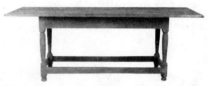

Federal cherry and mahogany veneer two-part dining table, New England, early 19th century, refinished, 88⅝in. wide.
(Skinner Inc.) $1,430

Painted pine and maple tavern table, probably New England, 18th century, base with red stain, top scrubbed, 72in. long.
(Skinner Inc.) $2,500

A Charles II oak bench with molded rectangular top and arcaded frieze, on splayed turned baluster legs joined by stretchers, 80¾in. wide.
(Christie's) $4,522

A George IV mahogany dining table with two D-shaped end-sections and one extra leaf, on fluted turned tapering legs and giltmetal caps, 79in. wide.
(Christie's) $2,479

Italian Renaissance walnut refectory table, on a baluster trestle support joined by a plain stretcher, 57in. wide.
(Skinner Inc.) $2,200

Flemish baroque oak drop-leaf table, the molded base raised on turned supports on flattened bun feet, 63½in. long.
(Skinner Inc.) $3,300

Painted and decorated Windsor table, New England, early 19th century, later orange paint with buff color accent, 29¼in. wide. (Skinner Inc.) $715

George II mahogany tilt-top tea table, second quarter 18th century, raised on three foliate-pierced cabriole legs carved at the knees with shells, ending in pad feet, 35¾in. diameter. (Butterfield & Butterfield) $1,980

Gustav Stickley table, circa 1902, no. 449, original dark finish, labeled with small decal of _Stickley_ in a rectangle, 24in. diameter. (Skinner Inc.) $3,900

A specimen marble and hardwood table, the associated circular top centered with a star within a radiating pattern, inlaid with various marbles, mid-19th century, 32in. diameter. (Christie's) $3,652

George III satinwood vitrine table, last quarter 18th century, the rectangular recessed glazed top within a cross-banded reserve opening to a red velvet-lined interior, 34½in. wide. (Butterfield & Butterfield) $3,300

Venetian rococo lacca contrafatta tilt-top table, early 18th century, the top tilting above a pierced baluster-form standard carved with acanthus and husk swags, 32in. high. (Butterfield & Butterfield) $4,950

Antique American tavern table in pine and other woods, oval top, cut-out apron, moulded square tapered legs, 25in. high. (Eldred's) $193

A late Federal mahogany serving-table, Boston, circa 1815, on spirally-turned legs with turned feet and casters, 39½in. wide. (Christie's) $4,400

Chippendale walnut tilt-top tea table, Pennsylvania, late 18th century, old surface, 27½in. diameter. (Skinner Inc.) $880

OCCASIONAL TABLES

Charles X walnut occasional table, circa 1820–1830, the circular shallow gallery top above a plain cylindrical shaft with slight entasis on lappet-carved and scrolled incised tripod supports, 28¹/₄in. high. (Butterfield & Butterfield) **$1,870**

Regency inlaid calamander pedestal table, the burlwood-banded circular top above a plain frieze with molded gilt-metal edge, 36in. diameter. (Butterfield & Butterfield) **$5,500**

A Chinese export black and gilt-lacquer tripod gaming-table, decorated with chinoiserie landscapes and centered by a coat-of-arms within a Vitruvian scroll border, 18th century, 42¹/₂in. wide. (Christie's) **$3,203**

A Victorian mother-of-pearl inlaid black lacquer night table, mid 19th century, with a serpentine rectangular molded-top above a conforming shaped frieze, 30in. high. (Christie's) **$4,800**

Louis XIV beech occasional table, raised on shaped molded supports joined by an undulating H-form stretcher, 32³/₈in. wide. (Butterfield & Butterfield) **$4,125**

A Regency green and gilt japanned tripod table with rounded rectangular top decorated with chinoiserie figures fishing by a pagoda, 23in. wide. (Christie's) **$6,969**

Chippendale mahogany carved tea table, Newport, Rhode Island, 1760–80, old surface, 33in. diameter. (Skinner Inc.) **$11,000**

Queen Anne figured maple tavern table, New England, 18th century, the oval top above a rectangular case on circular tapering legs, 36¹/₂in. wide. (Butterfield & Butterfield) **$1,650**

A French mahogany round table with marble top, 25¹/₂in. wide. (Dreweatt Neate) **$975**

OCCASIONAL TABLES

A mahogany tripod table with piecrust tilt-top and bird-cage support on fluted shaft with downswept legs, 27½in. high.
(Christie's) $3,291

A Louis XV/XVI transitional tulipwood and kingwood serpentine table en chiffonier inlaid with lines, the hinged top quarter veneered and enclosing a velvet lined interior, 1ft. 5in. wide.
(Phillips) $2,226

A George II mahogany tripod table with circular piecrust tilt-top on spirally-fluted baluster shaft with downswept legs, 26½in. high.
(Christie's) $18,392

A Napoleon III bronze gueridon after the monument to Henri II, with circular specimen marble top inlaid with various marbles including brocatelle, green and red porphyry, verde antico and Siena, 26½in. high.
(Christie's) $3,287

An Italian scagliola top signed by *Mannelli* and dated *1702*, centred by a roundel decorated with a seated figure in 17th century costume with a parrot and a dog, on an associated part-17th century oak base, 32in. high.
(Christie's) $148,500

A mahogany tripod table, with baluster gallery inlaid with a brass line and pierced at the centers with carrying-handle motifs, mid-18th century, 28¾in. high.
(Christie's) $12,656

A mid-Georgian fruitwood tripod table inlaid overall with bands of walnut squares, the circular tilt-top on bird-cage support and turned spreading shaft, 27¼in. diameter.
(Christie's) $3,291

A late George II mahogany architect's table, the rectangular molded top with re-entrant corners and book rest, adjustable ratchet and with hinged brass candlestands at the sides, 3ft. wide.
(Phillips) $7,120

A Chippendale birch tilt-top tea-table, New England, circa 1760–1780, the serpentine top with outset corners tilting above a ball and column-turned pedestal and tripartite base with cabriole legs, 26¼in. wide.
(Christie's) $2,420

354

OCCASIONAL TABLES

A brass and mahogany tripod table on scrolled channeled supports joined by a circular stretcher on paw feet, first half 19th century, 22in. diameter.
(Christie's) $4,259

A George III mahogany tripod table with circular tip-up top with raised piecrust scalloped border on later birdcage and partly-fluted foliate baluster support, 28in. high.
(Christie's) $81,774

A mid-Victorian rosewood tripod table, the shaft carved with lotus leaves with fluted cluster columns on downswept legs with pointed feet, 29¹/₂in. high.
(Christie's) $3,485

A fine Chippendale carved mahogany tea table, Philadelphia, 1760–1780, with circular dished and molded rim top revolving and tilting above a tapering columnar and compressed ball-turned pedestal, 27¹/₂in. high.
(Christie's) $27,500

A Roman circular micro-mosaic table-top inlaid with flowers including roses, a tulip, violets and lily-of-the-valley, mid-19th century, 26¹/₂in. diameter.
(Christie's) $23,760

A George III mahogany tripod table with chamfered square tip-up top and curved gallery pierced and carved with running foliate scrolls, 29¹/₂in. high.
(Christie's) $136,290

A mahogany tripod table the shaped rectangular tilt-top with brass-inlaid spindle gallery on turn shaft carved with a pagoda roof, 25¹/₄in. high.
(Christie's) $2,130

A Louis XV kingwood, crossbanded and marquetry tric trac table, by Pierre Migeon II, the rectangular detachable top inset with a panel of tooled leather, 2ft. 8in. wide.
(Phillips) $40,653

A mahogany urn table of George III style with pierced square galleried top, the frieze carved with blind fretwork and with candle-slide, 24in. high.
(Christie's) $2,323

OCCASIONAL TABLES

Chinese Zitan table, 19th
century, rectangular with
pierced apron, square legs and
box stretcher, 45in. wide.
(Skinner Inc.) $2,000

A mid Victorian papier mâché
and gilt decorated occasional
table, with central painted panel
depicting figures in a landscape,
24in. wide.
(Christie's) $2,111

'Walking Table' by Ron Arad,
the rectangular top composed of
aluminium honeycomb encased
between two glass sheets, 180cm.
wide.
(Christie's) $5,907

Italian micro-mosaic occasional
table in the rococo taste, the
base Alpine, third quarter 19th
century, the black circular top
centered by a spray of flowers,
30in. high.
(Butterfield & Butterfield)
$2,200

A late 18th/early 19th century
North Italian rosewood,
marquetry and bone inlaid
poudreuse, all over decorated
with formal scrolling bands and
panels with foliage masks and
mythological beasts, 2ft. 6in.
wide.
(Phillips) $2,136

Set of George III mahogany
quartetto tables, circa 1810–
1820, raised on simulated
bamboo-turned and blocked
double standards, 20in. wide.
(Butterfield & Butterfield)
$3,300

A George II mahogany wine-
table with circular top on turned
baluster shaft, downswept legs
and pad feet, 22¹/₂in. high.
(Christie's) $2,826

A Regency mahogany reading
table, on a square column and
stepped platform base with 'X'-
shaped legs, ring turned feet,
casters, 2ft. 4in. wide.
(Phillips) $1,602

George III mahogany tilt-top
table, third quarter 18th
century, raised on ball and claw
feet, 27¹/₂in high.
(Skinner Inc.) $5,500

OCCASIONAL TABLES

A Georgian mahogany and oak tripod table, the round tilt top on a turned column support, on cabriole legs.
(Bonhams) $498

Spanish baroque walnut table, late 17th/early 18th century, on double baluster-turned and blocked supports joined by incised tied stretchers, 43¼in. wide.
(Butterfield & Butterfield) $3,300

A George II mahogany occasional table, the circular snap-top with a birdcage action, with a ring turned baluster stem, 2ft. 3in. diameter.
(Phillips) $1,157

A Federal mahogany serving-table, New York, circa 1810, the rectangular top with outset rounded front corners and reeded edge, on turned tapering legs and brass feet, 35¾in. wide.
(Christie's) $3,300

A Gordon Russell walnut occasional table, twelve-sided molded top above octagonal section legs with ebony feet, 53.3cm. high.
(Christie's) $1,083

A Restoration mahogany gueridon with circular fossilised gray marble top, on three spiral supports, 32in. diameter.
(Christie's) $3,455

A good 18th century Dutch decorated tea table, the circular dished snap top with a contemporary painting of Ester swooning in the presence of King Ahasuerus, 2ft. 8in. diameter.(Phillips) $3,840

A Gordon Russell oak table, the rectangular overhanging top with chamfered edges, above plain frieze enclosing single drawer, with ebony chamfered feet, 80cm. wide.
(Christie's) $2,363

A late 18th/early 19th century Dutch mahogany and floral marquetry occasional table, the circular snap-top with a ribbon tied spray of flowers and a bird within a meandering border.
(Phillips) $1,246

Federal cherry breakfast table, New England, early 19th century, single drawer with beading and replaced brass, 36in. wide.
(Skinner Inc.) **$660**

A George III mahogany Pembroke table, 32¹/₂ in. x 38in., on splay feet with brass castors.
(Dreweatt Neate) **$1,853**

Federal cherry inlaid Pembroke table, New England, circa 1810, with stringing on the skirts and legs, 34¹/₂in. wide.
(Skinner Inc.) **$1,320**

A George III satinwood veneered Pembroke table, banded in tulipwood, the frieze with a mahogany lined drawer, the square tapering legs, on brass castors, 30in.
(Woolley & Wallis) **$4,334**

A fine George III satinwood and marquetry Pembroke table, attributable to William Moore of Dublin, on square tapering legs inlaid with paterae hung with husk chains united by an undertier with gaitered feet, 2ft. 9in. long.
(Phillips) **$15,350**

A Federal inlaid mahogany Pembroke-table, Mid-Atlantic States, 1790–1810, the hinged oval top with twin drop-leaves over a conforming cockbeaded frieze drawer flanked by tablet inlay on square-tapering legs, 38¹/₄in. wide.
(Christie's) **$3,080**

A George III mahogany Pembroke table, the frieze inlaid with ebonized banding and one drawer, on square tapering legs with brass caps, 38¹/₂in. wide.
(Christie's) **$1,646**

A George III mahogany Pembroke table, on associated quadripartite base with turned spreading shaft, the downswept reeded legs with brass caps, 48in. wide.
(Christie's) **$3,098**

A satinwood and rosewood banded Pembroke table, with shaped rectangular leaves above an end frieze drawer on square tapered legs.
(Bonhams) **$824**

PEMBROKE TABLES

A Federal cherrywood Pembroke table, New England, 1800–1810, the rectangular top with two D-shaped drop-leaves above a long drawer, on square tapering legs, 35½in. long. (Christie's) **$1,100**

Cherry inlaid Pembroke table, Connecticut River Valley, circa 1800, refinished, 36in. long. (Skinner Inc.) **$3,850**

An early Victorian mahogany Pembroke table, the rounded rectangular top above a square section column, on a concave plinth and scroll feet. (Bonhams) **$773**

George III inlaid mahogany Pembroke table, circa 1790, with a reeded edge and rounded drop leaves hinging above a line-inlaid drawer, 37¼in. wide open. (Butterfield & Butterfield) **$2,475**

Fine George III burl yew-wood and mahogany oval Pembroke table of small size, late 18th century, raised on boxwood strung square tapering supports, 27¼in. wide open. (Butterfield & Butterfield) **$4,125**

A Federal mahogany Pembroke-table, New York, 1790–1810, the oval hinged top with molded edge and D-shaped drop leaves over a cockbeaded bowed frieze drawer, on square tapering legs, 31¾in. wide. (Christie's) **$1,760**

A George III mahogany Pembroke table, of oval shape, a single drawer to the end, on tapered legs with reeded corners. (Bonhams) **$854**

A Federal mahogany Pembroke-table, New York, 1790–1810, the rectangular top with clover-leaf shaped drop leaves over a frieze drawer, on square tapering legs, 31in. wide. (Christie's) **$2,640**

A late George III 'plum pudding' mahogany Pembroke table with kingwood crossbanding and boxwood and ebonized stringing, 44¼in. wide. (Bearne's) **$4,988**

SIDE TABLES

A gilt-gesso and pine side-table of George II style with rectangular black fossil marble top, the frieze decorated with acanthus scrolls above a cartouche with female mask, 58in. wide.
(Christie's) $5,808

A George III mahogany side table, the rectangular top above a geometric blind-fretwork frieze, on canted square legs with pierced fretwork angles and on block feet, 60in. wide.
(Christie's) $7,964

Late 18th century Italian mahogany side table with rectangular yellow marble top, on lyre shaped supports joined by stretchers 156.5cm. wide.
(Finarte) $7,623

A fine 18th century Florentine scagliola panel table top, possibly attributable to Lamberto Gori, inset into a Regency ebonized and parcel gilt base, the top panel 3ft. 7in. x 2ft. 2in.
(Phillips) $35,673

One of a pair of George III harewood, sycamore and marquetry side tables possibly by Thomas Chippendale Senior or Junior, banded overall in mahogany and amaranth, on square tapering legs, 44in. wide.
(Christie's)   (Two)

                    $52,470

A fine George III mahogany inlaid and crossbanded side table, raised on slender cabriole legs with simple leaf-carved spandrels and stiff acanthus leaf to the feet, 28³/₄in. wide.
(Tennants) $8,370

A George III mahogany side table with rectangular top, the rim carved with entrelac, above a beaded molding, on square tapering fluted legs, 46in. wide.
(Christie's) $8,131

Italian walnut and burr walnut and marquetry side table, with one long drawer, on cabriole legs, Turin, early 18th century.
(Finarte) $40,477

A George III mahogany and marquetry side table, the eared serpentine top crossbanded in tulipwood and inlaid with a geometric pattern centered by an oval floral pattern, 42in. wide.
(Christie's) $17,228

SIDE TABLES

A George III giltwood side table attributed to George Brookshaw, with demi-lune white marble top decorated with bands of urns linked with anthemia and scrolling foliage, 60½in. wide.
(Christie's) **$46,222**

A George III mahogany side table banded overall in satinwood and inlaid with ebonized lines, on turned tapering feet, 56in wide.
(Christie's) **$10,844**

A George III satinwood, marquetry and white-painted and parcel-gilt side table, the serpentine top crossbanded in tulipwood and banded with scrolling foliate inlay divided by paterae, 44¾in. wide.
(Christie's) **$25,212**

A George III mahogany side table, the serpentine molded top with a flap at the back, on tapering cabriole legs mounted with gilt-lacquered brass foliage, 32in. wide.
(Christie's) **$24,338**

A classical green-painted and gilt-stenciled side-table, attributed to John Needles, Baltimore, early 19th century, on a quadripartite base with foliate bracketed X-shaped supports, on turned tapering feet, 37in. wide.
(Christie's) **$6,600**

A French brass-mounted floral marquetry side table, the rectangular top with molded edge and inlaid with a vase of flowers, wit two frieze drawers and on paneled square tapering legs, second half 19th century, 48in. wide.
(Christie's) **$7,227**

A George III mahogany side table with rectangular top, the frieze with three drawers divided by projecting panels carved with berried laurel wreaths, 52½in. wide.
(Christie's) **$223,905**

A William and Mary rosewood and kingwood oyster-veneered side table, the rectangular top inlaid with a star-pattern within circles, 26½in. wide.
(Christie's) **$5,597**

An early Georgian green and gilt-japanned side table decorated overall with chinoiserie scenes with people, birds and buildings in a landscape, 35¾in. wide.
(Christie's) **$10,505**

A Regency kingwood sofa table, with rounded rectangular twin-flap top, the frieze with two drawers to the front, the reverse with two simulated drawers, 59in. wide.
(Christie's) **$15,741**

A Regency brass-inlaid sofa table with rounded rectangular twin-flap top, the frieze with two mahogany-lined drawers and two simulated drawers, 61¹/₂in. wide.
(Christie's) **$6,776**

A Regency fiddleback mahogany sofa table inlaid overall with ebony stringing, on vase-shaped end-supports joined by a turned stretcher, 59in. wide.
(Christie's) **$8,855**

A Regency ebonized and bird's-eye maple sofa table, the rounded rectangular twin-flap top crossbanded in kingwood and centered by a burr-elm oval, on a U-shaped support, 58¹/₂in. wide.
(Christie's) **$6,030**

A George III mahogany and tulipwood banded sofa table, inlaid with boxwood and ebonized lines, the rounded rectangular hinged top containing two drawers, 5ft. x 2ft. 4in.
(Phillips) **$7,320**

A late George III rosewood and satinwood banded sofa table, the rounded rectangular top above two frieze drawers opposing two false drawers, 58¹/₂in. wide.
(Bonhams) **$9,900**

An elegant Regency calamander and satinwood banded sofa table, in the manner of George Oakley, outlined in brass stringing, 58in. wide.
(Bonhams) **$15,725**

A Regency satinwood and mahogany sofa table inlaid overall with ebony lines, on rectangular end-supports joined by a later turned stretcher, 61¹/₂in. wide.
(Christie's) **$4,899**

A Regency brass-inlaid sofa table on associated simulated rosewood quadripartite scroll supports and concave-sided platform base, 57in. wide.
(Christie's) **$5,034**

SOFA TABLES

A Regency mahogany and inlaid sofa table, the top with 'D'-shaped ends and crossbanded in rosewood, on lyre shaped twin end supports and splay legs joined by an undertier, 75cm. high.
(Phillips) $7,700

A William IV plum pudding mahogany sofa table, the rounded rectangular and crossbanded twin flap top fitted with two frieze drawers to one side, 49in. wide.
(Christie's) $3,350

Mid 19th century mahogany sofa table, the arched pedestals surmounted by giltwood eagle heads, 126cm. wide.
(Finarte) $10,222

A Regency mahogany sofa table, the figured top crossbanded in satinwood and rosewood above two drawers, 58in. wide, extended.
(Bonhams) $5,550

A Regency ormolu-mounted and brass-inlaid rosewood sofa-table, with a shaped rectangular twin-flap top inlaid with a line and fleurs-de-lys, 54in. wide.
(Christie's) $6,769

A Regency rosewood sofa table banded overall in satinwood, the paneled frieze with two mahogany-lined drawers to the front, 56³/₄in. wide.
(Christie's) $10,648

A Regency roseood, satinwood crossbanded and inlaid sofa table, the hinged top with rounded corners with scroll inlay, supported by lopers with roundels.
(Phillips) $9,250

A satinwood and floral painted sofa table, the rounded rectangular twin-flap top fitted with two frieze drawers to one side, 58in. wide.
(Christie's) $7,400

A George III mahogany sofa table with rounded rectangular two-flap top crossbanded with rosewood and inlaid with ebony and boxwood lines, 58in. wide.
(Christie's) $36,993

SOFA TABLES

A Regency mahogany sofa table with rounded rectangular twin-flap top crossbanded in kingwood and edged with gadrooning, on curved central supports, 56in. wide.
(Christie's) $3,769

A George III mahogany sofa table, on slender trestle supports and outswept legs tied by an inverted 'U'-shaped stretcher.
(Bonhams) $1,728

A Regency mahogany sofa table with reeded ornament, on standard dual splayed end supports united by a stretcher, 5ft. 5in. x 2ft. 4in.
(Phillips) $3,005

A Heal & Son oak sofa-table, designed by Sir Ambrose Heal, the frieze with two short drawers above twin column turned tapering legs, circa 1915, 158.5cm. wide.
(Christie's) $3,150

A Regency rosewood, ebony banded and brass inlaid sofa table, the rectangular twin flap top with a secrétaire frieze drawer, 4ft. 3in. extended.
(Phillips) $3,889

A Regency rosewood and brass inlaid sofa table, the hinged top with fleur-de-lis inlay to the corners, on rectangular column quatrefoil platform, 4ft. 10in. x 2ft. extended.
(Phillips) $5,406

A George III mahogany sofa table, on solid trestle ends joined by a later stretcher and splayed legs with brass caps, 59in. wide.
(Christie's) $3,099

A mahogany and rosewood crossbanded sofa table with two true and two false frieze drawers, on solid end supports and outswept legs, 19th century.
(Bonhams) $1,469

A Regency mahogany sofa table, crossbanded in rosewood and satinwood, and inlaid with boxwood and ebony lines, 5ft. extended.
(Phillips) $14,847

TEAPOYS

A Victorian rosewood teapoy, the hinged domed lid enclosing a divided interior above a turned baluster column, on three 'C'-scroll feet.
(Bonhams)   **$1,154**

William IV carved rosewood teapoy, circa 1838, opening to a storage area, raised on a petal-carved baluster-form pedestal on a coved square base on scrolled feet, 32in. high.
(Butterfield & Butterfield)   **$1,650**

A 19th century Anglo-Indian padoukwood teapoy, the scalloped sarcophagus top enclosing four hinged compartments above a foliate carved frieze.
(Bonhams)   **$777**

WORK BOX & GAMES TABLES

A Victorian inlaid walnut games table/work box, with octagonal tapered column on tripod base.
(Bonhams)   **$864**

A French Second Empire rosewood and brass inlaid traveling compendium with raised rectangular hinged lid and fitted interior with a variety of games.
(Christie's)   **$4,223**

Regency pen-work decorated work table, circa 1810, hexagonal hinged top centered by a painted classical scene, 28$\frac{1}{2}$in. high.
(Skinner Inc.)   **$2,640**

A Victorian burr-walnut and inlaid work table with rounded rectangular hinged top enclosing a tapering fitted well, above twin baluster-turned end-standards, 23in. wide.
(Christie's)   **$1,902**

A William IV rosewood work table, on a square waisted column with concave plinth and bun feet.
(Bonhams)   **$1,374**

A Victorian inlaid walnut combined games table and canterbury, on baluster-turned supports with slatted spindle-turned canterbury below, 33in. wide.
(Christie's)   **$1,456**

One of a pair of Regency ormolu-mounted calamander games-tables, each D-shaped top with stylized satinwood border enclosing a baize-lined playing-surface, 36in. wide. (Christie's) (Two)

$27,313

A Regency brass-inlaid rosewood games-table, the blue leather-lined top with sliding rectangular section, on paw feet headed by volutes, 55in. wide. (Christie's) $15,741

A Regency coromandel and brass strung combined games and work table, the stellar inlaid rosewood veneered hinged ratcheted top sliding to reveal a backgammon board, 2ft. 4in. wide. (Phillips) $4,882

A Regency rosewood and painted work-table, with hinged rectangular top with reading-support and concealed fitted mahogany-lined side drawer above a fixed green silk-lined and tasseled tapering work-basket, 19¾in. wide. (Christie's) $5,883

A Regency Chinese export lacquer decorated work table, with pagoda landscapes within a dragon border enclosing a fitted interior with ivory fittings, having a sliding well with armorial appliquéwork below, 2ft. wide. (Phillips) $3,450

A Federal mahogany sewing-table, Salem, Massachusetts, 1790–1810, the serpentine top above a conforming case with a cockbeaded drawer fitted with a velvet-lined writing surface over an additional drawer and sliding work-bag, 19½in. wide. (Christie's) $8,250

A Regency brass-mounted and inlaid rosewood combined work and games-table inlaid overall with foliage, the top centered by a rectangular glazed panel inset with a painting-on-vellum of a spray of flowers, 27¼in. wide. (Christie's) $10,925

Late 18th century Italian walnut and burr walnut games table inlaid with fruitwood, 101cm. wide. (Finarte) $6,812

A Regency ormolu-mounted rosewood, burr yewwood and simulated rosewood work-table with round rectangular green leather-lined pierced brass three-quarter-galleried top, 21in. wide. (Christie's) $4,202

WORK BOX & GAMES TABLES

A Regency ormolu-mounted rosewood games-table, the hinged square top sliding to reveal a backgammon board, on lyre-shaped end-supports, 28½in. wide.
(Christie's) $9,095

A Regency ebonized and penwork decorated games table, painted to simulate ivory marquetry in the Indian taste, the top decorated for chess with flowers and foliage, 1ft. 6in. square. (Phillips) $3,180

A Regency Chinese export lacquer card table, the hinged rectangular top with chinoiserie figures in a pagoda landscape within floral and foliate borders, 2ft. 7½in. wide.
(Phillips) $2,385

A Transitional ormolu-mounted tulipwood and marquetry gueridon, the kidney-shaped top decorated with trophies within scrolled and ribbon-tied foliate borders, on cabriole legs headed by simulated fluting joined by a conforming undertier, 22in. wide.
(Christie's) $55,440

A George II brass and mother-of-pearl-inlaid padoukwood concertina-action games-tables attributed to John Channon, the brass-inlaid rectangular eared top bordered by cartouches and engraved strapwork, 32½in. wide.
(Christie's) $42,020

An ormolu-mounted, marquetry and lapis lazuli work table, the hinged top centered by a foliate marquetry inlay on a sycamore ground, banded in harewood and boxwood, with a ribbon-tied foliate marquetry panel to each side, late 19th century, 24¾in. wide. (Christie's) $4,015

Late 18th century triangular walnut games table with two small drawers, on tapering legs, Genoese.
(Finarte) $5,727

A Regency rosewood games table, attributed to Gillows, the rounded rectangular top with re-entrant corners and central reversible sliding section inlaid with a chess-board, 34in. wide. (Christie's) $10,467

An early George III mahogany work-table with rectangular gadrooned top, a slide and partly-divided drawer on chamfered square legs, 28½in. wide.
(Christie's) $31,152

WORK BOX & GAMES TABLES

A Dutch Biedermeier vide poche with oval dished top and mahogany-lined divided drawer above a green silk-lined workbasket, 21½in. wide. (Christie's) **$1,936**

Classical carved mahogany veneer work table, Salem, Massachusetts, circa 1820, the top drawer fitted with writing surface, 18¾in. wide. (Skinner Inc.) **$770**

A Regency rosewood work table with rounded rectangular hinged top banded in calamander on spirally-reeded column support and quadripartite concave-sided base, 20½in. wide. (Christie's) **$6,195**

A classical carved mahogany work-table, attributed to A. Querville, Philadelphia, 1815–1825, the hinged rectangular top with molded edge above a fitted interior, on four carved paw feet with waterleaf-carved knees and casters, 23in. wide. (Christie's) **$3,850**

A Chinese Export padouk-wood games-table inlaid overall with ebony and satinwood lines, the rounded rectangular twin-flap top banded in satinwood with sliding central section, early 19th century, 48in. wide. (Christie's) **$17,336**

A George III mahogany work-table inlaid with satinwood and banded overall, with mahogany-lined drawer above a pleated green silk-lined work basket, 24in. wide. (Christie's) **$3,203**

A Federal mahogany work-table, New York, 1800–1815, on a turned pedestal and quadripartite base on downswept molded legs, on paw feet with casters, 25¼in. wide. (Christie's) **$3,300**

Victorian rosewood octagonal formed work box on a tapering octagonal pedestal with triple splay base, approx. 15in. wide. (G.A. Key) **$823**

A late Federal carved mahogany work-table, Salem, Massachusetts, 1800–1820, the rectangular top with outset rounded corners, on spirally-turned tapering legs and ball feet, 21¾in. wide. (Christie's) **$1,320**

A Victorian walnut games and work table, the burr-walnut fold-over top set with a Tunbridge-ware panel depicting Eridge Castle, 23in. wide. (Bearne's) **$1,651**

American Renaissance figured maple and rosewood sewing table by Herter Brothers, New York, circa 1872, on stylized feet, 34½in. wide. (Butterfield & Butterfield) **$1,045**

An early Victorian rosewood work table, the rectangular top with wide crossband, above a fitted drawer and a fabric-covered workbag, 23in. wide. (Tennants) **$1,105**

Federal mahogany veneer work stand, New England, circa 1810, old refinish, 16½in. wide. (Skinner Inc.) **$3,300**

A Victorian burr walnut work table, on shaped legs, 22in. wide. (Dreweatt Neate) **$741**

A Victorian burr-walnut work table, the banded hinged top above a well on a turned support on four carved cabriole legs, 20½in. wide. (Bonhams) **$885**

A classical mahogany work-table, New York, circa 1830, the square top with outset polygonal hinged ends opening to deep compartments over two cockbeaded small drawers, 30½in. high. (Christie's) **$935**

Directoire burl walnut sewing table, circa 1800, raised on X-form supports joined by a ring-turned stretcher, 26½in. wide. (Butterfield & Butterfield) **$2,090**

A William IV rosewood work table with hexagonal hinged top and upholstered well on scroll uprights carved with rosettes, 22in. wide. (Christie's) **$1,248**

WRITING TABLES & DESKS

A brass-mounted mahogany and partridgewood writing-table with ebonized banding, on lyre-shaped end-supports joined by double turned stretchers, 44in. wide.
(Christie's) $7,537

A Regency partridgewood, mahogany and ebony bonheur-du-jour, the mirror-backed glass-topped rectangular superstructure with a concave-fronted shelf, on turned tapering feet, 26½in. wide.
(Christie's) $2,093

A 19th century kingwood, mahogany ormolu mounted marquetry bureau plat, in the Louis XV style, crossbanded and veneered with 18th century panels, 4ft. wide.
(Phillips) $10,605

A Regency rosewood writing-table with rounded rectangular green leather-lined top with pierced brass three-quarter gallery, on downsplayed end-supports, 41in. wide.
(Christie's) $11,229

A George III ormolu-mounted writing-table, the eared rectangular red leather-lined top with molded edge, the inverted breakfront frieze with three mahogany-lined drawers, 49in. wide.
(Christie's) $12,606

A Regency brass-inlaid satinwood writing-table with rounded rectangular crossbanded top, on solid paneled end-standards centered by a flowerhead medallion and joined by an arched stretcher, 33¼in. wide.
(Christie's) $15,741

A mid-Victorian ormolu mounted mahogany burr walnut and marquetry bonheur-du-jour of Louis XVI style, with three-quarter pierced gallery, above a tambour shutter with book-ends, 34in. wide.
(Christie's) $5,113

A George III plumwood dressing-and-writing-table with serpentine hinged top inlaid with diagonally-quartered panels of plum bordered with rosewood and inlaid with lines, 20½in. wide.
(Christie's) $29,205

A giltmetal-mounted red-and-gilt Japanese lacquer writing-box-on-stand, the detachable box with hinged rectangular lid decorated with buildings and mountains beside a lake, 27½in. wide.
(Christie's) $2,904

A George III mahogany writing-table in the manner of Mayhew and Ince, on turned tapering legs headed by ovals and with brass caps, 53½in. wide.
(Christie's) $11,369

A Regency giltmetal-mounted rosewood and parcel-gilt Carlton House desk, the carved galleried superstructure with later geometric gallery and with six mahogany and cedar-lined drawers, 55in. wide.
(Christie's) $147,070

A Regency rosewood and brass-mounted writing table, in the Louis XVI taste, the rectangular crossbanded top inset with a green tooled leather panel, 4ft. 9in. x 2ft. 7in.
(Phillips) $4,452

A George III ormolu-mounted mahogany bonheur-du-jour possibly by John Okeley in the style of David Roentgen, the stepped top lifting to reveal a mirror and well flanked by two platforms with solid galleries, 36½in. wide.
(Christie's) $116,160

Louis XVI style gilt-bronze-mounted mahogany escritoire, after Weisweiler, circa 1900, raised on tapering square gilt-bronze legs headed by female herms, 33½in. wide.
(Butterfield & Butterfield)
$9,900

A Napoleon III ormolu and Sèvres-pattern porcelain-mounted, thuyawood and ebonized bonheur-du-jour, on fluted baluster supports joined by two undertiers, 53¼in. wide.
(Christie's) $5,478

A Regency amboyna and ebony bonheur-du-jour, the superstructure with shaped rectangular three-quarter galleried top above a central opening and cedar-lined drawer flanked by paneled bowfronted doors, 29¼in. wide.
(Christie's) $11,555

An Edwardian satinwood kneehole writing desk, the leather lined top of recessed serpentine outline with shelved superstructure and pierced brass gallery, 48in. wide.
(Christie's) $5,113

A French tulipwood, parquetry and ormolu-mounted serpentine bonheur du jour, decorated overall with geometric motifs, the crested and tiered mirror-backed top above two paneled doors, 33in. wide.
(Christie's) $11,517

371

An Edwardian inlaid satinwood bowfront desk, with ledged back and finials above a frieze drawer between two quarter-veneered paneled doors, 48in. wide.
(Christie's) $1,440

A Makers of Simple Furniture birchwood desk designed by Gerald Summers, the partly hinged rectangular top above two open shelves and single pedestal, 114cm. wide.
(Christie's) $788

Louis XV style parquetry bureau plat, late 19th century, the rectangular top with gilt-tooled leather writing surface over a central spiral ribbon-inlaid frieze drawer flanked by banks of two parquetry-inlaid drawers, 4ft. 11in. wide.
(Butterfield & Butterfield)
$4,950

A mid Victorian mahogany writing table, with hinged fitted compartment above two frieze drawers, on fluted tapering legs, stamped *Gillow*, 36in. wide.
(Christie's) $3,071

George III mahogany double-sided writing desk, circa 1800–1810, the drawers with lion mask ring handles, 42in. wide.
(Butterfield & Butterfield)
$2,750

A George III mahogany cylinder top writing table, inlaid with boxwood lines, the elliptical tambour shutter enclosing four small drawers and pigeonholes above a writing slide, 3ft. 6in. wide.
(Phillips) $6,360

A mahogany Carlton House desk inlaid with satinwood bands and ebony and satinwood lines, on square tapering legs, 55in. wide.
(Christie's) $8,638

An elegant George III mahogany lady's writing table, the crossbanded rectangular top inlaid with a boxwood oval, on ring turned tapered legs, 21³/₄ in. wide.
(Bonhams) $5,157

Louis XV style gilt-metal-mounted bureau plat, the shaped rectangular top inset with gilt-tooled leather within a banded reserve applied with a gadroon-cast edge, 5ft. wide.
(Butterfield & Butterfield)
$2,750

WRITING TABLES & DESKS

A mahogany partners' library table of Regency design with rounded rectangular leather-lined top and sides all carved with Greek-key designs, 19th century, 54¹/₂in. wide.
(Christie's) $38,390

An oak writing desk, designed by George Walton, the rectangular top above three drawers, on square tapering supports, circa 1900, 37in. high.
(Christie's) $1,181

A satinwood and inlaid kidney-shape desk, circa 1890, with leather inset top above a central drawer flanked by four small drawers.
(Tennants) $2,883

Louis Philippe brass and mother-of-pearl inlaid rosewood bonheur du jour, circa 1840, with mother-of-pearl and brass marquetry and gilt-bronze outline, raised on shaped cabriole legs, 31in. wide.
(Butterfield & Butterfield) $3,025

An 18th century Italian walnut and gilt copper applied kneehole dressing or writing table, the rectangular top with a hunting scene and palmette ornament to the corners, on later oak cabriole legs, 2ft. 10in. wide.
(Phillips) $2,544

Grain painted standing desk, probably Pennsylvania, circa 1825–40, original yellow ocher and burnt umber feather graining, 32in. wide.
(Skinner Inc.) $1,210

An Edwardian mahogany and marquetry writing table, the raised superstructure with broken scroll pediment above a hinged compartment inlaid with fan motif and cornucopiae, 42in. wide.
(Christie's) $3,839

Good Louis XVI style gilt-bronze-mounted mahogany and parquetry bureau plat, late 19th/early 20th century, the rectangular top with a leaf-tip cast gilt-bronze border, 45¹/₄in. wide.
(Butterfield & Butterfield) $9,900

An oak gate-leg writing cabinet designed by M.H. Baillie-Scott, rectangular top above fall-flap with pierced steel hinge plates designed by C.A. Voysey, 91.5cm. wide.
(Christie's) $5,900

FURNITURE

Northwest German gothic wrought-iron-mounted oak Fronstollentruhe, circa 1450–1500, the triple-planked rectangular top with strap metal hinges, 6ft. 9in. long. (Butterfield & Butterfield) $12,000

A French walnut cassone with hinged rectangular top edged with gadrooning, the front carved with twin panels with reclining figure of Juno, 16th century and later, 67in. wide. (Christie's) $20,790

Flemish late Renaissance carved walnut coffer, the rectangular hinged plank top with thumb-molded edge, 5ft. 1in. long. (Butterfield & Butterfield) $10,000

A paint-decorated poplar and maple blanket-chest, Pennsylvania, 19th century, the hinged and molded rectangular top opening to a compartment fitted with a till, 38^{5}/$_8$in. long. (Christie's) $15,000

An important large roironuri ground domed seventeenth century export coffer decorated in gold, silver and black hiramakie, takamakie, nashiji, hirame with a central lobed panel depicting stags beside rocks and autumnal flowers, 138cm. wide. (Christie's) $298,375

An Italian pietra paesina-mounted ebonised box with fielded paneled rectangular hinged lid centered by a rectangular panel, depicting the story of Noah, early 17th century, 16in. wide. (Christie's) $13,860

French gothic carved oak coffer, the rectangular triple plank hinged top opening to a till, the front with five gothic arched carved panels, 5ft. 7^{1}/$_2$in. long. (Butterfield & Butterfield) $12,000

A Momoyama Period rectangular coffer decorated in gold hiramakie and aogai, the flat overlapping top with a central rounded rectangular panel depicting a coastal scene with stags among trees, early 18th century, 50.5cm. wide. (Christie's) $40,450

A Momoyama period rectangular wood coffer with domed cover decorated with panels of samegawa-togidashi within shippo-hanabishi border, circa 1600, 45.5cm. long. (Christie's) $26,500

TRUNKS & COFFERS

An Italian walnut cassone
carved with scrolling foliage,
dolphins and classical urns, on
molded plinth base and block
feet, mid/late 16th century, 68in.
long.
(Christie's) $2,367

A 17th century Italian walnut
cassone, the front panel well-
carved with a vacant cartouche
surrounded by deeply carved
foliate scrolls and flowerhead
roundels, 68³/₄in. long.
(Tennants) $1,451

Louis XIII Provincial oak
armor chest, the long
rectangular hinged molded edge
top above fielded paneled sides
and front, 6ft. 11in. wide.
(Butterfield & Butterfield)
            $3,300

Antique American lift-top
blanket chest in pine, painted
black, two drawers, bracket feet,
37in. wide.
(Eldred's) $550

A pair of Italian walnut
cabinets-on-stand, the platform
base fitted with drawers, on
angled paw feet, adapted in the
19th century from 17th century
cassones, 55in. wide.
(Christie's) $3,455

Oak and pine carved and
paneled chest over drawers,
Hadley area, Massachusetts,
1690–1710, 49¹/₂in. wide.
(Skinner Inc.) $10,450

Grain painted and decorated
six-board chest, New England,
early 19th century, grained
ocher and umber original
decoration, 40in. wide.
(Skinner Inc.) $2,475

Grain painted and stencil
decorated six-board chest,
probably Schoharie County,
New York, circa 1830, red and
black graining in simulation of
rosewood, 40in. wide.
(Skinner Inc.) $440

Late 17th century oak paneled
coffer, the front with lozenge
carved detail, the top with three
panels and fluted molding,
approx. 4ft. 9in. wide.
(G.A. Key) $585

A Flemish oak coffer, the paneled front headed by an entrelac molding above flower-filled guilloche, on channeled stile feet, late 17th century, 46in. wide.
(Christie's) $1,036

Louis XIII carved oak chest, 17th century, the atlantes carved in the round and forming the front and return of the corner posts and standing on hippocampi, 4ft. 4¹/₂in. wide.
(Butterfield & Butterfield)
                               $2,750

A Charles I oak coffer with hinged molded rectangular top and frieze carved with foliage and sea-monsters, the front with three panels carved with flowerheads, divided by caryatid moldings, 48in. wide.
(Christie's) $3,769

An early 18th century South German oak marriage chest, the lid and front decorated with twin inlaid ivory crests and coats-of-arms representing the two families, 53cm. wide.
(Phillips) $1,414

A 17th century iron strongbox, of Armada design, the hinged top with nipple studs to release the key cover to a twelve shutter locking device, 58cm. wide, probably German.
(Phillips) $1,591

Painted blanket chest, New England, circa 1830, the top opens to paper lined interior, with lidded molded till above two drawers, 39in. wide.
(Skinner Inc.) $3,575

An 18th century Italian carved walnut cassone of small size, with a guilloche decorated hinged top and paneled sides on paw feet, 1ft. 8in.
(Phillips) $1,149

Oak chest, designed by George Washington Maher, circa 1912, green colored oak, cedar lined, brass handles, ends with fielded panels incorporating the motif of *Rockledge*, 60in. wide.
(Skinner Inc.) $2,000

An early Tudor iron-bound ash coffer, the hinged domed top enclosing an interior with false floor and till, 34¹/₂in. wide.
(Christie's) $9,045

TRUNKS & COFFERS

Carved and painted oak and pine chest over drawer, possibly by Peter Blin (1670–1710), 46in. wide.
(Christie's) **$12,100**

Continental late gothic carved oak box and cover of rectangular form, the cover with a stamped circular motif forming an allover trellis pattern, 12¼in. wide.
(Butterfield & Butterfield) **$522**

Painted pine blanket box, probably New Hampshire, first half 19th century, original blue paint, one original pull, 45¾in. wide.
(Skinner Inc.) **$1,430**

A Chinese black and gold lacquer coffer-on-stand, the rectangular hinged top decorated with peony, tits and junglefowl within panels of foliage, early 18th century, 53¼in. wide.
(Christie's) **$9,293**

Painted pine, oak and maple paneled joined chest, probably Hampshire County, Massachusetts, circa 1720, 30in. wide.
(Skinner Inc.) **$6,600**

A 17th century walnut cassone, of sarcophagus form, the paneled front carved in high relief with an urn of flowers flanked by winged female figures holding vacant cartouches, 6ft. 2in. wide.
(Phillips) **$6,678**

A Charles II oak coffer with rectangular hinged top enclosing an interior with till, the paneled front carved with *1671 IT*, on stile feet, 50in. wide.
(Christie's) **$1,884**

A handsome oak boarded coffer, the rectangular top above a foliate carved front, on trestle supports, 62½in. wide.
(Bonhams) **$1,425**

A Charles II oak coffer with molded rectangular hinged top above a frieze of stylized flowers and a central hobnail-bordered geometric panel flanked by two oval panels, 52in. wide.
(Christie's) **$1,225**

WARDROBES & ARMOIRES

Fine American Renaissance parcel-gilt, stained and burled maple armoire by Herter Brothers, New York, circa 1872, the mirrored door above a single drawer, 46¹/₂in. wide.
(Butterfield & Butterfield)
$5,500

A Gillow & Co. 'Stafford' satinwood and walnut wardrobe in three sections, painted in oil depicting Spring and Autumn, enclosing two slides above two short and three long drawers, 258cm. wide.
(Christie's) $8,860

A French mahogany collapsible armoire of Empire style with molded rectangular cornice above a pair of doors with two geometrically-glazed panels, on bracket feet, 54¹/₂in. wide.
(Christie's) $1,948

A George III oak wardrobe with molded rectangular breakfront cornice and Greek-key molding, on ogee bracket feet, 78¹/₄in. wide.
(Christie's) $4,522

Louis XV/XVI Provincial oak armoire, late 18th century, the pair of grilled doors centring a reserve carved with scrolling tendrils issuing foliage and flowerheads, 4ft. 9¹/₂in. wide.
(Butterfield & Butterfield)
$3,025

An oak checkered inlaid wardrobe, possibly designed by M.H. Baillie Scott, the molded cornice above a curved recess flanked by a pair of doors inlaid with flowers, 85in. wide.
(Christie's) $3,347

Régence carved walnut armoire, circa 1720, with a cavetto molded cornice of broken outline over a pair of metal grill doors, 5ft. 4in. wide.
(Butterfield & Butterfield)
$6,600

An antique English Victorian mahogany wardrobe with a tall pair of serpentine-fronted doors with conformingly shaped molded cornices, circa 1850, 7ft. 4in. high.
(Selkirk's) $3,100

An antique French Louis XV cherrywood bonnetière with two inset shaped panels and an outset cornice on scroll feet, circa 1760, 44in. wide.
(Selkirk's) $5,250

WARDROBES & ARMOIRES

A Robert 'Mouseman' Thompson oak and burr-oak carved paneled wardrobe, with one long cupboard door and one short enclosing two shelves, 119.5cm. wide.
(Christie's) $10,239

A Heal & Son mahogany wardrobe designed by Sir Ambrose Heal, from the 'Five Feathers Suite', London circa 1898, 191.5cm. wide.
(Christie's) $3,150

A Gordon Russell oak wardrobe, the molded rectangular top above two paneled doors with brass ring drop handles, on rectangular legs, 136.5cm. wide.
(Christie's) $4,529

Louis XV transitional pickled oak armoire, the cavetto cornice over triple panel sides and a pair of wire mesh double panel doors well carved with plumes, 4ft. 10in. wide.
(Butterfield & Butterfield) $9,900

A Regency mahogany breakfront wardrobe in the manner of Gillows, in four sections, the central section with two paneled doors enclosing trays, 99in. wide.
(Christie's) $3,896

A French Provincial oak armoire with molded rectangular cornice above two long paneled doors with waved moldings and carved with flowerheads and baskets of flowers, second half 18th century, 66in. wide.
(Christie's) $4,620

A pine wardrobe designed by E.W. Godwin, the paneled front with two studded brass bands and central cupboard door enclosing single fitted shelf, 241.5cm. high.
(Christie's) $23,628

A Regency mahogany wardrobe in four sections, the waved cornice centered by an anthemion and divided by turned finials above two paneled doors enclosing five trays, 98in. wide.
(Christie's) $4,522

A Victorian mahogany and satinwood banded wardrobe, the cavetto banded pediment above two fielded paneled doors and two base drawers, 49¼in. wide.
(Christie's S. Ken) $1,029

WARDROBES & ARMOIRES

An antique Italian rococo Venetian green painted wood armadio with silver-gilt highlights, 18th century, 7ft. 6in. wide.
(Selkirk's) $7,500

A fine antique French Régence oak armoirette with a pair of doors, each with arched tops and two scroll-carved fielded panels, circa 1730, 4ft. 4in. wide.
(Selkirk's) $5,250

A 17th century Flemish oak armoire, the projecting molded cornice above a frieze carved with scrolling foliage, on massive bun feet, 79in. wide.
(Bearne's) $3,956

George III Provincial oak bacon cupboard, second half 18th century, the concave-fronted high fielded paneled backrest enclosed by two pairs of shallow doors over two pairs of double paneled doors, 5ft. 5in. wide.
(Butterfield & Butterfield)
$1,870

An interesting gentleman's teak compactum, circa 1848, fitted with two short and five long graduated drawers with camphorwood linings.
(Tennants) $1,488

A mid-Georgian oak cupboard with molded rectangular cornice above three drawers and two fielded paneled long doors enclosing two shelves on stile feet, 59^{1}/$_{2}$in. wide.
(Christie's) $3,203

One of two rare wardrobes inscribed *Thine* and *Mine*, constructed in a rich variety of grain, with similar end panels and fitted interior, each 66in. high. (Tennants)   (Two)
$3,400

A Flemish oak and ebonized kas with molded cornice above acanthus scroll and putti frieze flanked by masks above four geometrically paneled doors, dated *1672*, 19th century, 70in. wide.
(Christie's) $8,408

An Edwardian mahogany breakfront wardrobe with two paneled doors, two short and three long drawers, flanked by full-length mirrored doors, 101^{1}/$_{2}$in. wide.
(Bearne's) $1,514

WASHSTANDS

A George III mahogany wash stand of square shape, the top with raised waved edge, inset with four recesses and basin well, 35in. high.
(Lawrence) $2,079

Federal mahogany and bird's-eye maple veneer corner chamber stand, Massachusetts, early 19th century, 21in. wide.
(Skinner Inc.) $2,090

A Federal carved mahogany wash basin stand, Boston, 1800–1810, with reeded and shaped splash board above a rectangular top with reeded edge fitted for three wash bowls, 30¹/₂in. wide.
(Christie's) $1,430

A late Regency gentleman's mahogany toilet stand inlaid with satinwood bands and boxwood geometric lines, 24³/₄in. wide.
(Christie's S. Ken)
                         $3,019

A Liberty & Co. oak washstand, the shaped superstructure with two tiled panels, above rectangular marble top flanked by two shelves, on bracket feet, 104cm. wide.
(Christie's) $716

A Federal inlaid mahogany and birch-veneered wash-stand, Portsmouth, New Hampshire, 1790–1810, the rectangular top pierced with three circular openings and edged with a three-quarter gallery, 35¹/₂in. high.
(Christie's) $22,000

Antique American Sheraton washstand in mahogany, shaped backsplash, drawer in base, turned legs, 18¹/₂in. wide.
(Eldred's) $220

Shaker painted pine washstand, Harvard, Massachusetts, 19th century, the hinged lid opens to a storage compartment above a cupboard, 36in. wide.
(Skinner Inc.) $11,000

An early 19th century mahogany washstand in the Gillows manner, on tapering reeded legs, 33in. wide.
(Bearne's) $740

A Federal mahogany etagère, Boston, 1790–1810, on turned tapering feet with brass cup feet and casters, 53in. high, 17½in. wide.
(Christie's) $3,300

A mid-Victorian calamander, ebonized and parcel-gilt three-tier whatnot with three-quarter galleried top, on fluted ebonized supports and toupie feet, 20in. wide.
(Christie's) $7,744

A George III satinwood whatnot with four canted rectangular tiers, the top tier with a mahogany and cedar-lined frieze drawer, 16¾in. wide.
(Christie's) $20,328

One of a pair of brass and mahogany three-tier whatnots, each with rectangular top with fluted edge and acorn finials, 39in. high.
(Christie's)   (Two)
                           $6,030

A Morris & Co. ebonised mahogany seven-tier whatnot, the design attributed to Philip Webb, on turned and square-section supports, circa 1875, 143.5cm. high.
(Christie's) $3,347

Mid to late 19th century four tier whatnot, each tier of serpentine form with turned pilaster supports, 22in. wide.
(G.A. Key) $183

A Regency mahogany three-tier lectern whatnot, the rectangular top above a finialed base with drawer, joined by turned supports and vertical cross stretchers, 45in. high.
(Christie's) $2,879

George III mahogany étagère, early 19th century, the two shelves with later diamond latticework sides and back, 32¾in. wide.
(Butterfield & Butterfield)
                           $2,475

A Regency mahogany whatnot of obelisk form, inlaid with ebony stringing, with acorn finials and five tiers on turned spreading supports, 67½in. high.
(Christie's) $6,776

WINE COOLERS

A late George III mahogany octagonal wine cooler with satinwood banded hinged top, on later stand with square tapering legs, 21in. wide.
(Christie's)   **$1,183**

A Regency brass-bound mahogany wine-cooler, with hinged oval fluted top centered by an oval stepped finial carved with a patera, on stand with paw feet, 26½in. wide.
(Christie's)   **$16,808**

A George III mahogany brass-bound hexagonal wine-cooler with geometrically-inlaid and banded hinged top enclosing an interior fitted with lead-lined divisions, 19in. wide.
(Christie's)   **$12,606**

A 19th century walnut cellaret or jardinière, stamped *Barbetti*, on tortoise feet.
(Dreweatt Neate)   **$4,680**

A George III mahogany wine cooler on stand, the brass-bound octagonal body with crossbanded segmentally-veneered hinged top, 28in. high.
(Bearne's)   **$6,536**

A George III brass-bound carved mahogany oval wine cooler, of coopered construction, with a broad brass band with molded edgings at the rim, 31½in. long.
(Tennants)   **$1,275**

A late George III mahogany and brass bound octagonal wine cooler, with a hinged lid and carrying handles at the tapering sides, 1ft. 7in. wide.
(Phillips)   .**$2,816**

A late 18th century Continental cellaret, the domed top and front inlaid with oval panels in various woods, on primitive cabriole legs, 18in. wide.
(Tennants)   **$2,325**

George III mahogany cellaret on stand, third quarter 18th century, the fluted stand with molded square legs, on casters, 30½in. high.
(Skinner Inc.)   **$3,850**

WINE COOLERS

A George III mahogany wine-cooler, on hairy-paw feet, the sides with brass carrying-handles, with later copper liner, 29¼in. wide.
(Christie's) £6,600

A late Victorian ormolu-mounted mahogany wine-cooler, the hexagonal lid with pomegranate finial, the sides with flower-filled entrelac-molding and laurel-wreath handles, 29in. high.
(Christie's) $3,203

William IV carved mahogany cellaret, second quarter 19th century, the coved rectangular top with canted corners opening to a metal-lined interior, 26in. wide.
(Butterfield & Butterfield) $2,200

A Regency mahogany wine cooler, the rectangular tapered body with a lead lined interior, canted angles and paneled sides with ebony scroll lines, 3ft. x 1ft. 10in.
(Phillips) $4,242

A George II mahogany wine-cooler, the oval brass-bound body with lion-mask carrying-handles with later brass liner on partly imbricated cabriole legs, 26¼in. wide.
(Christie's) $11,293

A William IV oak and ebonized wine-cooler with lead-lined interior above a gadrooned body and on spreading fluted shaft and square base, 26in. diameter.
(Christie's) $3,769

A George III plum-pudding mahogany cellaret, the sides with carrying-handles, the integral stand with square tapering legs and brass caps, 23½in. wide.
(Christie's) $3,872

A George II mahogany wine-cooler, the tapering body mounted with pierced carrying-handles, the waved shaped base edged with foliage centered by bunches of grapes, on hairy-paw feet, 27¾in. wide.
(Christie's) $292,050

A late George III mahogany and brass bound octagonal wine cooler, the hinged lid enclosing a later fitted interior and lining, on turned tapering legs, 20in. wide.
(Christie's) $2,879

WINE COOLERS

George III brass-mounted mahogany octagonal wine cooler on stand, late 18th century, the stand on slightly splayed square tapering supports ending in brass cappings, 17½in. wide. (Butterfield & Butterfield) **$4,125**

An Irish mid-Georgian mahogany bottle-stand, the tray-top with inverted lambrequin border and arched carrying-handle flanked by eight divisions, 28½in. wide. (Christie's) **$16,550**

George III mahogany hexagonal cellaret, the lid opening to a plain interior, the brass-banded sides fitted with two brass loop handles, 24½in. high. (Butterfield & Butterfield) **$1,320**

A George III brass-bound mahogany cellaret of canted rectangular shape, the hinged top inlaid with two satinwood octagonal panels each with a compass medallion, 26in. wide. (Christie's) **$23,232**

A George II oval brass-bound mahogany wine-cooler of bombé shape, the sides with giltmetal carrying-handles, on short cabriole legs and hairy paw feet, 28in. wide. (Christie's) **$104,016**

An early George II walnut cellaret, the molded hinged top with canted corners and divided interior, the sides with carrying handles, 1ft. 6in. wide. (Phillips) **$3,889**

George III brass-mounted mahogany wine cooler on stand, late 18th century, on a conforming stand above splayed square supports ending in casters, 19⅜in. wide. (Butterfield & Butterfield) **$3,850**

An early George III mahogany wine cooler, the oval brass banded body with carrying handles at the sides and zinc liner, the stand with square chamfered legs, 2ft. 1in. wide. (Phillips) **$3,498**

A George III brass-bound mahogany cellaret-on-stand, the hinged hexagonal top enclosing a lead-lined interior with compartments, 18½in. wide. (Christie's) **$10,615**

A Coalbrookdale fern and blackberry pattern cast-iron garden seat, scrolled arms with slatted wooden seat, 59¼in. wide.
(Christie's) $1,660

A bronze and rosso marble bird bath, centered by four addorsed dolphins, on a rusticated square base with stepped marble foot, on wooden plinth, 24in. wide.
(Christie's) $2,429

A white-painted cast-iron garden seat, the back with an arched top rail, with a wooden slatted seat on scrolled legs, 63in. wide.
(Christie's) $457

A fine English lead figure of Acis, attributed to the workshops of John Cheere, the young faun clad in a tightly-fitting bacchic goat-skin with curling hair and pointed ears, circa 1770, 52in. high.
(Christie's) $37,000

Fine pair of neoclassical lead urn-form gatepost or balustrade finials, probably English, late 18th century, 26½in. high.
(Butterfield & Butterfield) $3,575

One of a pair of red stoneware urns and pedestals, the waisted body raised with grapes and vine leaves, the lower part gadrooned on a spreading circular socle and stepped square base, the urns, 20½in. high.
(Christie's) (Two) $1,012

A stone sundial, with a circular stepped top, supported on four scrolled inverted volutes, with quadruped base, on stepped octagonal foot, the dial: 12in. diameter.
(Christie's) $1,720

A pair of patinated lead maquettes cast from models by George J. Frampton, for Queen Mary's Dolls House, of two young maidens in mediaeval costume, 26.2cm. high.
(Christie's) $1,378

A French limestone wall sundial, surmounted by a square stepped finial, the dial carved with the chapters above a molded arch, 18th century, 20in. wide.
(Christie's) $1,113

A large carved stone trough, of rectangular form, 87in. long.
(Christie's) $1,461

An unusual Coalbrookdale pattern cast-iron double-sided bench, with iron slatted seat, the arcaded back pierced with foliage, 56in. wide.
(Christie's) $3,441

A white marble bath, of tapering form with rounded ends, the front carved with two rings, 69in. wide.
(Christie's) $3,643

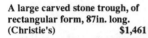

One of a set of four carved stone gothic finials, each of square tapering form and decorated with crockets, 18th/19th century, 48in. high.
(Christie's) (Four) $2,429

Pair of Regency lead jardinières, first quarter 19th century, with a ram's head projecting from each corner above festoons of berried foliage and flowers, 12½in. high.
(Butterfield & Butterfield) $2,200

A bronze armillary sphere on stone base, the interlocking rings pierced by an arrow, the inner edge of the primary ring engraved with the chapters, 59½in. high.
(Christie's) $1,619

A Doulton stoneware fountain, probably designed by John Broad, the quatrefoil base of serpentine outline with two putti astride dolphins between two swans, late 19th century, 62in. high overall.
(Christie's) $13,156

Pair of early Victorian tulip-form cast-iron garden urns, mid 19th century, each with a scalloped lip above a lappet-cast flat-reeded socle, 20½in. high.
(Butterfield & Butterfield) $935

One of a pair of white urns, the body with an egg-and-dart rim above a continuous band carved with foliate ribbon-tied swags, on a stepped socle and square base, 20th century, 32in. diameter.
(Christie's) (Two) $5,060

An Italian marble figure of Hebe, after Antonio Canova, her hair gracefully dressed and wearing a necklace, her right hand raised, 19th century, 50³/₄in. high
(Christie's) $3,846

A William IV lead cistern, of rectangular form, the front centered by a molded panel, the initials *F.T.* in a roundel and dated *1833*, 67³/₄in. wide.
(Christie's) $3,846

A white marble bust of Homer, his hair tied with a ribbon, on circular socle, late 18th/early 19th century, 26in. high.
(Christie's) $3,441

A wrought-iron bird cage, of circular form, surrounded by a domed canopy, with a pair of hinged doors, 101in. high.
(Christie's) $708

One of a pair of monumental white marble urns, after the Warwick Vase, each boldly carved in high relief with masks of Bacchus and Silenus, 20th century, 63in. high.
(Christie's)   (Two)
$17,204

A reconstituted marble group of the Three Graces, after Canova, on a shaped stepped rectangular base, 44in. high.
(Christie's) $850

A Victorian limestone pulpit, carved with bands of oak leaves and acorns, the foliate branches with pigeons, doves and squirrels, on spreading naturalistic foot, 87in. high.
(Christie's) $8,096

Large Victorian cast-iron two-handled garden urn, second half 19th century, with coved fluted sides and applied with side handles modeled as grosteque swans, 42in. high.
(Butterfield & Butterfield)
$2,200

One of a pair of lead urns, each with a waisted body flanked by stylized handles, raised in relief with cherubs, on a waisted socle and square canted foot, late 19th/20th century, the urns, 17³/₄in. high.
(Christie's)   (Two) $688

GARDEN STATUARY & FURNITURE

A white marble bust of the Apollo Belvedere, his tunic held by a circular brooch to the right shoulder, on circular socle, late 18th/early 19th century, 28¹/₂in. high.
(Christie's) $5,870

A rosso marble well-head, carved in high relief with figures, scrolling foliage and flower-filled vases, on molded foot, 33in. high.
(Christie's) $13,156

A lead fountain figure of a putto, holding aloft a dish with his left hand, the right supporting a festoon of flowers, late 19th/early 20th century, 35in. high.
(Christie's) $1,113

A cast-iron garden seat, with vine and grape pattern of curved outline with pierced seat, the legs united by stretchers, 36¹/₄in. wide.
(Christie's) $810

One of a pair of lead urns, each of circular tapering form with two ram's masks, the lower part with overlapping petals and acanthus, 30¹/₂in. diameter.
(Christie's)   (Two) $3,036

A Coalbrookdale laurel pattern cast-iron bench, of semi-circular form with pierced arched back, the arms with griffin head terminals, on winged monopodiae, 46in. wide.
(Christie's) $3,036

A cast-iron fountain, with two circular dishes, the first supported by two cherubs, shown facing each other, on a naturalistic base, 19th century, 57in. high overall.
(Christie's) $4,453

An Istrian gray-veined marble well-head, with a molded edge, and egg-and-dart below, banded by a geometric design with stepped base, 25¹/₄in. high.
(Christie's) $810

A Victorian cast-iron fountain, the octagonal bowl with a molded edge supported by a classically draped female figure, mid-19th century, 82in. high.
(Christie's) $5,060

A late 19th century carved white marble figure of a scantily-clad young man holding a lamp standard.
(Bonhams) **$2,419**

A cast-iron rustic pattern garden bench, with shaped back, the legs embraced by serpents, 52in. wide.
(Christie's) **$2,226**

An 18th century carved limestone pedestal, in the form of a naked kneeling boy supporting a rock, 38¹/₂in. high.
(Tennants) **$221**

An Italian green patinated bronze figure of Creugante, shown standing naked, his left hand with clenched fist raised above his head, inscribed *CRAOCANTE*, late 19th century, 28¹/₂in. high.
(Christie's) **$2,024**

A set of four circular bronze plaques, after Bertal Thorvaldsen, depicting The Ages of Man, 20th century, each 26¹/₂in. diameter.
(Christie's) **$4,048**

An Italian green patinated figure of the dancing faun, after the antique, shown naked, his hair garlanded, on a square stepped base, late 19th/early 20th century, 32in. high.
(Christie's) **$1,518**

A lead figure of a boy, in 15th century costume, his shirt raised with fleur-de-lys and with a purse suspended from his belt, on a stepped circular base, late 19th century, 50in. wide.
(Christie's) **$2,834**

A pair of Victorian stoneware urns, by Blanchard & Co., the waisted body with the head of Medusa to each side and a pair of entwined serpent handles, mid-19th century, 28in. wide.
(Christie's) **$3,036**

One of a pair of stoneware urns and pedestals, the waisted body with ribbon-tied floral pendants, on a fluted spreading circular socle, with square base, late 19th century, the urns, 30in. high.
(Christie's)   (Two)   **$3,846**

One of two Coalbrookdale nasturtium pattern cast-iron seats, with wooden slatted seats, the back stamped *C.B. Dale & Co.*, 51³/₄in. wide. (Christie's) (Two) $2,226

A bronze figure of Mercury after Giambologna, on circular green marble base, 75in. high. (Christie's) $7,123

A French green patinated bronze figure of a classical maiden, cast by Susse Freres, resting her left arm by a column, her hair tied in a chignon, on a rectangular base, 24in. high. (Christie's) $1,316

An Italian white marble figure of the Venus Italica, after Canova, the arms crossed and held to her breast with falling drapery about her, on an oval base, 20th century, 59in. high. (Christie's) $5,667

A pair of circular bronze plaques, after Bertal Thorvaldsen, depicting Day and Night, 20th century, each 31¹/₄in. diameter. (Christie's) $2,834

An Italian white marble fountain, centered by a baluster upright carved with acanthus and surmounted by a playful dolphin, late 19th/early 20th century, 87³/₄in. high. (Christie's) $12,144

An Italian white marble group of Ariadne and the Panther, after Johann von Dannecker, by G. Fettato, the naked Ariadne shown seated on the Panther, late 19th century, 18in. wide. (Christie's) $2,024

A stone gazebo, the domed scrolled wrought-iron rotunda above a frieze carved with fruit, foliage and ribbon-ties, on a circular base, 127¹/₂in. high; 76in. diameter. (Christie's) $60,720

A patinated bronze group of a knight on horseback, his hands held at prayer, the alert horse fully saddled, 38in. high. (Christie's) $8,217

BEAKERS

A Bohemian tumbler engraved within four oval panels with three quarter length figures symbolizing Africa, Europe, Asia and America, 11.5cm.
(Phillips) $860

A dated engraved barrel-shaped tumbler, one side with a view of Yarmouth Church, the reverse with the initials *JRP* above the date *1798*, 12.5cm. high.
(Christie's) $1,698

A German engraved beaker of cylindrical shape, intaglio and mattschnitt with a three-quarter length figure of St. Joanna, 11.5cm.
(Phillips) $748

A North Bohemian 'Lebensalter' cylindrical tumbler engraved with the 'Ages of Man', depicted as an arched bridge, each step supporting a pair of figures, circa 1820, 11.5cm. high.
(Christie's) $5,833

A North Bohemian 'Lithyalin' octagonal waisted beaker attributed to he workshop of Friedrich Egermann, the transparent green ground overpainted in an almost translucent dark-red and cut with wide flutes, Blottendorf, circa 1835, 10cm. high.
(Christie's) $1,525

Biedermeier lithyalin and gilded tumbler, circa 1830, with scene of Aesop before Croesus, signed, 4¹/₂in. high.
(Skinner Inc.) $4,400

An armorial cylindrical tumbler, engraved with a coat-of-arms and inscribed above *Prosperity to the House of Downing*, circa 1817, 10.5cm. high.
(Christie's) $1,653

A German green-tinted flared beaker applied with four milled bands, on a spreading foot and kick-in base, early 18th century, 17cm. high.
(Christie's) $1,458

A Baccarat cylindrical tumbler with an oval panel set with the Badge of the Legion d'Honneur enameled in colors on a gilt ground, 9.5cm. high.
(Phillips) $884

BOTTLES

W. & Co./NY pineapple shaped bitters-type bottle, olive yellow, double collared lip, iron pontil, 8¹/₂in. high, America, 1855–65. (Skinner Inc.) **$990**

Early pattern molded dog bottle, patterned in ribs, diamond and daisy designs, applied feet and head, colorless, 4¹/₄in. high, Germany or France, early/mid 18th century. (Skinner Inc.) **£286**

Blown ink bottle, deep emerald green with a tint of olive, whittled, sloping collar with flaring base-pontil scar, 5¹/₄in. high, America, 1820–50. (Skinner Inc.) **$83**

Early geometric smelling bottle, daisy pattern, corrugated edges, medium amethyst, 2in. high, possibly Keene Marlboro Street Glassworks, Keene, New Hampshire, 1815–30. (Skinner Inc.) **$308**

A sealed armorial 'onion' wine-bottle of olive-green tint, applied with a seal molded with a coat-of-arms, the tapering neck with string-ring and with kick-in base, circa 1710, 15.5cm. high. (Christie's) **$610**

Labeled blacking bottle, *Leonard and King's Sponge Blacking, Methuen, Mass*, deep olive amber, sheared lip-pontil scar, 5in. high. (Skinner Inc.) **$253**

Shaft and globe spirits bottle, circa 1650, with 4in. neck to shoulder, laid on ring below lip-pontil scar. (Skinner Inc.) **$825**

"Browns/Celebrated/Indian Herb Bitters" bottle, Indian queen figural, one of three known, aqua, 12¹/₅in. high, America, 1860–80. (Skinner Inc.) **$6,875**

A sealed and dated 'onion' wine-bottle of olive-green tint, applied with a seal inscribed *T. Burford 1718*, the tapering neck with a string-ring and with kick-in base, 16cm. high. (Christie's) **$1,525**

BOTTLES

"Greeley's Bourbon and Bitters" bottle, barrel shaped, pinkish amber, flattened collar-smooth base, 9¼in. high, America, 1860–80. (Skinner Inc.) **$358**

"Suffolk Bitters" figural pig bitters bottle, yellow amber, double collar, 10in. long, America, 1860–80. (Skinner Inc.) **$385**

Corset waisted cologne bottle, unusual shape, ten panels, medium amethyst, tooled lip-smooth base, 6½in. high, New England, 1850–70. (Skinner Inc.) **$286**

Early decorated spirits bottle, medium sapphire blue with white loopings, pewter threads, pontil scar, 7⅝in. high, Germany/Northern Europe, circa 1750. (Skinner Inc.) **$1,210**

An unusually large sealed green glass wine bottle, with onion-shaped body and kick-in base, 1719, 18cm. high. (Phillips) **$1,800**

Rare "Dr. Kilmer's Swamp Root Kidney Liver and Bladder Remedy", Binghamton, NY, light olive yellow, flat collar with smooth base, 8in. high, America, 1870–90. (Skinner Inc.) **$99**

A dated sealed wine bottle in dark olive glass, and of mallet shape with tapering neck, 1732, 22.5cm. (Phillips) **$1,445**

Pineapple figural bitters-type bottle, bright yellow amber, double collared lip-pontil scar, 8½in. high, probably Whitney Glassworks, Glassboro, New Jersey, 1850–60. (Skinner Inc.) **$275**

"H.P. Herb Wild Cherry Bitters" bottle, with original foil around lip and neck, medium amber, 10¼in. high, America, 1870's. (Skinner Inc.) **$231**

BOTTLES

"Bakers Orange Grove-Bitters" labeled bitters bottle, full front and back labels, olive amber, 9½in. high, America, 1870's. (Skinner Inc.) $374

Early pinch bottle, with sixteen vertical ribs, oval shape, light green, flaring lip-ironpontil scar, half-pint, 6¼in. high, Germany, mid 18th century. (Skinner Inc.) $275

Early looped bottle, medium grayish blue with white loopings, pewter threading, pontil scar, 6½in. high, probably Germany, mid 18th century. (Skinner Inc.) $1,650

"McKeevers Army Bitters" bottle, drum figural, amber, sloping collar-smooth base, 10½in. high, America, 1860–80. (Skinner Inc.) $1,980

Enamelled cordial bottle, colorless with enameled florals and Germanic inscription, metal threads, possibly silver, pontil scar, half-pint, 6¾in. high, Bohemia, mid 18th century. (Skinner Inc.) $176

'National Bitters' ear of corn figural bitters bottle, medium amber, 12½in. high, America, 1860–80. (Skinner Inc.) $225

Cathedral pickle bottle, square, fancy panels, rolled lip-smooth base, 12in. high, America, 1860–70. (Skinner Inc.) $55

Nailsea-type bottle, colorless with white loopings, sheared lip-pontil scar, 8½in. high, 1860–80. (Skinner Inc.) $132

'Browns/Celebrated/Indian Herb Bitters' figural Indian bitters bottle, patented February 11,1868, amber, 12³⁄₈in. high, America, 1870–80. (Skinner Inc.) $200

BOWLS

A J. Couper & Sons Clutha glass bowl, waisted circular form, green tinted glass striated with milky white and bronze colored streaks, 30.5cm. diameter.
(Christie's) $1,575

Webb gem cameo glass bowl, raisin-mauve bulb layered in white cameo cut and completely carved with scrolling floral repetitive design, 4³/₄in. diameter.
(Skinner Inc.) $7,150

A Gabriel Argy-Rousseau pâte-de-verre bowl, molded with four purple, green and red butterflies, with molded signature, 7.8cm. high.
(Christie's) $7,204

Early sugar bowl, galleried rim, solid applied foot, cover with large knop, deep blue, pontil scar, 6in. high, 1820–50.
(Skinner Inc.) $330

A Gabriel Argy-Rousseau pâte-de-verre bowl, the clear, mottled blue and purple glass molded with a band of stlized green buds suspended between blue and green leaf-like swags, 9.9cm. high.
(Christie's) $3,104

An Irish cut circular bowl with a wide band of honeycomb facets, the everted border with narrow flutes, early 19th century, 24.5cm. high.
(Christie's) $972

Swedish Kosta Art Glass bowl, heavy-walled colorless crystal cased to green with internal decoration of darker green, 5in. high.
(Skinner Inc.) $200

A Venni 'Vetro Pezzato Arlecchino bowl', designed by Fulvio Bianconi, the patchwork design comprising of irregular blue, green, red and clear glass, 15.1cm. high.
(Christie's) $6,208

Large white floriform Peking glass bowl with steep flaring sides molded in seven lobes terminating in a wide foliate edge and resting on a tall ring foot, 11in. diameter.
(Butterfield & Butterfield) $2,079

BOWLS

Tiffany favrile pastel blue centerbowl, rare ten-lobed transparent blue vessel striped with opaque opal-blue, 8¹/₂in. diameter.
(Skinner Inc.) $2,750

Steuben amethyst silverina centre bowl, elliptical form with mica-flecked diamond decoration, 12¹/₂in. wide.
(Skinner Inc.) $770

A Venetian footed bowl, the body with gadrooned underside and with two applied blue filigree threads to the folded rim, 16th century, 27cm. diameter.
(Christie's) $3,397

An Irish tripod turnover circular bowl, the rim with shallow diamond-within-lozenge ornament, Dublin or Cork, circa 1800, 28.5cm. diameter.
(Christie's) $2,041

A Stuart clear glass bowl designed by Graham Sutherland, flared shallow form on tapering foot, with waved bands of intaglio decoration, 35cm. diameter.
(Christie's) $2,760

Murano studio glass bowl, Barovier and Toso, designed by Ercole Barovier in the "Cathedrale" or "Athena" series, 8¹/₄in. diameter.
(Skinner Inc.) $4,400

'Bydling St Nicholas, Dorchester, Dorset' a landscape glass bowl by William Walker, bands of swirling earth colors beneath a band of pale blue 'sky', 23cm. wide.
(Christie's) $315

Early cut boat-shaped footed bowl, with starburst pattern, notched rim, large knopped stem, square base, pontil scar, 10in. high, Ireland, 1790's.
(Skinner Inc.) $715

Webb gem cameo glass bowl, bright cobalt blue sphere layered in both blue and white, 5in. diameter.
(Skinner Inc.) $6,050

'Cleones', a Lalique amber box and cover, the cover molded with beetles and foliage, 14cm. diameter.
(Christie's) $1,168

'Figurines et Violes', a Lalique circular box and cover, the exterior molded in relief with classical maidens dancing with scarves, stained green, 4in. diameter.
(Christie's S. Ken)
                                $2,356

'Roger'. A Lalique frosted glass powder box and cover, molded to the cover with circular clear glass protrusions in the form of berries, 13cm. diameter.
(Phillips) $438

French gilt-bronze-mounted enameled opaline glass box, mid 19th century, with canted corners molded with a diamond pattern, 9in. wide.
(Butterfield & Butterfield)
                                $2,475

'Amour Assis', a Lalique satin finished circular box and cover, the top surmounted by a seated cherub, 5³/₄in. high.
(Christie's S. Ken)
                                $3,855

A Louis Philippe ormolu-mounted baccarat toilet box with square cut facets and hinged lid, the border with bands of lotus leaves, 5¹/₂in. wide.
(Christie's) $1,517

A Gallé acid-etched and carved circular box and cover, pale gray glass overlaid in purple with trails of wisteria blossom, 6¹/₂in. diameter.
(Christie's S. Ken) $1,105

A rare and unusual Venetian glass jewel casket and cover of rectangular shape, the sides formed of rectangular filigree panels of trellis with circular florettes at the junctions, 18.5cm. x 14cm.
(Phillips) $2,431

A Gabriel Argy-Rousseau pâte-de-verre circular box and cover, of pale amber glass, the cover molded with yellow and purple stylized petals, 11.2cm. diameter.
(Christie's) $6,006

CANDELSTICKS

Tiffany gold iridescent candlelamp, twisted stem ten-rib candlestick with opal glass oil font, 12½in. high.
(Skinner Inc.) $1,320

Tiffany bronze and favrile candlestick, elaborate four branch candelabrum with green glass blown into slit candlecups, 11½in. high.
(Skinner Inc.) $3,025

Tiffany gilt bronze blown out candelabrum, three-branch candle holders with green favrile glass liners, 12½in. high.
(Skinner Inc.) $1,760

'Cariatide', a pair of Lalique frosted glass table decorations, with delicate pinky-brown tint, each modeled as the stylized torso of a young woman, 12in. high.
(Christie's S. Ken)
                    $30,401

A blue faceted taper-stick, the fluted nozzle with notched angles supported on a stem cut with diamond facets, circa 1790, 15.5cm. high.
(Christie's) $1,478

A pair of facet-cut tapersticks with barbed everted lips, flattened collars and central knops between diamond faceting, 15.5cm. high.
(Phillips) $1,020

Carder Steuben twisted candlestick, solid twist colorless shaft with dished pedestal foot and vasiform candlecup, 15in. high.
(Skinner Inc.) $550

One of a pair of George III Irish cut-glass twin-branch candelabra, each with a central hobnail-cut shaft with fleur-de-lys finial, 19¼in. high.
(Christie's)
          (Two) $15,488

Antique clear pressed glass candlestick, in dolphin form, height 10½in.
(Eldred's) $55

DECANTERS

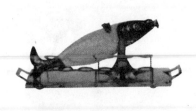

A large glass decanter and stopper, American, early 19th century, with a lobed stopper molded with diapering, 14³/₄in. high.
(Christie's) $1,210

An unusual liqueurs decanter modeled as a salmon with scale-cut body and black and white boot button eyes, overall length of tray 17³/₄in.
(Christie's S. Ken) $1,475

An engraved decanter and a stopper, for BEER, of club shape and named within a quatrefoil cartouche issuant with hops and barley, circa 1770, 36cm. high overall.
(Christie's) $6,805

A blue gilt-decorated decanter and a stopper, from the atelier of James Giles, of bell-shape decorated with a continuous frieze of garden statuary, circa 1765, 28cm. high.
(Christie's) $1,571

A pair of engraved and cut decanters and stoppers of club shape, decorated with a rounded turf stack flanked by two trees on a sward, early 19th century, 25.5cm. high.
(Christie's) $1,361

Thomas Cains-type decanter, two bands of broken chain decoration around body, two tripartite neck rings, inverted ring stopper, pontil scar, quart, 1815–30.
(Skinner Inc.) $330

German silver mounted glass decanter, 19th century, hexagonal form with rococo etching and chasing, 11in. high.
(Skinner Inc.) $825

Blown three-mold decanter, olive amber, sheared lip-pontil scar, pint, 1815–30.
(Skinner Inc.) $385

Blown three-mold decanter, stopper, colorless, pontil scar, quart, New England, 1825–40.
(Skinner Inc.) $154

DECANTERS

Blown three-mold decanter, pint, stopper, three pairs of quilled neck bands, colorless, pontil scar, New England, 1825–40.
(Skinner Inc.) $143

A 'Cyder' decanter and a stopper, of club shape, named within a quartefoil cartouche, circa 1770, 29.5cm. high overall.
(Christie's) $4,620

Early engraved decanter, thinly blown, well engraved with florals, pontil scar, 8³/₄in. high, possibly Pittsburgh district, 1820–40.
(Skinner Inc.) $176

An amethyst gilt-decorated decanter of club shape, the body with a meandering branch of fruiting-vine, the neck with traces of gilt spiral foliage decoration, circa 1780, 26cm. high.
(Christie's) $554

Pair of German silver and engraved glass decanters, 19th century, rectangular with rococo scenes, 10in. high.
(Skinner Inc.) $1,760

Gorham Sterling and ruby-colored cut glass decanter, repoussé melon-form cover on an ovoid body cut with fruiting vine, 9in. high.
(Skinner Inc.) $2,970

Blown three-mold decanter, with unusual ribbed Tam o'Shanter stopper, deep sapphire blue, flaring lip-pontil scar, 1825–40.
(Skinner Inc.) $660

Blown three-mold decanter, mint, stopper, colorless, pontil scar, New England, 1825–40.
(Skinner Inc.) $440

Early decorated bottle, decorated with quilled rigaree and prunts, two swirled rings around neck, 10in. high, probably Spain, late 17th/early 18th century.
(Skinner Inc.) $264

Almaric Walter pâte de verre tray, molded oval green dish centering darker freen figural fish with fanned gill fins, 9¼in. wide.
(Skinner Inc.) $2,200

Free blown milk pan, with pouring spout, aqua, folded lip-pontil scar, 18in. wide, America, mid 19th century.
(Skinner Inc.) $275

Swirling cut glass cheese dish, brilliant swirling pattern serving plate and matching high dome cover with faceted knob top, 8in. high.
(Skinner Inc.) $550

Tiffany silver and cut glass basket, flared horizontal stepped and cane cut flower basket mounted with floral handle, 13in. high.
(Skinner Inc.) $1,980

A J. & L. Lobmeyr large circular dish engraved by Karl Pietsch with 'The Marriage of Neptune and Amphitrite', the center with a running figure of Bacchus holding a goblet beside a leaping panther, 42.5cm. diameter.
(Christie's) $73,882

Hairpin pressed compote, with loop pattern base, wafer attachment, colorless, 5¾in. high, England, 1840–60.
(Skinner Inc.) $138

A baluster tazza, the stem with a triple annulated knop above a plain section enclosing an elongated tear and basal knop, circa 1725, 24cm. diameter.
(Christie's) $915

'Clos Sainte'Odile', a Lalique brown-stained statuette with dish, molded as a draped figure holding a book on her chest, 10.1cm. high.
(Christie's) $730

A Venetian 'ice glass' octagonal ice bucket or aspersory with ropetwist swing handle held in two applied loops, 20.5cm. high
(Phillips) $8,160

FIGURES

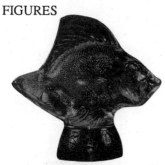

'Gros Poisson, Vagues', a Lalique sculpture, the clear glass molded as a large-finned fish, 39cm. high with base. (Christie's) **$4,867**

'Espagnole', a Sabino opalescent figure, molded as a Spanish dancer, poised holding a tambourine, with engraved signature *Sabino Paris*, 27.4cm. high. (Christie's) **$1,300**

Rare Steuben gazelle luminaire, molded Art Deco pressed glass figure mounted on conforming black plinth housing electrical fittings, 13in. high. (Skinner Inc.) **$495**

Gino Cenedese & Cie Studio glass figure, attributed to Alfredo Barbini, iridized opal mauve colored glass sculpture of bearded oriental fish vendor, 18in. high. (Skinner Inc.) **$1,485**

'Suzanne au Bain', a Lalique opalescent glass figure, molded as a nude girl poised on one leg, her arms outstretched supporting a drape, 22.5cm. high. (Christie's) **$1,762**

'Jeune fille aux colombes', a Sabino opalescent statuette, molded as a nude woman kneeling with three doves, with molded signature *Sabino Paris*, 15.8cm. high. (Christie's) **$815**

'Danseuse Drapée', a Sabino opalescent figure, molded as a nude female, walking arms outstretched with a long cloak flowing behind, 23.6cm. high. (Christie's) **$1,140**

'Thais', a Lalique statuette, the frosted glass molded in the form of a nude maiden, poised with her arms outstretched holding a drape, 27cm. high. (Christie's) **$6,230**

'Naïade', a Lalique mirror pendant, the gilded glass molded in relief with a sea nymph and swirling bubbles, the metal mount stamped *Lalique*, 9cm. long. (Christie's) **$584**

Eagle-tree historical flask, deep golden amber, sheared lip-pontil scar, half-pint, America, 1820's. (Skinner Inc.) **$1,210**

Sunburst flask, light olive amber, sheared lip-pontil scar, pint, Coventry Glassworks, Coventry, Connecticut, 1820's. (Skinner Inc.) **$275**

Hunterman-fisherman pictorial flask, aqua, round collar with ring-pontil scar, calabash, American 1850–60. (Skinner Inc.) **$70**

'Success to the Railroad' historical flask, bubbly glass, good color, deep forest green, possibly Mt. Vernon Glassworks, New York, late 1820's. (Skinner Inc.) **$150**

Sunburst flask, mint condition, no wear, medium apricot puce, sheared lip-pontil scar, half-pint, America, 1830–50. (Skinner Inc.) **$5,225**

'Biningers/Travelers Guide' pocket flask, teardrop shape, medium golden amber, double collared lip-smooth base, 6³/₄ in. high. (Skinner Inc.) **$180**

Baltimore/Glassworks sheaf of grain pictorial flask, calabash, medium sapphire blue, double collared lip-pontil scar, Baltimore Glassworks, circa 1850. (Skinner Inc.) **$3,960**

Free blown decorated flask, with four applied bands of quilled rigaree, deep olive amber, sheared lip-pontil scar, 5in. high, possibly South Jersey glasshouse, early 19th century. (Skinner Inc.) **$55**

'Travelers/Companion' historical flask, medium golden amber, dark striations throughout, possibly Westford Glassworks, Westford, Connecticut, 1857–73. (Skinner Inc.) **$125**

FLASKS

Kossuth-tree portrait flask, olive yellow, sloping collar with bevel-pontil scar, calabash, America, 1850–60.
(Skinner Inc.) $330

Nailsea-type flask, opaque white with large cranberry loopings, folded over lip-pontil scar, $7^{3}/_{4}$in. high, 1870–80.
(Skinner Inc.) $176

Waisted scroll flask, thinly blown, nice sharp impression, aqua, pint, probably Pittsburg district, 1830's.
(Skinner Inc.) $325

Washington-Taylor portrait flask, deep emerald green, sheared lip-pontil scar, quart, Dyottville Glassworks, Philadelphia, 1840's.
(Skinner Inc.) $880

Jenny Lind bust lyre flask, aqua, sheared lip-pontil scar, pint, McCarty & Torreyson, Wellsburg, West Virginia, 1840–60.
(Skinner Inc.) $825

'Lafayette' liberty cap portrait flask, medium olive green, sheared lip-pontil scar, pint, Covenry Glassworks, Coventry, Connecticut, 1820's.
(Skinner Inc.) $250

"Success to the Railroad" historical flask, deep green, sheared lip-pontil scar, pint, Keene Marlboro Street Glassworks, Keene, New Hampshire, circa 1830.
(Skinner Inc.) $209

Emil Larson type flask, inverted swirled diamond, amethyst, sheared lip-pontil scar, $5^{5}/_{8}$in. high, 1930's.
(Skinner Inc.) $110

Washington-Taylor portrait flask, medium sapphire blue, sheared lip-pontil scar, quart, Dyottville Glassworks, Philadelphia, Pennsylvania, 1847–55.
(Skinner Inc.) $1,700

GOBLETS

A baluster goblet with a deep funnel bowl, the inverted baluster stem enclosing a large tear above a folded conical foot, circa 1705, 21cm. high.
(Christie's) $875

A Bohemian dated portrait goblet and cover, the oviform bowl cut with wide flutes and engraved with the bust portrait of a gentleman, 1887, 46cm. high.
(Christie's) $1,167

A baluster goblet, the slender funnel bowl with a tear to the solid lower part supported on a cushion knop, circa 1720, 20cm. high.
(Christie's) $2,587

One of three baluster goblets, the bell bowls supported on angular knops above inverted baluster stems enclosing large tears, circa 1725, 18cm. high.
(Christie's)   (Three) $2,528

A 'Façon de Venise' latticinio goblet, the compressed oval bowl with a band of vetro a retorti between white threads, South Netherlands, second half of the 16th century, 13cm. high.
(Christie's) $11,666

A mammoth baluster goblet, the round funnel bowl with a solid base, the stem with a compressed baluster knop between two cushion knops, circa 1710, 28cm. high.
(Christie's) $7,392

A Dutch-engraved armorial pedestal-stemmed goblet, engraved with the crowned arms of Leiden flanked by lion supporters, on a folded conical foot, circa 1745, 17.5cm. high.
(Christie's) $1,069

A diamond-engraved light baluster portrait goblet, the funnel bowl with a bust portrait of Frederik Hendrik, Prince of Orange, the glass circa 1745, the engraving circa 1784, 18.5cm. high.
(Christie's) $2,528

A 'Façon de Venise' latticinio goblet, the clear flared funnel bowl terminating on a merese and supported on a baluster-knopped stem and conical foot, circa 1600, 13cm. high.
(Christie's) $1,653

A baluster goblet with a bell bowl, the stem with a beaded knop above an inverted baluster section and basal knop, circa 1730, 21cm. high.
(Christie's) $583

A German gold-ruby goblet and cover, the deep ogee bowl with a tear to the solid lower part, Bohemia or Saxony, circa 1740, 25.5cm. high.
(Christie's) $1,944

A Jacobite airtwist goblet, the bell bowl engraved with a rose, bud and half-opened bud, the reverse with a moth, circa 1750, 26.5cm. high.
(Christie's) $1,517

A large glass goblet, the bowl finely cut, on one side with the pre-Victorian version of the Royal coat of arms and on the other with the initials *P.P.*, 24.6cm., early 19th century.
(Bearne's) $3,235

A finely engraved Bohemian goblet, the faceted rounded funnel bowl engraved all-over with flowers and leaves, 16.8cm., early 18th century.
(Phillips) $972

A 'Façon de Venise' engraved goblet, the funnel bowl with the double-headed eagle of the Holy Roman Empire holding a scepter and sword and an orange branch, late 17th century, 22cm. high.
(Christie's) $1,361

A Dutch armorial goblet, the bell bowl engraved with the Dutch Lion surrounded by the arms of the Seven Provinces, on a conical foot, circa 1760, 23cm. high. (Christie's) $3,305

An opaque-twist 'King of Prussia' commemorative portrait goblet, the ogee bowl engraved with a bust portrait within a circular scroll and hatched cartouche, on a conical foot, circa 1765, 19.5cm. high.
(Christie's) $4,277

A Beilby opaque-twist goblet, the bucket bowl enameled in white with a growing fruiting-vine, the stem with two entwined threads, circa 1770, 17.5cm. high.
(Christie's) $3,694

JUGS & PITCHERS

A Roman green glass jug, a thick band of trail below the lip and at the base of the flaring neck, circa 4th century A.D., 6¼in. high.
(Bonhams) $750

A fine German lemonade set enameled by Stüdent, sign to one goblet, comprising: a tall jug and six goblets, each painted in opaque and translucent enamels, circa 1870
(Tennants) $1,302

A Hukin & Heath electroplated and glass 'crow's feet' decanter, designed by Christopher Dresser, on three metal feet, 24cm. high, October 1878.
(Phillips) $8,200

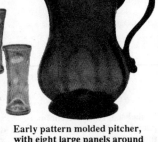

Art Nouveau lemonade set, green art glass tankard pitcher and six matching tumblers with raised gold enamel stylized blossoms, 12½in. high.
(Skinner Inc.) $413

Early pattern molded pitcher, with eight large panels around the lower portion, deep sapphire blue, pontil scar, 6in. high, possibly New England, 1840–50.
(Skinner Inc.) $495

A Richardson's opaque baluster jug, decorated in black monochrome heightened in white with Eastern figures, and a goblet en suite, circa 1846, 16.5cm. high.
(Christie's) $875

Early blown pitcher, eleven bands of threading around lip, applied handle, aqua, pontil scar, 6¼in. high, possibly a New York State glasshouse, 1830–50.
(Skinner Inc.) $231

A Venetian small ewer lightly molded with vertical flutes, the scroll handle applied with pincered ornament, late 17th century, 14cm. high.
(Christie's) $622

Early blown pitcher, double incised rim, applied foot and handle, deep sapphire blue, 6¾in. high, possibly South Jersey glasshouse, 1840–50.
(Skinner Inc.) $413

GLASS

JUGS & PITCHERS

An important pâté de verre glass jug by Walter Nancy, decorated with grapes on a yellow ground, 27cm. high. (Hôtel de Ventes Horta) $8,775

A Spanish condiment-set, the central two-handled column applied with opaque and dark-blue vermicular bands, 18th century, Granada or Almeria, 12¹/₂in. high. (Christie's) $1,200

A Spanish large cruet-jug of straw tint, the tapering oviform body with a slender slightly swelling neck, 17th century, Barcelona, 11in. high. (Christie's) $1,200

A Spanish 'Façon de Venise' latticinio baluster jug decorated with vertical marvered opaque-white threads, late 17th/18th century, 9in. high. (Christie's) $585

A Spanish 'ice-glass' small jug of straw tint, the 'ice-glass' globular body beneath a plain rim applied with turquoise trailed thread, late 17th century, Barcelona or Castile, 5¹/₂in. wide. (Christie's) $2,750

A W.M.F. lemonade jug, the tapering cylindrical glass body cut with diamonds and swags, 13¹/₂in. high. (Christie's) $428

A Schneider 'Le Verre Français' cameo glass jug of oviform, the mottled pink body overlaid with red glass shading to brown, 50cm. high. (Phillips) $695

A jug designed by E. Léveillé, with cylindrical neck and curved handles, internally decorated with mottled undulating stripes of white and maroon, 9³/₄in. high. (Christie's) $1,460

An Art Nouveau claret jug in silvered pewter mount, the pear shaped body acid-etched and enameled with a floral spray, 12³/₄in. high. (Christie's) $810

MISCELLANEOUS GLASS

Daum molded clear and frosted glass automobile sculpture, the long sleek boattailed two door vehicle with frosted detailing, 15¹/₄in. long.
(Butterfield & Butterfield)
$550

Nailsea-type rolling pin with trapped coin, 1883, English coin trapped inside colorless rolling pin with deep ruby loopings, 16¹/₂in. long, probably Nailsea district, England, 1880's.
(Skinner Inc.)
$385

'Escargots', a Lalique gray tinted glass domed circular inkwell and cover, the underside molded in relief with bands of snails, 6¹/₄in. diameter.
(Christie's S. Ken)
$964

A Vistosi metal and glass stylized bird, the free-blown smoky-gray glass internally decorated with a triple row of irregular blue and green rectangles, 26.5cm. high.
(Christie's)
$1,593

A Baccarat ormolu-mounted sulphide circular plaque set with a portrait of WASINGTON (sic) by Desprez, the ormolu mount molded with stiff leaves, circa 1830, 8.5cm. diameter.
(Christie's)
$1,069

One of a pair of early witch ball stands, hollow feet, with witch balls, golden amber, tooled lips-pontil scars, 12¹/₄in. high, possibly Whitney Glassworks, Glassboro, New Jersey, mid 19th century.
(Skinner Inc.)   (Two)
$495

Nailsea-type vase and witch ball, colorless with white loopings, pontil scar, 16in. high, possibly Pittsburgh or New Jersey glasshouse, 1840–60.
(Skinner Inc.)
$1,210

A laminated glass charger by Sara McDonald, circular with various metal inclusions forming geometric design, mottled and veined gray brown with mottled yellow and blue cross, 56cm. diameter.
(Christie's)
$788

A good mead-glass, the wide bowl with spiked gadrooning to the lower part, supported on a triple annulated knop, 14cm. high.
(Phillips)
$1,360

MISCELLANEOUS GLASS

Sinclaire cut glass scenic platter, 'silver thread' cutting centers moose medallion, rim features four game birds, 14½in. wide. (Skinner Inc.) **$3,100**

Phrenology head inkwell, milk glass head and font, cast iron frame, America, 1855–75. (Skinner Inc.) **$2,750**

End of day with mica marble, blues, reds, whites and yellows, excellent condition, 1⅝in., Germany, 1880–1915. (Skinner Inc.) **$413**

A flared épergne, engraved with trailing foliage on a drip pan suspending button and prism drops, 22in. high. (Christie's S. Ken) **$385**

'Sirène', a Lalique opalescent charger, the satin-finished glass molded in the center with a single sea-sprite, surrounded by bands of swirling bubbles, 36.7cm. diameter. (Christie's) **$10,043**

A clear glass obelisk designed by Loredano Rosin, on square plinth cut with beveled edges, surmounted by four spheres, engraved signature, 23in. high. (Christie's S. Ken) **$405**

Early pressed spillholder, inverted diamond with oval, amethyst, polished pontil, 4½in., New England, 1840–60. (Skinner Inc.) **$468**

A Wear Glass Works armorial cut-glass double-lipped wine-glass cooler from the Londonderry Service, of waisted form engraved with the Londonderry coat-of-arms, 1824, 17cm. wide. (Christie's) **$710**

A fish tank, by Tom Dixon, the glass body of pointed oval section, with polished steel cover and domed 'fish-eye' ventilation cover, 1990, 80cm. wide. (Christie's) **$1,280**

A Baccarat garlanded butterfly weight, the insect with translucent purple body, marbled wings, turquoise eyes and black antennae, mid-19th century, 6.5cm. diameter. (Christie's) $2,760

A Baccarat garlanded buttercup weight, the flower with a yellow stamen center surrounded by recessed cream petals, mid-19th century, 6.1cm. diameter. (Christie's) $4,666

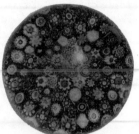

A Clichy close millefiori weight, the closely packed canes in predominant shades of dark-blue, green and pink and including a pink and white rose, mid-19th century, 6.5cm. diameter. (Christie's) $2,250

A St. Louis faceted upright bouquet weight, the bouquet with four gentian-type flowers in white, dark-blue, orange and pink and with three florettes in shades of pale-blue, pink and blue, mid-19th century, 8cm. diameter.(Christie's) $1,830

A St. Louis marbrie weight, the central concentric arrangement of dark-blue and pink canes enclosed within a circle of pale-pink hollow crimped tubes surrounded by large pale-green-centered dark-blue canes, mid-19th century, 7.7cm. diameter. (Christie's) $11,200

A St. Louis pink dahlia weight, the flower with five rows of ribbed pink petals about a pale-blue and ocher central cane and with five radiating green leaves showing from behind, mid-19th entury, 5.5cm. diameter. (Christie's) $2,250

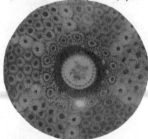

A St. Louis dated paneled carpet-ground sulphide weight, the center with a circular sulphide medallion painted with a bouquet within a circle of green-centered pink and white canes, 1848, 6.5cm. diameter. (Christie's) $19,107

A Clichy spray-weight, the large purple flower with red and white center surrounded by yellow dots growing from a slender dark-green stalk, mid-19th century, 7cm. diameter. (Christie's) $15,554

A St. Louis pelargonium weight, the flower with five heart-shaped pink petals edged in white about a green, yellow and brown dot center, the green stalk with two slender leaves, mid-19th century, 7cm. diameter. (Christie's) $1,830

412

PAPER WEIGHTS

GLASS

A St. Louis garlanded aventurine-ground pink double-clematis weight, the flower with two rows of ribbed petals about a yellow and blue 'match head' center, mid-19th century, 8cm. diameter.
(Christie's) $5,444

A Clichy blue-ground patterned millefiori weight, the large central pink rose set within a cinquefoil garland of green canes, mid-19th century, 7.7cm. diameter.
(Christie's) $2,916

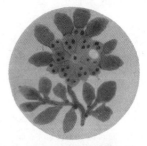

A Baccarat yellow wheatflower weight, the flower with twelve yellow petals spotted in black about a pink and white star center and with seven green leaves showing behind, mid-19th century, 8cm. diameter.
(Christie's) $4,277

A St. Louis concentric millefiori mushroom weight, the tuft with three circles of canes in shades of dark-green, white and pink enclosed by an outer circle of alternate pink and white canes, mid-19th century, 7.3cm. diameter.
(Christie's) $5,520

A St. Louis cruciform millefiori carpet-ground weight, the central blue, green, white and red cogwheel with four radiating spokes of red-centered white canes edged with red and green twisted ribbon, mid-19th century, 7.9cm. diameter.
(Christie's) $8,917

A Baccarat patterned millefiori weight, the central red, white and blue arrow's head setup within a circle of green-centered white star canes set within two interlocking trefoil garlands of red and dark-green canes, mid-19th century, 8cm. diameter.
(Christie's) $1,525

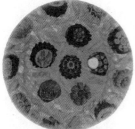

A Clichy initialed 'Barber's pole' checker weight, the central purple cane surrounded by two circles of colored canes including one with the letter 'C', mid-19th century, 6.3cm. diameter.
(Christie's) $4,666

A Clichy faceted patterned concentric millefiori weight, the central pink rose within three circles of canes in shades of red and green, turquoise and pink, mid-19th century, 7.9cm. diam.
(Christie's) $4,000

A Clichy blue-ground garlanded patterned millefiori weight, the central turquoise-centered white cane surrounded by seven pink pastry-molds and a circle of green-centered white canes mid-19th century, 8cm. diameter.
(Christie's) $1,525

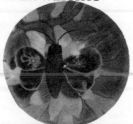

A Baccarat butterfly and white double-clematis weight, the insect with translucent purple body and marbled wings, mid 19th century, 6.6cm. diameter. (Christie's) $4,600

A St. Louis crown weight, the lime-green and cobalt-blue twisted ribbons radiating from a central cobalt-blue, white and pink setup, mid-19th century, 6.2cm. diameter. (Christie's) $2,750

A Baccarat butterfly weight, the insect with translucent purple gauze body, blue antennae, pale-blue eyes and marbled wings, mid-19th century, 5.8cm. diameter. (Christie's) $2,250

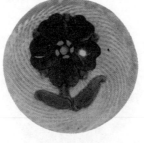

A St. Louis faceted panelled carpet-ground weight, the closely packed brightly colored canes divided by ocher and blue twisted ribbon into six triangular-shaped panels radiating from a central green and salmon-pink cane, mid-19th century, 7cm. diameter. (Christie's) $11,677

A St. Louis red Pelargonium weight, the flower with five heart-shaped petals about a yellow match-head and green center, mid-19th century, 6.7cm. diameter. (Christie's) $2,450

A St. Louis pink-ground white Pompom weight, the flower with many recessed petals about a yellow stamen center and with two green leaves and a bud showing behind, mid 19th century, 6.5cm. diameter. (Christie's) $1,850

A Clichy fruit weight, the three radiating ripe pears in shades of yellow and russet, mid 19th century, 6.8cm. diameter. (Christie's) $2,653

A Baccarat strawberry weight, the two ripe fruit and two bunches of green leaves pendant from a slender green stalk, mid-19th century, 7.2cm. diameter. (Christie's) $2,750

A Baccarat garlanded butterfly weight, the insect with trans-lucent purple body, marbled wings and blue eyes, mid 19th century, 7cm. diameter. (Christie's) $2,750

SHADES

Degaz art glass hanging shade, 13³/₄in. diameter, blue bird and branch overlay design cut to clear, signed.
(Du Mouchelles) $600

Tiffany bronze and favrile swirling leaf hanging lamp, raised rim and shaped beaded apron on leaded glass dome, 22in. diameter.
(Skinner Inc.) $9,350

Sabino French iridescent and frosted art glass plafonnier vasque, branch and thistle pattern, signed in center, 12in. diameter.
(Du Mouchelles) $4,500

A Loetz lampshade, oviform with foliate rim, the yellow ground internally decorated with iridescent silver wavy pattern, 12.4cm. high.
(Christie's) $1,416

A Gallé carved and acid-etched double-overlay plafonnier, the opaque yellow shade overlaid with lilac-colored flowers and green foliage, 15³/₄in. diameter.
(Christie's) $13,192

A Loetz lampshade, the yellow ground decorated with iridescent orange, green and silver trailed design above a band of silver rectangular dots, 13cm. high.
(Christie's) $2,336

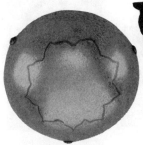

A Loetz plafonnier, the white ground decorated with iridescent orange oil spot design and central trailed star shape, 36cm. diameter.
(Christie's) $3,540

Tiffany bronze and favrile turtleback chandelier, half-round dome of amber and white striated ripple glass segments, 19in. diameter.
(Skinner) $15,000

A Le Verre Français acid-etched plafonnier, of circular section with green glass overlaid in mottled orange with snails, 13¹/₂in. diameter.
(Christie's) $975

415

Tiffany leaded glass window, with rare central monogram medallion of the original company *Louis C. Tiffany and Associated Artists*, 1878–82, 44¹/₂in. wide.
(Skinner Inc.) **$3,400**

Four late 19th century stained glass panels, two depicting the Sacrifice of Isaac, average dimensions 71 x 30cm.
(Phillips) **$1,480**

Pair of Tiffany leaded glass windows, bordered medallions incorporating colorful swirled rippled, confetti, opalescent glass, unsigned, 22in. square.
(Skinner Inc.) **$1,700**

'The Blessed Virgin Mary', a Morris & Co. stained glass window, designed by Edward Burne-Jones, the clear, blue, green, yellow and red glass, depicting the Virgin Annunciate, 105 x 66cm.
(Christie's) **$18,706**

A leaded and stained glass panel by George Walton, after a design by Charles Rennie Mackintosh, 133.6cm. high, 91.4cm. wide.
(Christie's)

'Minstrel with Cymbals', a Morris & Co. stained glass window, designed by William Morris, the clear, red, green and yellow glass depicting a young robed minstrel with cymbals amid fruit and foliage, 64.5 x 47.5cm.
(Christie's) **$16,737**

A Victorian stained-glass window depicting The Awakening of Bottom, a scene from A Mid-Summer Nights Dream, circa 1860, each panel, 35³/₄ x 18³/₄in.
(Christie's) **$2,834**

A 19th century stained glass panel depicting Christ Carrying the Cross, and another of similar size with two winged angels.
(Phillips) **$1,480**

George Washington commemorative glass pane, America, last quarter 19th century, acid etched cobalt blue to frost, 20in. wide.
(Skinner Inc.) **$468**

SWEETMEAT GLASSES

An opaque-twist sweetmeat-glass, the flared vertically ribbed bowl with waved rim, on a double-series stem and conical foot, circa 1775, 11cm. high. (Christie's) $594

A pedestal-stemmed sweetmeat-glass, the vertically ribbed double-ogee bowl with everted rim, circa 1750, 15cm. high. (Christie's) $680

An unusual pedestal-stemmed sweetmeat-glass, supported on a four-sided hollow molded stem above a folded conical foot, circa 1740, 13cm. high. (Christie's) $892

TANKARDS

A Russian (Imperial Glassworks) opaque-white feeding-mug, painted in purple monochrome on a powdered-blue ground with two figures in a continuous rustic landscape, circa 1795, 8cm. high. (Christie's) $1,653

A Bohemian ruby-overlay slender pewter-mounted tankard and cover, carved with a falconer wearing medieval dress, circa 1865, 24.5cm. high. (Christie's) $2,650

Early blown and decorated tankard, aqua with white loopings, applied solid handle, pontil scar, 7in. high, possibly a South Jersey glasshouse, mid 19th century. (Skinner Inc.) $413

TANTALUS

A Victorian burr oak and brass bound lift top tantalus and humidor fitted with three cut glass spirit decanters. (Langlois) $2,300

An electro-plate-mounted oblong walnut-veneered tantalus with scroll handle, fitted with three hobnail pattern cut clear glass shaped square decanters, 17in. wide. (Christie's) $777

19th century three bottle oak tantalus, plated handle and mounts, 14in. high. (G.A. Key) $405

Large dark blue Peking glass bottle vase, 19th century, the glass of a translucent violet-blue tone throughout, 15¹/_ in. (Butterfield & Butterfield) $4,675

A Loetz iridescent glass vase, with three applied scrolling handles, the blue glass decorated with a silver/blue oil splash pattern, 17cm. high. (Christie's) $1,096

A J. Couper & Sons Clutha vase designed by Dr. Christopher Dresser, the yellow glass with pink and vaseline striations and with silver foil inclusions, 26.3cm. high. (Christie's) $5,513

An important Tiffany 'Favrile' iridescent glass vase, decorated below the shoulders with a band of café-au-lait/lemon swirls against pale peacock blue with shades of green and violet, 29.5cm. high. (Phillips) $12,250

Good pair of green overlay Peking glass vases, 19th century, each of slender baluster form with a recessed circular foot and surmounted by a wide trumpet mouth, 8³/₈in. high. (Butterfield & Butterfield) $1,320

A Loetz iridescent vase, oviform with everted rim, the amber colored glass decorated with meandering iridescent silver and blue pattern, with engraved signature Loetz Austria, 13.7cm. high. (Christie's) $1,369

A Loetz cameo glass vase of almost conical shape, the pale-blue body shading through mauve and overlaid with amethyst, 29.5cm. high. (Phillips) $1,600

A Loetz iridescent glass vase, of squat baluster form with an irregular flared mouth, in clear glass covered with a golden iridescence, 13.5cm. high. (Phillips) $550

A large Gabriel Argy-Rousseau pâte-de-verre vase, the mottled white, purple and yellow ground molded with a wide band of blue scrolling design, 26.1cm. high. (Christie's) $8,217

VASES

A Schneider 'Le Verre Français' cameo glass vase, the mottled-orange and yellow body overlaid with shaded brown glass, acid-etched with pendant flowers, 23.5cm. high.
(Phillips) $870

A Daum wheel-carved and martelé cameo vase, the clear glass overlaid with pink flowering wild plants, with engraved signature *Daum Nancy* with the Cross of Lorraine, 24.9cm. high.
(Christie's) $6,574

'Oranges', a Lalique clear glass and back enameled vase, globular with thick everted rim, molded with oranges amongst, overlapping enamelled long, pointed leaves, 28.5cm. high.
(Christie's) $51,128

A Venini 'Vetro Pezzato Artecchino', designed by Fulvio Bianconi, composed of irregular squares of clear, blue, turquoise and red glass, 17cm. high.
(Phillips) $4,911

Pair of green Peking glass vases each of slender baluster form flaring towards the base and surmounted by a tall walsted neck, 11$\frac{1}{2}$in. high.
(Butterfield & Butterfield) $1,760

A Daum martelé cameo glass vase, of milky-white color overlaid with brown-acid-etched to leave a design of lily-of-the-valley flowers and leaves against a martele ground, 15cm. high.
(Phillips) $2,775

A Loetz octopus vase, globular with short neck, cased amber glass over white, decorated between layers with an air trap scrolling motif, covered with gilt and blue and white enamel floral decoration, with engraved marks *Pat. 9759*, 14cm. high.
(Christie's) $1,461

A Gallé carved and acid-etched double-overlay vase, the white ground tending towards amber at the base, overlaid with purple and amber flowering irises, with carved signature *Gallé*, 20.4cm. high.
(Christie's) $1,643

A Loetz octopus vase, cased amber glass over white decorated between the layers with an air trap scrolling motif, covered with a gilt painted scrolling design, 15.1cm. high.
(Christie's) $1,369

VASES

A Loetz shouldered ovoid vase the clear glass surface decorated with patches of white and random zig zags of red enamel, 8¼in. high.
(Christie's) $681

A Kosta vase, designed by Vicke Lindstrand, the purple glass heavily carved and etched with an abstract design, circa 1960, 23cm. high.
(Christie's) $1,012

A Loetz vase, the fluted oviform body with bulbous cylindrical neck and triangular section rim, green glass with iridescent turquoise splashes, 6½in. high.
(Christie's) $487

A Loetz vase, the yellow ground decorated with iridescent green, orange and silver running decoration with bands of rectangular dots below, 9.6cm. high.
(Christie's) $3,505

A Loetz vase, tapering cylindrical form with spiraled ridges and everted foliate rim, the clear glass internally decorated with green striations, 15.5cm. high.
(Christie's) $1,363

A Loetz white-metal mounted vase, with everted rim, the green ground decorated with silver/blue oil splash pattern, overlaid with white-metal scrolling, 27.7cm. high.
(Christie's) $1,655

A Loetz vase with brass mount, the blue ground decorated with iridescent oil splash pattern, the arched mounted with geometric openwork design, 20.5cm. high.
(Christie's) $3,310

A Loetz vase, designed by Koloman Moser, decorated with iridescent gold, blue and orange wavy bands, with engraved signature *Loetz Austria*, 8.5cm. high.
(Christie's) $8,762

A Daum acid-etched and enameled vase, the white, mauve and orange glass polychrome enameled with rosehip branches, 18.8cm. high.
(Christie's) $1,770

VASES

A Gallé enameled vase, the blue glass with a white, red, blue and black enamel painted shield shaped reserve, 15cm. high.
(Christie's) $1,770

A Loetz three-handled vase, applied with celery handles, the body in cased green, the handles in iridescent gold, 8¼in. high.
(Christie's) $681

A Kosta Boda rectangular vase designed by Vallien, the mottled blue glass surface decorated with irregular rectangular panels, 7½in. high.
(Christie's) $253

A Loetz vase, the pink glass internally decorated with iridescent silver craquelé design, 29.8cm. high.
(Christie's) $2,655

A Daum carved, acid-etched and enamel-painted winter landscape vase, the mottled orange and clear glass polychrome enameled with a snowy wooded winter landscape, 11.2cm. high.
(Christie's) $3,287

A Gallé enameled and gilded vase, with scrolling enameled designs within gilt reserves, incorporating stylized lions and other heraldic devices, 24.9cm. high.
(Christie's) $2,920

A Gallé carved, acid-etched and enameled vase, the clear acid textured ground decorated with gilded and polychrome enameled anemones, 15.2cm. high.
(Christie's) $1,168

A Pallme Konig vase, flaring cylindrical form with everted rim, the green ground decorated with iridescent pale blue trailing, 18.5cm. high.
(Christie's) $1,062

A Loetz vase, with everted rim and applied lattice decoration, the yellow ground with areas of rainbow iridescence, 18.5cm. high.
(Christie's) $1,416

VASES

Early Emile Gallé applied and enameled vase, with nine oval cabochons containing black and crimson red specks and inclusions, 8in. high. (Skinner Inc.) **$4,675**

René Lalique camaret vase, frosted molded sphere with repeating fish motif, 5¼in. high. (Skinner Inc.) **$798**

A late 19th century French silver-mounted engraved glass vase, on a chased silver stand on four feet, 6¾in. high. (Bearne's) **$404**

A very finely engraved 'rock crystal' style vase with pointed oviform body engraved with a nude muscular man standing in the sea and carrying a nymph over his shoulder, 20.5cm. (Phillips) **$2,988**

'Bacchantes', a Lalique opalescent glass vase of flared form, heavily molded in relief with a frieze of naked female figures, 24.50cm. high. (Phillips) **$14,004**

Tiffany red miniature vase, classic oval of brilliant red favrile, decorated with three gold and blue triple-pulled and hooked feather designs, 3½in. high. (Skinner Inc.) **$4,500**

'Paquerettes', a Lalique opalescent glass vase, molded in relief with stylized daisy-like blooms with seeded centers against a textured ground, 18.50cm. high. (Phillips) **$3,112**

A Webb 'rock crystal' style vase and cover of oviform on stepped octagonal foot, engraved by H. Boam, signed. (Phillips) **$1,309**

An Argy-Rousseau smoky gray glass vase, centered in enamel with a huddled group of white chicks flanked by similar solitary birds, 17.80cm. high. (Phillips) **$1,556**

VASES

Tiffany favrile cameo carved vase, rare double carved and applied baluster form vessel of frosted crystal, 10½in. high. (Skinner Inc.) $7,150

An impressive Art Deco Daum acid-etched green glass vase, the heavily molded vessel deeply etched with a frieze of circular volutes against a textured ground, 35.50cm. high. (Phillips) $19,061

Webb gem cameo glass vase, designed and hand carved by George Woodall, 8¼in. high. (Skinner Inc.) $23,100

A Gallé mold-blown cameo glass vase, the amber-tinted body overlaid with mauve-blue and reddish-amethyst glass, 30cm. high. (Phillips) $18,341

'Rampillon', a Lalique clear glass vase, of flared form molded with lozenge shape protrusions, 12.40cm. high. (Phillips) $1,167

A German 19th century vase pierced with arabesques and on a rising chased shaped circular base with bun feet, overall height 18½in., 19.25oz. free. (Christie's S. Ken) $1,280

Webb cameo glass lace miniature vase, rare transparent oval layered in white and cameo, 3½in. high. (Skinner Inc.) $2,970

Enamel decorated Art Deco vase, with stylized blossoms against splotched mustard yellow surface, 7½in. high. (Skinner Inc.) $165

Webb cameo glass vase, transparent crystal overlaid in yellow amber with rubrum lilies, 8in. high. (Skinner Inc.) $605

423

GLASS

A color-twist wine-glass, the stem with a laminated corkscrew core edged in translucent blue within two spiral opaque threads, circa 1765, 16.5cm. high. (Christie's) $2,250

A color-twist wine-glass, the stem with an opaque flat ribbon spiral edged in translucent red and green and entwined with a gauze spiral, circa 1765, 14.5cm. high. (Christie's) $4,850

A color-twist wine-glass, the stem with an opaque corkscrew core edged in purple and translucent spinach-green entwined by two opaque spiral threads, circa 1765, 17cm. high. (Christie's) $5,055

A color-twist wine-glass, the stem with an opaque corkscrew core edged in brick-red and translucent blue entwined by two opaque threads, on a conical foot, circa 1765, 15.5cm. high. (Christie's) $4,277

A small color-twist wine-glass, the short stem with a yellow multi-ply spiral core enclosed within an opaque laminated corkscrew edged in translucent pink, circa 1775, 9cm. high. (Christie's) $2,000

A tartan-twist wine-glass, the stem with an opaque corkscrew core edged in brick-red and translucent green within two opaque spiral threads, circa 1765, 16cm. high. (Christie's) $5,444

A Beilby opaque-twist wine-glass, the funnel bowl enameled in white with a pastoral scene of two sheep, one standing and the other recumbent flanked by foliage and a tree beside a fence, circa 1770, 15cm. high. (Christie's) $7,388

A color-twist wine-glass, the stem with an opaque gauze spiral entwined with an opaque corkscrew ribbon edged in translucent cobalt-blue, on a conical foot, circa 1765, 15cm. high. (Christie's) $3,694

An engraved color-twist wine-glass perhaps of Jacobite significance, the ogee bowl engraved with a meandering band of flowers including Scotch thistle and roses, circa 1765, 16.5cm. high. (Christie's) $2,645

GLASS

A color-twist wine-glass, the stem with an opaque corkscrew core edged in translucent mint-green and entwined by two spiral threads, on a conical foot, circa 1765, 14.5cm. high. (Christie's) $4,277

An initialed color-twist wine-glass, the ogee bowl engraved in diamond-point with the initials *M.P* above a foliate-spray, on a conical foot, circa 1765, 14.5cm. high. (Christie's) $4,277

An engraved color-twist wine-glass, the stem with two entwined opaque gauze threads enclosed within two translucent cobalt-blue threads, on a conical foot, circa 1765, 16cm. high. (Christie's) $3,964

A Beilby chinoiserie opaque-twist wine-glass, the funnel bowl enameled in white with a figure holding a staff and standing beneath a pagoda flanked by trees and shrubs, circa 1770, 15cm. high. (Christie's) $11,666

A tartan-twist wine-glass, the stem with an opaque corkscrew core edged in brick-red and translucent dark-green and entwined with two opaque threads, circa 1765, 16cm. high. (Christie's) $2,850

A tartan-twist wine-glass, the stem with an opaque corkscrew core edged in brick-red and translucent green and entwined by two opaque threads, on a conical foot, circa 1765, 17cm. high. (Christie's) $3,145

A color-twist wine-glass, the shoulder-knopped stem with a central translucent green core enclosed within a laminated opaque corkscrew edged in translucent red, circa 1765, 17cm. high. (Christie's) $2,850

A Beilby masonic opaque-twist firing-glass, the ogee bowl inscribed *Antient Operative Lodge DUNDEE.*, the short stem with a laminated corkscrew core, on a terraced foot, circa 1770, 9.5cm. high. (Christie's) $11,666

A small color-twist wine-glass, the stem with a central translucent green core enclosed within an opaque laminated corkscrew edged in translucent cobalt-blue, circa 1775, 10.5cm. high. (Christie's) $3,650

An engraved opaque-twist wine-glass decorated perhaps by a German hand, the bell bowl with three female masks suspending swags of fruit, late 18th century, 16cm. high.
(Christie's) $1,944

A deceptive baluster wine-glass, the thick funnel bowl supported on an inverted baluster stem above a folded conical foot, circa 1715, 11cm. high.
(Christie's) $2,236

A Beilby opaque-twist wine-glass, enameled in white with a border of fruiting-vine, the rim with traces of gilding, on a conical foot, circa 1770, 17cm. high.
(Christie's) $2,139

An Anglo-Venetian wine-glass, with spiked gadroons to the lower part, supported on a merese above a four-bladed propeller-knopped stem terminating in a basal knop, 1685–90, 14cm. high.
(Christie's) $4,277

A stipple-engraved facet-stemmed wine-glass attributed to David Wolff, of drawn shape, the ovoid bowl with two palm-trees on a large mound encircled by a wattled fence with a gate in the front, circa 1786, 15.3cm. high.
(Christie's) $11,666

An engraved wine-glass of drawn-trumpet shape, decorated probably by a German hand with a border of Laub-und-Bandelwerk, circa 1750, 19.5cm. high.
(Christie's) $739

A Beilby opaque-twist wine-glass, enameled in white with a border of fruiting-vine and with traces of gilding to the rim, circa 1770, 16cm. high.
(Christie's) $2,139

A light baluster water-glass, the bell bowl supported on a beaded inverted baluster stem and basal knop, mid-18th century, 14cm. high.
(Christie's) $739

A Beilby opaque-twist wine-glass, enameled in white with a border of fruiting-vine and with traces of gilding to the rim, circa 1770, 14.5cm. high.
(Christie's) $1,653

GLASS

An opaque-twist 'Cyder' glass, the slender funnel bowl engraved with a pendant branch of fruiting-apple, circa 1765, 18.5cm. high.
(Christie's) $3,500

An emerald-green incised-twist wine-glass with a generous round-funnel bowl, the stem with a swelling waist knop and incised with spiral twists, circa 1765, 14cm. high.
(Christie's) $1,361

A 'Façon de Venise' wine-glass, the flared funnel bowl supported on a merese above an hexagonally lobed inverted baluster stem, Venice, circa 1600, 14.5cm. high.
(Christie's) $875

A North Bohemian (Kronstadt) 'Schwarzlot' wine-glass painted by Ignatz Preissler, with three horses in various stances on a continuous grassy band, circa 1715, 12cm. high.
(Christie's) $11,666

A Jacobite portrait firing-glass of drawn-trumpet shape, engraved with a portrait of Prince Charles Edward within a circular double-line cartouche, mid-18th century, 10cm. high.
(Christie's) $9,332

A color-twist wine-glass, the double-knopped stem with an opaque gauze core within spiral translucent green, cobalt-blue, red and opaque threads, circa 1765, 15cm. high.
(Christie's) $2,722

A Jacobite airtwist wine-glass of drawn shape, the bowl engraved with a twelve-petaled rose and a bud, circa 1750, 17cm. high.
(Christie's) $2,139

A ratafia flute, the drawn trumpet bowl with basal fluting, the opaque twist stem with a central gauze, 18.2cm.
(Phillips) $956

An engraved faceted opaque-twist wine-glass, the ogee bowl cut with facets beneath a border of flowers and foliage, on a conical foot, circa 1770, 15cm. high.
(Christie's) $739

427

A Swiss oval gold snuff-box, engine-turned in various patterns, the cover set with a miniature of a gentleman, with prestige marks, circa 1780, 2¼in. wide.
(Christie's) $2,921

A George III Irish navette-shaped gold freedom box, the hinged cover engraved with the arms and motto of the city of Cork, by John Nicholson, Cork, 1787, 3³⁄₄in. wide.
(Christie's) $31,152

A Continental oval gold-lined piqué tortoiseshell snuff-box, the cover, walls and base piqué-posé with quatrefoils in dotted trelliswork, possibly Italian, circa 1760, 3¹⁄₂in. wide.
(Christie's) $5,841

A French Restoration rectangular gold snuff-box, set with six enameled panels showing scenes after David Teniers the Younger, by Gabriel Raoul Morel, marks for 1819–1838, 3¹⁄₄in. long.
(Christie's) $38,940

A fine very rare enameled gold musical snuff box, the lid signed *V. Dupont, 1815*, the box by Georges Reymond & Co., Geneva, the movement by Piguet and Meylan, No. 811, finely painted with scene depicting Rebecca and Eliezer at the well, circa 1815, 3¹⁄₄in. long.
(Christie's) $44,000

A George III oval gold snuff-box, engine-turned, the cover and base with Greek pattern borders, by Jacob Amedroz, 1805, 2³⁄₈in. wide.
(Christie's) $3,310

A Louis XVI oval vari-colored gold snuff-box, the borders applied with flowers and foliage in colored gold, by Jean-Charles-Marie Boudou, Paris, 1786, 2³⁄₄in. wide.
(Christie's) $4,868

A Continental oblong vari-colored gold and enamel presentation snuff-box, the cover with an oval miniature of Marshal Bernadotte, in the manner of Autissier, circa 1820, 3¹⁄₂in. wide.
(Christie's) $8,567

A Louis XVI circular gold-mounted aventurine quartz bonbonnière, with six aventurine panels, Paris, 1784, maker's mark indistinct, 2³⁄₈in. diameter.
(Christie's) $3,894

A George II cartouche shaped gold-mounted agate snuff-box, the cover and base with panels of striated mocha agate, circa 1750, 2¹/₄in. wide.
(Christie's) $2,434

A Continental rectangular gold snuff-box, engine-turned, the base chased with a laurel wreath, possibly Austrian, 19th century, maker's mark *B&C*, 3in. wide.
(Christie's) $1,460

A Swiss oval gold and enamel snuff-box, the center set with a miniature of a lady within three rows of diamonds, circa 1820, unmarked, 3in. wide.
(Christie's) $11,682

A George III octagonal two-colored gold and purpurine presentation table snuff-box, the cover set with an enamel miniature of John Iggulden with white hair and sideburns, by William Grimaldi, signed and dated *1816*, 4¹/₄in. long.
(Christie's) $15,576

A French circular gold-mounted tortoiseshell bonbonnière, the cover set with an enamel plaque of a young couple seated in a landscape, circa 1780, 3¹/₄in. diameter.
(Christie's) $1,408

A Mexican oblong vari-colored gold cheroot case, the cover with diamond-set pushpiece, *Ana Castillo* engraved on the base, Mexico City, early 19th century, assay master Cayetano Buitron, 1823–1843, 2¹/₂in. high.
(Christie's) $5,257

A George III rectangular gold snuff-box, the cover chased with Venus attempting to hold Adonis back from leaving her to go hunting with his dogs, by Alexander James Strachan, 1807, 2³/₄in. wide.
(Christie's) $9,346

An historical gold fob seal owned by Thomas and John Hancock, circa 1760, the citrine matrix carved with the Hancock arms within a rococo cartouche.
(Christie's) $6,050

A George III oblong vari-colored gold engine-turned snuff-box, the cover and base with applied acanthus leaf and scrolling foliage border terminating in shell corners, by Alexander James Strachan 1809, 3³/₈in. wide.
(Christie's) $14,018

A gutta ball, random hammered and inscribed 25 and in ink the inscription: *New kind of golf ball made of gutta percha in the ... year 1849.*
(Phillips) $36,500

A fine and rare gutty golf ball marker, stamped A. Patrick, the hinged handle with leather-covered roller and enclosing two grooved metal rollers, circa 1870.
(Christie's) $61,000

A mesh hand hammered gutta indistinctly numbered *27* and stamped *Swanst....*
(Phillips) $2,750

The Golf Match, A Poem, Broadsheet (Edinburgh or Leith), Blackheath, 5th March, 1783, this un-recorded and probably unique printed copy refers to a match between the Members of Leith and Blackheath.
(Christie's)   **$16,000**

After Victor Venner, a pair of chromolithographic prints by Wyman entitled, addressing the ball and lost ball, each 39 x 54cm.
(Phillips) $1,600

A mammoth niblick made by Cochrane of Edinburgh, the head stamped *Cochrane & Co, Edinburgh*, circa 1910, face 4$^{1}/_{2}$in. deep, 6in. toe to heel.
(Christie's) $13,783

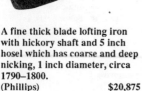

A fine thick blade lofting iron with hickory shaft and 5 inch hosel which has coarse and deep nicking, 1 inch diameter, circa 1790–1800.
(Phillips) $20,875

A good Edwardian inkstand of shaped outline, with two gutty ball inkwells surmounted by posy holder and Edwardian golfer, 23cm. high.
(Phillips) $490

A square toe curved face iron with rare alder shaft and later skin grip, 5 inch hosel, overall 41$^{1}/_{2}$in. probably early 18th century.
(Phillips) $108,500

GOLFING ITEMS

An unusual feather-filled golf ball by Allan Robertson, stamped *Allan* and numbered *28*, circa 1840.
(Christie's)   **$19,000**

A golden headed play club by T. Morris, with lancewood shaft in mid brown with 42½in. shaft.
(Phillips)   **$16,110**

A feather ball inscribed 27, *made and used by Allan Robertson, golf ball maker, St. Andrews 1849.*
(Phillips)   **$7,200**

A good albumen print of a group of golfers including Tom Morris and others, circa 1860, approx. 19 x 25cm.
(Phillips)   **$1,400**

A rare and unusual cross head playing club after the Hutchinson patent, one loft stamped ½ and the other loft ⅞in, the shaft stamped *Forgan, St. Andrews.*
(Phillips)   **$8,592**

Harry Vardon versus James Braid at Murrayfield Golf Club, Edinburgh on 30th July 1904, approximately 2½ minutes of film.
(Phillips)   **$20,875**

An extremely rare late 18th century long spoon in thornwood, stamped *McEwan*, overall 41in. with original grip.
(Phillips)   **$23,000**

An Edwardian silver vesta case, the fascia repoussé with a golfer with his club raised above his head about to strike the ball, London 1903, by H. Matthews, 32 grammes.
(Spencer's)   **$229**

A blacksmith-made iron club head with cut-off nose and curved sole, 5in. hosel, late 17th/ early 18th century.
(Christie's)   **$76,000**

Tanned Legs, RKO, 1929, one-sheet, linen backed, 41 x 27in.
(Christie's) $2,200

The Mummy, Universal, 1932, Title lobby card, 11 x 14in.
(Christie's) $10,450

Under the Yoke, Fox, 1918, one-sheet, linen backed, 41 x 27in.
(Christie's) $825

Queen Christina, MGM, 1933, three-sheet, linen backed, 81 x 41in.
(Christie's) $17,600

Atom Man vs. Superman, Columbia, 1950, six-sheet, linen backed, 81 x 81in.
(Christie's) $8,250

The Wizard of Oz, MGM, 1939, three-sheet, linen backed, 81 x 41in.
(Christie's) $25,300

Captain January, 20th Century Fox, 1936, one-sheet, linen backed, 41 x 27in.
(Christie's) $2,200

Son of Frankenstein, Universal, 1939, one-sheet, linen backed, 41 x 27in.
(Christie's) $14,300

Behind the Mask, Columbia, 1932, one-sheet, linen backed, 41 x 27in.
(Christie's) $770

The Old Dark House, Universal, 1932, one-sheet, 41 x 27in. (Christie's)   **$48,400**

King Kong, RKO, 1933, three-sheet, linen backed, 81 x 41in. (Christie's)   **$57,200**

The Wolf Man, Universal, 1941, one-sheet, 41 x 27in. (Christie's)   **$17,600**

An American in Paris, MGM, 1951, three-sheet, linen backed, 81 x 41in. (Christie's)   **$1,980**

A Dog's Life, First National, 1918, six-sheet, linen backed, 81 x 81in. (Christie's)   **$35,200**

Dracula, Universal, 1931, insert, 36 x 14in. (Christie's)   **$33,000**

The Bellhop, Vitagraph, 1921, one-sheet, linen backed, 41 x 27in. (Christie's)   **$715**

Citizen Kane, RKO, 1941, one-sheet, linen backed, 41 x 27in. (Christie's)   **$22,000**

Disraeli, Warner Brothers, 1929, one-sheet, paper backed, 41 x 27in. (Christie's)   **$770**

Alice the Peacemaker, Winkler, 1924, one-sheet, paper backed, 41 x 27in.
(Christie's) $22,000

Turning the Tables, Paramount-Artcraft, 1919, one-sheet, linen backed, 41 x 27in.
(Christie's) $1,650

Devil's Harvest, unknown, ca. 1940's, one-sheet, linen backed, 41 x 27in.
(Christie's) $990

The Cat's Meow, Pathe, 1924, one-sheet, linen backed, 41 x 27in.
(Christie's) $770

Devil Dogs of the Air, Warner Brothers, 1935, three-sheet, linen backed, 81 x 41in.
(Christie's) $5,720

The Fleet's In, Paramount, 1928, one-sheet, linen backed, 41 x 27in.
(Christie's) $2,200

The Phantom of the Opera, Universal, 1925, one-sheet, paper backed, 41 x 27in.
(Christie's) $38,500

The Pilgrim, First National, 1923, one-sheet, linen backed, 41 x 27in.
(Christie's) $6,600

20th Century, Columbia, 1934, one-sheet, linen backed, 41 x 27in.
(Christie's) $23,100

Dr. Jekyll and Mr. Hyde, Paramount, 1932, window card, 22 x 14in.
(Christie's) $7,700

City Lights, United Artists, 1931, three-sheet, linen backed, 81 x 41in.
(Christie's) $23,100

The Maltese Falcon, Warner Brothers, 1941, one-sheet, linen backed, 41 x 27in.
(Christie's) $5,500

The Oregon Trail, Republic, 1936, one-sheet, linen backed, 41 x 27in.
(Christie's) $10,450

Creature from the Black Lagoon, Universal, 1954, one-sheet, linen backed, 41 x 27in.
(Christie's) $4,620

The Unholy Three, MGM, 1925, one-sheet, linen backed, 41 x 27in.
(Christie's) $4,400

Casablanca, Warner Brothers, 1943, one-sheet, linen backed, 41 x 27in.
(Christie's) $5,720

The Grapes of Wrath, 20th Century Fox, 1940, one-sheet, linen backed, 41 x 27in.
(Christie's) $5,280

Star of Midnight, RKO, 1935, one-sheet, linen backed, 41 x 27in.
(Christie's) $7,700

Society Dog Show, Disney, 1939, one-sheet, linen backed, 41 x 27in.
(Christie's) $10,450

40,000 Miles with Lindbergh, MGM, 1928, one-sheet, linen backed, 41 x 27in.
(Christie's) $5,500

The Devil is a Woman, Paramount, 1935, one-sheet, linen backed, 41 x 27in.
(Christie's) $16,500

The Birth of a Nation, Epoch Producing Corp., 1915, one-sheet, linen backed, 41 x 27in.
(Christie's) $28,600

The War of the Worlds, Paramount, 1953, six-sheet, linen backed, 81 x 81in.
(Christie's) $5,280

The Westerner, United Artists, 1940, three-sheet, linen backed, 81 x 41in.
(Christie's) $5,500

East is West, First National, 1922, one-sheet, linen backed, 41 x 27in.
(Christie's) $880

The Red Shoes, J. Arthur Rank, 1948, original English poster, linen backed, 41 x 27in.
(Christie's) $1,760

Bluebeard's 8th Wife, Paramount, 1923, one-sheet, linen backed, 41 x 27in.
(Christie's) $14,300

The Master Mystery, Octagon Films, 1919, one-sheet, linen backed, 41 x 27in.
(Christie's) $16,500

Out West, Paramount-Arbuckle, 1918, one-sheet, linen backed, 41 x 27in.
(Christie's) $5,280

Sawing a Lady in Half, Clarion Photoplays, 1922, one-sheet, linen backed, 41 x 27in.
(Christie's) $2,420

Werewolf of London, Universal, 1935, insert, paper backed, 36 x 14in.
(Christie's) $4,620

Rebel without a Cause, Warner Brothers, 1955, six-sheet, linen backed, 81 x 81in.
(Christie's) $4,400

Moon Over Miami, 20th Century Fox, 1941, three-sheet, linen backed, 81 x 41in.
(Christie's) $13,200

Steamboat round the Bend, Fox, 1935, one-sheet, linen backed, 41 x 27in.
(Christie's) $1,100

Blonde Venus, Paramount, 1933, original Belgian poster, linen backed, 30 x 24in.
(Christie's) $10,450

Horse Feathers, Paramount, 1932, one-sheet, linen backed, 41 x 27in.
(Christie's) $5,280

A 19th century Russian icon of
St. Panteleimon the Healer, with
attributes, 12 x 10¹/₂in.
(Christie's) $801

An 18th/19th century Russian
icon of the Feodorovskaya
Mother of God, 14 x 12in.
(Christie's) $1,441

A 19th century Russian icon of
the Savior Painted Without
Hands, 21 x 17¹/₂in.
(Christie's) $1,602

An early 19th century Russian
icon of Saints Basil the Great,
Gregory the Theologian and
John Chrysostom, Hierarchs of
Orthodoxy, 11 x 9in.
(Christie's) $561

A late 18th century Russian
triptych icon, the center
depicting the Deisis, the side
panels with St. George and St.
Dimitri, 12 x 17in., extended.
(Christie's) $3,185

A Palekh School icon of Christ
Pantocrator, giving the Blessing
and holding the Gospels, 12 x
10¹/₂in.
(Christie's) $3,504

A 19th century Russian icon of
the Seven Holy Sleepers of
Ephesus, the All-Seeing Eye
above, within a silver riza,
10³/₄ x 8³/₄in.
(Christie's) $1,506

A 19th century Russian icon of
the Three Hierarchs of
Orthodoxy, Saints Basil, John
Chrysostom and Gregory the
Great, 12 x 10¹/₂in.
(Christie's) $801

A late 18th/early 19th century
Russian icon of the Nativity,
Christ's Birth within a surround
of angels, Wise Men and
shepherds, 13¹/₄ x 11¹/₂in.
(Christie's) $1,902

ICONS

A late 19th century Russian icon of five chosen saints, The Lord Sabaoth above, 12 x 10³/₄in.
(Christie's) $1,001

A 19th century Russian icon of the Hodigitria Mother of God Iverskaya, 17³/₄ x 15in.
(Christie's) $1,301

A late 18th/early 19th century Russian icon of St. George and the Dragon, 13¹/₂ x 11in.
(Christie's) $1,201

A late 18th/early 19th century Palekh style icon of the Descent into Hell and the Resurrection, within a surround of scenes of the Twelve Great Feasts, 14 x 12in.
(Christie's) $2,503

A Russian Imperial wood Easter egg, one side painted with the Resurrection, the other with a Cathedral, 6¹/₄in. high.
(Christie's) $6,406

A late 19th century Russian icon of Five Chosen Saints, including Sts. Constantine, Peter and Fevronia of Murom and the child saints Michael and Fedor, 7in. x 5³/₄in.
(Christie's S. Ken) $588

A 19th century Russian icon of the Archangel Michael, holding Cross and Sword, flanked by figures of Saints Catherine and Natalia, 13 x 11¹/₄in.
(Christie's) $901

A late 18th/early 19th century Russian icon, probably of the Archangel Michael, flanked by Saints George and Paraskeva Friday, 14 x 12in.
(Christie's) $1,602

A 19th century Russian icon of the Decollation of St. John the Forerunner, overlaid with a silver oklad with hallmark stamp for 1870, 9 x 7in.
(Christie's) $1,001

439

Red lacquer four-case inro, 19th century, signed *Moei* or *Shigenaga* with seal, 3¹/₂in. long. (Skinner Inc.) **$7,425**

A fundame ground three-case inro decorated in gold and iroe, hiramakie, kirikane and kimpun with Rosei dreaming, signed *Koma Kansai saku*, 19th century, 7cm. long. (Christie's) **$11,550**

A five case inro decorated in gold and silver hiramakie, takamakie, hirame and nashiji with a karashishi descending a waterfall among rocks and peonies, signed *Kyuhaku saku*, 19th century, 9.7cm. (Christie's) **$5,775**

A four-case kinji ground inro with rounded corners decorated in gold hiramakie, takamakie, kirikane and kimpun with a flying crane above a pine and a flowering plum tree, signed *Kajikawa saku*, 19th century, 9cm. long. (Christie's) **$8,663**

A four case somada style inro decorated in mother-of-pearl inlaid on a roironuri ground with a long tailed bird in a pine tree, 18th century, 8.9cm. (Christie's) **$4,620**

A four-case gold fundame ground inro decorated in gold and silver hiramaki-e with a hawk perched on a snow-covered pine tree, signed *Kajikawa saku*, 19th century, 8.5cm. long. (Christie's) **$7,700**

A five-case inro decorated in gold and silver togidashi on a roironuri ground with a spider weaving, and a wood netsuke of a bat with a spider, late 19th century, 7.8cm. long. (Christie's) **$32,000**

A fundame ground four-case inro with rounded corners decorated in gold and iroe hiramakie, takamakie, and kirikane with a shirabyoshi, an entertainer of the Heian period, 19th century, 8.5cm. long. (Christie's) **$3,850**

A sheath inro, the outer case in gold hiramakie, takamakie nashiji on a kinji ground, with two panels of irises, water-plants, peonies and chrysanthemums, 19th century, inro 8.3cm. (Christie's) **$17,000**

A three-case kinji ground inro finely decorated in Shibayama style with hanging flower baskets, unsigned, late 19th century, 10.2cm. long.
(Christie's) $17,325

A three case Shibayama inro in the form of a tied bag, decorated with a ho-o bird among flowers and foliage, late 19th century, 10cm.
(Christie's) $13,475

A two-case kuroronuri inro of flattened oval form decorated in gold and colored togidashi with a farmer and his wife caught in a sudden squall, 19th century, 8.3cm. wide.
(Christie's) $10,588

A four case kinji ground inro decorated in Shibayama style with a cockerel on a mortar beside a pestle, the reverse with a hen and a chick, late 19th century, 9.8cm.
(Christie's) $10,588

A three case inro decorated in gold hiramakie, hirame nashiji and inlaid in Shibayama style with insects beside two floral displays of irises, chrysanthemums and blossom, 19th century, 7.8cm.
(Christie's) $9,240

A three-case double gourd-shaped inro decorated in gold and silver hiramakie on a kinji ground, nashiji interiors with rats preparing the wedding feast, late 19th century, 11cm. high.
(Christie's) $14,000

A three-case nashiji ground inro decorated on one side with a gold ground inro with peacocks on a tree, signed *Kajikawa saku*, 19th century, 8.3cm. long.
(Christie's) $13,475

Lacquer single-case inro, inscribed and sealed *Zeshin*, in the form of a worn inkstone with archaic script and musical instruments in relief, signed *Mina Kiei* with seal.
(Skinner Inc.) $22,000

A three-case inro decorated in iroe togidashi on a roironuri ground with Masatsura at the tomb of Go-Daigo, signed *Toyo*, with Kakihan, late 19th century, 8.5cm. high.
(Christie's) $80,000

INSTRUMENTS

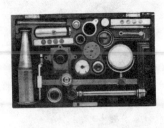

A rare mid 17th century horizontal sundial and nocturnal, unsigned, dated *1650*, and engraved with initials: *F/I C B DRID*, 4in. long.
(Christie's)   \$5,676

A 19th century lacquered brass 'Jones's Most Improved'-type compound monocular microscope, signed on the folding tripod stand *Cary LONDON*, 11¼in. wide.
(Christie's)   \$2,270

A late 17th/early 18th century silvered brass and ivory azimuth diptych dial, signed on the calendar volvelle *Jacques Senecal A Dieppe fecit*, 3in. long.
(Christie's)   \$3,406

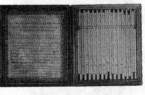

A French giltwood barometer, the paper dial signed in ink *Scatino, Opticien, Boulevarde St. Martini, à Paris*, 2ft. 8in. high.
(Bonhams)   \$990

A late 18th century lacquered and silvered brass universal equinoctial compass dial, signed on the hour ring *Jᵉ Ramsden London*, 7in. wide.
(Christie's)   \$2,270

A rare 18th century paper and card code/de-coder, by Mon: D'Montfort, the colored and inscribed sliders with instruction sheet, 7in. wide.
(Christie's)   \$4,730

An early 19th century lacquered brass 'Culpepper'-type microscope, unsigned, simple draw-tube focusing, the stage signed *Adams London*, 18in. high.
(Christie's)   \$1,892

An early 19th century? Persian steel saw; with a decorative cartouche, damascened in gold on the blade which reads: *Its owner is Aqa Muhammad, year 1245*, (H. = A.D. 1829–30); with mother-of-pearl handle, 10¾in. long.
(Christie's)   \$473

A 19th century lacquered brass compound binocular microscope, signed on the Y-shaped stand *ROSS London*, 25½in. high.
(Christie's)   \$3,027

INSTRUMENTS

Ship's wheel type kaleidoscope stamped, *C.D. Bush, Claremont, NH*, brass and leather wrapped barrel, 13¹/₂in. high.
(Eldred's) **$770**

A rare late 18th century French 'Loxocosme', with maker's label inscribed *Loxocosme or Demonstrateur*, 25¹/₂in. wide.
(Christie's) **$5,298**

A Thomason brass-barreled corkscrew decorated with fruiting vines and with turned bone handle, no brush.
(Christie's S. Ken) **$820**

A mahogany-body zograscope with 5 inch diameter magnifying lens and a 10 x 8in. mirror.
(Christie's S. Ken) **$1,025**

A rare early 17th century brass horological Compendium, unsigned; dated *1605*; comprising a nocturnal, magnetic compass, horizontal sundial and moon dial, 2in. diameter.
(Christie's) **$18,920**

A late 19th century desk barometer, the white circular dial with aneroid movement in cut glass surround with four ormolu supports, 9in. high.
(Christie's) **$795**

An early 17th century gunner's quadrant, the brass base frame stamped *C.T.D.E.M* and dated *1612* engraved with flowerand foliate decoration, 5¹/₄in. wide.
(Christie's) **$2,838**

An 8¹/₂-inch reflecting telescope, with painted steel tube, 76¹/₄in. long, brass eyepiece and viewer, thought to be by George Calver, Chelmsford, Essex.
(Tennants) **$850**

A good extensive set of drawing instruments by Elliott Brothers, The Strand, London, including a rolling rule, foot rules, pair of compasses, and curve patterns, 35cm. wide.
(Spencer's) **$3,321**

A Wimshurst-pattern
electrostatic plate machine, with
six segmented glass contra-
rotating plates, copper brushes
and brass conductor combs,
27in. wide.
(Christie's) $5,482

An extremely rare Crookes'
tube, the bulb containing a devil
molded in pale green glass,
mounted on a turned beechwood
stand, 13in. high.
(Christie's) $3,329

An unusually large electrostatic
barrel machine, unsigned,
possibly by Edward Nairne,
with mahogany and fruitwood
frame, 33¹/₂in. wide.
(Christie's) $979

Rare pair of Italian neoclassical
celestial and terrestrial globes
on urn-form stands with a pair
of faux-marble columnar
pedestals, the globes Gio. Ma.
Cassini, C.R.S. Inc., Roma,
1790.
(Butterfield & Butterfield)
                $18,700

A unique collection of one
hundred and twenty three
Geissler tubes, of various
patterns, designs, and sizes,
including liquid filled 'Multi-
Twist', 'Spiral', 'Multi-Bulb',
'Catherine-Wheel', 'Grecian-
Urn', 'Trumpet', 'Raspberry'
and other types many of tinted
glass, 1883.
(Christie's) $33,286

A pair of mid-Victorian globes,
labeled *NEWTON'S New and
Improved TERRESTRIAL
GLOBE*, London Published 1st
January 1872.
(Christie's) $27,110

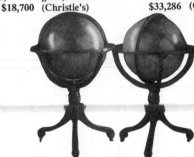

A most impressive and rare
Crookes' 'Windmill' tube,
containing a glass formed
windmill with mica sails, the
display demonstrates vividly the
mechanical properties of
electrons, 12¹/₂in. high.
(Christie's) $4,895

Good pair of William IV library
globes on stands by Newton, Son
& Barry, London, 1830 and
1832, each revolving in a
mahogany stand with ebonized
line decoration, 43in. high.
(Butterfield & Butterfield)
                $24,750

A rare American kaleidoscope
by G.C. Bush, Providence,
Rhode Island, "Patent reissued
Nov 11 1873", with textured
pasteboard tube and brass collar
incorporating object case filled
with colored glass, last quarter
19th century, 10¹/₄in. long.
(Christie's) $1,980

A Louis XV giltwood globe, now with terrestrial globe published by James Wyld, Leicester Square and dated *1855* and English chapter ring, 23in. high. (Christie's) **$10,400**

A rare Geissler 'Eye and Spiral' tube, the blown green glass center in oval-bulb on stand, 12½in. high. (Christie's) **$1,958**

A fine early 19th-century twin pillar duplex action vacuum pump, the rack gearing contained within the two lacquered brass pillars, 10¾in. long. (Christie's) **$1,175**

A pair of Regency mahogany globes by G. & J. Cary, the celestial globe calculated to the year 1820, each on turned shaft and tripod base, 40in. high. (Christie's) **$19,030**

An unusual late 14th (?), 15th (?), or early 16th (?) century brass astrolabe, from France or the Low Countries, with quatrefoil ornamentation on the rete and a dedication dated 1522, unique amongst known astronomical instruments in featuring "Chaldean" or "Astrologers'" numerals, 4⅝in. diameter. (Christie's) **$85,140**

A pair of globes of Louis XIV style with brass indicator rings, the terrestrial with dedicatory panel, on Italian ebonized and parcel-gilt stands, the stands and globes 33in. high. (Christie's) **$13,860**

A rare set of five auroraborealis discharge tubes, signed *J. King & Son, 2 Clare Street, Bristol*, with lacquered brass caps and spheres in fitted pine case, 28½in. long. (Christie's) **$2,154**

A fine pair of George III mahogany Cary's terrestrial and celestial globes, the basket stands on reeded tapered legs and united by stretchers below, 3ft. 9in. high. (Phillips) **$55,650**

A silver Butterfield dial signed *Butterfield a Paris, Premier Cadran*, inset with glazed compass, engraved with hour scales for 43–46–49–52 degrees, bird gnomon, mid 18th century, 78mm. long. (Christie's) **$2,420**

A rare Mickey Mouse cast white metal money box, indistinct registration number 50611?, 5¼in. high.
(David Lay) $1,080

A cast-iron stag, shown alert and looking forward, with five-point antlers, on a rectangular base, 19th century, 48in. wide.
(Christie's) $2,834

Cast iron Old South Church still bank, America, late 19th/early 20th century, with original paint and paper label, 13in. high.
(Skinner Inc.) $4,675

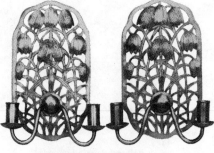

A wrought-iron porter's style chair, formed from horse shoes, with an arched top and waisted back, 66½in. high.
(Christie's) $370

A pair of Alfred Bucknell polished steel wall sconces designed by Ernest Gimson, with pierced decoration of fritillaries, the two curved branches with circular drip pans, circa 1940, 32cm. high.
(Christie's) $3,544

Cast-iron painted blackamoor tether, American, 19th century, the standing figure dressed in a white shirt and black pants, 44in. high.
(Butterfield & Butterfield) $1,650

Inlaid iron and mixed metal teapot, compressed globular form with panels of blossoms in gold and inlay, brass cover, signed, 3½in. high.
(Skinner Inc.) $1,760

A pair of Artificers' Guild wrought iron candelabra designed by Edward Spencer, supporting circular drip pans, numbered 3009, 28.5cm. high.
(Christie's) $2,363

A George III cast iron royal coat of arms, with flanking figures of the lion and unicorn, 50cm. wide approximately.
(Phillips) $1,300

'Alberto's Kettle', an aluminium, steel and blue painted kettle, by Ron Arad, the cut and angled form with curved spout and arched strap handle, 21cm. high.
(Christie's) $1,024

Cast iron doorstop in the form of a Scottie dog, 16in. high.
(Eldred's) $176

Fine large cast iron elephant doorstop painted black, 10in. high.
(Eldred's) $220

Hagenauer figure of a piano player, nickel-finish, flat stylised representation, impressed with Wiener Werkstatte mark, 8¹/₂in. high.
(Skinner Inc.) $1,100

'Spine Chair', a welded steel side chair by Andre Dubreuil, the scrolling profile terminating with tripod junction feet, the back and seat formed by slats tapering towards the back.
(Christie's) $1,575

Shaker iron stove, probably Harvard, Massachusetts, circa 1800, the lift lid above a base with canted corners on cabriole legs, ending in wrought penny feet, 26in. high.
(Skinner Inc.) $4,675

Cast iron garden ornament in the form of a Newfoundland dog, America, mid 19th century, 55in. long.
(Skinner Inc.) $23,100

Fine cast iron doorstop of a trained bear climbing a tree, marked *Warwick* on lower front, 13¹/₂in. high.
(Eldred's) $231

Antique American wood and iron candle mold, designed for twenty-four candles, 22in. wide.
(Eldred's) $633

A Japanese iron globular tripod koro and cover with bronze terrapin finial, silver inner liner and cover, 6in. high, signed *Chishinsai Katsunobu (Shoshin)*.
(Christie's)　　　　$35,000

A large russet-iron model of a carp, its body, tail, dorsal and ventral fins fully articulated, signed *Munekazu*, 19th century, 47cm. long.
(Christie's)　　　　$14,200

'Sailor', a painted iron figure of a Newfoundland, cast by Bartlett and Hayward, American, 19th century, 36³/₈ x 65¹/₂in.
(Christie's)　　　　$19,800

An unusual large russet iron cabinet formed in Chinese style with slightly splayed legs, the front with two hinged doors decorated with dragons, 18th century, 36cm. high.
(Christie's)　　　　$9,750

A pair of painted figures of hounds, cast by J.W. Fiske, American, 19th century, 48 x 46¹/₂in.
(Christie's)　　　　$38,500

'Le Cigognes d'Alsace', an Edgar Brandt wrought iron and bronze decorative panel, embellished in gilt bronze with three storks amid wirework clouds, 194 x 126cm.
(Phillips)　　　　$8,185

A pair of silver painted iron figures of seated grayhounds, English, 19th century, 17¹/₂ x 37³/₄in.
(Christie's)　　　　$1,760

A painted iron figure of Guanyin, seated on a lotus base with legs crossed and hands raised, the draping skirt polychromed with patterns of fire and cloud scrolls, Yuan Dynasty, 61.5cm. high.
(Christie's)　　　　$3,600

A pair of white painted iron figures of eagles, the birds staring straight ahead, their wings folded, on square bases pierced for mounting, 34in. high.
(Christie's)　　　　$3,300

IVORY

A fine silver-mounted ivory vase, maker's mark of *Tiffany & Co., New York 1889–1891*, 17³/₄in. high. (Christie's) $24,200

An ivory and stag antler okimono of a kingfisher with its catch on a lotus pod, a frog on the stem and a snail hidden among the pods, signed *Koho*, late 19th century, 23.5cm. long. (Christie's) $6,000

'Hoop Girl', a painted bronze and ivory figure, cast and carved from a model by Ferdinand Preiss, as a young girl wearing a greenish-silver bloomer suit and shoes, 20.5cm. high. (Phillips) $3,601

A finely patinated ivory netsuke of a magic fox dancing on its hind legs, the cord attachment formed by the tail, unsigned, 18th century, 11cm. (Christie's) $11,165

Fine pair of large ivory carvings of horses, Rajasthani style, 19th century, each depicting a majestic steed with flaring nostrils and large eyes accentuated by alert ears and long mane, 13³/₄in. high. (Butterfield & Butterfield) $30,250

A finely detailed and well carved ivory figure of Kannon standing in her elaborate headdress, holding a koro, signed *Nobuyoshi*, late 19th century, 27.7cm. high. (Christie's) $7,700

A German ivory pedigree in the form of a tree, the large oak tree carved as an ivory relief against a velvet ground, the pedigree listed on inlaid silver plaquettes, 19th century, 33 x 23in. (Christie's) $18,469

Two George IV silver-gilt and ivory beakers, each on spreading circular foot and with fluted borders, the mounts by Robert Garrard, 1825, the ivory probably Augsburg, mid 18th century, 7¹/₂in. high, 50oz. (Christie's) $10,560

A Dieppe silver-mounted ivory ewer and dish, the ewer carved in relief, the central panel showing the Triumph of Bacchus and Ariadne, 19th century, 19¹/₂in. high. (Christie's) $36,520

449

Goanese ivory figural Nativity group, 18th century, 10in. high.
(Skinner Inc.) $2,860

A German ivory relief of a battle scene, of curved rectangular form, the warriors mostly on horseback and wearing Roman armour, 19th century, 5 x 13³/₄in.
(Christie's) $6,625

An Italian ivory relief of Diana the Huntress, the goddess shown in a central panel striding forward armed with bow and spear, 19th century, 8 x 5in.
(Christie's) $1,405

A pair of fine ivory tusk vases, boldly carved with birds among flowers and foliage on wood bases, late 19th century, 46cm. high.
(Christie's) $10,346

French ivory inlaid marquetry wall plaque, third quarter 19th century, depicting a garden detail with an exotic bird with long plumage closely observing a grasshopper, 15³/₄in. diameter.
(Butterfield & Butterfield)
$4,400

Pair of carved ivory female musicians, 19th century, each slender maiden standing in layered robes and sashes with a musical instrument held to the front, 12¹/₄in. high.
(Butterfield & Butterfield)
$1,980

A finely detailed ivory okimono style netsuke depicting five Sika stags in a compact maple grove, signed *Masatoshi* (Shinkesai), 19th century, 4.2cm.
(Christie's) $846

A Japanese sectional carved ivory figure of a fruit seller, wearing a short patterned tunic, striped leggings and spats, small baskets and bags tied to his waist, 42.75cm. high.
(Spencer's) $2,383

A Dieppe carved ivory figure of a seated hound, 8.5cm. high.
(Spencer's) $526

IVORY

German silver gilt and ivory figure, in Renaissance style, 9in. high.
(Skinner Inc.) **$1,210**

Scottish staghorn and ivory inkstand, 19th century, mounted with an antler pen holder, a sander, inkwell and small dished tray, the whole raised on three carved ivory claw feet, 9in. wide.
(Butterfield & Butterfield) **$935**

A finely carved ivory okimono depicting an itinerant Buddhist priest with Rakan on his back having his foot bitten by a crab, unsigned, late 19th century, 37cm. high.
(Christie's) **$15,048**

Portuguese colonial carved ivory birdcage, early 20th century, of typical cylindrical form with dragon-carved hanging hook, enclosing carved and painted ivory birds, 12¼in. high.
(Butterfield & Butterfield) **$1,500**

A pair of Chinese carved ivory vases, of hexagonal section intricately carved with figures in landscapes, the necks with floral scroll handles, 19th century, 9in. high.
(Woolley & Wallis) **$648**

Fine Anglo-Indian etched ivory table bureau cabinet, Vizagapatam, first quarter 19th century, with an interrupted triangular pediment centering a turned finial above four drawers, 23³/₈in. wide.
(Butterfield & Butterfield) **$23,100**

A Dieppe ivory mirror with later oval beveled plate in a border of overlaid-leaves, the top with a coat-of-arms with supporters and flanked by eagles, late 19th century, 33 x 23in.
(Christie's) **$2,376**

German carved ivory figure of a horse and rider, late 19th century, the man wearing hunting gear of a riding hat, tunic, jacket, and high boots, inscribed *B. Rudolph, Stattgart*, 10³/₄in. high.
(Butterfield & Butterfield) **$3,300**

A fine ivory carving of a child on a wheeled hobby-horse, the details inlaid in mother-of-pearl, an uchiwa in his hand, signed *Kozan*, late 19th century, 13cm. high.
(Christie's) **$3,292**

JADE

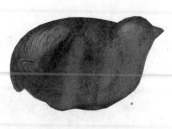

A white jade baluster vase and cover carved in high relief on one side with a phoenix perched on rockwork among flowers, 18th century, 19.5cm. high. (Christie's) $5,600

A white and brown jade quail, carved with a plump body resting on two thin legs tucked under and small head tilted upward, the long feathers well defined, 17th century, 7.2cm. long. (Christie's) $2,600

A pale celadon jade vase, carved as an upright hollowed curling lotus leaf issuing from ribboned leafy and flowering stems, 18th century, 21.5cm. high. (Christie's) $12,799

A very fine white jade table screen, Qianlong, carved according to the theme of Lanting Tsu by Wong Xizhi, to the front with scholars gathered along the bank of the winding stream, 9⁵/₈in. high. (Christie's) $170,680

A white jade mythical-beast vase, 18th century, well carved from a stone of lightly mottled pale celadon tone with a winged beast with dragon-like head, 4¹/₈in. high. (Christie's) $4,267

Fine carved nephrite brushpot, late 18th/early 19th century, carved in the form of a hollow tree trunk to simulate the natural pitting and knotting of wood, 7¹/₂in. high. (Butterfield & Butterfield) $59,400

A yellow jade vase and cover, of flattened baluster shape with elephant-mask handles and animal finial, the base carved with three goats amongst rockwork, early 18th century, 18.5cm. high. (Christie's) $22,000

A rare matched pair of celadon jade boulders carved from a single stone, one with Shoulao and a deer standing on a cliff, the other with a recumbent doe beneath a pine tree, 18th century, Qianlong, 19.5cm. high. (Christie's) $7,000

White jade cricket cage, 19th century, carved in shallow relief to depict a continuous landscape scene of flowering lily, prunus and chrysanthemum branches, 4¹/₂in. high. (Butterfield & Butterfield) $1,760

JADE

A celadon and brown jade recumbent horse, its front legs extended forward to support the head, the mane and tail defined by even incised lines, Tang Dynasty or later, 8.3cm. long. (Christie's) $4,400

A Moghul-style green jade stem-dish, 19th century, thinly carved from mottled green and spinach nephrite with irregular white inclusions as a petal-fluted saucer-dish, 5¹/₂in. diameter. (Christie's) $5,689

Lobed oval jadeite bowl carved to the well with a pair of carp encircling a fronted blossom amid further blossoms and leafy tendrils, 13¹/₄in. wide. (Butterfield & Butterfield) $27,500

Small white jade square form vase, Ming Dynasty, the sides carved in shallow relief to depict a band of stylized taotie masks bracketed by a leafy tendril and keyscroll band, 4¹/₂in. high. (Butterfield & Butterfield) $4,950

A pale celadon jade censer and cover carved around the lower section with taotie masks on a leiwen ground divided by two fixed-ring dragon-head handles, Qianlong, 15cm. wide. (Christie's) $3,400

A very fine jade monkey, late Ming Dynasty, ingeniously carved using the natural skin and inclusions of an irregular nephrite pebble as a crouching monkey, the posture naturalistic, 4¹/₈in. high. (Christie's) $64,000

A longquan celadon figure of Budai, Ming Dynasty, the seated figure in a casual attitude, resting one arm on a large peach, holding a tablet in the opposite hand, 6¹/₄in. high. (Christie's) $4,978

A fine jadeite globular bowl and cover, the spherical body raised on three cabriole legs and crisply carved with two mask handles suspending loose rings, 13.5cm. wide. (Christie's) $11,420

A celadon jade carving of double gourds carved and pierced with a large central double gourd and leafy tendrils with two smaller double gourds, 18th century, 10.5cm. high. (Christie's) $3,544

Art Deco sapphire and diamond double clip brooch, triangular-shaped clips set throughout with round and fancy-cut diamonds.
(Skinner Inc.) $10,175

An attractive 9 carat gold brooch, as a large and small owl perched upon a branch, with cabochon polished amethyst bodies.
(Spencer's) $364

Victorian Revival period brooch, of a sphinx emanating from a wrapped scroll, highlighted by granulation and wire twists, approx. 16ct.
(Skinner Inc.) $2,750

Enamel and diamond tiger head pendant, Alling & Co., highlighted by round diamonds, suspended from a 14ct. gold link chain.
(Skinner Inc.) $1,430

Victorian ear pendants, composed of hinged plaques, highlighted by wire twist and granulated gold completed by ball fringe, 14ct. gold.
(Skinner Inc.) $1,430

Carved shell cameo brooch, depicting the profile of a woman, mounted in a 14ct. gold frame with raised floral design.
(Skinner Inc.) $1,980

Victorian Egyptian Revival brooch, France, designed as a scarab set with rubies, emeralds and sapphires.
(Skinner Inc.) $2,200

Ruby and diamond fly brooch, set with carved rubies, round diamonds and cabochon-cut green onyx, 18ct. gold.
(Skinner Inc.) $1,540

Victorian hardstone cameo brooch, depicting the profile of a woman, mounted in a gold frame, 18ct. gold.
(Skinner Inc.) $880

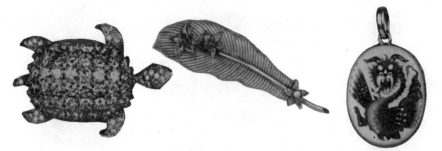

Diamond turtle brooch, set
throughout with round
diamonds, est. total weight
11.50ct., with emerald set eyes.
(Skinner Inc.) $9,075

18ct. gold, ruby and diamond
pin, Tiffany & Co., in the shape
of a feather, highlighted by
rubies and a diamond.
(Skinner Inc.) $440

Enamel locket, 1860s, depicting
a dragon, highlighted by
cabochon rubies and rose-cut
diamonds, 18ct. gold.
(Skinner Inc.) $6,600

Antique pink sapphire and
diamond pendant, centered by a
full Holland-cut pear shaped
pink sapphire, total weight
7.00ct.
(Skinner Inc.) $15,400

14ct. gold Madonna sandal clips,
attributed to Paul Flato, each set
with a garnet, originally
advertized in the October 15
1940 issue of Vogue magazine.
(Skinner Inc.) $1,980

14ct. yellow gold and ruby pin,
circa 1940's, Cartier, New York,
fluted leaf highlighted by five
round rubies.
(Skinner Inc.) $1,100

18ct. yellow gold knot brooch,
Tiffany & Co., Italy, 31 dwt.
(Skinner Inc.) $2,090

Art Nouveau locket, centered by
a cabochon-cut sapphire with a
raised floral design, 14ct. gold.
(Skinner Inc.) $770

18ct. yellow gold, emerald and
diamond frog pin, pavé-set
emeralds and diamonds with
cabochon-cut ruby eyes, signed
Fridel Virgilio.
(Skinner Inc.) $5,500

A mid-19th century gold, ruby, diamond and half-pearl-set circular crystal pendant.
(Bearne's) $2,880

A mid-19th century matted gold, turquoise and diamond-mounted hinged bangle with central target-shaped circular cluster of stones.
(Bearne's) $5,400

A 19th century gold oval locket with applied ruby, diamond and half-pearl star-shaped cluster, dated *1875*.
(Bearne's) $1,045

A fine emerald-green jadeite pendant, carved as a group of gourds with foliage and tendrils, the stone of even semi-translucent tone, 4.6cm. long.
(Christie's) $42,670

An enameled gold diamond-set lapel watch and a butterfly brooch signed *M. Scooler, New Orleans*, with nickel keyless lever movement jeweled through the center, 18ct gold cuvette, blue enameled dial with white enamel Arabic chapters, circa 1890, 23.5mm. diameter.
(Christie's) $3,520

A fine jadeite and diamond pendant, the stone of very large size and of very even emerald-green tone with good translucency carved to the front with four felines among a lingzhi branch.
(Christie's) $227,573

An oval shell cameo brooch, carved depicting a young woman within an engraved gold frame and in fitted case.
(Bearne's) $750

A German Art Nouveau brooch in the form of a woman with long flowing tresses, wearing cloche hat, 2¼in. long.
(Christie's) $6,230

An oval hardstone cameo portrait brooch, the carved agate depicting a woman within an enameled gold frame.
(Bearne's) $720

A diamond, sapphire, ruby and garnet butterfly brooch, the body set with carbuncles with diamond head and ruby-set antenna.
(Bearne's) $3,150

A 15ct. gold and Italian micro-mosaic oval brooch depicting 'Pliny's' doves within a millegrained and beaded scrolling wirework frame.
(Bearne's) $610

'Euphoria', a Memphis enameled chromed metal necklace on rubber cord, designed by Ettore Sottsass Jnr. for Acme.
(Christie's) $292

A platinum and diamond regimental brooch designed as the standard of The Royal Irish Fusiliers, pavé-set with rose diamonds.
(Bearne's) $1,620

A pair of lavender jadeite, pearl and diamond earrings, the jadeite of pear-drop form, the lavender bright with some inclusions, suspended from pearl and diamond cluster mounts, 4.7cm. long overall.
(Christie's) $13,512

A large and elaborate George Hunt Arts and Crafts brooch, with a central plaque of smoky quartz carved with the head of Medusa, 8.3cm. wide.
(Phillips) $3,274

A mid-19th century gold, emerald, diamond and gem-set crystal circular pendant, the wings pavé-set with emeralds and rose diamonds.
(Bearne's) $3,780

A late 19th century gold, sapphire and diamond crescent brooch with eleven graduated oval sapphires separated by pairs of brilliant-cut diamonds.
(Bearne's) $860

A late 19th century miniature portrait of F.W. Young as a boy, painted on ivory, mounted within a glazed frame of moonstones in gold settings as a pendant.
(Bearne's) $750

LACQUER

A rare 17th century oval barber's shaving bowl, the black lacquer ground decorated in gold hiramakie, kinpun and a little kirigane with lakeside buildings among trees, 31.6cm. wide.
(Christie's) $16,190

A red lacquer zushi containing a Shinto deity Dakini-ten mounted on a fox, late 18th/early 19th century, 22.5cm. high.
(Christie's) $3,010

A wood panel decorated with two fans, the open fan depicting the oil thief beside a temple lantern, the other birds among plum blossom, signed *Kongyokusai*, late 19th century, 70cm. wide.
(Christie's) $1,693

Unusual giltwood and red lacquer aviary, late 19th century, the three tiered structure composed of floral carved and pierced panels and columns, 63½in. tall.
(Butterfield & Butterfield) $3,300

A maroon lacquer suzuribako decorated in gold hiramakie, takamakie, kirikane, hirame and kimpun with Chinese scholars and children on a rocky path, unsigned, 19th century, 23.2 x 21.2cm.
(Christie's) $6,738

A finely modeled gold lacquered okimono of a macaque monkey wearing a sleeveless haori and sitting holding a peach, the back of his haori decorated in gold hiramakie with the other eleven zodiacal animals, late 18th/early 19th century, 19cm. high.
(Christie's) $44,480

A gold lacquer ground box and cover shaped as a persimmon decorated in hiramakie and kirikane, 19th century, 7.5cm. wide.
(Christie's) $1,693

A black roironuri ground suzuribako, the cover decorated in gold and silver hiramakie and kirikane with a pair of karashishi, 19th century, 22.7cm. long.
(Christie's) $5,800

A lacquer tobacco set decorated with panels depicting various landscapes, copper fittings and a kizerizutsu, late 19th century, 19.5cm. high.
(Christie's) $3,104

LACQUER

Lacquer box, 18th century, rectangular with single cabinet door, enclosing three drawers, 13in. wide.
(Skinner Inc.) **$1,320**

A lacquer saddle and stirrups decorated in gold hiramakie and takamakie and nashiji on a roironuri ground with ho-o birds, late 19th century.
(Christie's) **$5,267**

Japanese lacquer and metal tabako-bon, 19th century, fitted with tobacco containers and drawers, 7¼in. high.
(Skinner Inc.) **$3,400**

A black lacquer shrine decorated in iroe hiramakie, the exterior with crashing waves, the interior with numerous deities, dated on the reverse *4th Month Koka 2* (1845).
(Christie's) **$3,009**

A pair of Chinese export black lacquer and gilt painted papier mâché vases decorated overall with chinoiserie scenes, 19th century, 86in. high.
(Christie's) **$12,379**

A roironuri ground suzuribako with beveled corners, the cover decorated with shells scattered on a beach by breaking waves, pine trees in the foreground, late 17th/early 18th century, 27cm. long.
(Christie's) **$14,108**

A lacquer sagejubako of typical form decorated in gold hiramakie on a roironuri ground with plum, pine and bamboo, red lacquer interiors, late 19th century, 21.5cm. long.
(Christie's) **$1,411**

A lacquer table screen inlaid in the Shibayama style with Kidomaru beside a stream, the reverse with egrets in moonlight, metal mounts, late 19th century, 27.5cm. high.
(Christie's) **$6,019**

A lacquer kojubako modeled as a thatched house with an inner tray decorated in gold and silver hiramakie, takamakie and hirame, early 19th century, 12.5cm. high.
(Christie's) **$4,138**

A composite lacquer sage-jubako comprising a carrying frame, a small tray, a box, two sake bottles in a tray, a four-tiered jubako, late 17th/early 18th century, 24.5cm. high.
(Christie's) $5,643

A Momoyama Period small rectangular wood coffer and domed cover decorated with shippo hanabishi in gold lacquer, late 16th century, 23cm. long.
(Christie's) $5,643

A large fine Shibayama style kodansu, the silver ground carved in relief with massed chrysanthemum flowerheads, signed on the nashiji ground base *Masayoshi*, late 19th century, 30.5cm. high.
(Christie's) $37,620

A hexagonal gold ground lacquer box and cover on short shaped feet, the sides with panels decorated in Shibayama style with flowers and hanging flower baskets, late 19th century, 15.5cm. wide.
(Christie's) $11,130

A matched pair of Chinese export black and gilt lacquer dressing-tables decorated overall with chinoiserie scenes, each with serpentine top with conforming superstructure with pull-up shaped mirror, early 19th century, 25³/₄in. wide.
(Christie's) $7,871

An important seventeenth century ewer and basin decorated in gold hiramakie, 17th century, the ewer 25.5cm. high.
(Christie's) $182,875

A rare and fine double lozenge shaped sage-jubako connected by another lozenge-shaped piece, 17th century, 29.7cm. high.
(Christie's) $13,167

Good gilt lacquer decorated kodansu, Meiji period, ornamented with a flock of cranes amid pine and above a small hinged double-door compartment, 22¹/₂ x 24 x 14³/₈in. (Butterfield & Butterfield) $9,900

A six-case kimpun-scattered roironuri ground inro decorated with stylized ju characters against massed chrysanthemum flowerheads, signed *Shiomi Masanari*, early 19th century, 7.6cm. long.
(Christie's) $7,524

LACQUER

A two-case octagonal inro lacquered to imitate a cake of old Chinese ink in brown and dark olive green, signed *Zeshin*, 19th century, 3cm., and a stained ivory ojime.
(Christie's) $16,553

A superb suzuribako decorated with an Imperial ox-carriage in kinji takamakie and hiramakie, silver and aogai on a dark reddish-brown nunome-textured ground, unsigned, 19th century, 24.7cm. wide.
(Christie's) $23,100

A lacquered palanquin with gold hiramakie on a roironuri ground and gilt metal fittings incised with foliage, the exterior of the rectangular carrying case divided by horizontal bands, 19th century, 105cm. long.
(Christie's) $50,787

A fine lacquer vase and cover decorated in gold and silver hiramakie, takamakie, hirame, gyobu-nashiji and fundame with two panels elaborately decorated in Shibayama style, signed *Sadatoshi*, late 19th century, 26cm. high.
(Christie's) $34,650

A pair of important two-leaf gold lacquer screens decorated with figurative scenes, the panels bordered by a finely carved wood frame inlaid in mother-of-pearl and ivory, Meiji Period (1863–1912), each panel 225cm. high x 104.5cm. wide.
(Christie's) $376,200

A roironuri ground cylindrical sake flask, food container and cover decorated in gold hiramakie, kimpun and hirame with hydrangea, roundels and geometric pattern, 17th century, 29cm. high.
(Christie's) $11,286

A kimpun ground four-case inro, decorated with a group of butterflies on both sides, nashiji interior, unsigned, 19th century, an attached bead ojime, 7.5cm. long.
(Christie's) $1,693

A gold fundame and nashiji ground suzuribako in the shape of takarabune, a treasure boat, unsigned, 18th century, 22cm. long.(Christie's) $36,575

A composite lacquer sage-jubako comprising a carrying frame, a four-tiered jubako, two boxes and a sake bottle modeled as Jurojin with his stag, 18th century, 30.7cm. high.
(Christie's) $8,465

Handel treasure island lamp, textured glass dome shade reverse painted with tropical moonlit coastline scene, 27in. high.
(Skinner Inc.) **$10,175**

Hampshire pottery lamp, Keene, New Hampshire, circa 1910, with incised key device in matt green glaze, 10in. high.
(Skinner Inc.) **$413**

Handel-type floral table lamp, dome shade of green and amber leaded slag glass arranged with a wide band of violet blossoms, 23in. high.
(Skinner Inc.) **$650**

Tiffany bronze and favrile glass three-light lily lamp, tripartite upright stems hold gold iridescent blossom shades, 13in. high.
(Skinner Inc.) **$2,600**

A cameo giltmetal-mounted oil-lamp base, overlaid in opaque-white and carved with a branch of trailing prunus pendant from a band of stiff leaves, circa 1885, 24cm. high.
(Christie's) **$1,264**

Free blown petticoat oil lamp, wide flaring folded foot, large crimped handle, with thumb rest, pontil scar, 9$^1/_2$in. high, possibly New England, early 19th century.
(Skinner Inc.) **$770**

Pairpoint blown-out puffy lamp, squared molded Torino glass shade with rippled exterior surface design overall, 21$^1/_2$in. high.
(Skinner Inc.) **$13,200**

A William IV bronze colza oil lamp, in the form of a campagna shaped urn with fruiting cone finial, on a circular plinth, 39cm. high.
(Phillips) **$1,408**

Pairpoint puffy papillon lamp, quatriform blown out shade with four clusters of colorful rose blossoms centering multicolored butterflies painted within, 18in. high.
(Skinner Inc.) **$4,840**

A French gilt bronze bouillotte lamp, the conical tôle shade on adjustable stem issuing from a fluted half column, 84cm. high.
(Phillips) $2,581

Handel-type piano-desk lamp, adjustable roll cylinder shade of leaded green slag glass segments, 14in. high.
(Skinner Inc.) $605

Pairpoint scenic lamp, textured glass reverse painted featuring an antlered stag at lakeside, urn-form black metal base, 16in. high.
(Skinner Inc.) $1,870

Tiffany bronze and favrile seven light lily lamp, gold iridescent shades signed *L.C.T.*, 20¹/₂in. high.
(Skinner Inc.) $5,720

Pairpoint seascape table lamp, reverse painted flared *Exeter* shade with tropical island scene, 26in. high.
(Skinner Inc.) $2,090

Tiffany bronze lamp base, organic triple-stem shaft with hook above tendril looped socket, 24³/₄in. high.
(Skinner Inc.) $6,710

Tiffany abalone desk lamp, shade of twelve frosted colorless linenfold panels, mounted on gilt bronze shaft, 16¹/₂in. high.
(Skinner Inc.) $6,500

Muller Frères and Chapelle Stork lamp, composed of wrought iron reticulated cage in form of a stork, 15in. high.
(Skinner Inc.) $8,250

Tiffany bronze and turtleback desk lamp, mounted in ornate beaded bronze single-socket shade above molded platform base with sixteen inserted glass "jewels", 14in. high.
(Skinner Inc.) $3,100

LAMPS

A Regency bronze and giltmetal colza oil-lamp attributed to William Bullock, the circular molded top with removable burner, 11in. high.
(Christie's) $2,973

A Loetz and silvered brass table lamp, the spherical shade with an iridescent pale amber and oil spot pattern decorated with a band of green linear cells, 42cm. high.
(Christie's) $2,531

Early Tiffany blown-out bronze and favrile Tyler lamp, shaped dome shade of leaded glass segments arranged as twelve green swirling swags, 24in. high.
(Skinner Inc.) $44,000

Tiffany red poppy lamp, flared conical shade with brilliant and unusual striated glass segments depicting poppy blossoms, 26in. high.
(Skinner Inc.) $26,400

Daum cameo glass table lamp, mushroom dome shade and baluster shaft base of mottled yellow glass with green and red shadings, 26½in. high.
(Skinner Inc.) $15,000

Tiffany bronze and turtleback glass table lamp, nineteen iridescent green tiles bordered above and below by mottled green square and rectangular favrile glass segments, 24in. high.
(Skinner Inc.) $23,000

Tiffany bronze and favrile glass dragonfly lamp, on conical shade with seven turquoise blue, opal and red-winged dragonflies arranged on leaded glass segments, 22in. high.
(Skinner Inc.) $16,500

A Loetz and Osiris table lamp, the cylindrical shade with pinched quatrefoil rim, the yellow ground decorated with iridescent silver splashes and green and blue trailing.
(Christie's) $1,168

A Gallé carved and acid-etched triple-overlay lamp with bronze and ivory base, in the form of two perched eagles flanking a central rectangular column, 46cm. high.
(Christie's) $4,478

Pairpoint seascape table lamp, "Exeter", four ocean scenes enhanced by scallop shell and dolphin panels, 20in. high. (Skinner Inc.) $1,400

Mount Washington cameo glass lamp base, pink to white, mounted in brass and gilt metal lamp fittings, 8in. diameter. (Skinner Inc.) $375

Pairpoint butterflies and roses puffy lamp, quatriform blown-out glass dome, drilled and mounted to gilt metal petal-molded base, 20¹/₂in. high. (Skinner Inc.) $5,200

Pairpoint floral table lamp, large flared "Exeter" glass shade with broad apron of stylised blossoms of pink, blue, beige and amber, 22in. high. (Skinner Inc.) $1,600

A German electroplated two-division oil lamp with revolving boat-shaped reservoir supporting two burners, 25¹/₂in. high, stamped *Patent Wild & Wessel Berlin*. (Bearne's) $990

Rare Quezal twelve light lily lamp, gold iridescent ribbed blossom-form shades on slender stems arising from bronze leaf-pad base, 20in. high. (Skinner Inc.) $4,800

Leaded glass table lamp, Wilkerson-type amber-centered white clematis blossom leaded shade on two-socket black and gilt metal base, 20in. high. (Skinner Inc.) $325

Millefiore Art Glass miniature lamp, mushroom cap shade and matching glass lamp shaft, mounted with gilt metal and "Bryant" electrical fittings, 11in. high. (Skinner Inc.) $1,200

Handel daffodil table lamp, conical glass shade of sand-textured surface exterior painted with realistic daffodil, 27in. high. (Skinner Inc.) $4,250

One of a pair of leaded glass and patinated metal wall lanterns, possibly Handel, circa 1910, hexagonal verdigris framework, 18in. high.
(Skinner Inc.) $2,600

Late Louis XVI turned brass three-light bouillotte lamp, with three adjustable foliate scroll arms, 22¹/₂in. high.
(Butterfield & Butterfield) $3,025

One of a pair of Gustav Stickley wall lanterns, circa 1910, no. 225, wrought Iron lanterns with heart cut-out design, suspended from wrought iron hooks with spade shape mounts, 10in. high.
(Skinner Inc.) $2,000

Tiffany bronze and favrile crocus lamp, green and gold amber glass segments arranged in four repeating elements of spring blossoms, 21¹/₂in. high.
(Skinner Inc.) $8,250

German bronzed and metal glass figural lamp, designed as a tile-roofed outbuilding with three children gazing into a tub of water, 14in. high.
(Skinner Inc.) $880

Tiffany bronze and favrile apple blossom lamp, domed shade of transparent green segmented background for yellow-centered pink and white blossoms, 22¹/₂in. high.
(Skinner Inc.) $11,000

Tiffany bronze and favrile large linenfold lamp, twelve-sided angular gilt bronze lamp shade with amber fabrique glass panels, 24¹/₂in. high.
(Skinner Inc.) $12,100

A Tiffany Studios Art Nouveau bronze electric desk lamp, the shade inset with two amber iridescent turtle-back tiles decorated in the "Venetian style", 14¹/₄in. high.
(Selkirk's) $3,500

Leaded glass table lamp, attributed to Wilkerson, green and amber slag glass segments geometrically arranged with red jewel accent squares, 21¹/₂in. high.
(Skinner Inc.) $825

Wilkerson table lamp, leaded conical shade with red, yellow, orange and pink blossoms, 29in. high.
(Skinner Inc.) **$5,775**

Copper and mica table lamp, early 20th century, mica paneled shades, petal form sockets, 18¹/₂in. high.
(Skinner Inc.) **$1,210**

Handel scenic boudoir lamp, hexagonal ribbed textured glass, mounted on bronzed metal *Handel* signed base, 14in. high.
(Skinner Inc.) **$2,310**

Tiffany bronze and favrile blue dragonfly lamp, conical tuck-under shade of seven mesh-wing dragonflies with blue bodies and jewel eyes, 22¹/₂in. high.
(Skinner Inc.) **$22,000**

One of a pair of Handel wall sconces, early 20th century, oval hammered back plate, suspending cylindrical frosted glass buckle shade, 8¹/₄in. high.
(Skinner Inc.) **$850**

Handel scenic table lamp, textured glass shade reverse painted with riverside clusters of tall trees before a mountainous horizon, 24in. high.
(Skinner Inc.) **$7,150**

Miller paneled slag glass table lamp, extended on quatriform filigreed metal shade, mounted on metal base with green patina, 26in. high.
(Skinner Inc.) **$1,100**

Tiffany bronze and favrile lotus bell lamp, mottled green and white glass segments arranged in bell form geometric progression, 21in. high.
(Skinner Inc.) **$26,550**

Tiffany bronze and favrile glass pebble and cherry blossom lamp, dome shade composed of smooth 'stones' arranged as flowers below pink and red favrile glass jewels, 23¹/₂in. high.
(Skinner Inc.) **$40,700**

White marble figure of a shepherdess, attributed to Richard James Wyatt, 35in. high.
(Skinner Inc.)   **$2,695**

A 17th century Flemish alabaster relief panel of the Flight into Egypt, in the background soldiers carry out Herod's Edict, 6½ x 9in.
(Christie's S. Ken)   **$1,995**

Italian marble bust of a satyr, 19th century, 16½in. high.
(Skinner Inc.)   **$3,080**

Carved and painted marble bust of a maiden, signed *A. Cipriani*, circa 1900, the woman with a somber expression on her face, wearing a fringed scarf draped over her head and shoulders, 31in. high.
(Butterfield & Butterfield)
$2,200

Monumental Italian carved Carrara marble bust of a seventeenth century nobleman in the style of Roubilliac, Prof. Aetrilli, 19th century, the nobleman with moustache and projecting underlip with arrogant expression, 30½in. high.
(Butterfield & Butterfield)
$8,250

An English white marble figure of 'Young Romilly', by Alexander Munro, the young boy shown embracing his hound, wearing medieval tunic and breeches, circa 1863, 37in. high.
(Christie's)   **$5,478**

A white marble bust of the Apollo Belvedere, his hair tied with a ribbon, with gathered drapery about his shoulders, second half 19th century, 26½in. high.
(Christie's)   **$1,278**

Continental carved marble figural fountain, circa 1900, the figure of Cupid with a drape across his hips, looking down at a butterfly on his right arm, 37in. high.
(Butterfield & Butterfield)
$3,850

A carved white marble bust of Homer, shown bearded, weathered, damages, late 17th/ 18th century, on a 19th century socle, 20in. high.
(Christie's)   **$1,552**

An Italian white marble bust of a Roman emperor, by Leandro Biglioschi, his hair and physiognomy well modeled, 21¼in. high.
(Christie's) $1,004

An Italian white marble figure of the Sleeping Nymph, after the antique, shown reclining, her drapery falling about her in soft folds, her legs crossed, her head supported on her left arm with asp bracelet, 31in. wide.
(Christie's) $1,186

A white marble figure of a semi-naked dancing girl, holding a tambourine, her robes gathered about her waist on circular base, signed *Willm Physick Sculp 1868*, 39¾in. high.
(Christie's) $2,556

An English white marble figure of a nude woman, by Edwin Roscoe Mullins, the young woman shown standing gracefully, her drapery fallen about her legs, late 19th century, 32¾in. high.
(Christie's) $4,017

Pair of Louis XVI style gilt-bronze-mounted salmon-pink marble urns, of high shouldered ovoid-form with a pineapple finial, 20¼in. high.
(Butterfield & Butterfield)
                               $1,760

A white marble bust of Napoleon, as a young man portrayed looking straight ahead in deep contemplation, 23¾in. high.
(Tennants) $3,255

An Italian white marble figure of a naked woman, her right hand holding a lamp, on an oval base, 19th century, 41½in. high.
(Christie's) $1,461

A white marble bust of a gentleman, by Alexander MacDonald, his hair neatly modeled, signed and dated *Roma 1895*, 21¼in. high.
(Christie's) $639

An Italian white marble figure of the crouching Venus, her hair tied up in a headdress, her right hand sponging herself, 19th century, 37½in. high.
(Christie's) $4,565

Italian baroque design specimen marble and Botticino marble pedestal table, the thirteen sided circular top centered by a sunburst surrounded by inlaid fan shaped panels of various marbles, 4ft. diameter.
(Butterfield & Butterfield)
$4,400

Pair of Italian carved white marble figures of maidens in the neoclassical taste, third quarter 19th century, each standing contraposto against a treetrunk, 5ft. 10¹/₂in. high.
(Butterfield & Butterfield)
$24,200

Italian carved marble group of the Wrestlers, after the Antique, late 19th century, the two nude figures depicted locked in combat, height of group 38¹/₂in.
(Butterfield & Butterfield)
$27,500

An Austrian white marble figure of Venus, by Victor Oskar Tilgner, the goddess shown seated, her light robe falling off her shoulder and revealing her thighs, circa 1896, 50¹/₂in. high.
(Christie's)
$91,300

An Italian micro-mosaic black marble table-top, centered by an Arab hunting scene, the three hunters attacking a lion, mid-19th century, 33¹/₂in. diameter.
(Christie's)
$7,300

A Regency white marble occasional table, on a tapering gadrooned central column, the trefoil foot carved with acanthus scrolls, on claw feet, early 19th century, 26³/₄in. high.
(Christie's)
$2,374

'Awakening', a marble figure, carved from a model by Philippe, of a naked woman standing and stretching her arms, 32in. high.
(Christie's S. Ken)
$829

A pair of Louis XVI ormolu mounted white marble candlesticks, the campana-shaped nozzle cast with husk motifs and having separate bobèche, 25cm. high.
(Phillips)
$1,513

An Italian white marble and alabaster figure of Beatrice, in early Renaissance costume, her long alabaster robe richly decorated with foliate arabesques, late 19th century, 40³/₄in. high.
(Christie's)
$4,565

A late 19th century Italian alabaster bust of Galileo, unsigned, 14in. high.
(Christie's) $2,081

Italian specimen marble and agate table top, late 18th century, centered by a gameboard, surrounded by various stones, 47³/₄ x 27¹/₂in.
(Skinner Inc.) $6,050

A Napoleon III ormolu-mounted griotte marble urn with everted egg-and-dart rim flanked by beaded foliate scroll-handles, 20³/₄in. high.
(Christie's) $3,287

A fine English white marble figure of Eve, by John Warrington Wood, the graceful Eve shown naked and seated with her legs folded beside her on a grassy mound, signed *J. Warrington Wood Roma*, second half 19th century, 41in high.
(Christie's) $58,432

Fine Italian micro-mosaic and specimen marble table top on later base, circa 1900, centred by a circular scene depicting the Roman Forum, 29¹/₂in. high.
(Butterfield & Butterfield) $9,900

Italian carved marble figure of the Discus Thrower, after the Antique, late 19th century, raised on a mottled pink, brown and white marble pedestal, height of figure 5ft. 3in.
(Butterfield & Butterfield) $27,500

A white statuary marble figure of Diana, by Richard James Wyatt, the sandaled huntress shown striding forward, her robes falling revealing her right breast, 19th century, 53¹/₂in. high.
(Christie's) $8,217

A pair of black marble and pietra dura urns with pinched necks and baluster-shaped bodies decorated with scrolling floral ivy, 17in. high.
(Christie's) $3,287

A large Italian white marble group of a fisherboy, by Pietro Bazzanti, the young boy kneeling on a rock carved with waves, marine plants, and a frog, second half 19th century, 42¹/₄in. high.
(Christie's) $16,434

An Ami Continental II two hundred selection jukebox, circa 1962, with traditional domed glass cover and semi-circular selection panel.
(Bonhams) $2,387

A late 19th century Nicole Frères lever-wound cylinder musical box, the 13^{1}/$_{4}$in. cylinder playing eight tunes specified on the original tune sheet, 7^{1}/$_{2}$ x 22in.
(Tennants) $1,525

A 'Trade Mark' gramophone by the Gramophone Company, No. 5219, with March '98 Patent date, Clark-Johnson soundbox, lacquered brass horn, and cam-and-spring brake.
(Christie's) $4,280

An English chamber barrel organ with fifteen-key action, two ten-air barrels, one rank of wood and one of metal pipes, 51in. high, circa 1800.
(Christie's) $1,950

A key-wind forte-piano musical box by Nicole Freres, playing eight hymn tunes, with figured ash case with ebony stringing, 19^{1}/$_{4}$in. wide.
(Christie's) $5,000

A mahogany cased barrel piano, late 19th century, with twenty-two hammers striking piano strings before a pleated silk front, 37^{1}/$_{4}$in. high.
(Tennants) $1,116

A 19th century Swiss figured walnut, amboyna and ebonised cased 'Sublime Harmony' musical box, the 13in. interchangeable brass cylinder and two comb movement playing six airs.
(Spencer's) $3,590

An HMV Model 202 gramophone cabinet with quadruple-spring motor, 'antique silver' 5a soundbox and tone-arm, 49^{1}/$_{2}$in. high.
(Christie's) $4,250

An Edison Gem phonograph, with patent combination gear attachment, Walshaw-type turnover stylus in C reproducer and black 18-inch octagonal horn with crane, circa 1908.
(Christie's) $7,300

A Gramophone & Typewriter Ltd 'New Style No. 3' gramophone with top-wind motor, 7-inch turntable, plated zinc horn and oak case, 1904.
(Christie's)   **$2,140**

A 19th century Swiss rosewood musical box, the 44cm. brass barrel and double comb movement with pizzicato bar, 31in. wide.
(Spencer's)   **$1,580**

Rare Pathe Le Gaulois French phonograph with decorative red varnish and red aluminium horn, only produced for a short time up to 1903.
(Auction Team Köln)
$1,732

A Regina Sublima piano, with 73-note roll-operated mechanism, electric motor drive, coin mechanism with mercury switch, and oak case.
(Christie's)   **$4,250**

A Symphonion 'Lyra' 11⁷/₈-inch wall-hanging disc musical box with diametric combs on vertical bedplate, coin-slot mechanism and walnut-veneered case, 20in. high.
(Christie's)   **$1,850**

A Regina Corona 27-inch disc musical box with self-changing disc mechanism, double combs, magazine for twelve discs and mahogany case, 67in. high.
(Christie's)   **$21,000**

A Britannic gramophone with blue flower horn and molded classical Morning Glory pattern motifs to arm support, 17in. wide.
(Michael Newman)   **$601**

A Gramophone Company horn gramophone, circa 1920, with 12in. turntable and inlaid mahogany case, 17in. wide.
(Tennants)   **$1,711**

A Senior Monarch gramophone by the Gramophone & Typewriter Ltd with 12-inch floating turntable, triple-spring motor, and oak case, circa 1907.
(Christie's)   **$1,362**

An EMG Mark XB 'Tropical' hand made gramophone with four-spring soundbox, Paillard GGR double-spring motor, 29¹/₂in. diameter.
(Christie's) $4,880

A rare Gramophone Company de luxe gramophone with triple-spring motor, yielding turntable, Exhibition Junior soundbox and mahogany horn, 64in. high overall, circa 1920–22.
(Christie's) $7,150

An HMV Model II (Intermediate Monarch) horn gramophone with single spring motor in mahogany case, 17¹/₂in. diameter, dated on base *Nov. 1913.*
(Christie's) $2,000

A small Klingsor gramophone in oak case with pierced door to upper compartment containing horn aperture and strings, 27in. high.
(Christie's) $1,450

An 'Ideal Sublime Harmonie' inter-changeable cylinder musical box by Mermod Freres, playing six tunes on each cylinder, with tune selector and indicator, 41in. wide overall.
(Christie's) $8,500

A Cliftophone bijou grand gramophone in oak cabinet on twist-turned legs with Cliftophone horizontal soundbox, 32¹/₂in. high, circa 1924.
(Christie's) $800

A Dulcephone horn gramophone with Dulcephone single-spring motor in walnut case with carved moldings.
(Christie's) $775

An HMV Model 510 cabinet gramophone with Lumiere Pleated Diaphragm, quadruple-spring motor and quarter-veneered oak case, 43¹/₂in. high, 1924–5.
(Christie's) $2,650

Edison Standard Phonograph with large swan neck horn on gallows, oak case, circa 1905.
(Auction Team Köln) $2,756

Antique American lift-top miniature blanket chest in pine, 14½ x 8in.
(Eldred's) $633

A George III mahogany miniature tripod table with circular tip-up top on turned stem and cabriole base, 12½in. high.
(Christie's) $7,399

A miniature Georgian mahogany drop-flap oval dining table with gateleg action, raised on tapering turned supports and pad feet, 40cm. extended.
(Phillips) $3,382

A classical miniature carved mahogany chest-of-drawers, New York, 1830–1840, on carved lion's-paw feet, 23¾in. wide.
(Christie's) $1,980

Dutch silver miniature longcase clock by S. en H. Reitsma, Sneek, 1892–1949, Leeuwarden, 833 standard, 10in. high, gross weight 11oz. 10 dwts.
(Butterfield & Butterfield) $990

A mid-Georgian walnut miniature chest crossbanded overall in yewwood, the rectangular top above four graduated long drawers and on later bun feet, 15¼in. wide.
(Christie's) $2,986

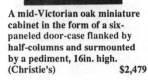

A mid-Victorian oak miniature cabinet in the form of a six-paneled door-case flanked by half-columns and surmounted by a pediment, 16in. high.
(Christie's) $2,479

A miniature Dutch bronze mortar in three stages, turned and molded at the muzzle, reinforce and rounded base, vent with shell-shaped pan behind the signature, *AD 1752*, 6in. barrel, 2¼in. bore.
(Christie's) $2,374

Miniature painted Chippendale tall chest, made by Jabez Rice, Massachusetts, early 19th century, painted brown, 15⅜in. high.
(Skinner Inc.) $8,800

MIRRORS

An early George III carved giltwood mirror of cartouche-shaped outline, inset with a contemporary plate, 3ft. 8in. high.
(Phillips) $1,511

A 19th century Dutch marquetry toilet mirror, decorated with scrolling foliage and floral sprays, on block feet, 1ft. 9¹/₂in. wide.
(Phillips) $623

Queen Anne looking glass, 18th century, in walnut veneers, gilt bezel, pierced gilt flower basket pediment.
(Eldred's) $770

A Federal giltwood verre eglomisé mirror, probably Boston, 1810–1820, with broken molded cornice above a frieze with vines and berries flanked by flowerheads over an eglomisé panel depicting a naval hero, 21in. wide.
(Christie's) $2,090

A giltwood mirror of George II style, the frame carved with acanthus scrolls, with scrolled cresting centered by a scallop shell flanked by acanthus above a mask of Diana, 59 x 36in.
(Christie's) $3,872

Louis XV parcel-gilt and painted pier mirror, circa 1725, in a narrow molded frame carved with upswept palm stems entwined with foliage beneath a shaped arched cresting, 2ft. 11in. wide.
(Butterfield & Butterfield) $12,100

An Italian rococo style giltwood pier glass, the rectangular plate flanked by two ormolu candelabra with petal sconces and mirrored border, 19th century, 91¹/₂ x 49in.
(Christie's) $7,646

An early 18th century carved walnut and strung swing-frame toilet mirror with ogee arched plate and cushion surround, 1ft. 5in. high.
(Phillips) $1,431

Louis XVI painted and parcel-gilt trumeau, late 18th century, surmounted by a painted arched oil-on-canvas panel of a female goat herder with her flock, 3ft. 7in. wide.
(Butterfield & Butterfield) $3,575

Polychrome painted pine
courting mirror, Northern
Europe, late 18th century, with
applied flowers and shaped
pendant, 21in. high.
(Skinner Inc.) $1,045

George III parcel-gilt and
carved mahogany mirror, circa
1780, the rectangular mirror
plate within a molded frame
with arched foliate cresting
centered by a gilt phoenix
perched on a branch, 47in. high.
(Butterfield & Butterfield)
$3,300

A George III giltwood mirror
with later oval plate, the frame
carved with climbing acanthus
and headed by an asymmetrical
ribbon-tied acanthus cresting,
44¹/₂ x 25in.
(Christie's) $10,890

Danish neoclassical parcel-gilt
mahogany small mirror, late
18th century, the ruffled scroll
crest enclosing a mahogany
panel mounted with a central
giltwood foliate sprig, 13in.
wide.
(Butterfield & Butterfield)
$495

Charles X carved pine
overmantel mirror, second
quarter 19th century, in a broad
paneled frame carved in high
relief with sprays of chestnuts
and foliage, 45in. wide.
(Butterfield & Butterfield)
$3,300

A classical giltwood mirror,
probably Boston, 1805–1830, the
broken molded cornice hung
with acorns over a frieze
centered by a fruiting grape vine
flanked by ogee-arched niches,
67¹/₂in. high.
(Christie's) $6,050

Labelled Federal giltwood and
eglomisé mirror, Cermenati &
Monfrino, Boston, circa 1806,
tablet with naval engagement,
32¹/₄ x 17in.
(Skinner Inc.) $660

George III carved giltwood
mirror, third quarter 18th
century, the oval plate in a
molded frame within a pierced
and carved border of unswept
palm leaves, 41in. high.
(Butterfield & Butterfield)
$7,700

Fine Spanish baroque painted
giltwood and gesso mirror, early
18th century, within an
elaborate gilt foliate scroll frame
interspersed with cherub heads,
4ft. 6in. wide.
(Butterfield & Butterfield)
$8,800

A giltwood mirror with arched beveled divided plate, the molded frame carved with foliate strapwork, the cresting headed by lambrequins, last quarter 17th century, 49 x 25in. (Christie's) $11,616

An ebonized and tortoiseshell toilet mirror, the cartouche-shaped frame inset with a Charles II stumpwork panel sewn with a man and woman, 30in. high. (Christie's) $7,970

A late Victorian gilded composition mirror of Adam style, the oval plate within a ribbon-tied laurel border and pierced mirror-backed surround of entwined leaves, 59$^{1}/_4$ x 34in. (Christie's) $4,453

Venetian rococo reverse engraved and painted giltwood mirror of large size, mid-18th century, within subsidiary mirrored borders with rounded outset corners decorated with trophies of arms, 8ft. 8in. high. (Butterfield & Butterfield) $12,100

A Queen Anne silvered-wood and walnut girandole in narrow walnut and molded silvered-wood frame, the plate with a small crack at the base, 34 x 23$^{1}/_4$in. (Christie's) $33,099

Venetian rococo parcel-gilt and stained mirror, third quarter 18th century, the divided mirror plate of irregular outline within a deeply concave molded frame outlined with elongated parcel-gilt S-andC-scrolls, 6ft. 8in. high. (Butterfield & Butterfield) $9,900

A George III giltwood mirror with oval plate in a Vitruvian scroll and rockwork surround and florally-entwined scroll frame, 52 x 33in. (Christie's) $8,291

A late 18th century Italian carved giltwood and decorated mirror, of Renaissance design, the cornice with foliate dentil and egg and dart moldings, 3ft. 3in. high. (Phillips) $6,010

A George II giltwood mirror with rounded rectangular divided plate, the frame carved with pilasters headed by acanthus capitals, 71 x 36in. (Christie's) $36,784

A George III giltwood mirror with oval plate and frame carved with unspringing foliage and flowerheads entwined with ribbons, 45 x 26¹/₂in.
(Christie's) $23,364

A late George II carved giltwood landscape mirror with triple plate surmounted by pierced trefoil and 'C'-scroll acanthus leaf cresting, 4ft. 5in. x 2ft.
(Phillips) $12,726

An early George III green-painted and gilded mirror with rectangular plate and frame pierced and carved with long and short C-scrolls entwined with foliage, 36³/₄ x 24in.
(Christie's) $52,569

Italian baroque giltwood and polychromed mirror, mid-18th century, the domed vertical plate flanked by winged figures upholding a canopy surmounted by a coronet, 5ft. 9in. high.
(Butterfield & Butterfield)
                    $7,700

Flemish School, early 18th century, a Bacchanalian scene, oil on shaped canvas, approx. 30 x 52¹/₂in., incorporated in a carved gilt wood overmantel mirror with three beveled plates, 56in. wide.
(Tennants) $9,300

A George II mahogany toilet-mirror in a narrow frame carved with scrolling foliage and rocaille between fluted and rusticated supports, 29¹/₄in. high.
(Christie's) $29,205

Federal mahogany veneered inlaid and parcel gilt looking glass, England/America, late 18th century, 57in. high.
(Skinner Inc.) $27,500

A classical giltwood convex mirror, American, early 19th century, the black-painted and carved spreadwing eagle perched on a plinth above a circular reeded frame, 45in. high.
(Christie's) $7,150

A fine Queen Anne carved giltwood and gesso pier glass, the beveled mirror border enclosed by two narrow giltwood bands, the border plates divided by leaf clasps, 5ft. 8in. x 2ft. 8in. overall.
(Phillips) $16,814

A giltwood mirror, the laurel-bound frame surmounted by a flaming urn flanked by trailing leaves, 63³/₄ x 41¹/₂in.
(Christie's) $3,203

A late Federal mahogany shaving mirror, William Fisk, Boston, Massachusetts, 1810–1825, swiveling between baluster and ring-turned supports with ball finials above a rectangular case, 24in high.
(Christie's) $935

A giltwood mirror with oval plate, the frame carved with rockwork, C-scrolls, acanthus and berried foliage, 44 x 30¹/₂in.
(Christie's) $5,421

A walnut and parcel-gilt wall mirror of George II design surmounted by a pierced scroll cresting with central acanthus cartouche with simulated drapery to the side and shaped apron, 53¹/₂in. high x 25in. wide.
(Christie's S. Ken)
                    $2,106

A Federal carved giltwood convex mirror, American, early 19th century, with carved spreadwing eagle perched on a rocky plinth flanked by scrolled leafage above a cylindrical molded frame, 34in. high.
(Christie's) $4,400

A North Italian giltwood wall mirror surmounted by a female mask, flanked by similar motifs within a flowerhead and C-scroll surround, late 18th century, possibly Venetian, 53in. high x 35in. wide.
(Christie's S. Ken)
                    $2,438

George II parcel-gilt walnut mirror, mid-18th century, the foliate-carved swan's neck cresting centered by a carved cartouche, 4ft. high.
(Butterfield & Butterfield)
                    $3,025

A North Italian giltwood mirror, the later rectangular plate in a molded frame surmounted by a bird amid scrolling foliage cresting, late 18th century, 28in. x 17¹/₂in.
(Christie's) $3,467

A Federal giltwood and verre eglomisé mirror, Boston, Massachusetts, 1790–1810, a large rectangular verre eglomisé panel painted with a romantic landscape, 48¹/₂in.
(Christie's) $3,850

A Venetian painted mirror, the shaped rectangular plate surmounted by a cartouche within a carved and molded frame, 29$^{1}/_{2}$ x 18$^{1}/_{2}$ in.
(Bonhams) $3,293

Florentine rococo style carved giltwood mirror within a border of deeply carved and pierced scrolling foliage and pendant fruit, 4ft. 1in. wide.
(Butterfield & Butterfield) $3,850

A George II giltwood mirror, the frame with broken cornice above an acanthus scroll frieze, the waved apron centered by a scallop shell, 54$^{1}/_{2}$ x 29in.
(Christie's) $5,227

Italian neoclassical parcel-gilt and cream painted mirror, circa 1790, the vertical plate flanked by half-round fluted column stiles supporting stiff leaf capitals, 4ft. 1$^{1}/_{2}$ in. high.
(Butterfield & Butterfield) $1,100

Rare Charles II metallic thread embroidered silk petit point traveling mirror, circa 1660–1685, 15$^{3}/_{4}$ x 15$^{1}/_{4}$ in.
(Butterfield & Butterfield) $3,025

Régence stripped pine mirror and a later copy, the first early 18th century, the outer edge with bead and chain-carved border, surmounted by an arched foliate-scroll-carved cresting, 6ft. 7in. high.
(Butterfield & Butterfield) $5,500

An early George III gilt gesso girandole, the cresting with swan-neck pediment and foliate ornament with central cartouche, inset with a later beveled plate, 3ft. 1in. high.
(Phillips) $1,590

Florentine rococo style carved and painted mirror in a deeply carved and pierced border of scrolling acanthus, 5ft. high.
(Butterfield & Butterfield) $3,025

Classical giltwood looking glass, Continental, early 19th century, the projecting molded cornice hung with spherules, 48$^{1}/_{2}$ in. high.
(Skinner Inc.) $1,100

A George II walnut and parcel-gilt mirror in a foliate border and flanked by trailing fruiting foliage, the broken swan's-neck cresting centered by a later helmet, 51¹/₂ x 28¹/₂in.
(Christie's) $5,421

A Regency giltwood convex mirror, with ebonized reeded slip within a fluted and acanthus molded surround with a shell carved foliate cresting and apron, 52¹/₄in. diameter.
(Christie's) $11,901

Country Queen Anne painted and decorated mirror, 18th century, painted black with white sprigs and flourishes, 17³/₈in. high.
(Skinner Inc.) $10,450

An Italian giltwood mirror with rectangular plate within elaborate shell, scrolling foliate and berry surround surmounted by armorial cresting with a crown, late 19th century, 36in. high.
(Christie's) $1,632

A classical carved giltwood verre églomisé mirror, New York, 1815–1825, the broken molded pediment above a verre églomisé panel depicting a tropical island and a ship, 47in. high.
(Christie's) $1,650

A George III giltwood mirror with later oval plate, the frame carved with ribbon-and-rosette entwined with acanthus, with acanthus-scroll cresting, 32 x 23in.
(Christie's) $2,904

A George I gilt-gesso mirror, the rectangular beveled plate in an acanthus-carved surround surmounted by an arched cresting, 50³/₄ x 30¹/₄in.
(Christie's) $15,741

A George III giltwood mirror, the oval plate in a naturalistic frame carved with climbing foliage, the cresting with a ho-ho bird on rocks, 47 x 27¹/₂in.
(Christie's) $10,494

A giltwood mirror with shaped rectangular plate, the pierced sides carved with foliate branches, the cresting carved with foliage above confronting C-scrolls, 53 x 37in.
(Christie's) $8,131

A George II giltwood mirror, the beveled rectangular plate in a molded acanthus-carved surround, surmounted by a swan-neck cresting, 54 x 26in.
(Christie's) $6,646

A giltwood mirror, the triple-divided rectangular plate in a beaded frame with lotus leaf-carved outer border headed by a foliate-scroll cresting surmounted by an urn, 38½ x 51in.
(Christie's) $3,678

Federal giltwood looking glass, America, early 19th century, projecting molded cornice hung with spherules, 45in. high.
(Skinner Inc.) $413

A George I gilt-gesso mirror in a molded foliate surround below a raised cresting with two scallop shells, centered by a later candle-holder, 36¾ x 19in.
(Christie's) $9,680

An early Victorian giltwood oval mirror frame of George III style, carved as two ribbon-tied acanthus fronds, 45 x 45½in.
(Christie's) $1,682

A giltwood mirror, the frame carved with scrolling acanthus beneath a cresting of opposing C-scrolls, mid 19th century, 90in. high.
(Christie's) $2,687

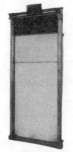

A silvered mirror with oval plate, the cresting carved with acanthus-scrolls and grapes centered by an oval medallion, late 17th century, probably German, 54 x 31in.
(Christie's) $6,776

A George III giltwood and gesso pier glass, surmounted by a husk-carved pediment, frieze set with three classical roundels, 36½in. wide.
(Bearne's) $1,686

Continental rococo giltwood mirror, in a deeply scalloped frame of slightly convex section molded in low relief with masks and bacchic scenes, 43½in. wide.
(Butterfield & Butterfield) $7,700

MISCELLANEOUS

A Florentine pietra dura plaque with a parrot on its perch on a table with an Etruscan krater vase, a vase of flowers and ewers on a black slate ground, circa 1870, 16 x 23$^{1}/_{2}$in.
(Christie's) $32,505

World Flyweight Championship belt: *Presented to W. Ladbury of Greenwich, by his numerous sporting friends in commemoration of his victory over Sid Smith for the Championship on the 2nd June 1913.*
(Phillips) $2,238

Roman brown basalt relief of an erotic scene, 2nd-3rd century A.D., the naked copulating couple carved in high relief, 9$^{1}/_{2}$in. high.
(Butterfield & Butterfield) $3,300

Rhinoceros horn libation cup, 18th/19th century, the honey brown horn delicately carved as an open peach issuing from a gnarled leafy branch, 3$^{3}/_{4}$in. high.
(Butterfield & Butterfield) $1,100

A French pull-along 'barking' Boston terrier, circa 1910, the papier mâché, nodding head and well molded body with black and white furze hide, 44cm. long.
(Spencer's) $600

One of a matched pair of American horn open armchairs, on quadripartite supports and sharply pointed feet, late 19th century.
(Christie's)   (Two) $3,360

Babe Ruth and Lou Gehrig autographed baseball, circa 1928, signed during spring training at the 'Al Lang Stadium', St. Petersburg, Florida.
(Du Mouchelles) $6,000

Late baroque carved limestone group of Europa, 17th century, with one of her infant sons at her breast, and two other children at her side, 12$^{1}/_{2}$in. long.
(Butterfield & Butterfield) $825

A Regency black-painted and gilt leather pitcher, decorated with a border of vine-leaves, with scrolling gilt-metal handle, 8in. high.
(Christie's) $555

An Italian pietra dura panel, entitled *GOLDEN WEDDING* depicting an old man and woman, signed *G. MONTELATIA 1910*, 40in. wide.
(Christie's)   **$17,347**

A Charles II polychrome beadwork basket with rectangular top, loop-handles and pierced trelliswork sides around a scene of an elegant couple in a garden, 21¼in. wide.
(Christie's)   **$10,364**

A mosaic topped table depicting Pliny's doves drinking from a bowl surrounded by a sunburst oval, mid 19th century, 52½in. wide.
(Christie's)   **$9,981**

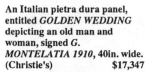

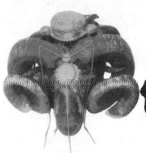

A Victorian ram's head snuff mull fitted with four various snuff containers, three decorated with thistles, the fourth decorated with thistles and also engraved with an armorial, crest and motto, 15½in. overall.
(Christie's)   **$2,251**

A fine pair of soapstone figures of lady Immortals on lions, 17th/ 18th century, each carved with a female Immortal figure seated 'side-saddle' on the back of a striding Buddhistic lion-dog, 14¼in. high.
(Christie's)   **$18,490**

French carved giltwood and lacquered cage d'ascenseur in the Louis XVI taste, late 19th/ early 20th century, painted with gilt-foliated line borders and floral bouquets, on a gold-speckled green ground, 4ft. 4½in. wide.
(Butterfield & Butterfield)   **$3,025**

An Italian haliotis veneered and gilt painted bowl, on a pinched socle and acanthus draped shaft with spreading circular base, 22¼in. diameter.
(Christie's)   **$5,700**

A lacquered pen decorated in iroe hiramakie, nashiji on a roironuri ground with a cart beneath cherry blossom, signed *Sosetsu "aged 69"*, 14.5cm. long.
(Christie's)   **$4,514**

Fine rhinoceros horn libation cup, 17th/18th century, the honey-colored matrix well carved and pierced with a continuous scene, 5¼in. high.
(Butterfield & Butterfield)   **$14,300**

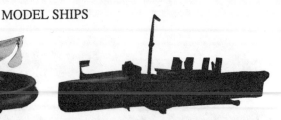

Painted wood model of a whaling boat, America, late 19th/early 20th century, mounted on a wooden base within a glass dome, 15½in. long. (Skinner Inc.) **$770**

A sleek Bing tinplate keywind torpedo boat, painted in Navy Gray with a dark red hull, single mast, dual lifeboat, 40in. long. (Christie's) **$15,400**

Wood model of a coastal steamer, America, 20th century, (possibly the Fall River line), 33in. long. (Skinner Inc.) **$385**

Shadow box with half-model of the three-masted ship "Lolo", signed *E. Ellard*, America, late 19th/ early 20th century, with painted background, 27¾in. wide. (Skinner Inc.) **$880**

Shadowbox with model of the brig "Alice", America, early 20th century, polychrome wood, with finely detailed painted backdrop, 27½in. wide. (Skinner Inc.) **$880**

Painted wood model of the "Constitution", America from Alma II' Alma, fully rigged, mounted in inlaid mahogany and glass case, 44½in. wide. (Skinner Inc.) **$2,860**

Painted wood canoe, "Old Town, Maine", early 20th century, the painted and stencil decorated wooden canoe with two caned seats, the body with stenciled line decoration, 47½in. long. (Butterfield & Butterfield) **$12,100**

A shipbuilder's 50in. model of the S.S.
'Cheniston' with brass and plated deck detail,
built by Bartram`& Sons, Sunderland for the
Century Shipping Co. Ltd., London, in 61in.
glazed mahogany display case.
(Anderson & Garland) $6,260

Scale model of the Titanic from the Bergamo
Collection, Italy, circa 1915.
(Hôtel de Ventes Horta) $10,000

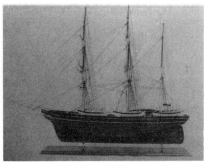

The whaleship "Sunbeam", plank on beam
construction using many fine hardwoods with
mahogany hull, pearwood deck, and basswood
masts, 67 x 23 x 52in.
(Eldred's) $3,850

A Top-of-the-Line French Radiguet tinplate and
copper live steam battleship "Inflexible", circa
1895, finished in black with copper trim, 40in.
long.
(Christie's) $11,000

A painted tinplate live steam replica four-funnel
battleship, with twin masts, fore and aft gun
turrets and six port and starboard facing turrets,
25in. long.
(Christie's) $839

Cased French Prisoner of War bone and ivory
model of the British Frigate "Fisgard 1796",
England, early 19th century, fully rigged and
finely detailed with polychrome figures of gun
crews and sailors, 35in. wide.
(Skinner Inc.) $16,500

A model hull of a fourth rater, painted planked
construction, carved and gilded stem, part of the
figurehead missing, Continental circa 1650–80,
29in.
(Woolley & Wallis) $4,320

Painted wood model of a whaleboat, early 20th
century, fitted with oars, harpoons, lances, tubs,
lines, etc., mounted on stand, 23in. long.
(Skinner Inc.) $715

MODEL TRAINS

A Märklin hand-painted 4 Volt electric LNER 4–4–2 'Atlantic' locomotive with original DC mechanism and six-wheel tender, Cat. Ref. CE3121, circa 1928.
(Christie's) $1,492

A finely engineered exhibition standard 7¹/₄in. gauge model of the Texas and Pacific Railroad 4–4–0 locomotive and tender No. 34 built by M. Pavie, 21¹/₂ x 84in.
(Christie's) $15,136

A finely engineered and detailed exhibition standard 5in. gauge model of the Great Western Railway Armstrong Queen Class 2–2–2 locomotive and tender No. 55 'Queen' of 1873, built by P. Rich, Rhiwderin, 14¹/₂ x 52in.
(Christie's) $9,460

A fine live steam Märklin cast iron and tinplate hand painted "King Edward" passenger train, gauge 3, comprising an engine and tender painted black with red and yellow piping, 68in. long overall.
(Christie's) $19,800

An extremely fine and very detailed exhibition standard 7¹/₄in. gauge model of the Great Western Railway 14XX Class 0–4–2 side tank locomotive No. 1450 built by I.R. Holder, 20¹/₂ x 45in.
(Christie's) $14,190

A fine 5 inch gauge model of the industrial 0–4–0 side tank locomotion No. 1 built by J.B. Aillot Ateliers de Construction de Montceau-les-Mines, 1871, 15¹/₂ x 27in.
(Christie's) $7,568

A painted and lithographed Leipzig station comprising, main building, front steps, 2 side ramps, 2 side walls, 2 curtain walls, 2 pairs of covered island platforms, station 92cm., circa 1919.
(Phillips) $14,920

A finely detailed and well presented exhibition standard 5in. gauge model of the British Railways (ex. Great Western Railway) Dukedog Class 4–4–0 locomotive and tender No. 9014, built by I.P. Watson, Herne Bay, 14 x 60in.
(Christie's) $7,568

A Scratch-built live steam 5-inch gauge model of B.R. Class '2' 2–6–0 locomotive and tender, No. 78019, by C.F. Palmer, finished in black, 58in. long, circa 1954.
(Tennants) $2,210

A Märklin hand-painted 20 Volt electric LMS 4–4–0 locomotive and six-wheel tender, Cat. Ref. E13020, in lake, black and gold livery, circa 1934.
(Christie's) $1,492

Bing, a finely engineered 4-4-0 spirit fired locomotive, boiler fed by multiple burner, finished in cream LSWR colours, circa 1903, some chipping to boiler.
(Phillips) $3,357

A Märklin hand-painted bogie pullman 'Car No. 4 Third Class', Cat. Ref. 2890, circa 1930.
(Christie's) $1,585

A magnificent Märklin hand-painted "Gare Centrale" major railway station, gauge one, circa 1910, finished in varying shades of tan as simulated stone, 34in. wide.
(Christie's) $22,000

A Bing clockwork 15194/0 GNR train set, comprising 0–4–0 No. 266 locomotive and matching four wheel tender, 3rd coach and passenger luggage van, circa 1906.
(Christie's) $1,119

A well engineered 5in, gauge model of the Great Western Railway River Class 2–4–0 locomotive and tender No. 76 'Wye' modeled as modified circa 1896 by R.F. Richards, Southsea, 13¹/₂ x 54in.
(Christie's) $7,190

A finely engineered and detailed 1¹/₃₂in.:1ft. scale 7¹/₄in. gauge model of the Great Western Railway Broad Gauge 2–2–2–2 locomotive and tender 'Iron Duke' of 1847, built by R.R. Davies and V.S. Hayward, Cheltenham, from Tredgold's drawings of 1851, 10¹/₂ x 48in.
(Christie's) $6,622

A late 19th century small full size single cylinder vertical reversing stationary engine, 25¹/₂ x 13¹/₂in., with brass bound wood lagged cylinder. (Christie's) $2,081

A finely engineered exhibition standard 4¹/₂in. scale model of the single cylinder two-speed general purpose traction engine 1981 'Beatrice', 44³/₄ x 72in. (Christie's S. Ken) $26,741

A finely engineered model 3in.:1ft. scale model Rider–Ericsson 8 inch hot air driven pumping engine built by J.P. Nazareth, 21¹/₂ x 16¹/₂in. (Christie's) $3,027

Painted brass and steel high wheel bicycle (Penny Farthing), American, late 19th/early 20th century, the red painted working model with handlebar grips above a curved frame with seat, 14in. high. (Butterfield & Butterfield) $3,850

A well engineered 2in. scale model of the Burrell Special Scenic Showman's Road Locomotive 'Thetford Town', Reg. No. E.L. 1988, built by E. Lofthouse, 23¹/₄ x 47¹/₂in. (Christie's) $8,514

Wood and brass silo by G. Elias & Bro., Buffalo, NY, circa 1900, the varnished model of cylinder shape with removable cone top, 25¹⁷/₂in. high. (Butterfield & Butterfield) $2,475

A well engineered model single vertical cylinder, floor mounted Watt boiler feed pump built by J.R. Arlett, 10in. high, with wood clad brass bound cylinder. (Christie's) $1,135

Painted and metal brass 'braker' electric car, American, circa 1896, the black painted working model with a spindle backseat, 10in. long. (Butterfield & Butterfield) $2,475

A late 19th century brass and copper vertical stationary steam plant, the cross tube boiler mounted on a brass base with fittings including water gauge, 25in. high. (Christie's) $946

A 1976 Peugeot 304 cabriolet, good running order, 69,000 miles, one lady owner, basically sound, requires cosmetic restoration.
(Tennants) $2,890

1969 Mercedes Benz 300 SEL, four-door sedan, vehicle odometer reading 46,446 miles, 6.3 litre, eight cylinder, automatic transmission, dark green.
(Skinner Inc.) $13,200

1961 Rolls-Royce Silver Cloud II standard saloon, engine: V8, alloy block and cylinder heads, overhead valves by pushrods and rockers from central camshaft, hydraulic tappets, 6230cc, bore and stroke 104mm. x 94.4mm., compression ratio 8:1, 200bhp at 5000rpm, twin SU HD6 carburettors, coil ignition, 12-volt electrics, brakes: four-wheel servo assisted drums with hydraulic front and combined hydraulic/mechanical rear, dual master cylinders, right-hand drive.
(Christie's) $23,000

1955 Rolls-Royce 'Silver Dawn' standard steel saloon, coachwork by Rolls-Royce Ltd., Crewe, color, burgundy and black coachwork with dark red leather upholstery, engine; six-cylinder in-line, cast-iron monobloc, alloy cylinder head, overhead inlet valves, side exhaust, single camshaft, 4566 c.c., bore and stroke 92mm. x 114mm., compression ratio 6.4:1, 145 b.h.p. at 4000 r.p.m., Zenith carburettor, twin SU petrol pumps, transmission; single dry plate clutch with four-speed automatic gearbox.
(Christie's) $22,950

1920/21 Rolls-Royce 40/50 HP Silver Ghost Doctors Coupe, coachwork by Windovers of London, engine: six-cylinder in-line, two groups of three cast iron blocks, non-detachable cylinder heads, two side valves per cylinder by rockers and rollers from single camshaft, 7428cc, bore and stroke 114mm. x 121mm., compression ratio 3.2:1, 65bhp at 1500rpm.
(Christie's) $81,500

1937 Bentley 4¼-litre sports saloon, coachwork by Park Ward, London, engine, six-cylinder in-line, monobloc, detachable cylinder head, overhead valves by pushrods, 4257cc, bore and stroke 88.9mm. x 114.3mm., compression ratio 6.8:1, 125bhp at 4500rpm, twin SU HV4 carburettors, coil and distributor ignition, 12-volt electrics.
(Christie's) $48,850

1971 Cadillac Eldorado convertible, engine: V-8 cylinder, cast iron block, bore and stroke 4.30in. x 4.30in., 8200cc, overhead valve, pushrod actuated, compression ratio 9:1, 365bhp at 4400rpm, transmission, Turbo Hydra-matic longitudinally mounted with transfer case, suspension: front, independent via torsion bar and A-arms.
(Christie's) $10,580

1964 Ferrari 330 GT 2+2 Coupe, coachwork by Pininfarina, engine: 209 series, V12, 60°, single overhead camshaft per bank, two overhead valves per cylinder, light alloy block and cylinder heads, 3,967cc, bore and stroke 77mm. x 71mm., compression ratio 8.8:1, 300bhp at 6,600rpm, triple Weber 40 DCN carburettors, twin Marelli distributors, right-hand drive.
(Christie's) $53,000

1926 Rolls-Royce 20HP Sedanca-de-Ville, coachwork by Barker & Co, London, engine, six-cylinder in-line, cast iron block and detachable cast iron cylinder head, two overhead valves per cylinder by pushrods and rockers from single crankcase mounted camshaft, 3127cc, bore and stroke 76.2mm. x 114.3mm., compression ratio 4.6:1, 53bhp at 3000rpm, single two-jet Rolls-Royce carburettor with starting carburettor, right-hand drive.
(Christie's) $32,500

1929 Chevrolet International Model AC 30 CWT Ranch Wagon, manufactured by General Motors, Australia, engine, six-cylinder in-line, overhead valve, cast iron block and cylinder head, 3200cc, bore and stroke 83mm. x 95.25mm., compression ratio 5.02:1, 46bhp at 2600rpm, Carter IV carburettor, 6 volts electrics, transmission: single dry plate clutch, four-speed straight cut gears with synchromesh on 3rd and 4th, right-hand drive.
(Christie's) $10,175

1963 Mercedes-Benz 220SE Cabriolet, engine, six-cylinder, single overhead camshaft, 2195cc, bore and stroke 80mm. x 72.8mm., 134bhp at 5000rpm, transmission: four-speed manual, suspension, front, wishbones and coil springs, rear, swing axles and coil springs, brakes; four wheel drums, right-hand drive.
(Christie's) $32,550

1959 Bentley 2 standard saloon, engine, V8, alloy block and cylinder heads, overhead valves by pushrods and rockers by central camshaft, hydraulic tappets, 6230cc, bore and stroke 104mm. x 94.4mm., compression ratio 8:1, 200bhp at 5000rpm, twin SU HD6 carburettors, coil ignition, 12-volt electrics.
(Christie's) $21,360

1971 Morris Minor 1100 Traveller, engine, four-cylinder in-line, overhead valve, cast iron block and head, 1098cc, bore and stroke 64.6mm. x 83.7mm., compression ratio 8.5:1, 48 bhp at 5100rpm, one SU carburettor, transmission: four-speed manual, suspension, front, wishbones and torsion bars, rear, semi-elliptic leaf springs, right-hand drive.
(Christie's) $2,445

1908 Maxwell two-cylinder Runabout two-seater, engine, front location two-cylinder, water-cooled, horizontally opposed cast iron cylinder barrels, cast iron crankcase, open mechanically operated inlet valves, open flywheel, 14HP, single Griffin downdraught carburettor, magneto and trembler coil ignition, right-hand drive.
(Christie's) $16,250

1937 Packard 'Super Eight' town car, coachwork by Brewster & Company, New York, color, silver and maroon coachwork with black leather top, salmon cloth and black leather interior, engine; eight-cylinder in-line, L-head, two side valves per cylinder, cast-iron block, detachable alloy cylinder heads, 5240 c.c. (320 cu. in.), bore and stroke 80mm. x 127mm., compression ratio 6.5:1, 135 b.h.p. at 3200 r.p.m., single coil ignition, Detroit Lubricator carburettor.
(Christie's) $65,445

1964 3.8-Litre Jaguar E-Type Series I Roadster, engine, six-cylinder in-line, seven bearing cast iron block and light alloy cylinder heads, twin overhead camshafts, overhead valves, 3781cc, bore and stroke 87mm. x 106mm., 265bhp at 5500rpm, triple SU HD8 carburettors, transmission: single dry plate clutch, four-speed manual, suspension: independent front wishbones, torsion bars, coil springs and anti-roll bar, right-hand drive.
(Christie's) $38,665

1902 Thomas Runabout, engine; water-cooled, single cylinder, 106.3 cu. in. (1,743 c.c.)), bore and stroke 121mm. x 152mm., transmission; three-speed, brakes; two wheels at the rear, single chain drive.
(Christie's) $24,200

1931 Ford Model A roadster, color, black coachwork with brown interior trim, engine; four-cylinder in-line, water-cooled, cast-iron block, detachable cylinder head, side valves, 3300 c.c., bore and stroke 98.0mm. x 107mm., compression ratio 4.2:1, 40 b.h.p. at 2300 r.p.m., Ford positive feed carburettor, electric start.
(Christie's) $23,757

1959 MGA Twin Cam, chassis No. YD 392–4 PHRZ–451, color, yellow with black upholstery, engine; four-cylinder in-line, twin overhead camshaft, 1588 c.c., wheelbase 7ft. 10in., length 13ft., width 4ft. 9½in., dry weight 2,185 lbs., left-hand drive.
(Christie's) $17,600

1926 Lincoln Sport Roadster Model L–151, coachwork by Locke & Co., engine; V.8 side-valve, cast-iron block and cylinder heads, 357.8 cu. in. displacement (5,865.5 c.c.), wheelbase; 12ft. 0in., price when new $4,500, left-hand drive.
(Christie's) $77,000

1935 Duesenberg Model SJ Convertible Coupe, coachwork by Bohman & Schwarz, engine No. J509 (formerly J572), color, burgundy coachwork with tan leather upholstery, engine; double overhead camshaft straight eight, 420.0 cu. in. (6,885 c.c.), wheelbase 11ft. 10½in., front track 4ft. 8in., rear track 4ft. 8in., overall length 16ft. 8in.
(Christie's) $1,155,000

1920 Moon 20 HP 'Six' Touring, chassis No. 42041, engine No. 253, color, yellow coachwork with black wings and black hood, brown leather interior, engine; six-cylinder in-line, cast-iron monobloc detachable cylinder head, overhead valves by pushrod, 3,208 c.c., wheelbase 10ft. 2in., front track 4ft. 4in., rear track 4ft. 4in., overall length 14ft. 0in., dry weight 3,200 lbs.
(Christie's) $16,500

1948 Alfa Romeo 6C 2500 Super Sport Cabriolet, coachwork by Pinin Farina, chassis No. 915716, engine No. 928020, color, red coachwork with dark blue upholstery, engine; six-cylinder in-line, cast-iron monobloc twin overhead camshafts, 2,443 c.c., bore and stroke 72mm. x 100mm., wheelbase 8ft. 10in., front track 4ft. 9in., rear track 4ft. 9½in., dry weight 3,300lbs, right hand drive.
(Christie's) $104,500

1957 Maserati 300 S Sports Racing Car, coachwork by Fantuzzi, chassis No. 3035, engine No. 3052, color, Italian racing red coachwork with black seats, engine; six-cylinder in-line, alloy block and cylinder heads, twin overhead camshaft, two overhead valves, 2,993 c.c., wheelbase 7ft. 8¼in., front track 4ft. 4in., rear track 4ft. 2in., dry weight 1,710 lbs, right-hand drive.
(Christie's) $1,028,500

1933 Lagonda 3-Litre Open Tourer, chassis No. Z10710, engine No. 2459, color, black with red upholstery, engine; six-cylinder in-line, overhead valve, 3,181 c.c., wheelbase 10ft. 9in., track 4ft. 8in., right-hand drive.
(Christie's) **$79,200**

1950 Jaguar XK120 Roadster, chassis No. 670505, engine No. 670505, color, black with red upholstery, engine; six-cylinder in-line, twin overhead-camshaft, 3,442 c.c., wheelbase 102in., front track 50⁵/₈in., rear track 50in., dry weight 2,800 lbs, left-hand drive.
(Christie's) **$44,000**

1952 Allard K. 2 Roadster, chassis No. 3126, silver metallic coachwork with deep red leather upholstery, engine; Cadillac Competition V.8 cylinder, 5,424 c.c., forged steel crankshaft, hydraulic Isky race cams, compression ratio 9:1. 300 b.h.p. at 6,000 r.p.m., overall length 14ft., dry weight 2,700 lbs., left-hand drive.
(Christie's) **$63,800**

1939 Packard Six (1700) Station Wagon (Woody), coachwork by J.T. Cantrell, chassis No. 1700–2192, engine No. B–18672A, color, black coachwork with wooden sectioned bodywork, engine; side-cylinder in-line cast-iron monobloc, six valve, L-head, 245 cu. in., wheel base 10ft. 2in., front track 4ft. 11¹/₄in., rear track 5ft., left-hand drive.
(Christie's) **$35,200**

1957 Mercedes Benz 300 SC Roadster, coachwork by Daimler Benz, Sindelfingen, chassis No. 75000 45100015 (45th of 53 produced), color, maroon coachwork with tan leather interior and top, engine; six-cylinder in-line, cast-iron block alloy cylinder head, two overhead valves per cylinder, single overhead camshaft, 2,996 c.c., wheelbase 9ft. 6in., front track 4ft. 10in., rear track 5ft., overall length 15ft. 5in., dry weight 3,924 lbs, left-hand drive.
(Christie's) **$550,000**

1936 Bentley 4¹/₄-Litre Airline Saloon, coachwork by Gurney Nutting, chassis No. B118 HK, engine No. K 2 BY, color, red coachwork with tan upholstery, engine; six-cylinder in-line, cast-iron cylinder block and detachable cast-iron cylinder head, two overhead valves per cylinder operated by pushrods and rockers from side-mounted camshaft, 4,257 c.c., wheelbase 10ft. 6in., front track 4ft. 8in., rear track 4ft. 8in., overall length 14ft. 6in., dry weight 3,920 lbs., right-hand drive. (Christie's) **$115,500**

1955 MG TF 1500 Sports two seater, color red coachwork with tan interior and beige hood, engine; four cylinder in-line, two overhead valves per cylinder operated by pushrods from single block mounted camshaft, 1466 c.c., bore and stroke 72mm. x 90mm., compression ratio 8.3:1, 63 b.h.p. at 5250 r.p.m., twin SU downdraught carburettors.
(Christie's) $20,620

1937 Aston Martin 15/98, 2-litre short chassis 2/4 sports tourer, coachwork by Abbot Coachworks, color, cream coachwork with cherry-red upholstery, engine; four-cylinder in-line, 1949 c.c., bore and stroke 78mm. x 102mm., overhead valves, single overhead camshaft, compression ratio 7.75:1, 98 b.h.p. at 5000 r.p.m., twin SU carburettors, twin SU fuel pumps.
(Christie's) $34,067

1971 Jaguar Series III V.12 'E' Type coupé, color, primrose yellow coachwork with black leather interior, engine; V.12 cylinder, two overhead in-line valves per cylinder operated by single overhead camshaft per bank, 5343 c.c., bore and stroke 90mm. x 70mm., compression ratio 9:1, 272 b.h.p. at 5850 r.p.m., four Zenith Stromberg 175 CDSE carburettors.
(Christie's) $17,930

1961 Jaguar 3.8-litre Mk II saloon, color, Old English white coachwork with blue Rexine upholstery, engine; six-cylinder in-line, cast-iron block, light alloy cylinder heads, overhead valves, twin overhead camshafts, 3781 c.c., bore and stroke 87mm. x 106mm., compression ratio 8:1, 220 b.h.p. at 5500 r.p.m., twin SU HD6 carburettors.
(Christie's) $12,551

1955 Mercedes Benz 300 SL gullwing coupé, color, black coachwork with red upholstery, engine; six-cylinder in-line, single overhead camshaft, two valves per cylinder operated by rocker arms, 2996 c.c., bore and stroke 85mm. x 88mm., compression ratio 8.55:1, 240 b.h.p. at 6100 r.p.m., Bosch direct fuel injection, dry sump lubrication, transmission; four-speed all synchomesh gearbox.
(Christie's) $259,985

1958 Jaguar XK 150 drophead coupé, color black coachwork with black leather interior and black hood, engine; six-cylinder in-line, twin overhead camshaft, straight port head, 3442 c.c., bore and stroke 83mm. x 106mm., compression ratio 8:1, 210 b.h.p. at 5750 r.p.m., twin SU H6 carburettors, transmission; single dry plate clutch and three-speed automatic gearbox, hypoid bevel 'live' axle.
(Christie's) $35,860

MOTOR VEHICLES

1979 Aston Martin V.8 Volante, color, Mexico red coachwork, tan leather interior, engine; V.8 cylinder, alloy block and cylinder heads, two valves per cylinder operated by two overhead camshafts per bank, 5340 c.c., bore and stroke 100mm. x 85mm., compression ratio 9.3:1, 330 b.h.p. at 6000 r.p.m., four Weber 42 DGNF carburettors.
(Christie's) $86,064

1971 Jaguar V.12 Series III E Type, 2 + 2 coupé, color, maroon coachwork, tan leather upholstery, engine; V.12 cylinder, two overhead in-line valves per cylinder operated by single overhead camshaft per bank, 5343 c.c., bore and stroke 90mm. x 70mm., compression ratio 9:1, 272 b.h.p. at 5850 r.p.m., four Zenith Stromberg 175 CDSE carburettors.
(Christie's) $32,722

1970 Alfa Romeo Giulia Junior Zagato coupé, coachwork by Zagato, color, red coachwork with black interior, engine; four-cylinder in-line, twin overhead-camshafts, two valves per cylinder, 1962 c.c., bore and stroke 84mm. x 88.5mm., compression ratio 9:1, 132 b.h.p. at 5500 r.p.m., twin Weber carburettors, transmission; single dry plate clutch with five-speed all synchromesh gearbox.
(Christie's) $15,241

1972 Maserati 4.2-litre Indy, coachwork by Vignale, color, red coachwork with black interior, engine; V.8 cylinder, four overhead camshafts, two valves per cylinder, 4136 c.c., bore and stroke 88mm. x 85mm., compression ratio 8.5:1, 260 b.h.p. at 5500 r.p.m., four Weber DCL N5 carburettors, transmission; single dry plate clutch, five-speed manual all-synchromesh gearbox.
(Christie's) $22,950

1962 BMW Isetta '300' coupé, built by Isetta of G.B. Ltd., Brighton, Sussex, color, red coachwork with black vinyl roof, engine; single cylinder four-stroke overhead valve, 298 c.c., bore and stroke 72mm. x 73mm., compression ratio 7:1, 13 b.h.p. at 5200 r.p.m., single Bing 22/98 carburettor, transmission; four-speed gearbox, primary drive by shaft, final drive by adjustable chain.
(Christie's) $4,124

1955 Simca Aronde 'Grande Large' two-door coupé, color, black/gray coachwork with gray/white interior, engine; four-cylinder in-line, overhead valve by pushrods, single camshaft, 1221 c.c., bore and stroke 72mm. x 75mm., compression ratio 7.8:1, 48 b.h.p. at 4500 r.p.m., Solex 32 carburettor, transmission; four-speed synchromesh gearbox with steering column gearchange, hypoid bevel back axle.
(Christie's) $5,738

497

A cloth-covered car trunk, 18in. wide.
(Christie's) $330

A spirit flask styled as a 1930s Rolls-Royce radiator, 7³/₄in. high.
(Christie's) $330

1950 Alfa Romeo Alfetta Tipo 158, a diecast ashtray inscribed Alfa Romeo Campione del Monde 1950, 11 Ciran Premi – 11 Vittorie, 7in. high.
(Christie's New York)
                                $1,100

Rene Lorenzi poster, XVIIIe Grand Prix Monaco 29 Mai 1960, 32 x 25cm.
(Onslow's) $876

A pair of wicker tonneau baskets shaped to fit on the running boards of a rear entrance tonneau motor car, circa 1903, 43in. long.
(Christie's) $770

German Grand Prix poster, Won On Texaco Brooklands Riley Model First in the 1100cc Class July 19th 1928, published by Texaco, 74 x 48cm.
(Onslow's) $412

Clincher Non-Skid Tyres, color lithographic poster, on original board, 35 x 25cm.
(Onslow's) $2,400

A large silver cigarette box, the lid engraved with the Barnato-Hassan Special racing car and inscribed *To Oliver Bertram from Woolf Barnato*, hallmarked *London 1919*.
(Onslow's) $4,200

Leonnetto Cappiello, Peugeot poster, lithograph in colors, printed by Devambez, Paris, backed on linen, 59 x 46in.
(Christie's) $1,000

'Special Retailers of Rolls-Royce Cars', a metal showroom advertising sign used outside one of the twenty-five showrooms in London during the 1920s, 28¼in. wide.
(Christie's) $1,870

Brooklands BARC badge, reverse stamped *980*.
(Onslow's) $432

An Oakland Auto trunk, the hinged lid and fall front opening to reveal fitted interior with four small cases, 18½in. wide.
(Christie's) $1,100

A black painted Shell two gallon can with Motor Oil insert complete with contents, fine original condition.
(Onslow's) $480

A fine picnic hamper by Brooks Bros., the wicker basket with lid opening to fitted interior, circa 1915, 12½in. wide.
(Christie's) $880

Lucas Lamps, We make Light of Our Labor, color lithograph advertisement, 74 x 49cm.
(Onslow's) $3,320

An Election timekeeper's chronometer, Swiss lever movement with matt silvered dial and Arabic numerals, in a fitted mahogany box, 6in. wide.
(Christie's) $810

An unrestored pair of Lucas King of the Road rear lights numbered 434 and 435, good condition, 32cm. high.
(Onslow's) $945

A large framed poster of a French family beside a vintage car, removing a spare tyre from the belly of the "Michelin Man", 158 x 116cm.
(Phillips) $835

An attractive Quinton attributed to Louis Guersan in Paris, circa 1750, body length including button, 13⁹/₁₆in. (Phillips)

$6,408

A fine violin by Antonius & Hieronymus Fr. Amati, Cremonen Andreae Fil. F (16--), bearing their label. (Phillips)

$47,655

A fine violin by Antonius & Hieronymus Fr. Amati bearing the maker's label *Cremonen Andreae Fil. F 1621.* (Phillips)

$141,200

A fine violin, attributed to Henry Lockey Hill, London, circa 1820. (Phillips)

$10,602

An interesting violoncello by a maker not recorded, bearing the label: *Made by Smith Sycamore Street Sheffield* and dated *1789.* (Phillips)

$7,524

A fine French violin labeled *Jean Baptiste Vuillaume à Paris/Rue Croix des Petits Champs* and numbered *1912* and signed on the inside back. (Christie's)

$53,130

An interesting violin, probably English, circa 1920, Stradivari model, bearing a reproduction label, the one-piece back of medium curl. (Christie's)

$15,054

An Italian violin, circa 1880, possibly Neapolitan, the two-piece back of small curl, the ribs and scroll similar, the table of medium to open grain. (Christie's)

$4,959

A fine viola by Charles Boullangier bearing the maker's label *Fecit London, dated 1885.* (Phillips)

$11,115

A violin by Giovanni Battista Rogeri bearing the label *Jo. Bap. Rogerius Bon: Nicolai Amati de Cremona Alumnus Brixiae fecit Anno Domini 1695.* (Phillips)

$40,595

An attractive dancing master kit or pochette, probably 18th century, with a 19th century one-eighth size violin bow. (Phillips)

$3,078

A fine violoncello of the Bernadel Paris School, circa 1840. (Phillips)

$25,650

A good Italian violin, influenced by Storioni, labeled *Laurentius Storioni Cremo-/nensis fecit ... /Anno 1802,* the one-piece back cut on the slab. (Christie's)

$24,794

A violin by Antonius and Hieronymus Fr Amati, bearing the maker's label *Cremonen Andrea fil f,* circa 1600. (Phillips)

$18,811

A French violoncello labeled and signed *Collin-Mézin,* the two-piece back of faint small curl, the ribs and scroll similar. (Christie's)

$5,313

A violin by Lorenzo and Tommaso Carcassi, bearing the maker's label, 1775, in a waterproof oblong case by W.E. Hill & Sons. (Phillips)

$14,240

A French violin by Honoré Derazey, the one-piece back of medium curl, the ribs of fainter figure, the scroll of plain wood. (Christie's) **$6,730**

A good violin by William Robinson, bearing the maker's label in *Plumstead, London AD 1920.* (Phillips) **$2,928**

A good violin by Petrus et Hipolitus Fratres Silvestre, bearing the label: *Fecerunt Lugdini anno 1842.* (Phillips) **$14,535**

A fine violin by Pierre Silvestre bearing the maker's label in Lyon dated 1857, in a shaped leather case, lined gold colored velvet. (Phillips) **$25,593**

A fine English violin by George Wulme Hudson labeled *Pressenda*, the two-piece back cut on the slab, the ribs and scroll similar. (Christie's) **$6,730**

An important and rare, small size violin by *Antonius & Hieronymus Fr Amati Cremonen, Andreae Fil. F 1588.* (Phillips) **$89,000**

A French violin by François Lupot Orleano anno 1772, the two-piece back of faint medium curl, the ribs similar. (Christie's) **$15,054**

A good French violoncello by Gustave Bernardel, Paris 1880, the two-piece back of handsome medium to small curl. (Christie's) **$28,336**

A rare tenor viol early 17th century bearing a manuscript label William Bowcliffe, with black wood case. (Phillips)

$11,570

A violoncello by Pierre Flambeau, in Paris, circa 1800, branded by the maker below the button. (Phillips)

$6,840

A good violin by Honore Derazey Pere in Mirecourt, bearing the maker's label and brands, circa 1870. (Phillips)

$12,825

A violoncello by Bernard Simon Fendt, London, circa 1830, in black hard carrying case. (Phillips)

$22,230

A fine viola made in the workshop of Charles Buthod, circa 1890, bearing the label *Buthod Luthier eleve Vuillaume a Paris.* (Phillips)

$2,394

A Swiss violoncello by Adolf König Zurich 1932, the two-piece back of handsome medium curl, the ribs similar. (Christie's)

$2,834

A fine violin by Charles Gaillard, bearing the maker's label *at 11 Boulevard Bonne Nouvelle Paris 1869.* (Phillips)

$15,390

A good violin by Bela Szepessy,London 1896/ N. 107, the two-piece back of handsome medium curl, the ribs and scroll similar. (Christie's)

$11,512

A stained boxwood netsuke of Shoki gripping oni tightly round the neck, signed *Tomochika*, early 19th century, 6.5cm. high. (Christie's) **$1,500**

Ivory netsuke of a doctor doll, early 19th century, unsigned, 4¹/₄in. long. (Skinner Inc.) **$605**

A pale boxwood netsuke of a long-haired mermaid with an infant at her breast, signed in an oval reserve Kokei, late 18th century, 4.6cm. high. (Christie's) **$4,235**

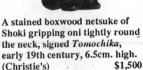

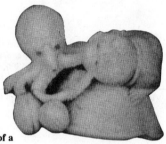

A finely detailed small ivory netsuke of a wild boar asleep on a bed of leaves beside a fallen oak branch, unsigned, late 18th century, 3.3cm. (Christie's) **$5,300**

An important wood netsuke of a foreigner standing with one hand on his head while holding a small dog in the other, his eyes inlaid in amber and the dog's in brass, *Suzuki Katsusuke*, 18th century, 12.8cm. high. (Christie's) **$26,950**

Ivory netsuke of an octopus and cat, 19th century, signed *Masakazu*, 1in. high. (Skinner Inc.) **$1,540**

Wood netsuke of a frog on a tree stump, signed *Masanao*, inlaid eyes, 1¹/₄in. high. (Skinner Inc.) **$1,045**

A well patinated ivory netsuke of a Korean musician holding a drum flung over his shoulder and a drumstick in his right hand, signed *Masakazu*, 19th century, 5.1cm. high. (Christie's) **$5,267**

Ivory netsuke of two skeletons wrestling, 19th century, signed *Gyokosai*, 2¹/₄in. high. (Skinner Inc.) **$880**

An ebony netsuke depicting two South Sea Islanders struggling with a large piece of red coral, their eyes inlaid in ivory, probably Tomoe, 19th century, 5.7cm. wide.
(Christie's) $4,235

An ivory netsuke of a karako holding a hobby-horse, engraved and stained detail, late 19th century, 5.6cm.
(Christie's) $658

An ivory netsuke of a mermaid, the creature holding a shell, stained facial and scale detail, signed *Ren* (Rensai), 19th century.
(Christie's) $19,360

An ivory netsuke of a snake, its body coiled into many loops, its mouth open and eye pupils inlaid, unsigned, 19th century, 3.5cm.
(Christie's) $1,750

An ivory netsuke of Daruma with arms folded inside his robe crossing the ocean on a reed, signed *Minkoku*, early 19th century, 4.5cm. high.
(Christie's) $1,084

A well-detailed ivory netsuke of a rat sitting holding a candle with its forepaws, its eyes inlaid in black horn, signed *Tomokazu*, 19th century, 3cm. high.
(Christie's) $1,400

A very fine boxwood and ivory netsuke depicting Choryo kneeling to put on Kosekiko's shoe, with lacquer and metal detail, late 19th century, 4cm. high.
(Christie's) $14,150

A finely patinated ivory netsuke of a temple servant holding an umbrella and carrying a lantern, unsigned, late 18th century, 10cm. high.
(Christie's) $3,200

Wood mask netsuke, early 19th century, grimacing male face, signed *Tadatoshi*, 1¹/₂in. long.
(Skinner Inc.) $523

A Loetz vase with white-metal mount, designed by Koloman Moser, slender flared stem with swollen bowl and everted rim, 23cm. high.
(Christie's) $6,230

A Liberty 'Tudric' rectangular pewter tray with arched handle, inset with rectangular panel decorated in 'Pomegranate' pattern, the tray chased in relief with stylized foliage, stamped marks, 12in. high.
(Christie's) $1,078

A rare York flagon, applied with a scroll handle and hinged lid with divided twist thumb-piece and pointed finial, 14³/₄in. high, circa 1725.
(Tennants) $5,208

A 'Tudric' twin-handled cylindrical pewter vase, cast in relief with sprays of honesty and bearing the inscription *For Old Times Sake*, 7³/₄in. high.
(Christie's) $325

A pair of Wolfer Frères Art Nouveau white metal vases, each of organic style with tapering ovoid reeded body, 12¹/₂in. high.
(Christie's) $5,841

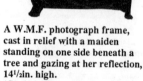

A W.M.F. photograph frame, cast in relief with a maiden standing on one side beneath a tree and gazing at her reflection, 14¹/₂in. high.
(Christie's) $1,752

Pewter coffee pot, Roswell Gleason (active 1822–1871), Dorchester, Massachusetts, mid 19th century, 11in. high.
(Skinner Inc.) $250

Liberty and Co. biscuit box, designed by Archibald Knox, 1904, hammered texture with raised geometric motifs in dark patina, 4¹/₂in. high.
(Skinner Inc.) $375

A late 17th century pewter half gallon measure by Richard Dunne, of baluster form with fluted eared thumbpiece, 27.75cm. high overall.
(Spencer's) $1,853

PEWTER

One of two pewter ladles, 19th century, the first marked *T.D. Boardman*, the strap handle arched and monogrammed *H.M.*, 14in. and 15³⁄₄in. long.
(Christie's) (Two) $308

A W.M.F. pewter tea service, of waisted hexagonal form cast in relief with whiplash foliage and sprays of berried foliage.
(Christie's) $2,531

A W.M.F. pewter sweetmeat dish of cylindrical form pierced and embellished with linear motifs, 17.2cm. high.
(Phillips) $220

A Wiener Werkstätte white metal hand mirror, the design attributed to Joseph Hoffmann, 9¹⁄₂in. long.
(Christie's) $3,894

A set of three post war Italian hollow white metal stylized figures of penguins, graduated in size, 7¹⁄₂, 9¹⁄₂ and 12¹⁄₂in. high.
(Christie's) $681

A Liberty 'Tudric' tray designed by Archibald Knox, of bowed rectangular section cast in relief with foliate roundels, 19¹⁄₄in. wide.
(Christie's) $712

A W.M.F. pewter centerpiece stand, cast as an Art Nouveau maiden in swirling dress, standing holding aloft an urn, 14in. high.
(Christie's) $545

A Liberty & Co. hammered pewter rose bowl, the design attributed to Oliver Baker, cast and applied decoration, set with five green glass studs, 15.8cm. high.
(Christie's) $730

Pewter candlestick, England, circa 1675, octagonal bobeche over conforming ringed standard, medial drip pan and base, 8¹⁄₂in. high.
(Skinner Inc.) $7,700

PEWTER

A pair of Art Deco white metal twin branch candlesticks, each on stepped circular base surmounted by asymmetric curved stems, 6in. high.
(Christie's) $443

A Liberty & Co. 'Tudric' pewter easel timepiece of irregular circular outline having a raised decoration of leaves and berries, 12cm. diameter.
(Phillips) $550

Three American pewter coffeepots, Josiah Danforth, Middletown, Connecticut, Boardman and Co., New York, R. Dunham, Portland, Maine, 19th century.
(Butterfield & Butterfield) $1,760

An 18th century Scottish pewter tappit hen lidded measure of mutchkin capacity, 6in. high.
(Christie's) $275

A Liberty & Co. 'Tudric' pewter inkwell, of capstan form with rounded rectangular lid on a canted square base, 9cm. high.
(Phillips) $550

A Federal pewter pitcher, Boardman and Hart, New York, fl. 1828–1877, with flaring lip and peaked applied handle, 7³/₄in. high.
(Christie's) $990

Two Liberty & Co. pewter vases designed by Archibald Knox, each bullet-shaped form chased with stylized floral decoration, on tripod bases, 18.8cm. high.
(Christie's) $770

An 18th century English pewter charger, 20¹/₂in. diameter, with reeded border, the centre later engraved with the Duke of Marlborough, initial *M* and date, *1704*.
(Bonhams) $1,575

A pair of Liberty & Co. Tudric pewter twin-branched candelabra designed by Archibald Knox, with pierced decoration of leaves and berries on tendrils, on rectangular flat foot, 27.8cm. high.
(Christie's) $3,272

A pair of W.M.F. pewter
candlesticks, the tulip-shaped
sconces raised on tall squared
columns flaring to the bases,
22cm. high.
(Phillips) $775

Pair of American pewter
teapots, William Calder,
Providence, Rhode Island, early
19th century, 9¹/₂in. high.
(Butterfield & Butterfield)
                              $550

A pair of Art Nouveau pewter
Kayserzinn candlesticks each of
triangular section, 11¹/₂in. high.
(David Lay) $479

A French Art Deco white metal
vase, the body stamped in relief
with dense geometric patterns,
French poinçon, 5¹/₂in. high.
(Christie's S. Ken) $240

A composite set of three 19th
century French pot bellied
lidded measures with spouts.
(Christie's) $1,150

A Kayserzinn pewter jug, the
body cast with fruiting oak
branches, the lid with a squirrel,
13in. high.
(David Lay) $370

A pair of W.M.F. pewter
candlesticks, the openwork
rectangular columns flaring to
the base, 15cm. high.
(Phillips) $260

An English 18th century pewter
charger, 20¹/₂in. diameter, with
wrigglework vitruvian scroll
border, dated 1694, by Richard
King Junior.
(Bonhams) $1,000

A pair of Liberty & Co. 'Tudric'
pewter candlesticks, the design
attributed to Archibald Knox,
the bullet shaped sconce with
flanged rim, 23.5cm. high.
(Phillips) $740

Dorothea Lange, "Company housing for cotton workers near Corcorn, California", 1940s, gelatin silver print, 7⁶/₈ x 9⁶/₈in. (Butterfield & Butterfield)

$715

W. Eugene Smith, "Doctors", circa 1950, gelatin silver print, 13¹/₈ x 19¹/₄in., photographer's name stamp in ink. (Butterfield & Butterfield)

$550

Jacques Henri Lartigue, "Horse races at Montreuil", 1911, printed 1972, 6¹/₂ x 9in., signed in ink on the mount. (Butterfield & Butterfield)

$440

Anon, Lady with large black dog, circa 1860, quarter-plate ambrotype, with gilt metal mount. (Christie's)

$391

Henri Cartier-Bresson, "Rue Mouffetard", 1954, printed later, gelatin silver print, 14 x 9³/₈in., signed in ink and the photographer's blindstamp in the margin. (Butterfield & Butterfield)

$3,300

Willard Van Dyke, "Nehi", circa 1931, gelatin silver print, 9¹/₂ x 7¹/₂in., signed, titled, dated. (Butterfield & Butterfield)

$1,210

Roger Mayne, Boy with gun, 1956, gelatin silver print, 9⁷/₈ x 7¹/₄in., photographer's ink copyright stamp on verso. (Christie's)

$548

Photographer unknown, Album containing 24 photographs of The Paris Exposition Universelle, 1889, albumen prints, each measuring approximately 8³/₄ x 11³/₄in. (Butterfield & Butterfield)

$495

W. Eugene Smith, "Spanish spinner", 1951, printed 1977, gelatin silver print, 12³/₄ x 9in., signed on the mount in ink. (Butterfield & Butterfield)

$1,650

Duane Michals, "Magritte's room", 1965, printed later, gelatin silver print, 6³/₄ x 9⁷/₈in., signed.
(Butterfield & Butterfield) $467

Nicholas Nixon, "Yazoo City, Mississippi", 1979, printed later, gelatin silver print, 7¹/₈ x 9³/₄in., signed.
(Butterfield & Butterfield) $935

Max Yavno, "Orson Wells", circa 1942, gelatin silver print, 7⁶/₈ x 9⁶/₈in., photographer's stamp in ink.
(Butterfield & Butterfield) $1,100

R. Lowe (Cheltenham), Caroline Georgina Colledge and her brother John, circa 1855, a 5 x 4in. daguerreotype.
(Christie's) $730

Andre Kertesz, "Wandering violinist", 1921, printed 1980 for "A Hungarian Memory" portfolio, gelatin silver print, 9³/₄ x 7¹/₂in., signed in pencil on verso.
(Butterfield & Butterfield) $1,320

Frank Meadow Sutcliffe, 'His Son's Son', late 19th century, carbon print, image size 7⁷/₈ x 6in., numbered 31 with photographer's initials in the negative, matted.
(Christie's) $548

Edward Steichen (1879–1973), Noel Coward, 1932, gelatin silver contact print, 10 x 8in.
(Christie's) $1,369

Photographer unknown, 2 albums containing 133 photographs: Chinese landscapes, portraits and genre scenes, 1880s, albumen prints.
(Butterfield & Butterfield) $2,200

Man Ray, 'Mrs Simpson', 1936, double exposure silver print, 8³/₈ x 6¹/₄in., matted, framed.
(Christie's) $2,465

PHOTOGRAPHS

S.L. Carleton, 'Young girl with King Charles spaniel', circa 1848, sixth-plate daguerreotype, folding morocco case.
(Christie's) $313

Jacques-Henri Lartigue, 'Avenue du Bois de Boulogne', 1911, printed later, gelatin silver print, image size 9⁵/₈ x 13⁷/₈in., signed in ink.
(Christie's) $2,349

Lewis Carroll (Charles Lutwidge Dodgson) (1832–98), Xie Kitchin, circa 1873, cabinet card, albumen print 5¹/₂ x 4in., numbered 2223 in ink in Carroll's hand on verso.
(Christie's) $2,349

Thomas Annan (1829–87), 'Close, No. 28 Saltmarket', 1868–77, carbon print, 11 x 9in., mounted on card, printed title and number 26 on mount.
(Christie's) $587

Herb Ritts, 'Men with Kelp', Paradise Cove, 1987, gelatin silver print, image size 19¹/₈ x 15¹/₄in., photographer's copyright blindstamp in margin, signed.
(Christie's) $587

G. Riebicke, 'Archer with borzoi', circa 1930, gelatin silver print, 6¹/₂ x 4³/₄in., photographer's ink credit stamp on verso, matted.
(Christie's) $783

Robert Doisneau, Pablo Picasso, 1952 printed 1989, gelatin silver print, image size 10³/₈ x 8¹/₈in., signed in ink in margin.
(Christie's) $1,174

Anon, Little girl holding puppy, mid 1850s, sixth-plate daguerreotype, lightly hand-tinted, gilt metal mount.
(Christie's) $332

Don McCullin (b. 1935), Melanesian portrait, 1983, gelatin silver print, image size 17 x 12in., matted, signed and dated in ink on mount.
(Christie's) $587

PHOTOGRAPHS

Robert Frank, "Paris, 1950",
printed later, gelatin silver
print, 8³/₄ x 13³/₈in., signed,
titled, and dated in ink in
margin.
(Butterfield & Butterfield)
$2,475

Frantisek Drtikol (1883–1961),
Nude, 1933, toned gelatin silver
print, 11¹/₂ x 9in.
(Christie's) $3,520

Aleksandr Rodchenko (1891–
1956), Red Square (early 1930s),
gelatin silver print, 7 x 9³/₈in.,
indistinct inscription in ink and
pencil on verso.
(Christie's) $5,874

Horst P. Horst (b. 1906), The
Mainbocher corset, Paris 1939
printed 1986–87, gelatin silver
print, image size 16¹/₄ x 13in.,
signed in pencil in margin,
matted, framed.
(Christie's) $4,699

Julia Margaret Cameron,
Alfred, Lord Tennyson, 1860s
printed 1875, carbon print, 13¹/₂
x 10in., printed by the Autotype
Company, mounted on card.
(Christie's) $587

Richard Avedon (b. 1923),
'Robert Frank, photographer
Mabou Mines, Nova Scotia',
1975, gelatin silver contact print,
10 x 8in., no. 29 of an edition of
50, signed in ink.
(Christie's) $2,545

Roger Mayne (b. 1929), Girl
seated on steps, Southam Street,
late 1950s, gelatin silver print,
14⁷/₈ x 10¹/₂in., mounted on card.
(Christie's) $1,468

Edward Weston (1886–1958),
D.H. Lawrence, 1924, gelatin
silver print, 9¹/₂ x 7¹/₂in., ink
credit stamp *The Carmelite* and
various pencil annotations on
verso.
(Christie's) $587

Frank Meadow Sutcliffe (1853–
1941), Portrait of a fisherman,
1880s, printed later, toned
gelatin silver print, image size
8¹/₂ x 6in.
(Christie's) $352

Roger Mayne, 'Two Jivers, Richmond Jazz Festival', 1962, printed late 1960s, gelatin silver print, 7 x 10½in. (Christie's) $639

Anon, Reclining nude with bird in her hand, 1850s, stereoscopic daguerreotype, hand-tinted, paper-taped. (Christie's) $3,652

Max Yavno, "Muscle Beach Los Angeles", 1949, printed later, gelatin silver print, 7⅞ x 13⅜in. (Butterfield & Butterfield) $4,400

Anon, Standing nude leaning on a chair, 1850s, stereoscopic daguerreotype, hand-tinted, paper-taped. (Christie's) $3,287

Ansel Adams, "Dogwood, Yosemite National Park, California", 1938, printed 1970s, gelatin silver print, 13½ x 9½in., signed in pencil on mount. (Butterfield & Butterfield) $3,850

Anon, Nude, 1850s, stereoscopic daguerreotype, lighly hand-tinted and with gilt highlights, paper-taped with label numbered *No. 14/209* on verso. (Christie's) $8,140

Lewis Hine, 2 photographs: "Baltimore cannery", and Four schoolboys, both circa 1910, gelatin silver prints, the first 4¾ x 6⅝in. (Butterfield & Butterfield) $605

Anon, Sleeping dog, mid 1850s, sixth-plate daguerreotype, gilt metal mount. (Christie's) $469

Pedro Meyer, "Boda en Coyoacan" (Wedding in Coyoacan, 1983, gelatin silver print, 8 x 12in., signed and titled in pencil on verso, framed. (Butterfield & Butterfield) $467

Larry Keenan Jr., "McClure, Dylan, Ginsberg, North Beach, S.F.", 1965, printed 1967, gelatin silver print, 9¾ x 13in. (Butterfield & Butterfield) $550

Robert Frank, "Daytona Florida", 1961, printed later, gelatin silver print, 8½ x 13in., signed, titled, and dated in ink in margin. (Butterfield & Butterfield) $935

Nicholas Nixon, "MDC Park, Brighton, Massachusetts", 1979, printed later, gelatin silver print, 7⅛ x 9⅝in., signed. (Butterfield & Butterfield) $880

514

PHOTOGRAPHS

Ralph Steiner, "Always- Camel AD", 1922, printed 1981, gelatin silver print, 3⁷/₈ x 5in., signed. (Butterfield & Butterfield)

$605

Anon, reclining nude with gilt head-dress, 1850s, stereoscopic daguerreotype, hand-tinted, gilt highlights, paper-taped. (Christie's) $7,669

Choumoff (Paris), Autographed portrait of Claude Monet, circa 1910, warm-toned platinum print, 6³/₈ x 8¹/₄in., signed in red ink. (Christie's) $2,556

Yousuf Karsh, "Jascha Heifetz", 1950s, gelatin silver print, 9⁶/₈ x 11³/₄in., signed in ink in the margin, framed. (Butterfield & Butterfield) $825

Anon, reclining nude reading a book, 1850s, stereoscopic daguerreotype, hand-tinted, paper-taped. (Christie's) $7,669

Ralph Steiner, "American baroque", 1929, printed 1949, gelatin silver print, 7⁷/₈ x 9⁷/₈in., signed and dated in pencil on verso. (Butterfield & Butterfield) $1,760

Lewis Carroll, 'Irene at Elm Lodge', July 1863, oval albumen print, 6⁷/₈ x 8⁷/₈in. (Christie's) $15,400

Anon, Group portrait of girls, 1850s–60s, half-plate daguerreotype, lightly hand-tinted, gilt surround, in thermoplastic union case with geometric and scroll design. (Christie's) $1,540

Alice Boughton, portrait of Robert Louis Stevenson, circa 1900, platinum print 6 x 8in. (Butterfield & Butterfield) $3,300

Anon, Reclining nude with a man in the background, 1850s, stereoscopic daguerreotype, hand tinted, paper taped. (Christie's) $18,601

Arthur Dunn, 'Mark Twain and Family at Dollis Hill', 1900, carbon print, 6 x 8in., mounted on card. (Christie's) $256

Jacques Henri Lartigue, Woman and dog, 1920s, printed 1972, 6¹/₂ x 9in., signed in ink on the mount. (Butterfield & Butterfield) $660

515

PHOTOGRAPHS

Howard Coster (1885–1959), T.E. Lawrence on his Brough Superior motorbike, 1925–26, gelatin silver print on textured card, 7³/₈ x 9¹/₄in.
(Christie's) $513

Ansel Adams, "Frozen lake and cliffs, Sierra Nevada, Sequoia National Park", 1932, printed later, approximately 8 x 10in.
(Butterfield & Butterfield) $12,100

Roger Mayne (b. 1929), Brenda Sheakey (screaming child), Southam Street, 1956, printed mid/late 1960s, gelatin silver print, 7¹/₄ x 9¹/₄in.
(Christie's) $1,643

Herb Ritts, 'Man holding shell', Australia 1986, gelatin silver print, image size 18⁵/₈ x 15¹/₄in., photographer's copyright blindstamp in margin.
(Christie's) $1,132

Irving Penn (b. 1917), 'Two Thin New Guinea Women', New Guinea, 1970, printed 1984, multiple-printed and hand-coated platinum-palladium print, 13¹/₄ x 13¹/₈in.
(Christie's) $2,739

Albert Watson (b. 1942), Untitled, (1970s), gelatin silver print, 39¹/₂ x 29¹/₂in., mounted on board, signed and numbered 34/35 in ink on verso, framed.
(Christie's) $365

Greg Gorman, Dave Michelak, 1987, gelatin silver print, 30¹/₄ x 24³/₄in., signed and dated in ink with the photographer's copyright stamp.
(Butterfield & Butterfield) $1,278

Izis (1911–1980), 'Jardin des Tuileries', Paris 1950, gelatin silver print, image size 11¹/₈ x 8⁵/₈in., titled and dated with photographer's credit stamp on verso.
(Christie's) $1,004

Horst P. Horst, 'Lisa Fonssagrives, New York, 1940', printed 1980s, platinum-palladium print, image size 18³/₄ x 15in., signed in pencil in margin.
(Christie's) $3,652

PHOTOGRAPHS

Anon, Family group portrait, circa 1895–97, mammoth carbon print, 29½ x 39½in., finely hand-tinted, contemporary gilt frame.
(Christie's) $694

Gustave Le Gray (1820–82), The Great Wave, Sète, 1856–59, albumen print from two negatives, 12³/₈ x 15½in.
(Christie's) $31,042

William Heick, "Hats, Seattle", 1952, gelatin silver print, 9½ x 12½in., signed and dated in pencil on the mount.
(Butterfield & Butterfield) $605

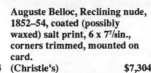

Edouard-Denis Baldus, 'Paris Saint-Eustache', circa 1860, albumen print, 16⁵/₈ x 13in., signed in the negative, mounted on card.
(Christie's) $7,304

Auguste Belloc, Reclining nude, 1852–54, coated (possibly waxed) salt print, 6 x 7⁷/₈in., corners trimmed, mounted on card.
(Christie's) $7,304

Bert Hardy (b. 1913), 'Maidens in Waiting, Blackpool', 1951, printed later, gelatin silver print, image size 13 x 10in., signed in ink in margin, framed.
(Christie's) $730

Lotte Jacobi (1896–1990), 'Peter Lorre', 'Grock' and other portraits, (1940s–50s), printed late 1950s, six gelatin silver prints, 6½ x 4³/₄in., to 9½ x 7½in.
(Christie's) $584

Robert Howlett (1831–1858), Attempted launch of the "Great Eastern", November 28, 1857, printed early 1900s, gelatin silver print, 10 x 8½in., arched top, mounted on card.
(Christie's) $511

Yousuf Karsh (b. 1908), Pablo Picasso, 1954, printed later, gelatin silver print, 23½ x 19½in., mounted on card, signed in ink on mount, matted, framed.
(Christie's) $2,008

517

PHOTOGRAPHS

Peter Stackpole, "Minsky's dressing room", 1937, printed later, gelatin silver print, 9³/₈ x 7³/₈in., signed in pencil. (Butterfield & Butterfield)

$550

Edouard-Denis Baldus, Pavillon Turgot, Louvre, circa 1855, salt print, 17⁵/₈ x 13⁵/₈in., signed and numbered *E. Baldus No. 47* in the negative, mounted on card. (Christie's)

$2,009

Philippe Halsman, "Dali skull", 1951, printed 1970, gelatin silver print, 12¹/₂ x 10¹/₂in., signed, titled, and dated in pencil. (Butterfield & Butterfield)

$1,540

Julia Margaret Cameron, "Sappho", circa 1866, albumen print, 14¹/₂ x 11¹/₂in., signed and annotated *from life not enlarged* in ink. (Butterfield & Butterfield)

$1,980

Roger Mayne, 'Ladbroke Grove – group watching car crash', 1958, printed circa 1960, gelatin silver print, 7¹/₄ x 9¹/₈in., photographer's ink copyright stamp and title on verso. (Christie's)

$456

Dorothy Wilding, HRH Princess Margaret, 1947, gelatin silver print, 18 x 14⁵/₈in., pencil border, mounted on tissue with photographer's printed signature. (Christie's)

$183

Photographer unknown, Portrait of a black woman with a white child, ¹/₂ plate tintype, gilt preserver, leather case broken at hinges. (Butterfield & Butterfield)

$385

William Heick, "Woman on bus, Seattle", 1951, gelatin silver print, 9⁷/₈ x 8in., signed and dated in pencil on the mount. (Butterfield & Butterfield)

$715

Philippe Halsman, "Nixon jumping in the White House", 1955, printed 1969, gelatin silver print, 14 x 11in., signed, titled, and dated in pencil. (Butterfield & Butterfield)

$935

PHOTOGRAPHS

Andre Kertesz, "Circus", 1920, printed for "A Hungarian Memory" portfolio, gelatin silver print, 9³/₄ x 7³/₄in. (Butterfield & Butterfield) $1,320

Barbara Morgan, "Martha Graham–Letter to the World", 1940, printed 1980, gelatin silver print, 10³/₈ x 13¹/₈in., signed. (Butterfield & Butterfield) $660

Man Ray, Head of a woman, 1946, solarized gelatin silver print, 8 x 6¹/₄in., includes signature and date. (Butterfield & Butterfield) $2,750

André Kertész, Snow street scene, New York, 1958, gelatin silver print, 6³/₄ x 4³/₄in., mounted as Christmas card on hand-made paper with untrimmed edges. (Christie's) $1,278

Marion Post Wolcott, "Transportation for 'Hepcats', Louisville, KY", 1940, printed 1978, gelatin silver print, 6⁵/₈ x 9¹/₈in. (Butterfield & Butterfield) $990

Dorothy Wilding, The Duke and Duchess of Windsor, autographed portrait, 1944, gelatin silver print, 9¹/₈ x 6¹/₂in., mounted on tissue, signed by sitters and dated in ink. (Christie's) $1,735

Alexander Rodchenko, "Portrait of Majakowski", 1924, printed 1989, gelatin silver print, 12 x 9³/₈in., titled and dated in pencil. (Butterfield & Butterfield) $1,100

George Bernard Shaw (1856–1950), Alvin Langdon Coburn, July 1906, photogravure, 8³/₈ x 6³/₈in., on tissue, then card, matted. (Christie's) $876

Cecil Beaton, "Lily Langtrey, Lady de Bathe", gelatin silver print, 10⁷/₈ x 8in., titled in white ink on image, signed in orange watercolor on mount. (Butterfield & Butterfield) $550

Philippe Halsman, "John Steinbeck", 1957, gelatin silver print, 19¹/₂ x 15³/₄in., signed and titled in pencil.
(Butterfield & Butterfield)
$2,090

Imogen Cunningham, "Magnolia blossom", 1925, printed circa 1979, gelatin silver print, 10⁵/₈ x 13¹/₂in.
(Butterfield & Butterfield)
$1,760

Margaret Bourke-White, "Frank Profitt, folk singer", 1940s, gelatin silver print, 13²/₈ x 9⁶/₈in., framed.
(Butterfield & Butterfield)
$2,475

Man Ray (1890–1976), Robert Winthrop Chanler, 1929, toned gelatin silver print, 10⁷/₈ x 8¹/₈in., signed *Man Ray Paris* in red crayon.
(Christie's) $639

Edward Weston, "White Sands, New Mexico", 1940, gelatin silver print, 7⁵/₈ x 9⁵/₈in., initialed and dated.
(Butterfield & Butterfield)
$12,100

Brian Griffin (b. 1948), George Melly', 1990, printed later, gelatin silver print, image size 14 x 14in., signed and dated in pencil on verso, framed.
(Christie's) $547

Yousuf Karsh, "Nikita Khrushchev", 1963, printed later, 19³/₄ x 15³/₄in., gelatin silver print, signed in ink on the mount.
(Butterfield & Butterfield)
$990

Gisele Freund, "Andre Malraux, Paris", 1935, printed later, gelatin silver print, 11³/₄ x 9¹/₂in., signed and dated in ink in the margin.
(Butterfield & Butterfield)
$302

Galerie Contemporaine series: Valery, "Victor Hugo", circa 1880, Woodbury type, 9 x 7¹/₂in., on the original letterpress mount.
(Butterfield & Butterfield)
$412

Berenice Abbott, "Portrait of Orozco", early 1930s, gelatin silver print, 13³/₄ x 11⁵/₈in, signed in pencil on mount.
(Butterfield & Butterfield)
$825

Irving Penn (b. 1917), Pablo Picasso, Cannes, 1957, probably printed early 1960s, gelatin silver print, 22⁷/₈ x 22⁷/₈in., flush mounted on plywood.
(Christie's) $2,191

Frederick Evans, Portrait of Aubrey Beardsley, circa 1894, photogravure, 5 x 4¹/₈in., credit printed in the margin.
(Butterfield & Butterfield)
$220

Bill Brandt (1906–1984), 'Hampstead, London 1953', printed later, gelatin silver print, 12³/₈ x 10³/₈in., singed in ink on verso, matted, framed.
(Christie's) $766

Judy Dater, "Nehemiah", 1975, gelatin silver print, 10³/₈ x 13³/₈in., signed in pencil on the mount, framed.
(Butterfield & Butterfield)
$715

Gisèle Freund, 'Samuel Beckett', n.d., gelatin silver print, image size 12 x 7⁷/₈in., photographer's blindstamp on image, signed in ink in margin.
(Christie's) $694

Philippe Halsman, "Marc Chagall", 1946, printed later, gelatin silver print, 13⁵/₈ x 10³/₄in., signed, titled, and dated in pencil.
(Butterfield & Butterfield)
$935

Irving Penn (b. 1917), Igor Stravinsky, 1948, printed 1970, multiple-printed and hand-coated platinum-palladium print, 19 x 13³/₄in., with aluminium backing, signed.
(Christie's) $4,382

(?) Herman, Toulouse Lautrec seated at his easel, 1894, gelatin silver print, 7³/₄ x 6¹/₄in., mounted on card, signed and dated by the photographer, matted and framed.
(Christie's) $1,461

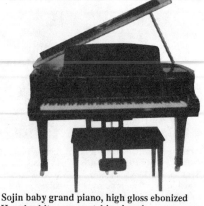

Square piano, by Frederic Beck of Broad Street, Soho dated 1790 in mahogany and inlaid case on stand with square tapering supports and brass patera headers.
(Lots Road Galleries) $2,775

Sojin baby grand piano, high gloss ebonized Hepplewhite case, matching bench.
(Du Mouchelles) $6,000

A John Broadway & Sons oak 'Manxman' piano, designed by M.H. Baillie-Scott, with hinged overhanging rectangular top, circa 1899, 142.6cm. wide.
(Christie's) $11,814

An orchestrion, with piano, xylophone, base and snare drums, cymbol, tamborine and wood block housed in an oak case with two leaded colored glass panels.
(Allen & Harris) $6,290

Erard carved and inlaid walnut and mahogany grand piano, circa 1890, the foliate and berry marquetry cover outlined in penwork above scroll and foliate-carved paneled sides, length 8ft. 7in.
(Butterfield & Butterfield) $5,225

A William IV satinwood cabinet piano by George Dunn, New Road, London, with ebonised moldings, having a molded cornice and foliate headed stiles and scroll candle branches.
(Phillips) $2,750

A Bluthner Boudoir grand piano with Aliquot scaling, the rosewood case on tapering turned and fluted legs with brass castors, 5ft. 10in. (Bearne's) **$3,145**

Bechstein model 'B' grand piano No. 105019, the ebonized case with tapering octagonal legs and brass castors, 6ft. 8in. (Bearne's) **$1,272**

An overstrung upright pianoforte by John Broadwood & Sons, the rectangular case decorated with inlaid satinwood, the paneled front with stylized foliage centered by a classical urn, 58½in. wide. (Christie's) **$3,361**

An early Victorian satin ash upright piano by John Broadwood and Sons with pierced fret carved upper panels on cabochon carved scroll uprights, 59in. high. (Christie's) **$2,250**

A grand pianoforte by John Broadwood & Son, in a crossbanded mahogany case with satinwood interior and inscribed nameboard, on a mahogany trestle stand with brass castors, circa 1806. (Christie's) **$5,313**

A Gothic Revival straight-strung upright piano by Gebrüder Knake, Munster, the oak case pierced and carved throughout with tracery, scrolling foliage, linenfold and strapwork, 5ft. 4in. wide. (Bearne's) **$1,800**

An Italian eighteenth century carved and gilded leaf frame, the border with cherubs and pierced scrolling acanthus leaves, 50¹/₄ x 43in.
(Christie's) $8,854

An Italian late eighteenth century carved and gilded hollow frame, 60¹/₄ x 80⁷/₈in.
(Christie's) $2,261

Charles II giltwood picture frame, late 17th century, with pierced and carved acanthus and husks, surmounted by a shield, 22¹/₂in. wide.
(Skinner Inc.) $770

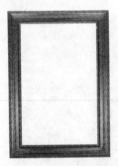

A Netherlandish seventeenth century carved ebonized frame, with various ripple and wave moldings, 35⁷/₈ x 51¹/₄in.
(Christie's) $14,128

A Dutch nineteenth century carved ebonized frame, decorated with ivory inlay figures and cherubs' heads, tortoiseshell geometric panels and mother-of-pearl dots, 30¹/₂ x 27in.
(Christie's S. Ken) $4,213

An Italian seventeenth century carved and gilded frame, with egg-and-dart outer edge, imbricated leaf center running to corners, 47¹/₂ x 40in.
(Christie's) $13,186

A German eighteenth century carved and gilded frame, with leaf-and-dart outer edge, the corners with opposed C-scrolls, 32 x 38in.
(Christie's) $1,319

A Spanish seventeenth century carved, gilded and painted frame, with scroling centers and corners on blue ground, 39¹/₂ x 35in.
(Christie's S. Ken) $3,370

A Continental nineteenth century carved and gilded frame, with egg-and-dart outer edge, the scrolling acanthus corners running to rosettes, 43³/₄ x 35³/₈in.
(Christie's) $1,507

A Venetian seventeenth century carved, gilded and painted frame, with marbled center and raised inner edge, 23¹/₈ x 17¹/₄in.
(Christie's) **$1,224**

American School, late 19th century, carved and painted watermelon frame and genre scene, signed *R.S.P. 98*, 21 x 14¹/₂in.
(Skinner Inc.) **$1,540**

A Dutch seventeenth century carved ebonized frame, with various ripple and wave moldings, 21¹/₂ x 19in.
(Christie's) **$1,507**

An Italian seventeenth century carved and gilded cassetta frame, with punched scrolling foliage and flowers, 27 x 22⁵/₈in.
(Christie's) **$3,579**

Spanish seventeenth century carved and gilded frame, with scrolling acanthus corners and foliate inner, 22¹/₄ x 19¹/₄in.
(Christie's S. Ken) **$5,034**

A Louis XIV carved and gilded frame with dentil outer edge, scrolling foliage, flowers and C-scrolls on cross-hatched ground, 79³/₄ x 99¹/₄in.
(Christie's) **$16,954**

An Italian eighteenth century carved and gilded leaf frame, the border decorated with acanthus leaves and pierced scrolling foliage, 40¹/₂ x 45¹/₂in.
(Christie's) **$2,543**

An Italian seventeenth century carved and gilded frame, with lotus outer edge, the central plate decorated with acanthus scroll corners and etched centers, 50³/₄ x 40³/₄in.
(Christie's) **$4,333**

A Louis XIV carved and gilded frame, the flowerspray corners flanked by acanthus leaves, foliage and flowers on cross-hatched ground, 10 x 8³/₄in.
(Christie's) **$1,601**

PICTURE FRAMES

A French Louis XIV carved and gilded frame with ogee sight edge, embellished to the corners, 15⁵/₈ x 12¹/₂ x 3¹/₄in.
(Bonhams) $428

A Roman 17th century carved gilded and varnished frame of reverse section with pearl sight molding, 9¹/₂ x 6¹/₄ x 1³/₄in.
(Bonhams) $650

An Italian 17th century carved and gilded frame of reverse section with an imbricated leaf sight edge, 18 x 13⁷/₈ x 4in.
(Bonhams) $770

A Louis XIV carved and gilded frame, the corners and centers carved with anthemia and ovals with flowers flanked by interwoven C-scrolls, 31⁷/₈ x 36¹/₂in.
(Christie's) $24,489

A Spanish early seventeenth century carved and gilded frame, the dentil outer edge surmounted by acanthus scroll and tulip motif cresting, 42⁷/₈ x 33¹/₈in.
(Christie's) $15,840

A French Regency carved and gilded frame, the anthemia corners and scallop shell centers flanked by opposed c-scrolls, foliage and flowers, 35¹/₂ x 41³/₄in.
(Christie's) $4,898

A fine French gilt composition frame of hollow section with lamb's tongue sight, pearl, and imbricated leaf top edge, 21 x 16⁵/₈ x 3¹/₄in.
(Bonhams) $445

A Spanish seventeenth century carved, gilded and painted cassetta frame, with scrolling foliate central plate, 23¹/₈ x 28¹/₄in.
(Christie's) $3,768

An Italian late 16th century black and gilt cassetta frame with scraffito cauliculi ornament to the centers and corners of the frieze, 19³/₈ x 14¹/₈ x 4in.
(Bonhams) $2,052

A Louis XIV carved and gilded frame, the anthemia corners and flowerspray centers flanked by opposed C-scrolls, 18½ x 21¾in. (Christie's) $3,579

A fine French Louis XV carved, gilded and pierced frame, the acanthus rail running to center cartouche, 11 x 9¾ x 4in. (Bonhams) $855

An Italian seventeenth century carved and gilded frame, with ribbon-and-stick outer edge, 38¼ x 32⅞in. (Christie's) $3,768

A Spanish eighteenth century carved, gilded and painted frame, with punched scrolling foliage and flowers running to similar corner panels, 29⅞ x 23⅞in. (Christie's) $7,912

An Italian seventeenth century carved, gilded and painted cassetta frame, with imbricated leaf outer edge, the central plate with cauliculi centers, 15¾ x 14¼in. (Christie's) $2,826

A Spanish eighteenth century carved, gilded and painted frame, with marbled central plate, foliate inner edge and bar-and-quadruple-bead sight edge, 30⅝ x 26½in. (Christie's) $2,261

A Louis XVI carved and gilded frame, with gadrooned raised outer edge and cartouche cresting flanked by foliage and flowers, 24¼ x 18⅝in. (Christie's) $3,960

A Lombard early sixteenth century carved and gilded tabernacle frame, the entablature supported by pilasters flanked by volutes, overall size 18½ x 14¾in. (Christie's) $7,524

An Italian seventeenth century carved and gilded frame, with scrolling acanthus outer edge and raking gadrooned knull raised inner edge, 20½ x 34in. (Christie's) $7,920

PLASTER

A composition and plaster overlaid on linen male torso, 51in. high, on a block plinth.
(Christie's) $2,250

An Art Deco silvered plaster figure of a naked female with a hoop, circa 1935, 11½in. high. $185

A plaster bust by Phoebe Stabler, of the head of a maiden, on an oval section cut-sided base, 1942, 31.5cm. high.
(Christie's) $788

A painted plaster-of-Paris bust of Thomas Edison, head and shoulders, signed *G. Tinworth 1888 and Doulton & Co., Lambeth*, the front inscribed *EDISON with Colonel Gouraud's compliments*, 22½in. high.
(Christie's) $2,000

An English patinated plaster bas-relief of 'Cathal and the Woodfolk', cast from a model by Charles Sargeant Jagger, satyrs, centaurs and nymphs in Bacchic abandon, circa 1912–14, 19⅞ x 31⅛in.
(Christie's) $4,216

A late 19th century French plaster bust of 'L'Espiegle', signed on the shoulder *J.B. Carpeaux*, 51cm. high.
(Christie's) $2,850

A plaster figure of a scantily clad classical lady running with her right arm raised holding a goblet, 98in. high.
(Christie's) $4,000

A pair of polychrome-painted plaster figures of Chinamen in court dress with nodding heads, both holding ceremonial staffs, early 19th century, 15¾in. high.
(Christie's) $8,910

A rare plaster figure of the young Charlie Chaplin standing dressed as a tramp, his oversized boots above named base, 15½in. high.
(David Lay) $708

A portrait miniature of Helen L. and Arthur V. Cunningham by Mrs. Moses B. Russell, 1852, on a shaded orange and brown field, in gold frame, 1¹/₂in. high.
(Christie's) $3,850

Gabriel Xavier Montaut (1798–1852), a lady, in green dress with double-frilled lace collar, two bands in her dark curls, signed and dated *1820*, 2¹/₈in. diameter.
(Christie's) $1,266

A portrait miniature of Mr. Thomas Chase by Robert Field, 1804, with brown wavy hair, black coat, on a shaded brown field, 3in. long.
(Christie's) $5,500

A portrait miniature of John Rutledge by Charles Fraser (1782–1860), with powdered wig, black jacket, and ruffled shirt, 4¹/₈ x 3¹/₂in.
(Christie's) $7,700

Attributed to James Sanford Ellsworth (active 1835–1855), a portrait of Elizabeth Jackson Hill, sitter identified on verso, embossed paper, 3 x 2¹/₂in.
(Skinner Inc.) $1,980

Miniature portrait of Captain Robert Thomas, 1815, unsigned, identified *Capt. Robert Thomas 1815* in ink below image, 3 x 3¹/₄in.
(Skinner Inc.) $935

A portrait miniature of J. Pringle attributed to Henry Benbridge, circa 1780, with powdered white wig, wearing a brown coat with blue waistcoat on a shaded blue field, 1³/₄in. high.
(Christie's) $440

A portrait miniature of Peter Augustus Jay, American, circa 1840, with brown hair and blue eyes, in engraved gold oval frame, 1³/₄in. long.
(Christie's) $880

Thomas Forster (fl. circa 1700), a lady, full face in décolleté dress with white underslip, foliage background, plumbago, signed and dated *1702*, oval, 4⁵/₈in. high.
(Christie's) $13,629

Richard Crosse (1742–1810), a gentleman, facing right, in green coat with brown buttons and brown waistcoat, powdered wig, gold frame with bright-cut border, oval, 2in. high.
(Christie's) $1,496

Moritz Michael Daffinger (1790–1849), a lady, facing right, in low-cut white dress, a ribbon around her waist, her dark hair held in large curls, signed on the obverse, oval, 3in. high.
(Christie's) $13,200

William Grimaldi (1751–1830), after John Hoppner, R.A. (1758–1810), H.R.H. Frederica, Duchess of York, facing right, in low-cut white dress, oval, 2³/₄in. high.
(Christie's) $4,400

Frederick Buck (1771–circa 1839/1840), an officer, possibly James Davidson, wearing the scarlet uniform of the Royal Irish Fusiliers, gold frame, the reverse with gold monogram J.D. on plaited hair, oval, 2¹/₂in. high.
(Christie's) $1,021

John Smart (1742–1811), a lady, facing right, in loose white dress with blue ribbon at shoulders, white plumed turban headgear, her brown curled hair falling to her shoulders, oval, 2³/₄in. high.
(Christie's) $28,160

John Smart (1742–1811), an officer, facing right, in the uniform of the 2nd Battalion of the Madras Presidency Foot Artillery, white waistcoat and frilled cravat, signed with initials and dated 1791, oval, 2¹/₂in. high.
(Christie's) $17,600

Dominicus du Caju (1802–1867), a lady, seated half length, in low-cut embroidered white dress edged in lace, a red shawl draped around her shoulders, signed on the obverse, circular 3³/₄in. diameter.
(Christie's) $5,280

John Smart (1742–1811), a lady, facing right, in white dress with ruffled collar, short dark hair, signed with initials and dated 1800, gold frame with glass reverse, oval, 3in. high.
(Christie's) $19,360

Attributed to Elizabeth Marie Delatour (1750–1834), Camille Desmoulins, facing right, in blue coat, black-spotted yellow waistcoat, signed on the obverse, gilt-metal frame, circular, 2³/₄in. diameter.
(Christie's) $1,760

Moritz Michael Daffinger (1790–1849), Princess Clementine Melterwich, full face, in white dress secured by a triple strand of pearls, signed on the obverse, oval, 3in. high. (Christie's) $7,040

Sampson Towgood Roch (1759–1847), an officer, possibly Henry Pottinger, facing left, wearing the scarlet uniform of the 38th Regiment of Foot with silver epaulettes, oval, 2³/₄in. high. (Christie's) $7,920

Abraham Daniel (died 1806), Masters Charles and Samuel Black, the younger boy held in his brother's arms, in brown jackets and white shirts with lace collars, oval, 4¹/₂in. high. (Christie's) $5,280

Samuel Cooper (1609–1672), a gentleman, facing left, wearing breastplate with gilt studs and white lawn collar, long brown curling hair and mustache, on vellum, dated *1645*, oval, 2¹/₂in. high. (Christie's) $14,080

Richard Schwager (1822–1880), a young girl, seated on a cushion, in low-cut white dress edged in lace, red sash and bows at shoulders, a straw hat and child's doll beside her, signed and dated *1868*, oval, 3⁷/₈in. high. (Christie's) $6,160

Bernard Lens (1682–1740), Anna Maria Whitmore, holding a fan, in gray dress sprigged in crimson and edged with lace, with gauze bodice and apron, signed with monogram and dated *1791*, oval, 3³/₄in. high. (Christie's) $10,560

Alexander Gallaway (fl. circa 1794–1812?), a lady, facing left, in gray-blue dress with black lace-border, white fichu, and white cap with gray ribbon and bow, signed and dated *1795*, oval, 2³/₈in. high. (Christie's) $1,584

Peter Paillou (died after 1820), a gentleman, facing left, in brown coat, white shirt and lace cravat, signed and dated *1790* on the obverse, oval, 2¹/₄in. high. (Christie's) $15,840

Nicholas Hilliard (1547–1619) and Lawrence Hilliard (1581–1647), a gentleman, nearly full face, in black doublet embroidered with leaves, on vellum, gold frame, oval, 2in. high. (Christie's) $21,120

531

George Engleheart (1750–1829), a gentleman, nearly full face, in black coat, white shirt and frilled cravat, sky background, oval, 3¹/₈in. high.
(Christie's) $2,640

Joseph Einsle (1794–died post 1850), a young boy, seated beside his wooden cart, full length on a grassy bank, signed and dated *1821*, 2¹/₂in. diameter.
(Christie's) $1,760

Richard Cosway, R.A. (1742–1821), a gentleman, facing right, in blue coat with gold buttons, white waistcoat, white shirt and cravat, oval, 2⁷/₈in. high.
(Christie's) $3,168

Charles Robertson (circa 1760–1821), a lady, facing right, in low-cut blue dress with lace edging, her curled brown hair upswept and falling to her shoulders, gold frame with plaited hair border, oval, 1³/₄in. high.
(Christie's) $1,056

Alexandre Lenoir (fl. circa 1810), Lady Campbell, facing left, in low-cut white dress edged with lace, a pink shawl around her shoulders, inscribed in pencil on the reverse, rectangular, 3⁵/₈in. high.
(Christie's) $704

John Thomas Barber Beaumont (1774–1841), Mr. Howing, facing right, in black coat, white waistcoat and cravat, signed with initials on the obverse, gold frame, the reverse with lock of hair tied with gold wire and seed pearls, oval, 2³/₄in. high.
(Christie's) $1,760

Richard Crosse (1742–1810), a gentleman, facing right, in blue coat, white waistcoat and tied cravat, powdered hair en queue, gold frame with bright-cut border, oval, 2³/₄in. high.
(Christie's) $5,280

Attributed to Francis Sykes (fl. circa 1746–1763), a lady, facing right, in low-cut green dress with lace edging, red stone and drop pearl brooches at corsage, oval, 2¹/₈in. high.
(Christie's) $616

Continental School, circa 1794, Emperor Francis I of Austria, facing right, in green coat with red facings, on parchment, indistinctly signed and dated, gilt-metal mount, 4in. high.
(Christie's) $1,144

Andrew Plimer (1763–1837), Christian, Lady Boston, facing left, in décolleté white dress and matching bandeau in her curling hair, gold frame, oval, 3¹/₈in. high. (Christie's) $2,288

George Engleheart (1750/3–1829), Colonel Black, facing right, in scarlet uniform with buff color facings and silver epaulette, oval, 1³/₄in. high. (Christie's) $2,288

Samuel John Stump (1778–1863), a gentleman, full face, in brown coat, white waistcoat and cravat, signed on the obverse and dated *1805*, oval, 2⁵/₈in. high. (Christie's) $2,464

English School, circa 1805, Elizabeth and Marianne Austen as children, three-quarter length, in white dresses, the latter wearing a sprigged bonnet and holding a basket of cherries, oval, 3¹/₃in. high. (Christie's) $1,848

William S. Doyle (1769–1828), Miss Mary Eliza Byrne, facing left, in low-cut white dress with lace edging, an embroidered shawl around her shoulders, gilt-wood frame, rectangular, 3¹/₂in. high. (Christie's) $1,232

Charles Jagger (circa 1770–1827), a gentleman, facing left, in blue coat with black collar and gold-colored buttons, white waistcoat and cravat, signed on obverse and reverse, gold frame, oval, 2¹/₂in. high. (Christie's) $1,144

Anna Tonnelli (née Nistri) (1763–1846), John Adamson Rice, facing right, in blue coat with gold buttons and black collar, white shirt and frilled cravat, inscribed on reverse *1798*, oval, 3¹/₈in. high. (Christie's) $1,672

Richard Crosse (1742–1810), a young man, possibly Edward Crosse, in profile, leaning against a table beside a globe, reading a book, in purple coat and white shirt, oval, 2³/₄in. high. (Christie's) $1,496

Abraham Daniel (died 1805), an officer, facing right, wearing the scarlet uniform of the 65th Foot, later the York and Lancaster Regiment, with silver epaulettes and white cross band, oval, 3in. high. (Christie's) $4,752

Christian Friedrich Carl Kleemann (1735–1789), a gentleman, in mauve coat with black collar and silver buttons, matching waistcoat and lace shirt, powdered hair en queue, signed, silver frame, oval, 1⅞in. high. (Christie's) $3,802

Johann Christian Schoeller (1782–1851), a lady, in low-cut blue dress trimmed with white lace, wearing a gold tiara with pearls in her curly hair, sky background, signed and dated 1823, oval, 4¾in. high. (Christie's) $6,336

Follower of Herman van der Mijn (1684–1741), a young girl, in white chemise and beige-lined blue cloak, oil on copper, oval, 2¾in. high. (Christie's) $676

Attributed to Friedrich-Georg Dinglinger (1666–1720), a gentleman, in purple coat with gold-laced buttons and white lace cravat, full-bottomed wig, enamel, gilt-metal frame, oval, 2¾in. high. (Christie's) $1,690

Maximilien (?) Villers (fl. circa 1790), a gentleman, in blue coat with two buttons bearing the initials *A* and *G* respectively, turquoise and yellow striped waistcoat, powdered hair, signed and dated 1789, circular 2⅝in. diameter. (Christie's) $13,728

Moritz Michael Daffinger (1790–1849), Lieutenant-Colonel Peter Delancey, in scarlet uniform of the 75th (Stirlingshire) Regiment of Foot, with buff facings, silver lace and epaulette, signed, oval, 3¼in. high. (Christie's) $15,840

David Logan (1635–1692), Sir Henry Blount, in doublet with small buttons, white collar and tied ribbon, full-bottomed wig, dated 1679, oval, 5¼in. high. (Christie's) $896

Andrew Plimer (1763–1837), Louisa Plimer, the artist's daughter, in lace trimmed décolleté white dress with short sleeves, curly brown hair, rectangular, 3⅜in. high. (Christie's) $8,959

Lorentz Lars Svensson Sparrgren (1763–1828), Benjamin Franklin, in gray-blue coat and waistcoat, white frilled shirt, signed, chiseled gilt-metal frame, oval, 3½in. high. (Christie's) $5,280

Sampson Towgood Roch (1759–1847), a lady, facing left, in low-cut pale blue dress with lace neckline adorned with a single strand of pearls, her brown hair up-swept and curls falling to her shoulders, signed and dated *1788*, oval, 2⅝in. high. (Christie's) $968

André-Leon Larue, called Mansion (1785–1834), a lady, in low-cut black dress and white fichu gathered in a high lace ruff, matching bonnet decorated with pink roses and buds, signed and dated 1821, oval, 2⅞in. high. (Christie's) $6,758

William Prewitt (fl. circa 1740), a lady, in décolleté pink dress with white underslip and blue stole, wearing a black hat decorated with large white plumes, oval, 1⅞in. high. (Christie's) $3,186

Louis-Marie Autissier (1772–1830), a lady, in décolleté mauve dress and white fichu gathered with pearl clasps, pink roses in her curly hair, signed and dated *Paris 1822*, oval, 3in. high. (Christie's) $1,394

Thomas Hazlehurst, a gentleman, in brown coat with black velvet collar, white waistcoat and white tied cravat, powdered hair, signed with initials, oval, 2⅝in. high. (Christie's S. Ken) $644

Fanny Charrin (fl. circa 1820), a lady, in low-cut black dress with white underslip, twisted gold colored ropes round her waist, signed in full on obverse, oval, 3in. high. (Christie's) $796

Jean Baptiste Isabey (1767–1855), Count Vassili Ivanovitch Apraksin, in green uniform of an Adjutant Suit of the Tsar, with scarlet facings, silver lace and epaulettes, on card, signed, oval, 5½in. high. (Christie's) $12,671

William Booth (1807–1845), a gentleman, half-length, facing left, in black coat and waistcoat, white shirt and cravat, gilt-metal mount within black frame, rectangular, 3½in. high. (Christie's) $493

Jean-Baptiste Singry (1782–1824), a lady, in elaborately frilled white dress with blue striped shawl, tied at corsage, her black hair upswept in curls, signed, oval, 6in. high. (Christie's) $2,389

Nathaniel Currier, publisher (active 1835–1907), Across the Continent, "Westward the Course of Empire Takes Its Way", by F.F. Palmer (Conningham 33; Peterz 2085), lithograph with hand-coloring, 1868, on wove paper, 17³/₄ x 27¹/₄in.
(Christie's) $14,300

Paul Revere (American, 1735–1807), *A View of the Obelisk erected under Liberty-Tree in Boston on the Rejoicings for the Repeal of the – Stamp-Act 1766*, signed in the plate *Paul Revere Sculp*, engraving on laid paper with fleur-de-lis watermark, plate size 10 x 13⁵/₈in.
(Skinner Inc.) $48,400

Pablo Picasso, Deux Femmes, linocut printed in colors, 1959, on Arches, a fine impression signed in pencil, numbered 19/50, 528 x 646mm.
(Christie's) $37,840

Roy Lichtenstein, Sweet Dreams Baby!, screenprint in colors, 1965, on stiff wove paper, an exceptionally fine, fresh impression, the yellow vibrant, signed in pencil, numbered 61/200, 906 x 651mm.
(Christie's) $32,164

Marie Laurencin, Les Trois Têtes, lithograph, printed in colors, on B.F.K. Rives, signed in pencil and numbered 64/75, 502 x 650mm.
(Phillips) $15,993

'Martini', by Louis Icart, etching and drypoint, printed in colors, signed lower right with artist's blindstamp, Copyright 1932, 34 x 44cm.
(Christie's) $9,130

PRINTS

Charles H. Crosby & Co., Boston, lithographer,
(American, 1819–1896), *Built by the Amoskeag
Manufacturing Company*/early fire engines,
identified in the matrix, chromolithograph on
paper, sheet size 24 x 31⁷/₈in.
(Skinner Inc.) **$4,675**

Bernard Buffet, St. Tropez la Baie, lithograph
in colors, 1977, on Arches, signed in pencil
and inscribed *E.A.*, one of thirty,
500 x 650mm.
(Phillips) **$13,861**

'Coursing III', by Louis Icart, etching and
drypoint, printed in colors, signed lower right,
with artist's blindstamp, Copyright 1930 by L.
Icart-Paris, 40 x 64,5cm.
(Christie's) **$6,939**

'Summer Dreams', by Louis Icart, etching and
drypoint, printed in colors, signed lower right
Copyright by L. Icart Sty. N.Y., 33 x 46cm.
(Christie's) **$12,782**

Pablo Picasso (1881-1973), Le Repas frugal,
etching, 1904, on wove paper, a very good
impression, one of 250 impressions, after steel-
facing printed on this paper by Vollard in
1913, 463 x 377mm.
(Christie's) **$184,195**

Paul Signac (1863-1935), Les Andelys,
lithograph printed in colors, 1895, on wove
paper, third (final) state, signed in pencil,
numbered 23 from the edition of 40,
303 x 453mm.
(Christie's) **$23,837**

Currier and Ives, Publishers (American, 19th century) after Arthur Fitzwilliam Tait (American, 1819–1905), "American hunting scene/An early start", 1863, image size 18³/₄ x 27⁵/₈in.
(Skinner Inc.) $3,850

Currier and Ives, Publishers, The American National Game of Base Ball, Grand Match for the Championship at the Elysian Fields, Hoboken, N.J., lithograph with hand-coloring, 1866, on wove paper, 19³/₄ x 29³/₄in.
(Christie's) $16,500

Framed colored lithograph, American, mid-19th century, *Washington Entering New York*, by Herline & Henzel, with original key, 28¹/₂ x 42in.
(Eldred's) $715

Paul Nash, A Shell Bursting, Passchendaele, lithograph, 1918, from the edition of 25, signed, dated and entitled in pencil, on cream antique laid paper, 386 x 534mm.
(Phillips) $2,488

Superb framed colored lithograph after a painting by W.L. Walton, *The International Contest of Heenan and Sayer at Farnsborough on the 17th of April, 1860*, by Bufford Sons, Boston, 31¹/₂ x 40¹/₂in.
(Eldred's) $2,200

Currier and Ives, publishers, Life in the Woods, "Returning to Camp", by L. Maurer, lithograph with hand-coloring and touches of gum arabic, 1860, on wove paper, with margins, 18¹³/₁₆ x 27³/₄in.
(Christie's) $3,300

QUILTS

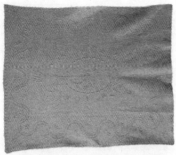

A white-on-white stuffed and quilted cotton coverlet, American, dated 1810, centered by a trapunto floral vase surrounded by a continuous scrolling trapunto princess feather vine design, 77 x 90in.
(Christie's) $3,850

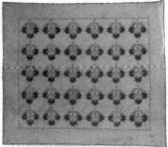

An appliqued and trapunto quilted coverlet, Maryland, circa 1850, worked in the Carolina Lily pattern on a white ground with repeating stuffed pineapples and leaves framed by a pieced sawtooth inner border, 83 x 95in.
(Christie's) $1,000

A pieced and appliqued cotton quilted coverlet, Pennsylvania, 1910, worked on a grid with thirty blocks of four repeating designs, the profiles of Abraham Lincoln and of George Washington alternating with a patriotic shield and a top hat, 76 x 86in.
(Christie's) $850

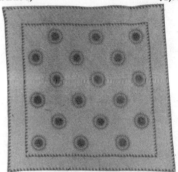

A pieced appliqued and trapunto quilted cotton coverlet, American, 19th century, worked in a mariner's compass pattern with eighteen squares of appliqued red-printed mariner's compass alternating with eighteen squares of trapunto scrolling wreath, 88¼ x 90in. (Christie's) $3,520

Pieced linsey-woolsey quilt, America, late 18th/early 19th century, worked in lavender and yellow diamond patches, heightened with basket weave quilting, 101 x 95in.
(Skinner Inc.) $495

Pieced and appliquéd quilt, America, second half 19th century, "basket of flowers" pattern worked in printed navy blue patches, 80 x 82in.
(Skinner Inc.) $900

QUILTS

Pieced quilt, America, late 19th/early 20th century, worked in red, green, yellow and pink printed cotton patches arranged in the "Star of Bethlehem" pattern, 74 x 85in.
(Skinner Inc.) $330

An Amish cotton quilted coverlet, Midwestern, circa 1930, worked in the flower basket pattern with lilac baskets on a black diamond-stitched ground, 77 x 84in.
(Christie's) $1,045

A pieced and appliqued cotton quilted coverlet, probably New York, circa 1860, worked in the Bethlehem Star pattern with green and red calico on a white diamond-stitched ground, 96 x 96in.
(Christie's) $2,200

A pieced and appliqued friendship quilt, South Carolina, circa 1850, the broderie perse quilt composed of twenty-five blocks separated by chintz sashing, the blocks of various designs including many floral motifs, a stag, a classical female equestrian, and Zachary Taylor, 93 x 91in. (Christie's) $4,400

A pieced and appliqued cotton quilted coverlet, American, circa 1840, the central star worked in a variety of cotton prints of green, red, blue, brown and purple shades surrounded by spandrels of chintz trophies and wreaths, 99 x 100in.
(Christie's) $4,620

A pieced and appliqued cotton album quilt top, New England, circa 1850, worked in twenty squares of various designs including a red brick house, a deer, crossed flags, an anchor, patriotic shields, and numerous fruit and floral motifs, 72 x 88in.
(Christie's) $2,860

QUILTS

A pieced silk coverlet, American, late 19th century, worked in the pineapple pattern with a variety of prints including plaid, polka dot, stripe, and floral, 60 x 62in.
(Christie's) $1,430

Unusual pieced and appliqued sunburst quilt, America, 19th century, each of the twenty squares with layers of appliqued triangular yellow, red and green cotton patches, 88 x 71in.
(Skinner Inc.) $523

A pieced and appliqued cotton quilted coverlet, American, early 20th century, worked in the schoolhouse pattern with blue, red, orange, and green cotton on a white ground surrounded by a wide blue border, 75 x 80in.
(Christie's) $2,970

An International Order of Oddfellows pieced and appliqued cotton quilted coverlet, American, circa 1865, worked in nine squares of a heart-and-hand design on a diamond-stitched white ground, 82 x 83in.
(Christie's) $1,430

An Amish cotton and wool quilted coverlet, American, circa 1930, worked in the grandmother's dream pattern with twelve blocks in violet, blue, burgundy, and black, 68 x 86in.
(Christie's) $2,860

Pieced quilt, America, late 19th/early 20th century, worked in yellow, red and white cotton patches arranged in the "Star of Bethlehem" pattern, 75 x 78in.
(Skinner Inc.) $715

A rare Amish or Mennonite pieced cotton quilted coverlet, Lancaster County, Pennsylvania, worked in the sawtooth diamond-in-the-square pattern with a central rose sawtooth diamond stitched *Martin M. Lichty 1879*, 84 x 86in.
(Christie's)   **$6,050**

A pieced cotton quilted coverlet, American, circa 1890, the central Lone Star worked in yellow, red, black and blue calico on a blue calico ground with Princess Feather stitching surrounded by a red calico sawtooth border, 82 x 81in.
(Christie's)   **$770**

A pieced and appliqued stuffed and quilted cotton coverlet, American, mid-19th century, worked in brown calico on a white cotton ground centered by a Rising Star with floral trapunto corner blocks, 95 x 97in.
(Christie's)   **$2,200**

An Amish pieced wool and cotton quilted coverlet, probably Ohio, dated *1914*, worked in twenty-four blocks of the Flying Geese pattern on a black ground, with an olive-green binding, 67 x 85½in.
(Christie's)   **$3,300**

An Amish pieced and appliqued quilted cotton coverlet, probably Ohio, circa 1920, worked in red and white in twenty blocks of Hole in the Barn Door pattern variation alternating with blocks of scrolling Princess Feather leaves, 89 x 72in.
(Christie's)   **$1,650**

A pieced and appliqued quilted cotton coverlet, American, mid-19th century, worked in eleven blocks of Mariner's Compass pattern with green, blue, orange, and red calico centred by halved Mariner's Compass blocks and quartered corner blocks of similar design, 84 x 95in.
(Christie's)   **$2,420**

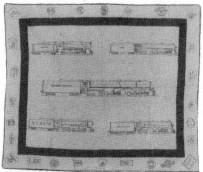

An embroidered cotton pictorial quilt, American, circa 1930, worked in red thread on a white ground framed by a wide red rectangular inner border, depicting numerous train engines and cars, 82 x 68in.
(Christie's) $2,090

A pieced and appliqued quilted cotton coverlet, American, mid-19th entury, centered by a scrolling bud and floral medallion of green, red, and yellow calico surrounded by a continuous scrolling floral and bud vine, 89 x 92in.
(Christie's) $4,400

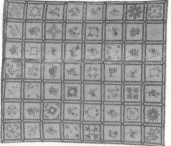

A pieced and appliqued cotton quilt top, Maryland, circa 1854, worked in fifty-six blocks of chintz and calico on a white ground with red sashing and depicting various designs including broderie perse floral bouquets, 94 x 81in.
(Christie's) $1,760

An Amish quilted wool coverlet, initialed A.S., probably Lancaster County, Pennsylvania, circa 1925, worked in the Diamond in the Square pattern with green and red wool on a diamond-stitched blue ground, 76½ x 78in.
(Christie's) $2,640

An Amish quilted wool and wool crepe coverlet, probably Lancaster County, Pennsylvania, circa 1940, worked in the Diamond in the Square design, the maroon diamond with Star, Princess Feather and Grape quilting on a jade diamond-stitched square, 75 x 74in.
(Christie's) $2,200

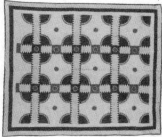

A pieced and appliqued cotton quilted coverlet, American, late 19th century, worked in green, red and yellow cotton on a white ground with six blocks of the New York Beauty pattern surrounded by echo stitching centered by rosettes, 76 x 90in.
(Christie's) $880

1930's period bakelite cased rocking ship clock, (electrically operated) in the form of a radio case.
(G.A. Key) $397

A 'bangle' radio for National Panasonic, yellow plastic.
(Bonhams) $75

A G.E.C. mottled brown bakelite electric radio, of rectangular form with white rectangular dial flanked by louvre speakers, $7^1/2$in. high.
(Christie's) $275

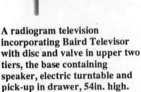

A radiogram television incorporating Baird Televisor with disc and valve in upper two tiers, the base containing speaker, electric turntable and pick-up in drawer, 54in. high.
(Christie's) $3,500

An S.O.E. agent's suitcase wireless receiver/transmitter (Transceiver no. 3 Mark II, known also as B2) with earphones and tap key, $16^1/2$ x $12^1/2$in.
(Christie's) $2,167

An English transparent plastic radio for Zarach 1971, of cube form, 15cm. high.
(Bonhams) $220

A Bush Model AC3 mains receiver with molded wood fret in 'Cathedral' style walnut-veneered cabinet, 18in. high, circa 1932.
(Christie's) $876

A Marconiphone Multivalve Type RB7 receiver in smoker's cabinet style mahogany case with BBC transfer, $20^1/2$in. high, circa 1923.
(Christie's) $6,500

A Philco 'People's Set' Model A527 5-valve mains receiver in brown bakelite case, $15^1/2$in. high, circa 1937.
(Christie's) $623

A piece of paper inscribed to a fan and signed *Love, love, love, love, love, love, love, love, love? Jimi Hendrix.*
(Christie's S. Ken) $1,264

A tooled leather guitar strap decorated with artist's name *Bill Haley* and a floral pattern, 49in. long, used by Haley in the late 1970s.
(Christie's) $817

An illustrated souvenir tour programme *Rolling Stones 1966* signed inside on fly leaf by all five members of the group in blue biro.
(Christie's) $817

John Entwistle, a Hamer Explorer twelve-string bass guitar, in cherry sunburst, rosewood fretboard, Schaller machine heads, active electronics, di Marzio pick-ups, flamed maple top and mahogany body, 48¹/₂in. in flightcase.
(Christie's) $1,452

Elvis Presley, an important autograph letter, signed, [n.d. but October 28th 1958] Hotel Grunewald, Bad Nauheim, Den, Terrassenstrasse 10, to Anita Wood, telling her of his intentions to marry her.
(Christie's) $7,260

A full-size Spanish classical acoustic guitar, with ebony fretboard, spruce top signed and inscribed *To Simon, Best Wishes, Bob Dylan, 10.12.86.*
(Christie's) $1,180

Madonna, a presentation 'Multi-Platinum' disc, *Presented to Kim Gifford in recognition of your outstanding efforts in helping to achieve sales of over 1,200,000 units in the UK of 'The Immaculate Collection'.*
(Christie's) $648

A portrait photograph of Jimi Hendrix by Jim Marshall 1967, printed in 1989, taken at the sound check for the Monterey Pop Festival 17th June 1967, signed, 11¹/₈ x 16¹/₄in.
(Christie's) $817

An American one sheet poster for Labyrinth, Tri-Star Pictures, 1986, signed and inscribed *Michael – Thank you, Jim Henson* and *For Michael with very best wishes, Bowie '91,* framed, 38¹/₂ x 26³/₄in.
(Christie's) $370

Elvis Presley, a boxer's robe of cream satin, the back with appliquéd clover leaf emblem and lettering *KID GALAHAD*, with copy of Elvis Monthly Star Special number one, circa 1962 featuring Elvis wearing the robe.
(Christie's) $8,712

A cream fun fur 'butcher boy' cap with printed label *Imitation Fourrure*, purchased for Cynthia by John Lennon on their honeymoon in Paris, September 16th, 1963.
(Christie's) $436

John Lennon, an autograph postcard, signed addressed to Melody Maker's Raver column using strong language in response to their article regarding the possibility of Yoko Ono working with Miles Davis.
(Christie's) $1,361

A printed menu for the B.O.A.C. ... BEATLES BAHAMAS SPECIAL 1965, signed on the cover by John Lennon three times and by Paul McCartney, George Harrison and Ringo Starr.
(Christie's) $1,452

An album cover, *Meet The Beatles!*, Capitol Records, 1964, signed on the back by all four members of the group in blue biro.
(Christie's) $2,178

A three-quarter length machine-print photograph of Paul McCartney cleaning his teeth circa 1964, signed *Love Paul McCartney* one front tooth reputedly colored-in, in blue biro by McCartney himself, 8¼ x 6in.
(Christie's) $472

John Lennon, an autograph postcard signed, frankmarked Singapore 25th October 1976, to Julian Lennon *Dear Julian, what happened to ya? love Dad & Yoko*.
(Christie's) $1,452

Janis Joplin, a pair of portrait photographs by Jim Marshall, 1968, printed in 1988 taken in subject's dressing room backstage at the Winterland Ballroom, San Francisco.
(Christie's) $581

A piece of paper signed and inscribed *J Morrison cheers THE DOORS*, in common mount with a portrait photograph of the subject, framed.
(Christie's) $1,271

An early group photograph of
The Beatles including Pete Best
circa 1962, signed by all four
members of the group on the
back, 7 x 8¹/₂in.
(Christie's) $1,089

An official fan club card, 1963,
signed on the Dezo Hoffmann
photograph by each member of
the group and inscribed *To
Gwen love from THE BEATLES*
in Paul McCartney's hand.
(Christie's) $944

An early black and white
portrait of the Rolling Stones,
signed on the front by all five
members of the band, including
Brian Jones, in black ink, 10 x
12in.
(Christie's) $635

A souvenir concert programme
for The Beatles/Mary Wells
tour, 1964, signed on the cover
by each member of the group in
black biro.
(Christie's) $1,543

A 'short' birth certificate issued
on the 12th August 1960,
inscribed John Lennon's details:
*Name and Surname: John
Winston Lennon, Sex: Boy, Date
of Birth: Ninth October 1940,
Place of Birth – Registration
District: Liverpool.*
(Christie's) $2,904

John Lennon, a rare typescript
letter, signed, *22nd June 1974,
1.W. & 72 NY. NY. apt.72*, to
Cynthia, annotated with a
caricature of a smiling face
between two flowers, in colored
felt pens. 1p.
(Christie's) $3,993

A souvenir concert programe
for The Beatles Show 1963,
signed and inscribed *To Marie...*
by all four members of the
group on the fly leaf.
(Christie's) $998

A rare English souvenir concert
program, 1958, signed on the
back cover by *Buddy Holly,
Jerry Allison* and *Joe Mauldin* in
blue and black biro.
(Christie's) $1,634

A portrait photograph of Rod
Stewart by Jim Marshall, the
subject sitting on a bed in
pyjamas and looking into a
teapot, 1974, 8 x 12in. framed.
(Christie's) $399

A rare Scottish Tour program, 1963, signed on the cover by each member of the group In blue biro.
(Christie's) $1,634

The Beatles, an album, *Please Please Me*, 1963, signed on the back cover by all four members of the group.
(Christie's) $1,316

An important hand-made and illustrated Christmas card given to Cynthia Powell in December 1958, including two pen and ink self-portraits of John and Cynthia.
(Christie's) $14,520

A monochrome concert poster, *The Who, The Grateful Dead, Oakland Stadium*, circa late 1970s, signed by Pete Townshend, Roger Daltry and John Entwistle, 18¼ x 15½in. framed.
(Christie's) $607

Jimi Hendrix, a black felt hat trimmed with an American Indian style band of leather and metal decorated with circular panels, worn by Hendrix on stage, circa 1963.
(Christie's) $9,108

A rare single-sided acetate for *Black Star, 20th Century Fox Film Corp.* white label with typescript details giving title of song by *Elvis Presley And Orchestra*, 78 r.p.m.
(Christie's) $4,655

An illustrated souvenir concert program for *The Beatles at the Royal Hall Harrogate, March 8th 1963*, signed on the cover by each member of the group in blue or black ink and biro, 8 x 5¾in.
(Christie's) $1,214

The Jam/Rick Buckler, a Union Jack jacket with maker's woven label, *Carnaby Cavern, London* stitched inside, worn by Rick Buckler for promotional purposes.
(Christie's) $850

A rare concert poster for *Hastings Pier Sunday, 22nd October 7.30–11*, 1967, featuring *Jimi Hendrix Experience plus full supporting program*, 29½ x 20in.
(Christie's) $3,441

Elvis Presley, a publicity photograph, signed.
(Christie's) $567

Bob Dylan, an album cover *The Times They Are A-Changin'*, 1963, signed on the front by Bob Dylan in black felt pen.
(Christie's) $486

A concert poster, *The Sensational Rolling Stones* at the *Odeon, Southend, Saturday, 10th October*, 1964, 18¹/₂ x 12in.
(Christie's) $2,024

Michael Jackson, a rhinestone stage glove of white cotton stockinette encrusted with sparkling hand-sewn imitation diamonds, with *Western Costume Co. Hollywood* woven label, printed with artist's name *Michael Jackson*.
(Christie's) $30,855

A black felt trilby signed and inscribed on underside of brim *All My Love Michael Jackson* and stamped with artist's name in gilt lettering on inside band.
(Christie's) $1,619

A pair of handcuffs made by Jay-Ree, Spain, 9in. long; accompanied by a photograph of Sid Vicious and Nancy wearing the handcuffs and a letter of authenticity from Sex Pistols' tour manager Boogie.
(Christie's) $769

Elvis Presley, a half-length publicity photograph circa early 1960s, signed and inscribed *To Linda Best Wishes Elvis Presley*, 6¹/₂ x 4¹/₂in. framed.
(Christie's) $445

A single-breasted three button jacket of multi-colored striped silk trimmed with scarlet collar and pocket flaps, worn by Keith Richards circa 1967.
(Christie's) $2,125

John and Yoko, a printed handbill *WAR IS OVER! If you Want It, Happy Christmas from John and Yoko* signed and inscribed *Love John Lennon and Yoko Ono Lennon*, 8¹/₄ x 6in.
(Christie's) $972

A half length publicity postcard Elvis Presley *in "Pulverdampf und heisse Lieder"* signed by subject in blue biro.
(Christie's) $508

The Beatles, an E.P., *Twist and Shout*, 1963, signed on the back cover by all four members of the group.
(Christie's) $972

A Coral Records promotional postcard, 1958, signed by Buddy Holly, Joe Mauldin and Jerry Allison, $5^3/4$ x $3^1/2$in.
(Christie's) $1,214

Jimi Hendrix and the Experience, a page from an autograph book signed and inscribed *Be good in whatever you do, Jimi Hendrix, Love Mitch, Noel Redding and Gerry (road manager)*.
(Christie's) $1,271

An early concert poster *Buddy Holly And The Crickets* at the *Philharmonic Hall, Hope Street, Liverpool, Thursday, 20th March, 1958*, $24^3/4$ x $17^3/4$in. framed.
(Christie's) $1,271

Four pieces of paper signed individually by Jim Morrison, John Densmore, Robby Krieger and Ray Manzarek, in common mount with a machine print photograph of the Doors, 22 x $27^1/2$in.
(Christie's) $1,720

A half-length publicity photograph circa early 1960s, signed *Best Wishes Elvis Presley* and inscribed in a different hand *To Wendy*, $9^1/8$ x $7^7/8$in.
(Christie's) $581

A self-published, limited edition book An American Prayer, 1970, signed on the title page *J. Morrison*, 20 unnumbered leaves, original boards, titled in gilt.
(Christie's) $3,086

A publicity photograph of The Beatles in The Bahamas, 1965, signed by each member of the group and inscribed *To Linda from The Beatles* in Ringo Starr's hand, $9^3/4$ x 8in. framed.
(Christie's) $648

An autograph letter signed, from Fats Domino to a fan *Dear David, to be honest with you I don't perticulary* (sic) *care for Rap* (?) *music*, 11½ x 8½in. (Christie's) **$648**

The Beatles, a E.P. cover, *All My Loving*, Parlophone, 1963, signed on the back in black ink by all four Beatles. (Christie's) **$2,530**

A Michael Jackson Phonograph, made by Vanity Fair, 1984, with instruction leaflet, in original box, 11 x 12½in. (Christie's) **$142**

George Harrison, a portrait photograph by Robert Whitaker, *Way Out*, 1965 (printed later), taken in the grounds of Chiswick House, May 20th, 1966, signed by photographer on margin, 20 x 16in. (Christie's) **$1,113**

A black leather jacket trimmed with black ribbed wool at the collar and hem, worn by John Lennon both on stage and as part of his personal wardrobe in Hamburg and Liverpool circa 1960–1962. (Christie's) **$44,528**

A piece of paper signed and inscribed *Love John Lennon* and *Yoko Ono*, additionally annotated with Lennon's characteristic portrait of their smiling faces, 16½ x 11in. framed. (Christie's) **$911**

A publicity photograph of the four Beatles in a recording studio circa 1963, signed by each member of the group in blue biro, 14 x 11in. (Christie's) **$1,316**

The Beatles, a single A Hard Day's Night Capitol Records, 1964, signed on the label by all four members of the group in blue biro. (Christie's) **$1,634**

Eric Clapton, a portrait photograph by Jim Marshall, 1967, printed later, signed, titled and dated by photographer, 20¾ x 16¾in. (Christie's) **$648**

Afshar Oriental rug, 5ft. x 9ft. 11in., with compartmented Tree of Life design on an ivory field, late 19th century.
(Eldred's) $1,210

Kuba long rug, Northeast Caucasus, late 19th century, 12ft. 7in. x 5ft. 4in.
(Skinner Inc.) $10,000

Heriz Oriental rug, 8ft. 5in. x 11ft. 8in., with central geometric medallion on a brick red field with geometric and floral elements.
(Eldred's) $3,080

South Caucasian long rug, late 19th century, the column of nine red, medium blue, red-brown, gold and teal octagonal medallions rest on the navy blue field, 10ft. 8in. x 4ft.
(Skinner Inc.) $1,100

Kurd village rug, Northwest Persia, early 20th century, with a narrow trefoil border, (small repairs, minor end fraying), 5ft. 4in. x 4ft. 6in.
(Skinner Inc.) $468

Shirvan Oriental rug, 4ft. x 8ft. 11in., with geometric elements on a navy blue field with animal and human figures, late 19th century.
(Eldred's) $2,860

Chinese rug, early 19th century, the circular open floral medallion surrounded by butterflies in shades of navy blue, ivory, rust and apricot, 6ft. 6in. x 3ft. 5in.
(Skinner Inc.) $7,500

A fine antique Sumak bag face, North East Caucasus, mid-19th century, the field covered with diagonal bands, 1ft. 7in. x 1ft. 9in.
(Phillips) $716

A Kashan rug, the ivory field with two columns of indigo and red floral medallions surrounded by flowerheads and vines, 6ft. 8in. x 4ft. 7in.
(Christie's S. Ken)

                              $2,217

A fine Lesghi rug, North East Caucasus, circa 1900, the dark indigo-blue field bearing a central row of characteristic Lesghi stars, 6ft. 3in. x 4ft. 4in. (Phillips) $2,385

Navajo Gray Hills rug, circa 1920, 48 x 84in. (Eldred's) $880

Oriental rug, Serab, 4ft. 5in. x 9ft. 11in., with central medallion on a natural camel hair ground with navy blue corners. (Eldred's) $1,320

Karabagh rug, South Caucasus, early 20th century, three large red, medium blue and abrashed camel octagonal medallions nearly cover the dark brown field, within a narrow ivory small scale "crab" border, (good condition), 7ft. x 4ft. 4in. (Skinner Inc.) $1,000

Hooked rug, America, 20th century, patterned in the manner of a prayer rug, 40 x 46in. (Skinner Inc.) $385

Eagle Karabagh rug, South Caucasus, early 20th century, two large sunburst medallions in shades of midnight and royal blue, 6ft. 8in. x 4ft. 3in. (Skinner Inc.) $1,320

Turkish prayer design Oriental rug, 3ft. 6in. x 5ft. 7in., with red and green design on a navy blue field, Western Anatolia, early 20th century. (Eldred's) $715

A fine antique Senneh Kelim, Persian Kurdistan, the sable field with a characteristic all over herati design in coral, powder-blue, celadon and ochre, 6ft. 4in. x 4ft. 4in. (Phillips) $1,272

Kazak rug, Southwest Caucasus, early 29th century, the large red and teal stepped diamond medallion with teal triangle pendants, 7ft. x 4ft. (Skinner Inc.) $770

Shirvan rug, East Caucasus, late 19th/early 20th century, two rust and gold stepped polygon medallions, 5ft. 3in. x 3ft. 5in. (Skinner Inc.) $990

A fine Persian Bidjar handwoven wool oriental carpet with a design of palmettes and flowering vines, 11ft. x 17ft. 6in., circa 1900. (Selkirk's) $8,500

An antique Kashgai rug, Southern Persia, the deep indigo-blue field decorated with a pattern of highly stylized camels, stags, peacocks and birds, 9ft. 9in. x 5ft. 1in. (Phillips) $4,094

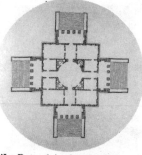

A rare antique Mongol saddle rug, probably 18th century, decorated with two round ornaments formed by groups of stylized tree peonies, 4ft. 7in. x 2ft. 2in. (Phillips) $875

'La Rotunda', a hand tufted woollen carpet by Nigel Coates, circular, a prototype by V'soske Joyce, design taken from the plan of Villa Capra by Palladio, 265cm. diameter. (Christie's) $5,119

Sultanabad rug, West Persia, early 20th century, the overall design of light rose flowerhead and teal vines, 6ft. 4in. x 4ft. 4in. (Skinner Inc.) $2,310

An antique Kashgai rug, South Persia, the rust field enclosing an indigo-blue and ivory diamond-shaped medallion surrounded by a pattern of characteristic rosettes, 6ft. 3in. x 4ft. 11in. (Phillips) $890

An antique Shirvan Pallas, South East Caucasus, flat-woven in the slit-tapestry technique, with multi-colored geometric motifs, 5ft. 7in. x 4ft. 3in. (Phillips) $1,602

An antique Tekke engsi, West Turkestan, the madder field decorated with a characteristic interpretation of the traditional compartmented design, 5ft. x 4ft. 1in. (Phillips) $2,492

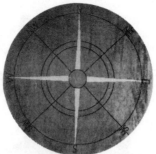

A Heriz carpet, North West Persia, the tomato-red field with flowering pale blue vines and feathered leaves, 9ft. 3in. x 6ft. 4in.
(Phillips) $3,560

A hand-tufted woollen carpet, circular, sage green ground with the points of the compass, circa 1945, 272.5cm. diameter.
(Christie's) $3,938

An antique Gerous carpet, Persian Kurdistan, the indigo-blue field decorated with an ascending lattice formed by bold multi-colored arabesques, 10ft. 6in. x 4ft. 8in.
(Phillips) $9,256

A Wilton hand-knotted woollen carpet designed by Edward McKnight Kauffer, abstract design in brown, pale green, dark and pale yellow, gray, red and black, circa 1929, 210 x 117cm.
(Christie's) $9,254

A rare 'Swan House' Hammersmith hand-knotted Morris & Co. carpet, designed by William Morris, dark blue ground with symmetrical quartered scrolling floral design incorporating a central medallion, circa 1890, 396 x 380cm.
(Christie's) $59,070

An antique Kashgai rug, South Persia, the indigo-blue field enclosing a central ivory diamond-shaped medallion surrounded by stylized floral stems, 7ft. 9in. x 4ft. 6in.
(Phillips) $2,492

Tabriz rug, Northwest Persia, early 20th century, with ivory scalloped diamond medallion, 5ft. 3in. x 3ft. 8in.
(Skinner Inc.) $2,200

'The Kinsale', a Liberty hand-knotted woollen Donegal carpet, the turquoise field with stylized pink and yellow rose flowerheads and leaves, circa 1903, 455 x 346cm.
(Christie's) $32,010

A Tekke Chuval, West Turkestan, the deep rose field decorated with six turreted guls in flame-red, 2ft. 6in. x 3ft. 5in.
(Phillips) $356

RUGS

An 18th century West Anatolian rug, the ivory field enclosing a shaped central panel divided into a flame-red central section, 5ft. 11in. x 4ft. 4in.
(Phillips) $7,950

An antique Kuba Dragon Sumak, North East Caucasus, circa 1880, the terracotta field decorated with a typical broad lattice, 10ft. 7in. x 8ft. 1in.
(Phillips) $6,678

An antique Bergama rug, West Anatolia, two golden yellow octagons from which radiate crimson rectangular panels, 6ft. 5in. x 4ft. 4in.
(Phillips) $2,862

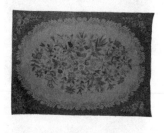

An antique Sejshour rug, North East Caucasus, the indigo-blue field decorated with a characteristic interpretation of the classical Oriental garden design, 6ft. x 4ft. 1in.
(Phillips) $6,764

A large hooked cotton rug, American, late 19th/early 20th century, the central floral medallion worked in pinks, blues, greens and browns on a cream ground, $146^1/2$ x 106in.
(Christie's) $6,050

A fine antique Ersari ceremonial trapping, the deep chestnut-brown ground decorated with a traditional lattice pattern depicted in dark indigo-blue, 4ft. 1in. x 5ft. 11in.
(Phillips) $4,094

A fine antique Motasham Kashan rug, Central Persia, the indigo-blue field arched at both ends and filled with flowering stems and weeping willows, 6ft. 10in. x 4ft. 3in.
(Phillips) $3,180

An antique Shahsavan storage bag, North West Persia, piled in natural camel hair, encloses a large tulip design in turquoise and coral rose, 2ft. 1in. x 2ft. 3in.
(Phillips) $1,113

A fine antique Motashem Kashan rug, Central Persia, the indigo field containing a stylized vine lattice work, 6ft. 7in. x 4ft. 4in.
(Phillips) $3,535

A fine antique Kashgai rug, the field decorated with an all over pattern of multi-colored chevrons filled with small blossoms, 5ft. 8in. x 3ft. 1in.
(Phillips) $10,680

A fine Tabriz prayer rug, North West Persia, the ivory mihrab decorated with a set of three trees and a pair of decorated columns, 6ft. 3in. x 4ft. 6in.
(Phillips) $4,984

An antique Konya Yastik, Central Anatolia, the coral rose field enclosing a central medallion in turquoise, ivory, wine red and indigo-blue, 3ft. 10in. x 2ft. 1in.
(Phillips) $1,272

An antique Daghestan prayer rug, North East Caucasus, second half 19th century, the ivory mihrab filled with an all over trellis enclosing stylized blossoms within a flame-red border, 4ft. 6in. x 3ft. 2in.
(Phillips) $3,916

A large pictorial cotton hooked rug, American, late 19th/early 20th century, in two registers; the upper depicting a farm scene with a barn, 97 x 129in.
(Christie's) $2,860

A Marasali rug, Shirvan, East Caucasus, the indigo field with a characteristic all over design of stylized botehs in turquoise, azure, terracotta and ivory, 5ft. x 3ft. 7in.
(Phillips) $3,382

A fine antique Kashgai rug, Southern Persia, the field divided into longitudinal bands depicted alternately in ivory and indigo blue, 8ft. 7in. x 5ft. 7in.
(Phillips) $9,721

An antique Chi Chi prayer rug, North East Caucasus, dated 1298 (A.D. 1881), the indigo field with geometric rosettes in ivory, azure, terracotta and ocher, 4ft. 7in. x 3ft. 9in.
(Phillips) $748

An antique Lambalo-Kazak, South West Caucasus, the deep rust-red field decorated with three rows of characteristic diamonds, 8ft. 6in. x 5ft. 7in.
(Phillips) $12,373

SAMPLERS

Needlework sampler *Rebecca Justice Aged 11 Years*, circa 1835, worked in silk threads, on linen ground, in original frame. (Skinner Inc.) **$9,625**

Needlework sampler *Wrought by Elizabeth Bigelow, Marlborough, Aged 11 Yeaf*, worked in silk threads in shades of green, pink, bittersweet, yellow and black on linen, 10 x 9¹/₂in. (Skinner Inc.) **$1,045**

Needlework sampler, *Wrought by Caroline Darling Marlborough August 1819 aged 11 years*, 17¹/₄ x 13¹/₂in. (Skinner Inc.) **$3,850**

Framed antique American sampler, verse reads, *This Sampler Is To Let You Know how Kind My Mother Was To Me She Learned Me To Read And Write And In Me Tok Great Delight*, signed *Elisabeth Laughlin, aged 14, 1841*, 17 x 17¹/₂in. (Eldred's) **$468**

A long sampler by Isbel Hall, 1653, embroidered in colored silks with bands of patterns, including trailing honeysuckle rows, stylized flowers and acorns, 26in. x 7in., English, 17th century. (Christie's S. Ken) **$2,972**

Rare needlework sampler, worked by Sally Johnson Age 12, Newburyport, Massachusetts, 1799, one of a small and important group of samplers worked in Newburyport from 1799–1806, 19 x 27in. (Skinner Inc.) **$33,000**

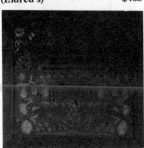

Needlework sampler, *Wrought by Adaline Libby Aged 16 1827*, probably New Hampshire, worked with silk threads, 20 x 21in. (Skinner Inc.) **$825**

Needlework sampler by Mary Ann Hartshorne, American, early 19th century, executed in polychrome silk threads on a linen ground, 16¹/₂in. high. (Butterfield & Butterfield) **$1,045**

One of a fine and rare pair of samplers, one signed *Ann Moorcroft* and one *Catherine Moorcroft*, and both *aged 12, 1812*, worked with Christian morality texts, 21 x 16in. (Tennants) (Two) **$1,488**

SAMPLERS

Needlework sampler by Hannah S. Pierce, Jamaica, circa 1829, executed in polychrome silk threads on a linen ground, 16¹/₂in. high.
(Butterfield & Butterfield)
$935

Needlework family record *Fanny Marks record and sampler wrought at the age of 15, 1825,* Keene area, New Hampshire, 24¹/₄ x 16¹/₄in.
(Skinner Inc.) $2,475

An attractive early 18th century child's needlework sampler, inscribed *Elizabeth Barclay her work finished 25th day of the seventh month 1725,* 12 x 11¹/₄in.
(Bearne's) $1,118

A silk-on-silk needlework sampler, American, late 18th/ early 19th century, depicting an alphabetic sequence above the poetic verse *While I am blest with Youthful bloom/I will adore the sacred lamb/If God inspires my heart with grace/And lets me see his shining face,* 12¹/₂ x 8¹/₂in.
(Christie's) $2,860

Unusual framed sampler, dated 1788, decorated with alphabets, birds, trees, flowers, houses, and more, height 47in.
(Eldred's) $550

A needlework silk-on-linen sampler by Desire E. Demmen, Scituate, Massachusetts, 1804, worked in polychrome silk threads on a linen ground, the upper register depicting an alphabetic sequence, 19¹/₄in. high, 15¹/₂in. wide.
(Christie's) $6,600

Needlework sampler by Charlotte Edwards, English, early 19th century, executed in polychrome silk threads on a linen ground centering a poetic verse, 12¹/₂in. high.
(Butterfield & Butterfield)
$1,045

Needlework sampler, inscribed *Mary Sheles work'd this in 1791* a variety of spot motifs worked in green, yellow, and brown silk, 14 x 10in.
(Skinner Inc.) $412

Needlework sampler, *Anna Brynbergs work done in the Eleventh Year of Her Age 1795,* Philadelphia, Pennsylvania, worked in silk threads in shades of blue, green, yellow, peach, cream and black, 15¹/₄ x 17¹/₂in.
(Skinner Inc.) $5,500

A gold-mounted scent-bottle and stopper of 'Girl in a Swing' type modeled as a Chinese family with a Chinaman embracing a Chinese lady holding an infant, 9cm. high.
(Christie's) $5,513

A Chelsea gold-mounted peach scent-bottle and stopper naturally modeled and colored, stamped gold mounts, circa 1755, 7cm. high.
(Christie's) $8,269

A Ruskin high-fired stoneware scent bottle, with hexagonal 'pointed' screw-fitting cover, the clouded flecking in green, yellow and red, 1927, 15.7cm. high.
(Christie's) $1,387

An unusual French frosted and clear glass perfume bottle and stopper for Caray, decorated in relief with a band of flies colored in green and gilt, 15.20cm. high.
(Phillips) $973

A cameo globular scent-flask with silver mount and hinged cover, the red ground overlaid in opaque-white and carved with a trailing prunus branch, probably Stevens & Williams, circa 1885.
(Christie's) $444

A Chelsea scent bottle and Girl-in-a-Swing stopper, the slender necked bottle encased in cream wicker work, a label bearing the name suspended from the neck, 9.5cm. overall.
(Phillips) $2,191

A Fürstenberg scent-bottle and gilt-metal stopper, after a Chelsea model, in a simulated wicker-basket, a gilt chain molded about the shoulders, circa 1770, 9cm. high.
(Christie's) $2,633

'Emeraude', a scent bottle and stopper made for Coty, in original fitted box, 4in. high.
(Christie's S. Ken) $300

A gold-mounted scent-bottle and stopper of 'Girl in a Swing' type modeled as a girl standing in flowered dress and white apron holding a dove, circa 1755, 7.5cm. high.
(Christie's) $7,876

A gold-mounted pug scent-bottle and stopper of 'Girl in a Swing' type naturally modeled as a seated pug bitch with black fur-markings, circa 1755, 6.5cm. high.
(Christie's) $5,907

A cut and enameled scent bottle and stopper, the front with a panel set with a crown enameled in colors on gilt foil, 10.3cm. high.
(Phillips) $1,530

A 'Girl in a Swing' scent bottle, as a figure of Shakespeare after the model by Scheemakers in Westminster Abbey, 8.2cm. high.
(Phillips) $1,200

One of a pair of Paris scent-bottle figures, modeled as American Indians on tree-stumps, 11in. high.
(Christie's S. Ken)
(Two) $564

'Voltigy', a Baccarat clear bottle for A. Gravier, modeled as a butterfly with outstretched wings, the body stained in pink and black, 3⅝in.
(Bonhams) $31,500

English cameo glass perfume, diminutive yellow bottle layered in white, cameo cut and carved with overall floral motif, 3¼in. high.
(Skinner Inc.) $900

'Pan', a Lalique frosted glass scent bottle, molded in relief with satyrs' heads enclosed in floral swags, stained blue, 5in. high.
(Christie's S. Ken)
$2,142

René Lalique "Amphytrite" parfum flaçon, frosted colorless crystal bottle in the form of a swirled snail shell with kneeling nude woman stopper, 3¾in. high.
(Skinner Inc.) $900

A Chelsea gold-mounted scent-bottle and stopper modeled as a cat with brown fur-markings, seated erect with a mouse in its mouth, circa 1755, 6.5cm. high.
(Christie's) $3,938

Lalique "Dans la Nuit" parfum, miniature sphere with molded stars and quarter-moon stopper, midnight blue patine overall, 3in. high.
(Skinner Inc.) $600

Baccarat, France, cameo conical shaped perfume atomiser bottle being royal-blue over clear glass with swan decoration, 9in. high.
(Giles Haywood) $180

'Shocking', a Schiaparelli scent bottle and stopper designed by Salvador Dali, modeled as dressmaker's dummy with a tape measure around the body.
(Christie's) $331

A Dubarry scent bottle and stopper, of rectangular form molded in relief with sunburst motif, 4¹/₄in. high.
(Christie's) $40

A Victorian silver scent flask of pointed fluted form with pendant chain, probably Birmingham 1885, 5¹/₂in.
(Tennants) $316

'Hantise', a Baccarat black enameled pink opaque bottle for A. Gravier, of multi-faceted ovoid form, with gilt metal bullet-shaped stopper and circular foot, 4⁵/₈in.
(Bonhams) $5,950

'Dans la Nuit', a Lalique display scent bottle and stopper, of spherical form molded in relief with stars, the reserve stained blue, 10in. high.
(Christie's) $1,363

'Parfum A', a black enameled frosted bottle for Lucien Lelong, of square section, each side molded with black enameled swags, 4¹/₈in. high.
(Bonhams) $8,000

'Le Jade', a Lalique pale green scent bottle, in the style of a Chinese snuff bottle, molded with an exotic bird amid tangled branches, 8.3cm. high.
(Christie's) $2,922

SCENT BOTTLES

A gold-mounted scent-bottle etui of 'Girl in a Swing' type modeled as The Three Graces scantily draped in flowered robes with flowers in their hair, circa 1755, 11cm. high.
(Christie's) **$4,922**

The Victorian novelty scent bottle, cast in the form of a fish, engraved to simulate fins, scales and gill detail, 9cm. long, by Drake & Lewis, 1884, 1¹/₄oz.
(Phillips) **$950**

'Origan', a Lalique clear glass atomiser made for 'D'Héraud, molded in relief with overlapping holly leaves, 6¹/₂in. high.
(Christie's S. Ken) **$343**

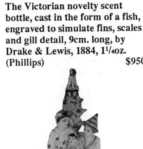

'Malice', a Baccarat enameled clear bottle for A. Gravier, of squared baluster form, the grooved edges enameled in blue, the front enameled in black, 4³/₈in.
(Bonhams) **$3,150**

A gold-mounted scent-bottle and a stopper of 'Girl in a Swing' type modeled as a Chinese family, the seated man with a child holding an apple on his lap, a woman standing beside, circa 1755, 9.5cm. high overall.
(Christie's) **$4,565**

'La Joie D'Aimer', a Baccarat enameled clear bottle for A. Gravier, of octagonal form, with swollen neck, enameled in black and orange with an abstract pattern, 5¹/₈in.
(Bonhams) **$2,450**

'Pluie D'Or', a Baccarat enameled clear bottle for A. Gravier, of triangular section, enameled in black, orange, green and yellow with flower sprays, with triangular domed stopper, 5³/₄in.
(Bonhams) **$7,350**

'Me Voici', a Baccarat enameled clear bottle for A. Gravier, of shoe form, with faceted stopper, the bottle enameled in green, blue, orange and yellow with Egyptianesque floral patterns, 4in. wide.
(Bonhams) **$10,850**

Abraham, Colomby, a late 18th century French gold, enamel and glass scent bottle containing a verge watch, the chased and engraved gold cap with blue, pink and white enamel decoration, 63 x 47mm.
(Christie's) **$5,422**

Polychrome engraved whale's tooth, 19th century, engraved with a woman and child enclosed by a leafy reserve, heightened with red and black ink, 4¹/₂in. high. (Skinner Inc.) $495

Pair of engraved polychrome whale teeth, 19th century, each engraved with ship at sea, enclosed by swag border, 6in. high. (Skinner Inc.) $1,100

Most unusual scrimshaw whale's tooth, 19th century, with cameo carving of a French naval seaman on one side, engraved *Donald McLaughton Mar 4, 1886* on the other, 5¹/₂in. long. (Eldred's) $715

Engraved whale's tooth, 19th century, engraved with a figure of a mother and child and *Lieut. Lovell*, 7in. high. (Skinner Inc.) $2,200

Pair of engraved whale's teeth, early 19th century, the first engraved with a cutting-in scene, the second also with a whaling scene, 7in. high. (Skinner Inc.) $1,320

Engraved whale's tooth, 19th century, deeply engraved with the figure of Liberty, a panoply of American flags and other patriotic devices, 4¹/₂in. high. (Skinner Inc.) $770

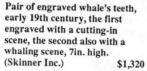

Scrimshaw Sperm whale's tooth, 19th century, decorated with the portrait of John Paul Jones on one side; a three-masted ship on the other, 4³/₄in. long. (Eldred's) $248

Pair of engraved whale's teeth, late 19th century, engraved with Liberty and Justice, Liberty heightened with red, 4³/₄in. high. (Skinner Inc.) $880

Engraved polychrome whale tooth, 19th century, engraved with American flags surmounting a spread eagle perched on a shaped foliate base, 5¹/₂in. long. (Skinner Inc.) $770

SEWING MACHINES

A Ward's Arm & Platform sewing machine, No 15851, with gilt and colored decoration. (Christie's S. Ken) **$847**

A rare Cookson's lockstitch sewing machine by Cookson's L.S.S.M. Co. Ltd., also stamped *G. Wallace Ash, Russell St., Landport,* 10in. high. (Christie's) **$2,441**

F W Müller No 6 child's sewing machine without a crank, drive rod and back cover plate, circa 1920. (Auction Team Köln) **$94**

A gilt decorated, black painted, hand operated sewing machine by Willcox & Gibbs, bears maker's plaque, contained in a wooden carrying case. (Spencer's) **$260**

A Newton Wilson 'Princess of Wales' lockstitch hand sewing machine with gilt decoration and wood carrying case. (Christie's) **$445**

A rare McQuinn lockstitch sewing machine, with scalloped base, partial gilt transfers, Britannia trade-marks, dated *October 20 1878.* (Christie's) **$7,750**

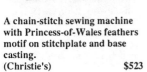

A chain-stitch sewing machine with Princess-of-Wales feathers motif on stitchplate and base casting. (Christie's) **$523**

A Cookson's lockstitch sewing machine with part-plated mechanism on cast iron base and wood cover. (Christie's) **$1,750**

A Weir chain-stitch sewing machine with gilt transfers, table clamp and original instructions. (Christie's) **$285**

A Komai style cabinet, the various doors and drawers inset with ivory panels inlaid in Shibayama style with various bird and floral scenes, late 19th century, 47cm. high.
(Christie's) $10,120

A lozenge-shaped lacquer tray decorated in iroe hiramakie, togidashi and nashiji with a central panel in Shibayama-style on a kinji ground with Jurojin seated reading a makimono, late 19th century, 25.5cm. long.
(Christie's) $2,650

A silver vase and domed cover, the lobed body suporting five convex panels decorated in Shibayama-style with birds in flight, signed *Kanemitsu*, late 19th century, 24cm. high.
(Christie's) $6,200

A silver and lacquer vase and cover decorated in Shibayama style with two shaped panels, one with egrets by wisteria and chrysanthemums, the other with Daikoku and Bishamonten, signed *Yoshiaki saku*, late 19th century, 25.5cm. high.
(Christie's) $10,600

A pair of small Shibayama style vases with massed flowerheads ground, each with the gold lacquer ground shoulder decorated in gold hiramakie with chrysanthemum flower and foliage, late 19th century, 16.2cm. high.
(Christie's) $8,450

A Japanese silver colored metal and Shibayama two handled vase, cover and liner, the melon fluted body inlaid in mother of pearl and polished hardstones, 26cm. high.
(Spencer's) $4,020

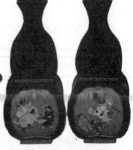

Pair of Shibayama School inlaid ivory tusks, signed *Masayuki*, late 19th century, with roosters and hens among flowers, 12in. high.
(Skinner Inc.) $6,600

A Komai style garniture, each of the vases inset with ivory panels inlaid in Shibayama style depicting various birds and floral designs, 36cm. high.
(Christie's) $16,200

A pair of faceted gourd-shaped tsuishu vases, decorated in Shibayama style with birds and flowers, brushes and books, signed *Ozeki sei*, late 19th century, 23.3cm. high.
(Christie's) $17,305

BASKETS

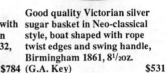

A Dutch 19th century silver sugar basket, oval chased with plinth, swags and scrolls, circa 1880, and a pair of sugar tongs.
(Bonhams) **$196**

An oval roll basket, 13in. diameter, bar-pierced sides with everted gadrooned border on raised oval base, Chester 1932, 28oz.
(Bonhams) **$784**

Good quality Victorian silver sugar basket in Neo-classical style, boat shaped with rope twist edges and swing handle, Birmingham 1861, 8¹/₂oz.
(G.A. Key) **$531**

A George III Provincial sugar basket of pedestal form, the body embossed with foliate festoons and tassies, and pierced with slots and lozenge motifs, 8cm. diameter, by Henry Tudor & Thomas Leader, Sheffield, 1777, 2³/₄oz.
(Phillips) **$657**

A pair of highly important George II two-handled circular baskets, each on pierced spreading foot with applied rope-twist band above, by Paul de Lamerie, 1734, 12¹/₂in. wide, 81oz.
(Christie's)

$1,012,440

Peter & Ann Bateman, a George III swing-handle sugar basket, the curved oval body finely pierced with an upper and lower frieze of bright-cut leaf motifs and festooning, 8in. high, 1791, 5oz.
(Phillips) **$864**

An attractive William IV sweetmeat basket, chased and embossed with scrolling foliage, 5in., maker's Taylor & Perry, Birmingham 1836, 3oz.
(Woolley & Wallis) **$550**

An attractive late Victorian basket by Martin Hall & Co., the beaded border enclosing pierced arcading and strapwork engraving, London 1877, 645 grammes, 30cm. wide.
(Spencer's) **$945**

A circular cake basket, the lobed body with engraved and repoussé decoration of game birds, London 1842 by Joshua Taylor probably, 34cm. diameter, 45oz.
(Langlois) **$2,398**

BASKETS

A Victorian shaped-oval bread basket, with applied border incorporating female masks, trailing vines, wheat ears and scrolls, by Robert Hennell, 1843, 16in. long, 61 oz. (Christie's) $8,800

An oval fruit basket, 8¼in. diameter, scroll pierced sides, leaf chased border on four pierced foliate feet, Sheffield 1919, by the Dixons, 17oz. (Bonhams) $818

A George II shaped-oval bread basket, the rim applied with wheat ears, fruits, vines and foliage and with dolphin's mask and scroll swing handle, by Samuel Herbert & Co., 1755, 14¼in. long, 48 oz. (Christie's) $8,096

German hallmarked silver fruit basket, 19th century, 800 fine, reticulated and chased figural and floral decoration, approximately 46 troy oz. (Skinner Inc.) $2,200

A pair of George III silver-gilt oval baskets and covers, the spreading sides and domed covers pierced and chased with fruit and vines, by William Pitts, 1808, 12½in. wide, 94 oz. (Christie's) $10,560

A sugar basket, pierced and chased with a cartouche, scrolls and paterae amongst pales and flutes, by Burrage Davenport, London 1772, 7³/₄oz., 5½in. high. (Tennants) $930

George II style silver cake basket, clover piercing and engraved crest, side bearing marks of Wm. Plummer, 1759–60, 13in. wide. (Skinner Inc.) $1,760

A pair of Dutch two-handled oval baskets, the wirework sides with applied vine leaves and grapes, with shell and scroll borders and vine tendril and leaf handles, Rotterdam, 1769, 12½in. overall, 1,253grs. (Christie's) $31,680

An attractive George III Irish swing handle sugar basket, the shaped oval body of bat's wing paneled fluting design, by Christopher Haines, Dublin, 1790, 12oz. (Phillips) $1,469

A sugar basket of hemispherical shape chased and pierced with flowers, scrolls, and a cartouche, by Richard Meach, London 1770, blue glass liner, 4¹/₂oz., 4¹/₂in. diameter.
(Tennants) $651

A George III oblong bread basket, chased with a broad band of flutes and with shell, foliage and gadrooned border and cornucopia, shell, fruit and foliage swing handle, by James Barber and William Whitwell, York, 1818, 12in. long, 39 oz.
(Christie's) $2,288

A silver cake basket, maker's mark of R&W Wilson, Philadelphia, circa 1830, with die-rolled Greek-key borders, 12in. diameter, 38 oz.
(Christie's) $1,100

Sterling silver handled basket by Watson Company made for Bailey Banks & Biddle, pierced edge, four feet, 10¹/₂in. long, 13.8 troy oz.
(Eldred's) $440

A pair of Edwardian baskets, the sides pierced in scroll and star designs, leafy borders and pierced scroll feet, by Messrs. Elkington, Sheffield, 1901, 21.5cm., 21.5oz.
(Lawrence Fine Art) $1,583

A fine George II shaped-oval bread basket, the everted border cast and pierced with wheat ears, flowers, scrolls and ribbons, by Paul de Lamerie, 1747, 13³/₄in. long, 72oz.
(Christie's) $207,273

A George III circular bread basket, with openwork basket-work sides, basket-weave border and twisted and foliage swing handle, by John Wakelin and Robert Garrard, 1795, 11¹/₄in. diameter, 42 oz.
(Christie's) $8,448

Large German silver basket, early 20th century, the flat oval base a cast plaque showing a group of winged putti gathering flowers, 14in. wide, 25oz. 12dwts.
(Butterfield & Butterfield) $2,475

A George II shaped oval bread basket, the sides pierced and chased with quatrefoils, scrolls and beading, by Edward Aldridge, 1759, with blue glass liner, 17¹/₄in. wide, 52oz.
(Christie's) $12,813

BEAKERS

SILVER

A William and Mary slightly flaring beaker on rim foot, scratch-engraved with stylized foliage, London 1692, 3¹/₄in., 3.75oz.
(Christie's) $3,407

A French mid 18th century inverted bell-shaped beaker on a fluted rising circular foot crudely engraved with two names, Orleans circa 1770, 4¹/₂in.
(Christie's S. Ken) $1,314

A Hungarian parcel-gilt beaker, engraved with initials and dated *1670*, the base inset with a medallic 1¹/₂-Thaler, 1541, struck at Kremnitz, 4in. high, 207grs.
(Christie's) $3,115

A Continental silver-gilt beaker, on domed spreading foot chased with fruit, flowers and foliage, inset with 16th century thalers, unmarked, 11¹/₂in. high, 1,304 grs.
(Christie's) $13,200

A pair of George III parcel-gilt beakers, engraved with panels of cupids between festoons and flowers, foliage and husks, by Thomas Balliston, 1818, 3¹/₂in. high, 9 oz.
(Christie's) $5,808

Russian silver Catherine the Great period beaker, Moscow, 1769, the sides densely chased in repoussé with exuberant rocaille, scrolls and vegetation, 8³/₄in. high, 10oz. 14 dwts.
(Butterfield & Butterfield)
                  $880

A late 18th century Channel Isles beaker, with an everting rim and a molded circular foot, 9.5cm. tall, by George Mauger, Jersey, circa 1780–1800, 3oz.
(Phillips) $777

A pair of late 18th century tapering beakers engraved with simulated staves and applied with hoops, possibly Joseph Walley, Chester, circa 1775, 3in., 8.25oz.
(Christie's) $1,167

A Swiss tapering cylindrical beaker, punched with a broad band of matting and with molded rim, Sion, circa 1700, maker's mark possibly that of Francois-Joseph Ryss, 3¹/₄in. high, 111grs.
(Christie's) $6,068

BOWLS

A Queen Anne circular punch bowl, chased with a broad band of flutes and with two applied grotesque male mask and drop-ring handles, by William Fordham, 1706, 11½in. diameter, 65oz.
(Christie's) $22,612

A George II circular sugar bowl and cover, engraved with a band of palm leaves and below the shaped rim with a band of strapwork, latticework and female masks, by John Le Sage, 1730, 4in. high, 17oz.
(Christie's) $14,698

Japanese silver repoussé punch bowl, Meiji period, with lush flowering kakitsubaki (iris) plants executed in high relief on a graduated ground, the base impressed STERLING K & CO., 54oz. 6dwts.
(Butterfield & Butterfield) $6,050

Danish silver circular bowl by Georg Jensen, Copenhagen, circa 1940, with lobed sides rising to everted horizontal border, 14in. diameter, 35oz. 4dwts.
(Butterfield & Butterfield) $2,200

A George III two-handled circular bowl with monteith rim, the body chased in high relief with oriental figures, flowers, scrolls and foliage, 11in. diameter, maker's mark W.B., London 1817, 100.8oz.
(Bearne's) $8,640

George III silver fruit bowl by John Parker & Edward Wakelin, London, 1761, the sides chased with swirling flutes, pierced in panels of alternating diaperwork and scrolls, 11in. diameter, 29oz. 4dwts.
(Butterfield & Butterfield) $4,000

A George II Irish plain circular bowl, on spreading foot and with molded rim, by Peter Racine, Dublin, 1734, 7½in. diameter, 19oz.
(Christie's) $5,276

A 19th century Continental shaped oval bowl and cover, with bulbous spiral reeded and fluted body, 5½in. long, 335gm.
(Bearne's) $720

A silver rose bowl, circular form with part swirl fluted decoration and gadrooned border, London 1899.
(Bonhams) $546

BOWLS

An Edwardian two-handled shaped oval jardinière, on four cast bracket feet, by Goldsmiths & Silversmiths Co., 1904, 19in. long, 134oz. (Christie's) $6,400

A Gorham Sterling and mixed metal punchbowl and ladle. (Skinner Inc.) $18,700

A circular two-handled bowl, the handles each formed as a child sitting astride a reeded scroll branch, by Omar Ramsden, 1937, 7¹/₄in., 10oz. (Christie's) $4,034

Large Victorian silver classical style Bacchic punch bowl by Elkington & Co., Birmingham, 1898, 16³/₄in. high, 178oz. (Butterfield & Butterfield) $6,600

Fine Sterling silver punch bowl by Old Newbury Crafters, engraved monograms and dates, 16¹/₄in. diameter, 107 troy oz. (Eldred's) $1,100

Rare Sterling silver bowl, circa 1930, by William Waldo Dodge, Jr. of Ashville, NC, hand hammered body, 10in. diameter, 20 troy oz. (Eldred's) $935

A silver Martele centerpiece bowl, maker's mark of Gorham Mfg. Co., Providence, circa 1905, the undulating rim repoussé with strawberries, leaves and flowerheads, 15¹/₄in. long, 58 oz. 10 dwt. (Christie's) $10,340

George II silver gilt bowl and cover, Phillips Garden, London, 1751, the upper body chased with flowers and a rococo scrollwork band incorporating two blank cartouches, 4¹/₄in. diameter, 9oz. 2dwts. (Butterfield & Butterfield) $1,540

A Hukin & Heath silver sugar bowl designed by Dr. Christopher Dresser, in the form of a basket with folded rim and loop handle, London hallmarks for 1881, 14.1cm. high, 195 grams. (Christie's) $630

A circular silver-gilt bowl, the lower part of the body with a detachable calyx of acanthus leaves, with everted reeded rim, unmarked, late 17th century, 7³/₈in. diameter, 16oz. (Christie's) $5,940

Fine Sterling silver centerpiece bowl marked *Tiffany & Co.*, applied spiral shell bosses, twelve-lobed rim, probably circa 1873–91, 10in. diameter. (Eldred's) $5,170

Sterling silver centerpiece bowl, circa 1896–1903, by Mauser Manufacturing Company, applied and pierced floral decoration, 14in. diameter, 64 troy oz. (Eldred's) $3,080

BOWLS

Sterling silver infant bowl and undertray by Gorham, with applied design of four children, date mark, 1903, bowl diameter, 5in. (Eldred's) **$1,760**

A rare silver barber basin, maker's mark of William Moulton IV, Newburyport, circa 1815, 10¹/₄in. diameter, 24 oz. 10 dwt.
(Christie's) **$5,500**

Austrian Jugendstil silver centerbowl with cut glass liner, F R, circa 1910, the vertical sides pierced with palmettes and scrolls, 12³/₄in. wide, 39oz. 12dwts.
(Butterfield & Butterfield) **$1,210**

Sterling silver centerpiece bowl by A. Stone & Company, maker's mark G, for Herman Glendenning (active, 1920–37), 30.4 troy oz.
(Eldred's) **$1,540**

A Charles I plain circular bleeding bowl, with pierced trefoil handle, 1632, maker's mark indistinct, but possibly that of Valerius Sutton, 6in. wide.(Christie's)

A fine silver bowl, maker's mark of Whiting Mfg. Co., circa 1890, the sides elaborately repoussé and chased with clam, oyster and mussel shells amid seaweed on a matted ground, 10⁵/₈in. diameter, 32 oz. 10 dwt.
(Christie's) **$13,200**

A silver punch bowl, maker's mark of Redlich & Co., New York, circa 1900, the openwork rims with trailing vine and flowerhead decoration, 10¹/₂in. diameter, 56 oz. 10 dwt.
(Christie's) **$2,860**

A silver footed bowl, maker's mark of Samuel Williamson, Philadelphia, 1795–1810, on a flaring pedestal base over a square foot, 6⁵/₈in. diameter, 15 oz. 10 dwt.
(Christie's) **$2,200**

A silver covered sugar bowl, maker's mark of Tiffany & Co., New York, 1870–1875, the lobed body repoussé with scrolls and stylized foliage, 10³/₄in. high, 22 oz.
(Christie's) **$2,200**

An Edwardian two-handled shaped-oval bowl, on four leaf-capped shell and scroll feet and with openwork mask and scroll handles, by Gibson and Co. Ltd., 1905, 28in. long, 157oz.
(Christie's) **$15,840**

A Hukin & Heath electroplated twin sweetmeat bowl designed by Dr. Christopher Dresser, the two bowls with straight collars and a strap handle positioned at the junction, 27cm. high.
(Christie's) **$985**

A good Edwardian gilt tazza, the incurved sides finely embossed with Bacchanalian masks, trophies and cartouches, by Christian Leopold Reid, London 1909, 37oz.
(Tennants) **$1,581**

Large German silver table box, early 20th century, the lid and long side panels decorated with cast scenes of putti at various pursuits, 12¼in. wide, 46oz. 18dwts.
(Butterfield & Butterfield)
$3,025

W.G. Connell, an Arts & Crafts Movement rectangular casket, the hinged cover with a female portrait medallion, the clasp with copper bolts, 5½in. overall, London 1899, 8¼oz.
(Woolley & Wallis) $797

A Spanish oval spice box, on four cast lion's paw feet and with central hinge, Valladolid, circa 1780 and with the mark of Juan A. Sanz de Velasco, 4½in. long, 438grs.
(Christie's) $6,336

A Guild of Handicraft hammered silver box and cover, the domed cover with painted enamel decoration of a river landscape at sunset, hallmarks for 1902, 11cm. diameter, 320 grams.
(Christie's) $2,363

One of a pair of George III spherical soap boxes, the circular spreading foot and cover border cast with a band of foliage, 1808, maker's mark W P, perhaps for William Pitts, 2½in. diameter, 7 oz.
(Christie's) $3,520

An early George V dressing table box, with escallop shell terminals, the hinged cover repoussé with figures in a public house interior, Chester 1911, 11cm. square overall.
(Spencer's) $563

A Victorian biscuit box on stand with hinged action opening to reveal pierced liners with cast handles and ornate cast legs, 19cm. wide.
(Phillips) $594

A Continental fan-shaped box decorated all over with cherubs, flowers and scrolling foliage, 6¾in. wide, import mark for London 1913, 7.9oz.
(Bearne's) $720

A Charles II plain oval silver tobacco-box, the detachable cover engraved with a coat-of-arms, the base engraved with a monogram, 1671, maker's mark indistinct, 3¾in. high.
(Christie's) $2,450

CANDELABRA

One of a pair of Victorian massive seven-light candelabra, the scroll stem entwined with vine tendrils and with frolicking putti, shamrocks and a harp, by John S. Hunt, 1844, 31¹/₂in. high, 741 oz.
(Christie's) $61,600

A pair of Continental seven-light candelabra, each supporting a naturalistic stem and one with a stag, the other with a hind, by L. Janesich, 19th century, 23in. high, 3,779grs.
(Christie's) $5,940

One of a pair Sheffield plate four light candelabra, English, early 19th century, with gadroon bands, fluted decoration and distinguished by square form knops, 23³/₄in. high.
(Butterfield & Butterfield)
(Two) $2,475

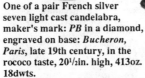

A pair of George III style three-light candelabra, with scroll branches terminating in circular drip-pans, chased with flutes and with reeded borders, 1933, 17in. high, weight of branches 50oz.
(Christie's) $5,940

One of a pair French silver seven light cast candelabra, maker's mark: *PB* in a diamond, engraved on base: *Bucheron, Paris*, late 19th century, in the rococo taste, 20¹/₂in. high, 413oz. 18dwts.
(Butterfield & Butterfield)
                               $16,500

Pair German silver five light candelabra, Friedlander, early 20th century, 800 standard modified reproduction of George III style, 19in. high, 111oz. 14dwts.
(Butterfield & Butterfield)
                               $1,980

A Victorian three-light candelabra, on three foliate and scroll feet and with floral border, by John S. Hunt, 1844, 18in. high, gross 99 oz.
(Christie's) $3,520

A pair of Victorian four-light candelabra, each on waisted circular base hung with foliage swags, by Smith and Nicholson, 1862, 23¹/₂in. high, 178 ozs.
(Christie's) $7,920

One of a pair of plated five-light candelabra, maker's mark of Tiffany & Co., New York, circa 1885, with foliate decoration, 15¹/₄in. high.
(Christie's) $4,180

CANDLESTICKS

A pair of Victorian desk candlesticks, the domed center and baluster stem cast and chased with masks, classical figures and foliage, by Robert Garrard, 1871, 6⁷/₈in. high, 24 oz.
(Christie's) $3,696

A pair of George II candlesticks, each on spreading octagonal base with slightly sunken center and with baluster stem and spool-shaped socket, by Paul de Lamerie, 6¹/₂in. high, 31oz.
(Christie's) $50,876

A very fine pair of late George III candlesticks by John Roberts and Co., with detachable circular sconces, Sheffield 1810, loaded, 32cm. high.
(Spencer's) $2,832

Pair of George III silver candlesticks by William Cafe, London, 1765, with spreading shaped stepped circular base chased with acanthus, 10¹/₄in. high, 38oz. 18dwts.
(Butterfield & Butterfield) $2,475

A pair of George I plain hexagonal cast candlesticks, engraved with a coat-of-arms within a scroll cartouche, by Matthew Cooper, 1719, Britannia Standard, 7in. high, 25oz.
(Christie's) $13,629

Pair of Continental silver candlesticks, apparently unmarked, 19th century, fitted with detachable nozzles, 12in. high, 18oz. 16 dwts.
(Butterfield & Butterfield) $1,100

A pair of columnar George III candlesticks, 12in. high, the cylindrical stems chased with spirally fluted masks, London, 1778, by Joseph Heriot.
(Bonhams) $2,518

A George II candlestick and matching snuffers and tray, the candlestick on spreading square base with incurved angles and baluster stem and spool-shaped socket, by James Gould, 1729, gross 22oz.
(Christie's) $17,900

A pair of Queen Anne candlesticks, each on spreading gadrooned octagonal base and slightly sunken center and with partly-fluted baluster stem and vase-shaped socket, by John East, 1702, 6³/₄in. high, 34oz.
(Christie's) $18,843

576

CANDLESTICKS

A pair George I candlesticks, engraved with a coat-of-arms with Bishop's miter above, by David Green, 1719, 7¹/₈in. high, 30 oz.
(Christie's) **$10,560**

Pair of Danish silver single candlesticks by Georg Jensen, Copenhagen, circa 1940, designer Harald Nielsen, both with circular stepped base, 2³/₄in. high, 10oz. 14dwts.
(Butterfield & Butterfield)
$2,200

A pair of candlesticks, the faceted knopped stem on stepped and cut square bases, gadrooned borders, Sheffield 1909. (Bonhams) **$1,110**

A pair of Queen Anne candlesticks, each on spreading decagonal base and with baluster stem and circular vase-shaped socket, by Ambrose Stevenson, 1711, 7in. high, 35oz.
(Christie's) **$12,488**

A set of four Sheffield plate candlesticks by Waterhouse, Hatfield & Co., Sheffield, circa 1840, 9¹/₄in. high.
(Butterfield & Butterfield)
$1,210

A pair of Edward VII table candlesticks, the octagonal bases, knopped stems and detachable nozzles with reeded edging, 7¹/₂in. high, Thomas Bradbury, London 1902, loaded.
(Bearne's) **$810**

A pair of George III candlesticks, decorated with vertical fluting, with vase-shaped sockets, detachable nozzles and gadrooned borders, by Matthew Boulton, Birmingham, 1801, 12in. high.
(Christie's) **$3,520**

A pair of modern, cast, desktop candlesticks with shaped square bases and knopped stems, 4¹/₄in. high, Asprey, London 1962, 27.81oz.
(Bearne's) **$504**

A pair of George III candlesticks, each on shaped square bases and baluster stem cast and chased with cherubs' masks, by Joseph Craddock and William Reid, 1810, 12in. high, 107oz.
(Christie's) **$7,537**

A baluster caster, the pierced domed cover applied with a band of flower buds and with stylized flower finial, by Omar Ramsden, 1936, 6¹/₂in. high, 11oz. (Christie's) **$2,972**

A set of three George III inverted pear-shaped casters, each on spreading circular foot, by James Mince and Jabez Daniell, 1771, 6³/₄in. and 8in. high, 20 oz. (Christie's) **$3,520**

A George I cast sugar dredger, the domed cover pierced and engraved and surmounted by a finial, 17cm. high, by Thomas Bamford I, 1721, 7.5 ozs. (Phillips) **$2,414**

A pair of 18th century Belgian casters of paneled baluster form with knop finials, probably by Ferdinandus Cornelius Carolus Millé, Brussels, 1747/9, 18.7cm. high, 19oz. (Phillips) **$16,416**

A rare and important silver sugar caster, maker's mark of Jacobus van der Spiegel, New York, 1690–1708, the domed cover pierced with fleurs-de-lys and florettes and varied shapes including hearts and scrolls, 8¹/₄in. high, 16oz. (Christie's) **$121,000**

A pair of George II plain octagonal sugar casters, with pierced domed cover and baluster finial, by Samuel Wood, 1737, 6in. high, 10 oz. (Christie's) **$1,760**

A Charles II caster, the cap pierced with a variety of scattered motifs below gadrooning and baluster finial, London 1679, 7¹/₂oz., 7¹/₈in. (Tennants) **$2,418**

A set of three Queen Anne octagonal casters, the pierced domed covers with bayonet fittings and baluster finials, unmarked, circa 1710, 5¹/₄in. and 4¹/₂in. high, 14 oz. (Christie's) **$1,232**

A caster with molded girdle and foot, the cap pierced with scrolls, maker probably S. Wood, London, 1728, 6¹/₂oz., 6³/₈in. high. (Tennants) **$744**

CENTREPIECES

Sheffield plate Regency épergne, unmarked, circa 1810–1820, supporting four oval glass dishes with scalloped borders and diapered sides, 12¹/₂in. high. (Butterfield & Butterfield) $1,320

'English Sterling' centerpiece, New York, circa 1870, the boat form bowl on a narrow waisted stem over a multi stepped expanding base, 8³/₄in. high, 42oz. (Butterfield & Butterfield) $770

Victorian Sterling reproduction of a George III épergne by Thomas Bradbury, London, 1897, on four foliate scroll feet, 14in. high, 112oz. 10dwts. (Butterfield & Butterfield) $8,250

Victorian silver three branch épergne with leaded glass liners by John Harrison & Co., Ltd., Sheffield, 1870, 21in. high, 123oz. 12 dwts. (Butterfield & Butterfield) $7,150

An antique German Renaissance Revival solid silver centerpiece in the form of a family tree, hallmarked *Posen* for Lazarus Posen, Frankfurt, circa 1880, 33¹/₂in. high, 339 troy oz. (Selkirk's) $8,500

A Victorian three-branch épergne, with acanthus leaf stem and three reed and foliage branches, by Robinson, Edkins and Aston, Birmingham, 1845, 15¹/₂in. high, 73oz. (Christie's) $5,653

A Victorian centerpiece of a putto riding a cornucopia drawn by swans, having a glass nautilus shell bough pot, the rectangular pond base engraved with a crest. (Woolley & Wallis) $1,029

A George V dessert stand centerpiece, supported on a paneled tapering stem, 13in. high, Walker and Hall, Sheffield 1920, 43.7oz. (Bearne's) $1,585

An antique English Sheffield George III style plated silver épergne with five lead crystal liners, 14in. high. (Selkirk's) $1,900

CHAMBERSTICKS

A George III chamber candlestick, the dished circular base with flying scroll handle and extinguisher, by Jonathan Alleine, 1777, 8cm., 14oz.
(Lawrence Fine Art) $483

A Victorian part-fluted and gadrooned boat-shaped chamber candlestick with rising curved spout and detachable conical snuffer, H.S., London 1895, 6³/₄in.
(Christie's) $545

A George III chamberstick, 4in. high, with reeded borders, and vase-shaped socket with detachable nozzle, London, 1807, by William Barrett II, 11 oz.
(Bonhams) $620

An early Victorian taperstick, of lobed flared cylindrical form with acanthus leaf sheathed double 'C' scroll handle, Sheffield 1841, by Henry Wilkinson & Co., 13.5cm. high.
(Spencer's) $361

A pair of William IV chamber candlesticks, the shaped circular bases and detachable nozzles with gadroon edging, 6¹/₂in. diameter, Paul Storr, London 1832, 28.9oz.
(Bearne's) $5,950

Matthew Boulton & Co, an early 19th century circular 'storm' chamber lamp with a matted, globular glass shade, a conical snuffer and gadrooned borders, 15cm. diameter, circa 1815.
(Phillips) $415

A George III chamber candlestick, with gadroon border and flying scroll handle, 1772 (no maker's mark but nozzle by Ebenezer Coker), 9.5cm., 7.5oz.
(Lawrence Fine Art) $347

A George III chamberstick, 6¹/₂in. diameter, with beaded borders, vase-form socket supporting detachable nozzle, London, 1778, by Richard Carter, Daniel Smith and Robert Sharp, 9 oz.
(Bonhams) $775

A William IV shaped circular chamber candlestick with reeded edging, 5³/₄in. diameter, Henry Wilkinson and Co., Sheffield 1835, 11.2oz.
(Bearne's) $684

CIGARETTE CASES

An amusing German enameled cigarette case, a gentleman with his female companion, both with cigarettes in their mouths, each smoldering where one touches the other, 9.5 x 7.5cm.
(Phillips) $650

An early Victorian cigar case, one side stamped with a view of Windsor Castle, the reverse stamped with a view of Kenilworth Castle, Nathaniel Mills, Birmingham 1839, 4.8in.
(Christie's S. Ken) $408

A Continental gilt-lined oblong cigarette case, the hinged cover enameled with a naked woman lying on a leopard skin rug, 3³⁄₄in. wide.
(Christie's S. Ken)

$2,161

A late 19th century Burmese cigarette case, the cover inset with an oval panel of polychrome enamel depicting a girl in Burmese National costume, 9 x 7.5cm., by S.C. Coombes, Rangoon, circa 1900, 4oz. (Phillips) $346

A William IV slightly curved oblong cheroot case, the front finely engraved with a standing sportsman and two grayhounds, by Henry Wilkinson & Co., Sheffield, 1832, 5¹⁄₄in. long, 10oz.
(Christie's) $6,501

A 9ct. gold engine turned cigarette case, rectangular form, engraved presentation inscription to interior.
(Bonhams) $580

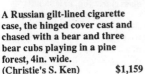

A Russian gilt-lined cigarette case, the hinged cover cast and chased with a bear and three bear cubs playing in a pine forest, 4in. wide.
(Christie's S. Ken) $1,159

A composite three piece smoking set, comprising a small cigarette box, a small ashtray and a cigarette case, Birmingham 1951, 113 grammes weighable silver.
(Spencer's) $203

Russian silver and gold cigarette case with gilt medallion, maker L P (Cyrillic), Moscow, 1908–1917, overstamped with Soviet mark 84, 7oz. 6dwts.
(Butterfield & Butterfield)

$1,320

CLARET JUGS

Continental silver claret jug, 19th century, probably French, mermaid handle and conch finial, apparently unmarked, 12in. high, approximately 33 troy oz.
(Skinner Inc.) $2,090

A silver and cut-glass claret jug, hinged domed cover with fruit finial, mask spout, vine chased scroll handle.
(Bonhams) $410

Gorham Sterling and two-color cut glass claret jug, ovoid body with green and ruby cutting, $10^{1}/_{2}$in. high.
(Skinner Inc.) $2,640

A Hukin & Heath silver mounted claret jug designed by Dr. Christopher Dresser, with hinged cover and ebonized bar handle, date registration lozenge for *9th May 1881*, 21.6cm. high.
(Christie's) $2,166

A pair of Victorian vase-shaped claret jugs, one engraved with the 'Triumphe of Venus', the other with a 'Sacrifice to Pain', by Roberts and Belk, Sheffield, 1866, $13^{3}/_{4}$in. high, 43 oz.
(Christie's) $4,400

A crested silver-mounted claret-jug, the flattened oviform body engraved with a crest within an oval cartouche flanked by scantily draped nymphs, London, 1891, 22.5cm. high.
(Christie's) $2,139

A late Victorian cut glass claret jug, engraved with flowers and scrolls in a rock-crystal effect, the silver top embossed with foliage and a humming bird, 11in. makers William Hutton & Sons, London 1894.
(Woolley & Wallis) $1,411

A George III vase-shaped claret jug, chased with alternate plain and matted vertical stripes, the shoulder with a band of rosettes and drapery festoons, by James Young and Orlando Jackson, 1774, $13^{1}/_{4}$in. high, gross 29 oz.
(Christie's) $2,992

German silver mounted cut glass claret jug, Friedlander, late 19th century, 750 standard silver, compressed spherical base with oval and diamond cut panels, $12^{1}/_{2}$in. high.
(Butterfield & Butterfield) $990

582

COASTERS

A pair of early Victorian silver-gilt wine coasters with scroll pierced sides and turned wood bases, Henry Wilkinson and Co., Sheffield 1847.
(Christie's) $1,385

A set of four George IV Irish circular wine coasters in the mid-18th century manner, pierced and chased with various animals, fruiting vines and scrolls, by W. Nowlan, Dublin, 1824, diameter 13cm.
(Christie's) $7,750

Four Sheffield plate shaped circular wine coasters with shell and foliate scroll edging on turned wood bases with crested inset plaques, 7in. diameter.
(Bearne's) $720

A pair of Old Sheffield plate wine coasters, circular with encrusted scroll and foliate borders, central crest engraved bosses to later wooden bases.
(Bonhams) $264

A pair of George III reeded, pierced and bright-cut circular wine coasters with turned wood bases, Richard Morton and Co., Sheffield 1793, 5in. diameter.
(Christie's) $3,175

A pair of William IV silver wine coasters with fluted and slightly flared sides, S.C. Younge and Co., Sheffield 1830.
(Christie's) $2,020

A set of four George III silver-gilt wine coasters, the sides pierced with arcading and applied with husk swags, rosettes and oval cartouches, by Robert Hennell, 1774.
(Christie's) $7,920

A pair of George III pierced and gadrooned circular wine coasters applied with paterae and floral and foliate swags, 4½in. diameter.
(Christie's) $1,730

A pair of early Victorian silver wine coasters with scroll pierced waisted sides, Joseph and Joseph Angell, London 1843.
(Christie's) $1,445

583

COFFEE POTS

A George III coffee pot, decorated with scrolls, flowers and foliage and with wood handle on spreading base, 10¼in. high, maker's mark *W.C.*, London 1762, 715gm., 22.9oz.
(Bearne's) $1,585

Antique American empire silver coffee pot, circa 1800–1830, raised petal decoration, wooden handle, ball feet, 11½in. high, 32 troy oz.
(Eldred's) $440

A George II chocolate pot, engraved with a crest and with swan neck spout, 9¾in. high, Isaac Cookson, Newcastle 1732, 29.2oz.
(Bearne's) $7,380

George III Sterling coffee pot by John Robins, London, 1793, with leaf capped spout, a stepped domed lid with urn finial and fitted with a wooden handle, 12½in. high, 29oz. 18dwts.
(Butterfield & Butterfield) $1,980

A Queen Anne Irish plain tapering cylindrical coffee pot, on molded rim foot, the partly octagonal curved spout at right angles to the wood scroll handle, by Thomas Bolton, Dublin, 1706, 9½in. high, gross 29oz.
(Christie's) $6,783

A Belgian pear-shaped coffee pot, with fluted curved spout, detachable hinged domed cover with scroll thumbpiece and flower finial, by Jacques-Hermann Le Vieu, Mons, 1753, 11¾in. high, gross 1,180 grs.
(Christie's) $21,120

A George II plain tapering cylindrical coffee pot, the curved spout with scroll base, the domed cover with acorn finial, by Richard Gurney and Thomas Cooke, 1747, 9½in. high, gross 27 oz.
(Christie's) $2,640

A George II pear-shaped coffee pot, chased with foliage festoons and rocaille ornament, the cover with an unusual mask, by John Swift, 1744, 10¼in. high, gross 35 oz.
(Christie's) $3,520

A Victorian coffee pot of George I design, with domed cover and side handle, by Goldsmiths and Silversmiths Co., 1899 (Britannia standard), 23cm., 19oz.
(Lawrence Fine Art) $1,448

COFFEE POTS

George II silver coffee pot by Thomas Farren, London, 1736, with cast faceted swan neck spout, 8³/₄in. high, gross weight 24oz.
(Butterfield & Butterfield)
$3,575

A silver coffee biggin, stand and lamp, maker's mark of Gale & Willis, New York, 1859, the body with elaborate foliate decoration, 11¹/₄in. high, 43 oz.
(Christie's) $1,650

A George II pear-shaped coffee pot, the body chased with flowers, foliage and scrolls, the curved leaf-capped spout cast with vacant rococo cartouche, by Thomas Whipham, 1757, 10in. high, gross 32oz.
(Christie's) $4,711

A George II tapering cylindrical coffee pot, with curved octagonal spout, the upper part of the body engraved with masks, foliage and trellis-work, 1732, 8⁵/₈in. high, gross 26 oz.
(Christie's) $3,520

A fine George II tapering cylindrical coffee pot, the curved spout terminating in bird's mask and with hinged stepped cover and baluster finial, by Paul de Lamerie, 1734, 8¹/₄in. high, gross 25oz.
(Christie's) $31,152

A George III vase-shaped coffee pot, chased with flowers, foliage and scrolls, with beaded and foliage curved spout and domed cover, by Charles Whipham and Thomas Wright, 1764, 11¹/₄in. high, gross 37 oz.
(Christie's) $3,520

George III Irish silver coffee pot by Charles Townsend, Dublin, 1772, on spreading circular base with scroll spout and wooden handle, 12in. high, gross weight 29oz. 6 dwts.
(Butterfield & Butterfield)
$3,575

A rare silver coffee biggin, maker's mark of Garrett Eoff, New York, circa 1820, with a scroll spout chased with acanthus and a carved wood handle, 9¹/₂in. high, 32 oz. 10 dwt.
(Christie's) $3,080

A George III coffee pot, with gadroon edging, leaf-capped spout, wrythen finial and wood scroll handle, 11³/₄in. high, maker's mark I.K., London 1772, 29.5oz.
(Bearne's) $3,330

CREAM JUGS

A George III cow creamer, engraved with hair along the ridge of back, the cover chased with flowers and applied with a fly, 9.5cm. high overall, by John Schuppe, 1767, 4 ozs. (Phillips) $12,474

A cream jug, helmet form with beaded border, loop handle and square pedestal base, Birmingham 1922. (Bonhams) $132

A William IV melon pattern milk jug, 4¼in. high, Jonathan Hayne, London 1792, 258 gms, 8.2 oz. (Bearne's) $481

A silver cream jug, maker's mark of John Myers, Philadelphia, 1790–1804, helmet-shaped, with a molded strap handle, on a flaring pedestal base with a square foot, 7⅛in. high, 5 oz. 10 dwt. (Christie's) $2,640

Sterling Arts and Crafts style cream pitcher and open sugar bowl by Whiting Mfg. Co., Providence, Rhode Island, 1913, 8oz. 14 dwts. (Butterfield & Butterfield) $302

A silver cream jug, maker's mark of John Baptiste Dumoutet, Philadelphia, circa 1800, helmet-shaped, the spreading circular foot on square pedestal base, 7³⁄₈in. high, 5 oz. 10 dwt. (Christie's) $1,760

A George IV cream jug, 3in. high, banded to belly with everted gadrooned border and florally-chased reeded strap handle, London, 1829, by Robert Hennell, 3.5 oz. (Bonhams) $165

A George III cream jug, the sides later chased with scrolls and foliage, London 1801, by Samuel Hennell. (Bonhams) $198

Russian silver cream pitcher, maker T Sokha, St. Petersburg, 1845, 84 standard, melon shaped body on conforming shaped oval foot, 6oz. 8dwts. (Butterfield & Butterfield) $220

CREAM JUGS

A George II cream jug, the upper part of the shaped-oval body chased with shells, scrolls and foliage on a matted ground, by Paul de Lamerie, 1742, 7oz. (Christie's) $7,537

A Dutch silver miniature cow creamer, the loop tail forming the handle, London import mark 1906, maker's mark *B.H.M.*, 107gm., 10.5cm. long. (Spencer's) $828

A late Victorian cream jug, with reeded borders and reeded angled handle, London 1892. (Bonhams) $149

A fine George II pear-shaped cream jug, on three female mask and claw-and-ball feet, chased with two shaped-oval panels, one enclosing goats, the other cows and a milkmaid, by William Cripps, 1749, 5¹/₄in. high, 9oz. (Christie's) $21,669

A pair of Victorian shaped-oval silver-gilt cream boats, each supported by a merman, by Andrew Crespel and Thomas Parker, 1869 and 1870 and two Old English pattern silver-gilt cream ladles, 1793 and 1795, 4¹/₂in. high, 28 ozs. (Christie's) $8,096

A silver cream jug, maker's mark of Daniel Van Voorhis, New York, circa 1795, with cast double-scroll handle, on a pedestal foot, 5¹/₂in. high, 4 oz. 10 dwt. (Christie's) $2,200

A fine George II cast cream jug, decorated with cows and a milk maid in naturalistic surroundings, by Elias Cachart, London 1740, 7¹/₂oz., 5in. (Tennants) $7,068

A George III cream jug, with prick engraved borders, and bright-cut bands, London, 1806, by John Merry. (Bonhams) $387

A rare George II cast boat-shaped cream jug, the body cast and chased with goats, a cow, bull's masks, shells, scrolls and foliage, by Louis Hamon, 1738, 5¹/₄in. high, 17oz. (Christie's) $16,017

CRUETS

A George II reeded broad boat-shaped cruet stand on fluted semi-ovoid feet, fitted with seven silver-mounted cut glass condiment bottles and jars, London 1792, 19.25oz. free.
(Christie's) $2,345

A George III boat-shaped oil and vinegar stand, on four shell-and-scroll feet with gadrooned border, by John Parker and Edward Wakelin, 1774, 11in. long, 22 oz.
(Christie's) $5,280

A silver boat-shaped four-cup egg cruet on reeded curved legs and with central openwork scroll handle, London 1912, 8½in. high, 21oz.
(Christie's) $376

Russian silver and glass mustard set by Nichols and Plinke, St. Petersburg, 1843, the frame with threaded octagonal holder for two glass mustard jars supported by four vertical supports, 6in. high, 16oz. 14dwts.
(Butterfield & Butterfield)
$1,100

A James Dixon & Sons electroplated condiment set designed by Dr. Christopher Dresser, the lozenge shaped holder with central handles and four square section compartments, with four faceted clear glass bottles and stoppers, 15.5cm. high.
(Christie's) $748

A late George III seven bottle cruet, the bombé boat shaped gallery repoussé and chased with scrolling foliage, raised upon four tapering flared feet, London 1866, by Hyam Hyams.
(Spencer's) $466

Silver five-bottle caster frame with scrolled legs, leaf-form feet, turned handle with bright-cut engraving, possible American, 10¼in. high, 36.6 troy oz.
(Eldred's) $220

A Belgian altar cruet, comprising shaped oval tray and two ewers and covers, by Johannes Moermans, Antwerp, circa 1660, the tray 15½in. wide.
(Christie's) $34,969

A Regency part-fluted rounded square cruet frame on foliate feet and with egg and dart border, Paul Storr , London, 1818, 10¾in., 35.50oz. free.
(Christie's) $7,009

CRUETS

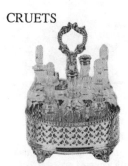

A silver plated cruet set, the seven cruet bottles in a pierced oval stand with beaded border, on four scroll feet.
(Bonhams) $460

A fine French silver-gilt two-handled boat-shaped oil and vinegar stand, fitted with two detachable openwork bottle holders, by Robert-Joseph Auguste, Paris, 1770, 12in. long, 44 oz.
(Christie's) $10,560

Silver six bottle revolving caster stand fitted with six glass castors by W.K. Vanderslice & Co., San Francisco, California, circa 1875, 14½in. high, 52oz.
(Butterfield & Butterfield) $2,090

An early George III cruet, the cinquefoil frame with central handle and engraved with a coat of arms on a rococo tablet, maker's mark *ID*, 1763, 23cm., frame 15.5oz.
(Lawrence Fine Art) $2,124

George III Sterling seven bottle cruet set by Robert Hennell, London, 1793, with seven original silver mounted glass cruets, the piece properly hallmarked with full and part marks, 10¼in. high.
(Butterfield & Butterfield) $2,750

A George I oil and vinegar frame, the open work sides formed as alternating pillars and brackets, by Paul de Lamerie, 1723, the bottle mounts unmarked, 7¾in. high, 18oz.
(Christie's) $19,470

A Victorian large shaped-circular egg frame, chased with flowers and scrolling foliage, with central foliage ring handle and six cups with shellwork borders, by John S. Hunt, 1846, 11in. high, 58 oz.
(Christie's) $2,288

A George III oblong egg cruet, on four shell and vine feet, fitted with six egg cups, each with shell and gadrooned everted rim, by Philip Rundell, 1818, 8in. long, 28oz.
(Christie's) $2,970

An unusual six cup egg cruet on bun feet with a part-spiral-fluted domed hinged cover with foliate handle, the latter turning to open arabesque-decorated panels concealing the egg cups, 10½in. high.
(Christie's) $540

CUPS

A rare Queen Anne Irish Provincial two-handled cup, with a molded rim, the campana-shaped body with a reeded girdle, 13cm. high overall, by William Clarke, Cork, circa 1714, 12oz. (Phillips) $2,938

A Commonwealth wine cup, the hexafoil slightly tapering bowl punched with beading and chased with matted arches, 1652, 3³/₄in. high. (Christie's) $11,440

A late 18th century two-handled cup with a domed pedestal foot and reeded handles, the campana shaped body decorated with bands of horizontal convex fluting, 14cm. tall, circa 1780. (Phillips) $276

Important Sterling silver trophy, 19th century, by Tiffany, cast handles in the form of angels holding children, either side with applied full, two-dimensional figures of women in diaphanous clothing, 24.8 troy oz. (Eldred's) $3,300

A pair of German wager cups, in the form of a Jungfrauenbecher and her male companion, Birmingham Import marks for 1902, maker's mark *IS* over *G*, 1187gm. total. (Spencer's) $4,799

A William IV two-handled silver-gilt cup and cover, the campana-shaped body decorated with acanthus leaves, flower-heads and with an applied horse, engraved *RICHMOND RACES 1834*, by Bernard & Co, 17¹/₄in. high, 115oz. (Christie's) $10,929

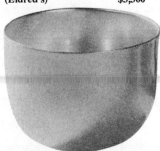

A George III tumbler cup, plain, of circular form with a rounded base, 5.5cm. high, inscribed *S.K*, by James Waters, 1770, 2¹/₂oz. (Phillips) $588

Sterling silver loving cup by Gorham, applied leaf and vine design, gold washed interior, 9³/₈in. high, 21.4 troy oz. (Eldred's) $495

A silver tumbler cup, maker's mark of Andrew Billing, Preston, Connecticut, Poughkeepsie area, 1775–1808, engraved with script monogram *JWK* within circular bright-cut reserve, 2¹/₈in. high, 1 oz. 10 dwt. (Christie's) $1,430

A George III rare Irish Provincial two-handled cup, the campana-shaped body chased with a foliate festooned classical frieze, by Daniel McCarthy, Cork, circa 1760, 14oz. (Phillips) $950

A Charles I shallow wine cup, the hexafoil bowl chased with stylized shells each within shaped-oval surround, 1640, maker's mark *GM*, a bird below, 2¹/₄in. high. (Christie's) $13,200

A late 19th century Australian silver, rare mounted coconut cup, the body finely carved with Aborigine fish motifs and supported by a calyx of silver-fern-like leaves, 14cm. high, by H. Steiner, circa 1882. (Phillips) $1,210

An Elizabeth I wine cup, the waisted stem with plain knop, the tapering bowl engraved with a band of strapwork and stylized foliate scrolls, 1571, maker's mark *HW*, 7in. high, 8 oz. (Christie's) $14,080

Pair of Sterling silver loving cups by Gorham, applied grapevine and Indian chief's head design, 8in. high, 39 troy oz. (Eldred's) $2,310

George III Sterling mounted ostrich egg cup and cover by Allen Dominy, London, 1798, the cup set on trumpet form pedestal base with reeded edge and bright-cut decoration, 12¹/₂in. high. (Butterfield & Butterfield) $1,100

Theodore B. Starr Sterling repoussé loving cup, 10¹/₄in. high, approximately 82 troy oz. (Skinner Inc.) $4,675

A mid 19th century Australian cup, cast in the form of a naked part kneeling Aborigine supporting on his head and with his left arm the cup, circa 1880. (Phillips) $864

A Charles II large tumbler cup, engraved with crest and beneath the lip, *The Gift from the owners of The Reliant*, 1683, maker's mark *IC*, 3in. high, 6 oz. (Christie's) $7,040

DISHES

A Hukin & Heath electroplated double bon-bon dish designed by Dr. Christopher Dresser, each oval basket with inverted rim, with loop handle, circa 1881, 14cm. high.
(Christie's)   **$827**

A chased silver fruit dish by Michael Lloyd, on four short cylindrical feet, the grooved central quatrefoil with four wells and a centered medallion of stylized overlapping fruit, 29cm. square, 98 grams.
(Christie's)   **$3,446**

A silver vegetable dish, maker's mark of Gorham Mfg. Co., Providence, circa 1870, with two stag-head handles, the domed cover with fawn finial, 13³/₄in. wide, 44 oz. 10 dwt.
(Christie's)   **$2,640**

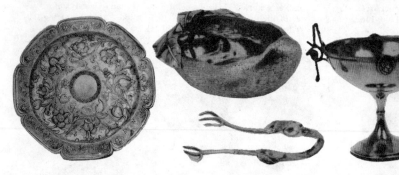

A Spanish silver-gilt shaped-circular dish, chased with birds, flowers and foliage, with raised molded border, late 17th century, possibly Palencia, 17³/₄in. diameter, 1,098 grs.
(Christie's)   **$2,640**

A parcel-gilt silver olive dish and tongs, maker's mark of Gorham Mfg. Co., Providence, 1887, formed as a cured olive with stem, 5³/₄in. long, 5 oz. 10 dwt.
(Christie's)   **$1,320**

Coin silver compote by Goodnow & Jenks, Boston, cameo reliefs at rim, classical style handle, conical foot with Greek key motif, 8¹/₂in. high, 14 troy oz.
(Eldred's)   **$468**

A silver Martele meat dish, maker's mark of Gorham Mfg. Co., Providence, circa 1905, the rim repoussé with flowers and leaves, the center engraved with a monogram, 20¹/₂in. long, 66 oz.
(Christie's)   **$6,600**

A silver covered vegetable dish, maker's mark of Gorham MFG, Co., Providence, 1916, with foliate scroll side handles, length over handles 12¹/₂in., 36 oz. 10 dwt.
(Christie's)   **$1,650**

A set of four Victorian shaped-oval meat dishes, each with gadrooned border and engraved with a crest, by J.C. Edington, 1838, 12in. long, 102 oz.
(Christie's)   **$2,816**

DISHES

A silver butter dish, maker's mark of Gorham Mfg. Co., Providence, circa 1860, with two bifurcated foliate scroll side handles, 9¹/₄in. wide, 14 oz. 10 dwt.
(Christie's) $715

Silver chafing dish, Jacob Hurd, Boston, circa 1745, pierced bowl with everted rim and removable pierced grate raised on three molded scrolled supports, 16³/₄ troy oz.
(Skinner Inc.) $22,000

A silver butter dish and cover, maker's mark of Bigelow, Kennard & Co., Boston, circa 1880, in the Persian taste, eleborately repoussé with foliate scrolls and fluting, 8in. wide, 16¹/₂ oz.
(Christie's) $880

A parcel-gilt silver compôte, maker's mark of Gorham Mfg. Co., Providence, 1870, one end forming a handle, elaborately clad with an entwined foliate frosted grape vine and applied gilt fox, 12¹/₂in. long, 39 oz.
(Christie's) $3,520

Two leaf-shaped dishes, chased to simulate acanthus-leaves, with matted decoration and tendril handle, Sheffield, 1829 and 1834, one by Robert Gainsford, the other by John Watson, 9¹/₄in. wide, 25 oz.
(Christie's) $3,168

A German silver-gilt two-handled wine taster, the base chased with a flower, by Wolff or Georg Rotenbeck, Nuremberg, 17th century, 4⁵/₈in. diameter, 60 grs.
(Christie's) $1,760

A Spanish oval dish, the well and border repoussé and chased with flowers and foliage, by Jose Asteiza, Bilbao, circa 1760, 20in. wide, 1,097 grs.
(Christie's) $2,816

A Louis XVI shaped-oval shaving dish, with detachable neck-notch and reeded borders, engraved with a coat-of-arms, by Jean-Antoine Gallemant, Paris, 1780–81, 13in. wide, 820 grs.
(Christie's) $4,576

A parcel-gilt silver covered butter dish, maker's mark of Tiffany & Co., New York, 1881–1891, the spot-hammered surface applied with silver-gilt leaves and thistles, 5⁷/₈in. diameter, 15 oz. 10 dwt.
(Christie's) $2,860

SILVER

Paul Storr, a George III entrée dish and cover, of plain circular form, the base-dish with a finely applied border of scallop and oak leaf motifs with gadrooning, 20.5cm. high overall, 1810, 61oz.
(Phillips) $12,096

A pair of electroplated rounded rectangular entrée dishes with detachable acanthus handles and gadroon edging, 14in. over handles.
(Bearne's) $810

A French two-handled silver-gilt circular écuelle and cover, chased with bands of flowers, scrolls and shell ornament, Paris, circa 1785, the bowl maker's mark *JDB*, perhaps for Jacques du Boys, 12in. wide, 839 grs.
(Christie's) $3,520

Pair of Sheffield plate covered dishes with liners, by Mappin Bros., circa 1850, the handles reeded and ribbon tied, the covers lifting to reveal removable liners, 10¹/₂in. diameter.
(Butterfield & Butterfield) $1,210

Two George I octagonal meat dishes, each with ovolo border, engraved with a coat-of-arms, by David Willaume I, 1725, Britannia Standard, 75oz.
(Christie's) $5,276

A pair of electroplated shaped oval entrée dishes and covers with detachable handles, 14in. over handles, Martin Hall and Company.
(Bearne's) $990

A pair of German plain circular vegetable dishes and covers, with detachable wood handles, engraved with a coronet and initial *W*, by Christian Drentwett, Augsburg, 1795–97, 8³/₈in. diameter, 2,240 grs.
(Christie's) $7,040

A George III Irish strawberry dish, of circular form with a scalloped rim, 24cm. diameter, by William Hughes, Dublin, 1772, 16oz.
(Phillips) $3,802

A George III oval entrée dish and cover, engraved with contemporary armorials, each dish with reeded handles, maker Robert Jones, London 1795, 41oz.
(Woolley & Wallis) $697

FLATWARE

SILVER

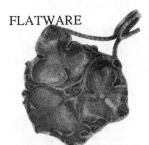

A large George IV "Lily Pad" pattern caddy spon, the looped handle formed as twigs, Robert Hennell, London 1829.
(Christie's S. Ken) $1,265

Hunt and Roskell, fine Victorian caddy spoon, the fig shaped bowl with a cast and pierced grape vine handle, London 1867.
(Woolley & Wallis) $542

A Victorian naturalistic leaf bowl caddy spoon with a hollow vine decorated handle, George Unite, Birmingham 1869.
(Woolley & Wallis) $232

A Charles II trefid end rat tail pattern spoon, with prick-worked initials *F* over *IM*, London 1672, possibly by Joseph Simson, 45gr., 19cm. long.
(Spencer's) $497

A rare early period fish slice with a feather edge stem and a shaped oval blade, engraved with a fish and pierced with floral scrollwork, 33cm. long, circa 1780.
(Phillips) $276

Two of a set of twelve Queen Anne cannon handled table knives, each engraved with a crest, two handles struck with indistinct maker's mark only, early 18th century.
(Christie's)   (Twelve) $7,399

Two of a set of twelve William III dog-nose pattern table forks, each with three prongs and engraved with a coat-of-arms, by Isaac Davenport, 1701, 21oz.
(Christie's)   (Twelve) $9,735

An early 18th century dog nose or wavy end spoon with elongated rat tail bowl, engraved with initials, marker's mark *IH*, 59gr.
(Spencer's) $331

A late Charles II trefid end rat tail pattern spoon, engraved *VH*, London 1680, maker's mark *IB* in shield, 51gr., 18.5cm. long.
(Spencer's) $364

A pair of parcel-gilt silver fish servers, maker's mark of Gorham Mfg. Co., circa 1880, the ivory handles carved with swirling flutes, 12in. long.
(Christie's) $1,320

A pair of silver scissors, the tapering blades joined through a figure-of-eight-shaped spring-handle, Tang Dynasty, 14.7cm. long.
(Christie's) $14,768

A rare pair of large silver ragout spoons made for Moses Michael Hays, maker's mark of Paul Revere, Boston, 1786, 12in. long, 8 oz.
(Christie's) $46,200

FLATWARE

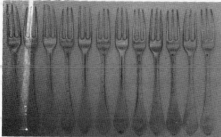

A set of twelve Queen Anne dog-nose pattern table forks, engraved with a coat-of-arms, by Joseph Barbutt, 1706, marks worn, 21 oz.
(Christie's) $2,992

Georg Jensen sterling partial flatware service, cactus pattern, approximately 149 troy oz., 120 pieces.
(Skinner Inc.) $6,050

A set of four George II silver-gilt dessert spoons, with shell-back bowls, the handles with shell terminals, each engraved with the royal cypher, garter motto and monogram, by Paul de Lamerie, circa 1730, 7oz.
(Christie's) $6,783

Empire silver gilt flatware service, Paris, early 19th century, maker *JPD* in lozenge, twelve each: tablespoons and dinner forks, knives with silver-gilt and steel blades, all mother-of-pearl handles, 44 troy oz.
(Skinner Inc.) $2,420

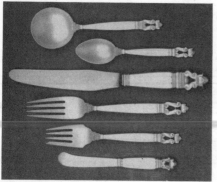

A silver fish slice, maker's mark of James Conning, Mobile, Alabama, 1842–1862, engraved with a fish amid foliate scroll decoration, 11¾in. long, 5 oz.
(Christie's) $1,760

Georg Jensen Sterling flatware service, Acorn pattern, twelve each: dinner forks, salad forks, soup spoons, dinner knives, butter knives, twenty four teaspoons, pair of salad servers, cake server, sauce ladle, two piece carving set, 107 troy oz.
(Skinner Inc.) $5,225

A rare silver soup ladle, maker's mark of William & George Richardson, Richmond, Virginia, circa 1782–1795, with a downturned pointed-oval handle, 12¼in. high, 4 oz. 10 dwt.
(Christie's) $1,870

596

FLATWARE

An Elizabeth I silver-gilt seal top spoon, the
partly-fluted baluster top, pricked with initials
SM, 1587, maker's mark a chanticleer.
(Christie's) $2,200

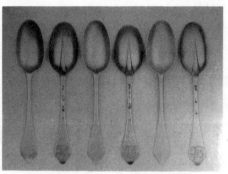

A set of twelve Queen Anne dognose pattern
table spoons, the reverse of the handles each
engraved with a monogram, *RSC*, by Isaac
Davenport, 1703, 24oz.
(Christie's) $4,899

A silver ladle, maker's mark of Joseph Anthony,
Philadelphia, 1785–1810, with downturned
rounded-end handle, 10in. long, 3 oz.
(Christie's) $1,320

Silver ladle, Benjamin Burt, Boston, circa 1780,
with tapered ivory tipped wooden handle, 14³/₄in.
long.
(Skinner Inc.) $715

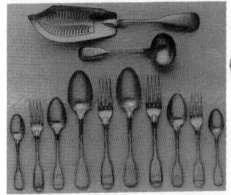

A fiddle and thread-table service, the majority
by William Eaton, 1826, 1834, 1837, etc.,
comprising 63 pieces, 131oz.
(Christie's) $7,160

A Dutch fish slice, pierced and engraved with
flowers, foliage and trelliswork, the shaped
handle with flower and foliage top, by Barend
Swierink, Amsterdam, 1778, 15¹/₄in. long,
214 grs.
(Christie's) $2,816

A Mary I silver-gilt apostle spoon, surmounted
by the figure of St. James the Greater, engraved
with initials *M.T.*, 1555, maker's mark a crescent
enclosing a mullet, possibly for Nicholas
Bartholomew.
(Christie's) $7,040

Kirk Sterling flatware service, 1880-90, repoussé
pattern, 104 pieces, monogramed, approximately
93 troy oz. weighable silver.
(Skinner Inc.) $1,430

GOBLETS

Fine antique American coin silver goblet, mid-19th century, with chased hunting decoration, marked *Pure Coin, Boston*, 8in. high, 11 troy oz.
(Eldred's) $715

A very attractive Victorian Aesthetic Movement wine ewer and two goblets en suite, in the Japanese style with cranes chasing butterflies amidst foliage and bamboo, by E.C. Brown, 1875, goblets 16.5cm. high, ewer, 29.5cm. high, 26.5 ozs.
(Phillips) $3,119

American silver goblet with chased decoration, cast vintage design base, unmarked, 8in. high, 11.2 troy oz.
(Eldred's) $303

Victorian silver goblet and beaker by William Hunter, London, 1870, and Henry John Lias & James Wakely, London 1881, 14oz. 8 dwts.
(Butterfield & Butterfield) $550

Assembled and matching silver three piece presentation water set, pitcher marked *Vanderslice & Co., San Francisco, Cal.*; goblets unmarked, dated *1866*, 44oz. 2 dwts.
(Butterfield & Butterfield) $2,200

Coin silver goblet and a cup with handles and salt cellar, third quarter 19th century, by Peter L. Krider, Philadelphia, circa 1850–1860, 15oz. 14 dwts.
(Butterfield & Butterfield) $440

A Victorian gilt-lined goblet on a rising circular foot and with a spherical knop, Messrs. Barnard, London 1887, 10¹/₂in., 22oz.
(Christie's) $675

A pair of George III goblets, each on a circular bead edge stem foot, 5.65in., one maker Charles Wright, London 1788, the other maker Stephen Adams, London 1808, 14oz.
(Woolley & Wallis) $1,129

Israeli silver Kiddish cup, Stanetzky, of goblet form, with applied filigree work on base, stem and lip, 5³/₄in. high, gross weight 3oz. 4 dwts.
(Butterfield & Butterfield) $193

SILVER

A Victorian inkstand, with central taper holder and two cut ruby overlaid glass bottles, by Yapp and Woodward, Birmingham, 1850, 19cm., weight of taper holder and base 10 oz.
(Lawrence Fine Art)　　$889

A silver inkwell, maker's mark of Shiebler & Co., New York, circa 1900, elaborately repoussé with scrolls and rocaille, the fitted silver-mounted glass bottles with fluted swirls, 10in. long, 19 oz. 10 dwt.
(Christie's)　　$3,080

A Victorian shaped rectangular ink stand with beaded edging, central rectangular reservoir with dog finial and two cut-glass wells, 10¼in. long, Birmingham 1890, 11.3oz.
(Bearne's)　　$1,350

A late Victorian small ink stand of lozenge form, set with a pair of slice cut glass ink wells of globular form, with silver mounts and pierced covers, Sheffield 1888, by Henry Wilkinson and Co., 261 grammes weighable silver.
(Spencer's)　　$783

A Victorian shaped oblong bright-cut inkstand, molded with two pen rests and fitted with two silver-topped cut-glass inkwells, Messrs. Barnard, London 1868 and 1869, 9³/₄in., 16.75oz. free.
(Christie's S. Ken)　　$1,652

George II Sterling inkstand by William Cripps, London, 1749, set on four incurvate scrolled supports, the stand with a single penwell, 11¹/₂in. wide, 48oz. 2dwts.
(Butterfield & Butterfield)　　$8,250

A George IV inkstand, with gadrooned borders, and scroll and shell corners, supporting foliate mounted paw feet, Sheffield, 1825, by John and Thomas Settle.
(Bonhams)　　$1,846

A George III inkstand, 8³/₄ x 6in., with reeded borders and two pen depressions, on four ball feet, London, 1800, by John Emes, 14oz.
(Bonhams)　　$1,464

A Victorian three-division rounded rectangular ink stand, on a stand with four tapering supports, 9in. long, Martin Hall and Co., London 1876, 466 gms, 14.9 oz.
(Bearne's)　　$1,194

A silver-plated inkstand, the shaped rectangular tray top surmounted by a figure of a golfer, 9¹/₂in. wide.
(Christie's)　　$1,871

A commemorative silver inkwell, circular with detachable glass liner, London 1935, Garrard & Co. Ltd.
(Bonhams)　　$546

An Edwardian gadrooned and foliate-pierced oblong gallery inkstand in the 18th century taste, Martin Hall and Co., Sheffield 1909, 8¹/₄in., 19oz. free.
(Christie's S. Ken)　　$1,200

JARS

An unusual Victorian silver-mounted ebony tobacco jar modeled as a barrel with simulated staves and applied hoops, George Fox, London 1864, 6in. overall.
(Christie's) $700

Dutch silver-gilt and carved mother-of-pearl tobacco jar and cover, Barend van Mecklenburg, Amsterdam, 1786, with protruding gadroon edge rim fitted with a lift off lid with matching rim flaring a full shell, 5⁵/₈in. high, 21oz. 8dwts., all in.
(Butterfield & Butterfield) $1,980

A cylindrical parcel-gilt trompe l'oeil caviar cooler, with simulated wood cover and bracket handle, by P. Ovchinnikov, Moscow, 19th century, containing stand and glass liner, 6¹/₂in. high, 714grs.
(Christie's) $3,762

A silver and mixed-metal ginger jar, maker's mark of Whiting Mfg. Co., circa 1885, the matted surface applied with a copper fish and with silver and copper foliage, 5¹/₂in. high, 10 oz. 10 dwt.
(Christie's) $1,980

A Victorian large ginger jar and cover and two similar trumpet-shaped vases, each chased with acanthus leaves and ribbon-tied fruit swags, by W.W. Williams, 1869, 224oz.
(Christie's) $18,706

Cut glass and silver jar, brilliant hobstar and oval cut, with rose decorated flared silver rim, 9in. diameter.
(Skinner Inc.) $750

Mount Washington Crown Milano covered jar, blue background melon ribbed bowl with gold enhanced floral decoration, 6³/₄in. high.
(Skinner Inc.) $330

An unusual silver and enamel powder jar, maker's mark of Gorham Mfg. Co., Providence, circa 1895, repoussé with foliate and drapery swags below a laurel band, 4¹/₂in. diameter, 6 oz. 10 dwt.
(Christie's) $1,210

Sterling ginger jar by Howard & Co., New York, New York, 1885, the body and lid allover chased and embossed with scrolling foliage and various flowers, 6in. high, 10oz.
(Butterfield & Butterfield) $522

JUGS

A German parcel gilt wine jug, the cover with bayonet fitting, formed as the head of a sphinx, with foliage finial, by Jacques Louis Clement, Kassel, 1793, 11³/₄in. high, gross 915gm. (Christie's) $7,399

A late Victorian novelty milk jug modeled as a bedroom hot water jug with wicker-covered handle, Heath and Middleton, Birmingham 1895, 7¹/₄in., 13.50oz. gross. (Christie's) $902

English Sheffield silver plated covered flagon, 18th century, inscribed on base, *Green Dragon Tavern, 1760, Boston*, 10in. high. (Eldred's) $303

A late George III jug by Edward Edwards, with everted gadrooned rim and hinged flat domed cover, with polished treen handle, London 1817, 737gm. gross. (Spencer's) $662

A silver covered hot-milk jug, maker's mark of Tiffany & Co., New York, 1891–1902, the spot-hammered surface etched with foliage and thistles, 7in. high, 20 oz. 10 dwt. (Christie's) $3,300

A large Tiffany and Co. japanesque jug, the copper baluster body applied with three Sterling silver fish, stamped *Tiffany and Co.*, 21.5cm. high over frog. (Spencer's) $18,205

A George II plain pear-shaped beer jug, with leaf-capped double scroll handle and molded rim and spout, by Fuller White, 1748, 6³/₄in. high, 29oz. (Christie's) $7,537

An Elizabeth I silver-gilt mounted tiger-ware jug, the box hinge and neck mounts engraved with stylized scrolling foliage and engraved strapwork, the domed cover with winged mermaid and cornucopia thumbpiece, 1573, 8¹/₂in. high. (Christie's) $17,820

A late George III jug, with gadrooned border and hinged slightly domed cover with globular finial, London 1810, maker's mark *HN*, 695gm. gross, 19cm. high. (Spencer's) $596

MISCELLANEOUS

SILVER

Baltic silver Scroll of Esther case with amethyst stones, late 19th century, boldly embossed and chased with rocaille work, 13¹/₂in. long.
(Butterfield & Butterfield)
$3,575

Plated lady's dressing table mirror with easel back, late 19th century, with wire easel back, 13¹/₂in. high.
(Butterfield & Butterfield)
$495

Sterling Smith Corona typewriter by Gorham Mfg. Co., Providence, Rhode Island, 1930, 10³/₄in. wide.
(Butterfield & Butterfield)
$8,800

Victorian three bottle plated decanter stand, registration marks for 1870, with three cut glass pear shaped bottles, 16in.
(G.A. Key)
$575

A Victorian dessert stand, cast in high relief with entwined scaly dolphins and putti holding reins, by Frederick Elkington, 1875, 12¹/₂in. high, 84oz.
(Christie's)
$9,045

A German silver-gilt mounted nautilus shell, chased and applied with flowers and foliage, the stem formed as a standing wood figure of a blackamoor, by Paul Solanier, Augsburg, 1690–1695, 14in. high.
(Christie's)
$7,920

A silver punch strainer, maker's mark of John David, Jr., Philadelphia, circa 1785, with pierced scrollwork handle engraved with initials *TSC* on front, 4¹/₂in. high, 1 oz.
(Christie's)
$8,250

A fine silver and enamel desk set, maker's mark of Tiffany & Co., New York, circa 1886, decorated with polychrome enamel in the Islamic taste, in original fitted leather box dated *1886*.
(Christie's)
$6,600

A Victorian model group of two girls, wearing windswept diaphanous garments, one holding a basket of flowers, by Elkington & Co. Ltd., 1891, 16¹/₂in. high.
(Christie's)
$5,653

MISCELLANEOUS

A model leopard, realistically chased with fur and engraved with spots and with detachable head revealing a gilt-lined well, 1928, 10½in. long overall, 33 ozs.
(Christie's) **$3,168**

Polish silver Torah pointer, maker's mark: *W.S.*, circa 1840, of heavy gauge, 84 standard, the upper section applied with filigree panels, 10½in. long, gross weight 7oz. 6dwts.
(Butterfield & Butterfield) **$1,540**

A Sheffield plate Argyle with engraved ribbon-tied festoons and fronds, with beaded edging, detachable cover and wood scroll handle, 4¾in. high.
(Bearne's) **$990**

A Hukin & Heath electroplated biscuit barrel, designed by Christopher Dresser, of spherical form on three feet, 20cm. high, March 1879.
(Phillips) **$5,000**

Bezelel silver bound prayer book, 20th century, one side etched with symbols of the Twelve Tribes and four filigree rondels, 7in. high.
(Butterfield & Butterfield) **$2,200**

German silver bun warmer, 19th century, tripartite globular form, with figures of Bacchic putti, 800 fine, 9½in. high, approximately 62 troy oz.
(Skinner Inc.) **$2,420**

A silver figural bell, maker's mark of Tiffany & Co., New York, circa 1875, the handle formed as a classical maiden, marked 5½in. high, 6 oz. 10 dwt.
(Christie's) **$1,045**

A pair of rare William IV circular silver-gilt spittoons, the detachable spreading rims with lobed borders, by Paul Storr, 1834, 7in. diameter, 32oz.
(Christie's) **$6,595**

Sterling silver cocktail shaker by Shreve, Crump & Low, hammered Art Deco style, San Francisco, circa 1910, 10¼in. high, 12.6 troy oz.
(Eldred's) **$1,210**

MISCELLANEOUS

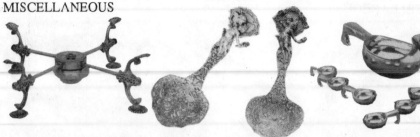

A George III dish-cross, on three openwork sliding shell feet and with similar supports and vase-shaped lamp with detachable beaded cover, by John Swift, 1768, 14in. long, 29 oz.
(Christie's) $2,816

A pair of silver bonbonnières, maker's mark of Tiffany & Co., New York, circa 1910, each with openwork scroll and flower stem terminating with cherub amid rocaille, 13½in. long, 34 oz.
(Christie's) $3,520

Russian 84 standard silver seven piece Kovsh form punch set, maker's mark *AK* (in oval), assay master's initials *AP*, circa 1899–1908, 62oz. 2dwts.
(Butterfield & Butterfield) $4,400

A late George V six piece dressing table set, with engine turned striped decoration and foliate chased borders, Birmingham 1929, in an apricot satin and velvet lined case.
(Spencer's) $331

A Victorian silver visiting card case by George Unite, of shaped vertical rectangular form, bright cut engraved with strap work panels, Birmingham 1876, 67gm., 10cm. high.
(Spencer's) $199

A George III plain cylindrical argyle, with elongated curved spout, short curved spout with hinged flap, wicker-covered scroll handle, and reeded borders, by Andrew Fogelberg and Stephen Gilbert, 1791, 4¾in. high, gross 11oz.
(Christie's) $4,868

A George IV silver-gilt cast table bell designed as layered acanthus leaves, 5¼in. high, Charles Fox, London 1826, 8.8oz.
(Bearne's) $3,060

A matched pair of Edward VII Art Nouveau comports, supported on openwork pedestal supports of whiplash scroll design, 6¾in. high, Birmingham 1907, 20.6oz.
(Bearne's) $575

A silver book-mark made for the Columbian Exposition of 1893, maker's mark of Tiffany & Co., 11½in. long, 8 oz.
(Christie's) $1,760

MISCELLANEOUS

A composite set of six napkin rings, each cast and applied with the figure of a dog, Birmingham 1935/6/7, 96gm. total. (Spencer's) $331

An early George V silver novelty pin cushion in the form of a boot, Birmingham 1912, by S. Blanskensee and Son Ltd., 12.5cm. long. (Spencer's) $248

A novelty silver plated condiment set, in the form of a small boy seated on a gate, above a pail, the gate flanked by two glass condiments. (Bonhams) $188

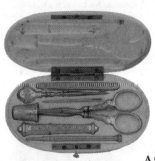

A 19th century French seven-piece silver-gilt nécessaire-à-coudre with engraved decoration in fitted and ivory case, circa 1870. (Phillips) $691

A George III plain cylindrical flagon, with scroll handle, corkscrew thumbpiece and hinged domed cover, by Thomas Whipham and Charles Wright, 1765, 12in. high, 42 oz. (Christie's) $3,520

A cased set of four silver gilt menu holders, depicting putti in a scrolling and floral decoration, Chester 1911. (Bonhams) $307

A George IV silver-gilt nutmeg grater, with hinged rasp and container, engraved with Garter Motto, by Philip Rundell, 1823, 7in. long, 5oz. (Christie's) $8,316

A good pair of meat dish covers of pleated domed form, by Joseph Cradock & William K. Reid, 1824, height overall 26.5cm. (Phillips) $1,555

Sterling muffinier by Tiffany & Co., New York, New York, circa 1891–1902, raised on four ball supports, 6³/₈in. high, 6oz. 18 dwts. (Butterfield & Butterfield) $605

MUGS & CANNS

A silver mug, maker's mark of Tiffany & Co., New York, 1875–1891, baluster form on spreading rim foot, elaborately repoussé with flowers, 6in. high, 18 oz.
(Christie's) $2,200

Antique American .900 fine silver mug by Wood & Hughes of New York City, chased and applied decoration, gilt interior, dated 1872, 3³/₄in. high, 6 troy oz.
(Eldred's) $363

A rare silver cann, maker's mark of John Bayley, Philadelphia, 1760–1770, the double scroll handle with acanthus-leaf grip, on molded circular foot, 5in. high, 13 oz. 10 dwt. (Christie's) $3,080

A pint mug with molded lip and foot, the scroll handle of tapering semi-circular section, by Langlands and Robertson, Newcastle, 1778, 10oz., 5in. high.
(Tennants) $707

An attractive Victorian silver-gilt christening mug, the baluster body with an overlapping rim embossed on either side with an oval 'disc' cartouche, 12cm. high, E. & J. Barnard, 1862, 7oz.
(Phillips) $864

Silver mug, George Hanners, Boston, circa 1740, tapering cylindrical form with molded mid-band and base band, scroll handle, 10 troy oz.
(Skinner Inc.) $5,500

A attractive Victorian christening mug, the cylindrical body paneled and engraved with floral sprays against a shaped background, 13cm. high, by Atherly & Sillwell, 1858, 6oz.
(Phillips) $484

A George I mug with molded foot, scroll handle of tapering semi-circular section, maker's mark C enclosing R, London 1717, 9¹/₂oz., 4¹/₄in. high.
(Tennants) $781

A silver cann, maker's mark of William Homes, Sr., Boston, circa 1750, the S-scroll handle with molded drop and bud terminal, 5¹/₄in. high, 10 oz. 10 dwt.
(Christie's) $1,320

A late Victorian molded circular mustard pot in the mid 19th century taste, chased with flowers and foliage, George Adams, London 1891, 2³/₄in. high.
(Christie's) $325

A French 19th century openwork mustard pot on a laurel leaf and berry-decorated shaped triangular base with foliate feet, 5¹/₂in., 13oz.
(Christie's) $1,635

A Victorian barrel-shaped mustard pot realistically decorated with simulated staves and hoops and with an engraved bung hole, George Fox, London 1864, 3¹/₄in. high.
(Christie's) $540

An early Victorian gilt-lined molded circular mustard pot on mask and lion's paw feet and with elaborate head and foliate-decorated scroll handle, William Brown, London 1838, 3¹/₂in. high.
(Christie's) $845

A novelty mutard pot modeled as an owl with yellow and black glass boot button eyes and detachable liner, 3¹/₄in. high.
(Christie's) $338

A late George II large mustard pot by the Barnards, of squat baluster form, repoussé with acanthus leaves and flowerheads and with a rococo scroll cartouche, London 1810, 131 grammes.
(Spencer's) $300

A George III gadrooned drum mustard pot pierced with birds on flowering branches and with a blue glass liner, London 1767, 3in. high.
(Christie's) $540

An unusual Victorian novelty mustard pot in the form of a pineapple standing on a scrolling foliate base, E.H. Stockwell, London 1876, 3³/₄in., 5.25oz.
(Christie's) $1,140

A Regency tapering circular mustard pot chased with a frieze of foliage and standing on leaf-capped lion's paw feet, Paul Storr, London 1801, 3¹/₂in. high.
(Christie's) $865

Dominick and Haff Sterling pitcher, late 19th century, chased vintage decoration, retailed by Bigelow Kennard and Company, 13³/₄in. high, 44 troy oz.
(Skinner Inc.) $1,320

Fine Sterling silver and cut and engraved crystal pitcher by Gorham, ornate leaf and berry decoration, 14¹/₂in. high.
(Eldred's) $1,980

A silver water pitcher, maker's mark of S. Kirk & Son., Baltimore, 1846–1861, elaborately repoussé with architectural landscapes amid flowers and foliage, 12in. high, 30 oz. 10 dwt.
(Christie's) $1,540

American Arts and Crafts hand beaten silver pitcher by LeBolt, Chicago, Illinois, circa 1915–1920, applied with cypher monogram on the side, 8¹/₄in. high, 22oz. 6dwts.
(Butterfield & Butterfield) $1,540

A pair of silver presentation ewers, maker's mark of Forbes & Son, New York, circa 1836, with elaborate foliate scroll handles, 11³/₄in. high, 78 oz.
(Christie's) $6,600

American silver octagonal pitcher by Whiting Mfg. Co., Providence, Rhode Island, 1921, on four cushion feet, hollow harp handle, 6³/₄in. high, 21oz. 8dwts.
(Butterfield & Butterfield) $440

A Victorian wine ewer, 12in. high, with scrolling borders and leaf-chased scrolling side handle on domed, circular base, London, 1856, by William Hattersley or William Hewit, 26.5oz. (Bonhams) $1,555

A fine silver and mixed-metal pitcher, maker's mark of Gorham Mfg. Co., Providence, 1880, the spot-hammered surface applied with a brass turkey, bamboo leaves, and a bronze fruit-tree branch, 7³/₄in. high, 30 oz.
(Christie's) $9,900

A silver water pitcher, maker's mark of Arthur J. Stone, Gardner, Massachusetts, 1908–1937, the body repoussé and chased with irises, 10³/₄in. high, 33 oz. 10 dwt.
(Christie's) $3,300

PITCHERS & EWERS

A silver-mounted 'craquelle' glass ice pitcher, maker's mark of Gorham Mfg. Co., Providence, circa 1880, with glass rope-twist handle and silver collar, 12¼in. high. (Christie's) $1,870

A silver water pitcher, maker's mark of John W. Forbes, New York, circa 1830, with foliate scroll handle and gadrooned rim, 12in. high, 31 oz. 10 dwt. (Christie's) $1,540

A silver water pitcher, maker's mark of S. Kirk & Sons, Co., Baltimore, 1903–1907, eleborately repoussé with architectural landscapes amid flowers and foliage, 12in. high, 43 oz.
(Christie's) $3,300

A silver water pitcher, maker's mark of Whiting Mfg. & Co., circa 1885, elaborately repoussé with flowers on a matted ground, 7¼in. high, 23 oz. 10 dwt.
(Christie's) $1,870

A fine silver and mixed-metal pitcher, maker's mark of Tiffany & Co., New York, circa 1880, the spot-hammered sides and handle applied with a dragonfly and butterflies amid a trailing vine of gold and copper, 7¾in. high, 26 oz. 10 dwt. (Christie's) $28,600

Mexican silver water pitcher by William Spratling, Taxco, circa 1931–1945, fitted with a carved wooden handle with an abstracted bird mask design, 6⅝in. high, 19oz., all in. (Butterfield & Butterfield) $3,025

Silver ewer, Robert and William Wilson (active 1825–1846), Philadelphia, baluster form with foliate and acanthus decoration, 45 troy oz.
(Skinner Inc.) $1,400

American silver hand wrought water pitcher by Herbert Taylor for Arthur Stone, Gardner, Massachusetts, circa 1935, with mild harp thumbrest, helmet brim spout, 40oz. 4dwts.
(Butterfield & Butterfield) $1,320

A silver water pitcher, maker's mark of Krider & Co., Philadelphia, circa 1851, elaborately repoussé with flowers enclosing a presentation inscription, with foliate scroll handle, 11in. high, 29 oz. 10 dwt. (Christie's) $990

PLATES

A set of twelve William IV shaped-circular soup plates, by William Eaton, 1832, 9³/₄in. diameter, 255oz.
(Christie's) **$10,709**

A Victorian set of twelve dinner plates, plain with shaped gadroon borders, engraved with a crest, 24cm. diameter, by Robert Garrard, 1854. 195oz.
(Phillips) **$8,294**

Twelve George III shaped-circular dinner plates, with gadrooned shell and foliage borders, by William Bennett, 1816 and 1817, 10¹/₂in. diameter, 332 oz.
(Christie's) **$14,080**

A set of twelve William IV shaped-circular dinner plates, each with a gadrooned and foliage border, by William Eaton, 1832, 9³/₄in. diameter, 229oz.
(Christie's) **$18,497**

A parcel-gilt silver wheat-pattern serving plate and cake knife, maker's mark of Gorham Mfg. Co., Providence, 1871, the rim applied and chased with gilt wheat sheaves amid foliage, 10¹/₄in. diameter, 22 oz. 10 dwt.
(Christie's) **$2,860**

Twelve George III shaped circular dinner plates, with molded gadrooned borders, engraved with two coats-of-arms and a Ducal coronet, by Andrew Fogelberg, 1773, 9¹/₂in. diameter, 203oz.
(Christie's) **$18,497**

German silver Pidyon Haben plate, mid 19th century, in the late 17th century style, the oval dish embossed and chased, struck with pseudo-Augsburg and other marks, 13³/₄in. wide, 18oz. 10dwts.
(Butterfield & Butterfield) **$4,125**

A set of twelve silver dinner plates, maker's mark of Howard & Co., New York, dated *1907*, the center engraved with a coat-of-arms and crest, 10in. diameter, 292 oz.
(Christie's) **$6,600**

Twelve American Sterling service plates by International Silver Co., Meriden, Connecticut, Trianon, 10¹/₂in. diameter, 234oz.
(Butterfield & Butterfield) **$3,850**

PORRINGERS

A silver porringer, maker's mark of Joseph Loring, Boston, 1770–1810, with pierced keyhole handle engraved with initials *ET*, 8¹/₈in. high, 8 oz. 10 dwt.
(Christie's)   **$2,420**

A James II silvergilt two-handled porringer and cover, on flattened reeded foot, with scroll handles and domed cover with acorn finial on a gadrooned rosette, by Robert Cooper, 1688, 7¹/₂in. high, 32oz.
(Christie's)   **$8,270**

A silver porringer, maker's mark of Benjamin Burt, Boston, 1760–1800, with a pierced keyhole handle engraved *WMc to FH*, 8in. high, 7 oz.
(Christie's)   **$1,760**

A Queen Anne Provincial two-handled porringer, the campana-shaped body chased with upper beaded girdle and below with 'hit and miss' floral motifs and spiral fluting, by Richard Freeman, Exeter, 1706, 2¹/₂oz.
(Phillips)   **$1,469**

A Charles II two-handled porringer, flat chased with European figures, exotic birds and flowering trees, probably by Samuel Dell, 1684, 3³/₄in. high, 8 oz.
(Christie's)   **$8,800**

A William III part spiral-fluted porringer, stamped with stylized acorns and foliage and with an oval cartouche surrounded by scale and scroll-work, Edward Wimans, London 1698, 8in. overall, 10.25oz.
(Christie's S. Ken)
                    $3,168

A Queen Anne porringer, chased in typical style with a vacant scrolling cartouche, the handles beaded, maker probably John Cowsey, London 1706, 11oz., 5¹/₂in. diameter.
(Tennants)   **$2,232**

Silver porringer by Thomas Dane, Boston, Massachusetts, circa 1760, with slightly domed base and bombé sides, cast pierced 'keyhole' handle, 7¹/₂in. long, 6oz. 2 dwts.
(Butterfield & Butterfield)
                    $1,210

A porringer, 7¹/₈in. wide, double scroll handles and cut cardwork to base, London, 1905 by D. & J. Welby, 14oz.
(Bonhams)   **$220**

611

SALTS & PEPPERS

A pair of early Victorian salt cellars, each cast in the form of a scallop shell on three dolphin feet, 1837, maker's mark overstruck with that of Joseph and Albert Savory, 3¼in. wide, 14oz.
(Christie's) $6,336

Victorian silver salt and spoon, R. Garrard, London, 1851–52, cast as a scallop shell supported by waves, approximately 17 troy oz.
(Skinner Inc.) $2,310

A pair of Victorian salt cellars, each on cast simulated coral and seaweed base, by John Mortimer and John S. Hunt, 1845, 3¾in. wide, 22oz.
(Christie's) $6,930

A rare trencher salt, maker's mark of Richard Conyers, Boston, circa 1700, with gadrooned rim and foot rim, 2¹⁄₈in. high, 1 oz. 10 dwt.
(Christie's) $18,700

Set of four Victorian silver-gilt figural salts by Walter, John, Michael & Stanley Barnard, London, 1898, 6½in. high, 59oz. 13 dwts.
(Butterfield & Butterfield)
                $6,050

A silver and mixed-metal pepper mill, maker's mark of Tiffany & Co., New York, circa 1889, inlaid with niello and copper tear drops and flowers, with bud finial, 3¾in. high, 5 oz.
(Christie's) $2,200

A fine and rare pair of silver salt cellars, maker's mark of Simeon Coley, New York, 1767–1769, on four scroll feet with scallop-shell knees and stepped pad feet, 3¼in. wide, 6 oz.
(Christie's) $3,080

A set of four George III large circular salt cellars, each on dished circular stand with three bracket feet chased with anthemion ornament, by Benjamin and James Smith, 1810, 4½in. diameter, 74oz.
(Christie's) $19,785

A pair of French shaped-oval trencher salts, each on scroll base and with quatrefoil rims, Arles, 1750, 130 grs.
(Christie's) $2,112

SAUCE BOATS

Danish Sterling sauceboat, Georg Jensen, Copenhagen, circa 1925–1930, plain long oval vessel with twisted flat wire handle, 6½in. high, 14oz. 8 dwts. (Butterfield & Butterfield)
$1,760

A pair of silver sauce boats, on three hoof feet, foliate capped scroll handles, Sheffield 1892, weight 17oz.
(Bonhams)
$602

Paul Schofield, oval sauce tureen, with two loop handles, the cover with an urn finial, London 1789, 20 oz.
(Woolley & Wallis)
$2,129

Pair of French silver sauce boats, late 19th century, helmet form with mythical beast handle, 8³/₈in. high, approximately 52 troy oz.
(Skinner Inc.)
$4,950

Swedish silver sauceboat, Bengt Fredrik Tellander, Jonkoping, early 19th century, with applied classical medallions on the sides, 5³/₄in. high, 5oz. 12 dwts.
(Butterfield & Butterfield)
$715

A pair of George II shaped-oval sauceboats, each with quilted double-scroll handle and gadrooned rim, by William Cripps, 1750, 8¼in. long, 29oz.
(Christie's)
$7,399

Pair of Kirk Repousse sterling sauce boats, Baltimore, 1903, chased floral design, 8¾in. long, approximately 18 troy oz.
(Skinner)
$1,100

A pair of George III Irish plain shaped-oval sauceboats, each on cast spreading foot and with leaf-capped scroll handle, by Robert Calderwood, Dublin, circa 1760, 8in. long, 33oz.
(Christie's)
$12,870

A pair of George III oval sauce boats, each on three pad feet, 7in. long, maker's mark W.S. possibly that of William Skeen, London 1768, 20.1oz.
(Bearne's)
$1,650

TANKARDS

Victorian silver gilt tankard, 19th century, unmarked, 8in. high, approximately 28 troy oz. (Skinner Inc.) **$1,650**

Silver tankard, Nicholas Roosevelt, New York, circa 1740, with molded base band, scrolled thumbpiece with oval shield terminal, 7in. high, 39 troy oz. (Skinner Inc.) **$880**

An antique American silver tankard by Thomas Fletcher and Sidney Gardiner of Boston and Philadelphia, circa 1812, 10¹/₂in. high, 43.6 troy oz. (Selkirk's) **$9,250**

A George II plain baluster tankard, with scroll handle, hinged domed cover and openwork scroll thumbpiece, by John Payne, 1754, 7³/₄in. high, 30oz. (Christie's) **$4,752**

A Queen Anne plain tapering cylindrical tankard, with scroll handle, hinged domed cover and bifurcated thumbpiece, by Seth Lofthouse, 1705, 7¹/₄in. high, 27oz. (Christie's) **$5,940**

A George III plain tapering cylindrical tankard, the body with applied rib and with scroll handle, hinged domed cover and corkscrew thumbpiece, by Charles Wright, 1772, 7³/₄in. high, 24oz. (Christie's) **$3,762**

A George I plain tapering cylindrical tankard, with scroll handle, hinged domed cover and corkscrew thumbpiece, the handle engraved with initials, by Henry Jay, 1718, 7in. high, 27oz. (Christie's) **$6,732**

A silver tankard, maker's mark of John Hastier, New York, circa 1740, with a flat-domed cover and a corkscrew thumbpiece, 7in. high, 29 oz. 10 dwt. (Christie's) **$15,400**

A George II plain tankard and cover, with scroll handle and domed cover with openwork thumbpiece, by Francis Spilsbury, 1741, 7¹/₂in. high, 28 oz. (Christie's) **$4,576**

TANKARDS

A Charles II tapering cylindrical tankard and cover, the lower part of the body chased with acanthus leaves and with a similar narrow band above, 1680, maker's mark C over W, 8¼in. high, 38oz. (Christie's) **$9,045**

A silver tankard, maker's mark of Josiah Austin, Charleston and Boston, Massachusetts, circa 1765, with a scroll handle applied with a molded drop, 8⅝in. high, 28 oz. 10 dwt. (Christie's) **$8,800**

A Charles II plain tapering cylindrical tankard, the handle pricked with initials, the body later engraved with a coat-of-arms within plume mantling, by John Sutton, 1672, 6in. high, 22oz. (Christie's) **$9,422**

A George II plain tapering cylindrical tankard and cover, with a molded rib around the body with scroll handle, by Robert Williams, 1728, 7¼in. high, 24oz. (Christie's) **$3,769**

A Hukin & Heath electroplated tankard designed by Dr. Christopher Dresser, tapering cylindrical form with ebonized bar handle, 21.5cm. high. (Christie's) **$748**

A George II plain baluster tankard, the body with applied rib and with scroll handle, hinged domed cover and scroll thumbpiece, by John Langlands, Newcastle, 1757, 7½in. high, 25oz. (Christie's) **$3,762**

George III Sterling tankard by Sutton & Bult, London, 1768, the domed lid set with chair back thumb piece, fully marked on base and lid, 8¼in. high, 29oz. 8dwts. (Butterfield & Butterfield) **$3,300**

German parcel gilt silver tankard by Dominikus Saler, Augsburg, circa 1700, with domed cover set on collet base, applied cast scrolling handle with bifurcated thumbpiece, 8¼in. high. (Butterfield & Butterfield) **$6,600**

A rare silver tankard, maker's mark of Eleazer Baker, Ashford, Connecticut, circa 1785, with an applied midband and a molded circular base, 8in. high, 29 oz. 10 dwt. (Christie's) **$37,400**

TEA & COFFEE SETS

Dominick and Haff sterling five-piece coffee set, retailed by Shreve, Crump & Low Co., early 20th century, chased scroll and floral decoration, approximately 91 troy oz.
(Skinner Inc.) **$1,980**

Austrian silver six-piece tea service, 19th century, Signer & Donath, neoclassical design, approximately weight 95 troy oz. weighable silver.
(Skinner Inc.) **$2,310**

Three-piece silver tea set, John Vernon, New York, circa 1800–10, each of bulbous oval form engraved with herringbone border and shields, 44 troy oz.
(Skinner Inc.) **$2,860**

Towle sterling seven-piece tea and coffee service, water kettle and stand, tea and coffee pots, creamer, sugar, waste bowl and sterling tray, approximately 270 troy oz.
(Skinner Inc.) **$4,400**

An unusual Victorian silver-gilt tea service, in the German taste, each chased with broad flutes and engraved with panels of scrolls, by William Cooper, 1842, height of teapot 5in., gross 25oz.
(Christie's) **$2,826**

Three piece German silver tea set, early 20th century, 800 standard octagonal forms with incurvate shoulders and raised on scroll supports at the corners, 53oz. 14dwts.
(Butterfield & Butterfield) **$1,210**

Victorian four piece associated silver tea snd coffee service, coffee pot S. LeBass, Dublin, 1869; teapot London, 1890, creamer London, 1893, and sugar Sheffield 1898, each by R.Martin & E. Hall, 83 troy oz.
(Skinner Inc.) **$2,200**

A three-piece Chinese export silver tea service, maker's mark *WHL*, late 19th/early 20th century, the bodies repoussé as bamboo stalks applied with foliate bamboo branches and dragonflies, height of teapot 5⁷/₈in. high, 34 oz.
(Christie's) **$1,870**

TEA & COFFEE SETS

A Walker & Hall four-piece electroplated tea-service, designed by David Mellor, the teapot of ovoid form with concave cover and ebonized handle and finial, 16cm. high.
(Christie's) $886

Silver tea and coffee service, Edward Lownes, Philadelphia, with applied bands of rococo decoration, with three pinwheel devices between marks, 146 troy oz.
(Skinner Inc.) $3,850

A Victorian four piece tea and coffee service, each on spreading circular foot and chased overall with scrolls, foliage and scalework, by George Richard Elkington, 1856, gross 84oz.
(Christie's) $4,899

Three-piece Sterling silver tea set, circa 1854–55, made by the John C. Moore Company for Tiffany, Young & Ellis, chased floral decoration, 26.6 troy oz.
(Eldred's) $1,760

Tiffany sterling three piece tête à tête, circa 1864, pear form, pineapple finial, chased ivy decoration, together with a pair of small Whiting sugar tongs, approximately 28 troy oz.
(Skinner Inc.) $2,640

Whiting repoussé sterling five-piece tea and coffee service, mid 19th century, floral decoration, approximately 85 troy oz.
(Skinner Inc.) $2,640

Assembled and matching English Victorian Sterling tea and coffee set together with a plated kettle on lampstand by William Hunter, London, 1854/5, embossed with flowers and diaper panels, and melon finial, 63oz. 12dwts.
(Butterfield & Butterfield) $3,850

Important silver gilt three-piece tea set by Mauser Manufacturing Company, chased floral and acanthus decoration, inscribed on base, *From the first run of the Mill of the 'Eleventh Hour' Gold Mining Co., April 1906*, 32.8 troy oz.
(Eldred's) $1,210

TEA CADDIES

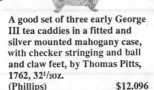

A tea caddy, the hammered body chased and embossed with tulips, signed *Gilbert Marks 1898*, 4³/₄in., London 1897, 10oz. (Woolley & Wallis)

$2,241

A good set of three early George III tea caddies in a fitted and silver mounted mahogany case, with checker stringing and ball and claw feet, by Thomas Pitts, 1762, 32¹/₂oz. (Phillips)

$12,096

American Aesthetic movement Sterling tea caddy by Kennard & Jenks, Boston, Massachusetts, circa 1880, engraved in the Japanese taste on the four sides and lid, 5in. high, 12 oz. 6 dwts. (Butterfield & Butterfield)

$5,500

Fine George III Sterling tea caddy by Robert Hennell, London, 1793, the body and lid with tooled decoration retaining original crispness, 6¹/₄in. high, 11oz. 8dwts. (Butterfield & Butterfield)

$3,850

A pair of George II oblong tea caddies and a matching square sugar box, the caddies each with sliding base and cover, 1756, maker's mark *W.A.*, contained in a silver-mounted shagreen case, height of caddies, 4³/₄in., 43oz. (Christie's)

$21,780

A silver tea caddy, maker's mark of Tiffany & Co., New York, 1891–1902, elaborately repoussé with flowers on a matted ground, 4¹/₂in. high, 7 oz. 10 dwt. (Christie's)

$935

George III Sterling tea caddy by Charles Chesterman, London, 1795, with ivory finial, bright cut decorative borders, a crest on the front and a coat-of-arms on the back, 5¹/₂in. high, 12oz. 2dwts. (Butterfield & Butterfield)

$2,750

George II Sterling tea caddy set by Thomas Blake, Exeter, 1741, each box engraved with a coat-of-arms on one side and a crest on the shoulder, 5in. high, 33oz. (Butterfield & Butterfield)

$8,800

George III Sterling tea caddy by Thomas Heming, London, 1779, the straight sided oval form with flat hinged lid centered with a stirrup handle, 4in. high, 11oz. 18dwts. (Butterfield & Butterfield)

$1,650

TEA CADDIES

A George III oval tea caddy, engraved with bright-cut flowers and foliage, with domed cover and cone finial, engraved with a crest, by Robert Hennell, 1788, 12 oz.
(Christie's) $4,048

A pair of George II vase-shaped tea caddies and sugar box, chased with flowers and foliage between swirling fluting, by Samuel Taylor, 1753, in fitted silver mounted wood case, 31oz.
(Christie's) $7,537

A silver tea caddy, rectangular with cut corners, melon fluted circular pull-off cover with fruit finial, London 1897, by William Comyns.
(Bonhams) $273

A George III shaped-oval tea caddy, the sides bright-cut engraved with festoons of flowers within stylized borders, by Thomas Chawner, 1786, 5³/₄in. high, gross 12oz.
(Christie's) $2,826

A pair of George II oblong tea caddies, each chased with bands of scrolls, foliage and rocaille ornament and engraved with initials, by William Soloman, 1758, 4¹/₂in. high, gross 46oz.
(Christie's) $8,291

A George III oval double tea caddy, engraved at the shoulder with a band of stylized foliage, with centrally hinged cover and reeded loop handle, by John Emes, 1800, 17 oz.
(Christie's) $3,520

A silver tea caddy, maker's mark of Tiffany & Co., New York, 1879–1891, the shoulder and slip on cap chased with scrolls, 8¹/₈in. high, 9 oz.
(Christie's) $1,320

A fine set of three George III tea caddies, chased with vertical sprays of flowers and similar looped cartouches, in the original tortoiseshell case, by W. Vincent, London 1770, the case relined by Lambert in the 19th century, 28oz.
(Tennants) $10,788

A George III plain oval tea caddy, with domed cover and foliage and ball finial, engraved with a coat-of-arms and presentation inscription, by Robert Sharp, 1796, 14 oz.
(Christie's) $2,288

SILVER

Large Victorian plated spirit kettle of reverse pear form, with ornate handle and lid finial. (G.A. Key) $795

Victorian electro-plated kettle-drum form hot water kettle on stand, maker T.H, last quarter 19th century, 7¹/₂in. high. (Butterfield & Butterfield) $605

George V silver kettle on stand, Hunt and Roskell Ltd., London, 1933–34, stand with shell feet, 13in. high, 44 troy oz. (Skinner Inc.) $880

American style silver hot water kettle on stand, marked *Old Friend*, 20th century, similar to Gorham's Plymouth, possibly Chinese, the kettle with swing handle over urn form body, 11³/₄in. high, 60oz. 10dwts. (Butterfield & Butterfield) $880

A silver kettle on stand, maker's mark of *Gorham Mfg. Co., Providence, 1885–1895*, the sides elaborately repoussé and chased with flowers on a matted ground, 12in. high, gross weight 66oz. (Christie's) $1,430

A George II spherical tea kettle, stand and lamp, the stand on three leaf-capped shell and scroll feet and with openwork apron, the kettle by Paul de Lamerie, 1736, the stand by Lewis Pantin, 1736, 13¹/₄in. high, gross 61oz. (Christie's) $8,762

A good George I tea kettle-on-stand, 12in. high, compressed pear-shape with faceted spout, fully hallmarked for London, 1723, by Thomas Farrer, 70 ozs. all in. (Bonhams) $30,000

An early George V small tea kettle on stand with burner, with swept shoulders and hinged domed cover, London 1913, 1302gm. total gross. (Spencer's) $695

A George II silver inverted pear-shaped tea-kettle, stand, lamp and triangular stand, by Hugh Mills, 1746, 15³/₄in. high, gross 90 oz. (Christie's) $9,346

TEAPOTS

George III silver teapot by Robert Hennell I, London, 1793, the oval body with vertical fluted ribbed sides, 6in. high, gross weight 14oz. 10 dwts. (Butterfield & Butterfield) $1,650

Silver teapot, 18th century, pear form with median molding, double scrolled ebony handle, 7³/₄in. high, 24 troy oz. (Skinner Inc.) $1,980

George III silver teapot by Joseph Scammel, London, 1791, with ebony pineapple finial on a silver leafy calyx, 6in. high, gross weight 14oz. 6 dwts. (Butterfield & Butterfield) $1,100

A George I plain pear-shaped teapot, on circular rim foot and with curved decagonal spout, hinged domed cover and baluster finial, engraved with a crest, by John Gorsuch, 1726, 6in. high, gross 19oz. (Christie's) $17,901

A Queen Anne plain pear-shaped teapot, stand and lamp, with octagonal curved spout and hinged flap, the domed cover with baluster wood and silver finial, by Simon Pantin, 1709, the stand and lamp by Nathaniel Lock, 1713, 8in. high, gross 22oz. (Christie's) $29,205

Silver teapot, Fletcher and Gardner, Philadelphia, circa 1810, applied mid band of grapevine on a pedestal base, 8¹/₂in. high, 28 troy oz. (Skinner Inc.) $715

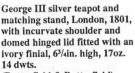

George III silver teapot and matching stand, London, 1801, with incurvate shoulder and domed hinged lid fitted with an ivory finial, 6³/₄in. high, 17oz. 14 dwts. (Butterfield & Butterfield) $1,430

A Victorian squat circular teapot engraved with armorials, the elaborate spout with blackamoor mask, by Robert Garrard, 1859, 40¹/₄oz. (Phillips) $2,246

George IV Scottish silver teapot by John McKay, Edinburgh, 1827, with a knopped leaf-wrapped berry finial, the body chased in repoussé with rocaille, scrolls, flowers and a scroll framed cartouche, 27oz. 10dwts. (Butterfield & Butterfield) $770

A George I bullet tea pot, with tapering nine-sided spout, upon molded collet foot, maker possibly Thomas Burridge, circa 1720, 4¹/₂in. to finial, 16oz. (Tennants) $2,604

A German decagonal pear-shaped teapot, with curved spout and shaped domed cover, probably by Heinrich Bohlens II, Bremen, circa 1735, 5³/₄in. high, 433grs. (Christie's) $7,160

A silver teapot, maker's mark of Isaac Hutton, Albany, 1790–1810, with straight spout, hinged domed cover, and urn finial, 6¹/₄in. high, 19 oz. (Christie's) $4,950

Silver teapot, Joseph Lownes, Philadelphia, circa 1800, engraved with foliate monogram on circular pedestal foot with square base, 11in. high, 26 troy oz. (Skinner Inc.) $2,310

A George I plain pear-shaped teapot, on circular rim foot and with decagonal curved spout, by Humphrey Payne, 1714, 6in. high, gross 13 oz. (Christie's) $8,800

An electroplated teapot on stand, the design attributed to Dr. Christopher Dresser, the circular cover with cylindrical ebonized finial, on tripod stand, with spirit burner, 19.7cm. high. (Christie's) $748

A George III hexagonal teapot, on rim foot and with angular handle and spout and detachable cover with seated Chinaman finial, 5in. high, gross 26 ozs. (Christie's) $2,640

A George III teapot, with ivory finial and angular handle on four ball feet, 6³/₄in. high, Thomas Robins, London 1805, 19.2oz. (Bearne's) $595

Fine George III Sterling teapot by Andrew Fogelberg, London, 1795, with straight sides, stepped domed cover, straight spout, ivory C-form handle and finial, 12 oz. 6 dwts., all in. (Butterfield & Butterfield) $2,750

TOAST RACKS

A George III toast tray, 10in. long, the oval body with molded border and scroll end grips, the four triple hooped bars detachable, London 1785, possibly by John Tweedie, 7oz. (Bonhams) $550

A Victorian silver toast rack, the seven reeded scroll divisions on a chased shell and scroll base on four foliate scroll feet, London 1839, 12oz. (Bonhams) $550

A Victorian toastrack, designed as openwork fans of foliate design on four bun feet, by Yapp & Woodward, Birmingham, 1850, 16cm. (Lawrence) $300

A Guild of Handicraft silver toast rack, on bun feet, with repoussé decoration of stylized fish and cabochon turquoises, London hallmarks for 1904, 12.5cm. high, 230 grams. (Christie's) $2,560

A Hukin & Heath electroplated toast rack designed by Dr. Christopher Dresser, on pad feet, the arch base with seven supports, 14cm. high. (Christie's) $630

A James Dixon & Sons electroplated toast rack designed by Dr. Christopher Dresser, with seven triangular supports, on four spike feet and with raised vertical handles, 13.5cm. high. (Christie's) $3,287

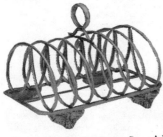

A George IV seven bar butterfly toast rack, of plain rounded rectangular form with central spade handle, by James Barber, George Cattle and William North, 308 grammes, 16cm. long, 1828. (Spencer's) $583

A Hukin & Heath electroplated letter rack designed by Dr. Christopher Dresser, the wire frame with seven adjustable supports joined by small spheres, with date lozenge for *9 May 1881*, 12.5cm. high. (Christie's) $886

A rare James Dixon & Sons electroplated toast rack designed by Dr. Christopher Dresser, on four pin feet supporting seven parallel hexagonal sections, 16.7cm. long. (Christie's) $5,907

A Victorian two-handled octagonal tray, with foliate pierced rim and bracket handles, by Martin Hall & Co. Ltd., Sheffield, 1899, 23½in. long, 99oz.
(Christie's) $3,366

A George II snuffer's tray, the angles with projecting shells, scroll side handle, on shell pattern feet, by John Priest, 1754, 21cm., 9oz.
(Lawrence Fine Art) $1,062

A George IV shaped-rectangular two-handled tray, with shell, foliage and gadrooned border and similar detachable handles, by Samuel Hennell, 1823, 28½in. long, 165oz.
(Christie's) $8,316

A George II shaped circular salver, on four scroll feet, with molded border, engraved with a coat-of-arms and motto, by John Tuite, 1733, 12¾in. diameter, 30oz.
(Christie's) $3,580

A fine silver and mixed-metal salver, maker's mark of Tiffany & Co., New York, circa 1880, the spot-hammered surface inlaid with three butterflies of copper, gold, platinum, and brass, 11in. diameter, 26 oz. 10 dwt.
(Christie's) $13,200

A George II silver-gilt shaped-circular salver, the border cast and chased with Bacchanalian masks and applied with trailing vines, by Charles Frederick Kandler, 1738, 13½in. diameter, 50 oz.
(Christie's) $4,576

An Edwardian dressing table tray, with stamped and pierced scroll and flower work folded border, Birmingham 1907, 284 grammes, 12in. wide.
(Spencer's) $448

Coin silver tray, Newel Harding & Co., Boston, circa 1855, engraved with the arms of the Bates family, 21in. wide, 103 troy oz.
(Skinner Inc.) $4,400

A fine silver chrysanthemum-pattern tea tray, maker's mark of Tiffany & Co., New York, 1902–1907, with cast chrysanthemum border, 29in. long, 270 oz. 10 dwt.
(Christie's) $22,000

Victorian Sterling galleried and footed tea tray by Bradbury & Henderson, Sheffield, 1887, with scrolled cast bracket handles applied at ends, the face tooled with decorative borders, 24in. long, 157oz.
(Butterfield & Butterfield)
$8,250

A pair of William IV shaped rectangular snuffers trays, with gadroon, acanthus and foliate edging, 9³/₄in. long, maker's mark *W.E.* possibly that of William Eaton, London 1830, 798 gms, 25.6 oz.
(Bearne's)
$1,579

Sterling silver asparagus tray in "Virginia Carvel" pattern, by Towle, pierced liner, applied border, 10 x 15in., 34.4 troy oz.
(Eldred's)
$605

A Victorian large shaped-circular salver, the openwork border cast and chased with Bacchanalian masks, by Robert Garrard, 1856, 25in. diameter, 210 oz.
(Christie's)
$8,448

A George III gadrooned and shell-decorated octafoil salver on scroll feet, probably David Bell, London 1763, 14in., 47 oz.
(Christie's S. Ken)
$2,023

Mixed metal salver in the Persian taste by Tiffany & Co., New York, New York, circa 1880, of shaped octagonal form, 12in. wide, 26oz. 14 dwts.
(Butterfield & Butterfield)
$9,350

A George III oval gallery tray, on four claw and ball feet, by John Crouch and Thomas Hannam, 1792, 24¹/₂in. wide, gross 290 ozs.
(Christie's)
$11,440

A large fine quality plated tray, with leaf-capped scroll handles, gadrooned borders and bun feet, 27in. over handles.
(Woolley & Wallis)
$890

A George III plain oval salver, on four scroll feet, with reeded border, later engraved with a coat-of-arms, 1781, maker's mark over-struck with that of Thomas Daniell, 15¹/₄in. wide, 48 oz.
(Christie's)
$2,992

TUREENS

A George III partly-fluted two-handled oval soup tureen and cover, the slightly domed cover with detachable entwined snake and foliage handle with beaded surround, by Paul Storr, 1808, 17¹/₂in. wide, 164oz.
(Christie's) $45,223

Early Victorian plated covered soup tureen by Elkington & Co., Birmingham, circa 1868, with a crown finial on a cushion with tassels, 12in. wide.
(Butterfield & Butterfield)
                        $412

A silver covered sauce tureen, maker's mark of Gorham Mfg. Co., Providence, 1868, the angular handles surmounted by alligators and terminating in a flowerhead and ribbon, 7¹/₄in. wide, 15 oz. 10 dwt.
(Christie's) $3,080

One of a pair of silver sauce tureens, maker's mark of Edward Lownes, Philadelphia, circa 1825, the sides applied with cast vintage decoration and two cast handles, 48 oz.
(Christie's)   (Two)
                        $17,600

Hester Bateman, a pair of sauce tureens and covers, the plain oval or boat-shaped bodies on pedestal bases, 19cm. high, 1784, 42¹/₂oz.
(Phillips) $4,493

Victorian plated covered soup tureen by Elkington & Co., Birmingham, circa 1850, the pinched neck with everted lip applied with scrolling foliage and flowers, 15¹/₂in. wide.
(Butterfield & Butterfield)
                        $770

A silver covered tureen, maker's mark of Tiffany & Co., New York, 1875–1891, the foot and lower body repoussé with spiral flutes, 11in. wide, 41 oz.
(Christie's) $3,850

'Japanese Movement' Sterling soup tureen with cover and associated ladle by Tiffany & Co., New York, New York, circa 1881, 13in. wide, together with a Tiffany & Co. soup ladle.
(Butterfield & Butterfield)
                        $13,200

S. Kirk and Son repoussé silver covered tureen, circa 1885, round with pineapple finial, 10¹/₂in. high, approximately 49 troy oz.
(Skinner Inc.) $4,290

URNS

Silver covered sugar urn, Philadelphia, 1790–1800, on square pedestal base, beaded border, bright cut with festoons and shields, 9in. high, 9³/₄ troy oz. (Skinner Inc.) **$825**

Sheffield plate coffee urn, circa 1820, on a stepped circular base raised on a square platform with four bun feet, 16¹/₂in. high. (Butterfield & Butterfield) **$477**

George III silver coffee urn by John Robins, London, 1784, on square platform base supported by four ball feet, 13¹/₂in. high, 38oz. 6 dwts. (Butterfield & Butterfield) **$1,760**

A George III tea urn, the body with embossed ribbon tied floral swags, beaded edges and fluted neck, 21in., Charles Hougham, London 1770, 98.5oz. (Woolley & Wallis) **$4,179**

A silver tea urn, New York, circa 1810; maker's mark indistinct, probably those of John and Peter Targee, with a domed cover, ball finial, two ring handles, faceted spout, and flaring stem with square base, 15³/₄in. high, 68 oz. (Christie's) **$4,180**

A George III two-handled vase-shaped tea urn, with foliage rosettes and with reeded, foliate scroll handles, by Daniel Smith and Robert Sharp, 1771, 19³/₄in. high overall, gross weight excluding wood base 107oz. (Christie's) **$5,940**

A George III two-handled vase-shaped coffee urn, with fluted body, ivory handle to the spigot and bright-cut engraved borders, by John Denziloe, 1792, the heater-holder and cover, 1903, 13³/₄in. high, gross 42 oz. (Christie's) **$2,464**

Sheffield plate tea urn, first third 19th century, with flattened top, pinched neck above and domed lid with leafy knop finial, 17¹/₂in. high. (Butterfield & Butterfield) **$440**

George III silver tea urn by Jacob Marsh or John Moore, London, 1769, with spiral fluting on waisted stem and square form base with cast scroll supports, 22in. high, 99oz. 12 dwts. (Butterfield & Butterfield) **$4,400**

A Victorian two-handled campana-shaped vase, body and handles formed as entwined grape-laden vine tendrils, by John S. Hunt, 1852, fitted with frosted glass liner, 21in. high, 225 oz.
(Christie's) $13,200

Gorham Sterling vase, circa 1878, repoussé decoration, chased stag's head handles, 9½in. high, approximately 19 troy oz.
(Skinner Inc.) $715

A silver vase, maker's mark of Gorham Mfg. Co., Providence, circa 1910, applied with acanthus leaves and acanthus and geometric strapwork, 12¾in. high, 52 oz.
(Christie's) $3,850

A Victorian Scottish two-handled vase, cover and rose-water dish, the dish on four shell feet and applied with four oval plaques with heads between, by Mackay Cunningham and Co., Edinburgh, 1880 and 1881, 30in. high, 213 ozs.
(Christie's) $6,688

A Chinese export silver vase, maker's mark of Wang Hing & Co., Hong Kong, late 19th/early 20th century, elaborately chased with Chinese figures at battle within an architectural landscape, 15in. high, 59 oz. 10 dwt.
(Christie's) $2,200

A William IV two-handled silver-gilt vase, the body of shaped outline with applied horses' heads and foliage, by Paul Storr, 1837, 9¼in. high, 96oz.
(Christie's) $16,582

A George III pierced and engraved wing-handled sugar vase with blue glass liner and corded rim, William Plummer, London circa 1780, 7in. overall.
(Christie's S. Ken) $553

A 19th century French silver incense burner as a vase and cover of paneled baluster form, cast with putti within cartouche, the domed cover with urn finial, 4in. high.
(Spencer's) $373

A fine silver, enamel and stone-set "Viking" vase, maker's mark of Tiffany & Co., New York, circa 1901, designed by Paulding Farnham, the shoulder applied with stylized masks, 12in. high, 30 oz.
(Christie's) $22,000

Fine silver plated champagne bucket, 20th century, with applied vintage decoration, engraved inscription, 11¹/₂in. high.
(Eldred's) $743

Pair of Sheffield plate wine coolers, early 19th century, crested, bracket handles with foliate attachments, gadroon edge, 11in. high.
(Butterfield & Butterfield)
$1,980

A Victorian two-handled campana-shaped wine cooler, on spreading circular foot and with dolphin and scroll handles, by Benjamin Smith, 1840, 11¹/₂in. high, 74 oz.
(Christie's) $7,040

American Sterling Arts and Crafts wine cooler by Shreve & Co., San Francisco, California, circa 1909–1922, with pair bracket handles at sides, overall peened finish, 8¹/₂in. high, 45oz. 12dwts.
(Butterfield & Butterfield)
$2,475

Pair Sheffield plate wine coolers, first third 19th century, comprising coolers, liners and collars, the baluster shaped body mounted on four floral and rocaille capped scrolling feet, 10¹/₂in. high.
(Butterfield & Butterfield)
$2,750

Art Nouveau Sterling wine cooler by Mauser Mfg. Co., New York, circa 1900–1910, with outwardly tapering sides rising to an irregular pierced lip applied with grape clusters and leaves, 10in. high, 72oz. 9 dwts.
(Butterfield & Butterfield)
$2,000

Sterling silver two-handled champagne cooler by Shreve, Crump & Low, chased medial band, 10³/₄in. high, 36.8 troy oz.
(Eldred's) $853

Pair Sheffield plate wine coolers by J. & T. Creswick, Sheffield, circa 1815, with reeded side handles, 9¹/₂in. high.
(Butterfield & Butterfield)
$1,320

Sheffield plate wine cooler, early 19th century, with border of applied foliage, scrolls and rocaille, 10¹/₂in. high.
(Butterfield & Butterfield)
$1,540

An extremely rare Imperial porcelain snuff bottle, molded in relief and decorated in famille rose enamels with a continuous landscape scene.
(Christie's) $17,772

Good Peking glass overlay snuff bottle, the milky-white body overlaid in rose, purple and lavender.
(Butterfield & Butterfield)
                                      $6,600

A glass snuff bottle, 19th century, the clear body with spots of pale caramel tone beneath others of dark chocolate color imitating tortoiseshell, stopper.
(Christie's) $1,998

A four-color glass overlay snuff bottle, 19th century, carved with overlay of tones of orange, yellow, lime-green and blue to depict butterflies in flight, stopper.
(Christie's) $5,627

An unusual Beijing glass snuff bottle, late Qing dynasty, naturalistically molded as a lychee with characteristic bosses and leaves issuing from below the neck.
(Christie's) $1,926

A fine agate snuff bottle, 18th/ 19th century, cleverly carved to emphasize the honey-colored banding as an oblong melon with smaller fruit growing from a vine on each side, stopper.
(Christie's) $2,221

A fine agate snuff bottle, 19th century, relief carved with a tethered horse beneath a tree, the stone of rich honey tone, stopper.
(Christie's) $7,243

A glass snuff bottle, 19th century, the bubble-suffused glass body with layers of amber and ocher spots imitating realgar.
(Christie's) $888

A small glass snuff bottle, 19th century, the opaque glass body with a mottled run of yellow, brown, white and blue spots, stopper.
(Christie's) $1,185

A Napoleon III shaped-rectangular gold snuff-box, the cover chased with War Trophies and foliage in four-color gold surrounding the initial *N*, circa 1855, 3³/₈in. wide.
(Christie's) $24,640

A Victorian oblong snuff-box, the cover cast with a view of York Minster, with foliage borders, by Nathaniel Mills, Birmingham, 1841, 3in. wide.
(Christie's) $5,104

A Victorian oblong snuff-box, the center engraved with two huntsmen in a landscape, the sides chased with flowers and scrolls and with engine-turned base, by Nathaniel Mills, Birmingham, 1849, 4¹/₂in. wide, 10oz.
(Christie's) $2,073

A French porcelain snuff box and cover with silver mounts, probably St. Cloud, painted with birds, flowers and foliage, 8.2cm. wide, 18th century.
(Bearne's) $845

A South Staffordshire enamel snuff-box formed as a finch, the hinged cover painted with parrot pecking grapes, with gilt-metal mount, circa 1765, 2³/₈in. long.
(Christie's) $3,520

A Louis XV cartouche-shaped blond tortoiseshell snuff-box, the hinged cover, walls and base piqué posé in gold and mother-of-pearl with trees, dogs, vases and flowers, circa 1740, 3in. wide.
(Christie's) $7,040

A St. Cloud silver-mounted snuff-box modeled as a swan with white feathers, a yellow beak, light-green eyes and brown eyebrows, décharge mark for Louis Robin, Paris 1738–44, circa 1740, 8cm. wide.
(Christie's) $6,695

A Berlin gilt-metal-mounted rectangular snuff-box, the interior of the cover finely stippled in colors with a lady at her dressing table trimming her pigtail accompanied by a gallant, circa 1780, 8.5cm. wide.
(Christie's) $5,513

A cartouche-shaped piqué blond tortoiseshell snuff-box, the cover piqué posé with a couple dancing within an elaborate strapwork and scroll border, circa 1740, 3¹/₄in. wide.
(Christie's) $3,894

Flemish baroque verdure tapestry, depicting a fortified town in middle distance in a wooded landscape including flowering plants and exotic birds and animals by a stream, 6ft. 6in. x 9ft. 11in.
(Butterfield & Butterfield) $4,950

A 19th century Flemish verdure tapestry, a landscape filled with tall trees with a peacock in the right forefront in shades of blue, biscuit, sepia and dark brown, 10ft. 6in. x 14ft. 10in.
(Phillips) $17,490

Flemish baroque tapestry fragment, third quarter, 17th century, depicting an Eastern potentate seated on his throne, before him a supplicating woman handing him a missive, 7ft. 6in. x 5ft. 1in.
(Butterfield & Butterfield) $6,600

A mid-Victorian Windsor tapestry, from the series of eight The Merry Wives of Windsor, woven in wools and silks depicting the legend of Slender and Anne Page, 76¹/₂ x 87¹/₂in.
(Christie's) $10,626

Flemish verdure tapestry of Diana and Actaeon, 19th century, the goddess striding with a staff in her hand and looking over at Actaeon as he emerges from bushes holding a dog by its collar, 6ft. 4¹/₂in. x 5ft. ¹/₂in.
(Butterfield & Butterfield) $3,575

An early 20th century tapestry depicting a hawking scene, in the lower left outer slip there is a woven shield containing an eagle and the letters *BPF*, this mark has been found on tapestries dated 1911 and 1913, but as yet the workshop is unidentified, 8ft. 8in. x 6ft. 8in.
(Phillips) $9,858

A 17th century Flemish verdure tapestry, possibly woven in Oudenarde, with a pair of swans swimming on a pond in the left hand corner of a wooded landscape, 8ft. 6in. x 14ft. 2in.
(Phillips) $20,670

Aubusson mythological tapestry, late 17th century, the rectangular panel with a mythological scene in a formal garden with a fountain before a pergola screen, a group to its left composed of four figures, a woman wearing a floral garland and classical style clothing standing with arms outstretched, 13ft. 7in. x 9ft. 8in.
(Butterfield & Butterfield) $22,000

An 18th century Flemish verdure tapestry, depicting a characteristic woodland scene with a waterfall running into a stream, 6ft. 10in. x 8ft. 7in.
(Phillips) $9,014

Flemish baroque verdure tapestry, woven in a palette of blues, greens, browns and ocher depicting a country house in mid-stance with a park and peahen in a clearing, 8ft. 6in. x 7ft. 4in.
(Butterfield & Butterfield) $3,850

Brussels baroque tapestry: Marcus Aurelius reprimanding Faustina, circa 1670, woven in tones of reds, blues and beige, 10ft. 10in. x 11ft. 10in.
(Butterfield & Butterfield) $13,200

An 18th century Flemish tapestry, probably Brussels, depicting a hawking scene with a group of three ladies, watching a falconer with a falcon on his hand, 10ft. 6in. x 11ft.
(Phillips) $10,335

A Steiff rich golden plush covered teddy bear, with brown glass eyes, pronounced snout, black stitched nose and claws, 11in. high, 1908–1910. (Christie's) $1,750

A golden plush covered teddy bear, with black stitched nose, glass eyes, slight hump, 22in. high, circa 1925, probably by Farnell. (Christie's) $540

An early 20th century excelsior filled blond plush teddy bear with black button eyes, long snout and beige colored felt paw pads, 25.5cm. tall. (Spencer's) $435

A large Steiff golden plush covered teddy bear, with boot button eyes, wide-apart ears, pronounced snout, black stitched nose and claws, 28in. high, 1906–08. (Christie's) $3,650

'The Dancing Bears': a rare joined couple, the white plush lady-bear with elongated limbs, dancing with a golden plush covered gentleman-bear with elongated limbs, 12in. high, both with Steiff buttons in ears, circa 1910. (Christie's) $6,500

A golden plush covered teddy bear with boot button eyes, cut muzzle, hump and elongated limbs, with Steiff button in left ear, 19in. high. $1,575

Tan mohair teddy bear with shoe button eyes, circa 1910, 12¾in. high. $370

A chubby long blonde mohair teddy bear, fully jointed with glass eyes, 20in. high. $370

An English gold plush teddy, with amber glass eyes, wide apart ears and pronounced stitched snout, 30in. high. (Bonhams) $166

TEDDY BEARS

'Bill Winky', a Deans golden plush covered teddy bear, with brown glass eyes, cut muzzle, brown stitched nose and claws and jointed limbs, 17in. high. (Christie's) **$600**

A Steiff bright golden curly plush covered teddy bear, with brown glass eyes, pronounced snout, black stitched nose and claws, 18in. high, circa 1926. (Christie's) **$1,050**

A Steiff golden plush covered center seam teddy bear, with boot button eyes, stitched nose and claws, hump and button in ear, 16in. high, circa 1906. (Christie's) **$1,800**

A large golden plush covered teddy bear with elongated limbs, boot button eyes, wide apart ears, felt pads, and Steiff button in ear, 1906–08, 28in. high. (Christie's) **$6,500**

An early 20th century Excelsior filled blond plush Steiff teddy bear, with black boot button eyes. Until recently, this bear was the Mascot for Gainsborough Rugby Club. (Spencer's) **$1,998**

A white plush-covered teddy bear with elongated limbs, pronounced snout, boot-button eyes, and Steiff button in ear, 12½in. high. (Christie's S. Ken) **$602**

A Steiff golden plush covered teddy bear, with elongated limbs, boot button eyes, cut muzzle, wide apart ears, felt pads and growler, 12in. high, 1910–15. (Christie's) **$935**

A Deans gold plush teddy bear with large wide apart rounded ears, and soft filled limbs and elongated felt pads, 22½in. (Phillips) **$460**

An early 20th century Steiff Excelsior filled mid-brown colored plush teddy bear, with black boot button eyes, 60cm. tall. (Spencer's) **$2,331**

TERRACOTTA

One of two Cretan terracotta oil jars, of bulbous form, each with three carved handles and waisted decoration, 19th century, 43¼in. high. (Christie's)   (Two) $913

Hellenistic terracotta figure of Dionysus, circa 300 B.C., depicted as the god of the vine, with long curly hair and beard and wearing a wreath of leaves on his head, 7¾in. high. (Butterfield & Butterfield)
$3,025

A terracotta oil jar, of circular tapering form with molded lip, 72in. high. (Christie's) $810

Louis XVI terra cotta figure of a maiden, late 18th century, the standing figure depicted with flowers in her upswept hair, wearing a laced bodice and long skirt, 43in. high. (Butterfield & Butterfield)
$17,600

A large pair of Italian terracotta busts of the rivers Reno and Zena shown as a god and goddess, by Andrea Ferreri, signed and dated, circa 1704, 35¾ and 37½in. high. (Christie's) $22,770

Hellenistic terracotta figure of a woman, circa 300 B.C., modeled with a classical head and long neck, her waved hair drawn back in a chignon, 9½in. high. (Butterfield & Butterfield)
$1,870

A French terracotta bust of a lady, cast and worked by Albert-Ernest Carrier-Belleuse, crowned by an elaborate tiara, ringlets and veil falling to her shoulder, 19th century, 26¼in. high. (Christie's) $7,304

A pair of eighteenth century glazed terracotta figures, each in two sections, with detail picked out in purple, in the form of a smiling bewigged footman with neckerchief, late 18th century, probably Italian, 64½in. high. (Christie's) $96,000

A French terracotta group of 'Le Fleuve', after Jean-Jacques Caffiére, the bearded river-god shown seated, his left leg over an urn flowing with water, 19th century, 23½in. high. (Christie's) $2,810

Two cushions each of rectangular shape with tasseled ends, covered in Aubusson tapestry, one with a shepherd boy, the largest 21in. wide.
(Christie's) $1,936

A letter case of brown silk woven with gilt threads and colored silks with episodes from the Fables de La Fontaine, 4 x 7in., French, third quarter of 17th century.
(Christie's) $1,791

An antique Saryk bridal asmalyk, 19th century, decorated with rows of stylized lilies depicted in indigo-blue and madder-red, 2ft. 9in. x 4ft. 8in.
(Phillips) $35,600

A late 16th century panel of undyed linen with regular repeat design of crowned hearts, with a linking motif worked in chain stitch, possibly French circa 1590's.
(Phillips) $1,840

An Imperial German embroidered War Association banner, one panel side of dark blue silk finely worked with Prussian eagle, the other panel with field gun with laurel wreath, 49 x 54in.
(Wallis & Wallis) $416

Embroidered friendship bed cover, Massachusetts, late 19th/early 20th century, square muslin patches embroidered with various motifs, 65 x 76in.
(Skinner Inc.) $412

A fine small Charles II silk needlework cushion, worked in a variety of stitches with the King and Queen beside a pool with fishes, $9^{1}/_{2}$ x $6^{3}/_{4}$in.
(Tennants) $5,022

Fabric panel, attributed to C.F.A. Voysey, early 20th century, comprised of silk and cotton jacquard woven fabric in green and cream, 93 x 84in.
(Skinner Inc.) $600

Pictorial hooked rug, 20th century, an American ship at sea, worked in shades of blue, purple, red, yellow, green and tan, 37 x 58in.
(Skinner Inc.) $450

A mid 17th century embroidered picture worked in silk and metal threads showing King Charles II and Catherine of Braganza, 27cm. x 37cm., English, circa 1660.
(Phillips) $1,288

A fine and large needlework picture, probably a firescreen banner, signed at the bottom *Mary Davidson, aged 13, 1706*, 27 x 19½in.
(Tennants) $8,928

An early George III silk picture, of a shepherdess and child with dogs, rabbits, birds and insects, walnut frame, 10½ x 13in.
(Tennants) $3,720

Beauvais tapestry pillow, 18th century, with one rounded side, sewn in shades of ocher, brown, tan, various shades of green and blue, crimson and burgundy, 19 x 18½in.
(Butterfield & Butterfield) $1,100

'Daffodil', a Morris & Co. curtain, designed by J.H. Dearle, printed cotton with braid border, repeating pattern of daffodils and wild flowers between waved stylized vines, 45 x 181cm.
(Christie's) $689

One of a pair of George II gros and petit point panels, worked in colored wools and heightened in silks, one with a gardener, the other with his companion, 19 x 22¾in.
(Tennants) (Two) $1,953

A silk-on-linen needlework picture, signed *Martha D. Ball*, American, early 19th century, worked in polychrome silk threads on a linen ground with a house surmounted by a flag on a hillock, 14¼ x 12⅛in.
(Christie's) $2,090

A George I panel, possibly from a large chair seat worked with a shepherdess beside a pond with swans, framed, 24in. square.
(Tennants) $5,580

A needlework picture, embroidered in colored silks and metal wire, with Bathsheba and her attendants, with King David watching from his castle, 12 x 17in., unfinished, mounted, English, mid 17th century.
(Christie's) $4,478

TEXTILES

Knitted appeal to President Andrew Johnson, Washington Insane Asylum, February, 1868, worked with yarns in brown, red, grey, blue and natural wool, 20 x 28in.
(Skinner Inc.) **$1,100**

'Bird', two pairs of Morris & Co. curtains, woven wool, repeating pattern, pairs of birds amid foliage, with two tie backs, 223 x 84cm.
(Christie's) **$4,725**

A needlework picture, embroidered in colored silks with two figures by a well, possibly Rebecca and Eliezer, 8 x 10in., English, mid 17th century.
(Christie's) **$5,257**

A good Charles II needlework panel, worked with a group including a young man riding a camel watching a young woman being baptized by immersion, 9 x 7¹/₂in.
(Tennants) **$2,604**

A late 18th century needlework oval picture, of a kneeling girl playing a harp, 12¹/₄ x 9¹/₂in.
(Tennants) **$521**

'The Four Seasons', a wall hanging designed by Walter Crane, woven silk on cotton, repeating design of roundels enclosing classical figures, circa 1893, 216 x 111cm.
(Christie's) **$6,695**

An early 19th century embroidered picture portraying a classical archway with view to colonnades beyond and surrounding ruins, 33 x 45cm., English, circa 1810.
(Phillips) **$221**

A woven wool curtain, the design attributed to B.J. Talbert, repeating floral design, dark olive green ground with sage green, rust red and beige, 272cm. long x 125cm. wide.
(Christie's) **$985**

A needlework picture, worked in colored silks and metal threads, with a central medallion depicting Rebecca and Eliezer at the well, 16 x 21in., English, mid 17th century.
(Christie's) **$12,850**

One of a pair of yellow and gilt-painted tole verrieres of oval shape, each painted with chinoiserie scenes, with waved rim and looped handles, 12¹/₂in. wide.
(Christie's)   (Two)

$1,693

Paint decorated shaped tin tray, Continental, 19th century, salmon reserve centering a portrait medallion of a Hessian officer, 20¹/₂ x 16in.
(Skinner Inc.) $330

Empire tin-lined zinc baignoire, circa 1820, with rounded tapering and slightly arched ends, 5ft. 4in. wide.
(Butterfield & Butterfield)
                                    $1,100

Punchwork decorated tin coffee pot, Pennsylvania, early 19th century, with potted tulip design, hinged lid with brass finial, 11in. high.
(Skinner Inc.) $1,400

Pair of paint decorated tin shields, possibly Pennsylvania, late 19th century, each with a patriotic emblem, 10¹/₂ x 15in.
(Skinner Inc.) $3,850

Tole decorated tea dispenser, 19th century, advertizing *Van Dyke*, 27¹/₂in. high.
(Eldred's) $154

A set of three japanned metal cylindrical tea canisters, the fronts decorated with armorials, 17in. high.
(Christie's) $1,650

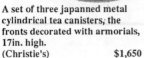

A Lucie Attwell's fairy tree biscuit money box tin.
(Dee & Atkinson) $160

A pair of early 19th century japanned metal chestnut urns and covers, each body with twin lion mask ring handles, decorated with gilt heightened sprays of flowers, 30cm. high.
(Phillips) $1,660

A Hess lithographed tinplate crank-operated flywheel-drive four-seat rear-entrance tonneau, with composition driver and pierced artillery wheel, circa 1908, 11in. long.
(Christie's) $895

A Märklin hand-painted kitchen, circa 1900, featuring a sideboard, sink, shelves, pots, pans and elaborate cookstove, 37in. wide.
(Christie's) $9,900

A fine oversized early Märklin tin-plate horsedrawn hansom cab, the cast lead white and black horse on wheels, 28in. long overall.
(Christie's) $18,700

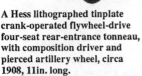

A Günthermann lithographed tinplate spring-motor four-seat open tourer, with chauffeur, crank-handle spring-wind and four opening doors, circa 1912, 11$^{1}/_{2}$in. long.
(Christie's) $1,025

A Carette tinplate keywind open phaeton, circa 1914, lithographed in yellow and black, with driver and rear passenger, 12$^{1}/_{2}$in. long.
(Christie's) $5,060

A red and black roadster having rear end differential, 14$^{1}/_{2}$in. long.
(Butterfield & Butterfield) $550

Lehmann Uho car with driver having lithographed plate mounted on hood marked with cities around the world, 7$^{1}/_{2}$in. long.
(Butterfield & Butterfield) $715

A rare and unusual tinplate castle, probably German, featuring steps leading to spires, towers, turrets and tiled courtyards, 31in. high.
(Christie's) $4,400

A Carette tinplate four-passenger keywind open tourer, circa 1910, lithographed in red, gold and black, and all four original passengers, 8$^{1}/_{2}$in. long.
(Christie's) $5,060

A Tippco lithographed tinplate clockwork electrically-lit 'Graf Zeppelin DLZ 127', with three-blade metal propeller, early 1930's, 17in. long.
(Christie's) $466

A painted wooden Noah's Ark, containing brightly painted animals and figures, 15in. wide, Sonneberg, mid 19th century.
(Christie's) $2,797

A German ocean liner with three stacks, having single mast and painted red and black with a tan deck, 11in. long.
(Butterfield & Butterfield) $413

A German painted tinplate clockwork cricketer, with red blazer and cap, yellow trousers and brown pads, 7in. high.
(Christie's) $2,424

A Lehmann lithographed tinplate yellow EPL No. 575 'Auto Post' mail van, with opening rear doors, espagnolet latch, steering and driver, 5½in. long.
(Christie's) $895

A Martin painted tinplate and fabric clockwork 'L'Artiste Capillaire', hairdresser with bald customer, 8in. high.
(Christie's) $1,641

Taybar No. 23 miniature model 'Baker and Barrow' in original box.
(James) $240

A Märklin tinplate 'Aeropal" hand or steam operated lighthouse roundabout, circa 1909, with stairways and many flags aloft, 19in. high.
(Christie's) $22,000

A German painted tinplate and fabric clockwork clown, with two flies on nose and operating fly-swatter in right hand, 8in. high.
(Christie's) $839

A Günthermann keywind tinplate vis-a-vis, circa 1902, lithographed in blue, tan and black, with large rubber-tyred wheels, original driver, 10in. long.
(Christie's) $14,300

K9, scratchbuilt to a high standard, with battery operation causing his eyes to light up giving him an intelligent countenance.
(Bonhams) $375

A German painted tinplate clockwork Negro 'Cake-Walking' Couple, with reciprocating-action wheeled mechanism, circa 1910, 6in. high.
(Christie's) $1,492

A Martin painted tinplate and fabric clockwork 'La Blanchisseuse', laundry woman bent over tub with scrubbing action, 7¹/₂in. long.
(Christie's) $1,342

A Lehmann lithographed tinplate flywheel-drive EPL No. 723 'Kadi', two Chinamen with tea chest, 7in. long.
(Christie's) $895

A German painted tinplate clockwork rifleman, in field gray uniform and box pack, with kneeling, standing and firing action, 7¹/₂in. high.
(Christie's) $1,305

A Günthermann lithographed tinplate clockwork 'Toonerville Trolley', with 'comic' oscillating and stopping action, 1920's, 5in. long.
(Christie's) $970

A fine early Doll et Cie ferris wheel ride, entirely hand-painted, consisting of six swinging gondolas, each with two passengers, 13¹/₂in. high.
(Christie's) $4,180

A Lehmann lithographed tinplate EPL No. 590 autobus, with original price label and tags for securing string handle, in original box with pencil inscription *Motor Buss*.
(Christie's) $3,356

A Martin lithographed tinplate flywheel-drive 'Le Livreur', delivery man and two-wheeled cart, 6in. long.
(Christie's) $336

A Lehmann painted tinplate and fabric EPL No. 500 'Paddy and the Pig', 5¹/₂in. long.
(Christie's) $1,025

Antique child's hobby horse, late 19th/early 20th century, in pine and other woods, mounted on wheels, 24in. long.
(Eldred's) $770

A painted wooden toy grocer's shop, with named drawers, fitted counter, bell, windows, mirror and stock, 34in. wide.
(Christie's) $709

Compagnie Industrielle du Jouet, clockwork P2 Alfa Romeo racing car finished in red, treaded tires, 52cm., with key.
(Phillips) $2,872

A painted wooden toy kitchen, with furnishings including tinplate kitchen range, water holder, cupboard, saucepans, and pottery jugs and bowls, 33in. wide.
(Christie's) $559

A French bicycle racing game, circa 1920, in fitted box which opens to reveal circular race course with four cyclists, 18 x 18in.
(Christie's) $2,420

A Kico lithographed tinplate clockwork 'Little Billy Scores!' billiards player, with red and yellow table, 6in. long.
(Christie's) $410

A Stock lithographed tinplate spring-motor 'Paddy's Pride', with original box lid, 8in. long.
(Christie's) $746

A large Tippco lithographed tinplate clockwork sixteen-seat charabanc with folded tinplate hood, with driver, 1920's, 18in. long.
(Christie's) $2,610

An extremely rare boxed "Buck Rogers" set of six figures, circa 1935, made by Britains Ltd. exclusively for the John Dille (USA) Company, all approximately 2¼in. tall.
(Christie's) $3,740

A Märklin Third Series painted tinplate clockwork Ship of the Line, with twin masts, single main funnel and six gun turrets, circa 1930, 14in. long.
(Christie's) $2,610

A Keystone aerial ladder truck, finished in red and having twin side ladders and bell on the hood, the sides having partial decals, 30in. long.
(Butterfield & Butterfield) $660

An early Märklin tinplate keywind Zeppelin, circa 1908, with twin silvered open gondolas, having passenger cabin in between, and four motors, 18in. long.
(Christie's) $9,900

Painted wood model of a milk wagon, New England, early 20th century, each side decorated with seal of *H.P. Hood & Sons Dairy Products*, 22in. wide.
(Skinner Inc.) $2,090

A magnificent early French tinplate horse-drawn open double decker tram, circa 1890, pulled by a pair of brown metal horses in livery, 42in. long overall.
(Christie's) $71,500

Spot-On No. 0 Presentation Set including Rolls Royce Silver Wraith, MGA, Ford Zodiac, Aston Martin, Austin Prime Mover articulated flat truck, in original box, circa 1960.
(Christie's) $653

A large Ohio pressed steel roadster finished in red and black with gray and red wheels, 18½in. long.
(Butterfield & Butterfield) $523

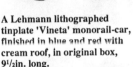

A Lehmann lithographed tinplate 'Vineta' monorail-car, finished in blue and red with cream roof, in original box, 9½in. long.
(Christie's) $1,025

A Lehmann lithographed tinplate clockwork EPL No. 790 'Nina' cat and mouse.
(Christie's) $1,025

An "Automatic Rower" keywind oarsman toy, circa 1915, constructed of wood with a jointed cloth dressed sailor having a composition body and celluloid face, 23in. long.
(Christie's) $3,520

Triang painted and lithographed tinplate clockwork Captain George Eyston's Magic Midget, finished in green and white rubber tires, in original box, circa 1935, 15in. long.
(Christie's S. Ken) $1,128

A French painted cast metal and steel single-seater military biplane, finished in khaki with French markings, circa 1917, 12in. long.
(Christie's) $447

A Lineol painted tinplate farm wagon, finished in gray, with painted composition driver and two-oxen team, on wheeled bases, circa 1934, 15in. long.
(Christie's) $653

A Nomura battery operated electrically lit tinplate Cadillac, with forward and reverse action, in original box, circa 1952.
(Christie's) $1,492

A Meier penny toy lithographed tinplate three-funnel battleship 'Emden', 5¼in. long.
(Christie's) $597

A German painted tinplate clockwork billiards player, the brown table with circular feed action, circa 1910, 11in. long.
(Christie's) $559

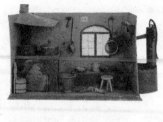

A Carette tinplate keywind two-passenger roadster runabout, circa 1910, handsomely lithographed in white and gold, and two tinplate painted passengers, a driver and a lady companion, 10in. long.
(Christie's) **$8,250**

A painted tin plate kitchen, the corner stove with hood, a painted glass window at the back and with utensils including a copper hot water bottle, 11½in. wide, late 19th century, possibly Märklin.
(Christie's) **$1,025**

A Lehmann painted and lithographed tinplate spring-motor EPL No. 345 'New Century Cycle, 5in. long.
(Christie's) **$485**

A Bing clockwork propeller-driven Polar Explorer on tinplate wheeled skis, with plush coat, felt gloves and boots, circa 1920, 7in. high.
(Christie's) **$1,771**

The famous George Brown tinplate "Charles" hose reel, circa 1875, finished with beautiful hand-painted decorative scroll work, probably the rarest early American tin toy known to exist, 23in. long.
(Christie's) **$231,000**

A Märklin painted iron and brass coastal or fortress gun, finished in gray with black lining and rivets, 1920's, 9½in. long.
(Christie's) **$653**

A Lehmann lithographed and painted tinplate EPL No. 640 Zig-Zag, rocking boat in rolling wheel.
(Christie's) **$746**

Dinky: a No. 249 Display Set 'World Famous Racing Cars' on easel-backed retailer's board, circa 1962.
(Christie's) **$522**

A Lehmann painted and lithographed tinplate spring-motor EPL No. 520 'Li La Hansom Cab', 5in. long.
(Christie's) **$1,342**

A Lehmann lithographed tinplate spring-motor EPL No. 773 'Masuyama', Japanese coolie pulling rickshaw, 1930's, 7in. long.
(Christie's) $839

A rare Märklin refreshment trolley, with red wheels and undercarriage, complete with painted composition food products, tin and glass tableware, 9in. long.
(Christie's) $3,740

A rare Lehmann lithographed tinplate EPL No. 585 Royal Mail van, finished in red, opening rear doors, 6¹/₂in. long.
(Christie's) $3,356

A Lehmann lithographed tinplate spring motor EPL No. 770 'Express', railway porter, 6¹/₂in. long.
(Christie's) $336

A Marklin toy kitchen range, finished in black and partly nickel-plated, the top with five apertures and fitted with a chimney, 20¹/₂in. high, early 20th century.
(Tennants) $680

A rare Märklin rabbit automaton with carriage, circa 1910, featuring a fur covered rabbit fitted with an on/off clockwork mechanism, 11in. tall.
(Christie's) $9,350

A Lehmann lithographed and painted tinplate EPL No. 490 'Tut Tut' motor car, comic motorist with bellows horn, 7in. long.
(Christie's) $1,212

A Britains lead and tinplate flywheel-drive rajah on walking elephant, circa 1890.
(Christie's) $839

A large Bing tinplate keywind transitional open phaeton, circa 1902, hand-painted in yellow with maroon piping, 13³/₄in. long.
(Christie's) $24,200

TOYS

A 'Hillclimber' ship with four lifeboats and twin stacks, the boat finished in light gray with stylized green waves around base, 12½in. long.
(Butterfield & Butterfield)
$330

A child size cutter sleigh, finished in yellow and black with stenciled decoration and upholstered seat, 33in. long.
(Christie's) $715

A Lincoln pedal car, circa 1935, finished in lime green with fenders/running boards, features include chrome plate steering wheel, 45in. long.
(Christie's) $8,800

An extraordinary Märklin tinplate fire set, circa 1919, consisting of three keywind matched fire trucks, each hand painted in red, black and yellow with rubber tires, all thre bear the Märklin metal embossed shield on the front panel, firehouse 21in. wide.
(Christie's)
$79,200

An early German hand painted tinplate swimming pool and changing shed, finished in light blue-gray with ticket window, 19½in. long.
(Christie's) $1,320

A German painted tinplate clockwork Negro Lady, dressed in long skirt and bonnet, with bellows and rotating wheeled action, 8in. high.
(Christie's) $1,771

A Carette painted and lithographed tinplate four-light landaulette, with chauffeur, opening doors, handbrake, start/ stop lever and luggage rack, circa 1911, 13in. long.
(Christie's) $2,424

TOYS

A Carette tinplate two-seat runabout, circa 1908, a handpainted white keywound runabout with composition figure, stop and go lever, 10¹/₂in. long.
(Christie's) $9,350

A Lehmann painted and lithographed tinplate spring-motor EPL No. 170 'Afrika' ostrich mail cart, 8in. long.
(Christie's) $709

A rare Märklin pullalong automotive water tanker, circa 1912, consisting of a larger water reservoir with indicator showing depth of water, 22¹/₂in. long.
(Christie's) $19,800

German painted tinplate clockwork, probably Günthermann: a lady in long skirt with hat and muff, with wheeled oscillating walking action, 8in. high.
(Christie's) $466

A large hand-enameled tinplate phaeton, circa 1885, attributed to Lutz, candle-powered front lantern, complete with store label from Paris, 20in. long.
(Christie's) $22,000

Fernand Martin, 'La Sentinelle Orientale', clockwork painted tinplate figure in tan uniform with red sash and cap, circa 1902.
(Christie's S. Ken) $2,052

A Lehmann Tap Tap porter featuring a man in blue jacket pushing a yellow cart marked *Tap Tap*, 6in. long.
(Butterfield & Butterfield) $468

A splendid Märklin tinplate hand-painted castle with revolving moat, finished in tones of tan and green, with red and blue accents, 13in. high.
(Christie's) $3,520

A Lehmann 'Adam' porter featuring a man in a blue jacket and red print trousers pushing an orange suitcase, 8in. high.
(Butterfield & Butterfield) $935

A number "7" American national pedal car, circa 1910, of tin, wood and brass, finished predominately in red with cream and green rectangular striping, 42in. long.
(Christie's) $9,900

An unusual Märklin pond, circa 1900, the circular base molded and painted to resemble a grassy slope with boat and cupola at center, 16in. wide.
(Christie's) $1,760

An early Günthermann tinplate keywind hook and ladder fire truck, circa 1910, hand-painted in red and yellow, with four original firemen, 14in. long overall.
(Christie's) $4,620

A Distler lithographed tinplate clockwork motorcyclist, with belt-driven rear wheel and oscillating steering action, 1920's, 7¹/₂in. long.
(Christie's) $1,715

A Bing painted and lithographed workbench, with two 'flat' articulated workmen operating a hand saw and a plane, circa 1912.
(Christie's) $522

An airship musical go-round, possibly French, circa 1915, featuring three bisque-headed doll aviators suspended from dirigibles.
(Christie's) $3,080

A Burnett lithographed tinplate spring-motor motor taxi, finished in yellow over black, with open cab and driver, 1920's, 7in. long.
(Christie's) $1,678

Lehmann lithographed tinplate Express cart, featuring a porter dressed in blue and yellow pulling a red and black "Express" cart, 6in. high.
(Butterfield & Butterfield)
                    $440

A Günthermann lithographed tinplate streamlined car (Stromlinienauto), finished in red and yellow with driver and 'Autobahn-Kurier'-style tail, circa 1938, 10in. long.
(Christie's) $317

A Mohr and Krauss lithographed tinplate clockwork motorcycle combination, finished in gray and red with blue lining, circa 1914, 8in. long. (Christie's) **$2,237**

An early French game tinplate windup circular bicycle race, comprising three articulated riders, wearing official striped shirts, 10in. diameter. (Christie's) **$3,080**

A Bing black-painted tinplate clockwork Ford Model T doctor's coupé, circa 1923, 6in. long. (Christie's) **$932**

A Bing painted and lithographed tinplate Continental windmill, in original A W Gamage box, circa 1912. (Christie's) **$354**

A rare Bing hand-enameled tinplate clockwork 'Brake' four-seat motor car, black mudguards, plated wheels, rubber tires and mechanism operating eccentric steering, circa 1902, 10in. long. (Christie's) **$7,458**

A Müller and Kadeder painted tinplate wind-up roundabout, with four painted cream-color canoes with painted figures of children and paper propellers, 11¹/₂in. high. (Christie's) **$2,640**

A Distler lithographed tinplate electrically-lit clockwork fire brigade turntable ladder truck, with driver and five seated crew, 1930's, 14¹/₂in. long. (Christie's) **$485**

A French tinplate horse-drawn double decker omnibus, circa 1890, painted red, yellow and black with driver, rear stairs, seats atop, passengers, and cast wheels, 18in. long. (Christie's) **$4,180**

An Arnold lithographed tinplate clockwork motorcycle, with civilian rider, luggage rack and sparkling-flint headlamp, late 1930's, 7¹/₂in. long. (Christie's) **$522**

Copper and lead painted repoussé running
horse, American, 19th century, the full-bodied
figure painted yellow over old gilt, 42in. long.
(Butterfield & Butterfield) $1,100

Copper airplane weather vane, 20th century,
25in. long.
(Skinner Inc.) $770

Fine antique American horse weather vane, in
copper and zinc, no pole, 26in. long.
(Eldred's) $1,210

Sheet metal weather vane, America, 19th
century, in the form of a logger with traces of
original paint, 35in. long.
(Skinner Inc.) $1,100

A cast zinc weathervane, possibly A.L. Jewell &
Company, Waltham, Massachusetts, circa 1850–
1867, in the form of a running centaur with bow
and arrow and serrated tail, 27in. high, 33in.
long.
(Christie's) $2,090

Molded copper black hawk weather vane,
America, 19th century, bole surface with traces
of gilt, 25in. long.
(Skinner Inc.) $2,530

Molded gilt copper Gabriel weather vane, attributed to Cushing & White, Waltham, Massachusetts, late 19th century, 30¹/₂in. long. (Skinner Inc.) **$1,760**

Molded copper weather vane, Cushing and White, Waltham, Massachusetts, second half 19th century, full-bodied figure of Dexter, fine verdigris surface, 43¹/₂in. long. (Skinner Inc.) **$4,250**

American molded and painted copper rooster weathervane, 19th century, with cut copper comb, crop and tail, the rooster with repoussé body painted green, yellow, brown and white, 32in. wide. (Butterfield & Butterfield) **$5,225**

A molded and gilded copper and zinc weathervane, attributed to J. Howard and Company, Bridgewater, Massachusetts, circa 1850–1868, the farmhouse form with uplifted ears above a modeled head and mane over a full body with raised right foreleg, 27in. high. (Christie's) **$5,500**

A gilded and molded copper cow weathervane, American, circa 1875, the standing cow with upswept horns and lifted ears above a modeled face, 27⁵/₈in. long. (Christie's) **$3,800**

Moulded copper rooster weather vane, America, 19th century, verdigris surface with traces of gilt, 20in. high. (Skinner Inc.) **$1,870**

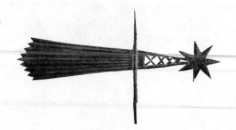

Molded copper and zinc weather vane, stamped *A L Jewell & Co Waltham, Mass* 1852–1861, in the form of Ethan Allen, (bullet holes, imperfections), 42in. long. (Skinner Inc.) $4,400

A molded copper weathervane, American, late 19th/early 20th century, modeled in the form of a shooting star continuing to a serrated and fluted banner mounted on a spire, 41in. long. (Christie's) $7,150

American molded and patinated zinc trotting horse weathervane, late 19th/early 20th century, with flowing mane and tail, 39in. high. (Butterfield & Butterfield) $1,210

A silhouette sheet iron weathervane, American, 19th century, depicting a horse with cut ears, full tail, and raised foreleg and a standing groom holding his reins, 28³/₄in. long. (Christie's) $1,870

A molded copper weathervane, American, late 19th century, modeled in the form of a full-bodied running horse with rippled mane and outstretched tail, 30¹/₄in. long. (Christie's) $3,000

Gold leafed molded copper trade sign in the form of a horse, America, in the half round, 60in. long. (Skinner Inc.) $4,675

Molded copper weather vane, New England, late 19th century, in the form of Smuggler, fine verdigris surface, traces of bolle, 24 x 41in. (Skinner Inc.) $2,640

Carved and painted trumpeting angel weathervane, America, 19th century, the figure of a woman with trumpet painted white, black, pink and blue-green, 33¼in. wide. (Skinner Inc.) $2,200

Molded copper and zinc cow weather vane, attributed to Cushing and White, Waltham, Massachusetts, late 19th century, verdigris surface, 27½in. long. (Skinner Inc.) $2,640

Molded copper stag weather vane, attributed to Harris & Co., Boston, 19th century, with fine verdigris surface, (bullet holes), 31in. long. (Skinner Inc.) $4,675

A gilded and molded copper weathervane, American, late 19th century, the Angel Gabriel form with spreadwings rising above the figure attired in a loose shift blowing a horn and on raised foot balanced upon a ring-turned sphere, 39in. high. (Christie's) $148,500

A molded copper and zinc weathervane, American, late 19th century, cast in the form of a copper running horse with windswept mane ridden by a cast zinc jockey mounted on an iron rod, 33¼in. long. (Christie's) $9,350

Carved and painted feeding rocking head black duck decoy, attributed to A.A. (Gus) Wilson, South Portland, Maine, 19³/₄in. long.
(Skinner Inc.)   **$2,090**

A New Caledonia ceremonial axe with disc shape blade of nephrite, pierced twice towards one edge and bound to the wood shaft with strings of plaited fiber, 72.5cm. high.
(Phillips)   **$1,758**

A 14in. Georgian carved wooden toby jug figure of a seated auctioneer holding a gavel, in the form of a money box.
(R.H. Ellis)   **$4,800**

A pair of Italian walnut baroque style figural brackets each in the form of a winged cherub holding aloft a tazza, 29in. high.
(Christie's)   **$1,902**

Flemish oak figure of a classical woman, late 17th/early 18th century, standing on later base, 31in. high.
(Skinner Inc.)   **$2,640**

An exceptionally finely carved pair of life-size wooden figures representing Grenadiers of circa 1801–08, possibly those of the Royal East India Company Volunteers, with bearskin caps, 78in. high.
(Christie's)   **$14,685**

A substantial gilded cartonnage mummy head-dress with long lappet wig, winged scarabeus and sun disc above forehead, late period, 20¹/₂in. high.
(Bonhams)   **$12,000**

Shaker turned bowl with mustard wash, probably Harvard, Massachusetts, late 19th century, 9in. diameter.
(Skinner Inc.)   **$8,250**

Baule wood mask, Ivory Coast, the heart-shaped face bearing protruding slit eyes, elongated nose and tiny mouth, 14in. high.
(Butterfield & Butterfield)   **$1,650**

WOOD

Ashanti wood stool, Ghana, the flattened rectangular base surmounted by a carved depiction of a full-maned lion devouring its prey, 22in. wide. (Butterfield & Butterfield)

$660

Carved wood bird group of hen, drake and quail with three chicks by Gordon Clark, Jr., 28in. long. (Eldred's) $660

One of a pair of Continental baroque style parcel-gilt and gray painted carved wood corner wall brackets, 19th century, 19¹/₂in. wide. (Butterfield & Butterfield) (Two) $1,980

A wooden sculpture, by Sergeff, of a nude woman with her head to one side, touching her long hair, 114cm. high. (Christie's) $1,947

A fine pair of George III giltwood wall brackets, with beaded moldings on acanthus leaf carved spreading supports and guilloche ornament below with foliate pendants, 1ft. 9in. x 1ft. 4in. (Phillips) $10,812

A Regency mahogany clock bracket with later mottled brown marble top and five-part scrolled support, 14¹/₂in. wide. (Christie's) $5,452

Dan wood mask, Liberia, the oval face with eye slits opening from almond-shaped orbs, the projecting mouth bristling with sharp curved teeth, 10¹/₂in. high. (Butterfield & Butterfield) $550

A fine William III limewood and giltwood bracket, in the manner of Daniel Marot, hung with lambrequin ornament supported on central palmette and flanked by putti heads, 1ft. 9in. high. (Phillips) $4,452

Madagascar wood funerary figure, depicting a nude female personage, the hair pulled back in a double chignon, 30in. high. (Butterfield & Butterfield) $550

WOOD

A gilded, painted, and carved pine eagle attributed to John Bellamy, Portsmouth, New Hampshire, mid/late 19th century, 43¹/₂in. wide.
(Christie's) $39,600

South Germany neoclassical giltwood watch holder, 18th century, surmounted by a lion, 16in. high.
(Skinner Inc.) $1,540

Egyptian polychrome wood solar barque with canopy, Eleventh/Twelfth Dynasty, 2134–1785 B.C., the long riverboat with lotus-bud stern and Anubis head prow, 19¹/₂in. long.
(Butterfield & Butterfield) $3,300

A late 19th century Venetian ebonized and polychrome blackamoor, the turbanned figure with inset glass eyes, 62in. high, overall.
(Christie's S. Ken) $2,384

Sunburst Celebration attributed to John Scholl (1827–1916), Germania, Pennsylvania, 1907–1916, painted in red, white, and blue with a carved and turned spoked and honeycomb-shaped wheel, 62¹/₄in. high.
(Christie's) $7,150

South German baroque carved and polychromed figure of the Archangel Michael, circa 1600, the figure of the Devil prostrate beneath his feet, raised on a coved rectangular base, 32in. high.
(Butterfield & Butterfield) $6,600

Decorative carved wood redhead decoy carving by Bob Mimms of Annapolis, 6¹/₂in. high.
(Eldred's) $110

Venetian baroque parcel-gilt, carved, and polychromed wood crest, early 18th century, the top half with a spread-winged eagle on yellow ground above craggy white peaks, 5ft. 3³/₄in. high.
(Butterfield & Butterfield) $4,950

Unusual wooden jack-o-lantern, 19th century, with handpainted face, 13¹/₂in. high.
(Eldred's) $440

WOOD

An early 19th century carved giltwood relief of a winged lion, gardant, his front paw resting on an open book, 81cm. wide. (Phillips) $2,121

A painted wood figure of a worshipping Chinaman with glass eyes, wearing a green cloak with polychrome floral decoration, 19th century, 21in. wide. (Christie's) $2,798

Carved wood duck decoy by J. Lapham of Dennisport, MA., 10in. long. (Eldred's) $143

Good Continental baroque carved pine group of three putti, Italian or German, circa 1700, the scantily draped infants frolicking together, 41½in. high. (Butterfield & Butterfield) $12,100

A pair of dummy boards of 17th century style, depicting a girl holding a parrot and a young boy holding a spaniel, the boy 37¾in. high. (Christie's) $4,380

Carved and painted figure of Uncle Sam on horseback, America, late 19th/early 20th century, 19in. high. (Skinner Inc.) $4,400

Snowflake stand attributed to John Scholl (1827–1916), Germania, Pennsylvania, 1907–1916, painted in white and gold with a spoked snowflake-shaped wheel, 68in. high. (Christie's) $8,800

A French giltwod wall applique with pierced ribbon-tied cresting suspending an overturned basket of flowers, a cage with billing birds and crossed garden tools, 29 x 23in. (Christie's) $3,762

Carved wooden panel, by Adelaine Alton Smith, Boston, 1909, mahogany relief carved grape clusters and vines, signed, 24in. high. (Skinner Inc.) $660

WOOD

A milliner's dummy, of composition, with a kid bonnet shape, inscribed *DANJARD, Paris, Brevete SGDD*, 19in. high, 19th century.
(Christie's S. Ken) $700

Scandinavian carved and painted wood beer bowl, 19th century, the red-painted oval bowl with two handles carved in the shape of horse's heads, 16¼in. long.
(Butterfield & Butterfield) $825

New Mexican Santo figural group, Jose Benito Ortega, 1875–1890, depicting San Ysidro Labrador, of "flat-figure style", standing with one arm raised, 20¾in. long.
(Butterfield & Butterfield) $15,400

A James I pearwood armorial standing cup with circular slightly-tapering body with four panels divided by twin-pilasters with heart-filled spandrels, the panels incised with the royal coat-of-arms, lacking cover, 9½in. high.
(Christie's) $15,074

Pair of Venetian parcel-gilt and polychromed blackamoor monkeys on pedestals, late 18th/early 19th century, each figure depicted wearing a perruque, 4ft. 6in. high.
(Butterfield & Butterfield) $33,000

Polychromed wood anthropoid mummy case, Ptolemaic Period, circa 300 B.C., wearing a wide striped tripartite wig, traces of original polychroming on the cover, 6ft. high.
(Butterfield & Butterfield) $9,350

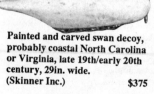

Painted and carved swan decoy, probably coastal North Carolina or Virginia, late 19th/early 20th century, 29in. wide.
(Skinner Inc.) $375

New Ireland wood malanggan figure, the slender human figure with oversized head marked by squared-off beard and mouth, 20in. high.
(Butterfield & Butterfield) $1,210

Carved and painted mermaid tavern sign, America, 19th century, 22in. long.
(Skinner Inc.) $3,190

WOOD

A Victorian treen tobacco jar, carved in the form of a boxer dog's head, with inset eyes and leather collar, 6in. high.
(Christie's) $895

Carved and painted eagle, New England, late 19th century, painted yellow and green, 36in. wide.
(Skinner Inc.) $880

Carved and painted tavern figure of King Gambrinis, America, 19th century, 26½in. high.
(Skinner Inc.) $2,860

Spanish carved and polychromed wood crèche figure, 19th century, the standing bearded figure wearing a short gray fur cape over his white chasuble and black robes, 19¼in. high.
(Butterfield & Butterfield) $715

Pair of German baroque parcel-gilt and polychromed wood figures of putti, 18th century, each seated figure carved with wavy brown hair wearing a gilt cloth about his loins, 17½in. high.
(Butterfield & Butterfield) $3,025

A late Elizabeth I pearwood cup and cover with circular slightly-domed cover surmounted by a stepped turned finial carved with ogee-leaves and surrounded by a band carved with a lion, a unicorn, a dove and an antelope, 10¾in. high.
(Christie's) $16,959

An 18th century Venetian carved walnut figure of a turbanned blackamoor, a towel fastened around his waist, 1.06m. high.
(Phillips) $1,849

French carved and polychromed wood tailor's trade sign, circa 1900, the tailor depicted in shirtsleeves, waistcoat and trousers wearing gold spectacles beneath bushy brows, 22½in. high.
(Butterfield & Butterfield) $660

Attributed to the Workshop of John and Simeon Skillin (1746–1800) and (1756/57–1806), a carved and painted figure of Ceres, 22in. high.
(Skinner Inc.) $23,100

Paint and gilt decorated sled, America, late 19th century, painted blue and gilt inscribed *Elaine* at sides, 23¹/₂in. long. (Skinner Inc.) $935

Carved and painted American eagle, circa 1900, attributed to John Hales Bellamy (1836–1914), Kittery Point, Maine, wings heightened with gilt, 73in. wide. (Skinner Inc.) $8,250

Carved and painted preening black duck decoy, attributed to A.A. (Gus) Wilson, South Portland, Maine, first quarter 20th century. (Skinner Inc.) $4,125

A Tyrolean carved pine hallstand in the form of a standing bear holding a tree trunk with young bear on the upper most branch, 79in. high. (Phillips) $2,600

Pair of Venetian rococo style carved silvered and giltwood blackamoor torchères, the figures, naked but for a swirling kilt, 6ft. 6¹/₂in. high. (Butterfield & Butterfield) $3,850

A carved and painted tobacconist's trade figure, America, circa 1875, in the form of a standing Indian maiden with plumed headdress, long articulated hair and a fringed robe, 68¹/₄in. high. (Christie's) $8,800

A monumental parcel-gilt, carved wooden panel by Professor A.H. Gerrard, from R.M.S. Britannic, deeply carved and incised with a frieze of eight wild horses amid stylized foliage, 270cm. wide. (Christie's) $13,783

INDEX